I0817995

ASTRONAUT II

MORE PAINTINGS BY **SCOTT LISTFIELD**

ASTRONAUT II
More Paintings by Scott Listfield
was designed in Oakland, California by Shaun Roberts
for Paragon Books. The text was composed using
'Futura PT' from Paratype.

Hardcover Edition
2000 copies
ISBN: 978-1-952251-38-2

June 2025
Printed in China

Paragon Books
929 Camelia Street
Berkeley, CA 94710-1419
paragon-books.com

$50.00
ISBN 978-1-952251-38-2
55000>
9 781952 251382

ASTRONAUT II

MORE PAINTINGS BY **SCOTT LISTFIELD**

JOURNEYS IN
TIME & SPACE

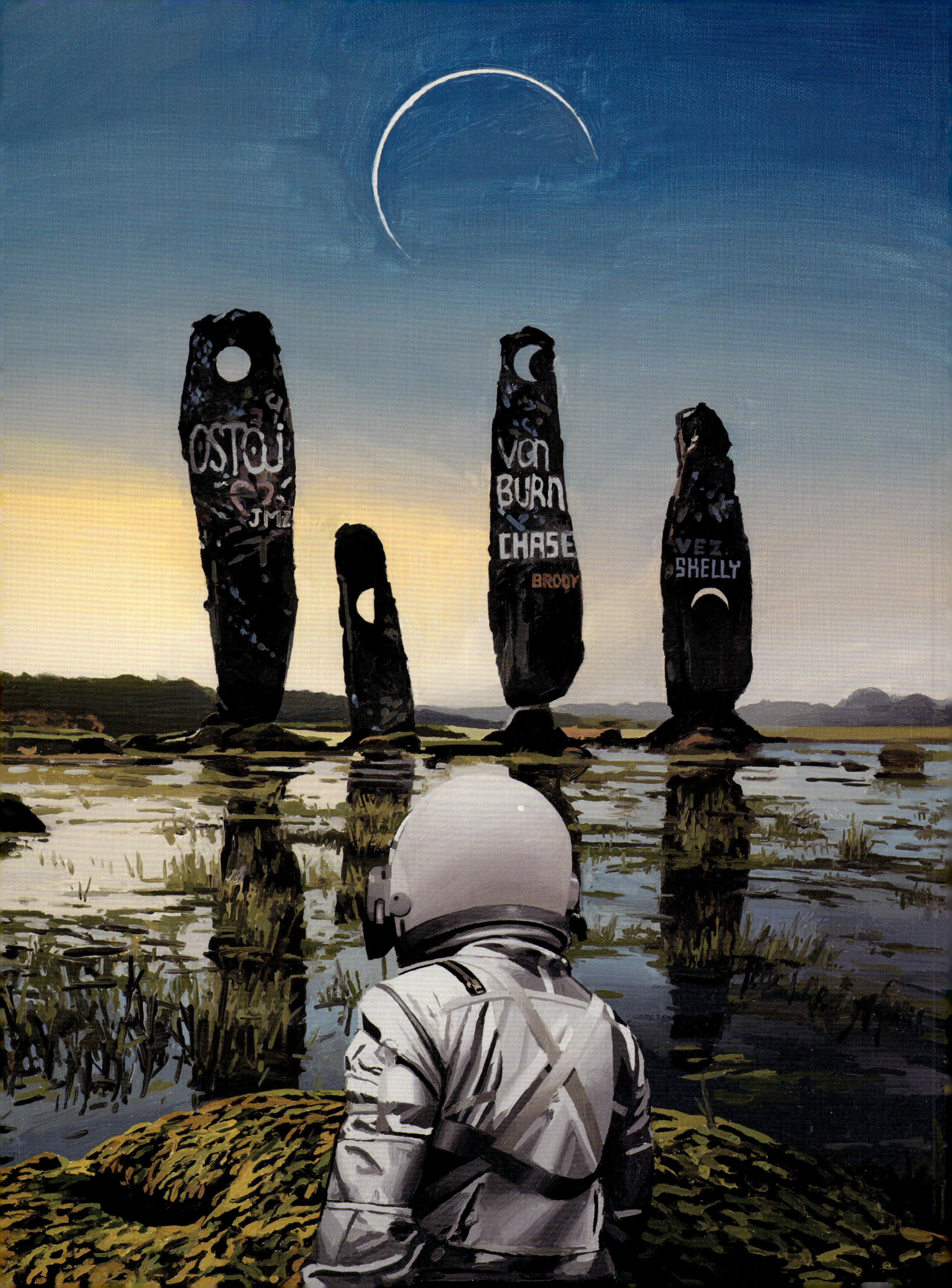
OSTOJ
JMZ
VEN
BURN
CHASE
BRODY
VEZ
SHELLY

Dedicated to **Joanna Zimmer**
and **Bob** & **Robin Listfield**

And in memory of:

Christopher Ostoj
Wesley Von Burn
Jason Chase
Susannah Kelly
Shawn Vezinaw Hosner

and Brody

#711
FOUR STONES [2024]

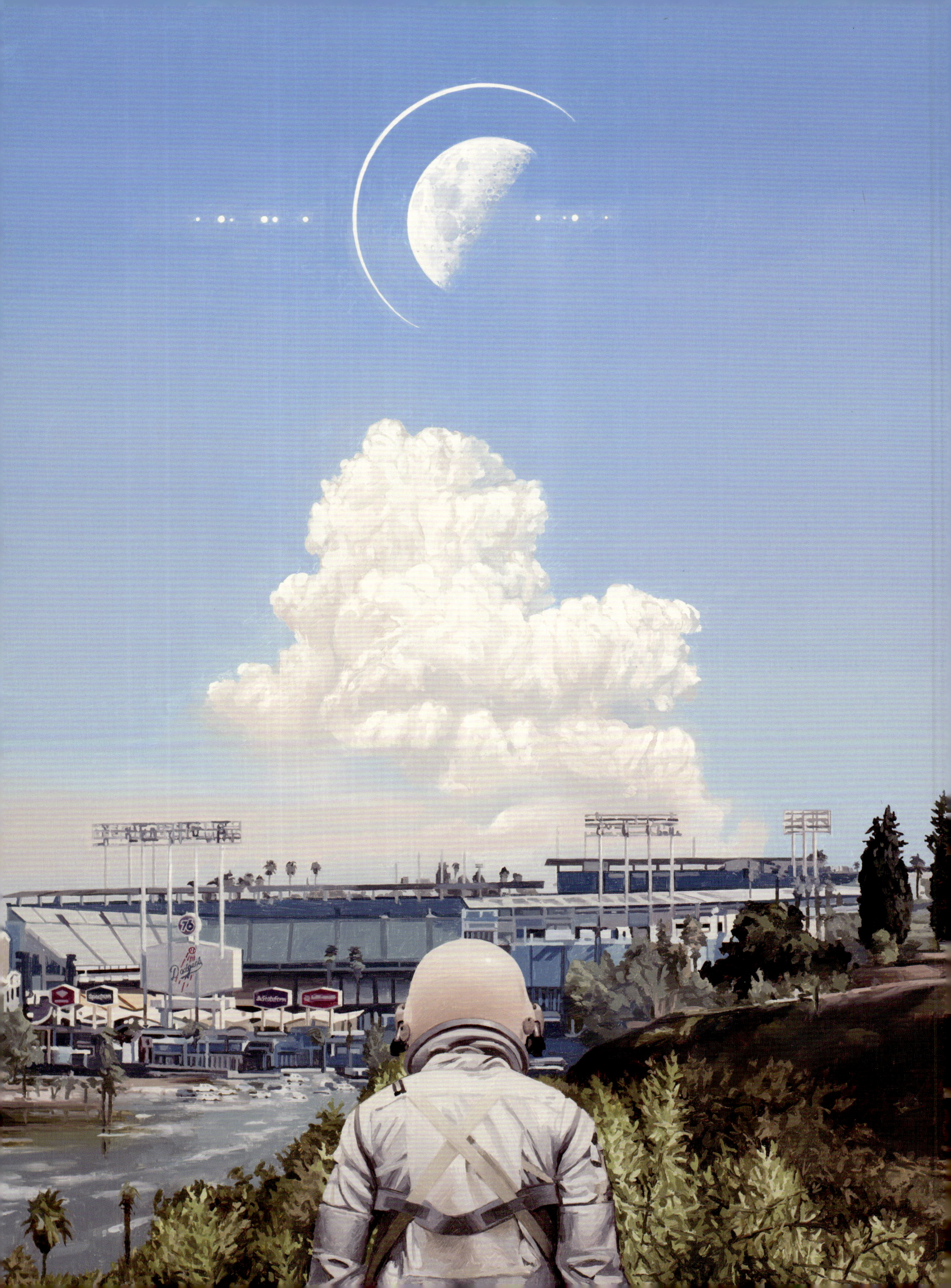
76
Dodgers

TABLE OF CONTENTS

#507
DODGER STADIUM [2020]

PREFACE

SCOTT LISTFIELD

Hi, my name is Scott Listfield. I paint astronauts and, sometimes, dinosaurs. Welcome to my second book.

My last book was published at the end of 2018, and it covered the first 19 years and 377 astronaut paintings of my art career. In it I wrote at length about why I paint astronauts, and then delved into some of the more prominent themes in my work: nature, music, pop culture, technology, and dystopia.

This second book covers the next 6 years of my career, from the end of 2018 up until the start of 2025, and includes 357 more astronaut paintings for you. During this time, unlike in the previous 19 years, most of my work was going towards solo shows. These typically include somewhere between 10 and 24 new paintings, which I would create around a central theme. These shows started to feel like discrete chapters in an ongoing book I was writing. Sometimes they bled naturally from one to another, and other times something would happen in the world—or in my life—and I would use that show as an opportunity to talk about those things. This book is organized around those solo shows, in chronological order. Each one is a chapter in my life, and now they will also each serve as a chapter in this book.

Back in 2018, my first book was completed over a very hectic few weeks while I was in the process of moving from my native Boston to Los Angeles. As it happens, moving cross country is not an ideal time to also be writing a book. Huh. Go figure. This time around, I'm thankfully staying in one place as I work on this. But that move created a natural break between the two halves of my career. The early part, spent mostly in Boston, where I slowly figured out what I wanted to say and how I wanted to say it. And this next part of my life, where I'm a bit more established, where I focused more on the larger stories I was telling, and where I'm living in a city with a much larger art community. It's a huge inflection point in my life. And while it is almost entirely coincidental that things happened this way, it makes a lot of sense that it serves as the break in between my two books.

I also started to get a lot more directly autobiographical in my work during this part of my career. While you will still find plenty of pop cultural references in these pages, I'm now a bit older, and have naturally become more reflective on my life. And look, the past 6 years have been crazy. Like, all time historically crazy. There were elections. And protests. And a pandemic. Oof, the pandemic. During this time, in very unsettling ways, the outside world began to resemble the dystopia I depict in my work. These paintings touch on those things. They talk about the losses I've experienced, the grief that comes

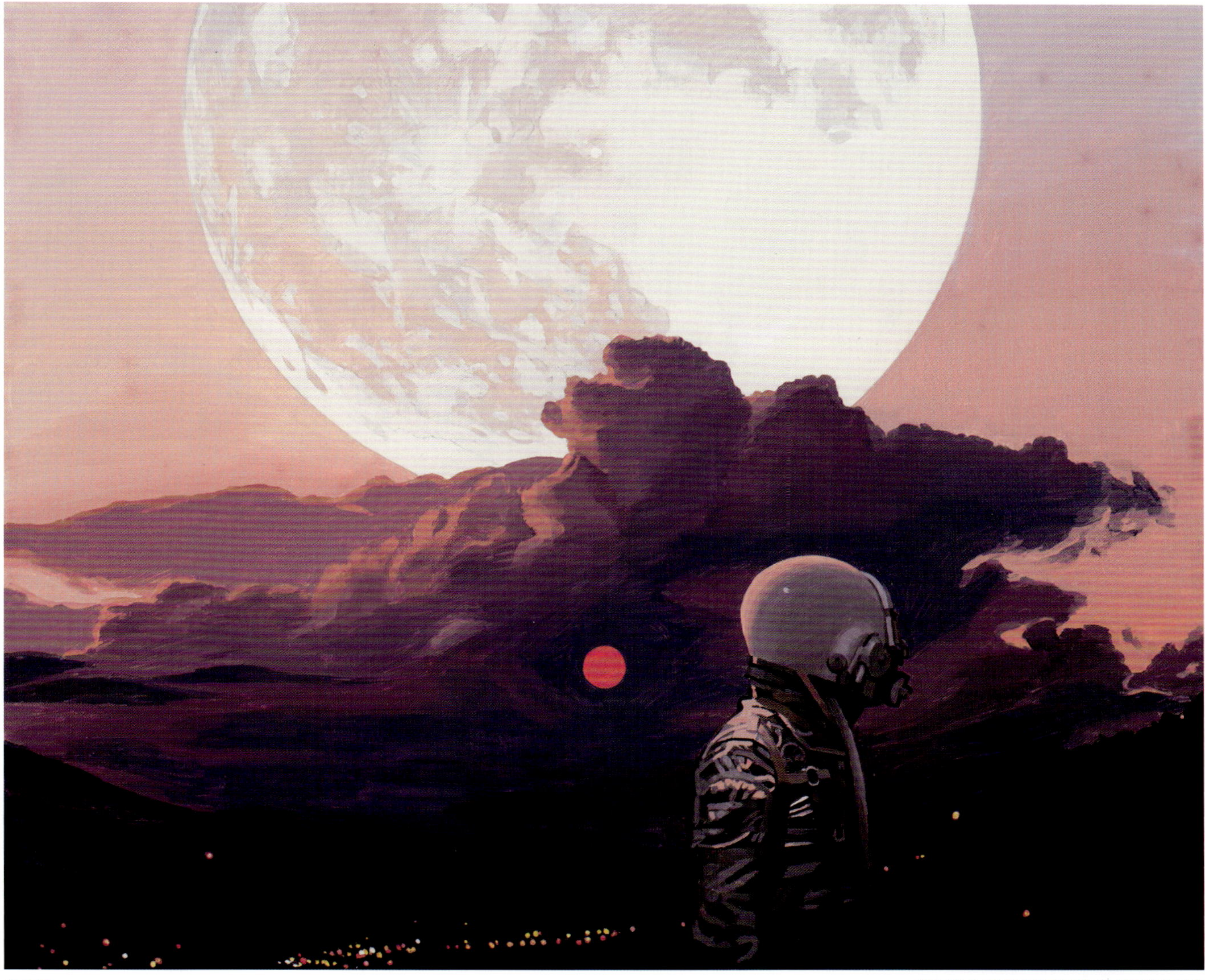

#675 PINK & PURPLE EVENING [2023]

with it, the social and political movements of this time, and of course the pandemic, and the feelings of isolation it brought to all of us. But don't worry! I also made a painting about *The Humpty Dance*. So I haven't become entirely serious.

I have, however, spent a lot more time looking back at my own life. And my astronaut, usually existing in some indeterminate future, has also begun to travel forwards and backwards, in both time and space: revisiting old paintings, revisiting places I've been, going back into the timeline of my own life, and escaping the turmoil of the present.

While I've begun to more deeply consider my own personal legacy, I've also been thinking about the legacy we will all leave behind after we're gone. What will last of the things we have created? Will people remember us? Will there be people at all? Will there be anything left of us beyond a handful of decaying monuments and a whole lot of microplastic? In other words, I'm getting older. We all are. (Sorry). I've been sending my astronaut further afield, to tell increasingly personal stories about the world around me. As for the future? Things feel very uncertain. It's been a tumultuous 6 years, hasn't it?

So buckle up. I hope you enjoy *Astronaut II*. We'll be traveling backwards and forwards in time. Adjust your helmets accordingly.

INTRODUCTION

KEN HASHIMOTO HARMAN

Harman Projects

All great literature is said to be one of two stories: a man goes on a journey, or a stranger comes to town. —Attributed to Leo Tolstoy

Though likely apocryphal, this oft-cited quotation endures for its easily understandable universal truth: as human beings, we are drawn to the thrill of adventure but are also scared of the unfamiliar.

This duality forms a persistent tension within the human condition. Since the earliest epochs of human history the oscillation between exploration and security has shaped both our psychological makeup and sociocultural evolution. Humanity, in this view, can be characterized as a composite of hunters and gatherers—adventurers and conservators.

In contemporary popular culture, these archetypes remain deeply embedded. From the mythopoetic journeys in Tolkien's world building to the enigmatic arrivals in Kurosawa's *Yojimbo* (later reinterpreted in Leone's *A Fistful of Dollars*) the binary of the journey and the stranger retains its narrative potency. More than a century after Tolstoy's death, the endurance of these motifs reflects their deep resonance within our collective imagination.

The work of contemporary American artist Scott Listfield exemplifies this enduring dichotomy, situated at the intersection of speculative fiction and art historical inquiry. His recurring protagonist, The Astronaut, traverses a constructed universe that is simultaneously recognizable and alien. Whether navigating lush terrestrial landscapes or dystopian urban wastelands, The Astronaut remains an impartial observer, faceless and voiceless. His presence adheres to an aesthetic principle akin to the Prime Directive of science fiction: to witness without interference.

Through this device, Listfield invokes both narrative and visual tropes. The Astronaut is at once a voyager into uncharted symbolic terrain and a perpetual outsider. Encased in a retrofuturistic space suit evocative of the 1960s Mercury missions, The Astronaut appears protected yet emotionally and physically distanced. The suit symbolizes both the Cold War-era anxieties of nuclear war and utopian aspirations alike as man ventured out for the first time into the cosmos.

Formally, Listfield's compositions frequently position The Astronaut from behind, suggesting a contemporary extension of the *Rückenfigur* tradition of German Romanticism. This compositional device, emblematic in the works of Caspar David Friedrich, invites the viewer into a shared contemplative experience. In so doing, Listfield establishes a lineage extending from the 1800s to today, though through a speculative, futurist lens.

In Friedrich's oeuvre, the faceless figure turned away from the viewer facilitates a meditation on the sublime. The Astronaut becomes a proxy, not merely a narrative device, but a psychological surrogate allowing the viewer to not only contemplate the sublimity of the scene, but also transposing the viewer into the painting itself.

As art history progressed, German Romanticism gave way to a new world and even newer ways of looking at that world. Darwin's *On the Origin of Species* (1859) demystified the sublimity of the natural order, while the Second Industrial Revolution (1870–1914) shifted focus away from the rural to the urban, giving rise to Modernism which then of course led to Post-Modernism and to the Contemporary art movements of today.

One quote we can confidently attribute to Leo Tolstoy, as found in his 1897 treatise *What is Art?*, offers a prescient and opinionated stance:

Art is that human activity which consists in one man's consciously conveying to others, by certain external signs, the feelings he has experienced, and in others being infected by those feelings and also experiencing them.

In this sense, Listfield's Astronaut is not a solitary entity but rather a shared vessel that represents us all. The figure's alienation and wonderment are infectious, producing a postmodern condition we've all contracted.

At the very end of his life, Tolstoy famously renounced his familial and material ties, disappearing in pursuit of spiritual and ascetic clarity. His last written words were this brief but poignant note left behind as he slipped out of his family home under the cover of darkness:

I am doing what old men of my age are wont to do. They escape worldly life to live out their final days in solitude and silence.

Perhaps Listfield's Astronaut, like all great protagonists, is doing the same. Venturing out on his own endless journey—though maybe he's just arrived, a stranger in a world not quite his own.

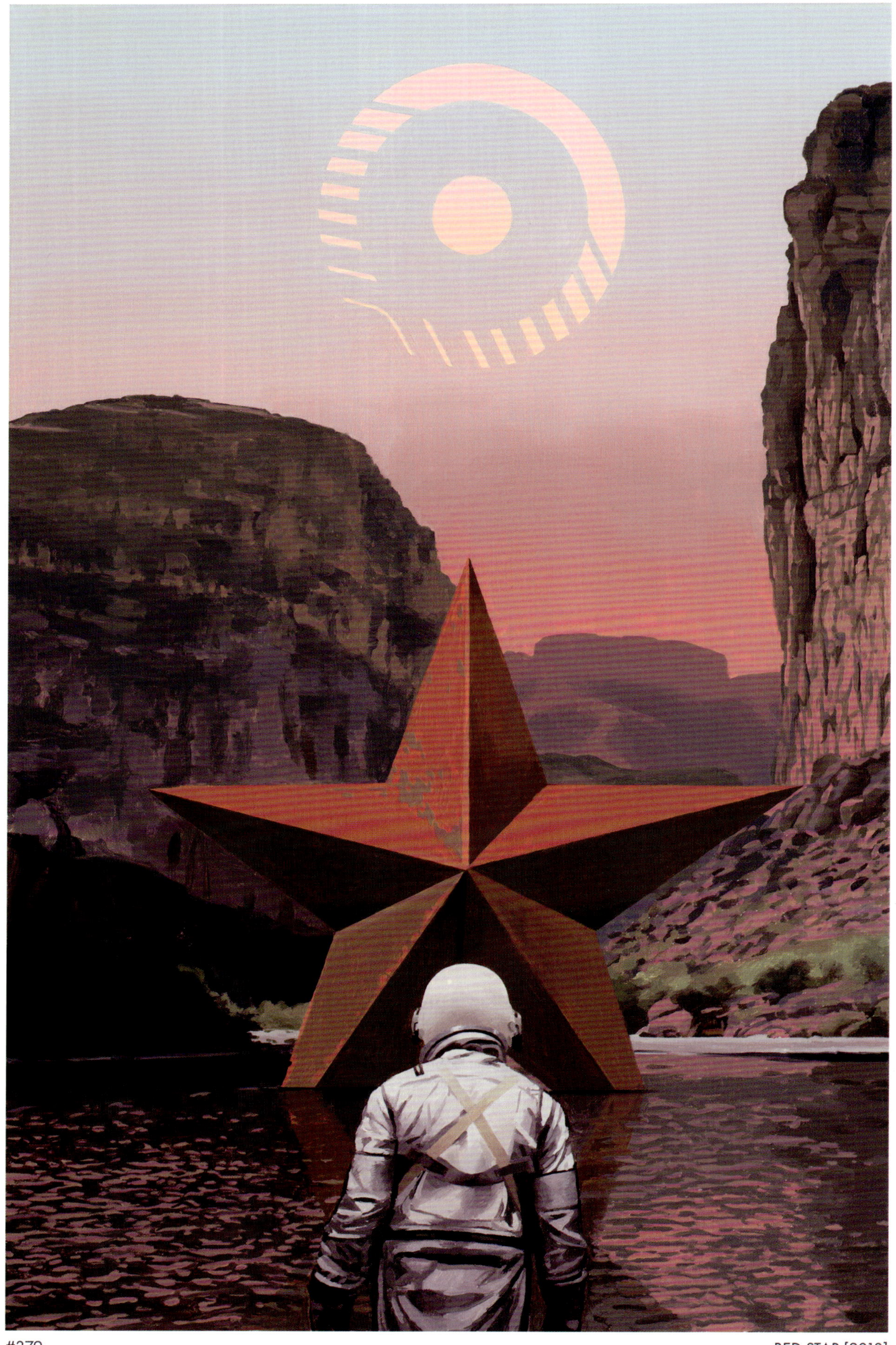

#379

RED STAR [2018]

LONE STAR

//

Preacher Gallery, Austin, TX
May, 2019

This is the first show of new paintings I made since relocating to Los Angeles. Is it the start of something entirely new, or is it very much a continuation of what came before? Kinda yes to both. It was also the first show I had in Texas, and I leaned into it a bit:

I have heard that the stars at night are big and bright, deep in the heart of...well, you know. My paintings are known for the singular astronaut lost in a landscape cluttered with pop culture icons, corporate logos, and tongue-in-cheek science fiction references. In my first large scale show in Texas, at Austin's Preacher Gallery, I wanted to send the astronaut in my work out to explore the vast Texan landscape. The canyons and mountains of Big Bend, the empty roads and dusty train tracks of the expansive interior, the oil wells and longhorns, the stars at night and, of course, "Houston, we have a problem," and everything else that makes Texas, well, Texas. I also found myself inspired by the sculpture of the large bronze star outside the Bullock Texas State History Museum in Austin. It is—extremely literally—a lone star. It became a recurring theme in the work, appearing in riverbeds, on the crests of hills, and far off on the distant horizon. It led me to what is perhaps an obvious title and theme for this show but one I couldn't stop thinking about: *Lone Star*.

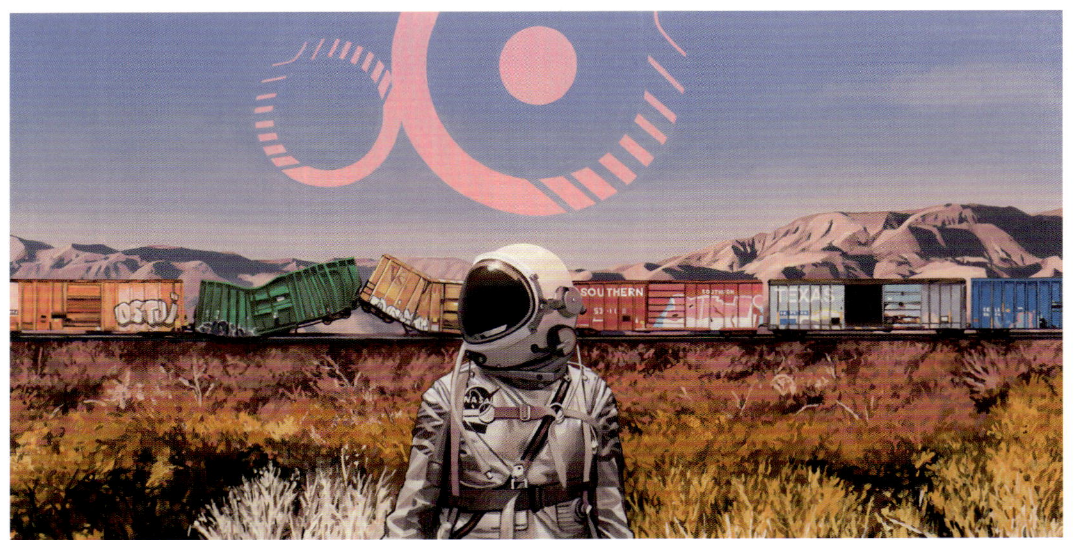

#389 THE RAILROAD [2019]

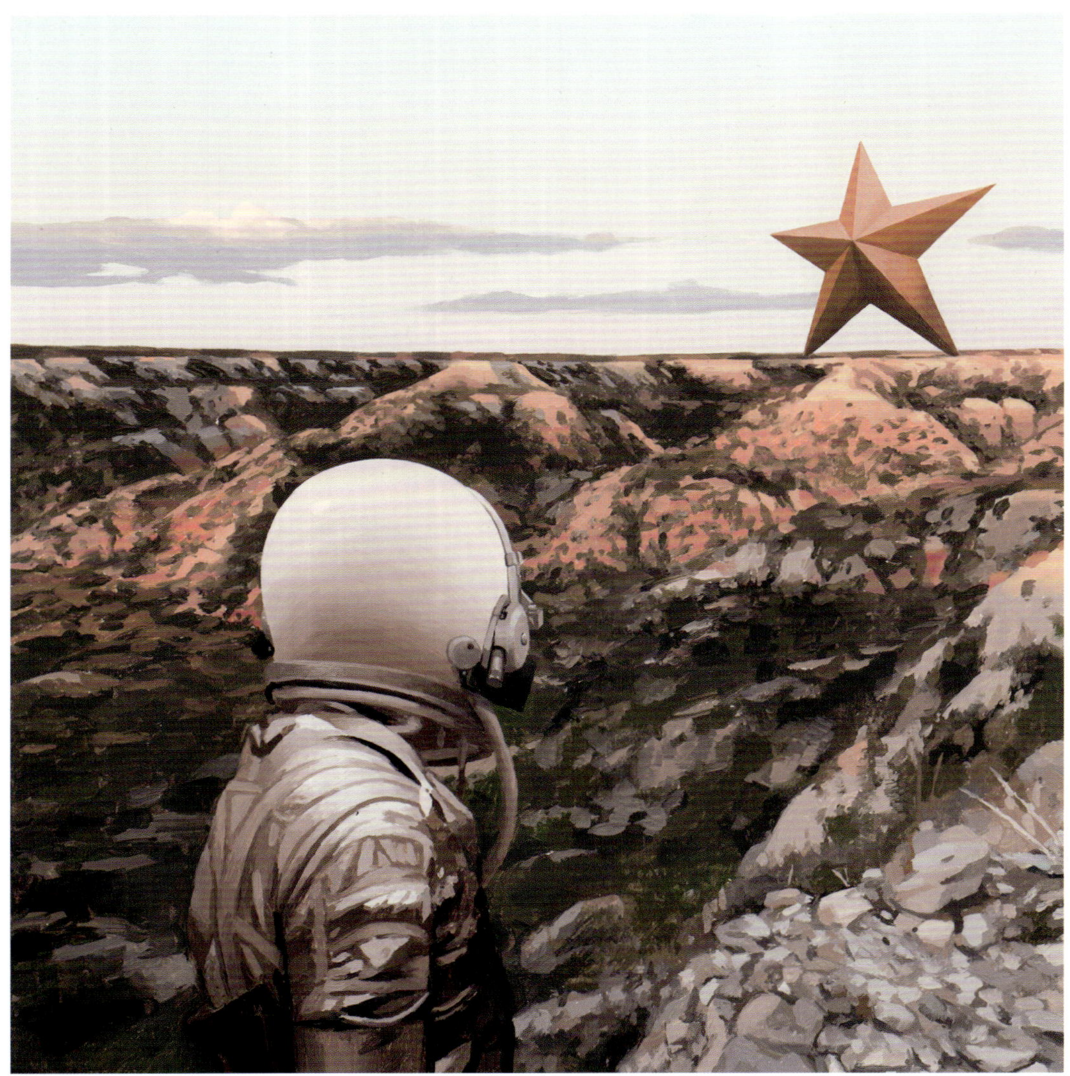

#383 SUNSET STAR [2018]

#395
LONGHORNS [2019]

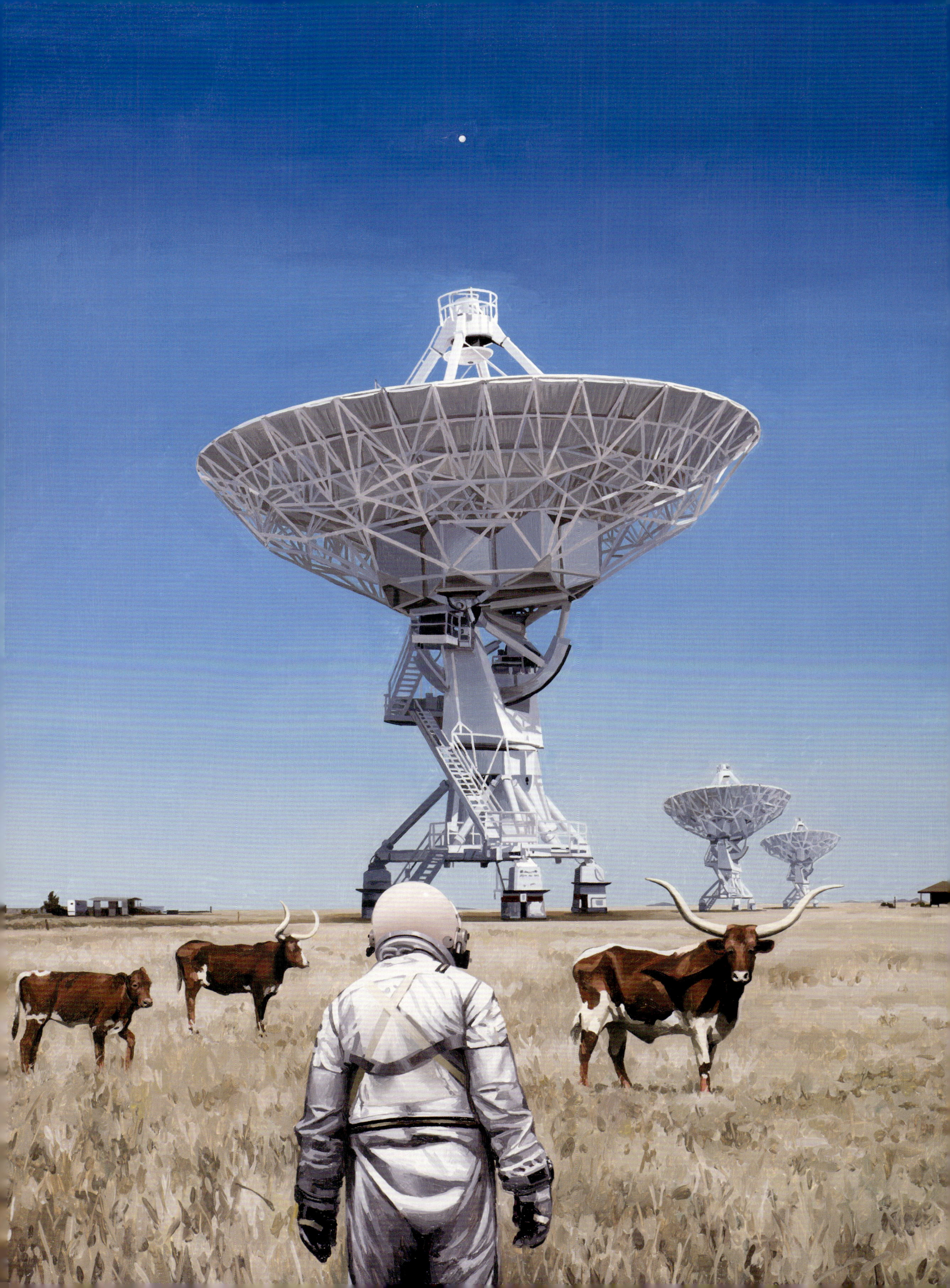

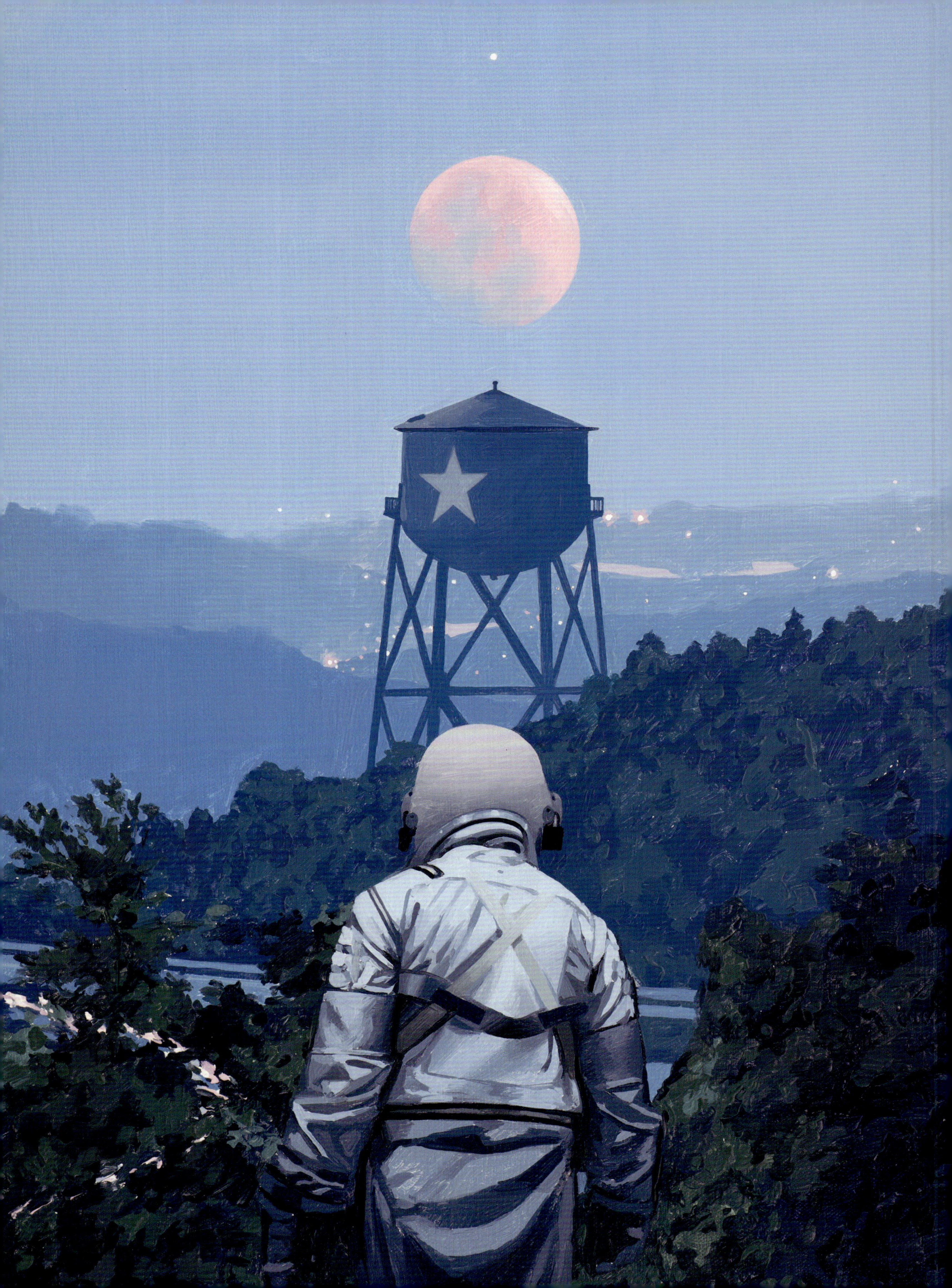

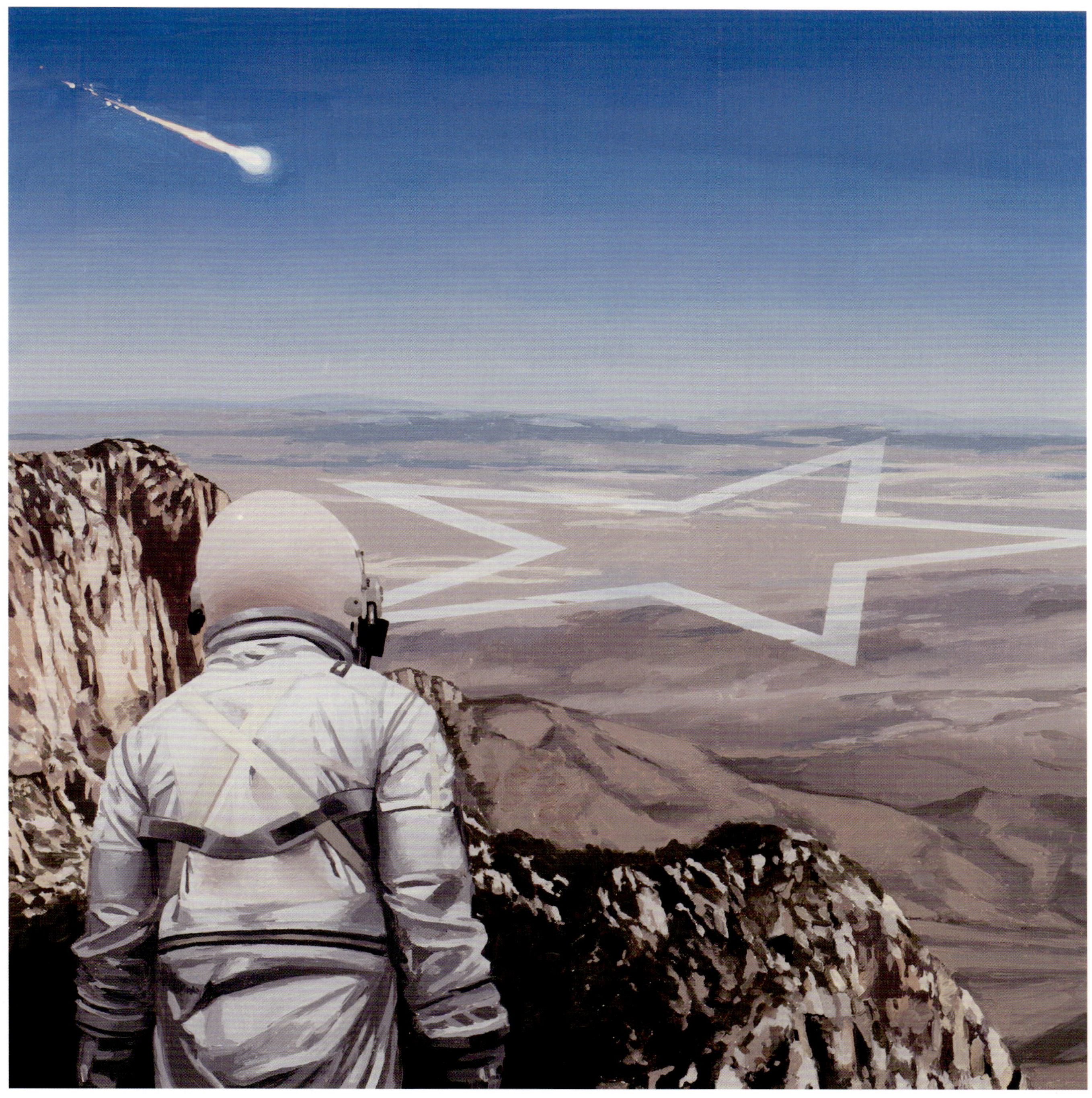

#385

SHOOTING STAR [2018]

#387

PINK MOON [2019]

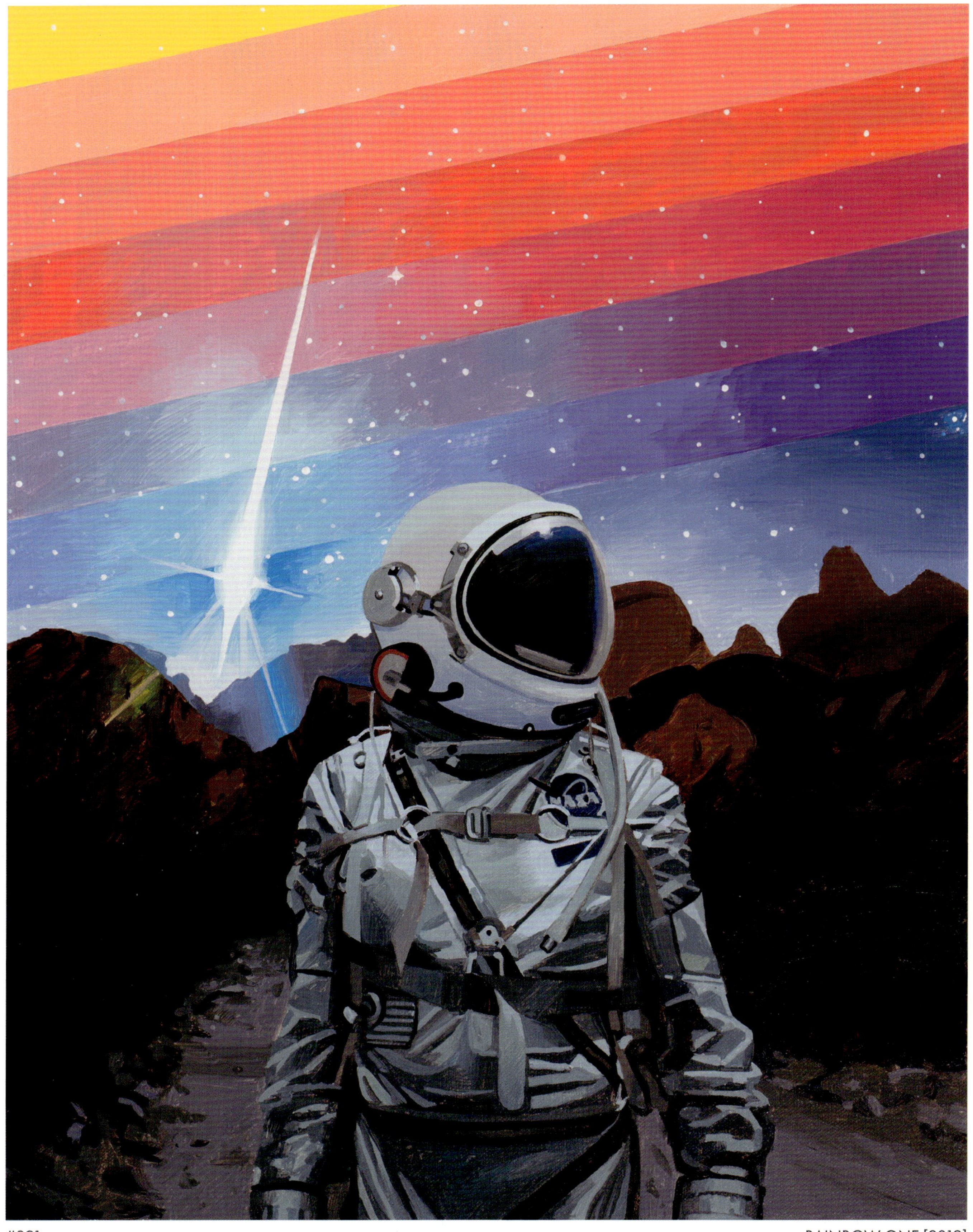

#391

RAINBOW ONE [2019]

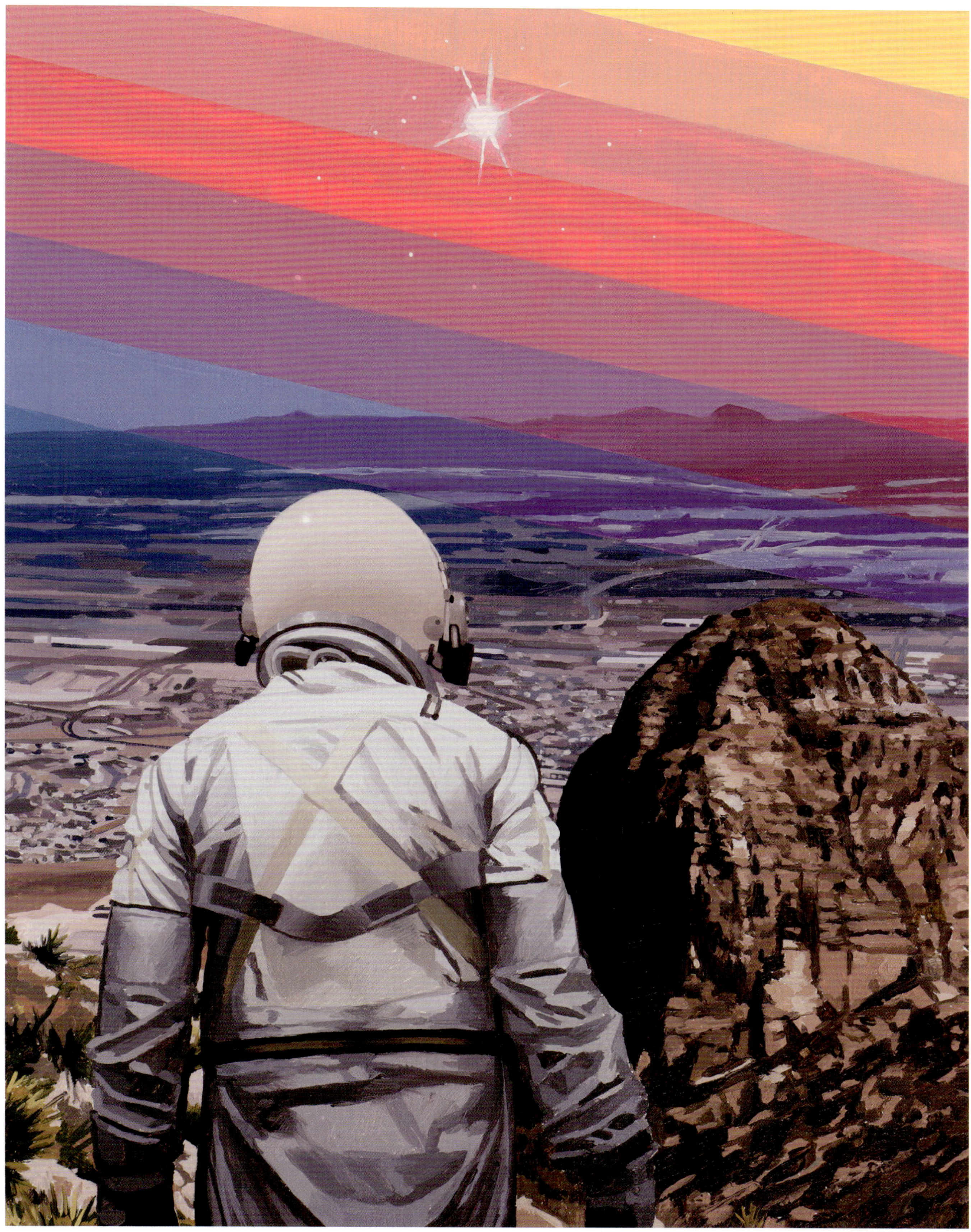

#392

RAINBOW TWO [2019]

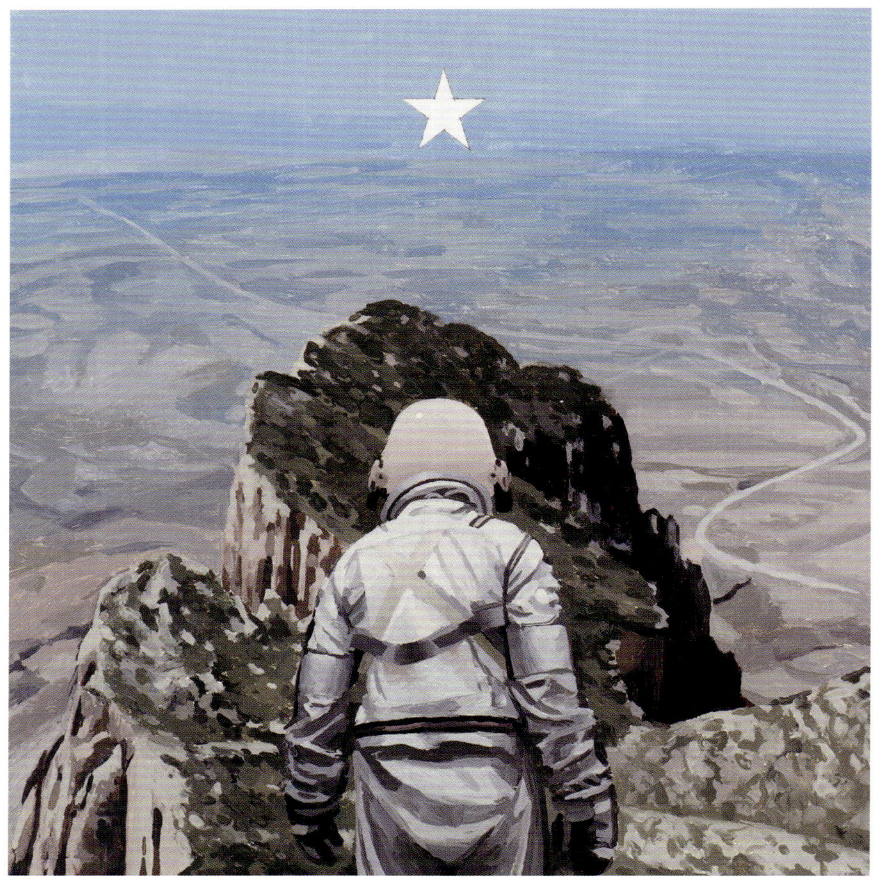

#394 CLIFF STAR [2019]

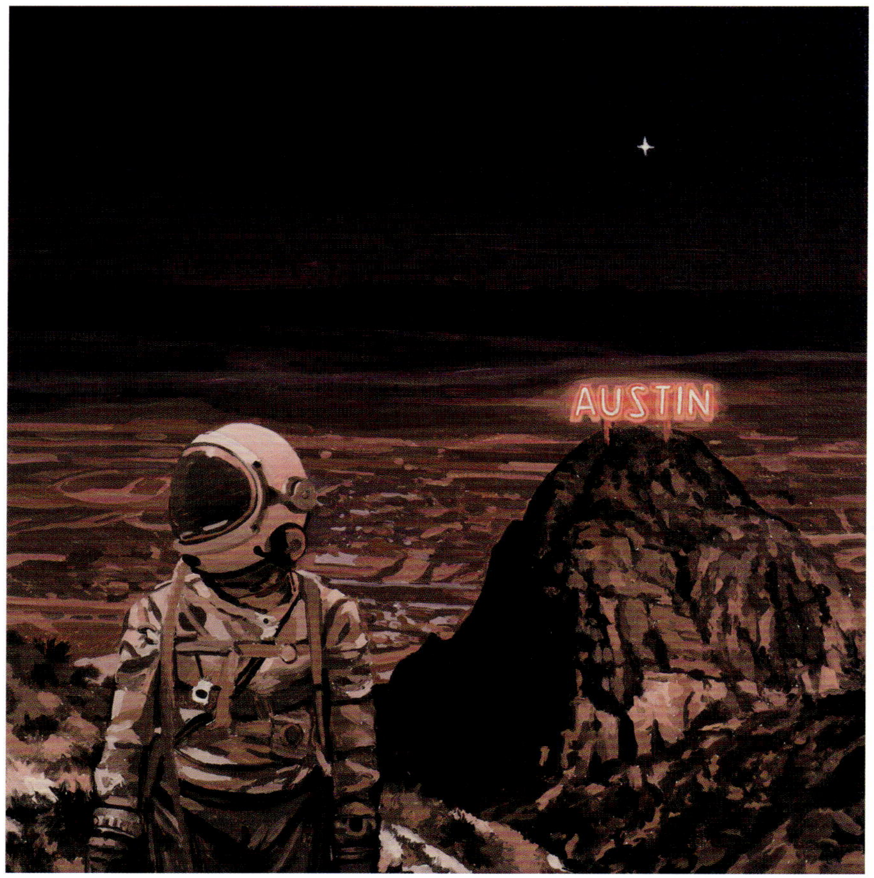

#390 AUSTIN [2019]

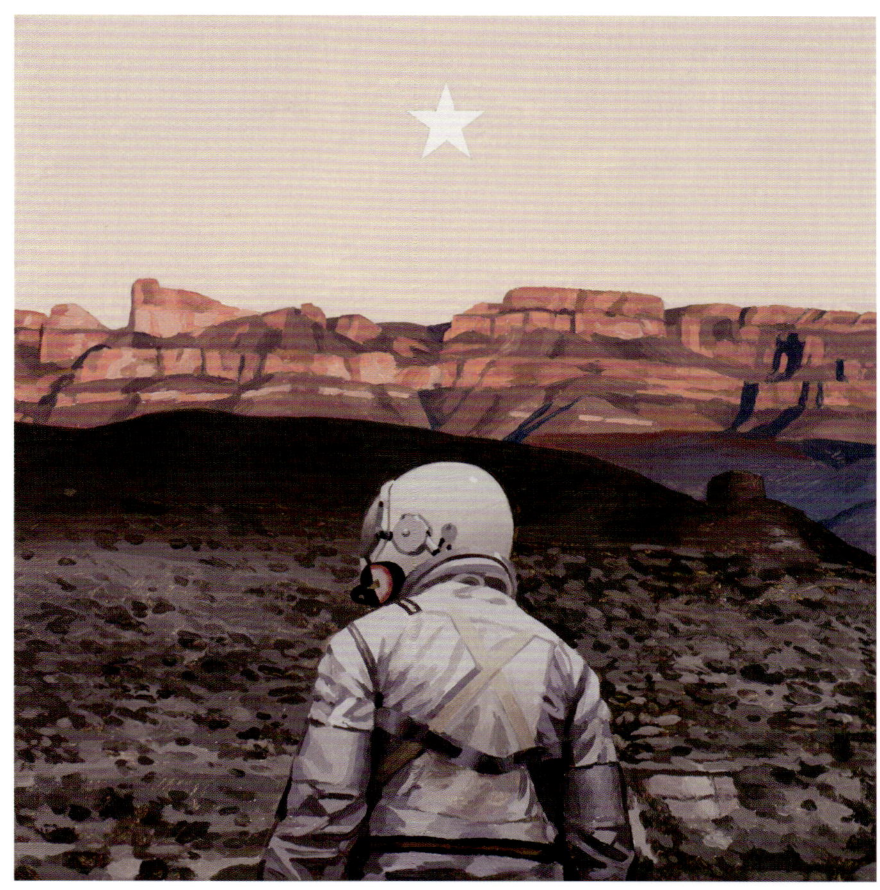

#397 PINK CANYON [2019]

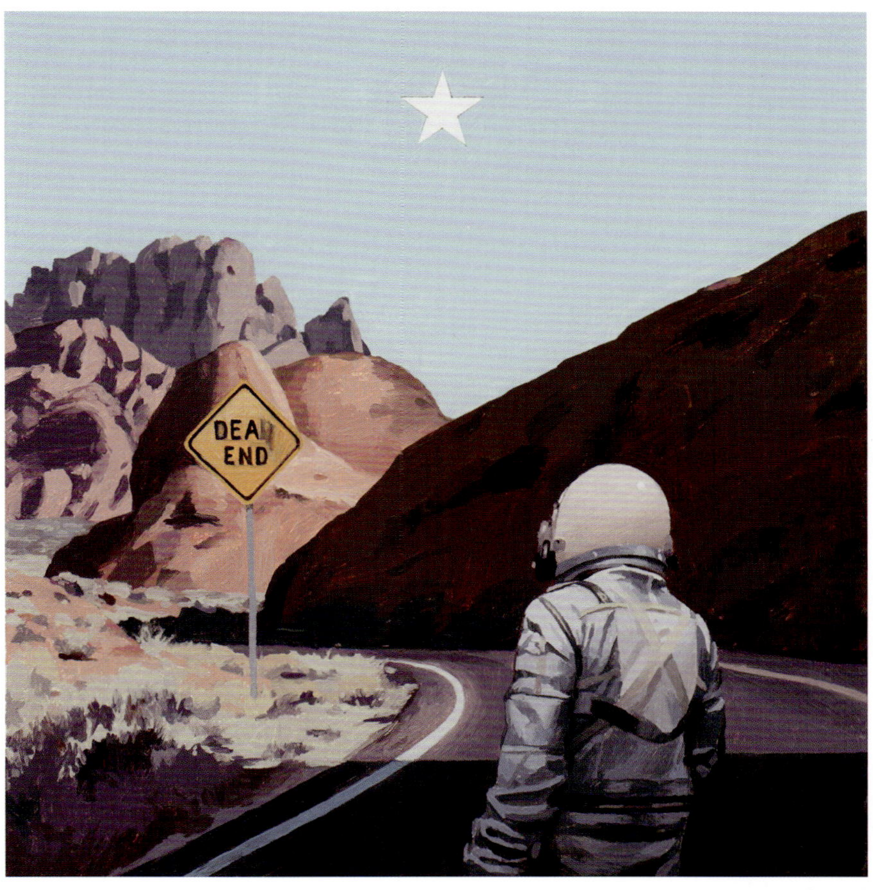

#396 DEAD END [2019]

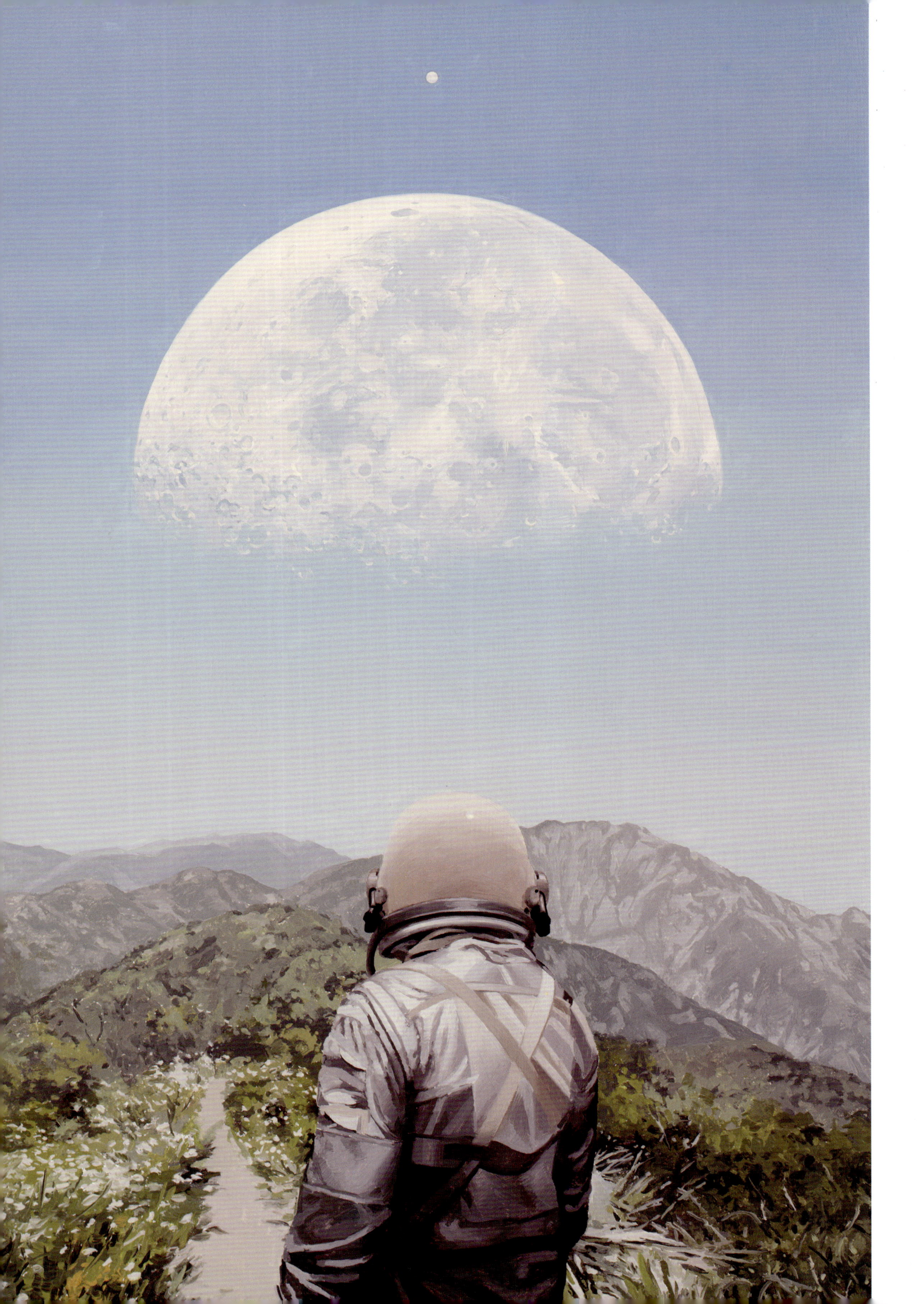

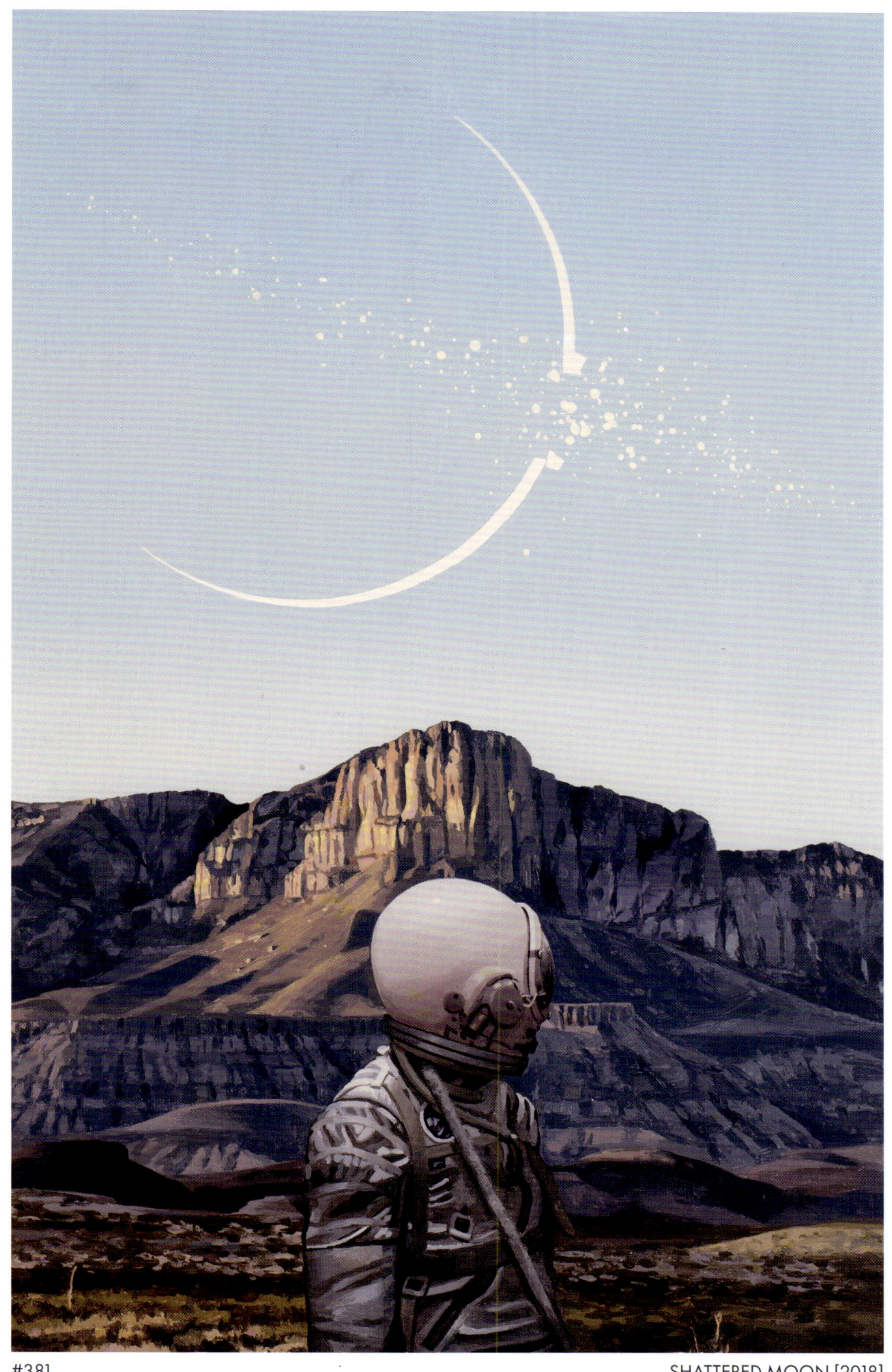

#381 SHATTERED MOON [2018]

#380
WHITE MOON [2018]

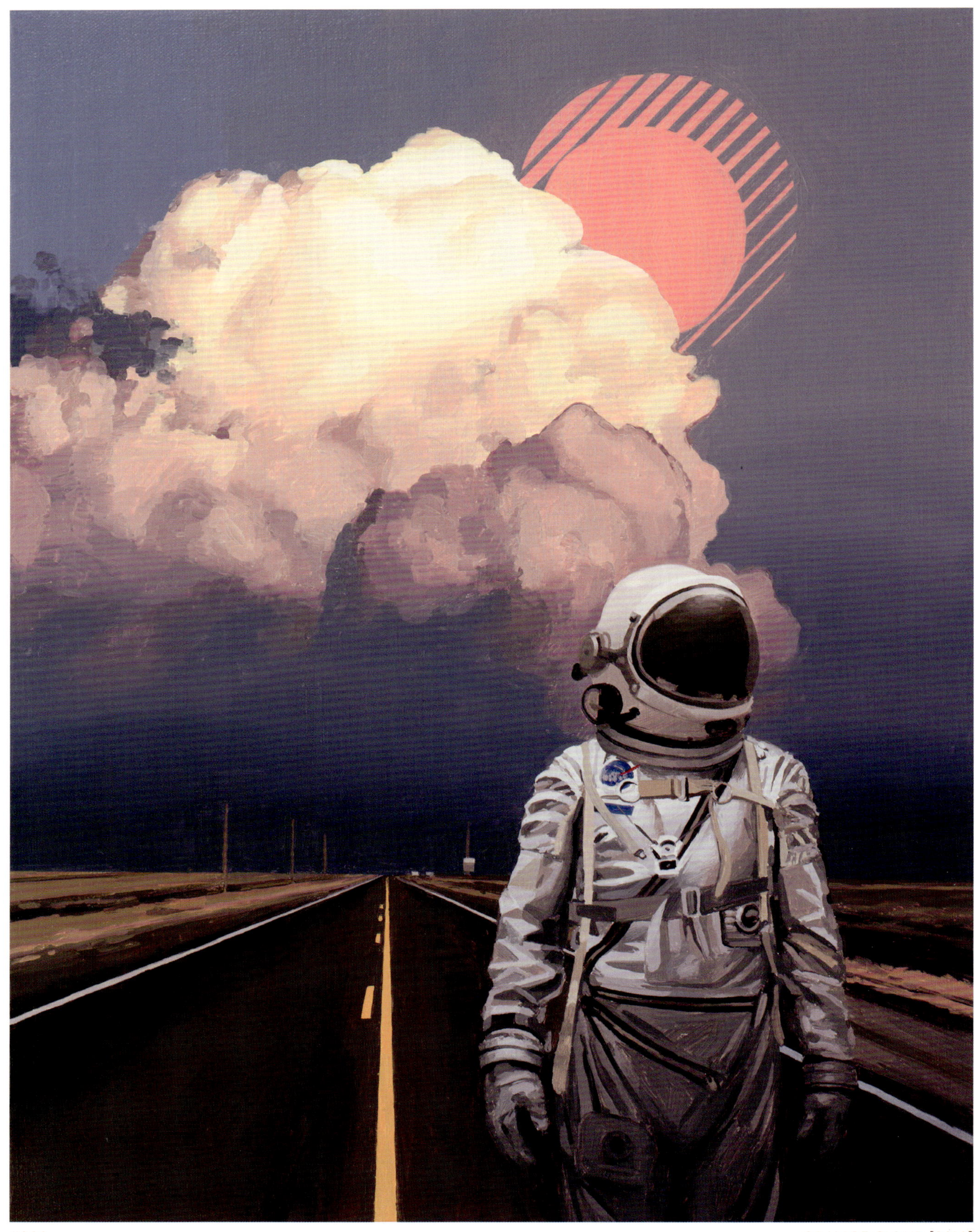

#388 ORANGE CLOUD [2019]

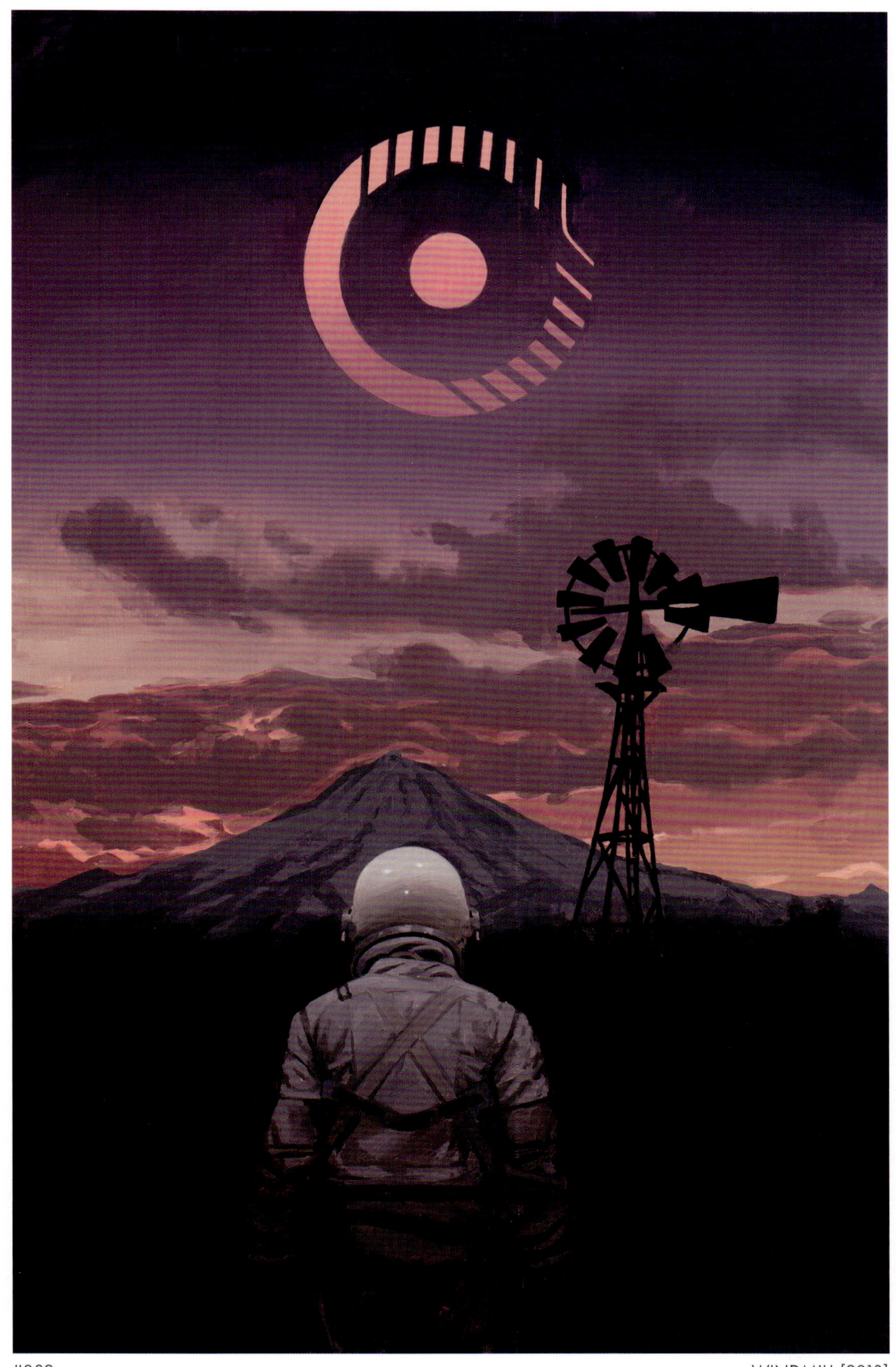

#382 WINDMILL [2018]

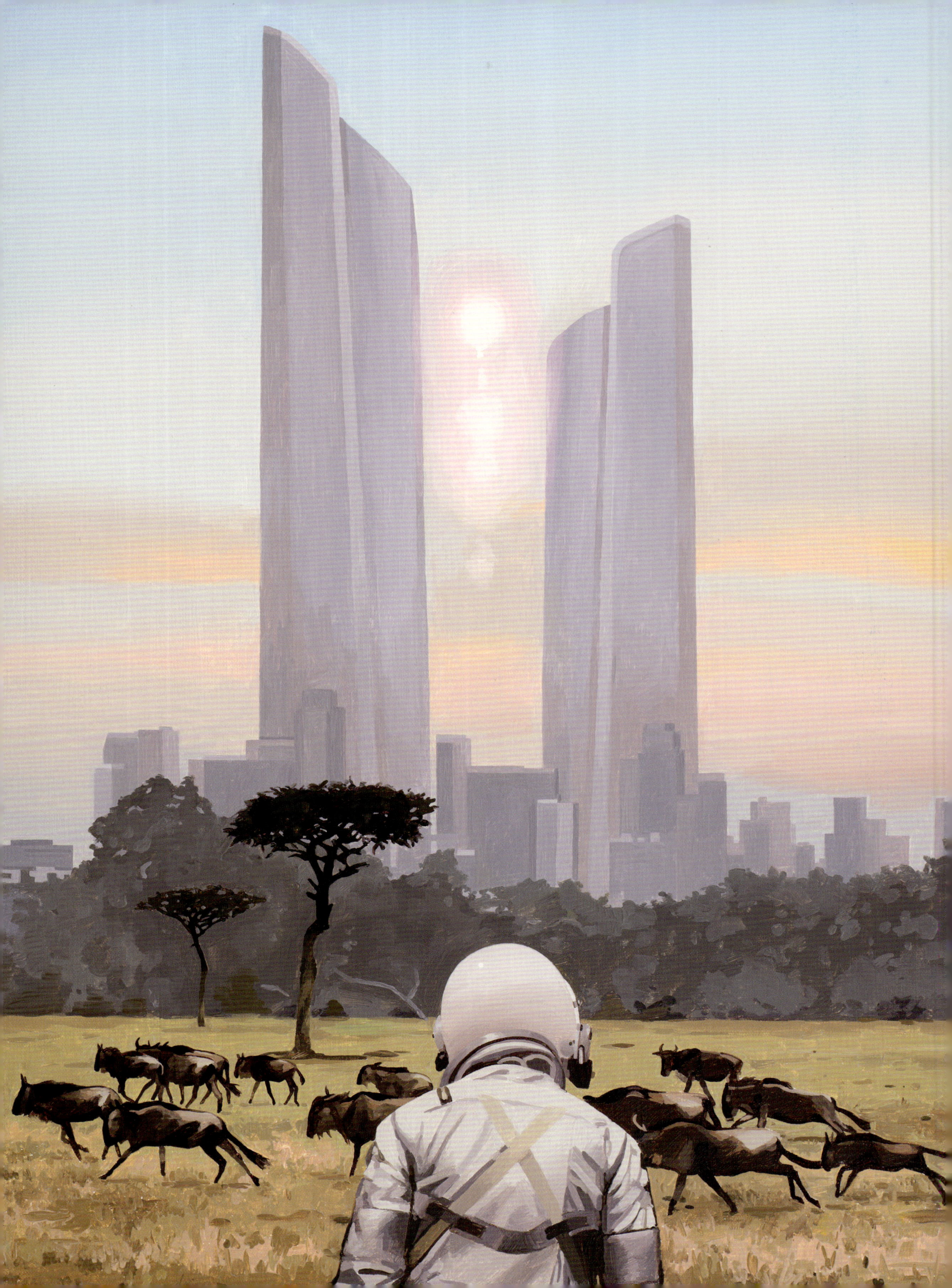

RE-ENTRY

//

Antler Gallery, Portland, OR
April, 2019

When I show with Antler Gallery, I often paint animal or nature themes. For this show, I had just relocated to Los Angeles and I was thinking about the effect that new environment had on my view of the world. I was suddenly in a much larger city, a sprawling place where I didn't know where I was going most of the time. I felt excited, sure, but also very lost and disconnected. I started to paint some of the places I had walked by or driven past. A landscape that was alternately dusty or flooded, representing the particularly wet winter in LA that year. The animals in these paintings all seem to have made a home for themselves in this unusual environment, perched on cars or running under overpasses. They, not coincidentally, seem a lot more comfortable here than the astronaut. After all, nature adapts. Humans? We have to do a bit of molding the landscape around us to fit our needs instead.

#407
WILDEBEEST [2019]

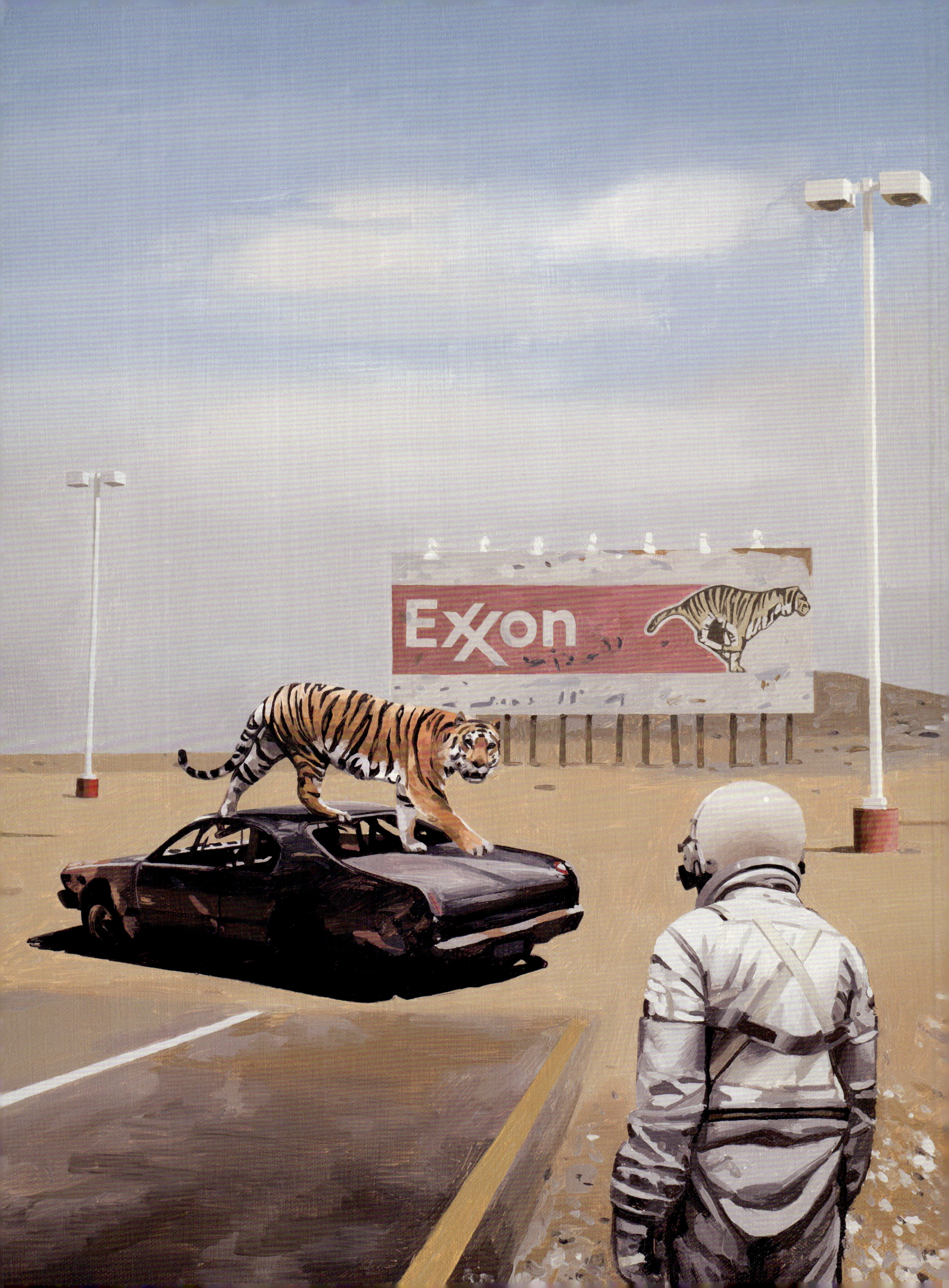
Exxon

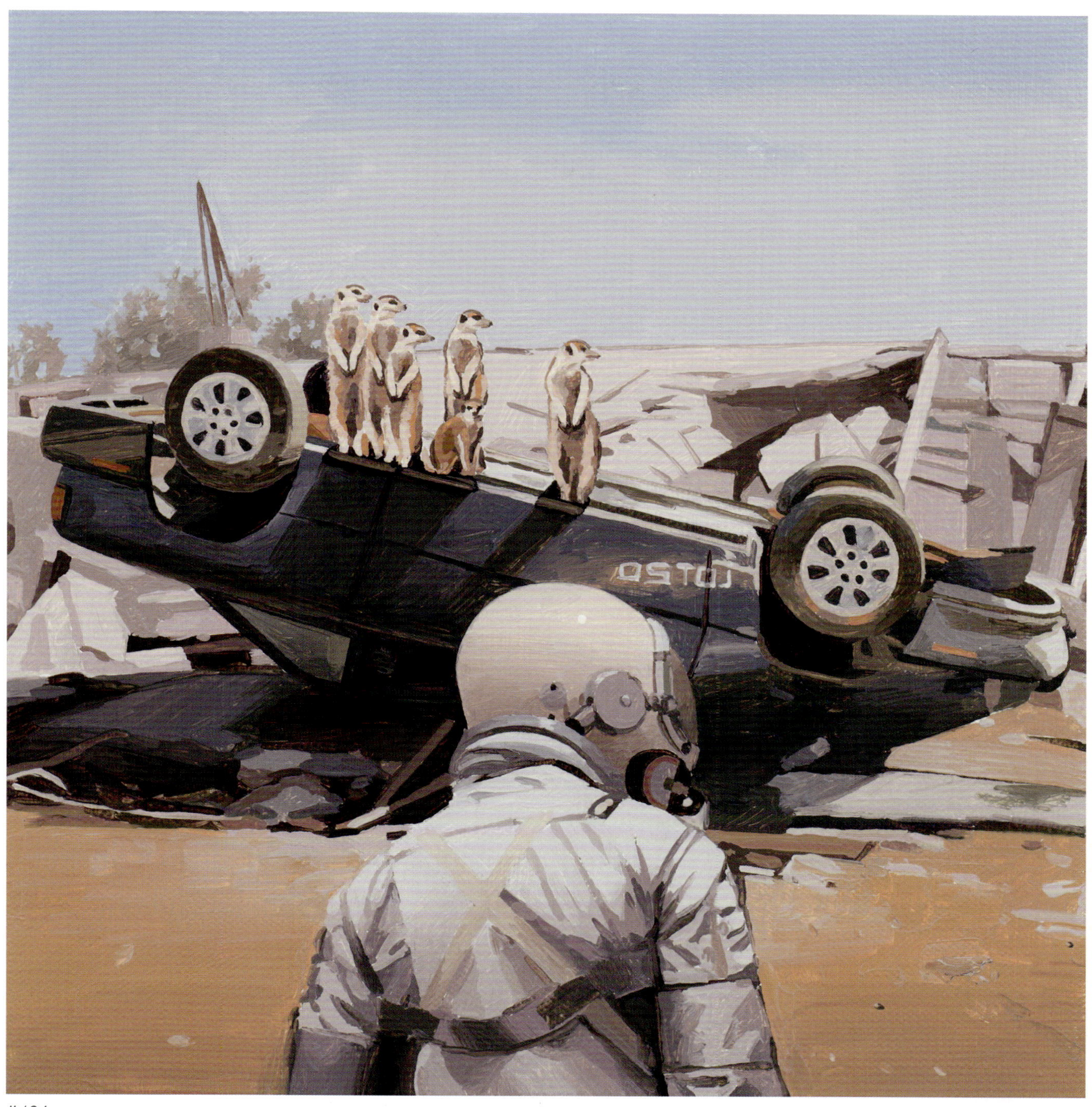

#406

MEERKATS [2019]

#405

TIGER [2019]

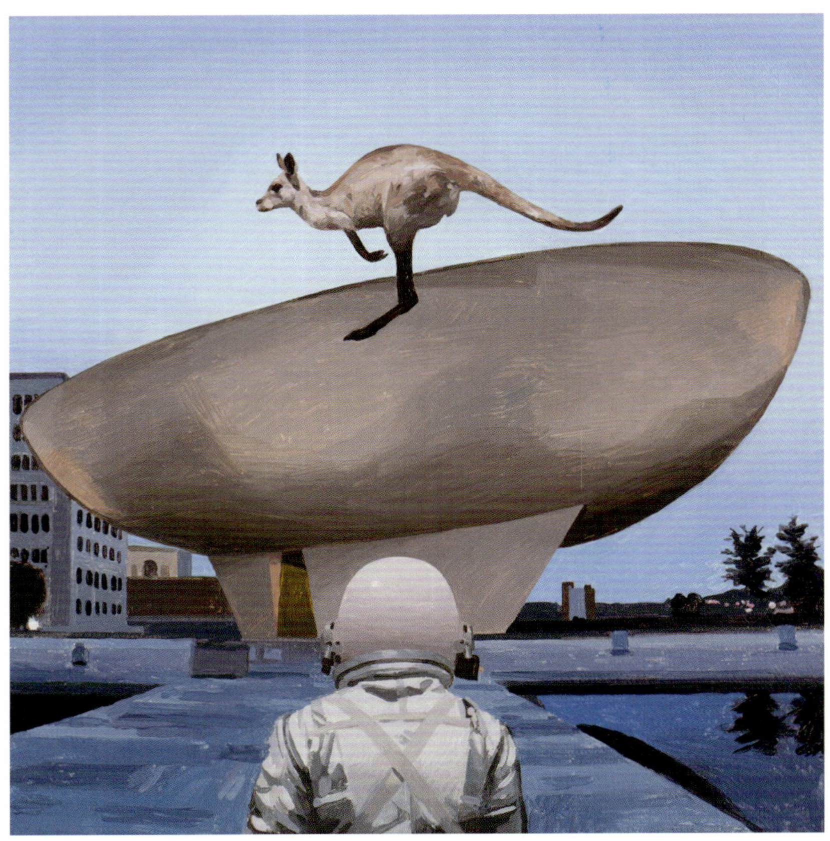

#409 KANGAROO [2019]

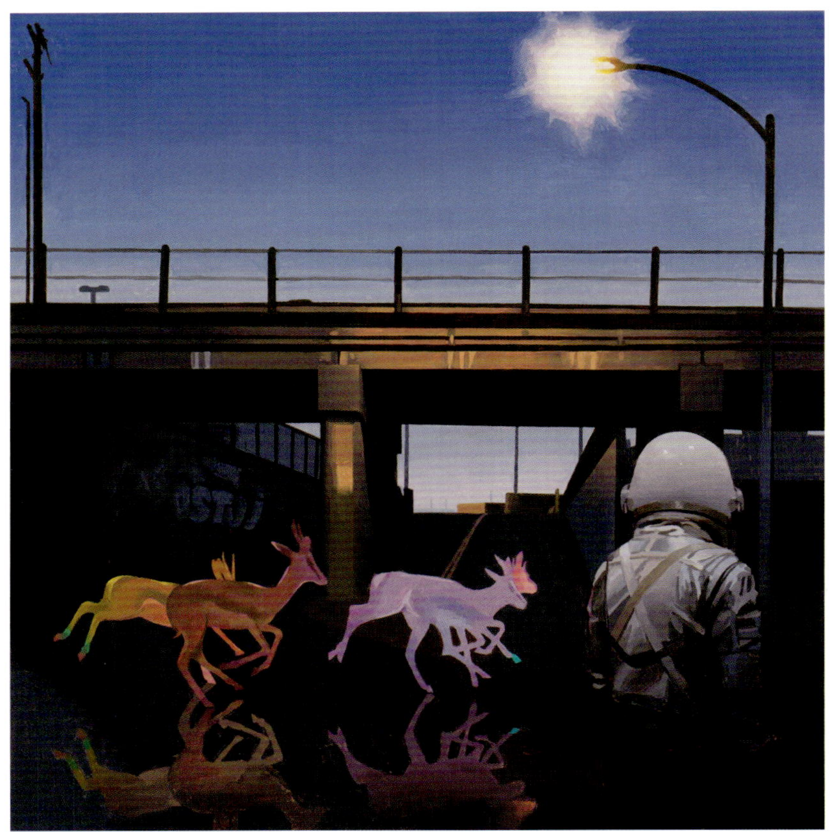

#404 DEER [2019]

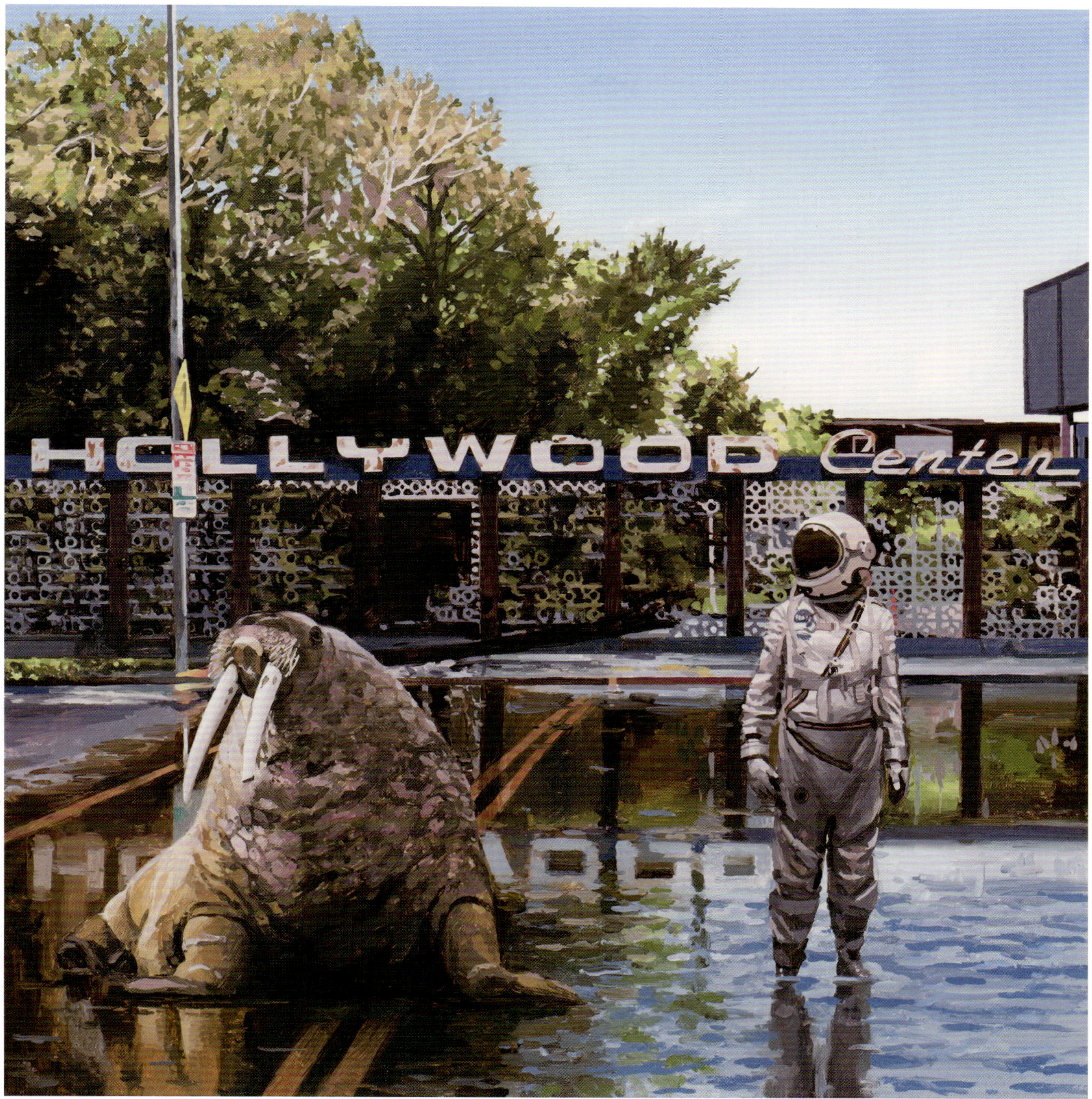

#408

WALRUS [2019]

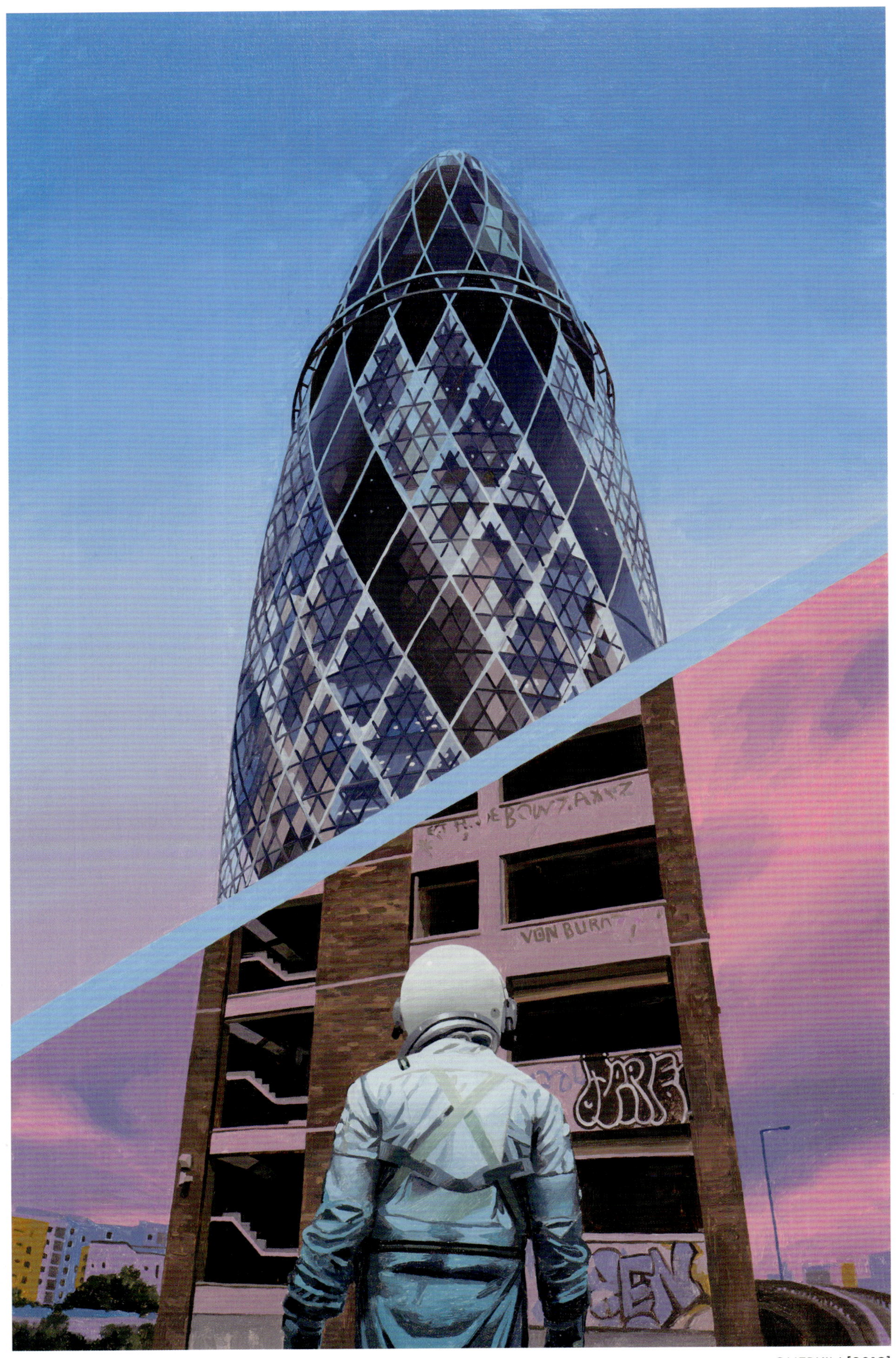

#414

GHERKIN [2019]

DIVIDE: AN ASTRONAUT STORY

//

StolenSpace Gallery, London, UK
June, 2019

In my previous show at StolenSpace Gallery in London, I created a series of paintings where the astronaut in my work explored a lost or parallel London from the '90s. The show was about London's past, it's present, and about my two decade old love affair with British music and culture from that time. And then, right after that show wrapped, Brexit happened.

Of course, I'm an American and am pretty ill-equipped to make intelligent statements on anything that has been going on in UK politics. And so, for my second show at StolenSpace Gallery, I didn't want to make a show that was literally about Brexit. But it all feels eerily similar to political and cultural movements that have recently been dividing people here in the US, and in many other places around the world. And the more I thought about it, it was that divide, the one between regular people and those in power, the left and right, the old and young, the extremely wealthy and everybody else, the skewing of what's real and fake—it was those things which I couldn't stop thinking about. It feels like we're all teetering on the edge of a great divide, with everyone fearful of both the present and the future.

And so I created a series of paintings split in half with a hard line, where two separate worlds appear to be connecting or disconnecting, and I've used the landscape and architecture of modern London as a kind of language between those two worlds. The lone, singular astronaut who appears in each of my paintings explores this fractured place. Sometimes slipping between the two and sometimes stuck in one half, able to see both partitions but unable to make sense of the two halves together.

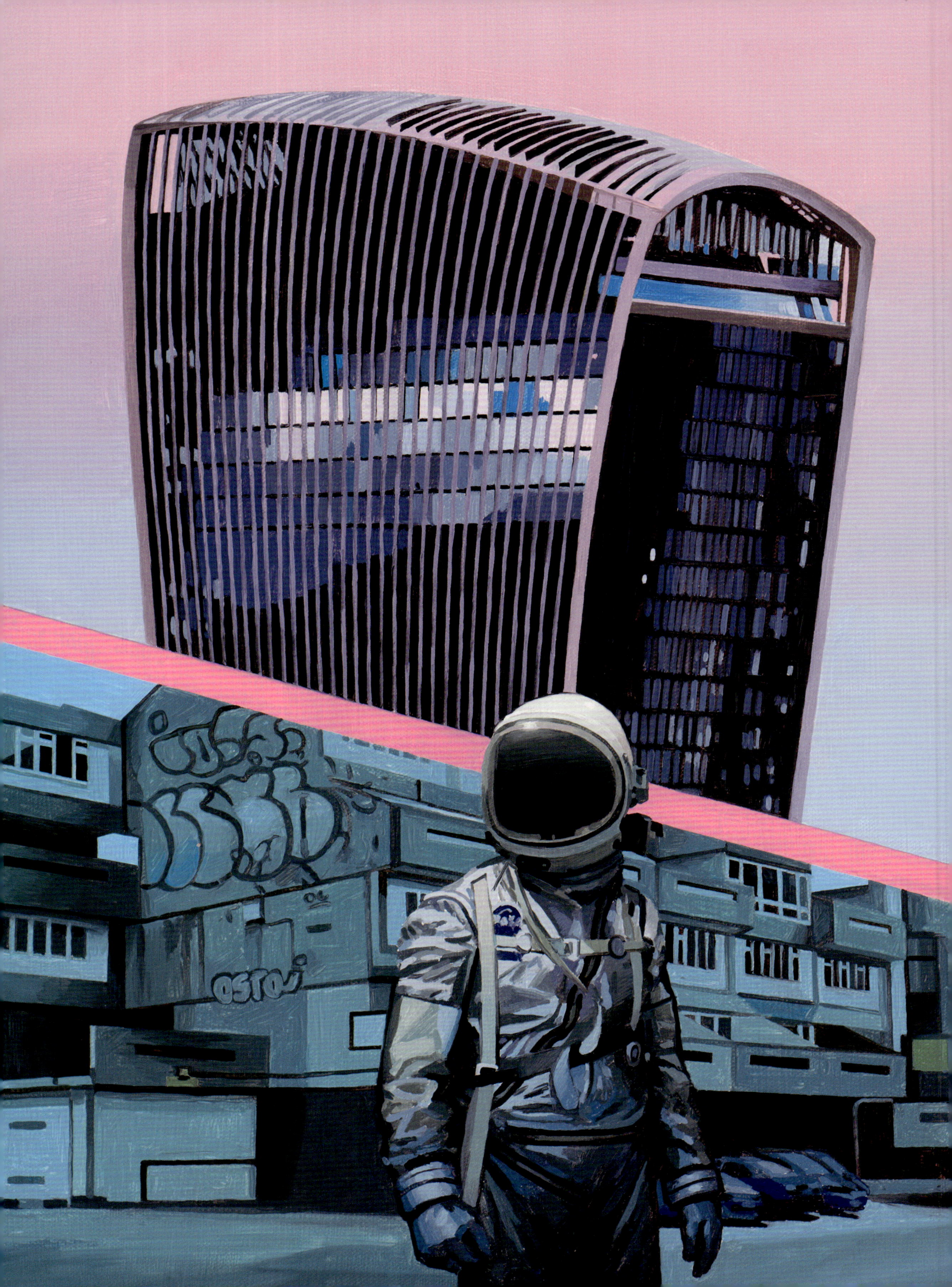

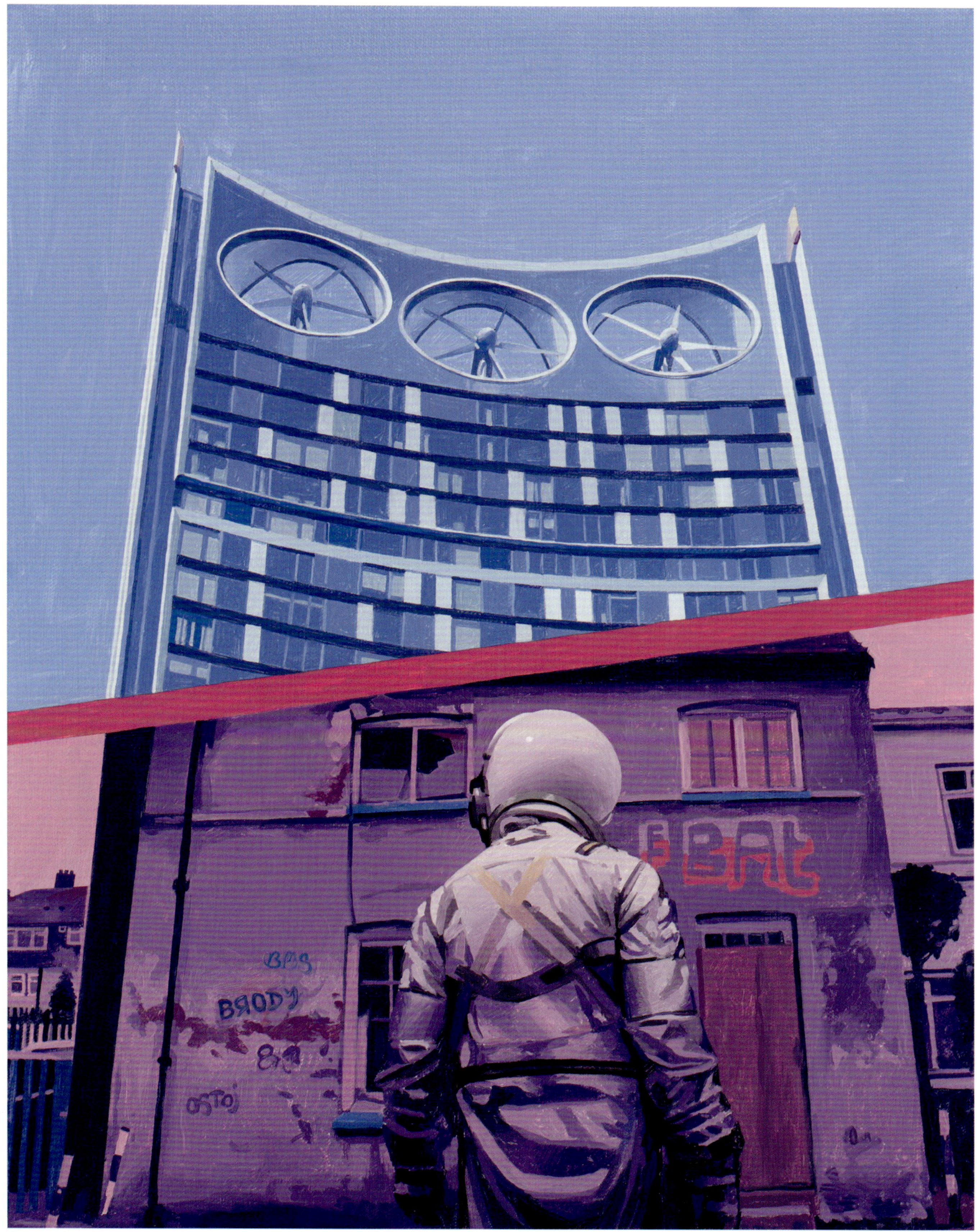

#417

RAZOR [2019]

#413

WALKIE TALKIE [2019]

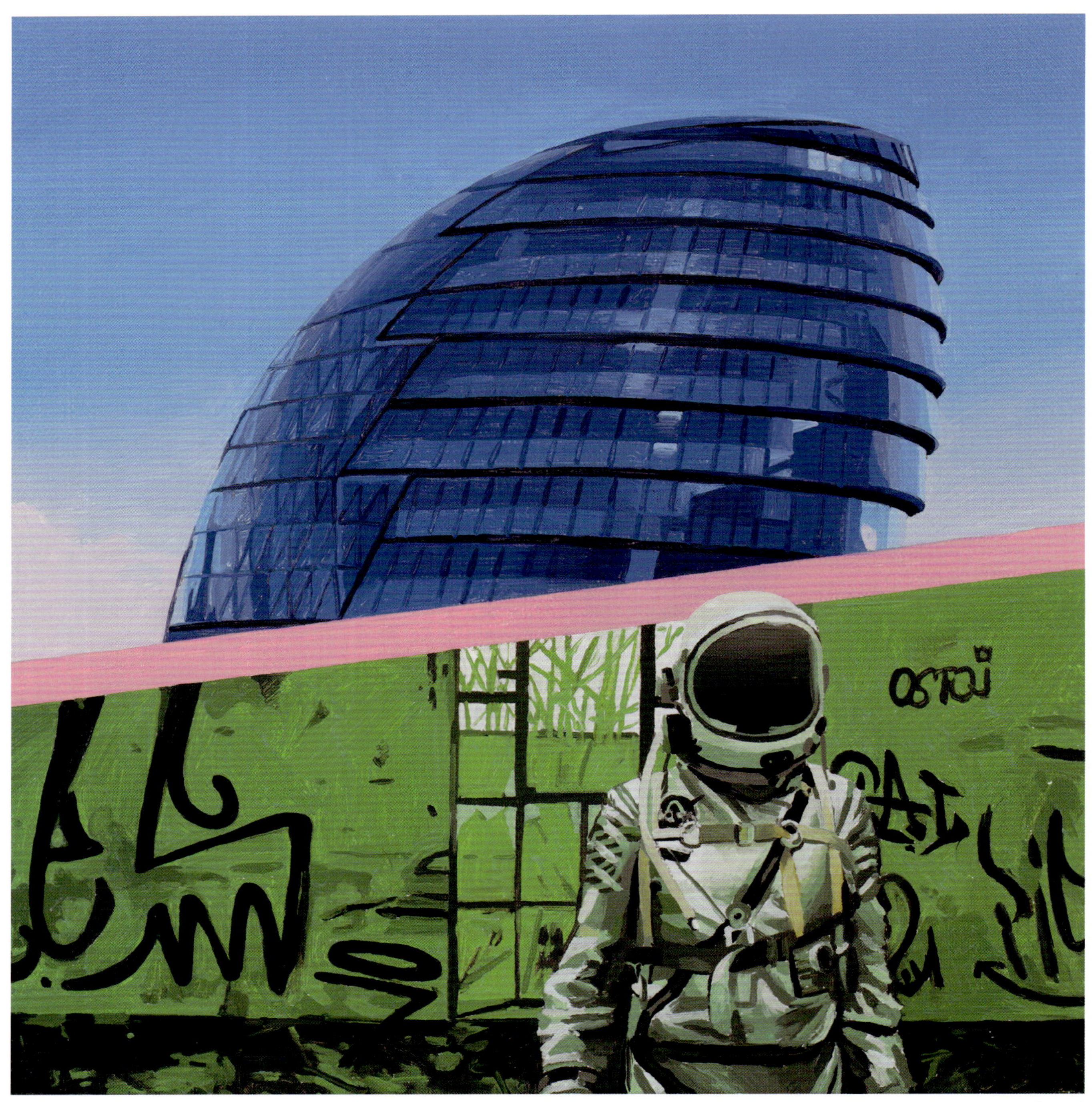

#418 THE SNAIL [2019]

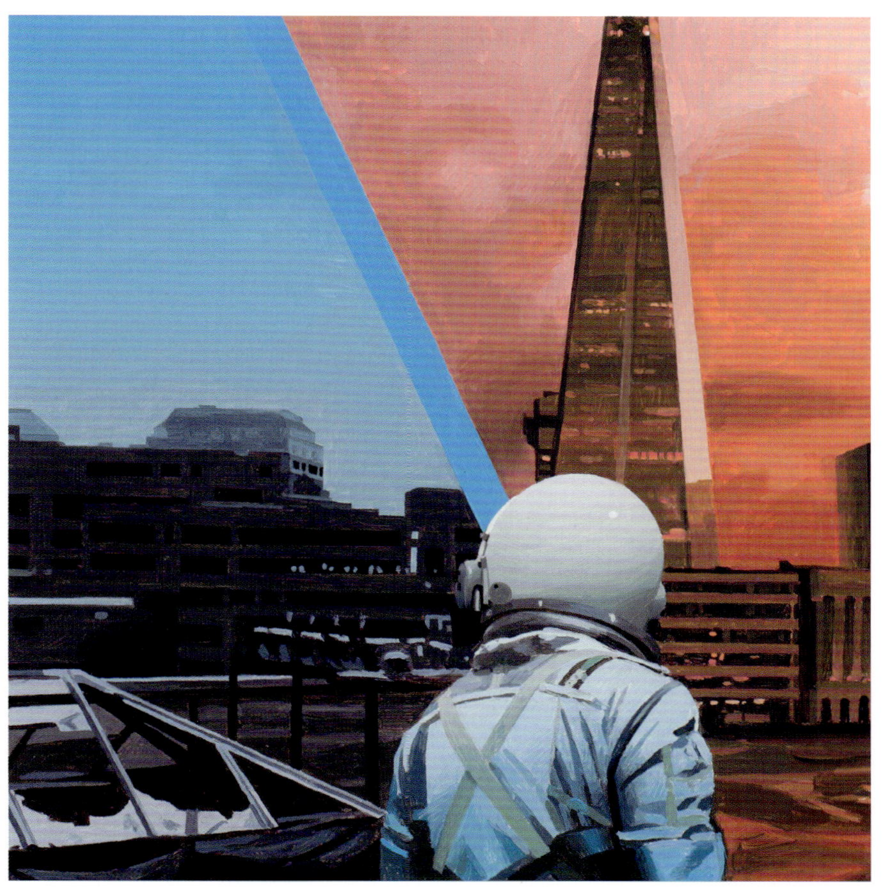

#416 SHARD [2019]

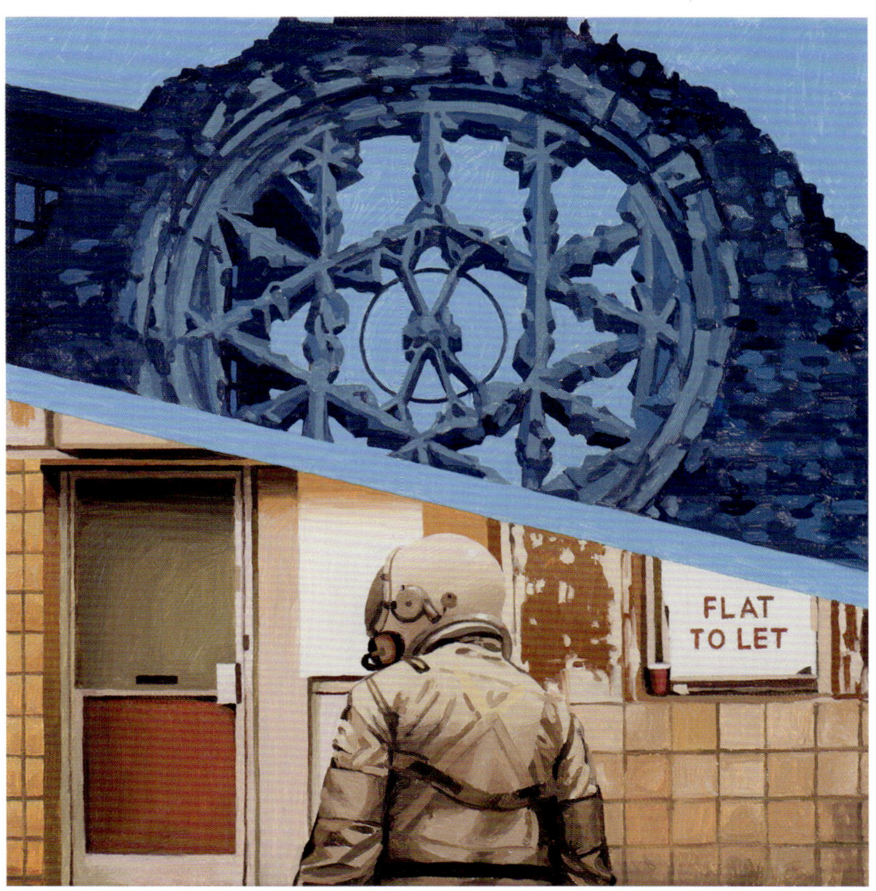

#415 WINCHESTER PALACE [2019]

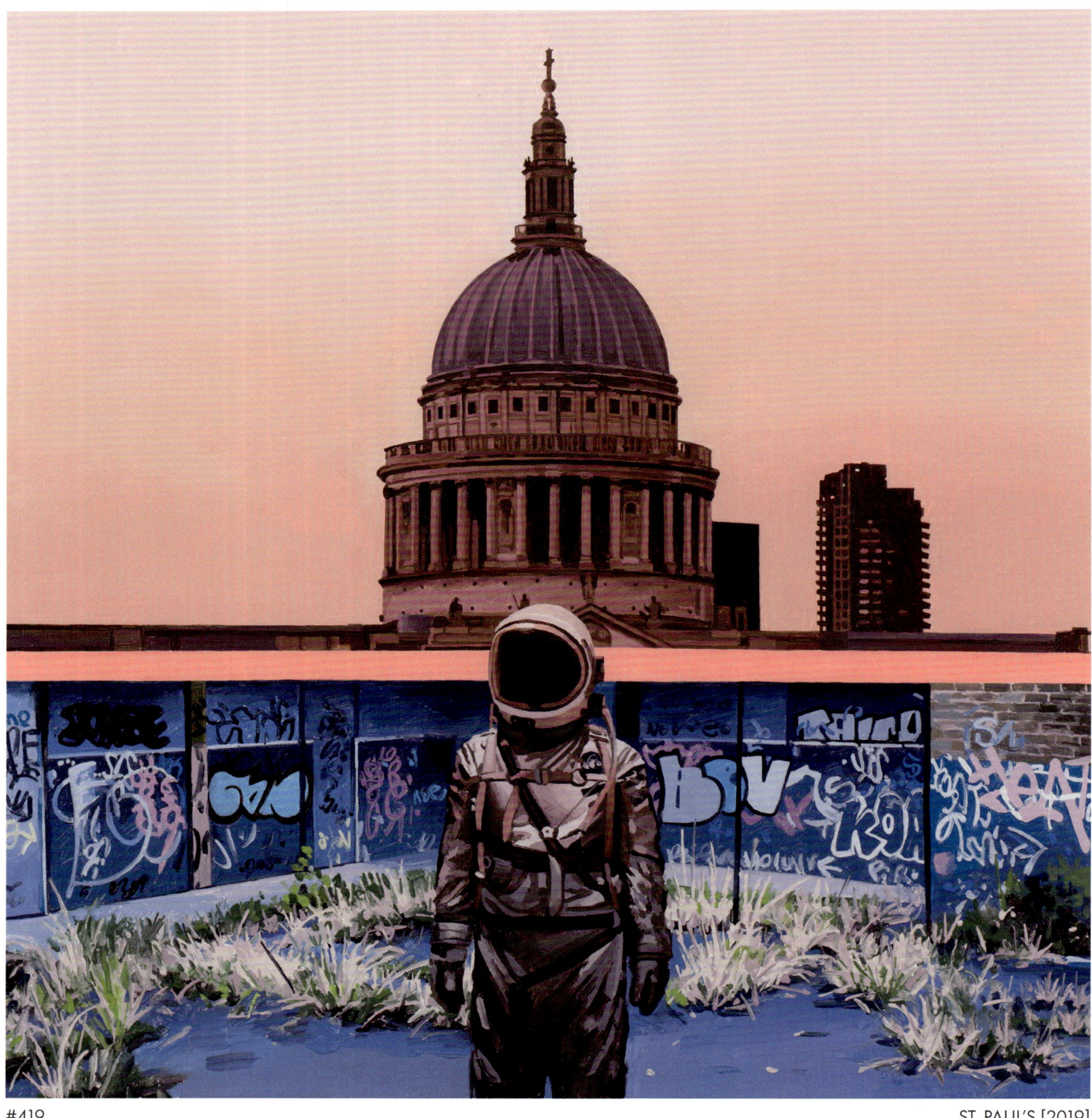

#419

ST. PAUL'S [2019]

#420

THE SCALPEL [2019]

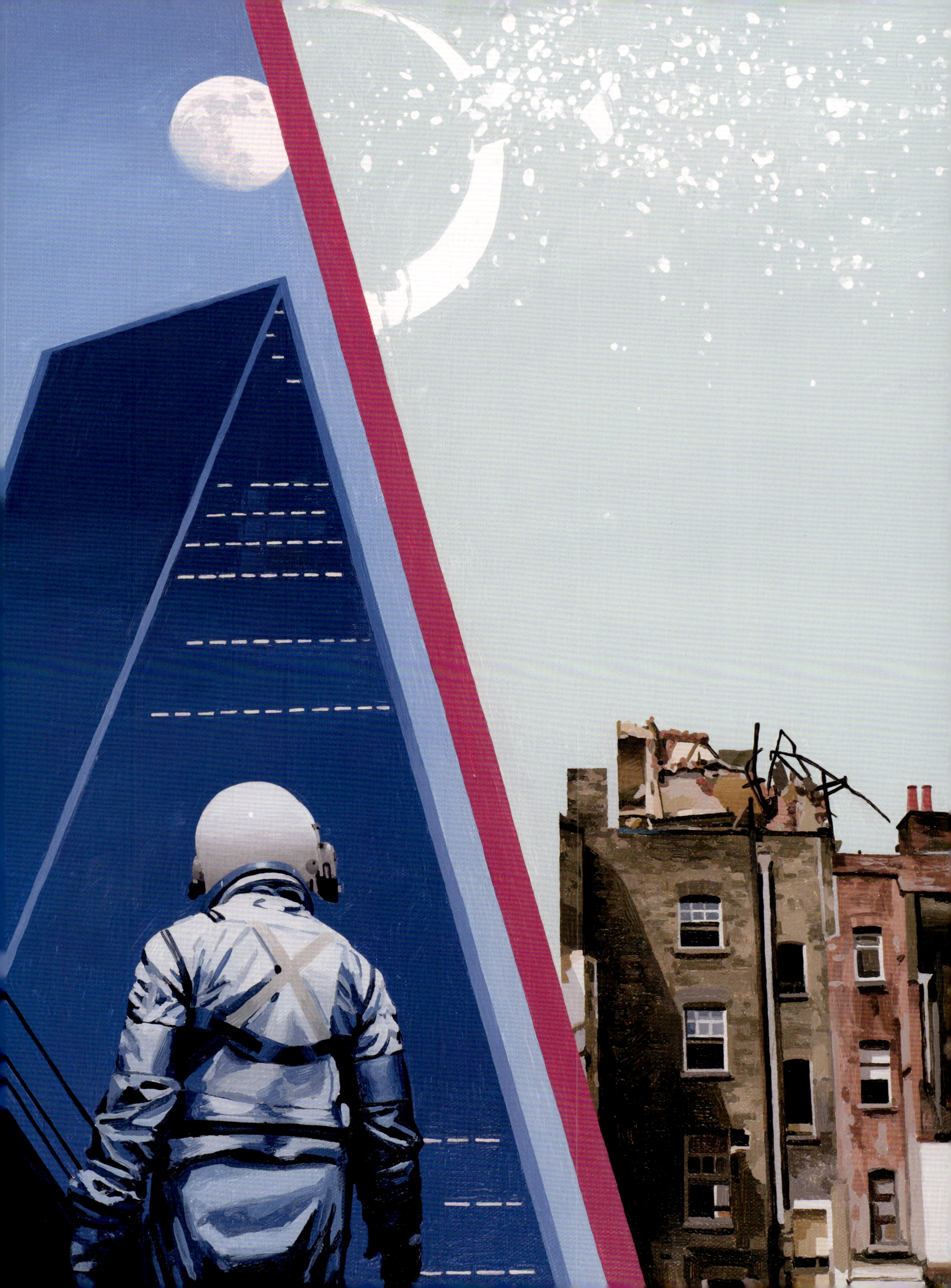

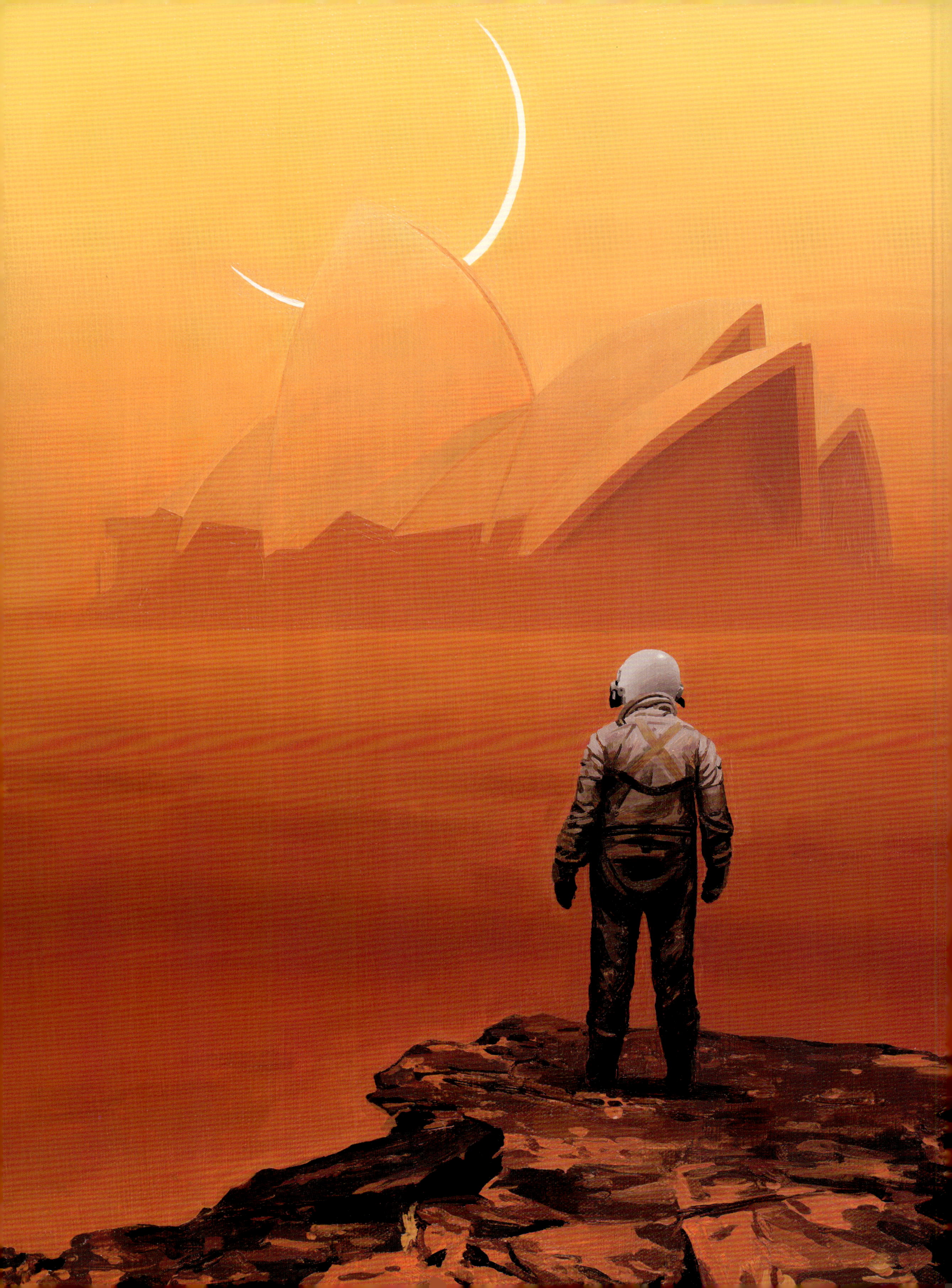

FURY ROAD

Beinart Gallery, Melbourne, Australia
October, 2019

A very long time ago I graduated from college. Three days later I hopped a plane to Sydney. I wanted to very literally get as far away as I could from the small town I went to school in. I had a place to stay but pretty much no plan what to do with my life, and I ended up spending a lot of my time in Australia wandering alone in an unfamiliar country where I barely knew a soul. I explored. I took some classes. I took a very long bus trip to Melbourne. I painted a few exceedingly mediocre landscapes. I was 21 years old and had no idea what the next chapter in my life might look like. It was a brief and strange pause between childhood and adulthood that I knew would not last long. Eventually I went back home.

A lot of my experiences from this time ended up inspiring my very first astronaut paintings. Upon returning home from Australia, I still felt like a stranger, an explorer, an alien. I've been painting astronauts now for a while but those feelings still inspire me today.

And so, for my first solo show in Australia I wanted to make paintings about a very wild and beautiful place. But, like the astronaut in my work, I'm not from there. And so I made a series of paintings for my show at Beinart Gallery in Melbourne, which all take place in a desert continent where everywhere there are signs of a civilization that has been left to rot and rust away. Cars, boats, and buildings turning to dust. There are animals here, still, but they seem out of place and, perhaps, out of time. Polar bears and humpback whales left in places they never should have been. The last remnants of a coral reef, trapped like long extinct creatures in amber.

Wandering amidst it all is the astronaut from my paintings. Following what used to be roads and river ways but are now just dry and dusty paths to nowhere.

#425
DESERT OPERA [2019]

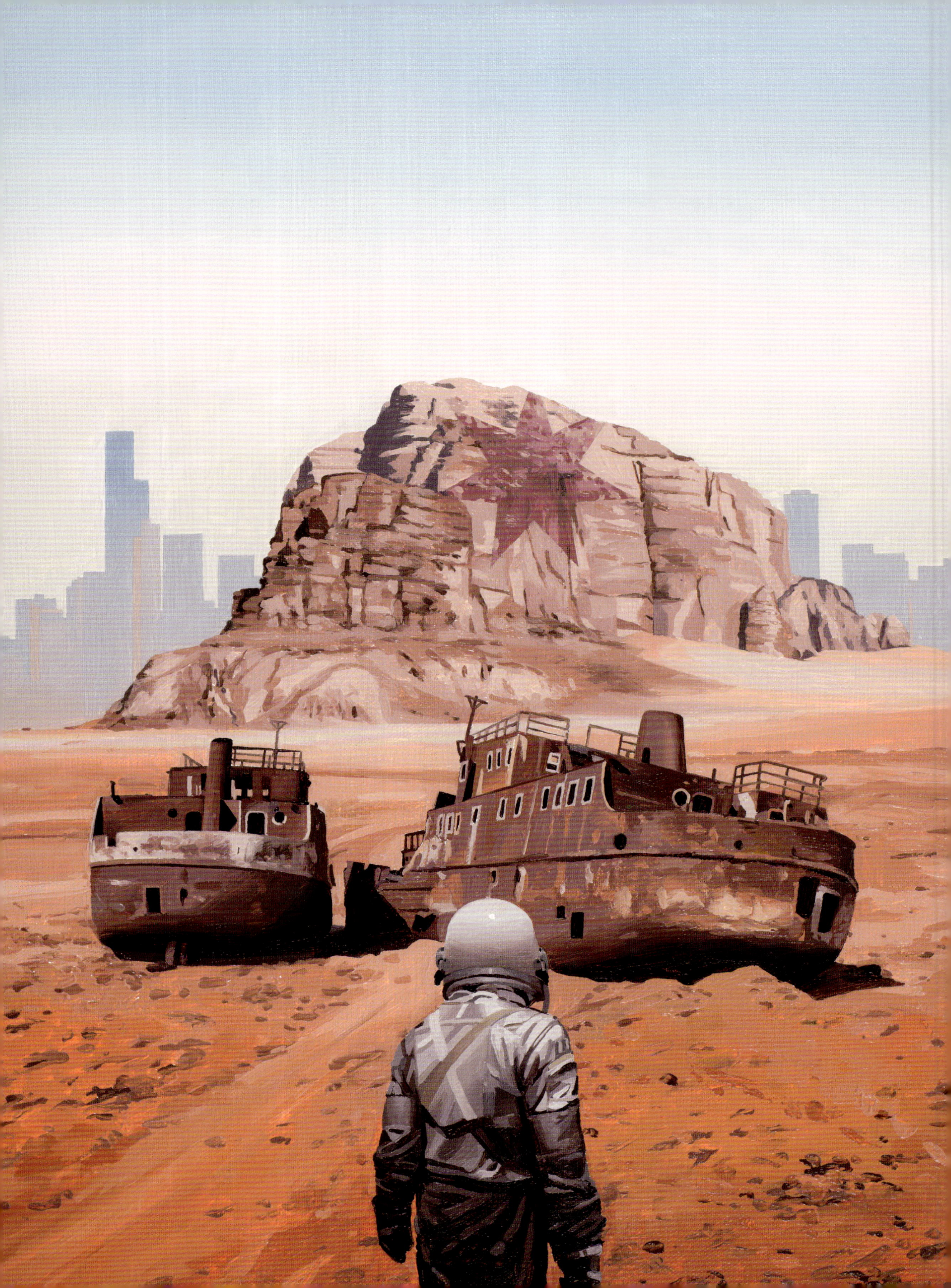

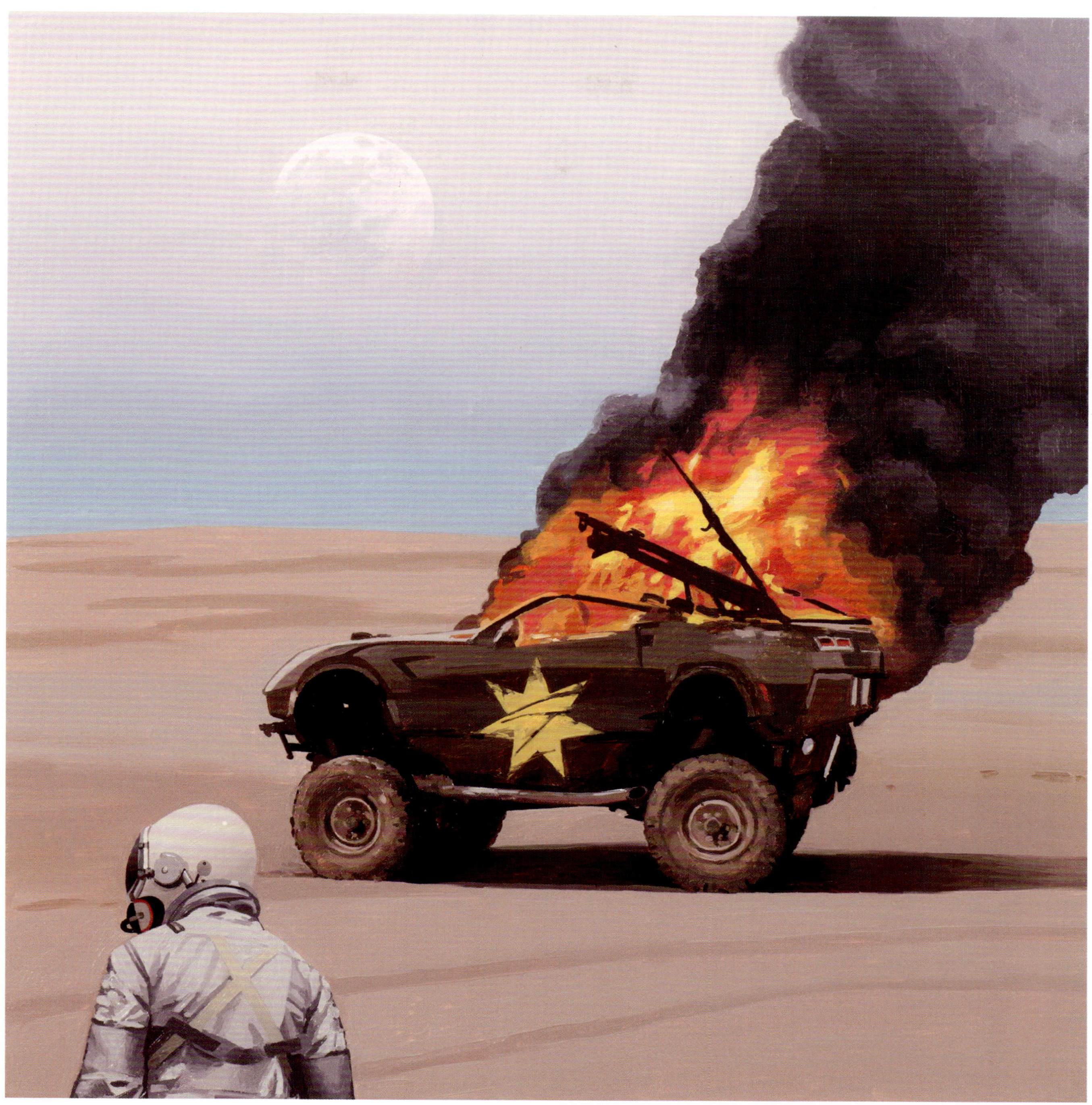

#437

BURNING [2019]

#424

THE SEA [2019]

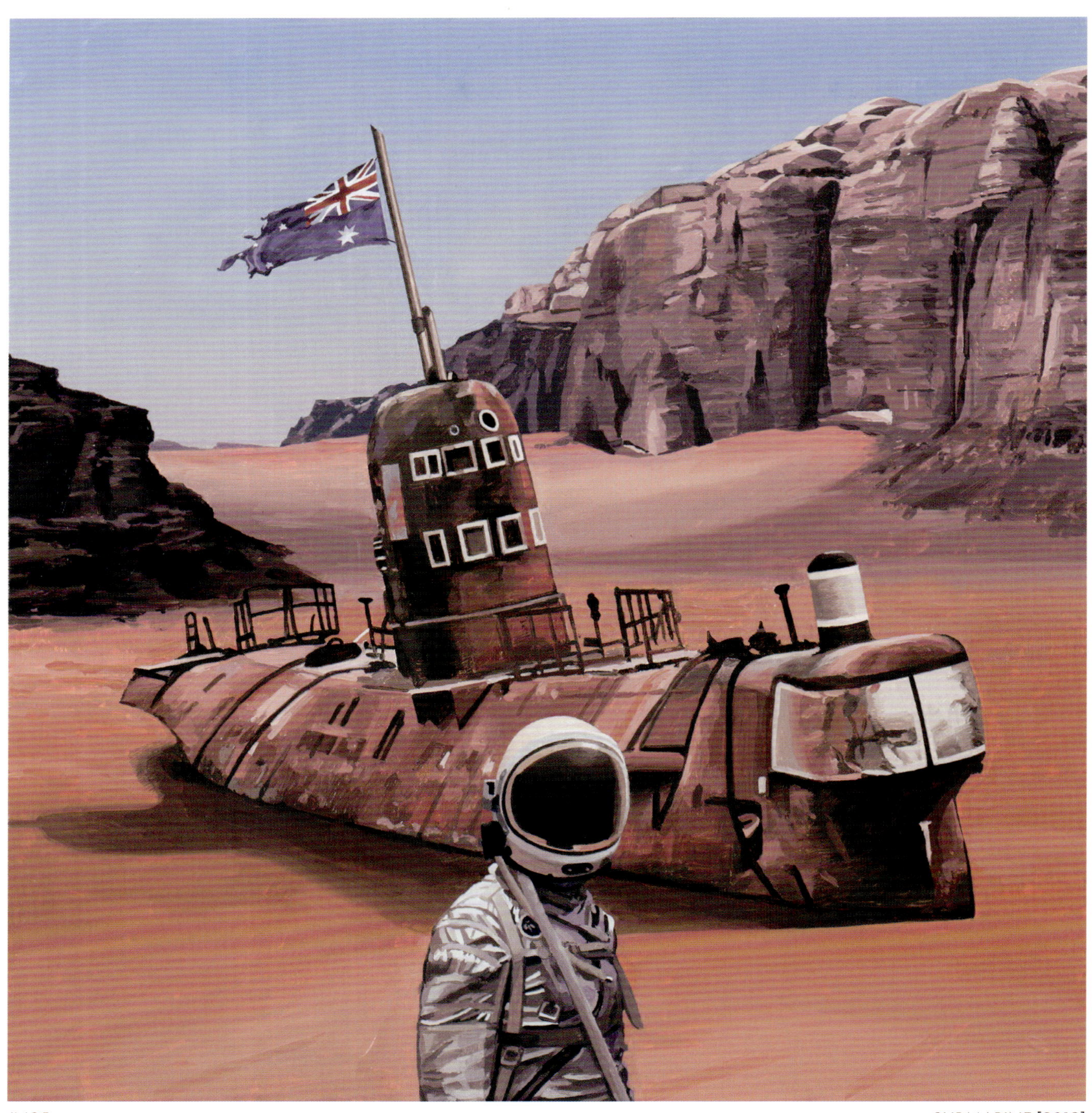

#435

SUBMARINE [2019]

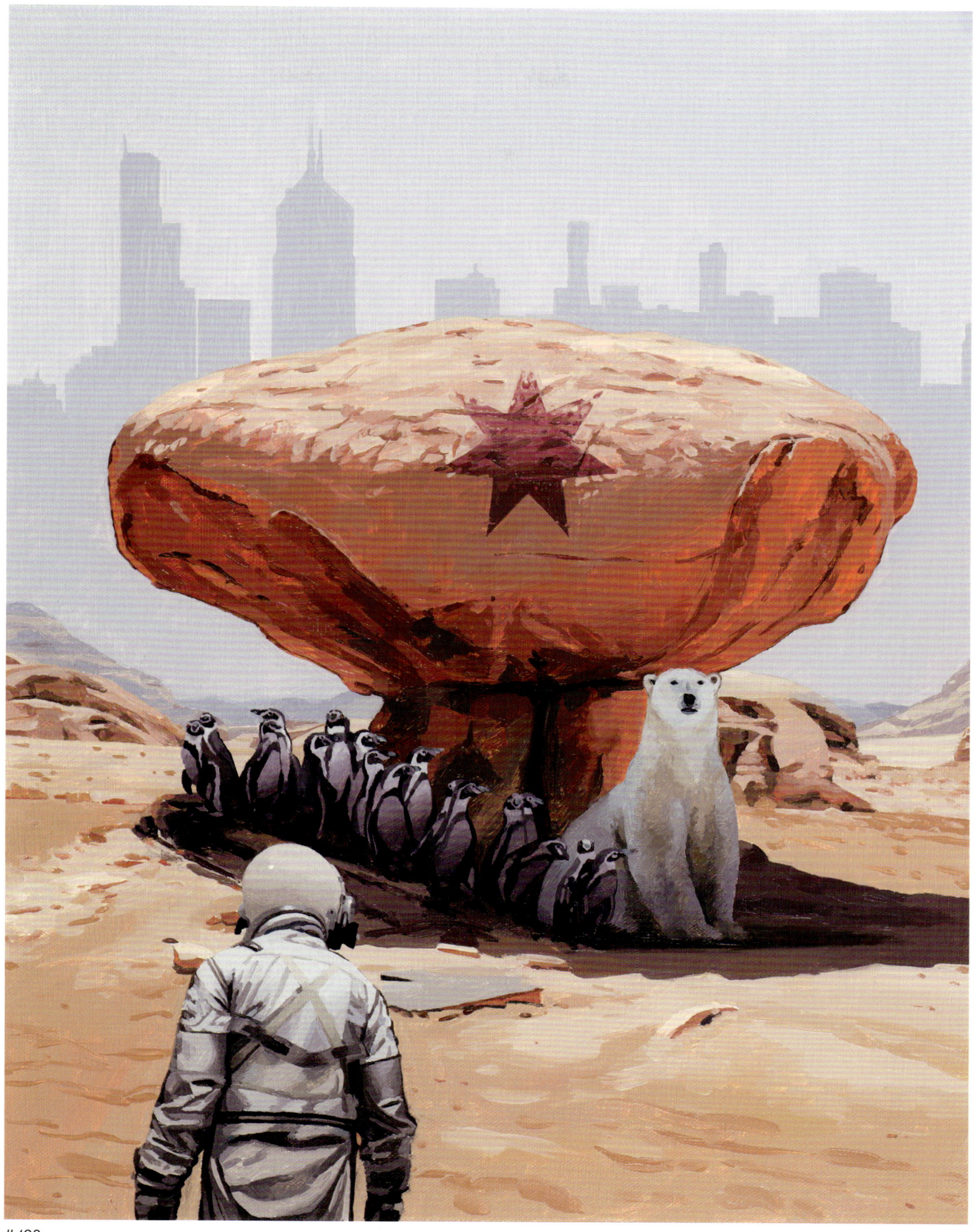

#423

SHELTER [2019]

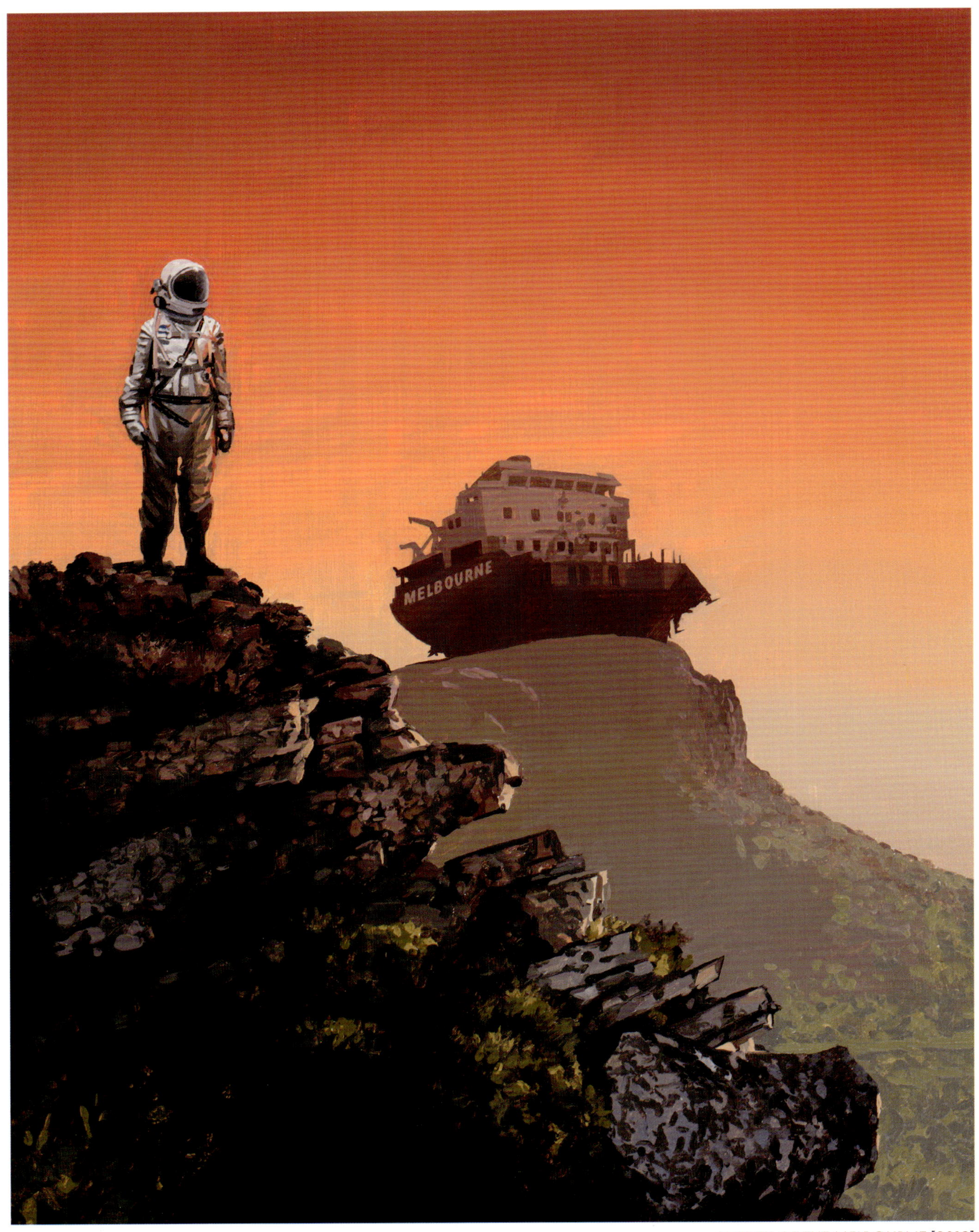

#432

WRECK OF THE MELBOURNE [2019]

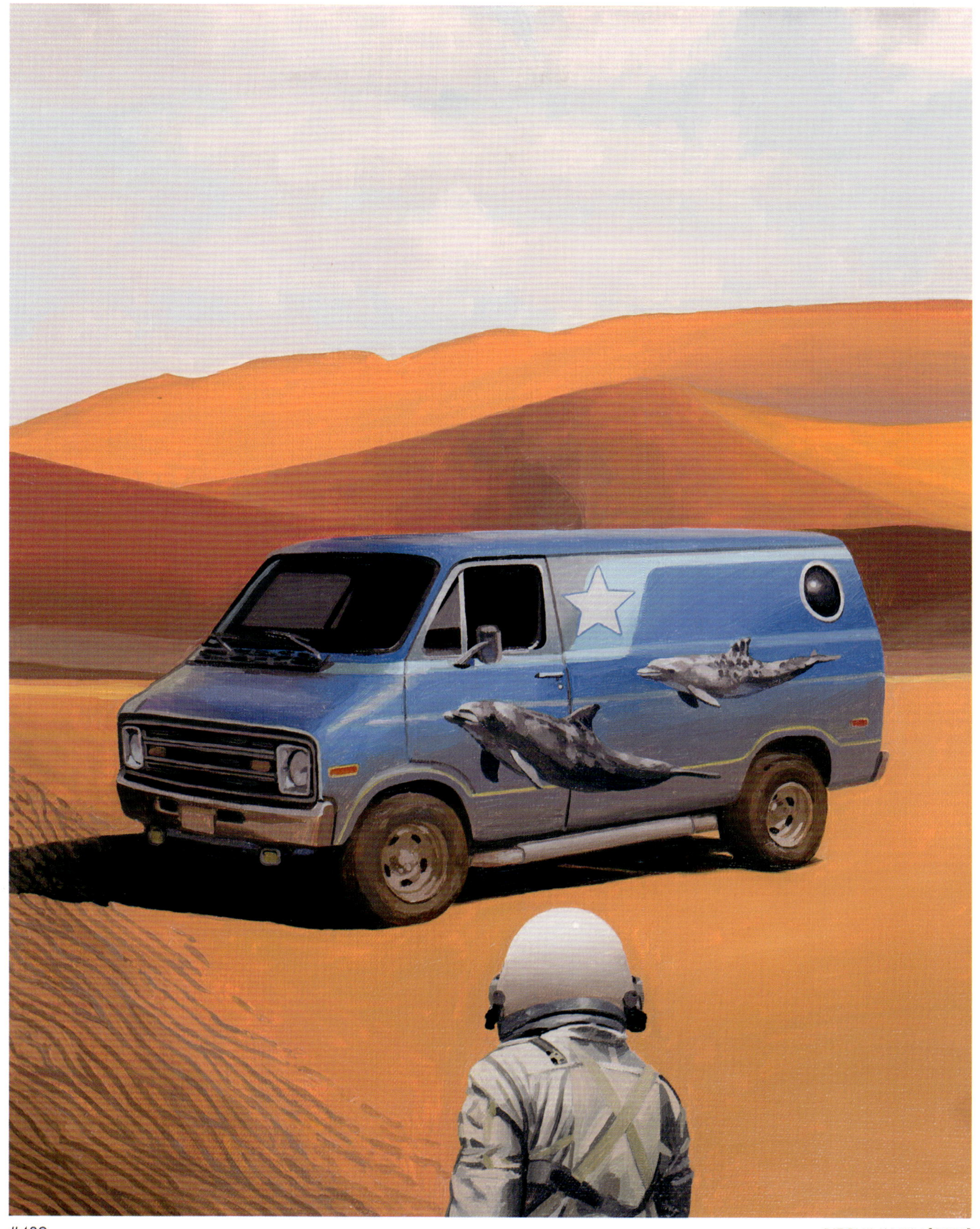

#439

BITCHIN' VAN [2019]

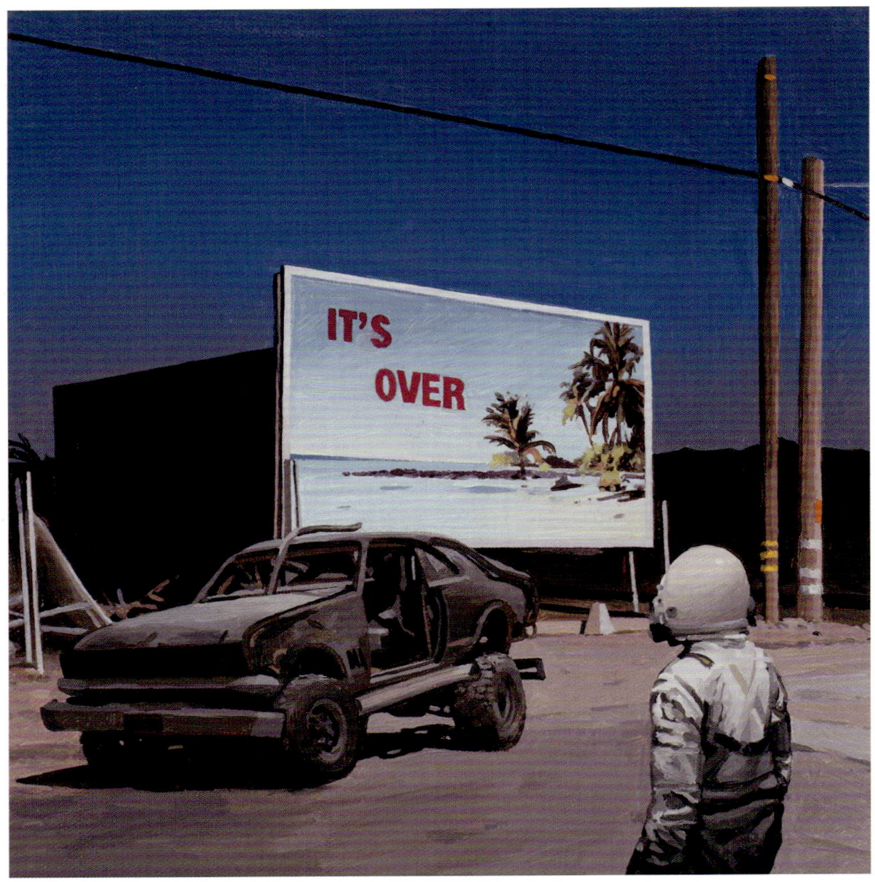

#427 IT'S OVER [2019]

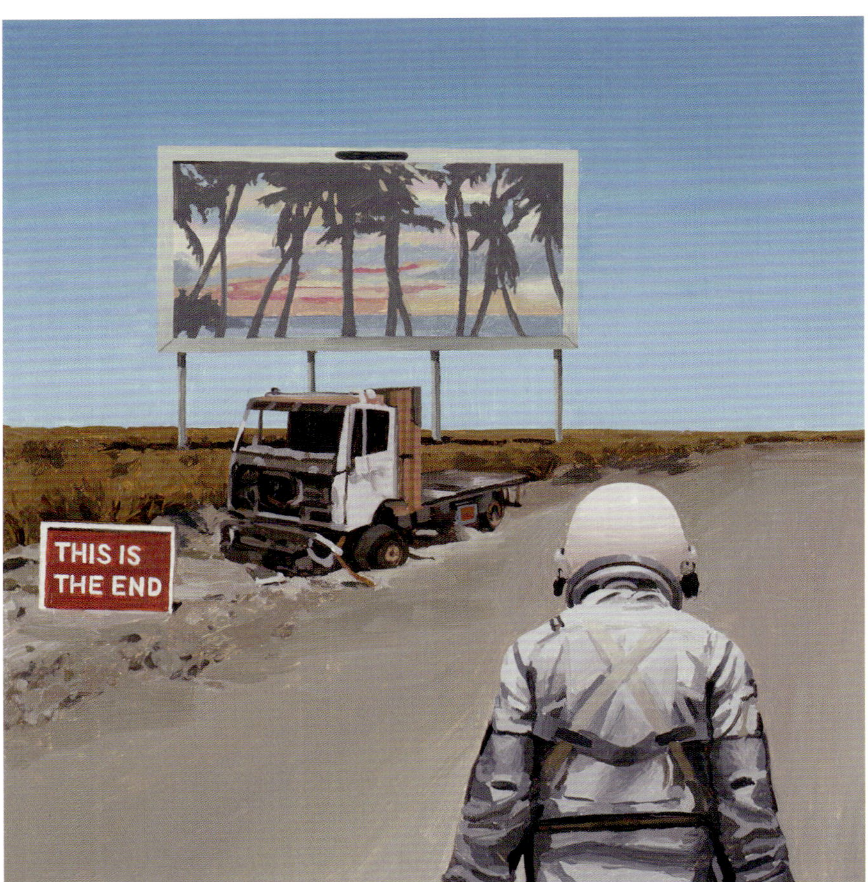

#428 THIS IS THE END [2019]

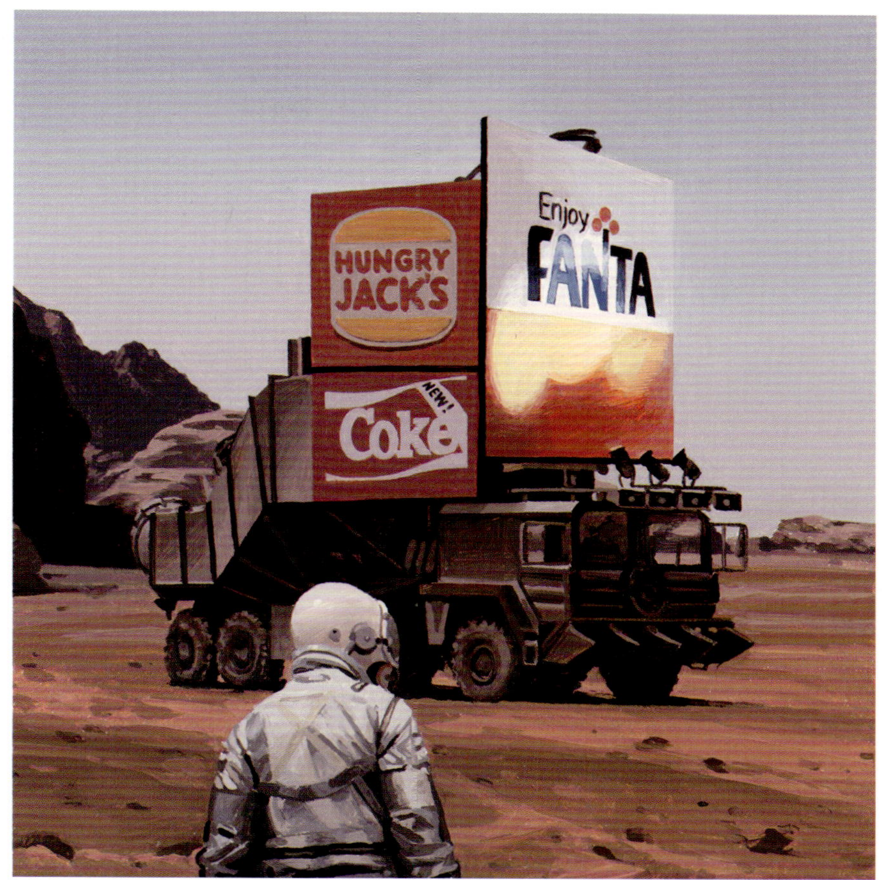

#429 DOOF WAGON [2019]

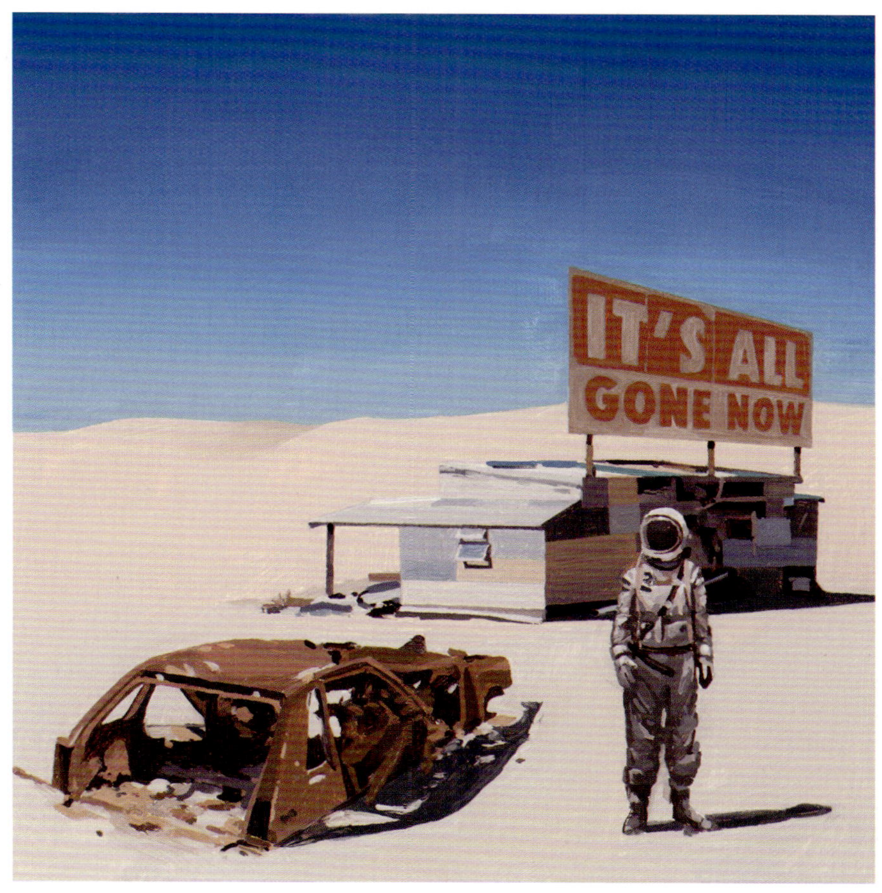

#430 IT'S ALL GONE NOW [2019]

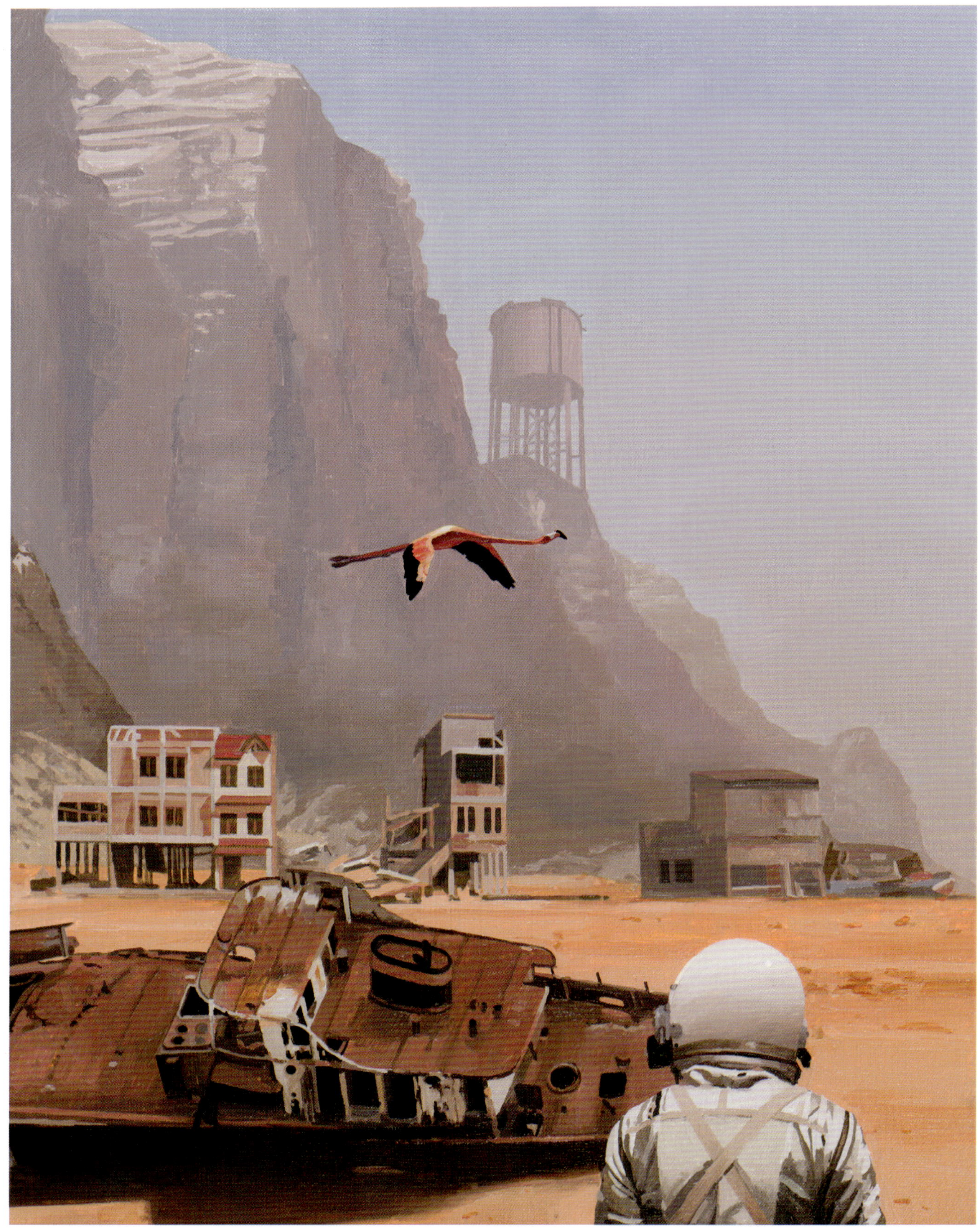

#440

FLAMINGO [2019]

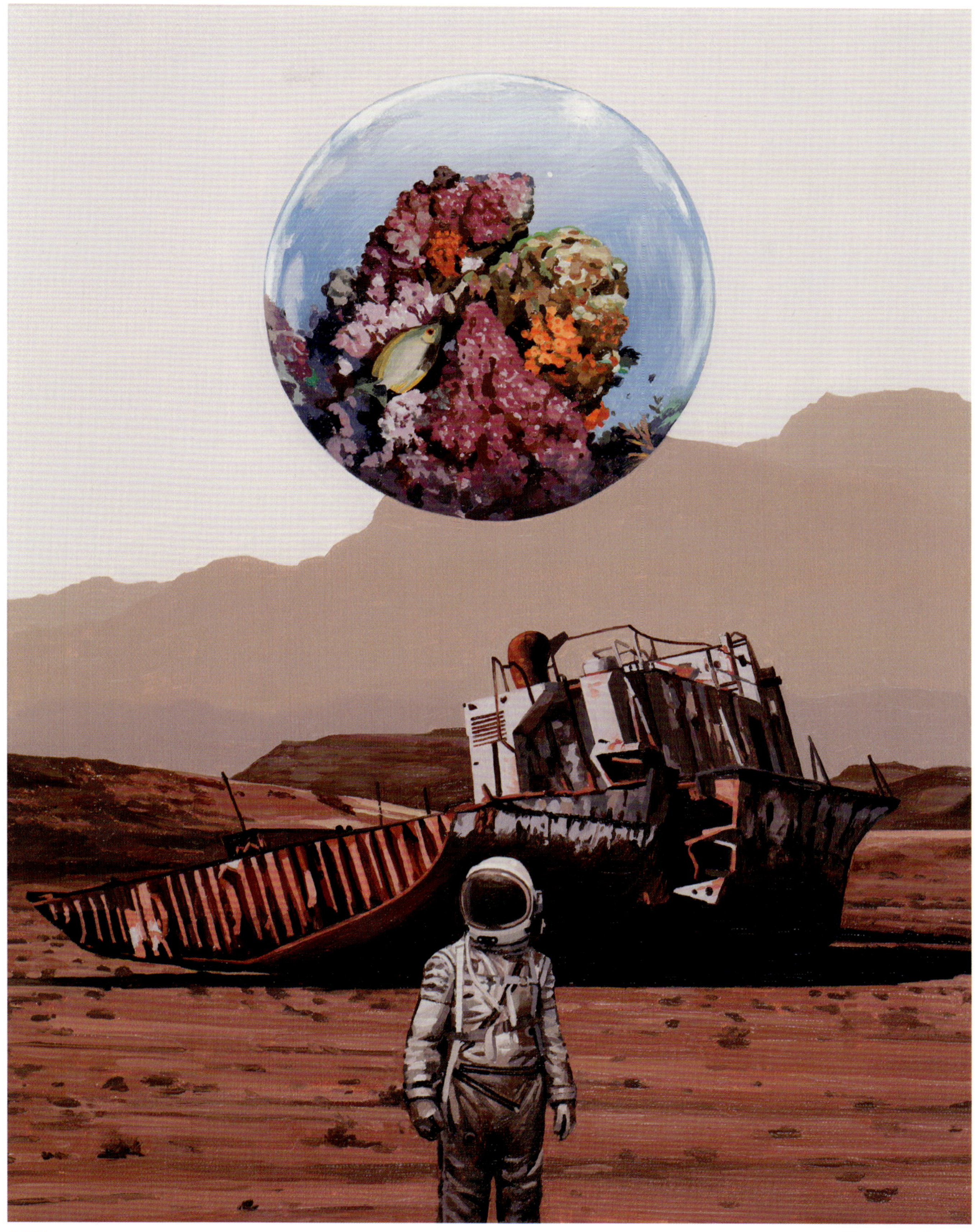

#438

CORAL REEF [2019]

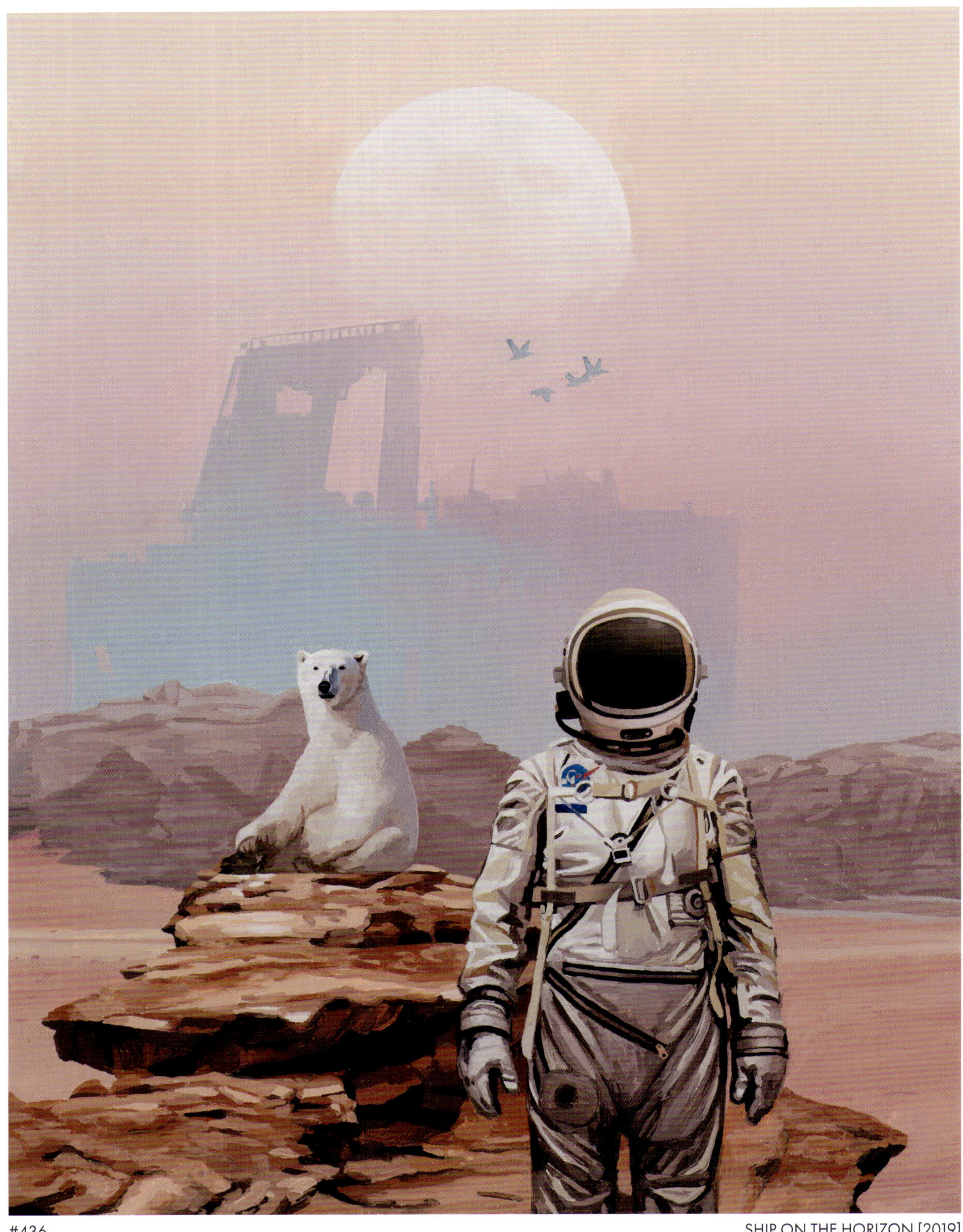

#436

SHIP ON THE HORIZON [2019]

#431

BALL'S PYRAMID [2019]

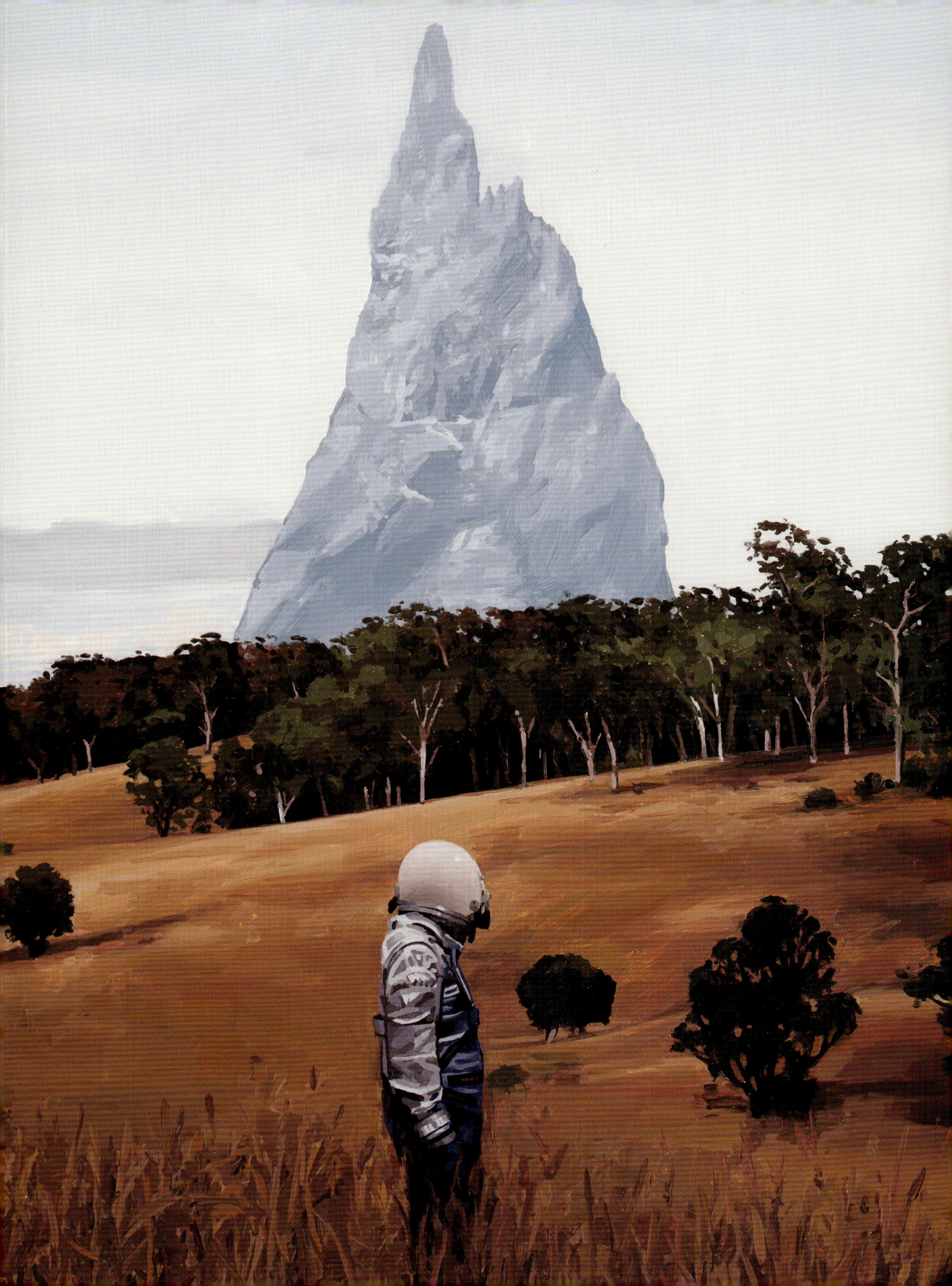

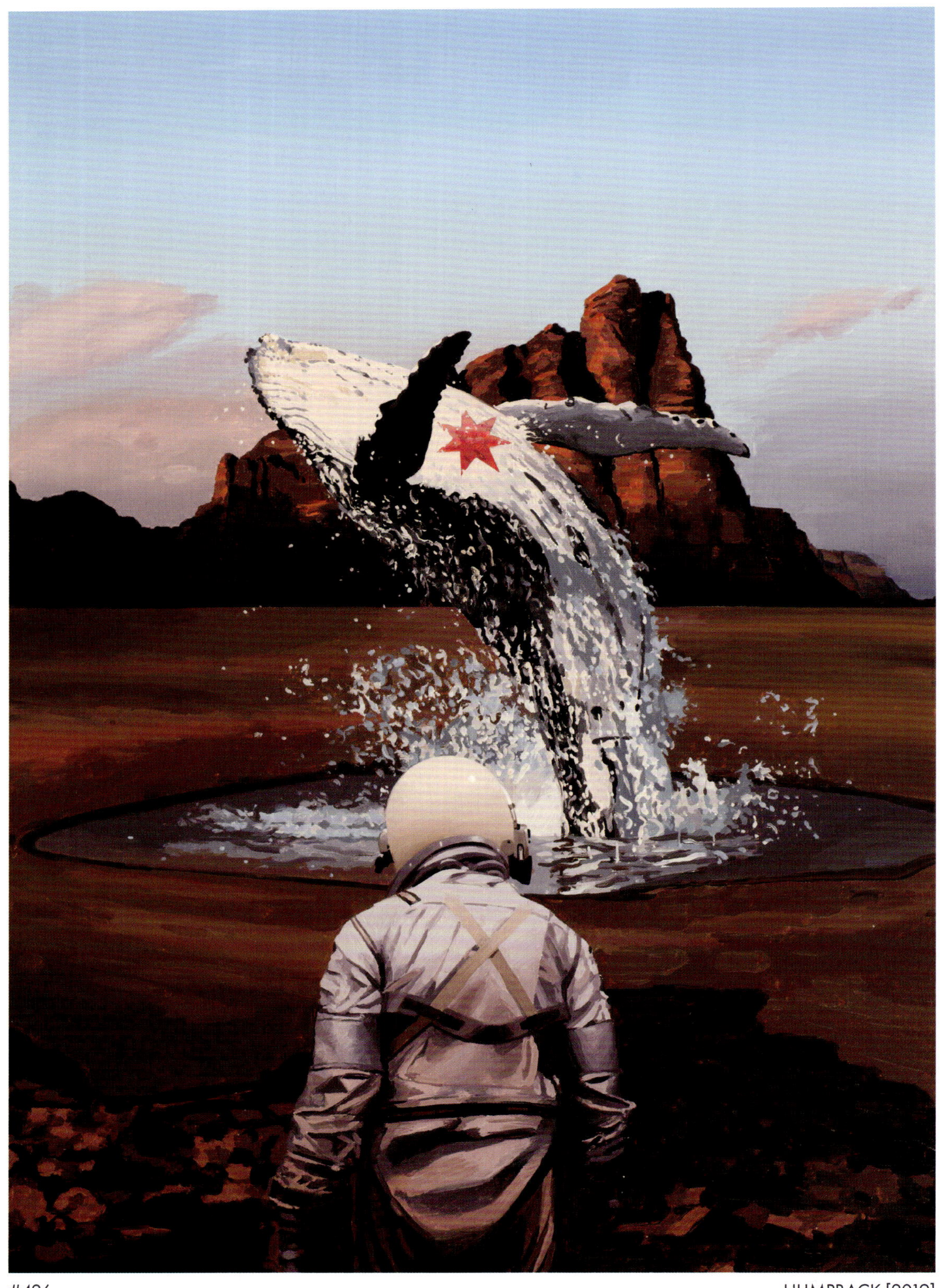

#426 HUMPBACK [2019]

#434
SPOONBILL [2019]

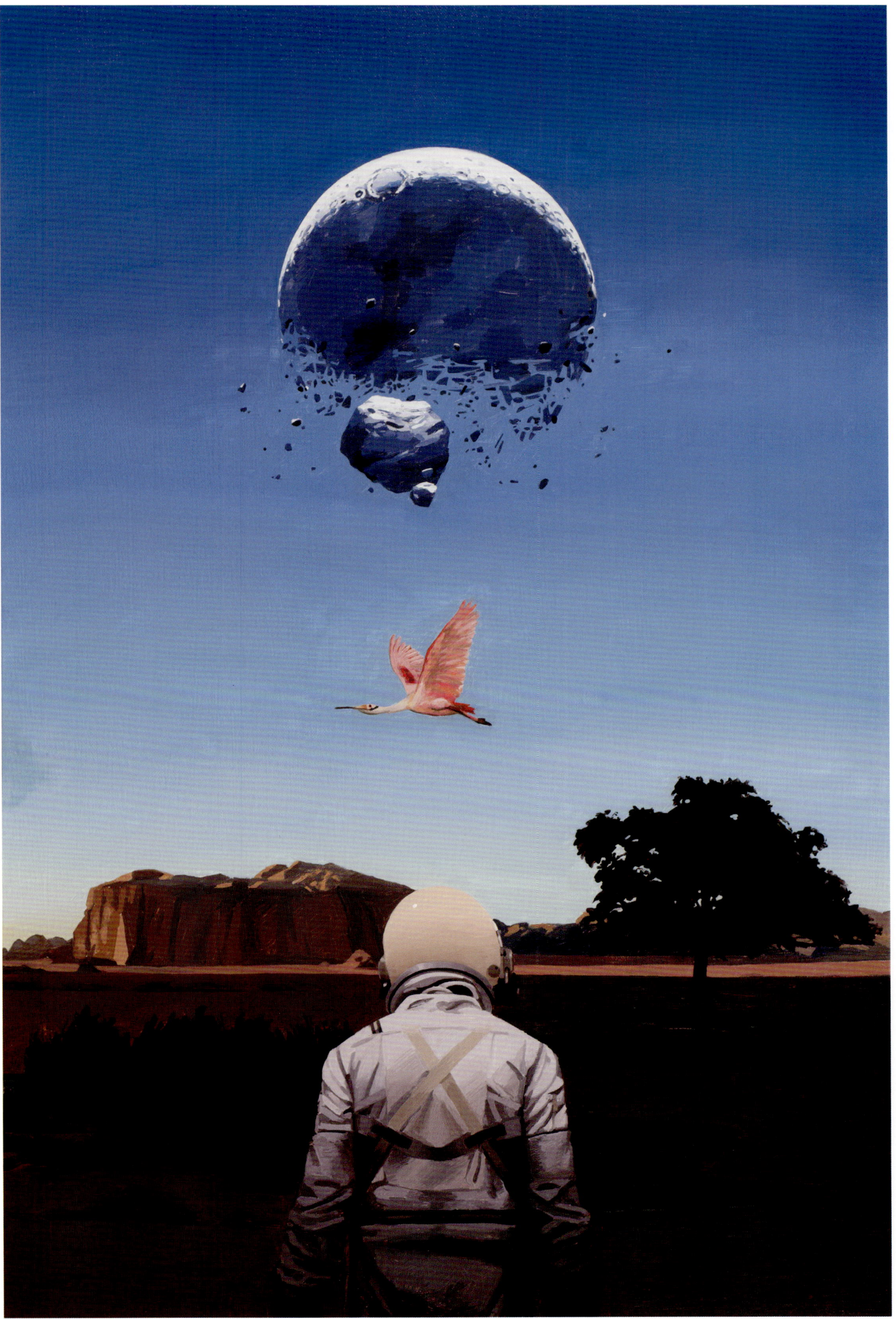

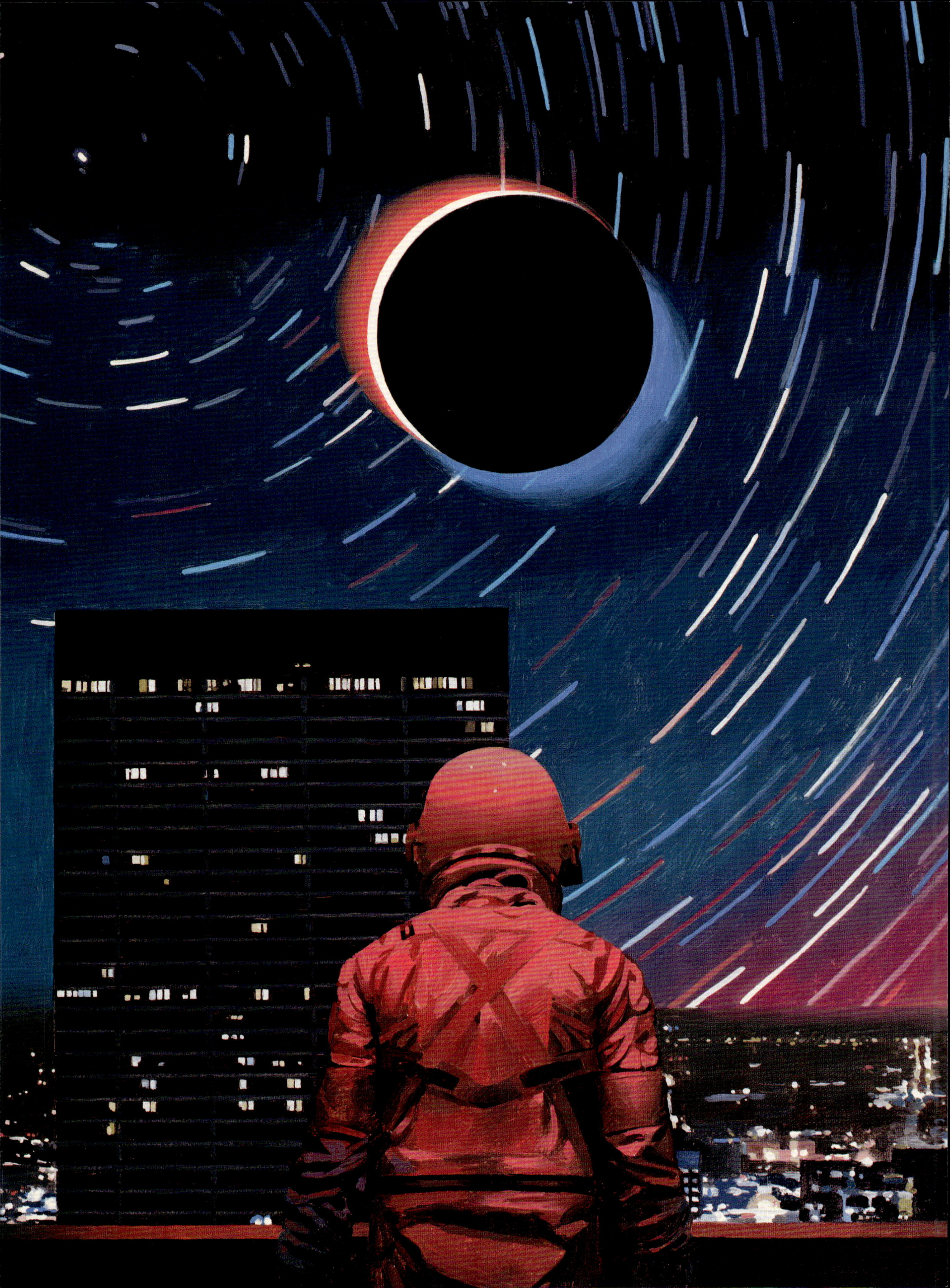

CAUTION:

TIME TRAVEL CAN BE UNPLEASANT

////////////////////////

Spring, 2020

Hey! Who wants to travel back in time to Spring 2020? What's that? Nobody at all? I can take my time machine and shove it where? Oh, ok. Yeah, I get it.

You know this, but in March of 2020 the world fell apart. I had a show that May. It was supposed to be about the upcoming election and how broken America felt. Looking back now, it's still about that, but it also in real time became about the entire world being broken as well. I had a number of additional shows over the following couple of years, most of which (obviously) in some way deal with the fallout of the pandemic. I've decided to keep my original statements for these shows mostly intact, which now read as semi-incoherent dispatches from a time of utter chaos. Fun! If you want to close this book for a bit and go look at pictures of puppies, I mean, maybe I'll join you.

#399
ECLIPSE [2019]

THIS IS AMERICA

Thinkspace Projects, Los Angeles, CA
May, 2020

It's 2020 and we're living in the future. We can't go outside and there's no more toilet paper. This is America.

« **In 2018** I had my last show at Thinkspace Projects in Los Angeles. It was titled *1984* and was a reimagining of George Orwell's haunting book, which had recently spiked to the top of the Amazon best seller's list because it was suddenly, and alarmingly, relevant again. But I set each piece in a fluorescent colored version of Los Angeles in the '80s, filled with Rubik's Cubes, vintage Lamborghini's, and Phil Collins. Things in America were looking dark but I wanted the paintings to feel almost impossibly light in contrast to their dark overtones.

» **It's 2020** and an election is looming. Like a lot of people I've been wondering if this is a turning point in American history. But which way are we turning?

« **In 2018**, after living most of my life in Boston, I moved across the United States to Los Angeles. I've been thinking about the long divide between my old life which I left behind and the new city I've just arrived in. I've never felt the vastness of America as much as I do now. All the widely varied places, people, and landscapes that lie between the places I've lived. I wanted to make paintings about the open expanses, the purple mountains, the Grand Canyon, the monuments we've built on purpose and by accident to the history of our nation.

» **It's 2020** and I've watched everything in my Netflix queue. Like a lot of Americans, I worry about the future. Unlike a lot of Americans, I make paintings about the future. I'm inspired by scenes of dystopian movies and novels, and I'm always curious why we're so drawn to the end of things. Why do we have that dark impulse to see our civilization washed away by tidal waves, by asteroids, by terminators, by apes in clothes, by Thanos? Often enough those scenes feel like nothing more than CGI. But other times it's hard to shake the feeing that we're inevitably crashing towards the future that we've already predicted. That we have no real control over it, like the extras in a Godzilla movie watching helplessly as a giant monster tears down our city.

« **In 2018**, after my *1984* show wrapped up, Andrew Hosner, the co-founder of Thinkspace, reached out to me and pitched an idea for my next show—national parks.

#450
STATUE OF LIBERTY [2019]

This seemed like a good idea—the astronaut in my work can, after all, go anywhere, and I liked the idea of exploring the natural beauty here in America. Of doing my take on a landscape show. At the time, the president was talking about selling off parts of the national park system and it seemed an apt metaphor for the way we were trading the most visible and beautiful parts of our country for short term profits. As I started working on the paintings that would become this show, though, it quickly grew to something beyond national parks. I started thinking about the landscapes and monuments of America and what they represent, to the believers and to the cynics. To the people this country has helped in so many ways, and to the many it has pushed aside or displaced. I thought about the endless scenes from movies where our recognizable landmarks are washed away or blown up. I thought about the Hudson River school and Edward Hopper and the countless other

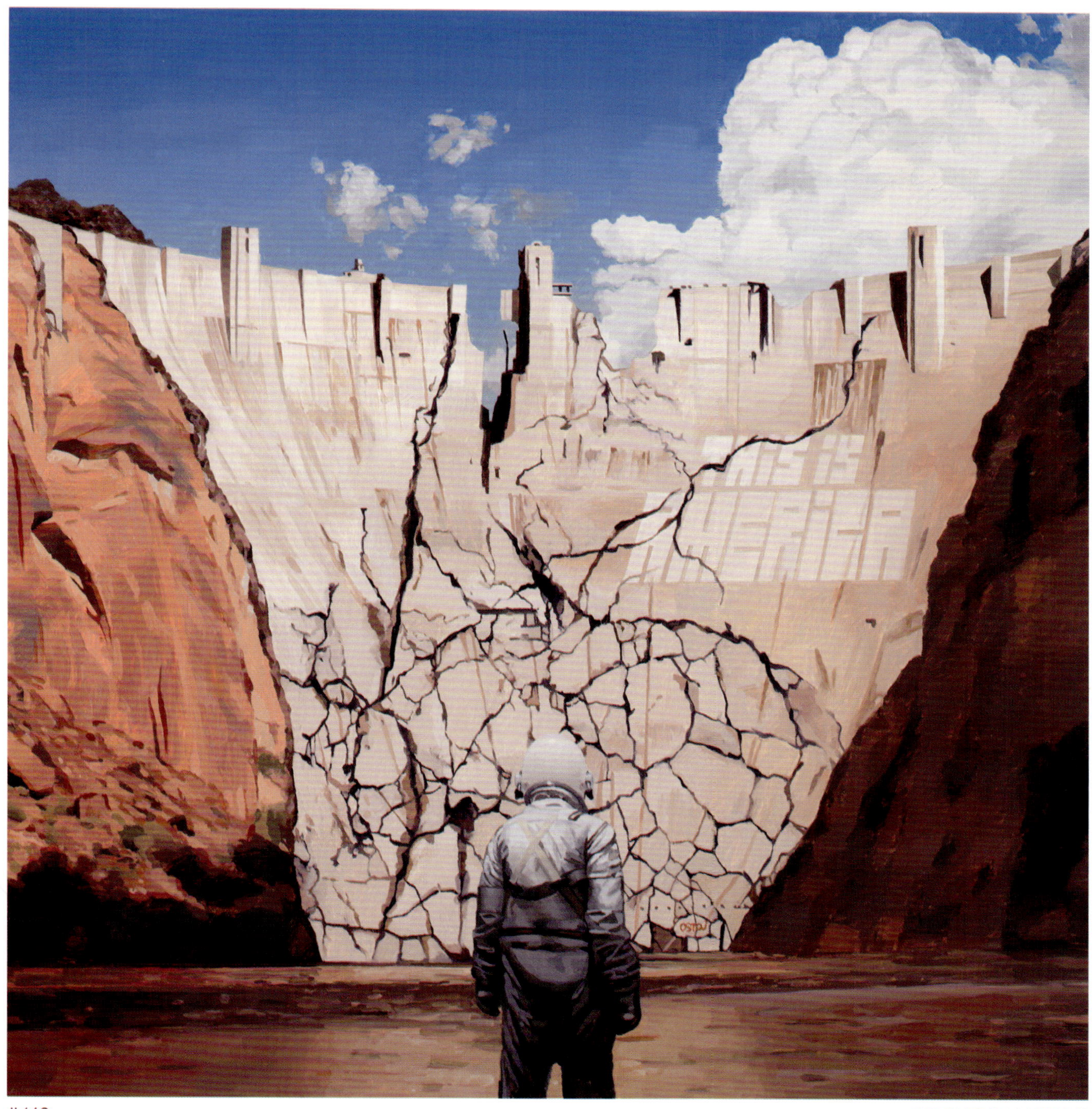

#462

HOOVER DAM [2020]

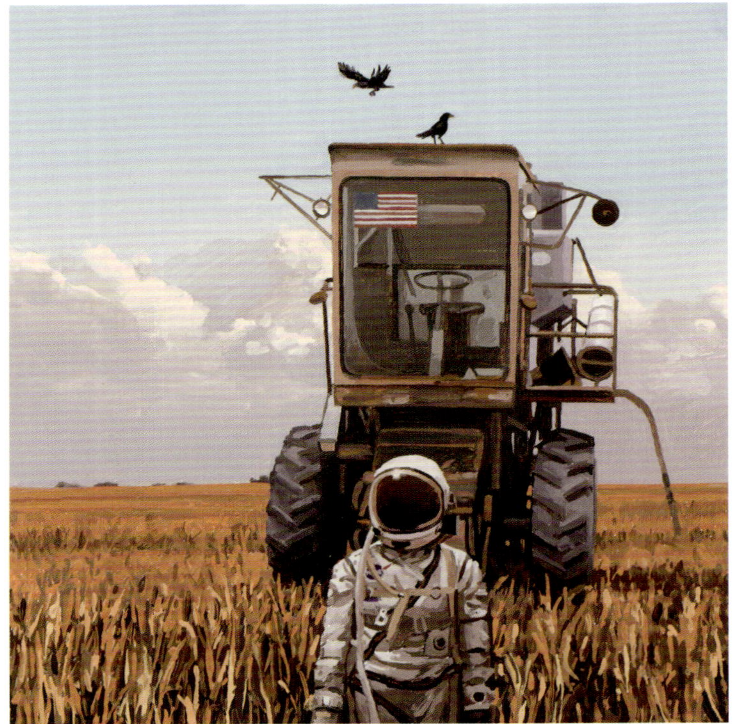

#467 CORNFIELD [2020]

American artists over the years who have painted the American landscape in a way which said something about the times they lived in. I thought about being part of that long tradition.

» **It's 2020** and we're awaiting a pandemic to pass us by. I've been thinking about this show for two years now and it never occurred to me that when it arrived, it would do so silently and quietly, all of us hunkered away at home, looking at my story of America on screens. All those movies, all those novels, all of my paintings depicting a lost and empty future suddenly feel a bit too real.

« **In 2018** Donald Glover, under his musical alias Childish Gambino, released a video for his song titled *This is America*. It's cinematic. It's a beautiful and deeply scathing indictment of violence and race in our country. It feels chaotic and claustrophobic and weirdly, confusingly, beautiful. It's also thickly layered with cultural references, with everything from Jim Crow era imagery to Michael Jackson videos. There's a sense of menace in it that feels hard to escape.

» **It's 2020** and I'm not sure I recognize the America I live in. There's a sense of menace in this country that feels hard to escape. And yet despite that feeling, the future is not yet written.

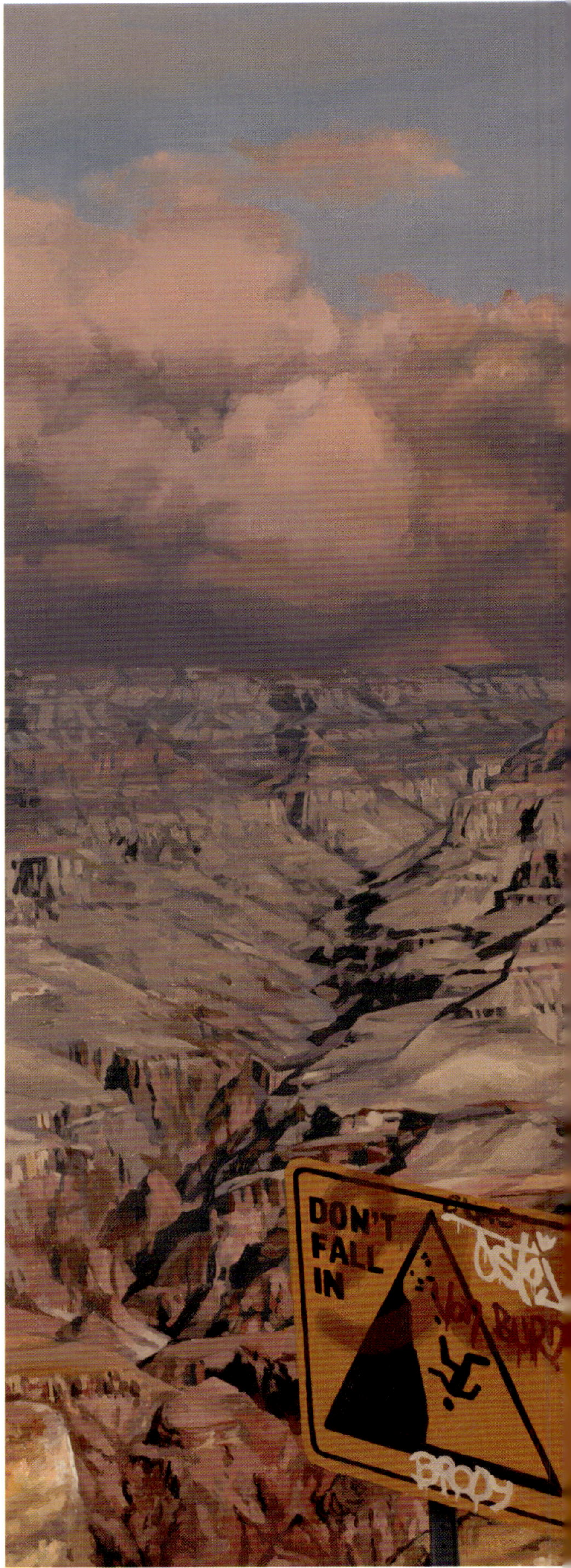

#449

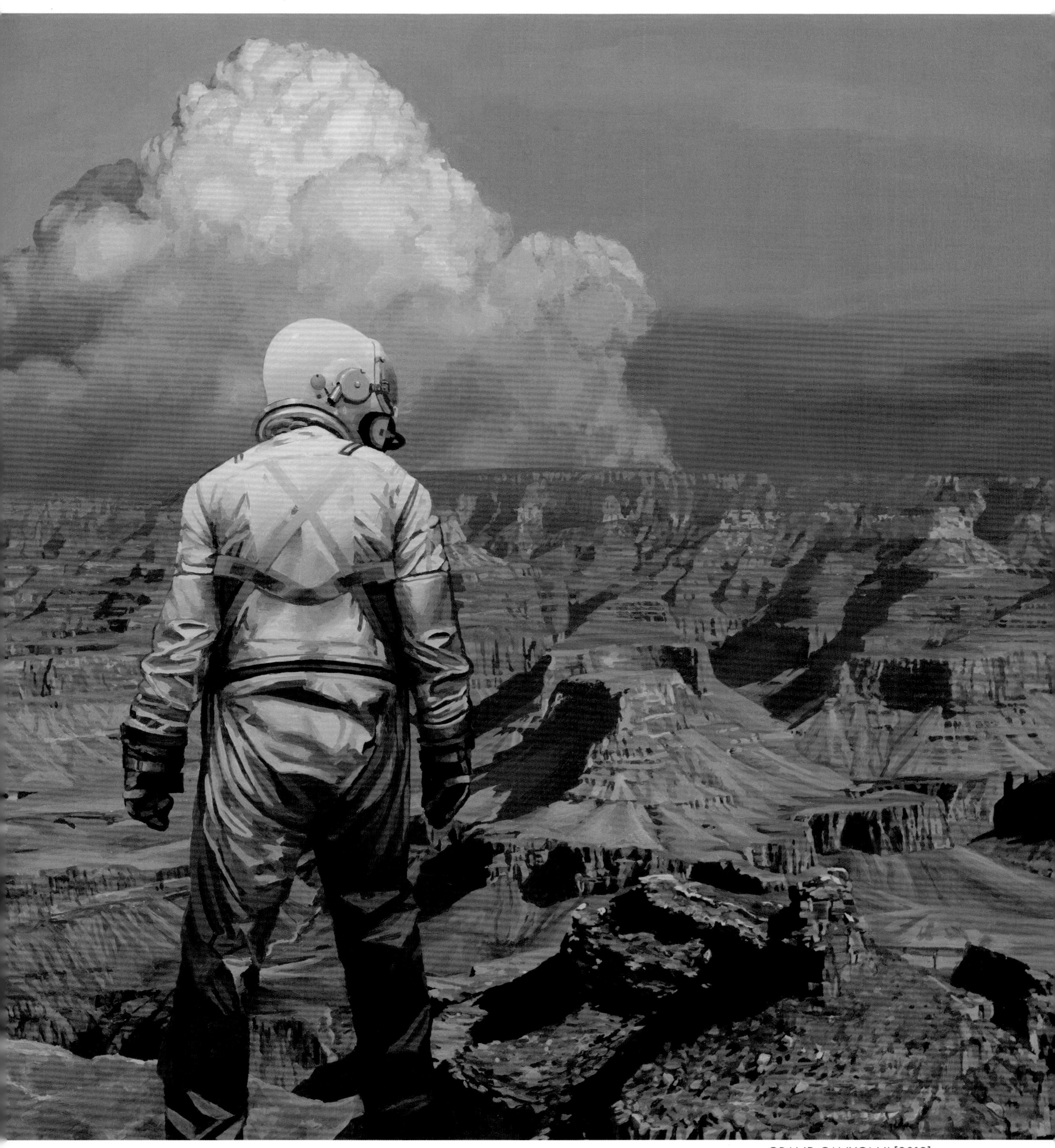

GRAND CANYON II [2019]

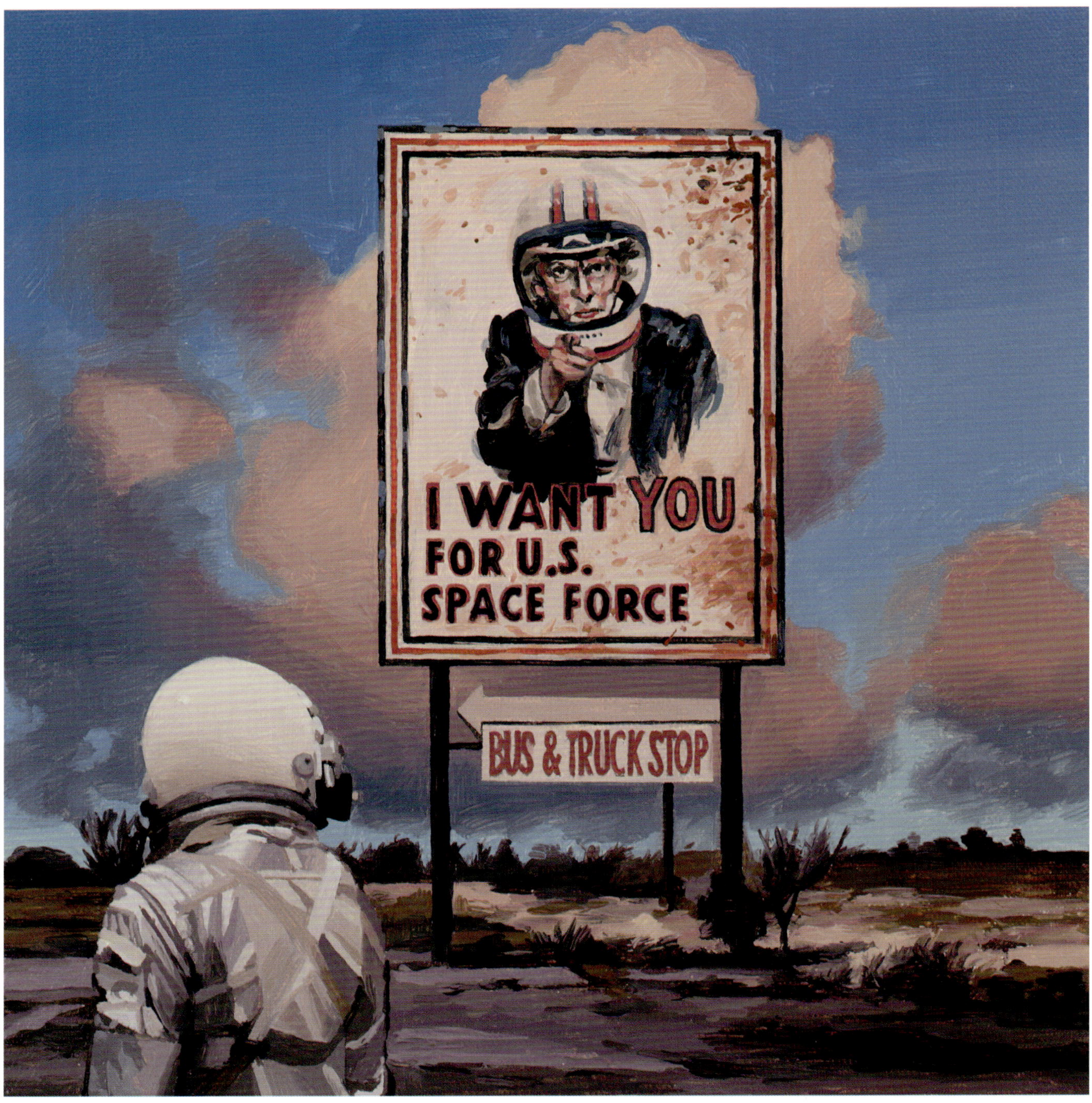

#457

JOIN THE SPACE FORCE [2020]

It's not over for us. We still live in an endlessly beautiful country. We've chipped away at it, through deliberate efforts and our own carelessness. But it's still there. It's not too late to do something and I wanted to capture that sense of hope amidst some dark times.

» **It's 2020**. Welcome to the dystopia of your choosing.

This is America.

#463

SAGUARO [2020]

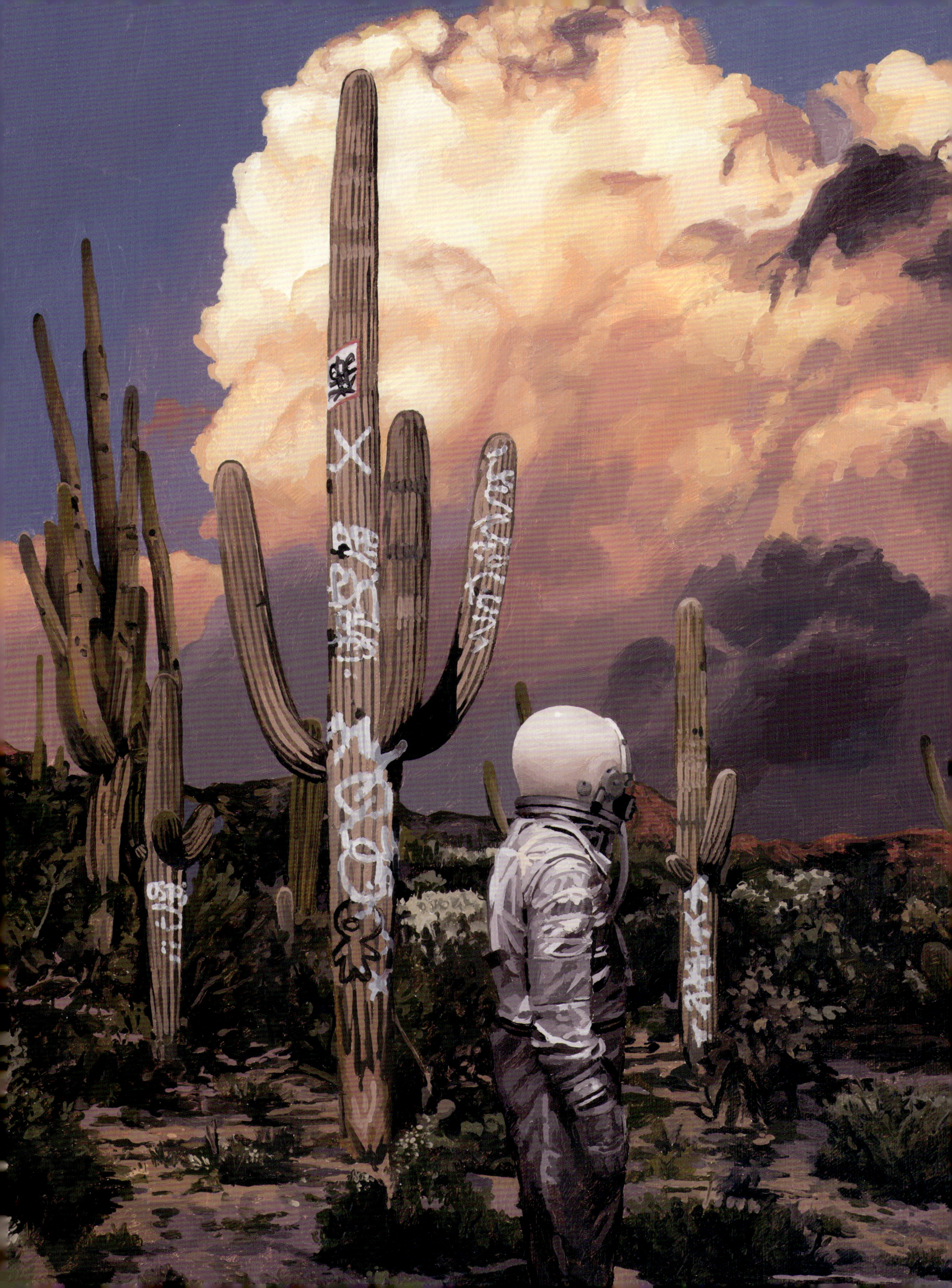

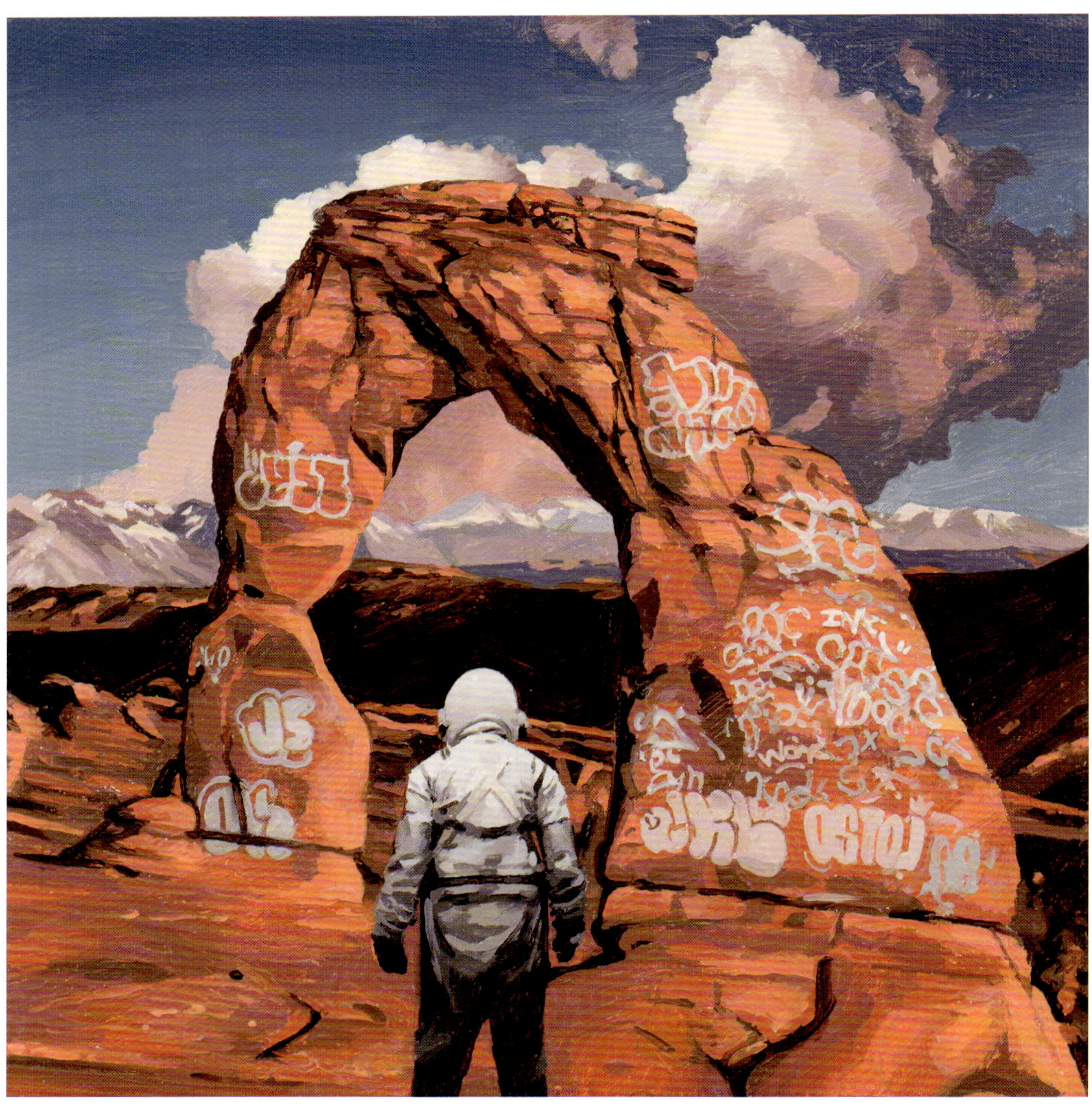

#465 ARCH [2020]

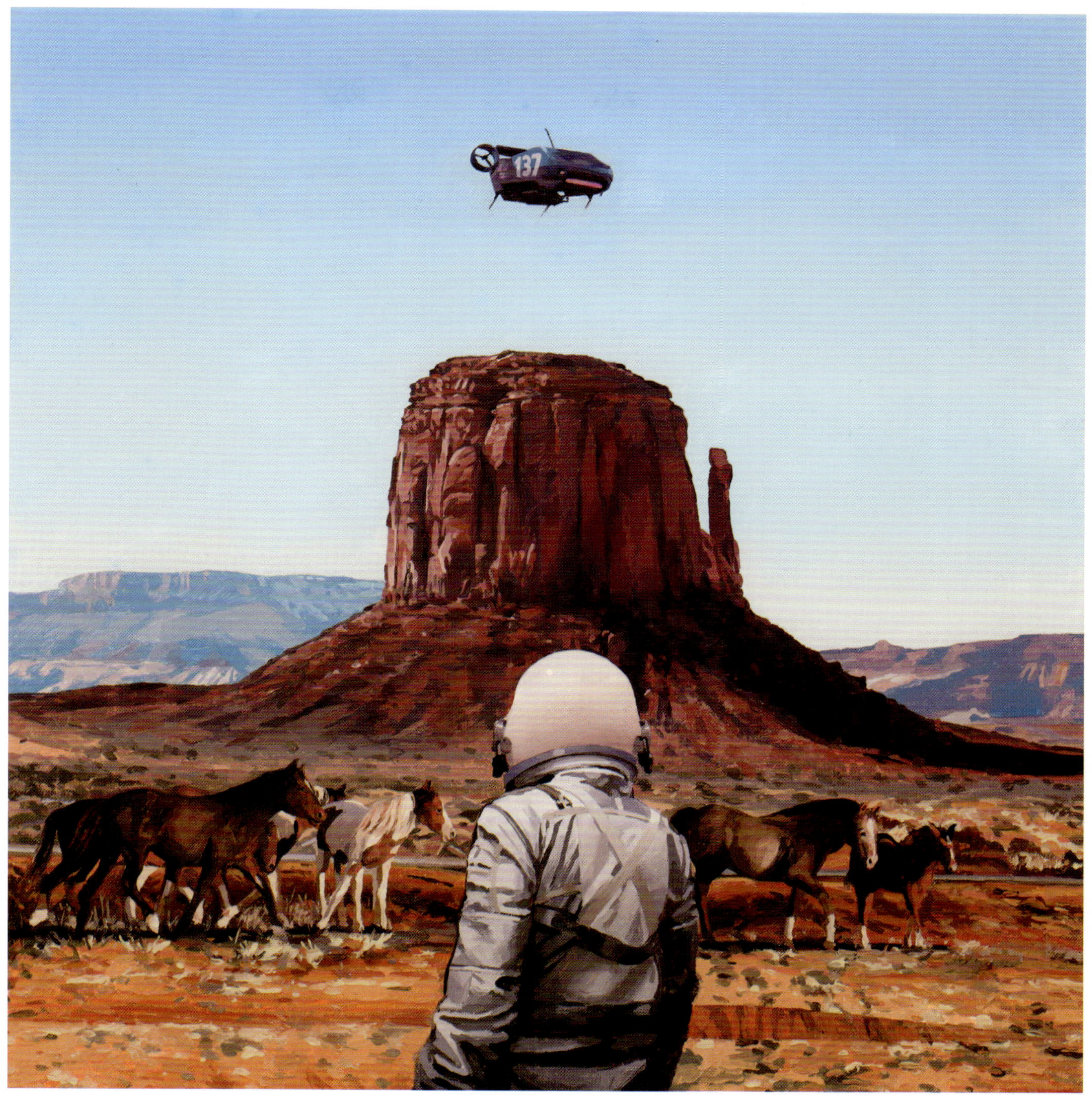

#447

MONUMENT VALLEY [2019]

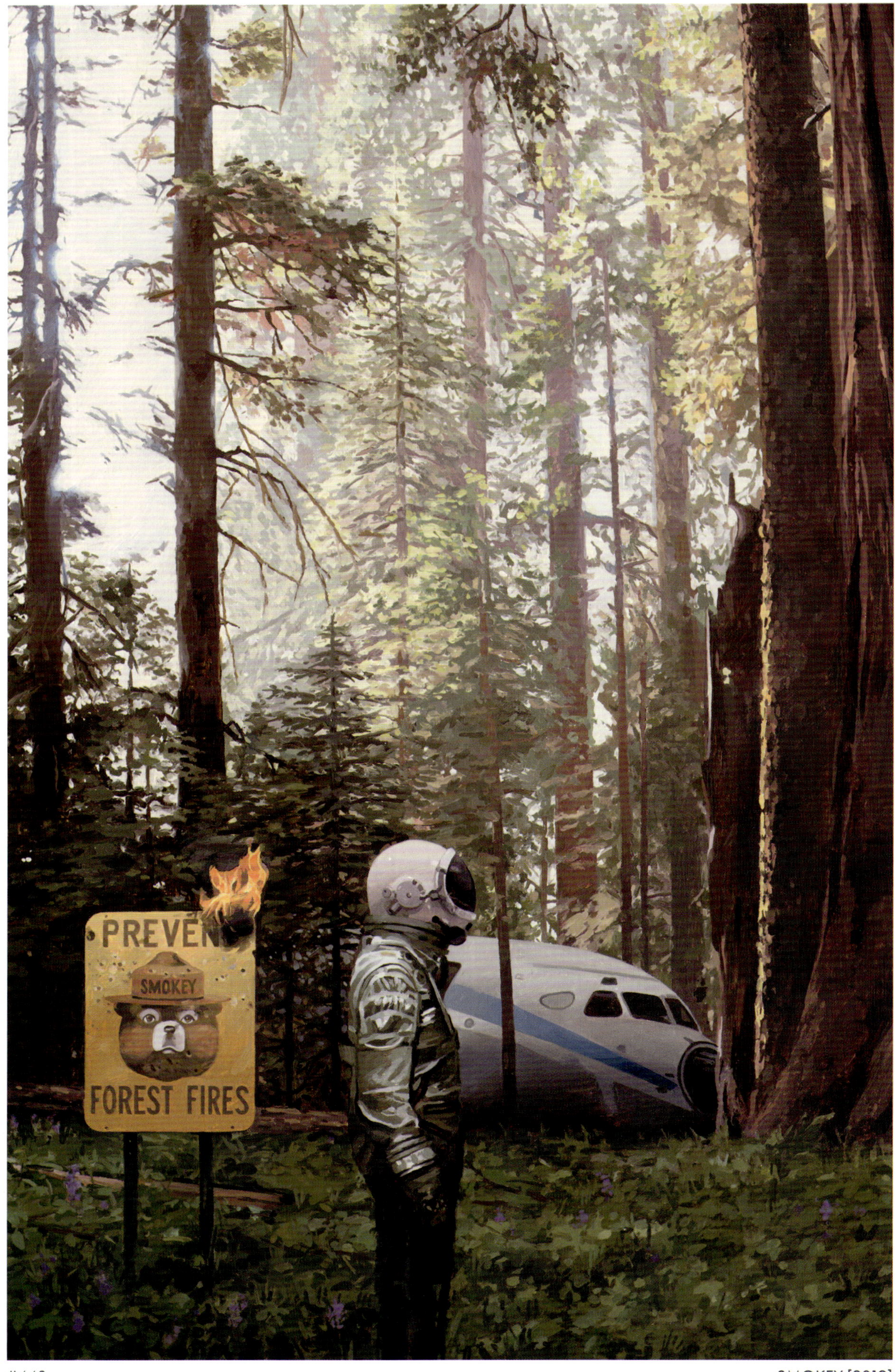

#448

SMOKEY [2019]

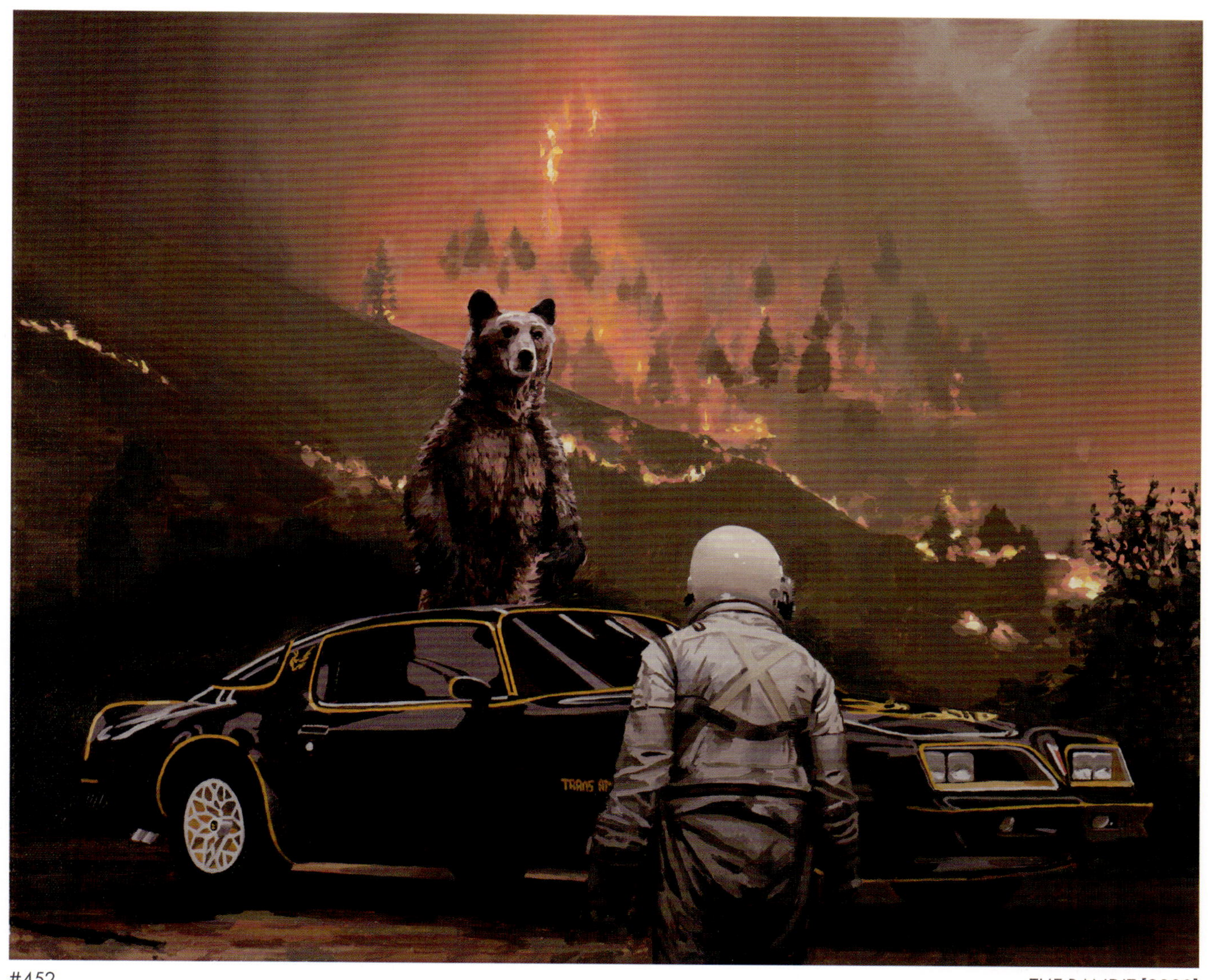

#452

THE BANDIT [2020]

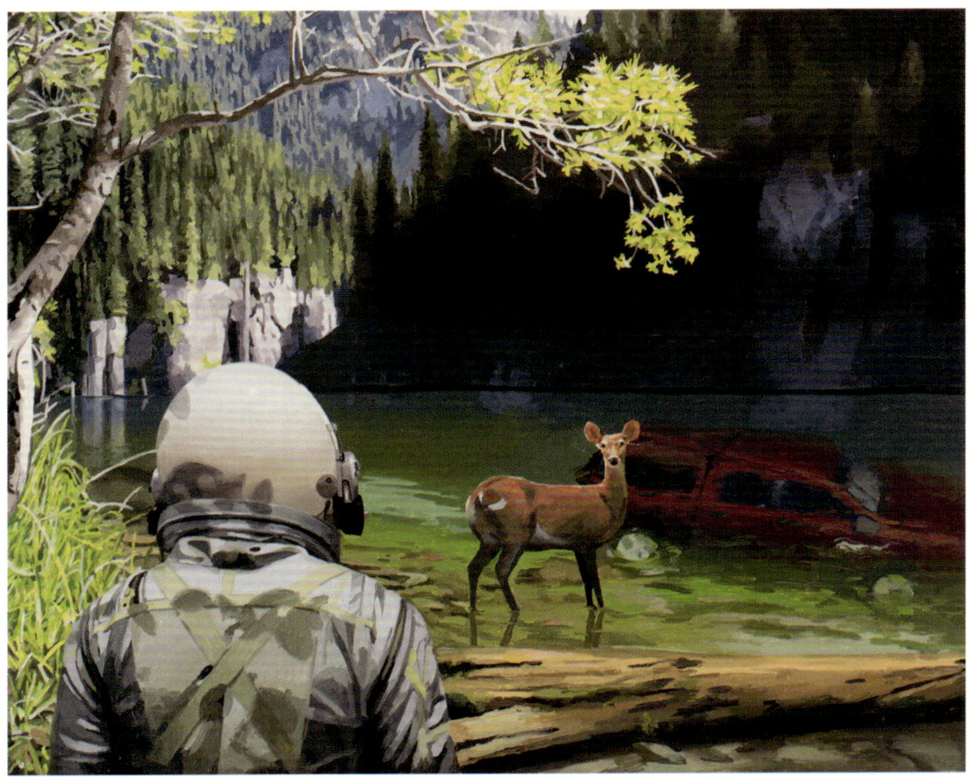

#453 SUBMERGED [2020]

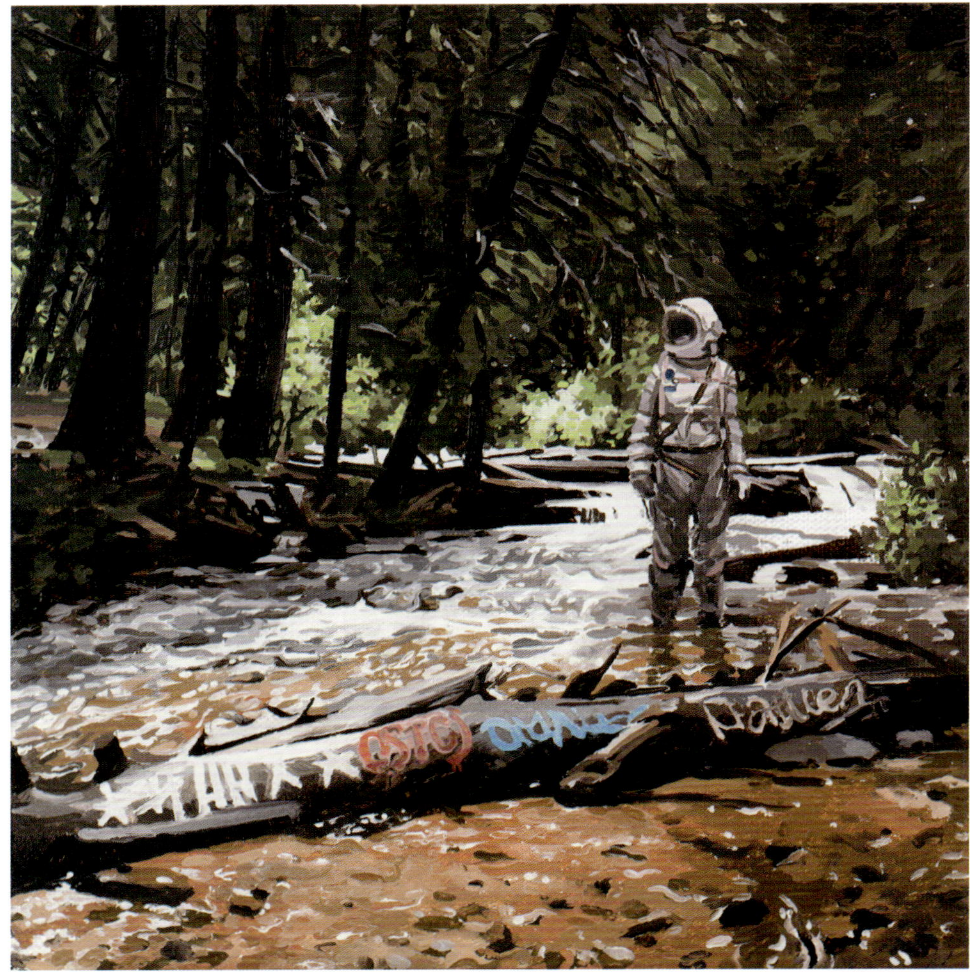

#469 THE STREAM [2020]

#466
HOLLYWOOD FOREVER [2020]

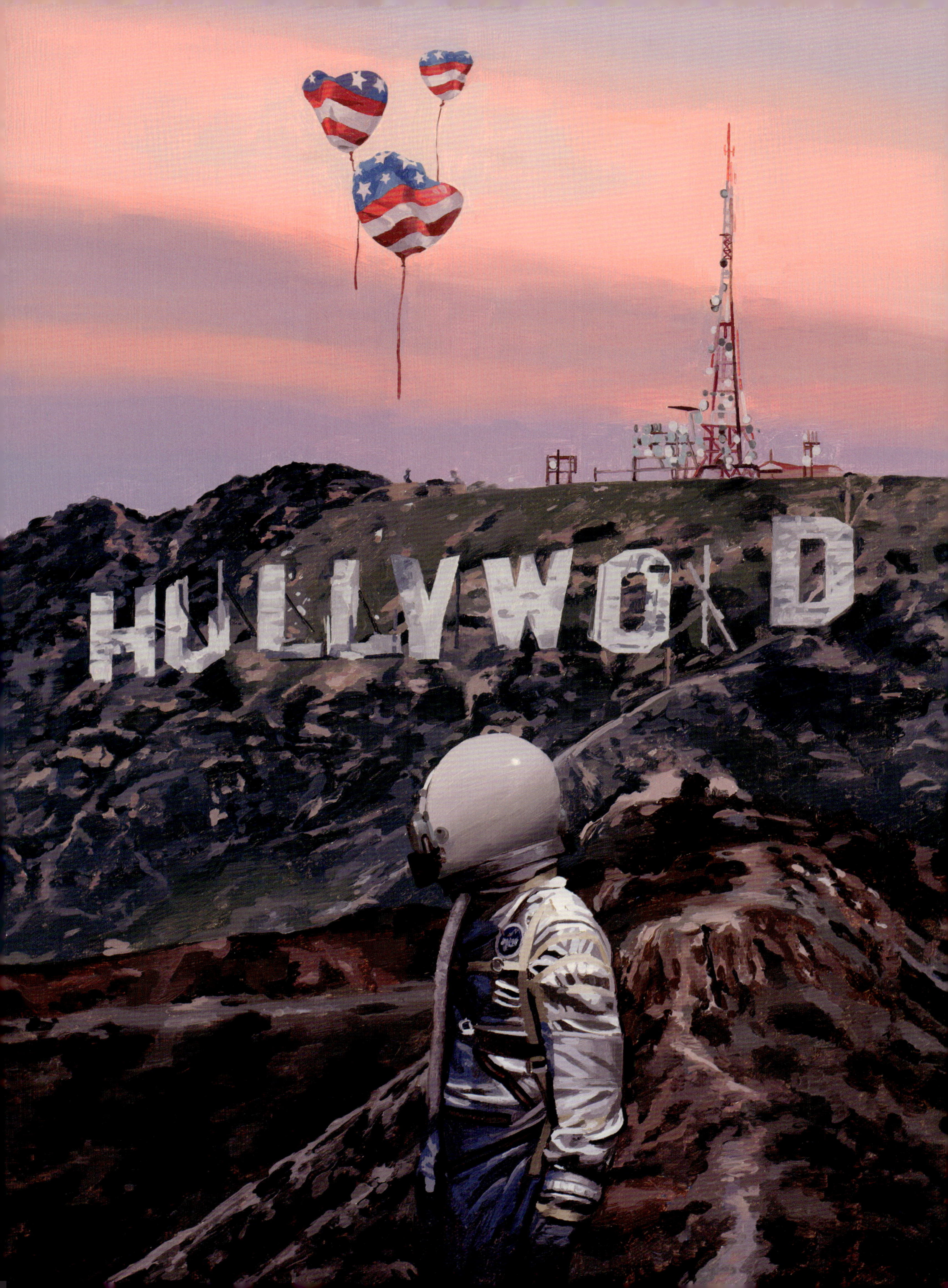

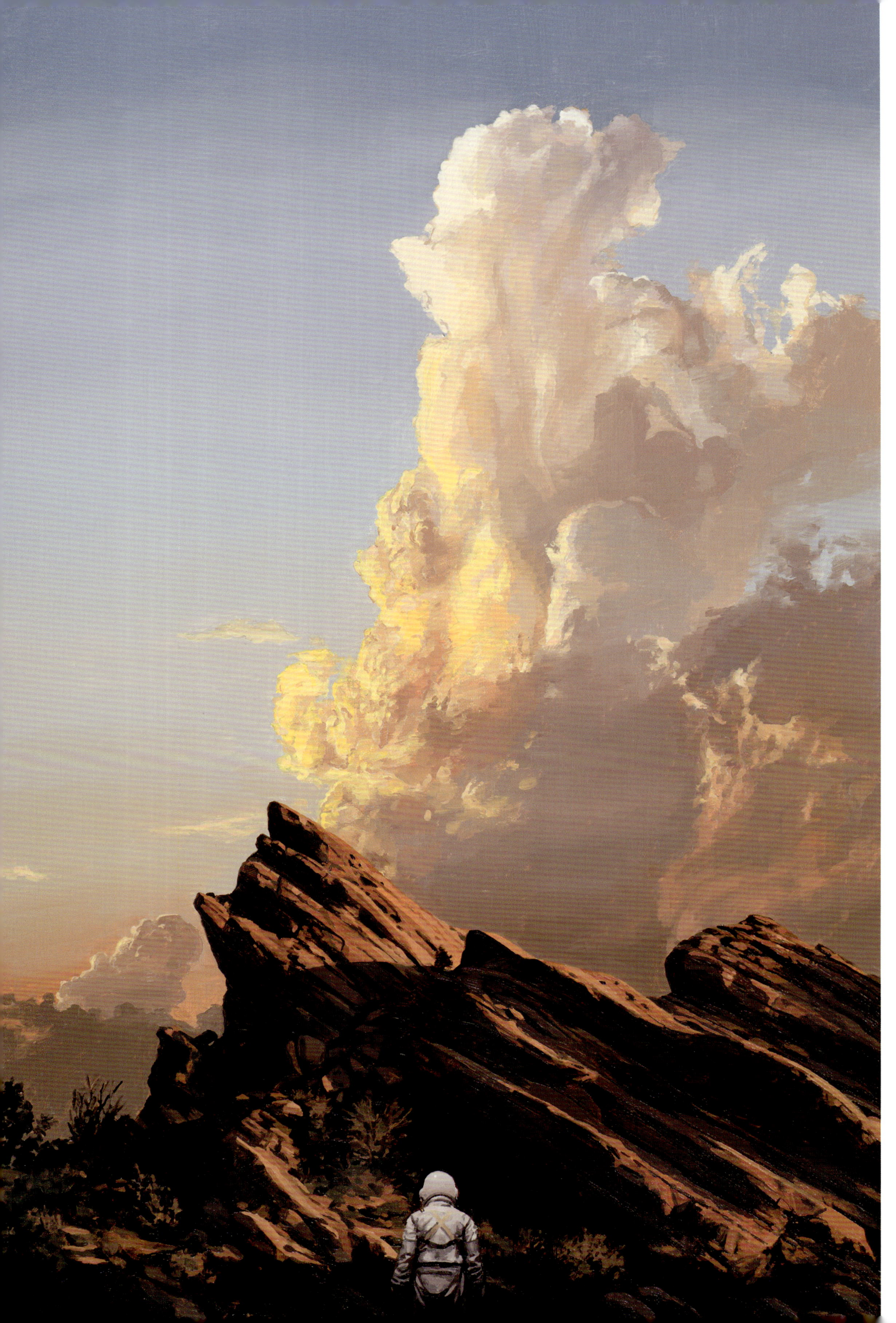

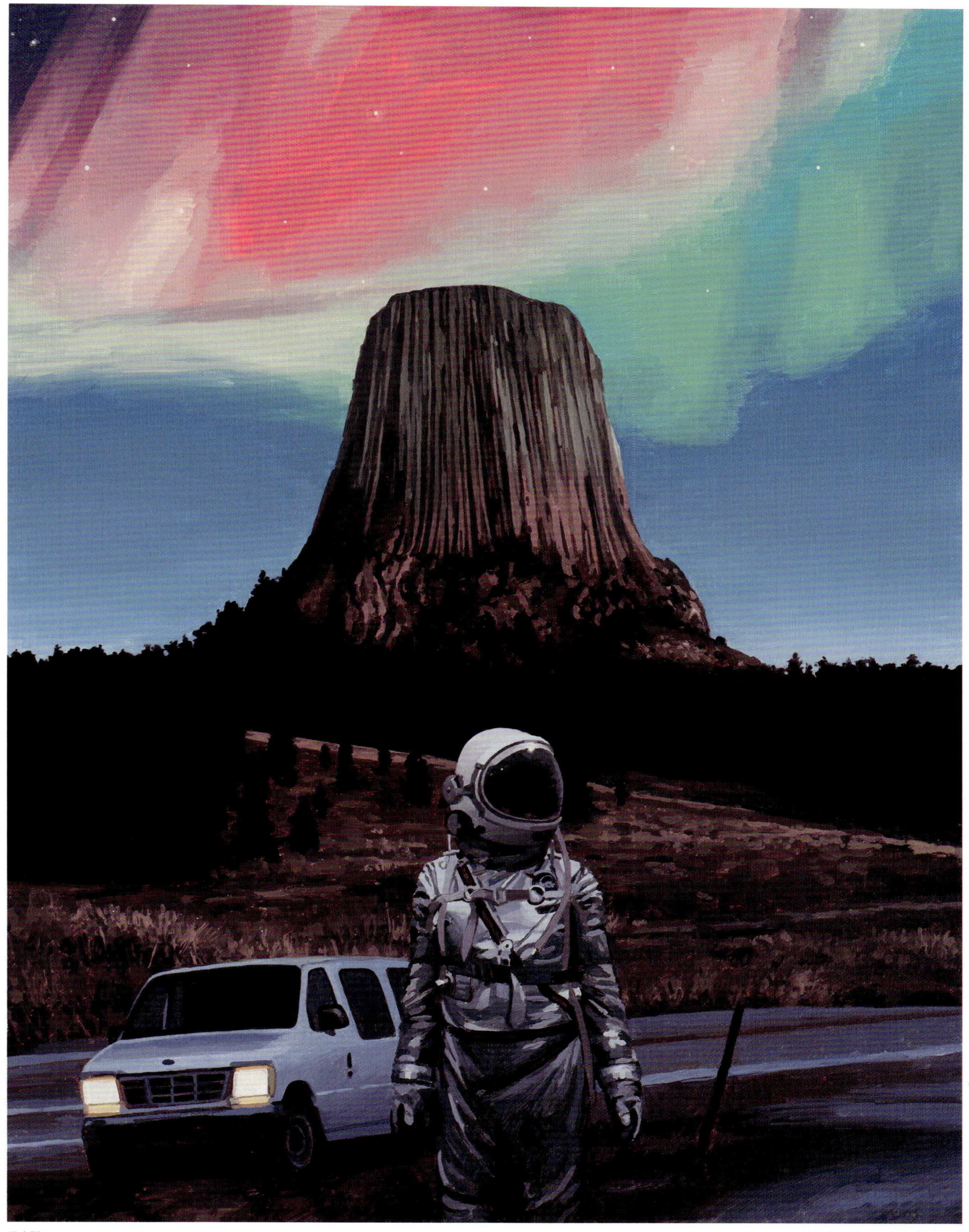

#451

DEVIL'S TOWER [2020]

#468

VASQUEZ [2020]

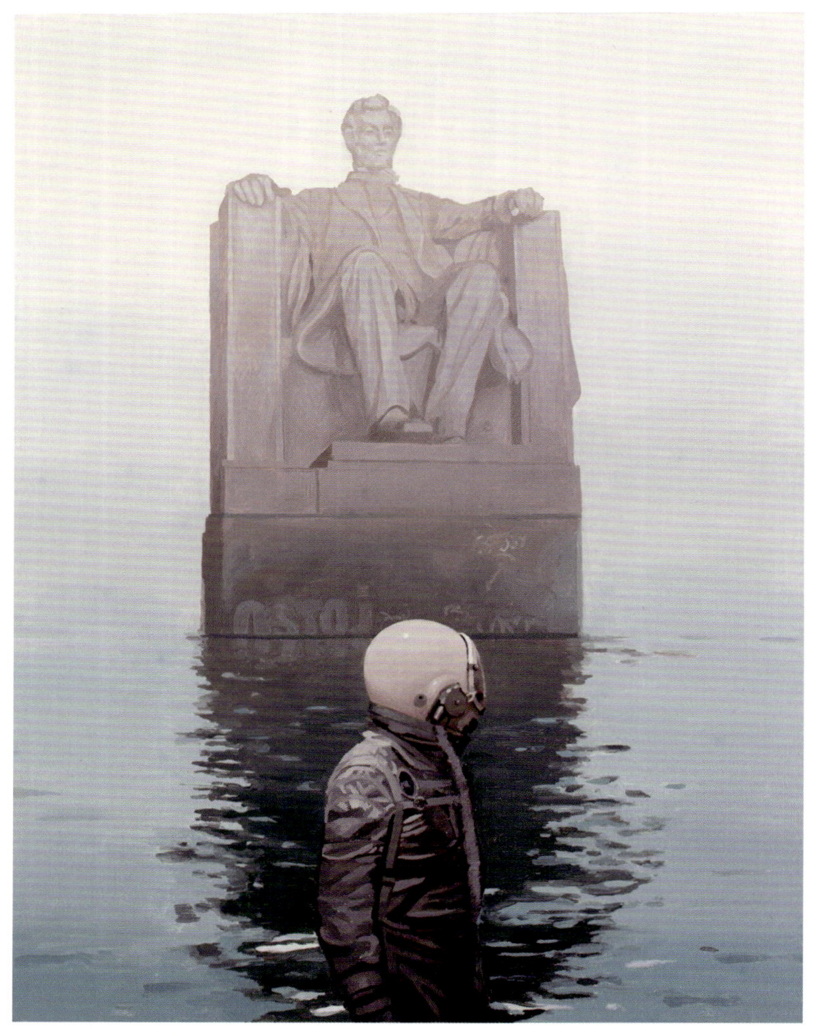

#459
ABE [2020]

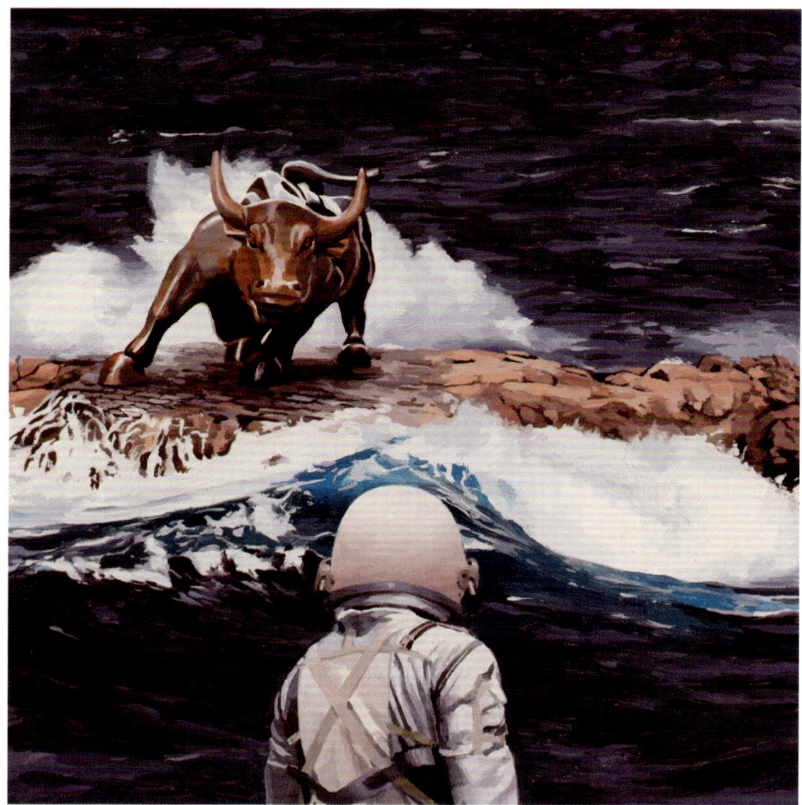

#455
BULL [2020]

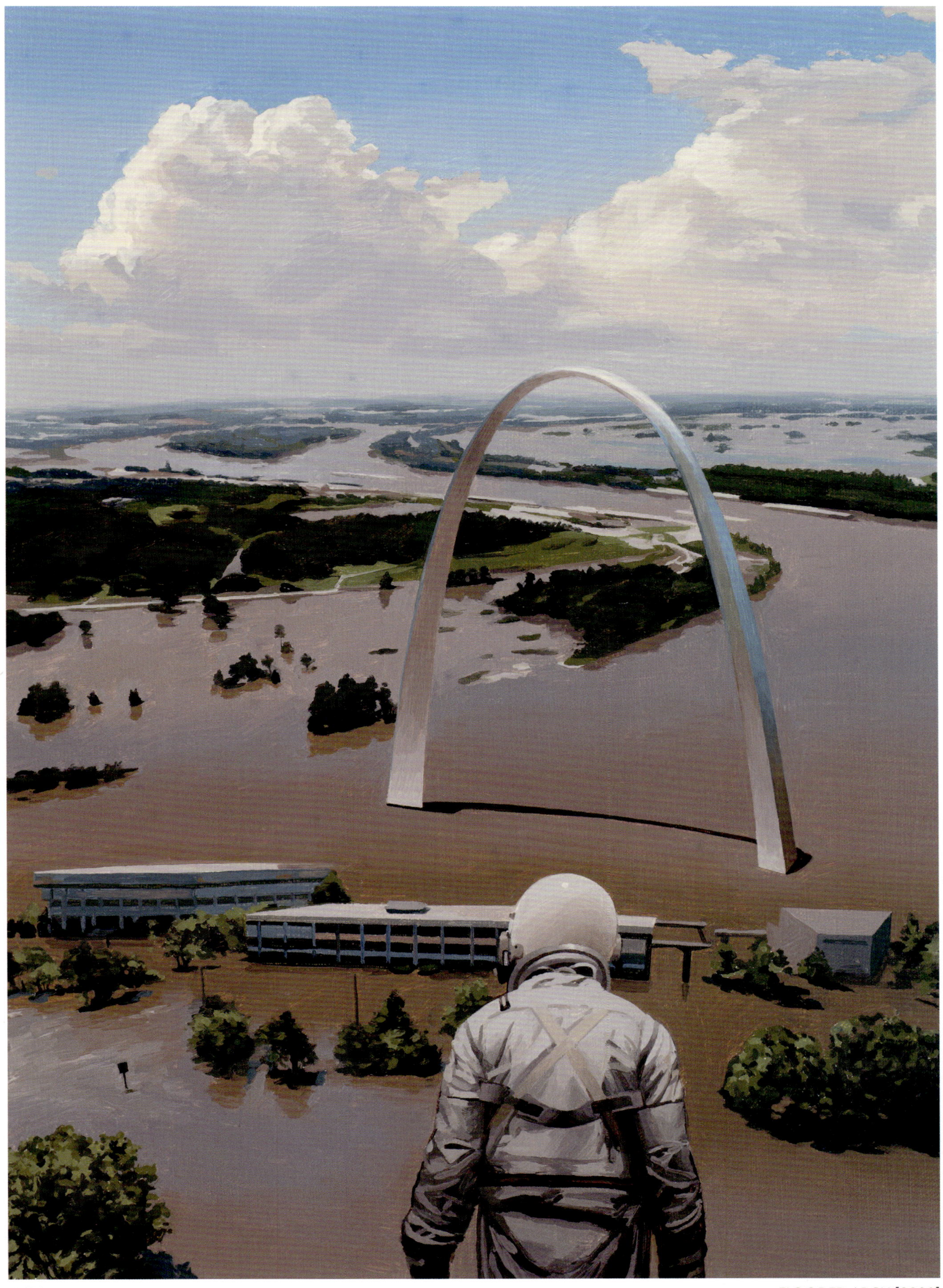

#458

FLOODED ARCH [2020]

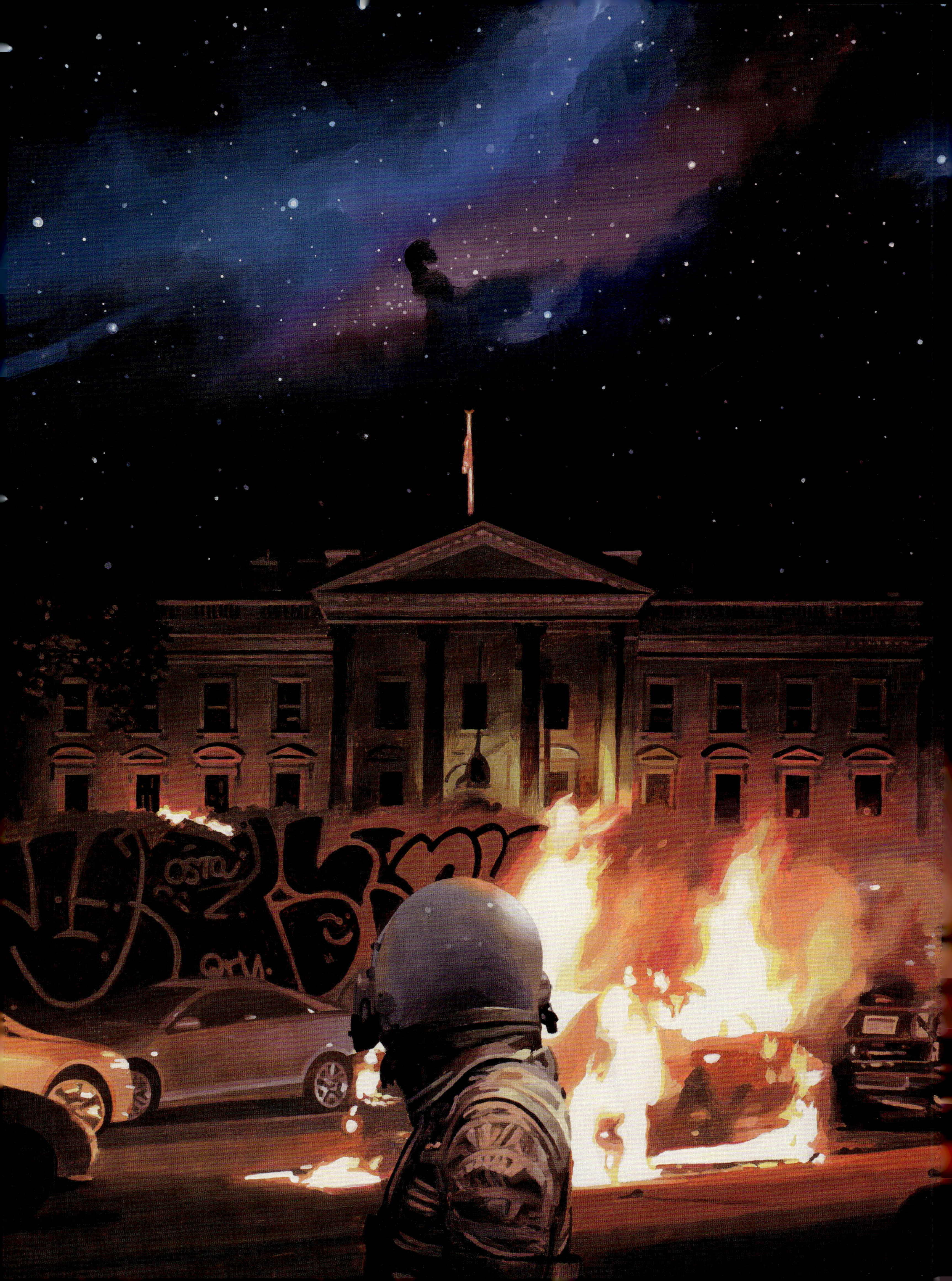

QUARANTINE

//

Spoke Art Gallery, New York, NY
September, 2020

I began working on this series of paintings while the world was in lockdown. Most of the planet was stuck at home riding out a pandemic unlike anything we've experienced in 100 years.

City streets were empty, buildings boarded up, coyotes and tumbleweeds inhabited downtown. I began to hear from people that the real world was looking more and more like one of my paintings. Needless to say, this gave me pause. It's always good as an artist to feel like you're in the zeitgeist. That you're capturing the time you're living in. It's another thing entirely to get the uneasy feeling that you've predicted a fairly bleak present. I was struggling with what to do with this knowledge. I had people asking me, only half jokingly, to make paintings of a future that was considerably more pleasant than the one we were living through. How about rainbows instead of deserts? Unicorns and ice cream instead of empty and abandoned city streets?

And I, like many people, struggled with how to talk about this time we were all living through. How do I continue to make paintings when real life was stranger than anything I could imagine? And as weird and unprecedented as it all was, the longer I lived in quarantine, the more my actual life became mundane and borderless. I didn't see friends. I didn't see family. I barely left the house. Days became weeks became months. Time almost entirely ceased to have real meaning. There were no singular events in my life to delineate the passage of time. Things I watched on Netflix felt real and my real life felt unreal. The edge between things felt blurry. To compensate for lack of activity, my brain set me off wandering into increasingly surreal dreams at night, leaving me groggy and confused in the morning. Reality itself was bending. It was starting to lose meaning.

And then, in the midst of it all, George Floyd.

The world seemed to tip on its axis. Cities that had been empty were now filled with fire and protest. Months of nothingness suddenly became too much. The blurry and surreal dreamscape I was floating through was filled with an endless barrage of news and news and news and news. Almost all of it bad. And yet there was the feeling that we were moving towards something. Finally.

#480
WHITE HOUSE [2020]

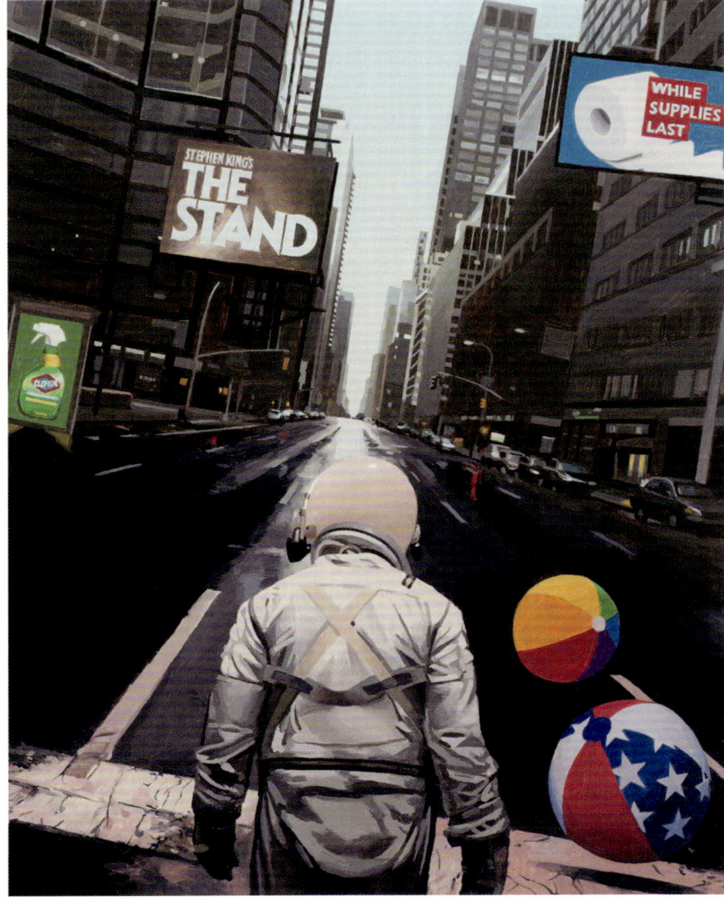

#474 THE STAND [2020]

Hundreds of years of oppression were, if not ending, at least facing a reckoning. Maybe? Hopefully. Statues toppled and fell. Fires, literal and metaphorical, continued to burn.

And the virus picked up steam again. And we're all trapped inside of a snow globe being shaken every few days. The things that felt essential a few months ago seem meaningless now, and those three months might feel like three decades or three minutes, depending on how you look at it.

I've struggled to try and stay motivated during this time. So much has happened and yet I've barely left my house. Wandering daily from my downstairs studio to my upstairs living room couch and then back again. My work is very much about exploration. All I've had to explore recently is the darker depths of my own mind.

And so in these new paintings, the astronaut that roams my work wanders through deserted cities literally tipping and falling. Where gravity has its own free will. Bits and pieces of a recognizable pop culture landscape tumble through these scenes sideways, toppling along with statues. Things break. Things burn. But the astronaut, like us, keeps going.

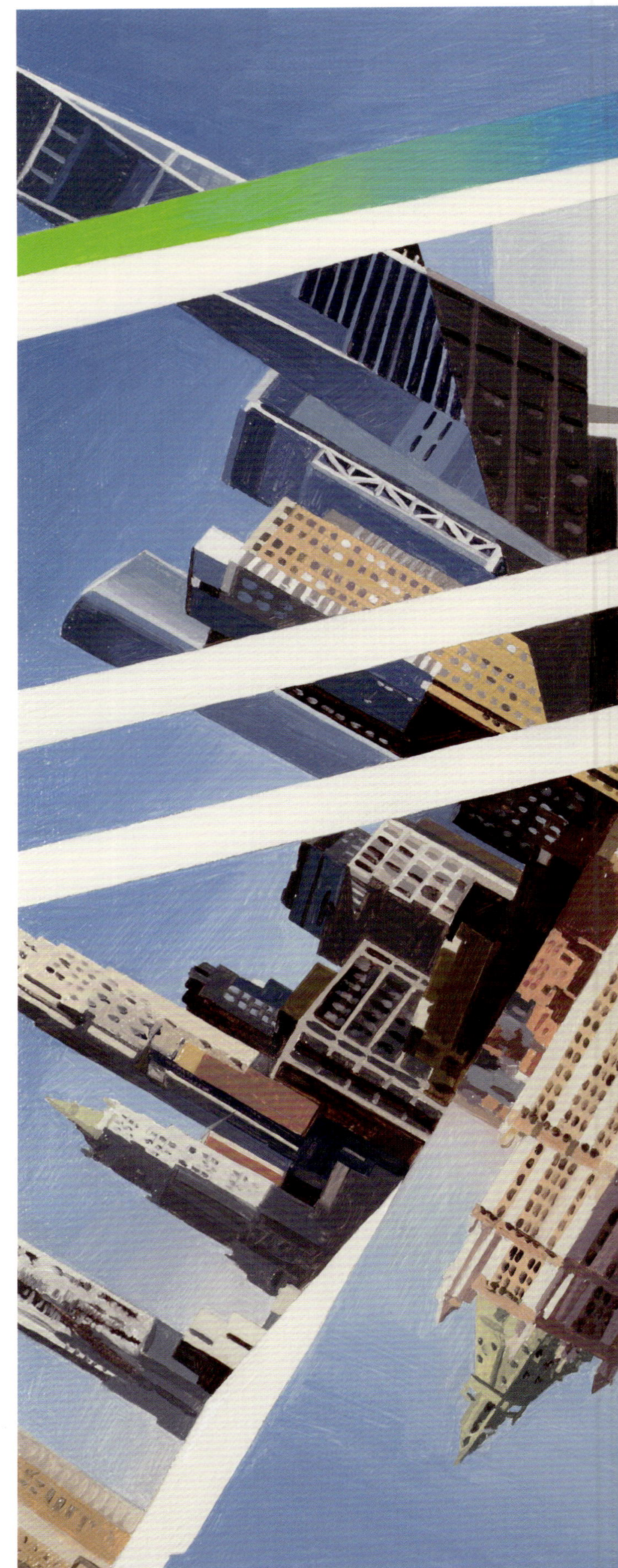

#491

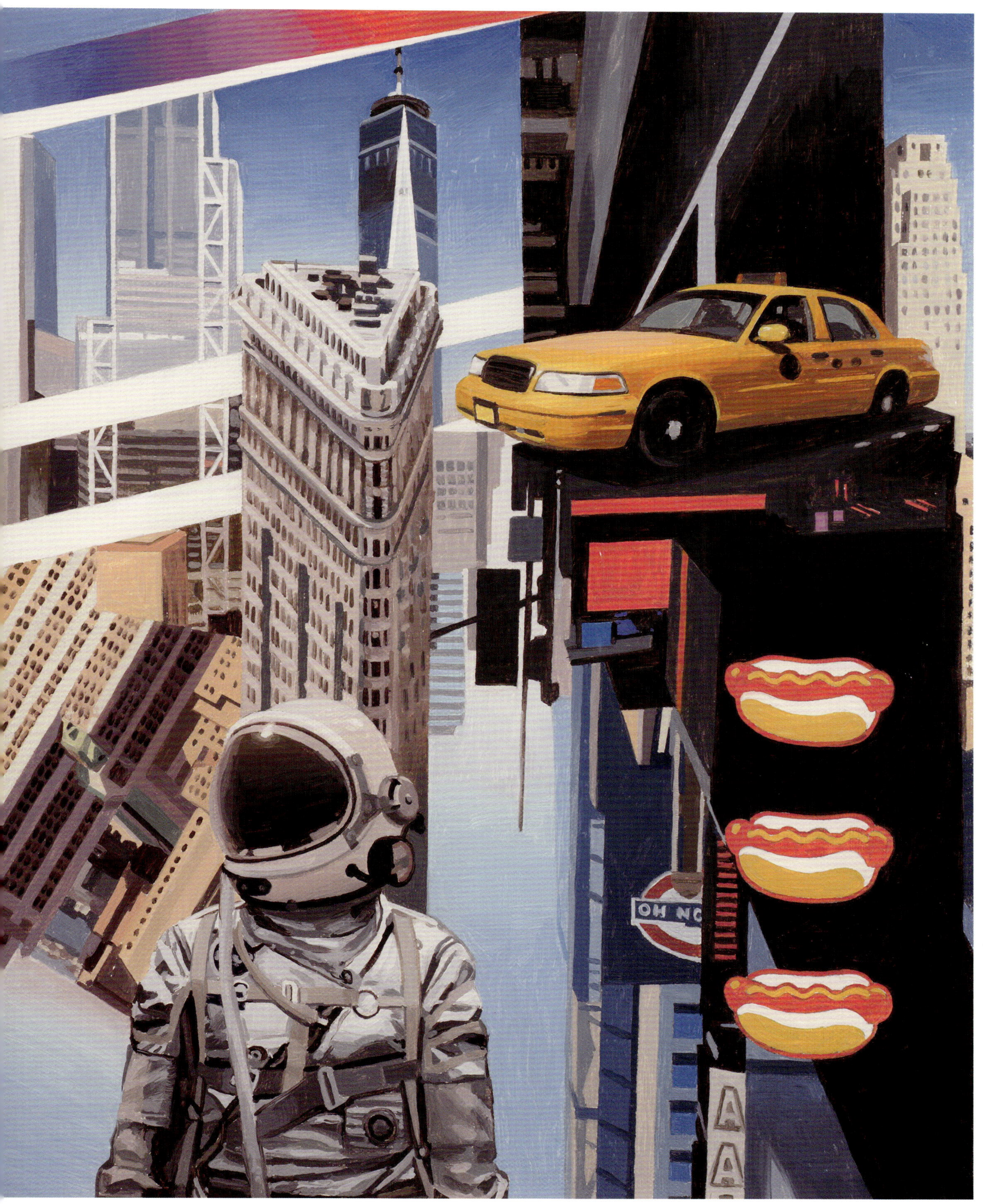

TAXI [2020]

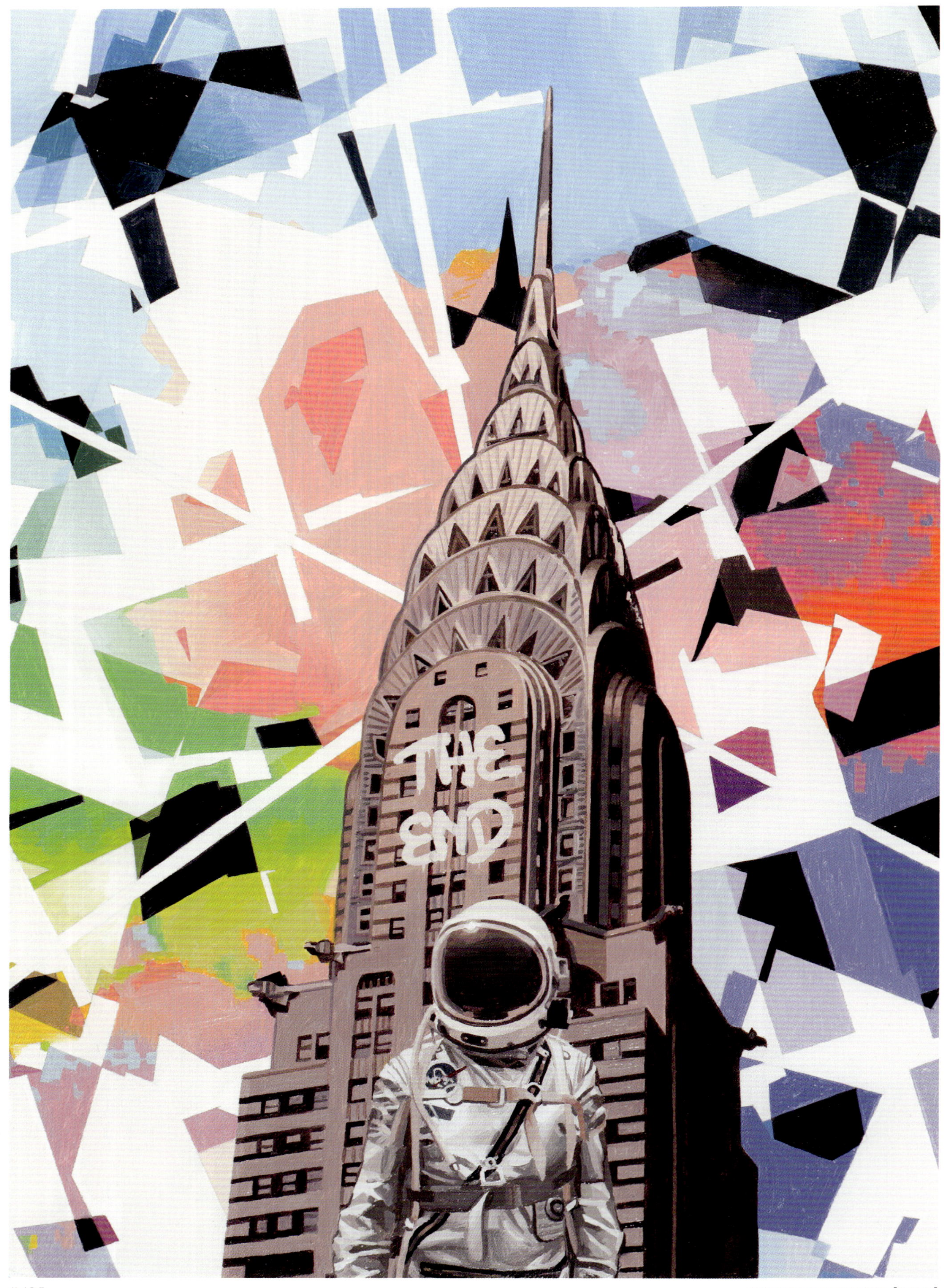

#495

CHRYSLER BUILDING [2020]

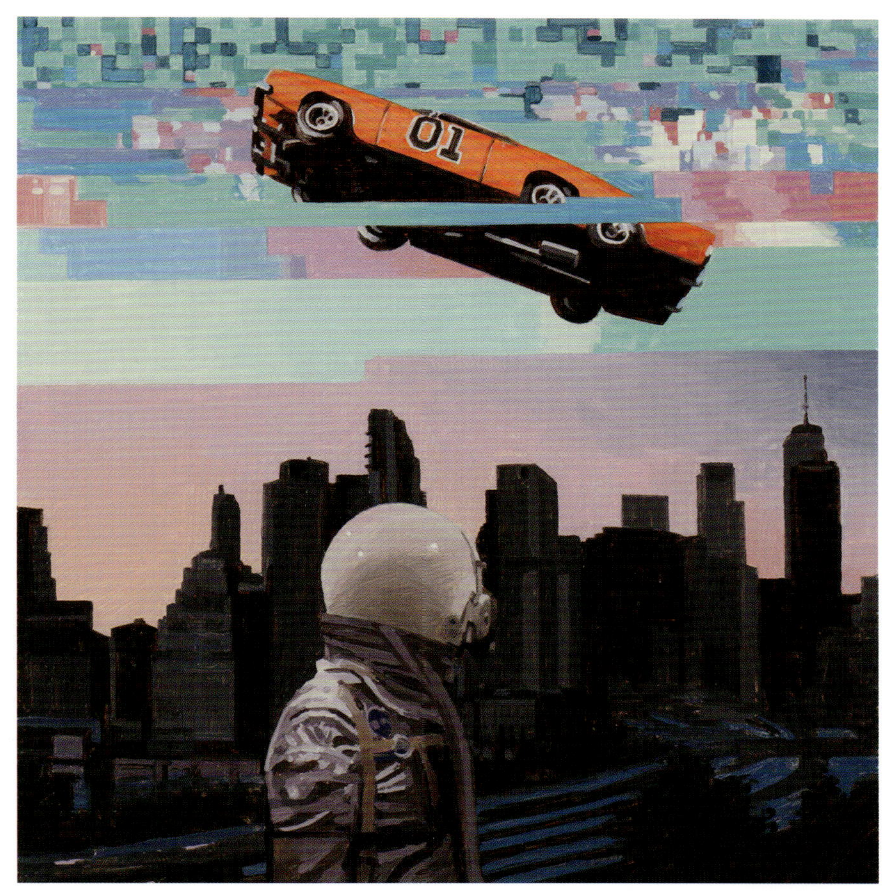

#487 GLITCH [2020]

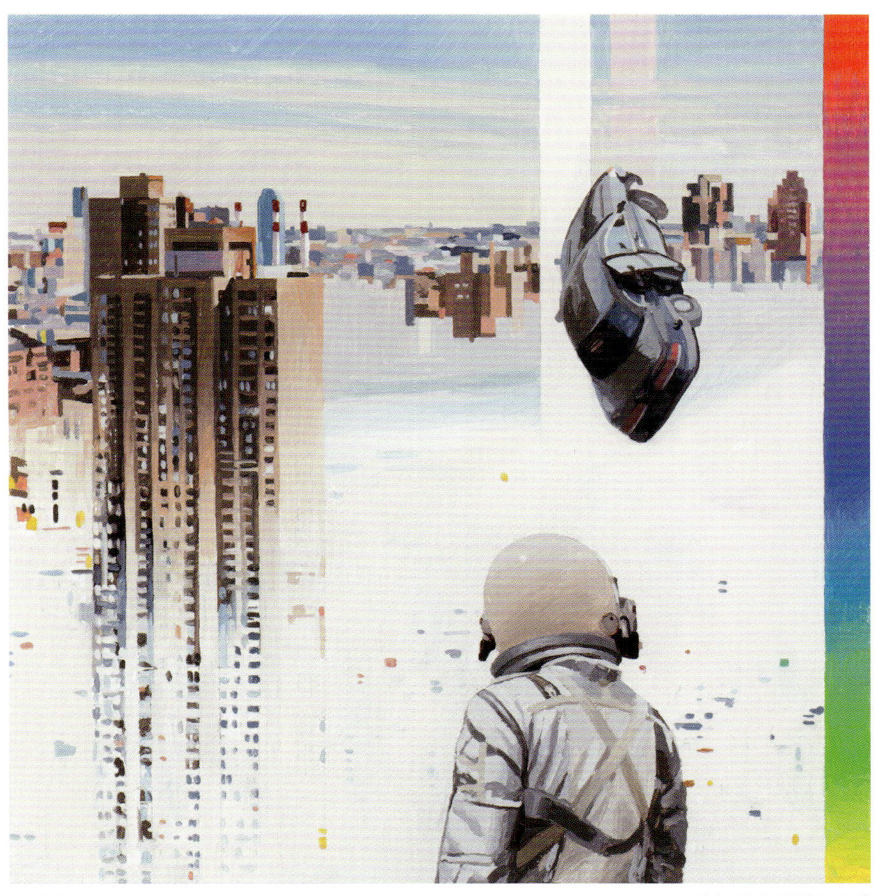

#494 FADE OUT [2020]

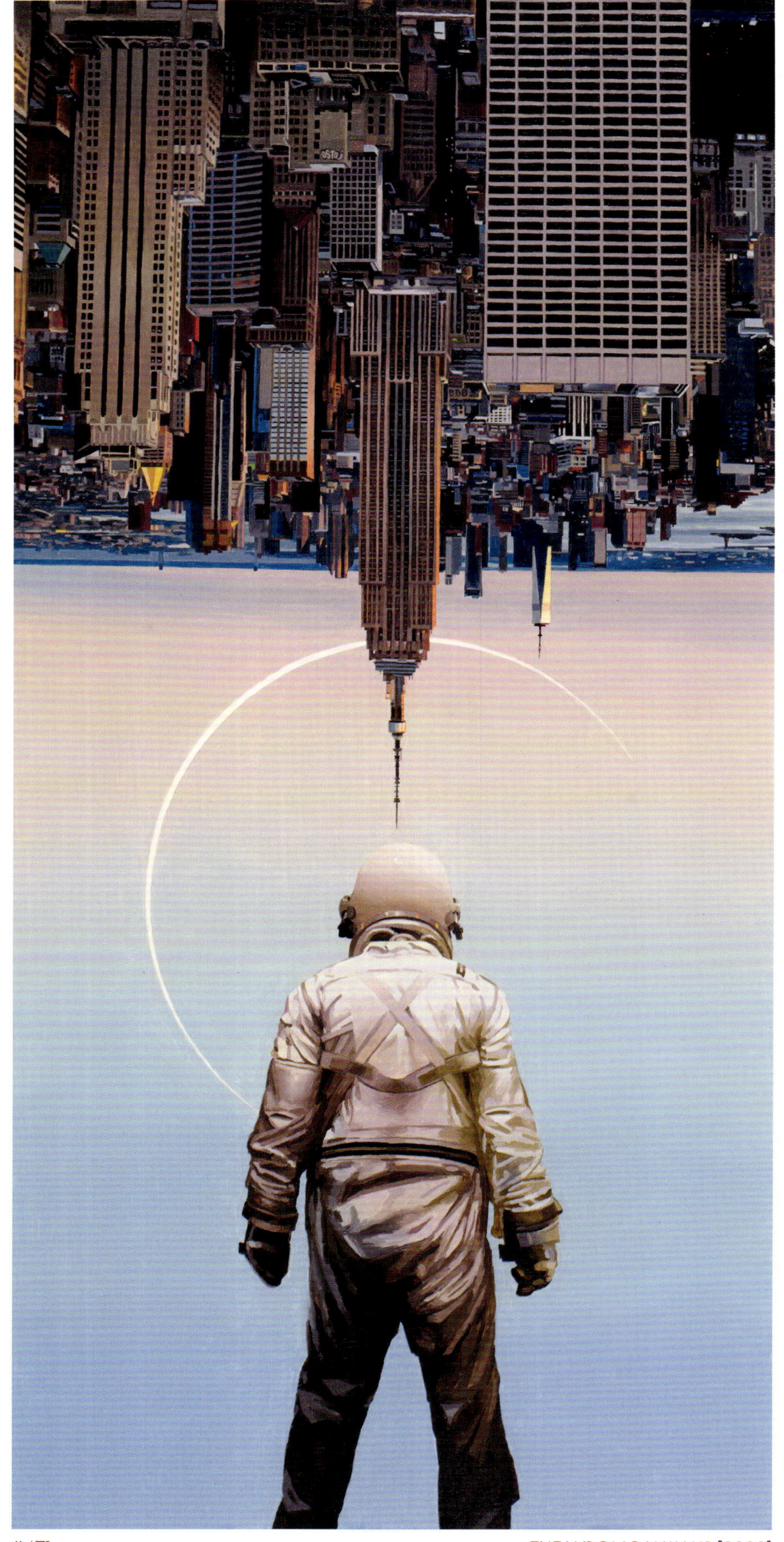

#471 THE WRONG WAY UP [2020]

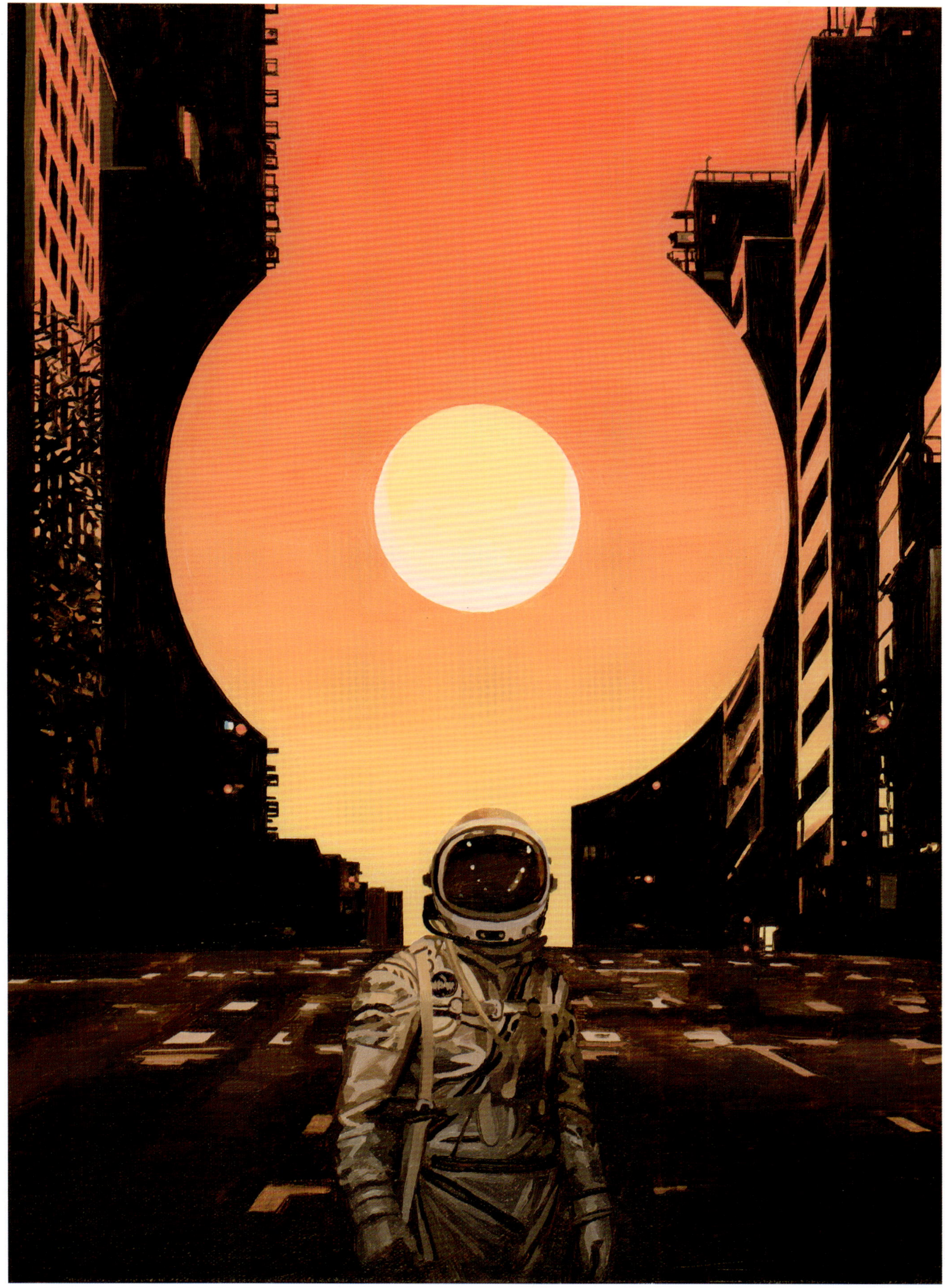

#473

HOLE [2020]

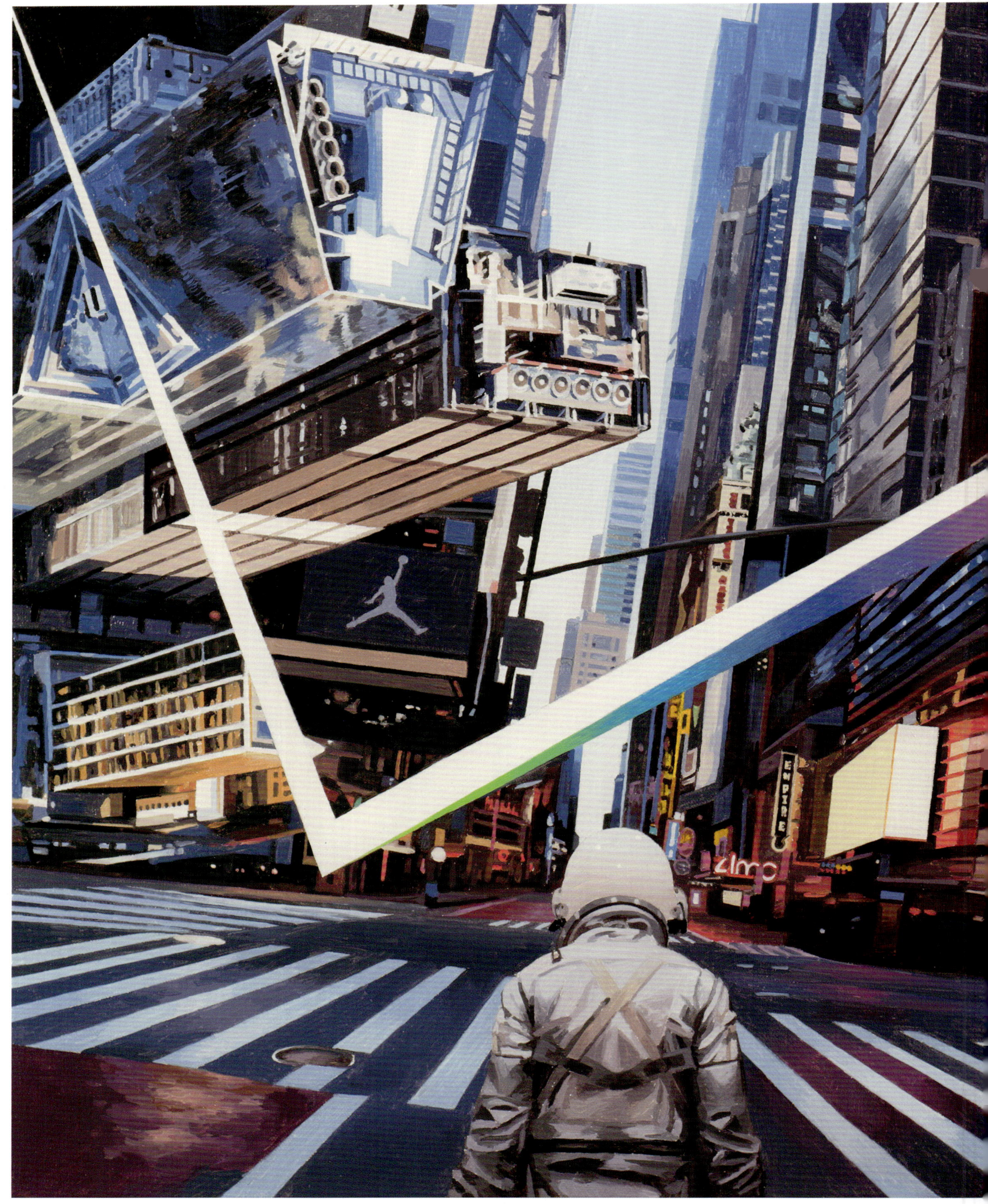

#490

EMPTY CITY [2020]

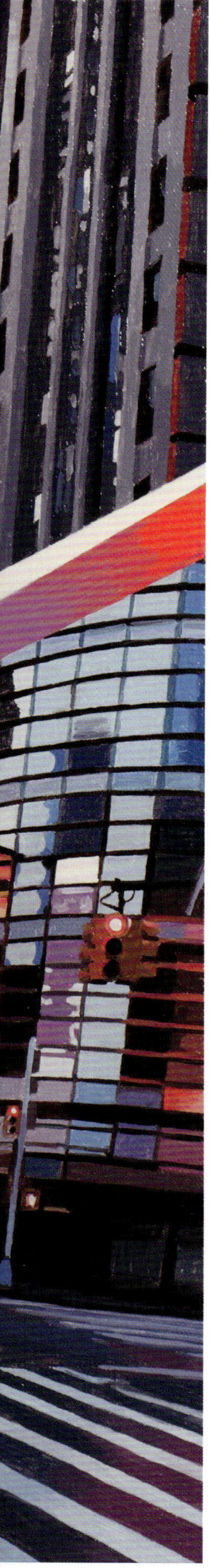

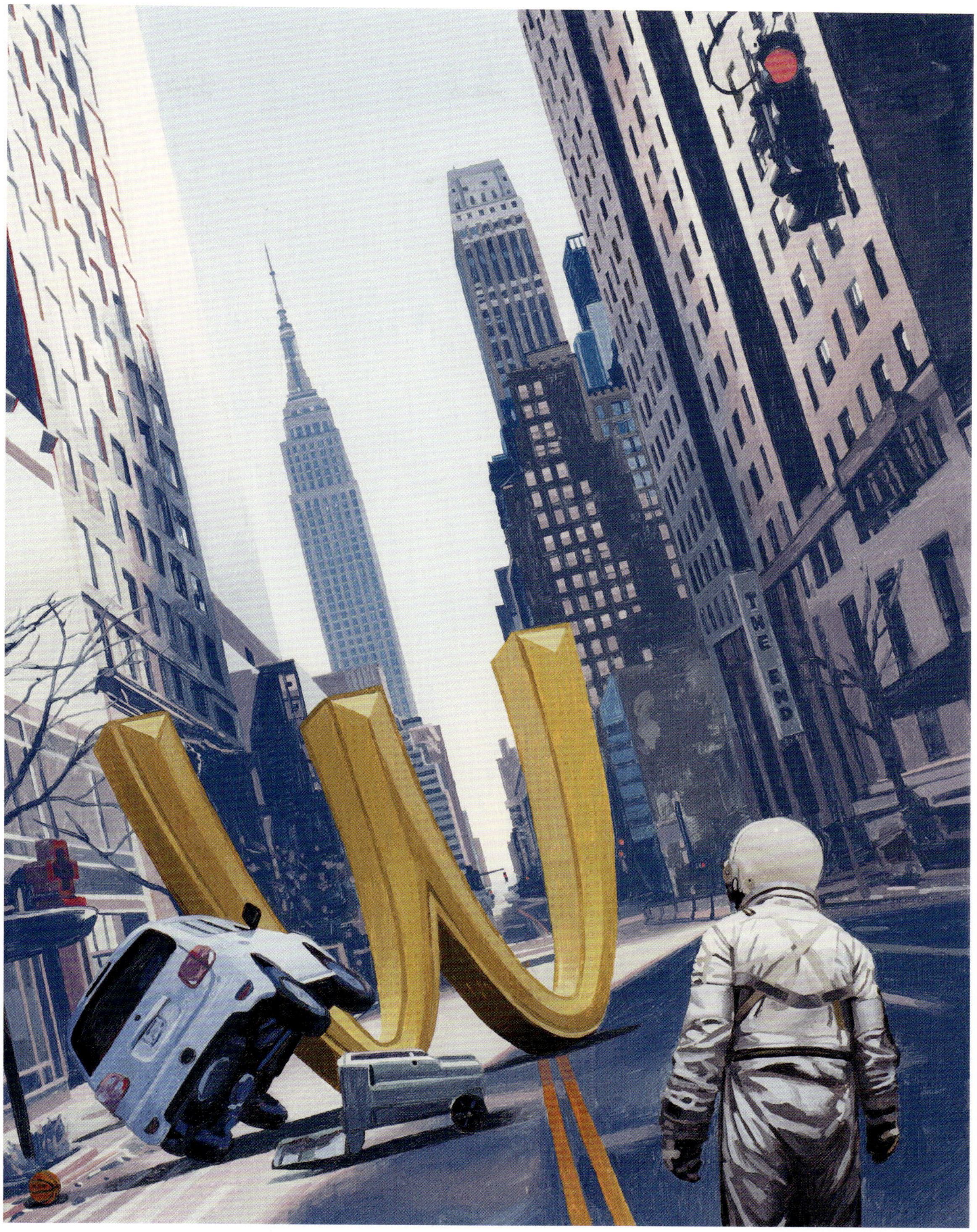

#472

M IN THE STREET [2020]

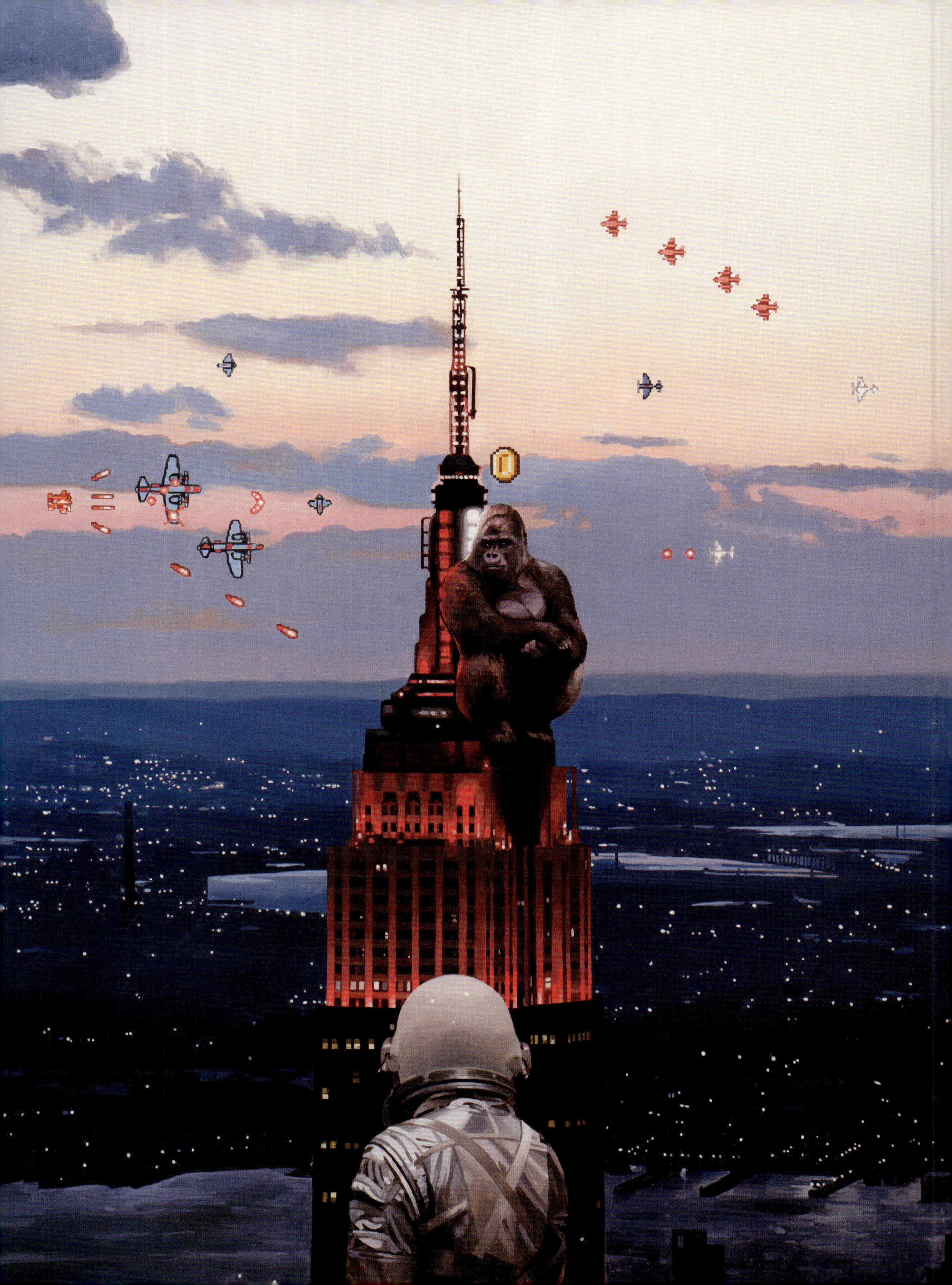

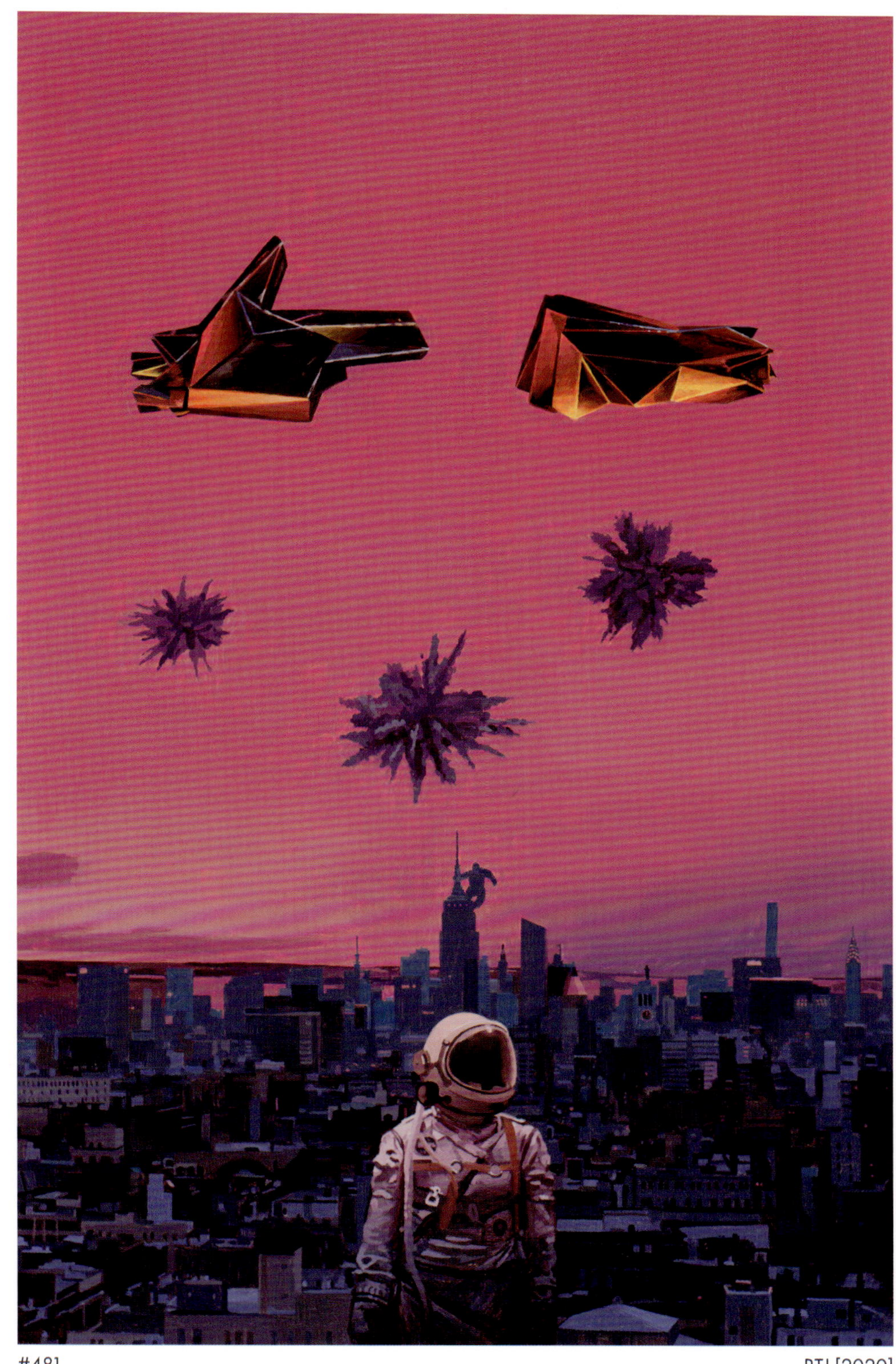

#481 RTJ [2020]

#482
KONG [2020]

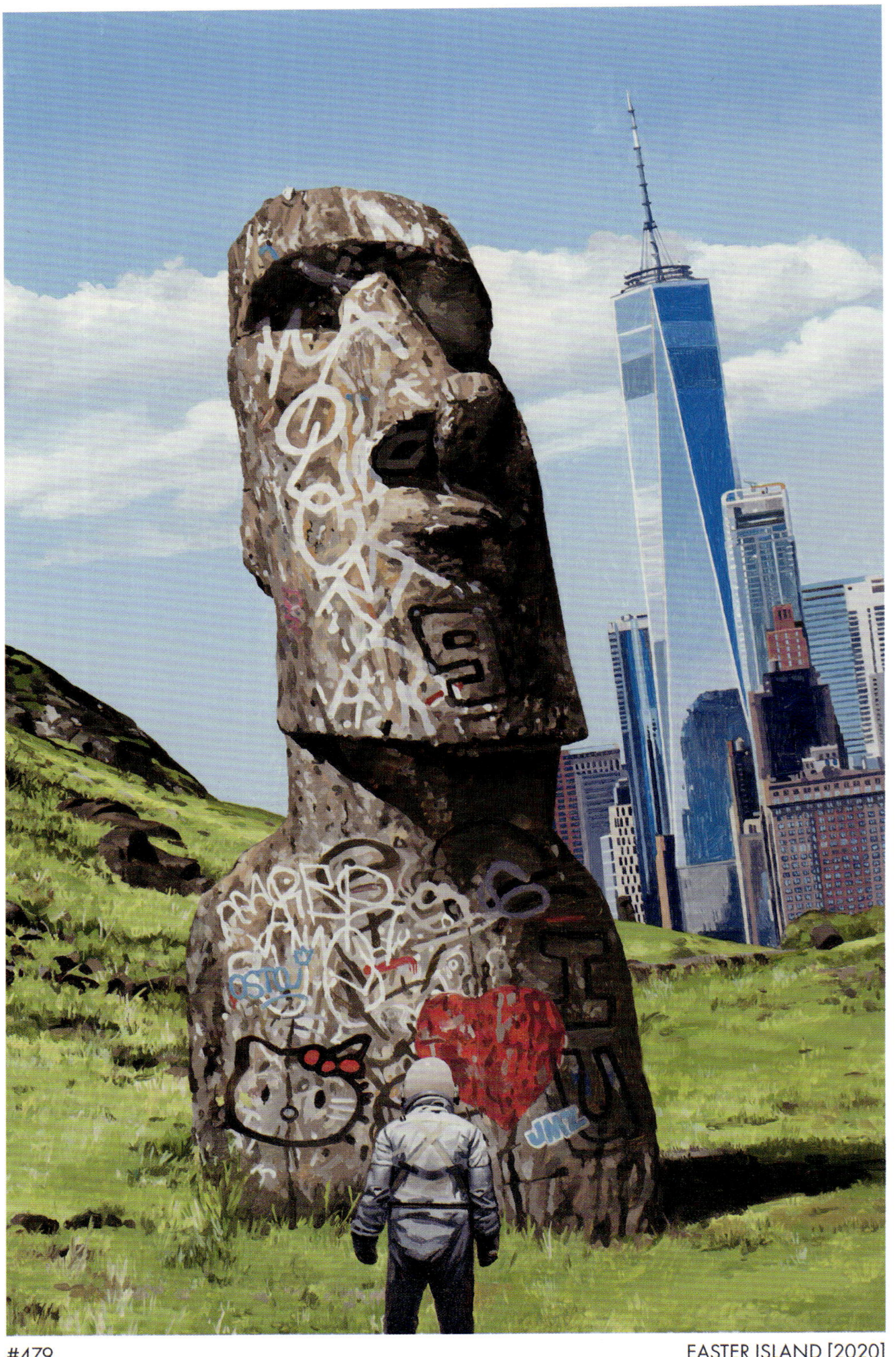

#479

EASTER ISLAND [2020]

#483

HEADLESS HORSEMAN [2020]

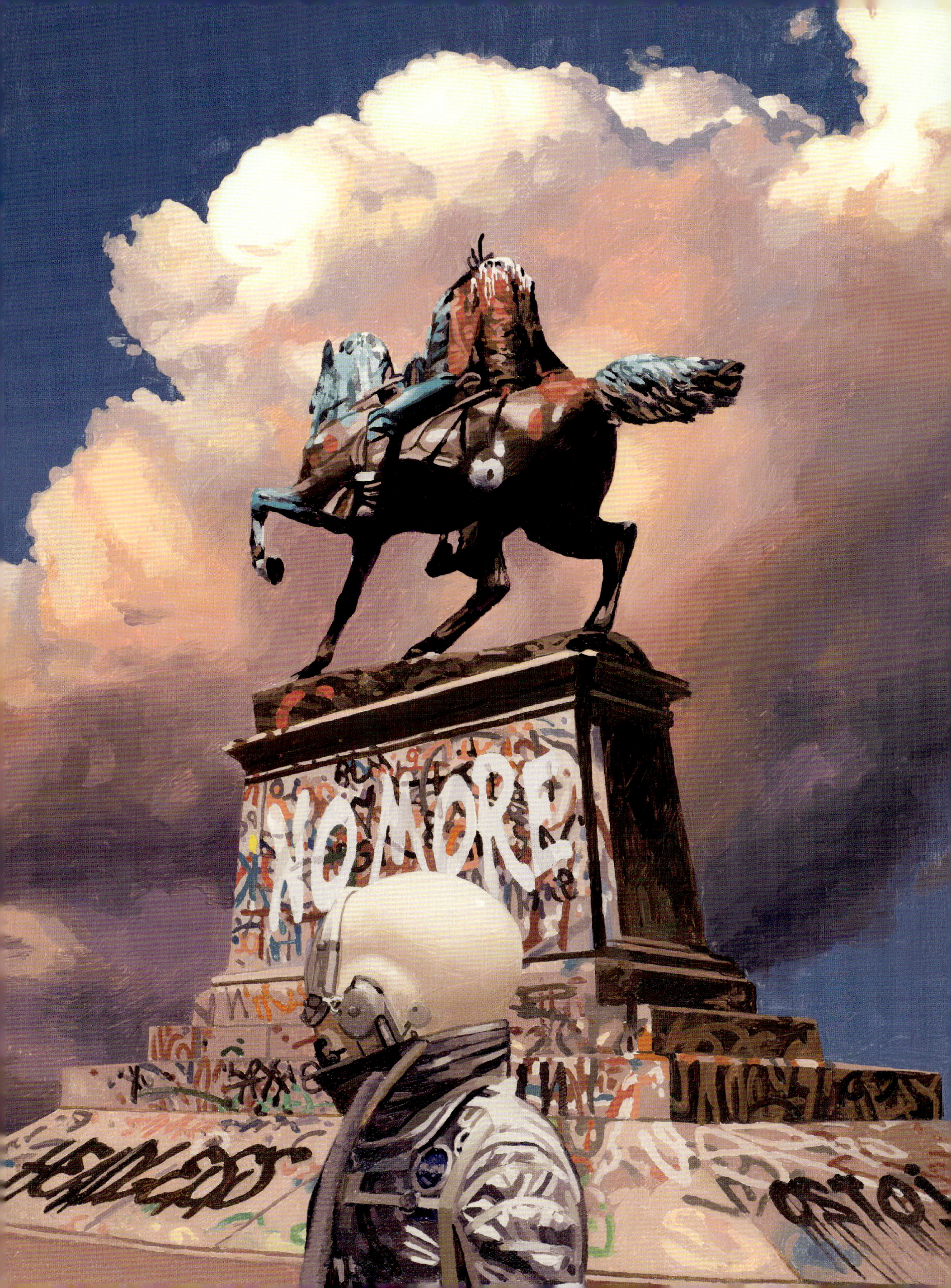
NO MORE

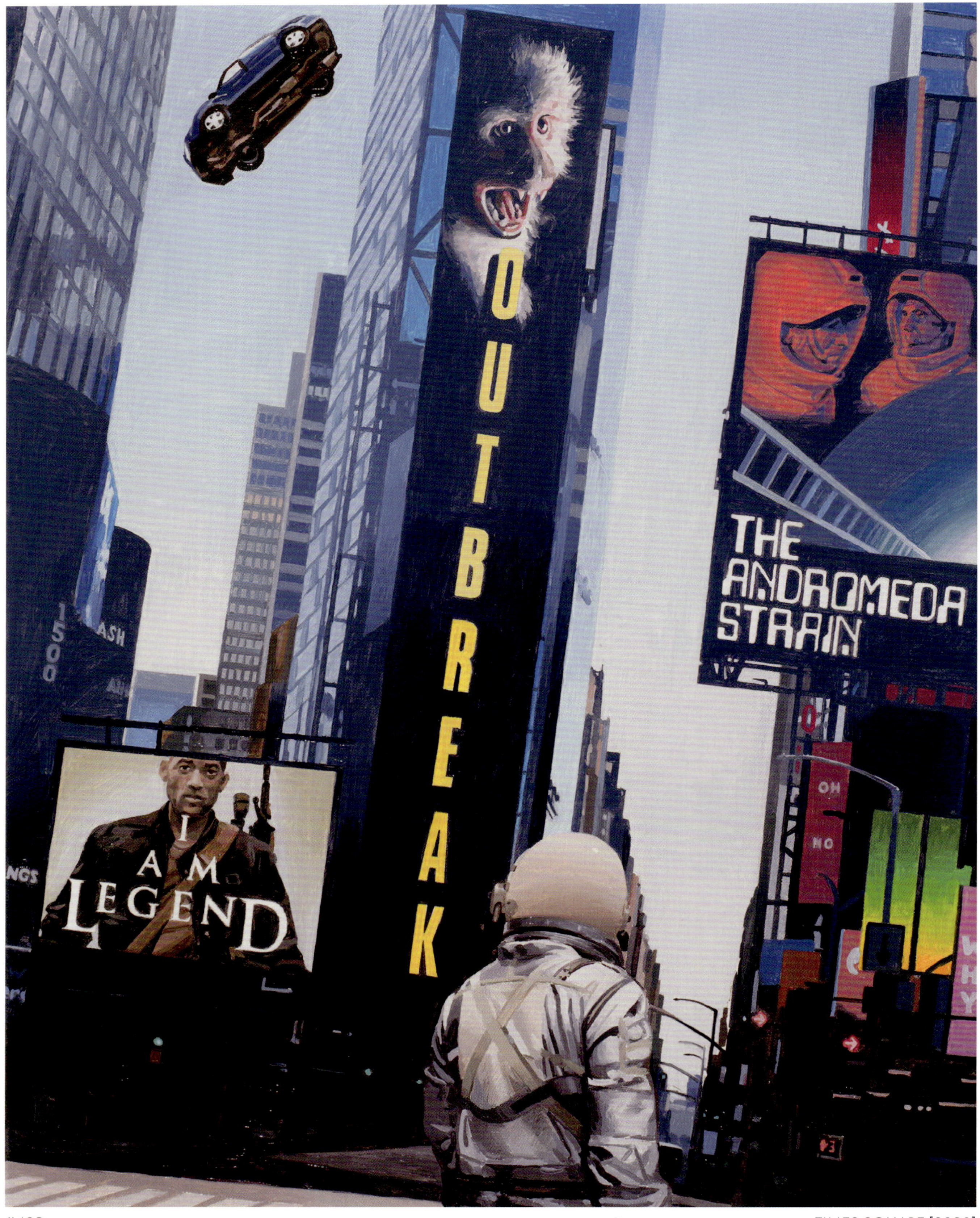

#489 TIMES SQUARE [2020]

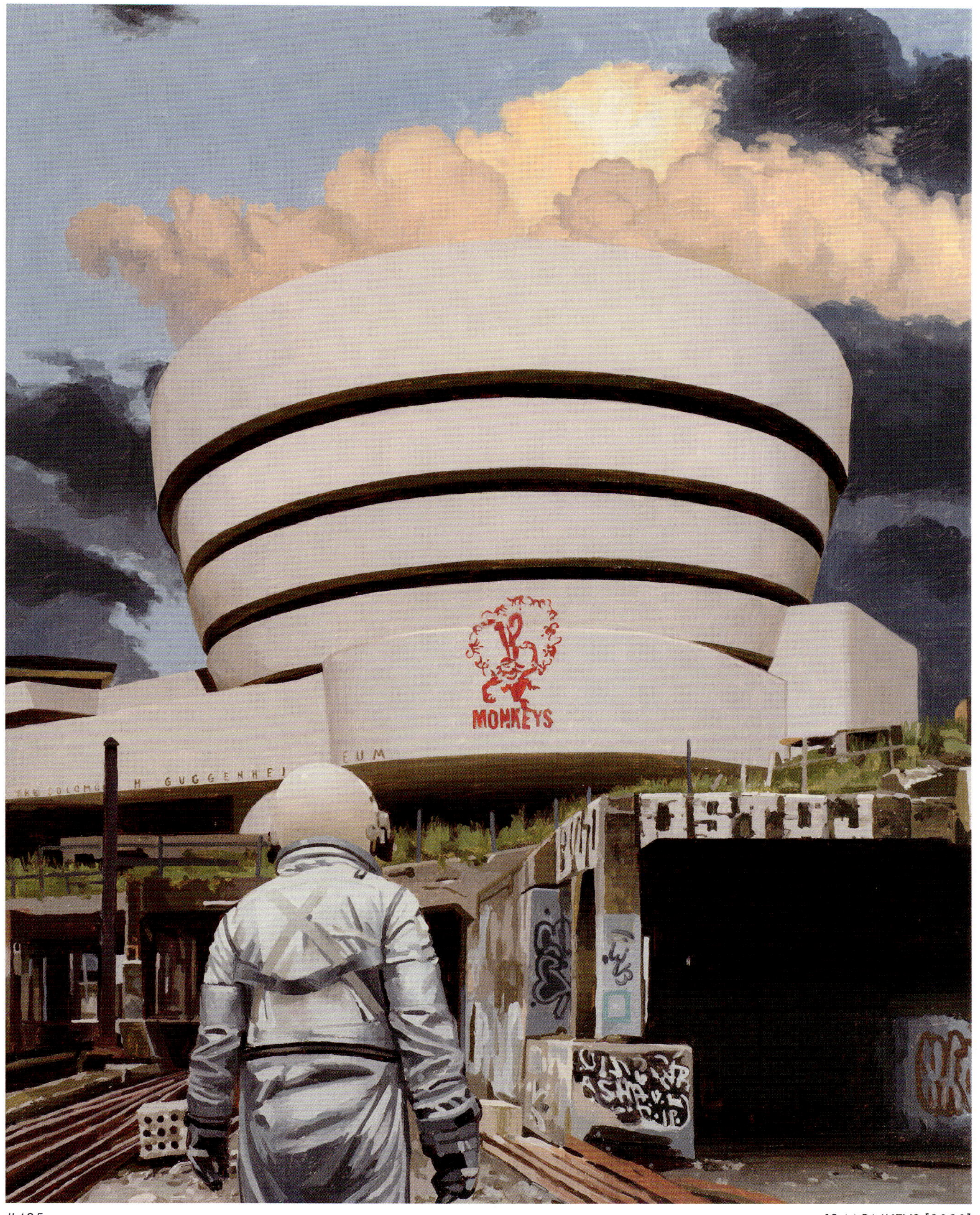

#485

12 MONKEYS [2020]

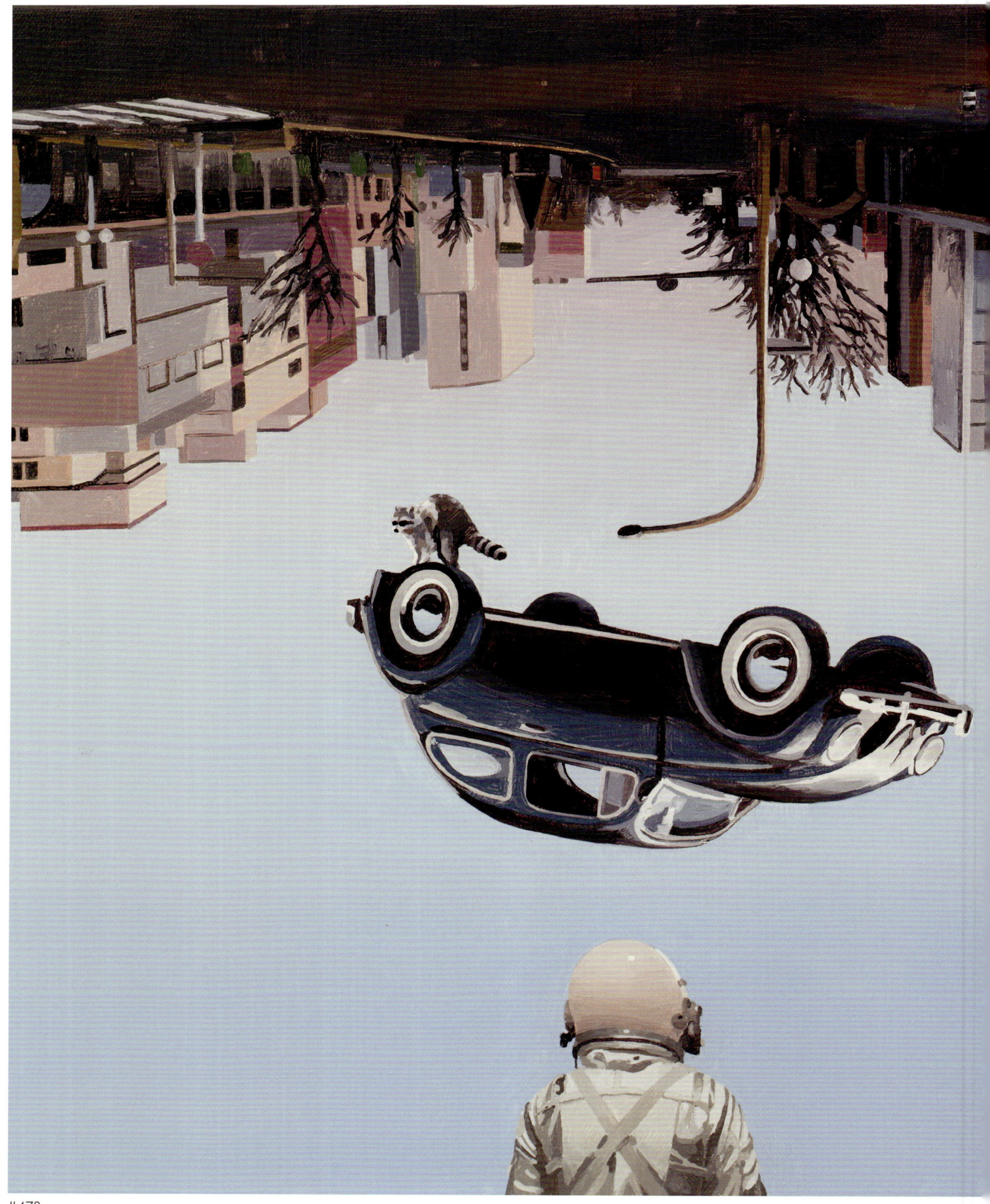

#478

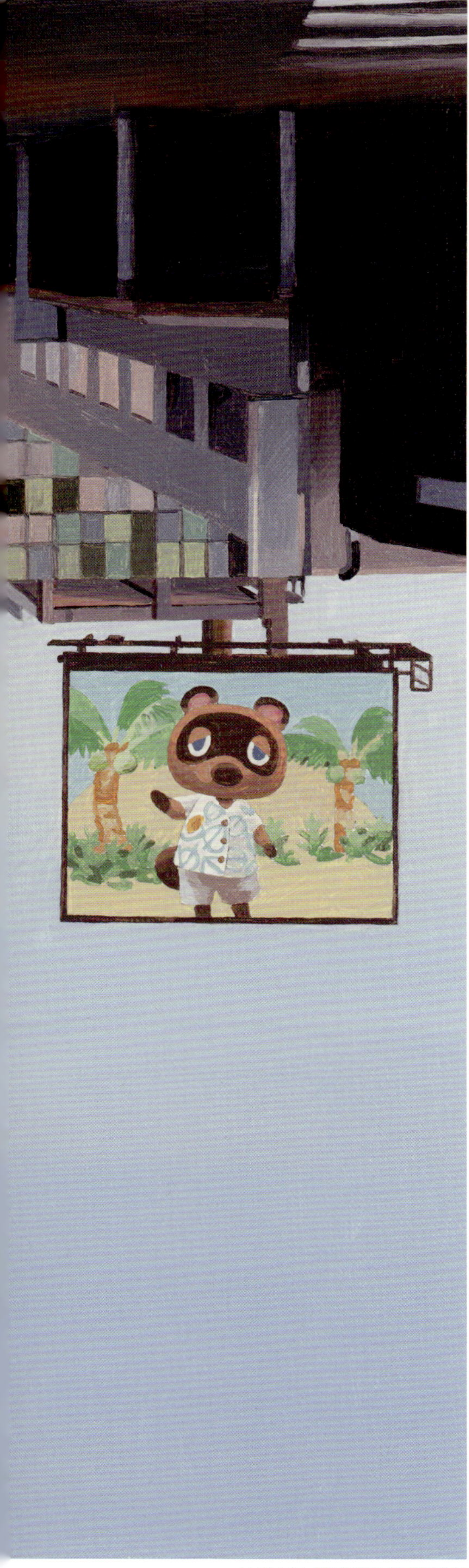

ANIMAL CROSSING [2020]

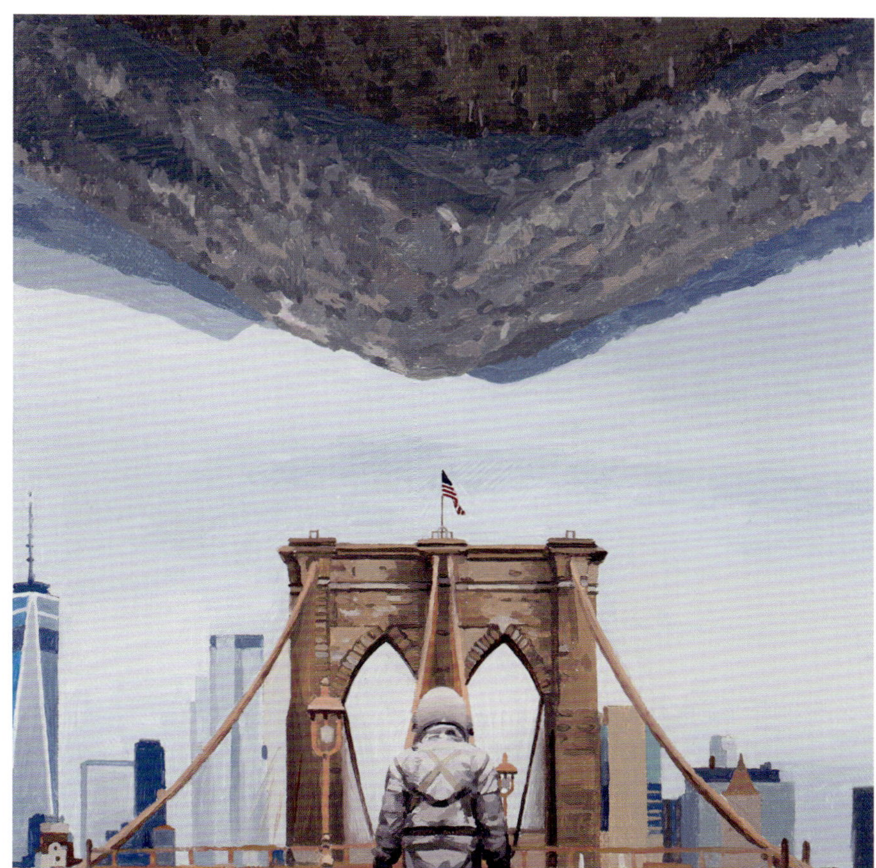

#484 BROOKLYN [2020]

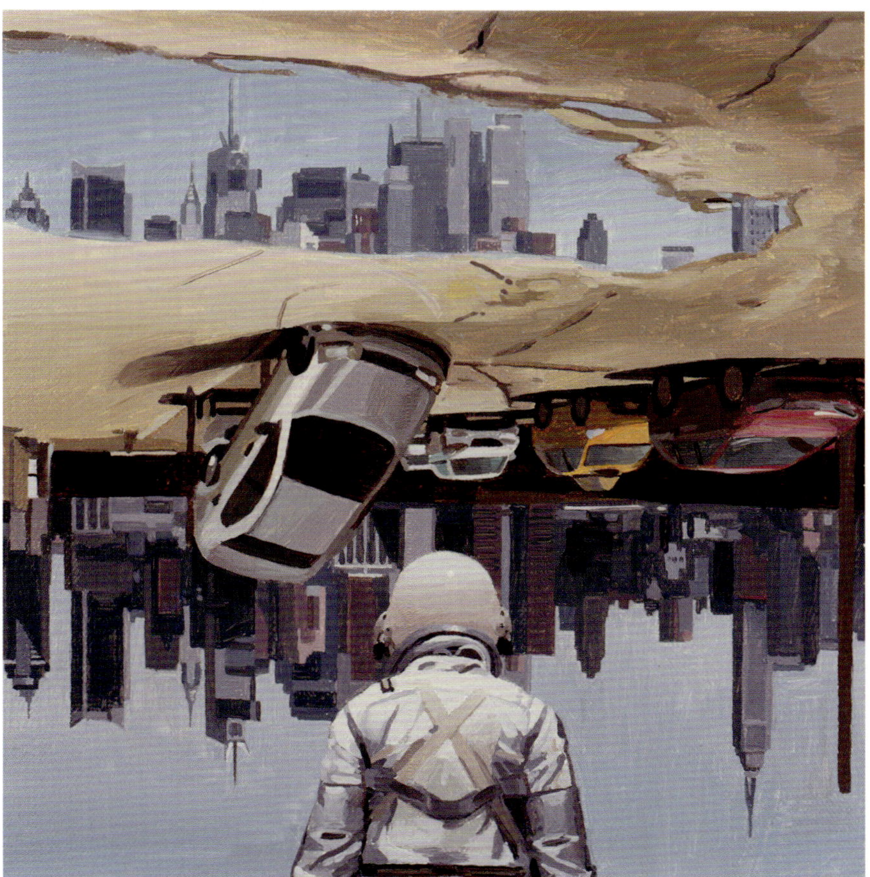

#486 PUDDLE [2020]

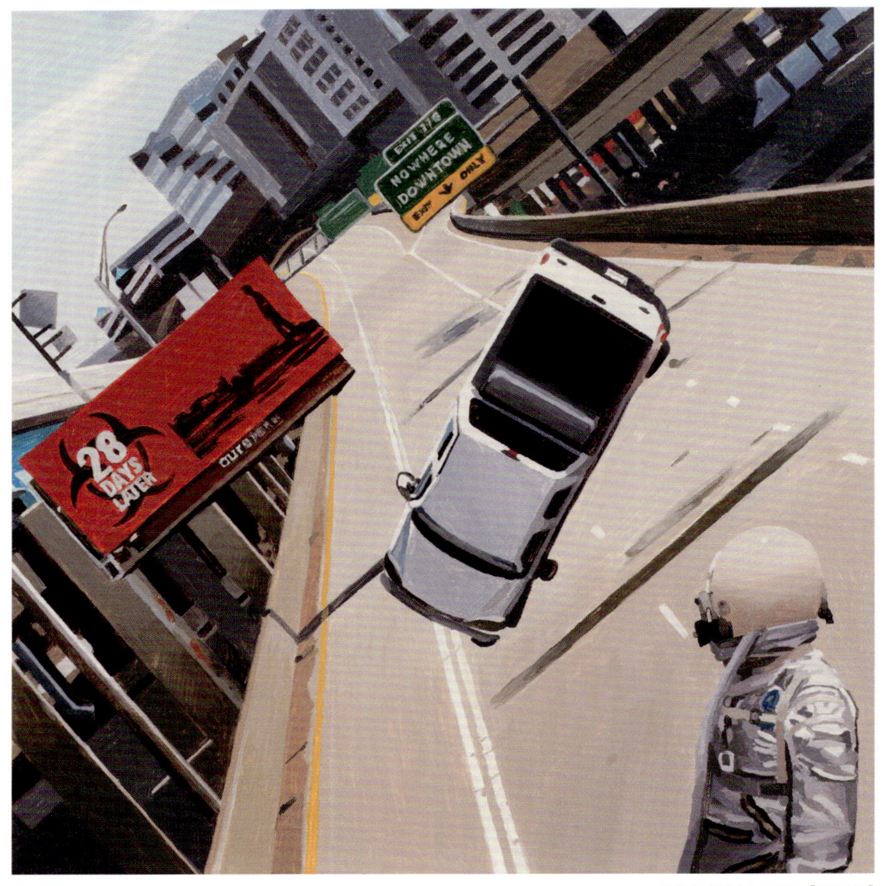

#477 28 DAYS LATER [2020]

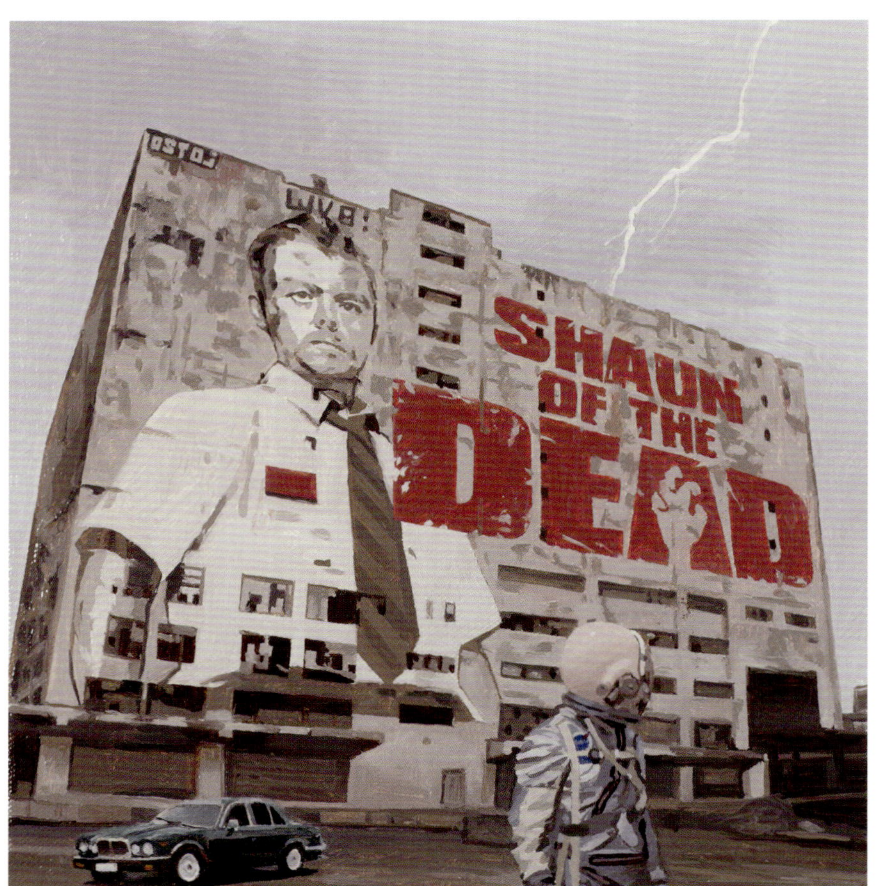

#492 SHAUN [2020]

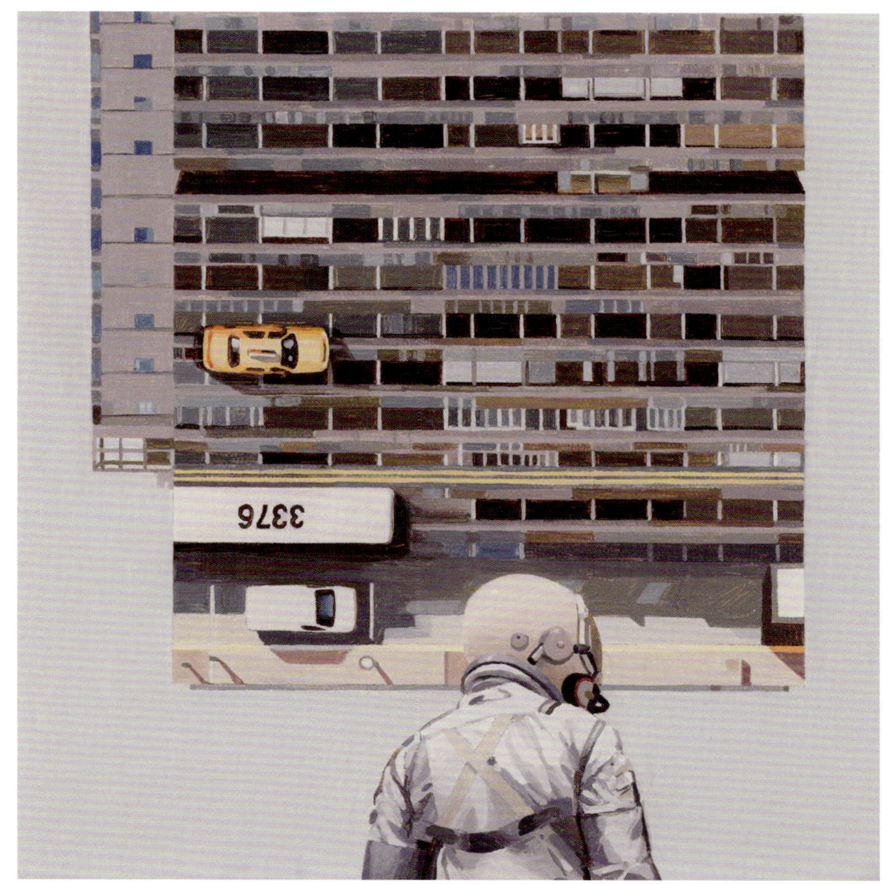

#476 RIGHT OF WAY [2020]

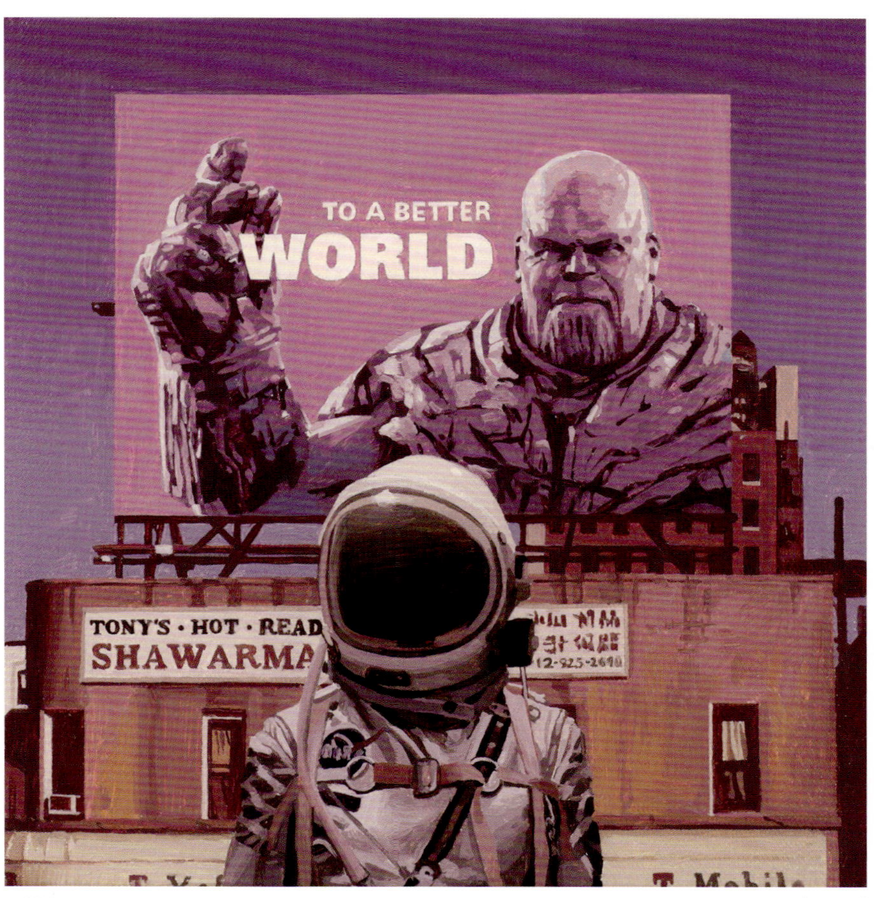

#488 TO A BETTER WORLD [2020]

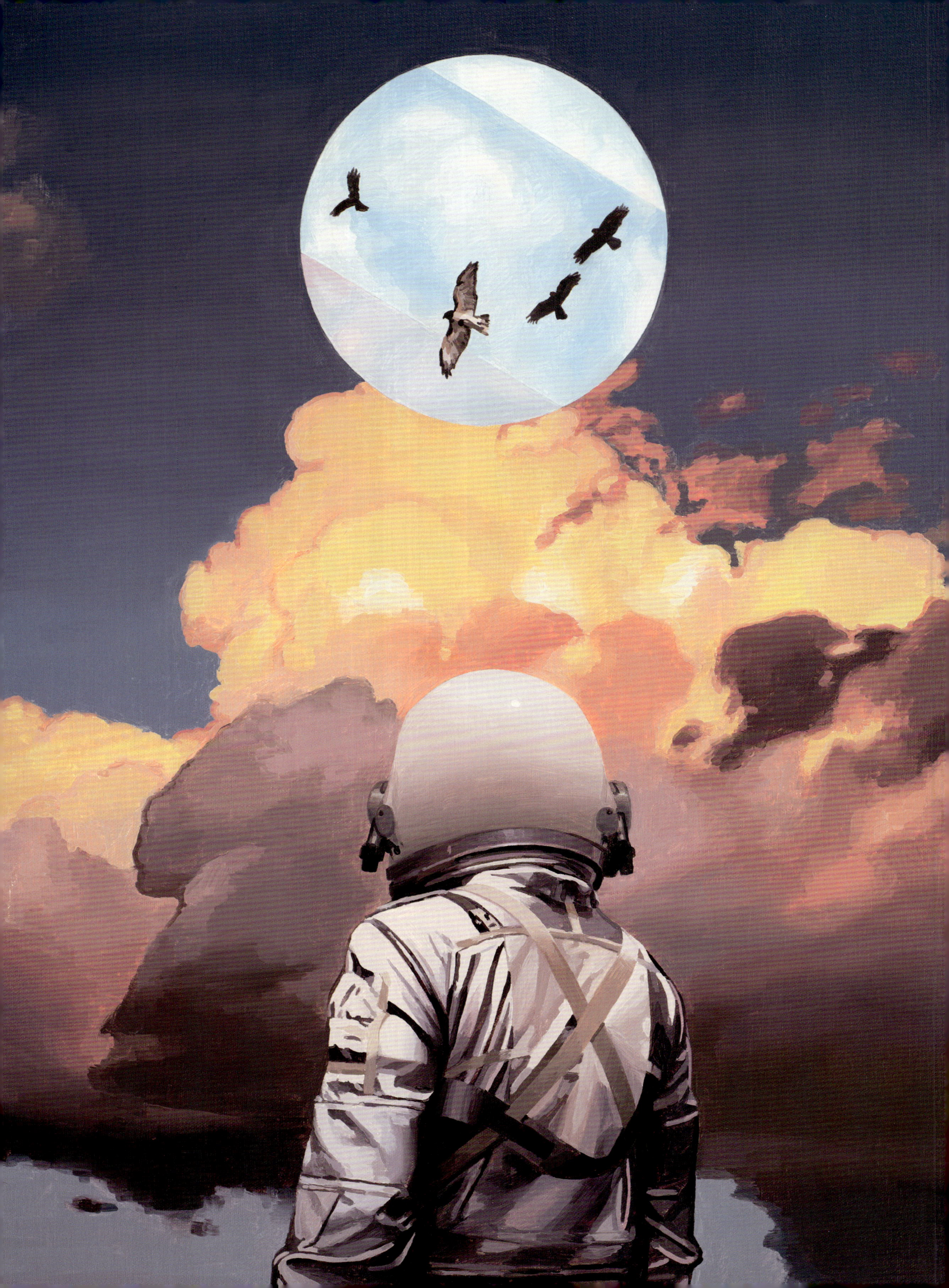

DO ANDROIDS DREAM

Antler Gallery, Portland, OR
March, 2021

For my latest show with Antler, I found myself trying to retain some attachment to the outside world after spending most of the last year indoors. At various points during that time, when it's been relatively safe to do so, I've found myself going on increasingly long and meandering walks through the winding hilly streets and neighborhoods near my home in Los Angeles. It's given me some sense of purpose, and at least a rough facsimile of the feeling of exploration that often inspires my paintings.

This outside world feels very much like a dream to me. One I experience in short bursts before returning to my living room and my studio, where I hunker down and make some paintings in between episodes of Wandavision.

I've also been lately revisiting some of the works of Philip K. Dick, who has long been an inspiration in my paintings. When I walk outside, it sometimes feels like I'm entering the hallucinogenic semi-futuristic California often depicted in his books. I've lately been hearing an owl in my neighborhood, and I can't help but wonder if it's real, a replicant, or just a recording.

But I'm also feeling hopeful for the first time in a long while. Vaccines are circulating, and I hope that one day soon we'll be able to return to something resembling normal. It will be a strange experience though, living life again after so long putting it on hold. This series of paintings are about what I hope is the last days of this period of unreality we've been living in, and looking beyond it to something new.

#516
CIRCLE IN THE SKY [2021]

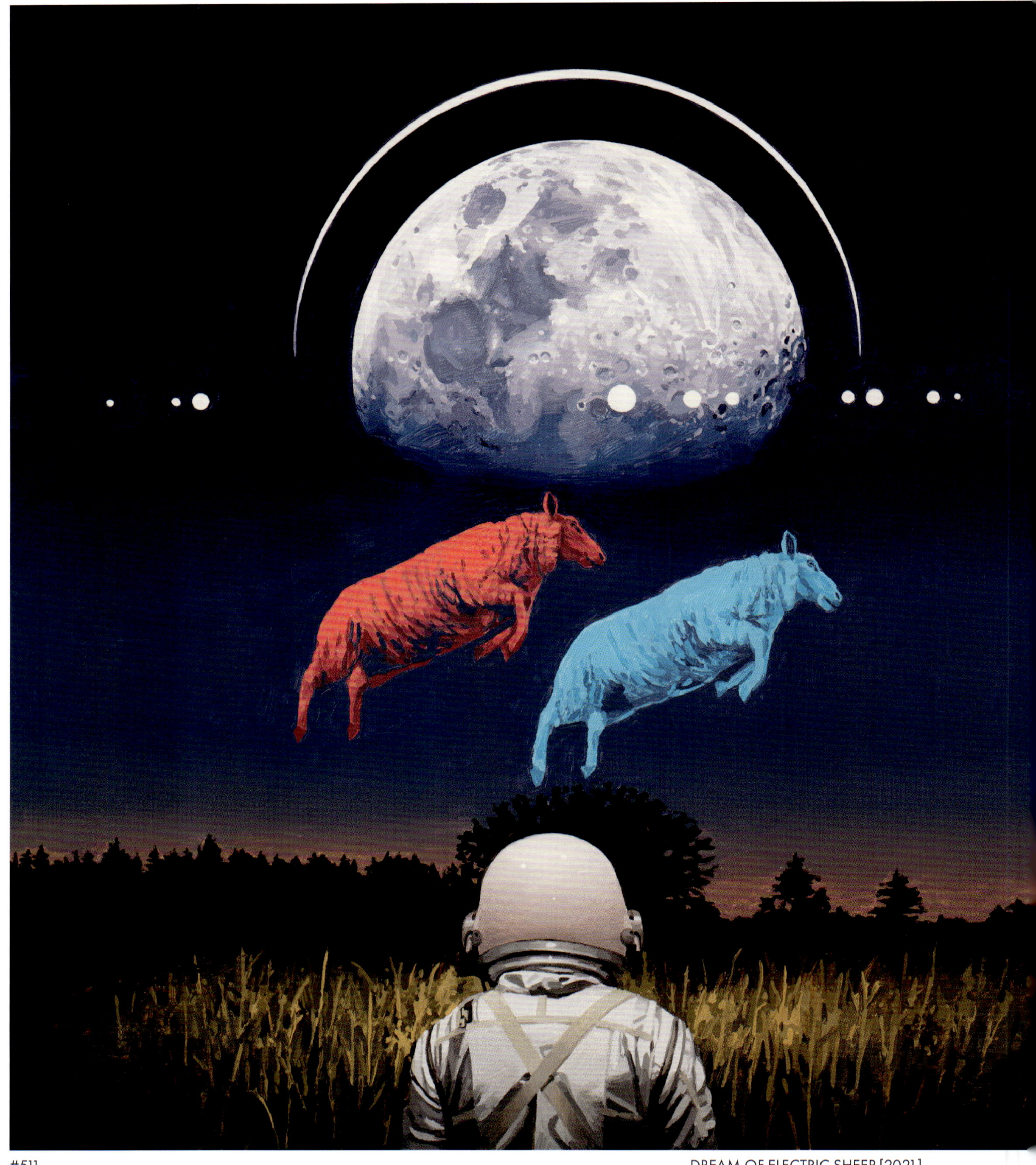

#511 DREAM OF ELECTRIC SHEEP [2021]

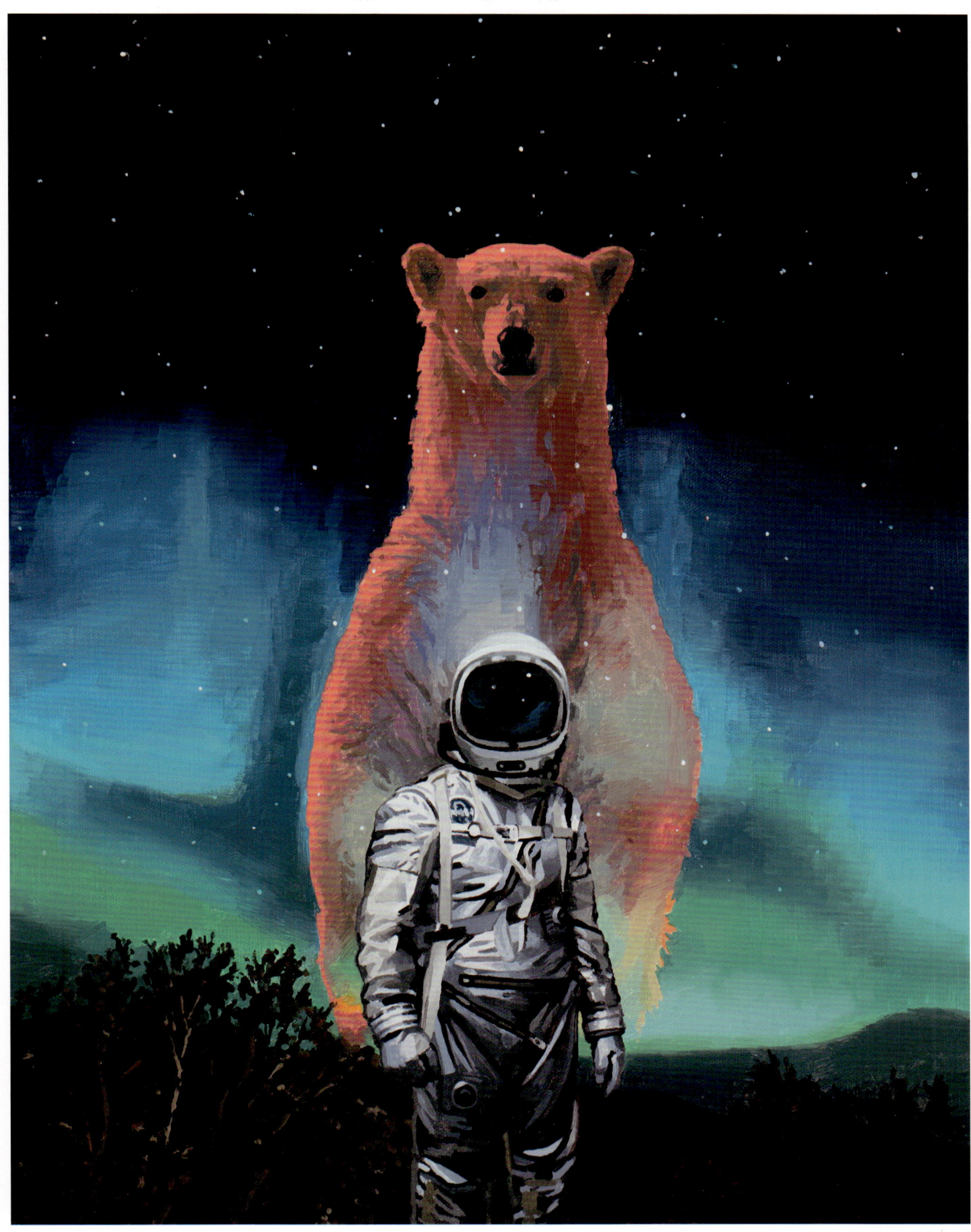

#512

NIGHT BEAR [2021]

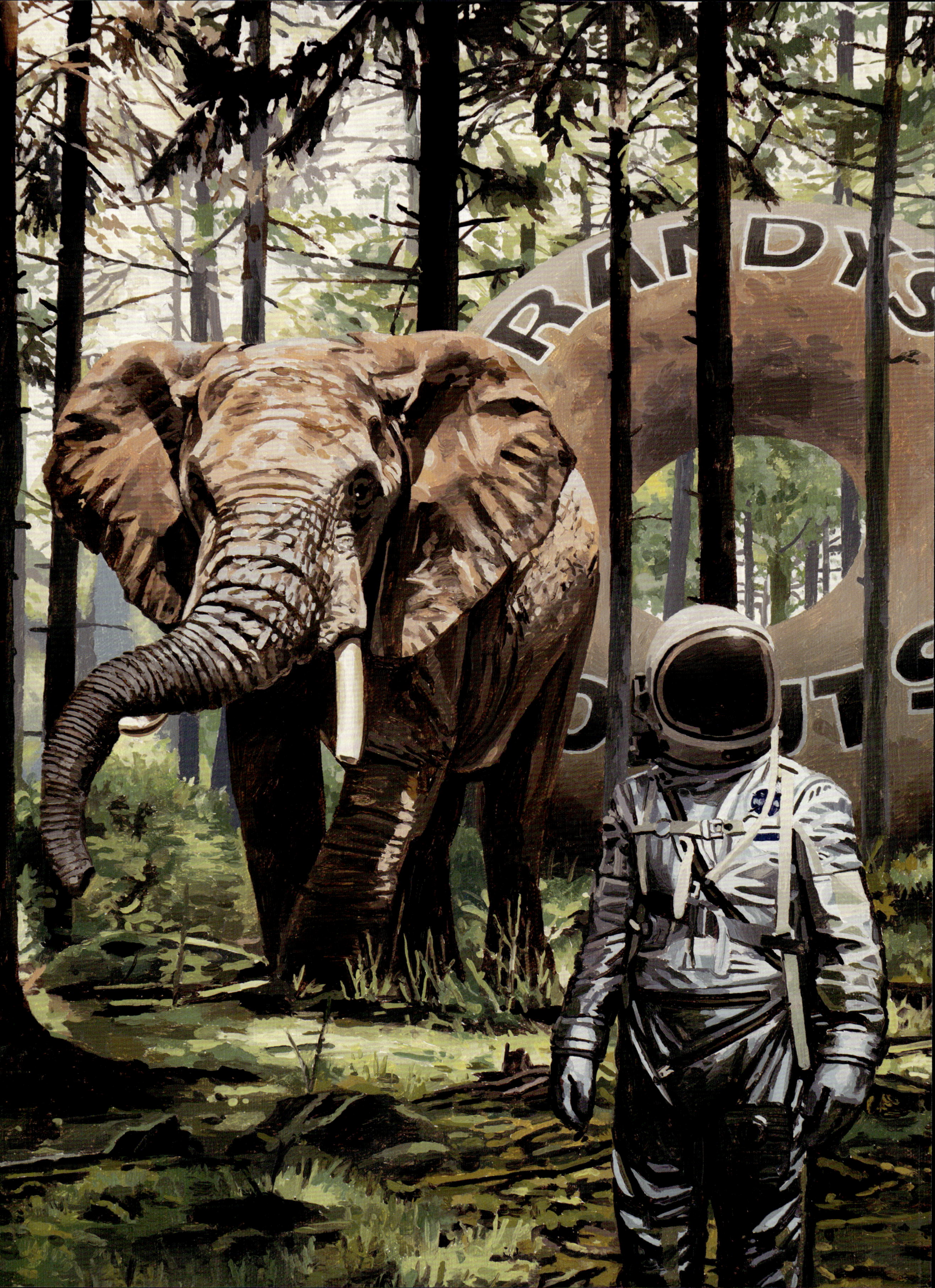
RANDYS

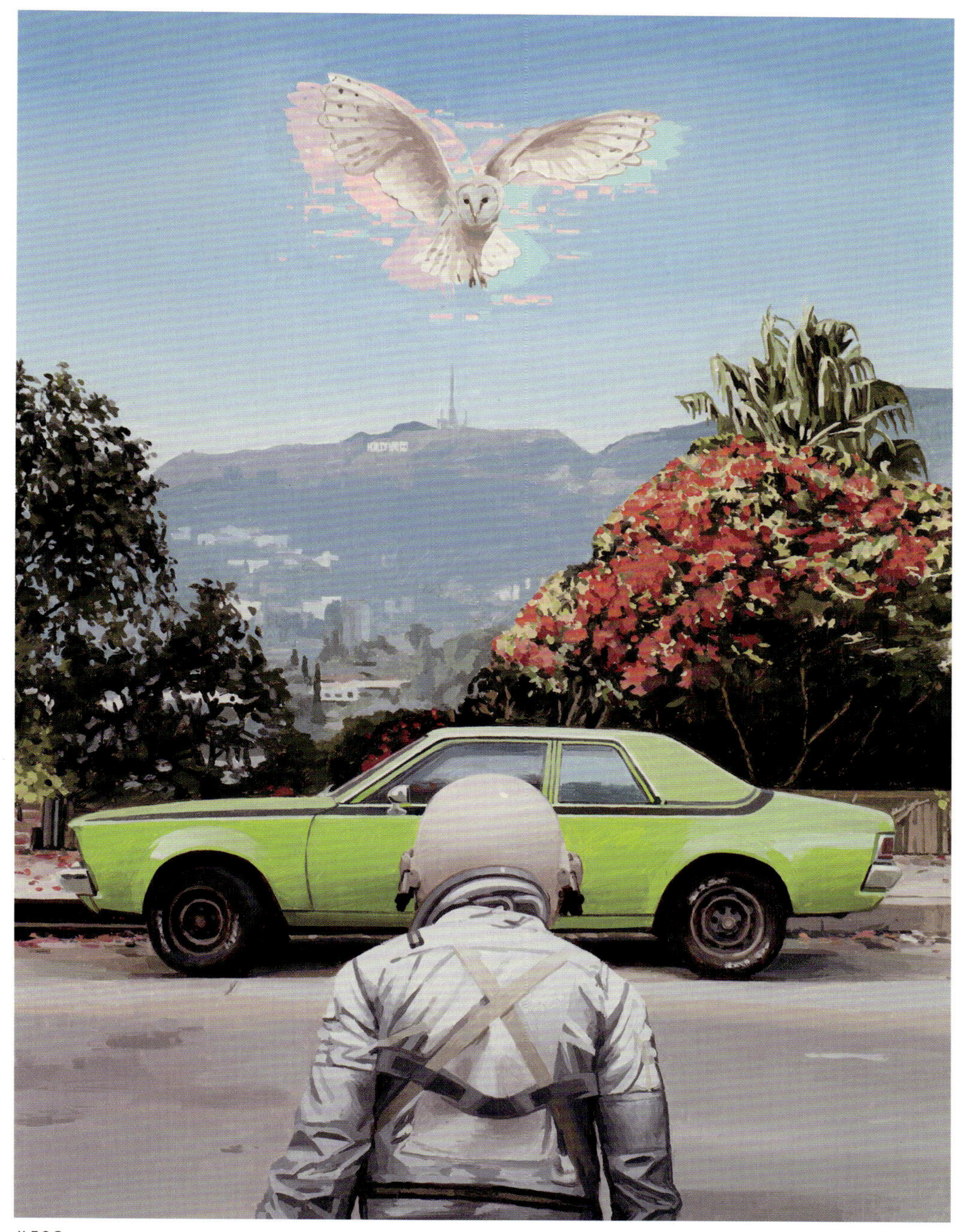

#509

OWL [2020]

#517

ELEPHANT [2021]

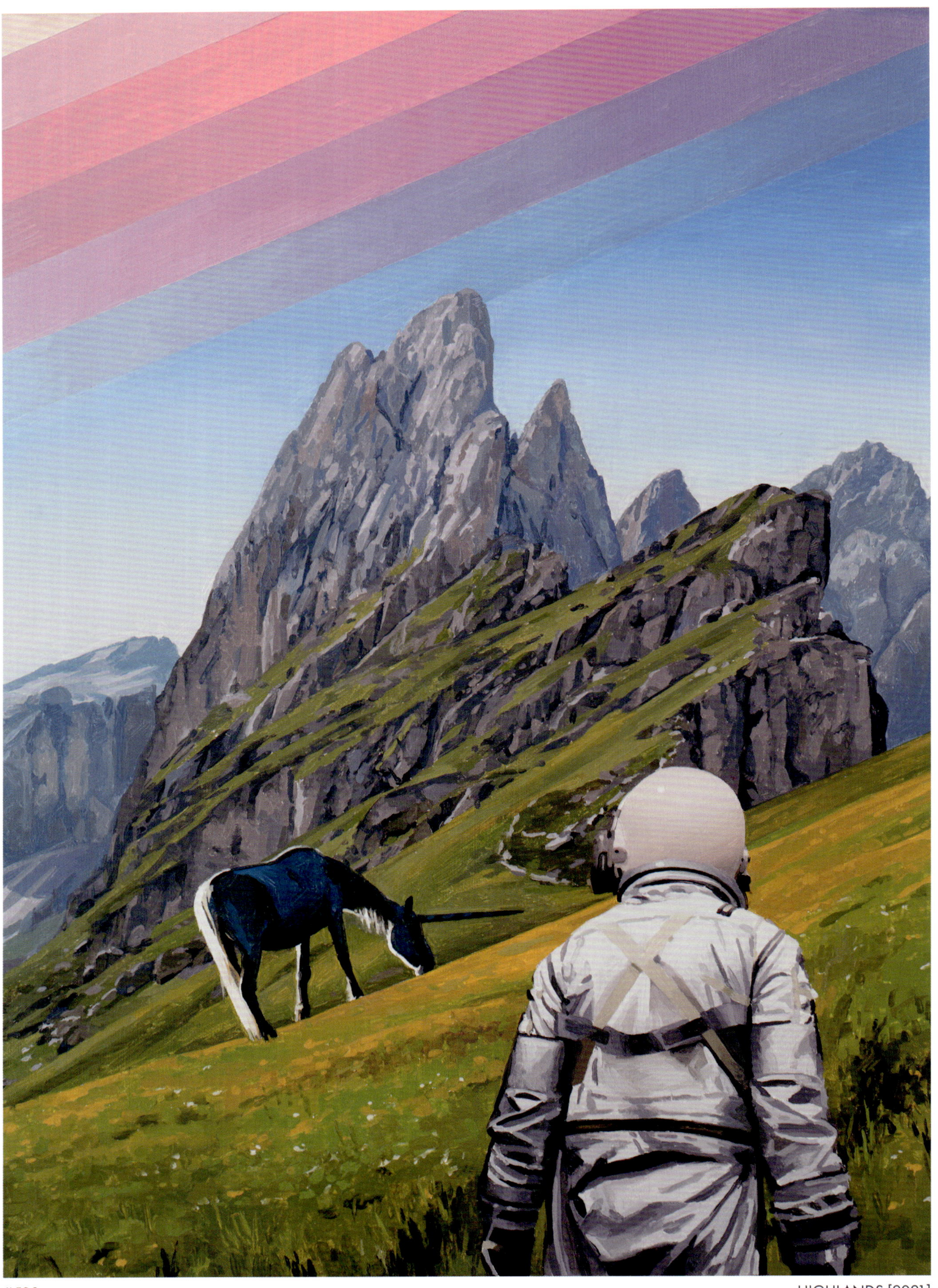

#520

HIGHLANDS [2021]

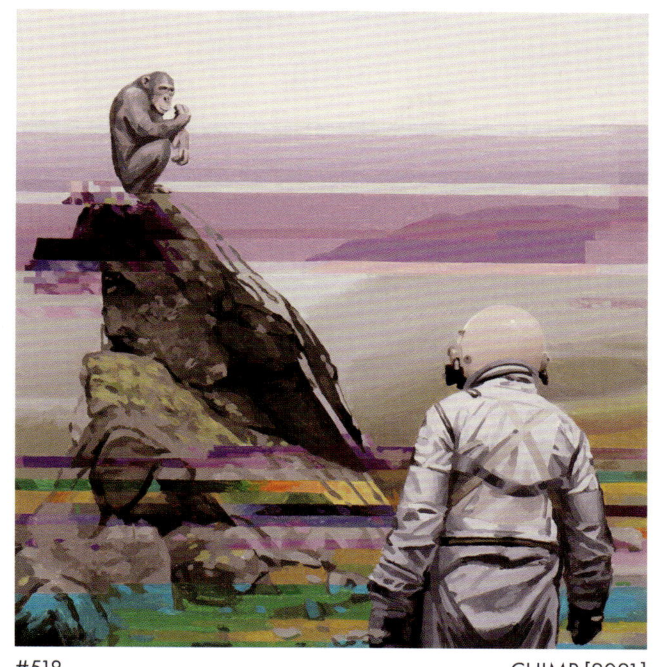

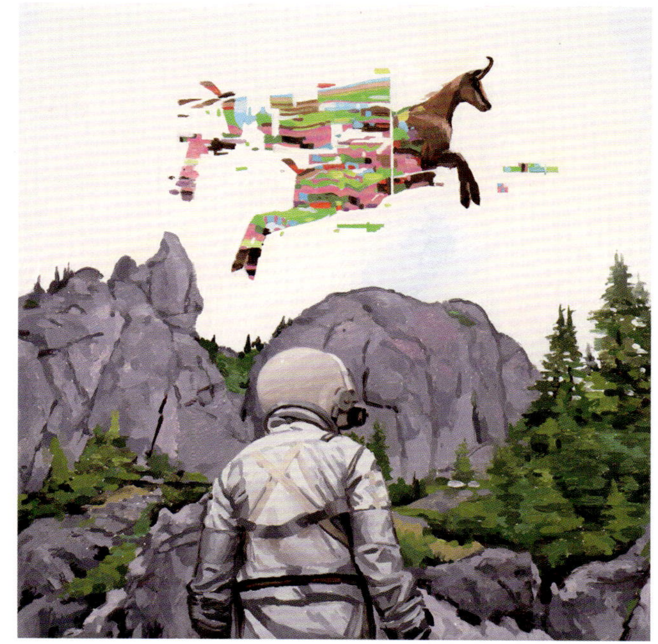

#518 CHIMP [2021]

#510 MID JUMP GLITCH [2020]

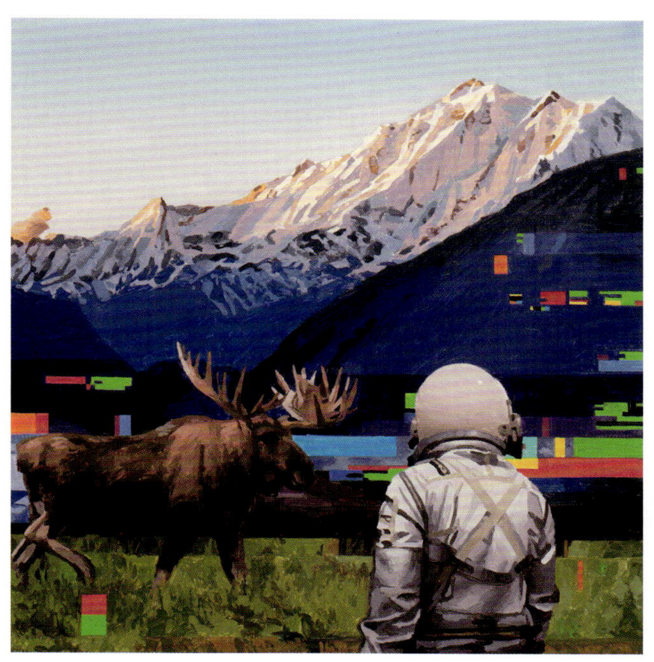

#514 MOOSE [2021]

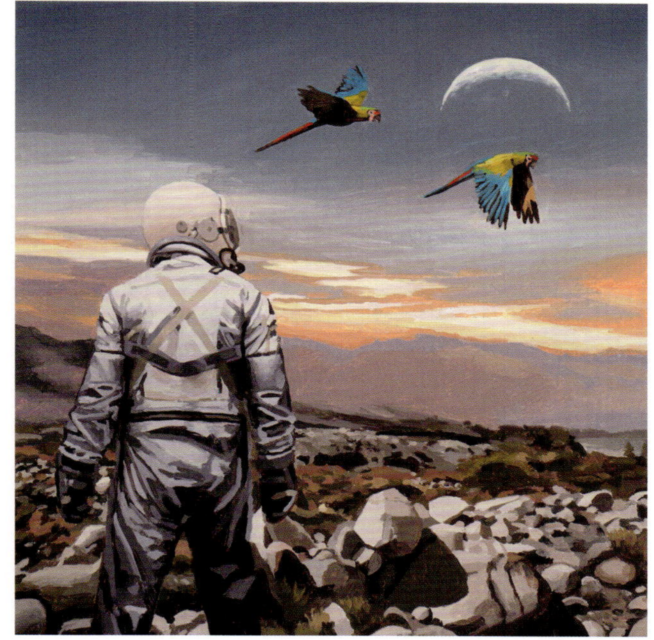

#513 PARROTS [2021]

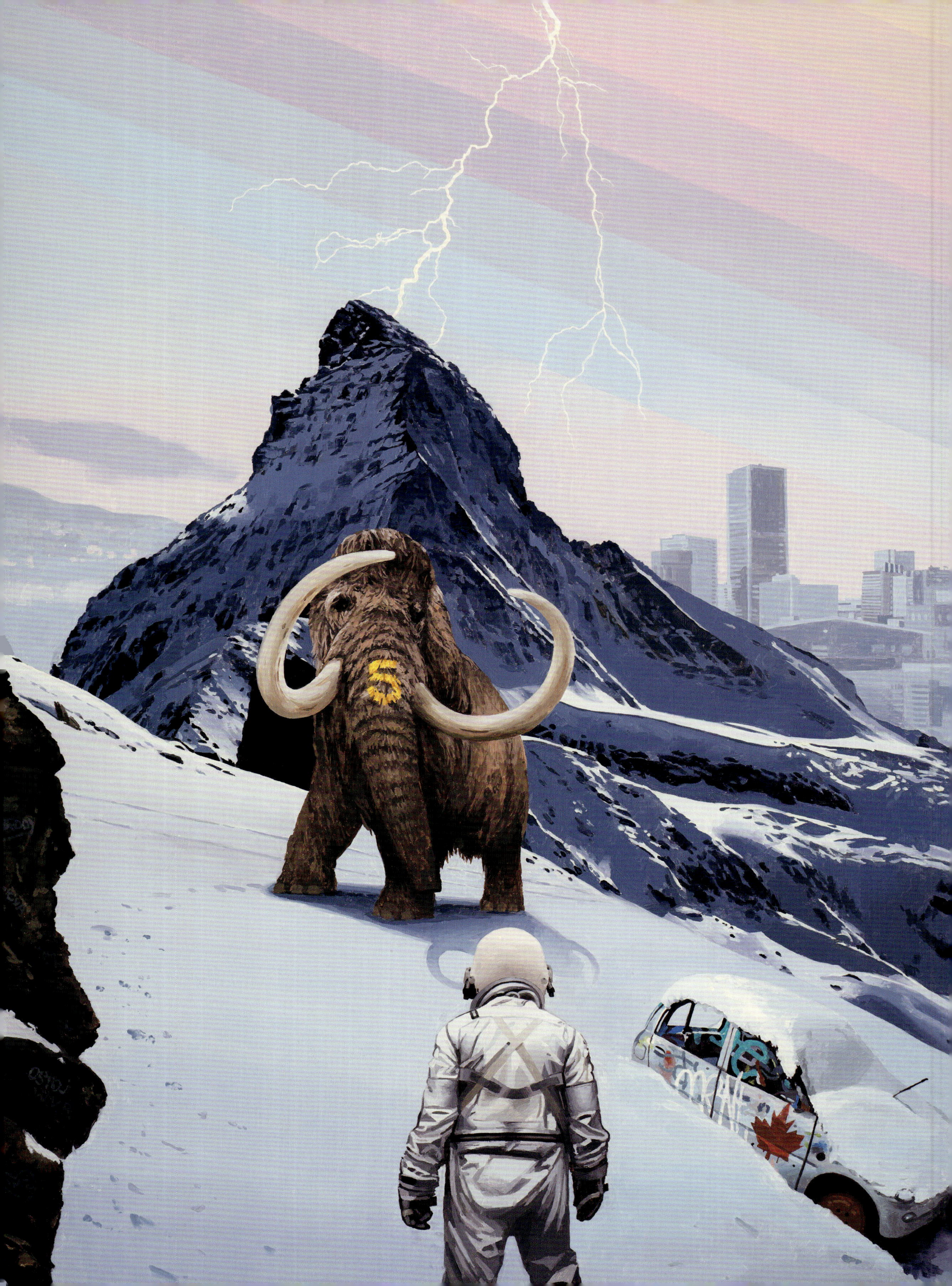

HEAVY METAL

S16 Gallery, Montreal, Canada
August, 2021

I spent most of the previous year and a half making paintings about the quarantine, about politics, literally painting the crumbling bonds between us, and the fractured sense of reality I experienced being largely trapped at home for the duration. I'm glad I did. I think I made some of the most important work of my life during that time. But I'll be honest. Man, did the last year and a half suck. I know, I know. Hand me the pulitzer right now for that sentence. Very profound. Nothing we haven't all thought a million times.

But when it came time to make paintings for my show at S16 Gallery in Montreal, for the first time in forever I felt a twinge of something unfamiliar. Call it hope, call it optimism, call it just having SOMETHING on my calendar for the first time in ages. But I was feeling surprisingly ok. I left behind some of the darker and more introspective themes of my recent work and instead turned to...*Heavy Metal Magazine*? Well, yes, sort of. I've long been inspired by classic sci-fi illustration from the '60s and '70s, although more so in concept than execution. But for this latest show, I had some fun and dove into woolly mammoths, pyramids, asteroids, spaceships, and laser beams. I painted caves, moons, saber tooth tigers, lime green skies, and giant monolithic rocks. I had some fun, some actual FUN, and it was great. Here's to better things in the future. Famous last words, I know.

#526
MAMMOTH [2021]

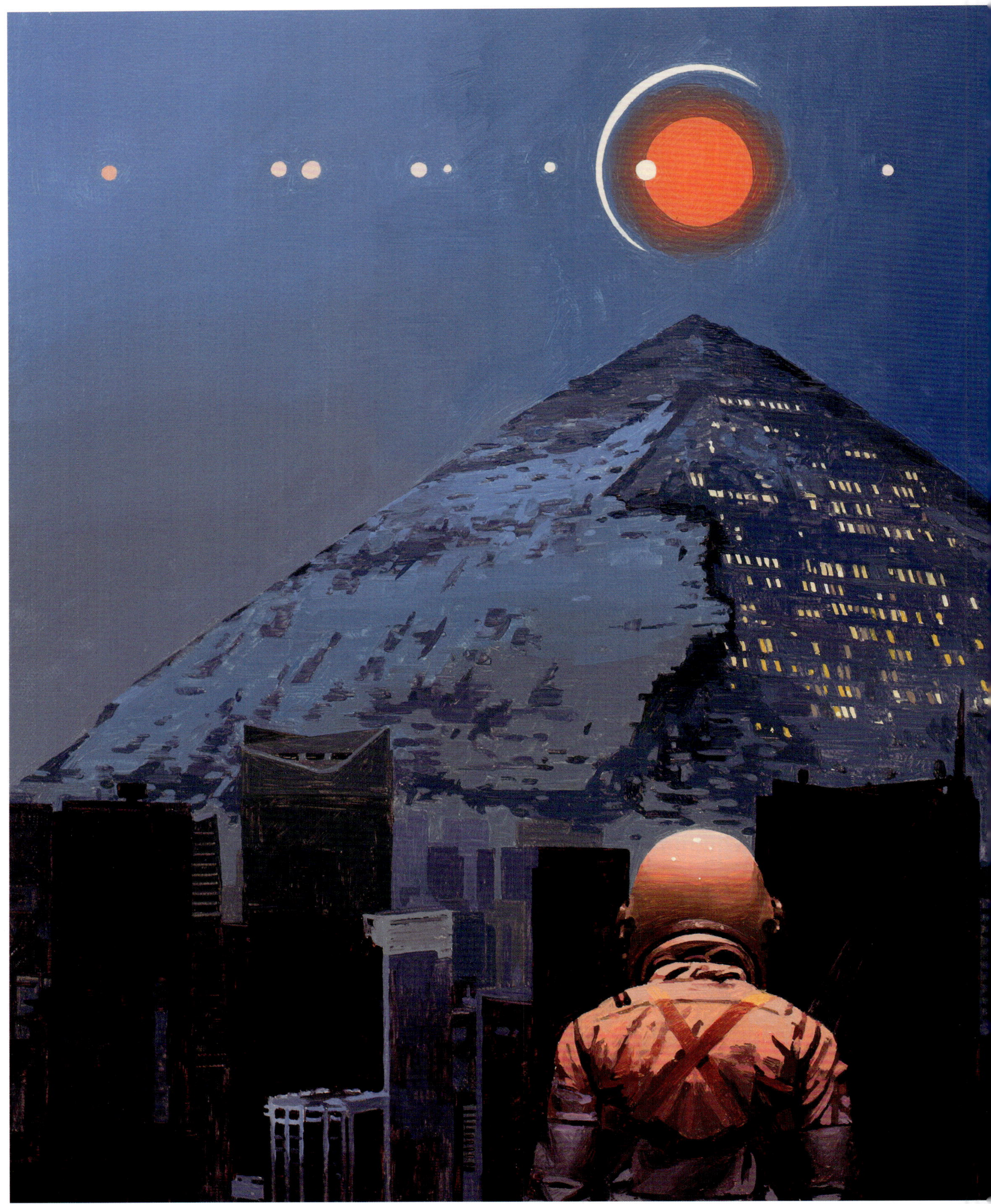

#531

PYRAMID [2021]

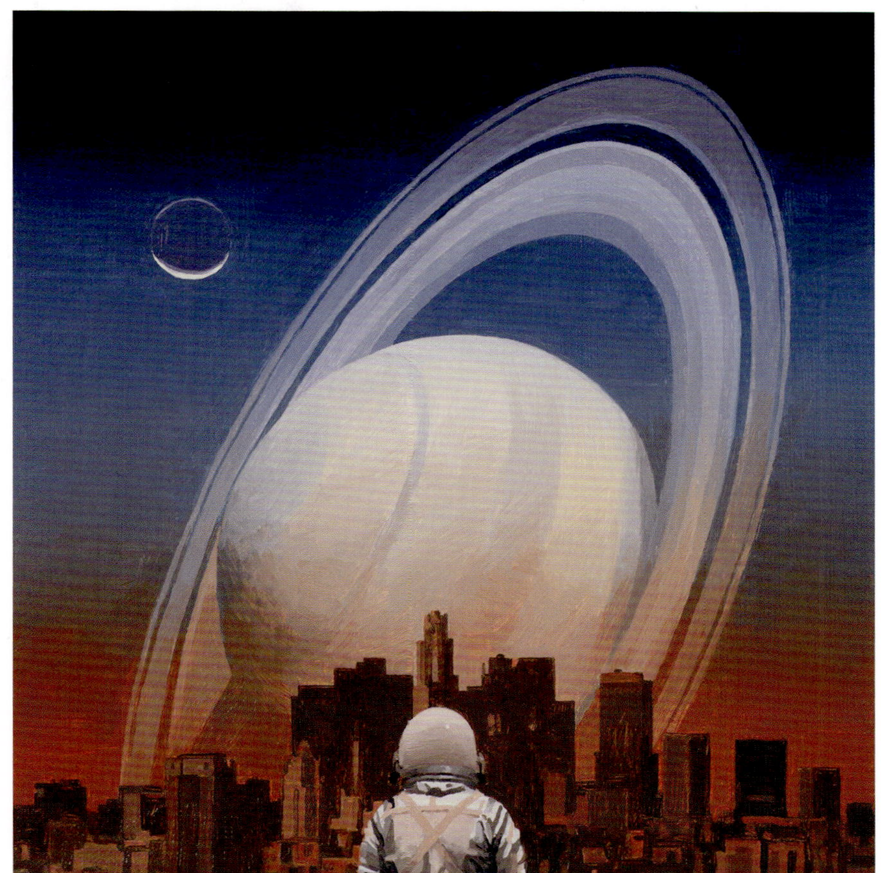

#529 SATURN RISES [2021]

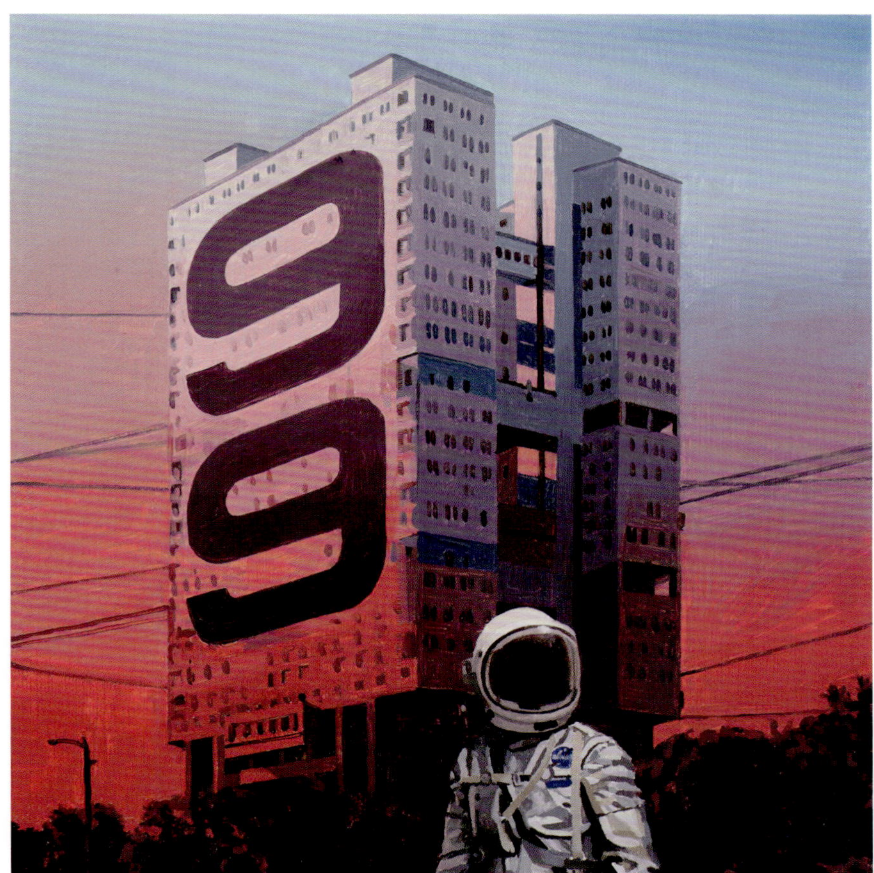

#536 NINETY NINE [2021]

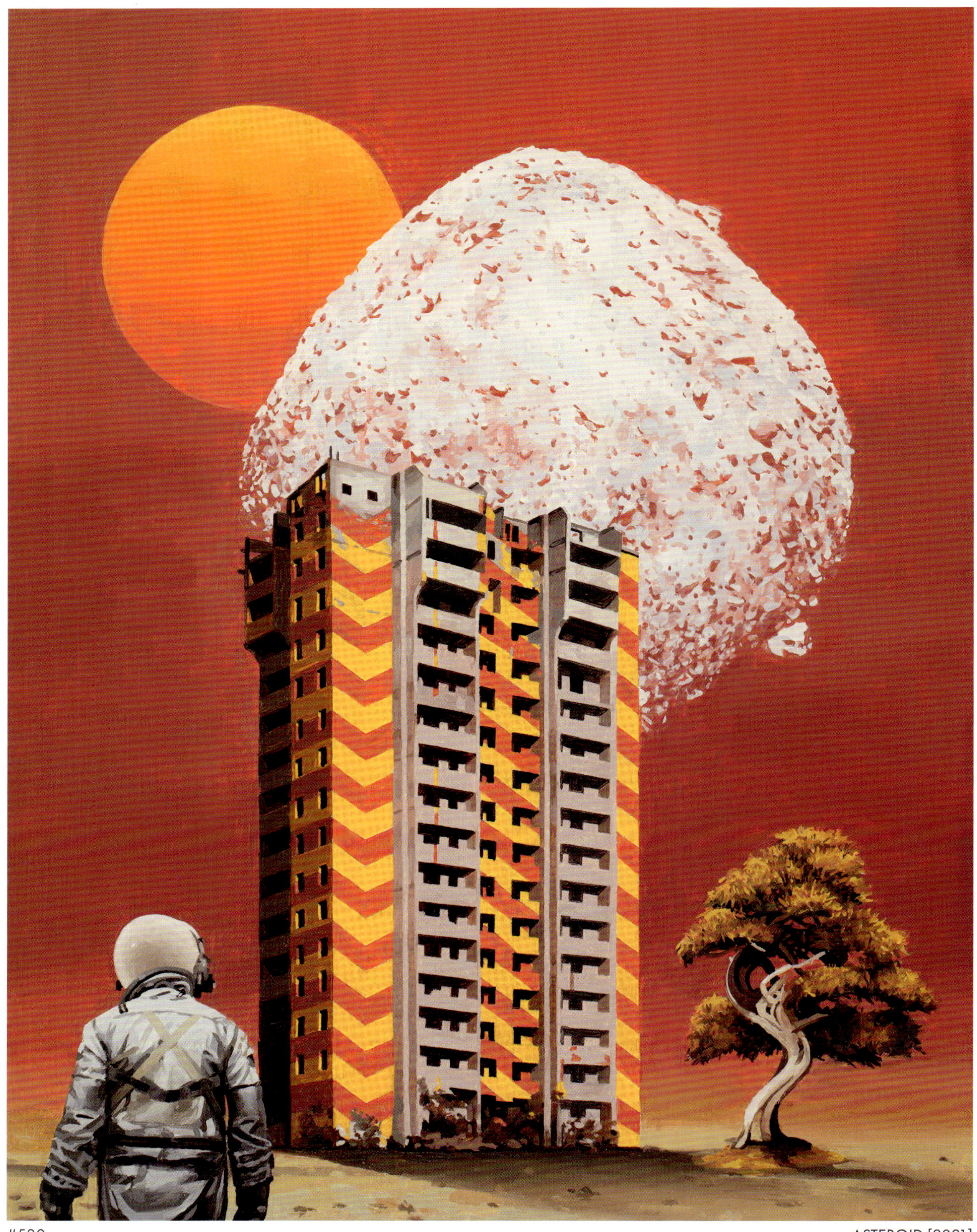

#530 ASTEROID [2021]

#535
SUN STAGES [2021]

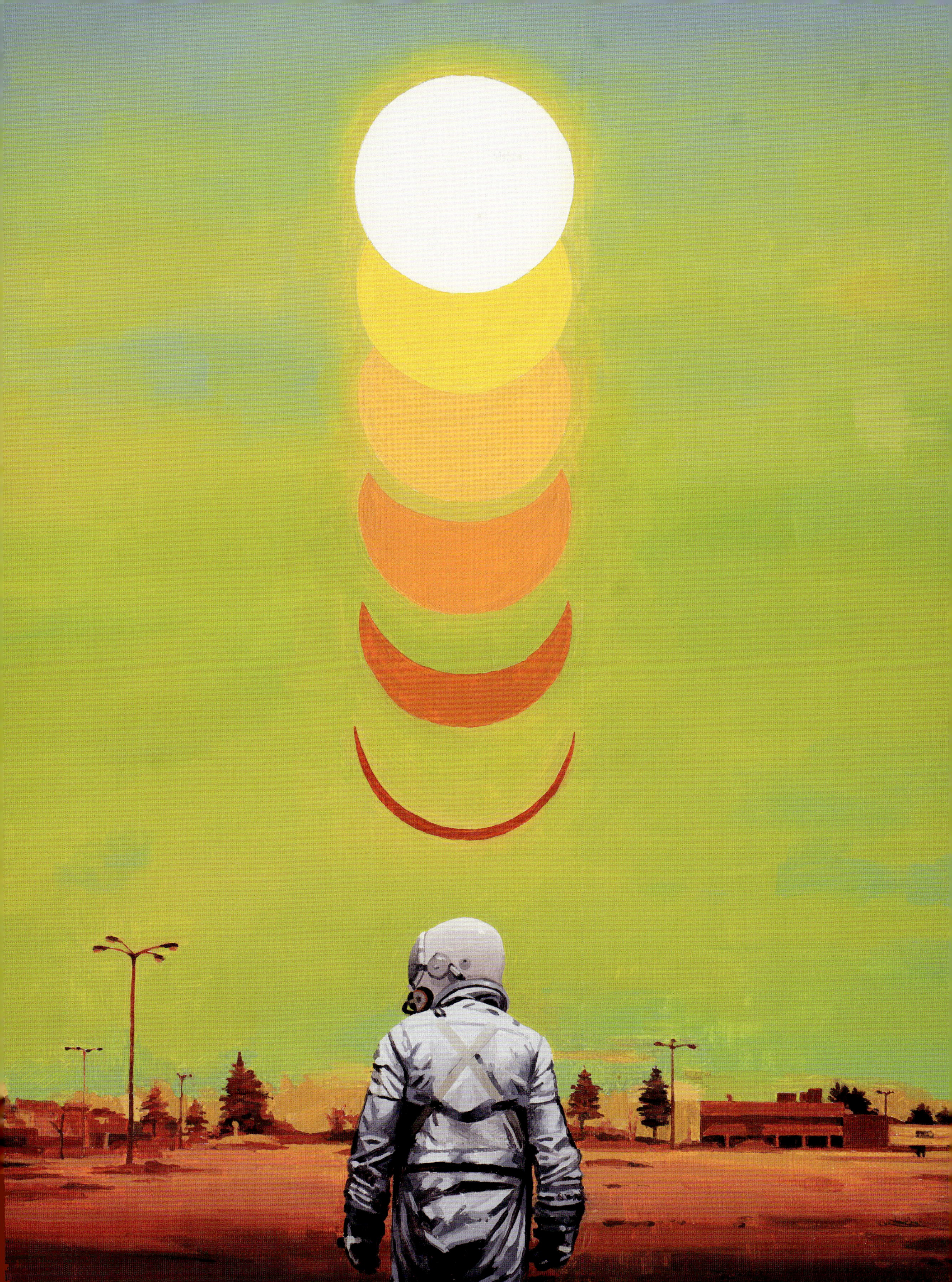

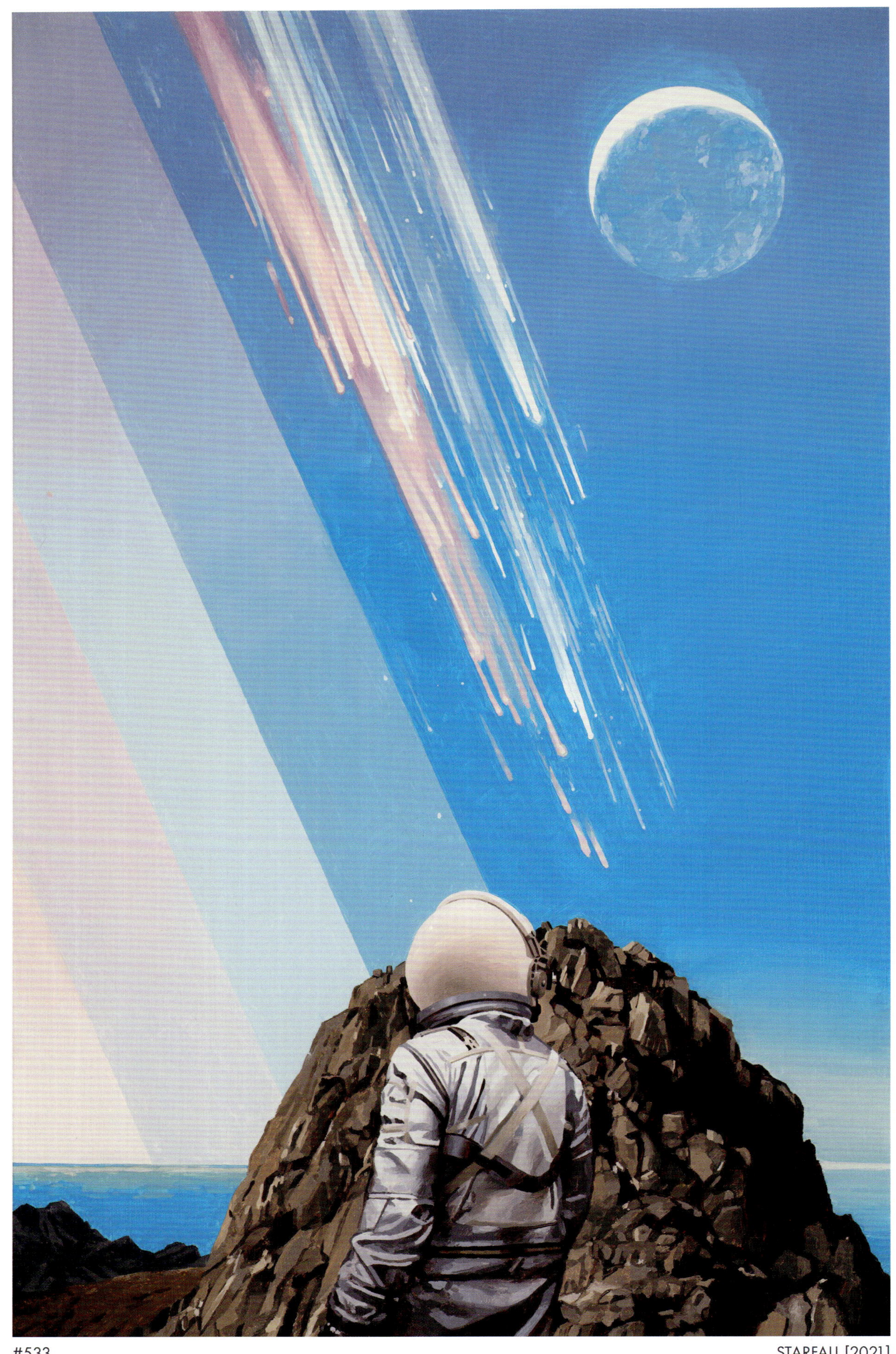

#533 STARFALL [2021]

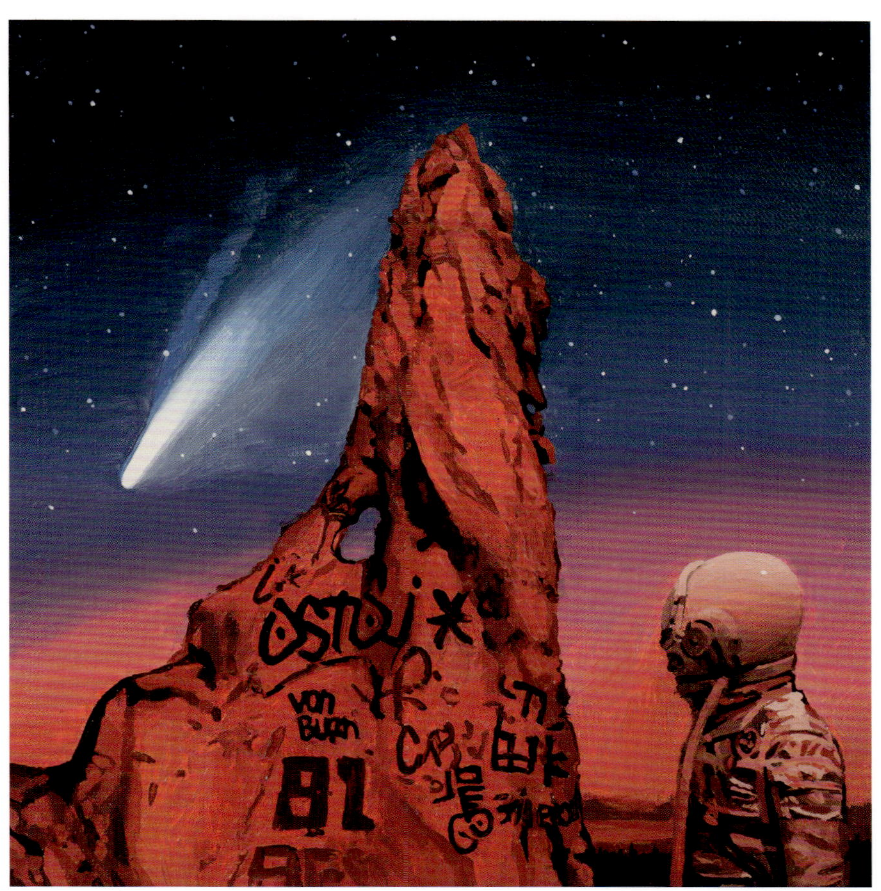

#532 OUTCROP [2021]

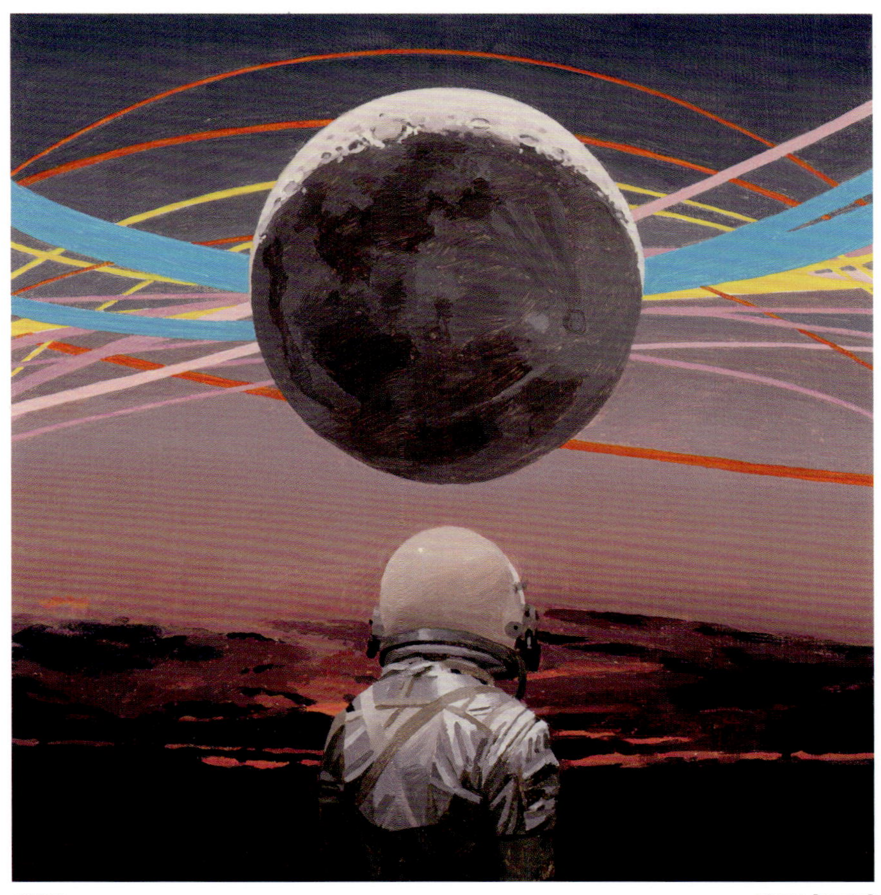

#527 ARCS [2021]

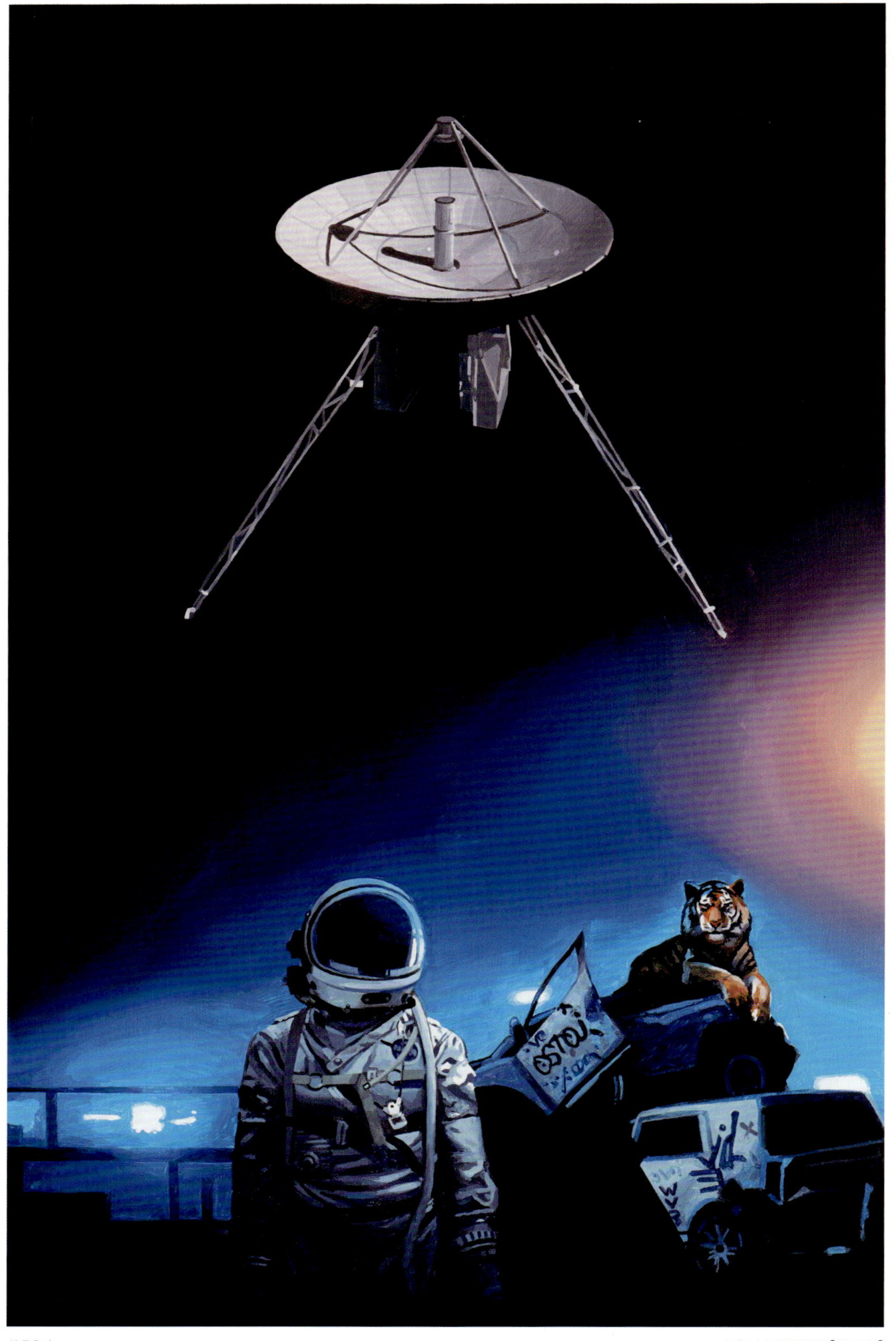

#534 LOW ORBIT [2021]

#528
BIG ROCK [2021]

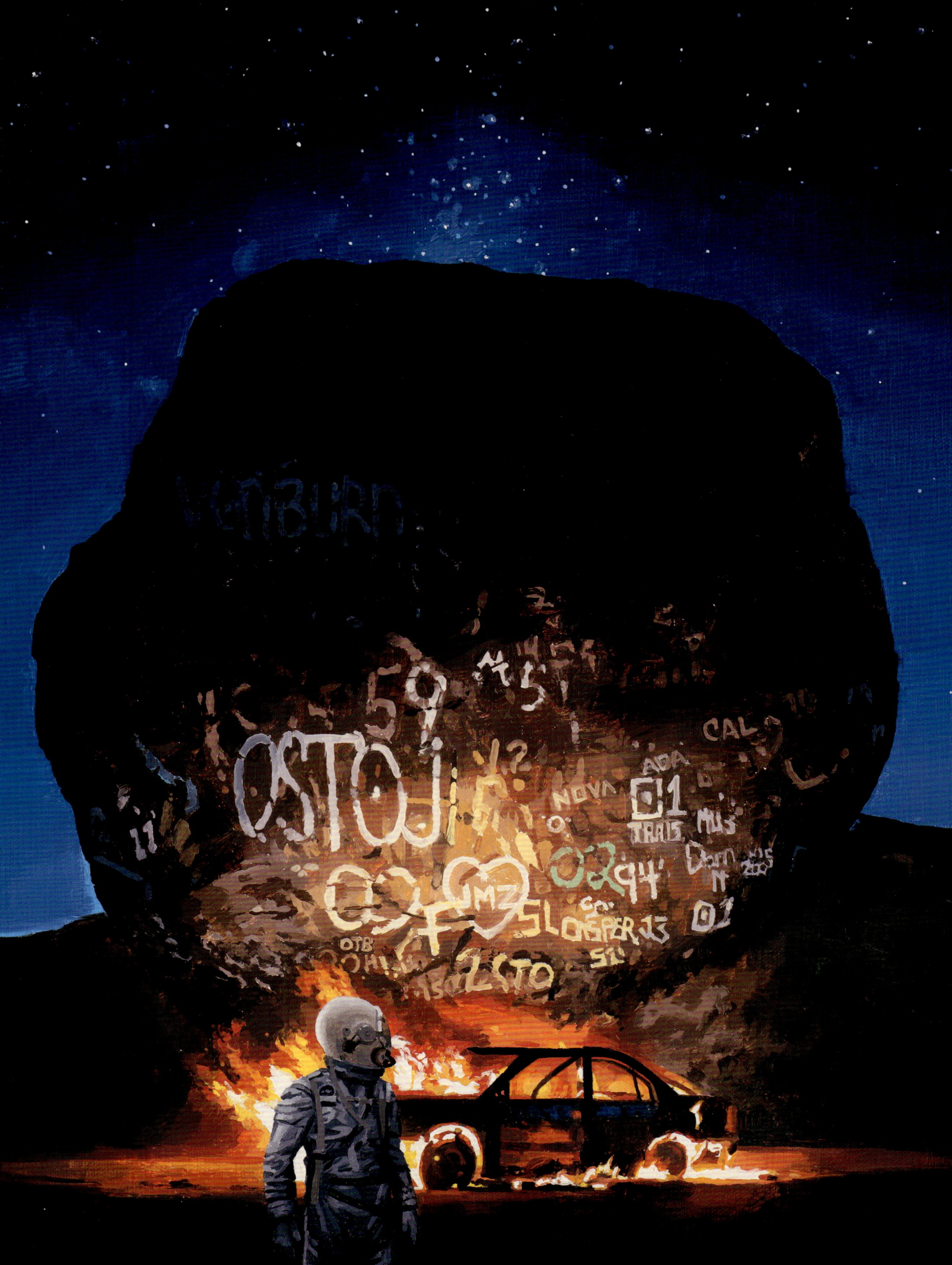

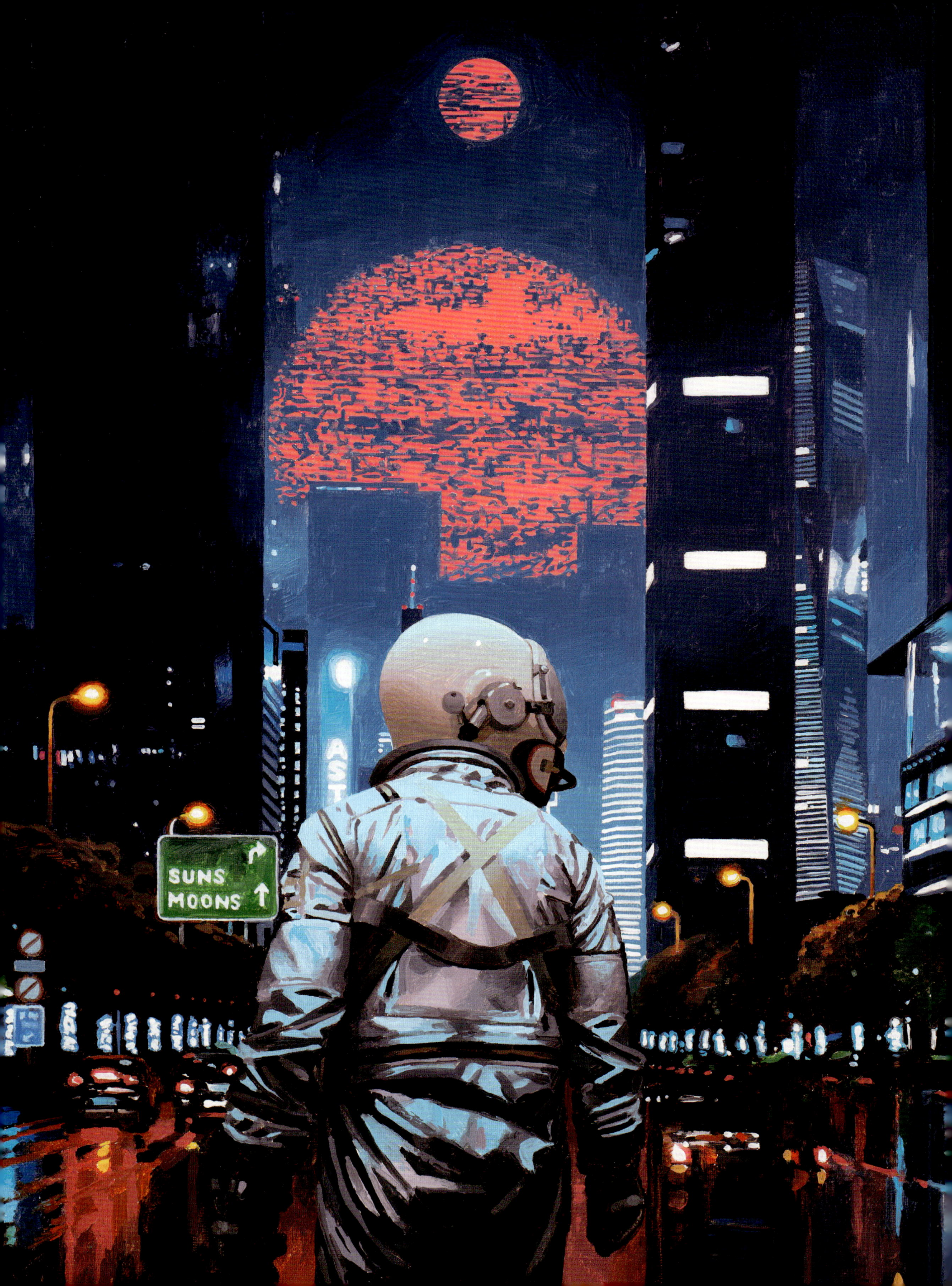
SUNS
MOONS

SUNS & MOONS

Beinart Gallery, Melbourne, Australia
December, 2021

Exploration has always been an important theme in my work. Without being able to do hardly any of that, of course, painting through the COVID era has been a bit of a challenge. I mean, just living through the COVID era has also been "a bit of a challenge," which is, I hope, the dumbest and most obvious thing I ever have to say. By now I've settled into the fits and starts stage of this global pandemic, where things are good and then bad, and then bad, and then bad, and then maybe good? And then bad again.

During this "late-period pandemic" or whatever we want to call it, I've increasingly been drawn to visuals that go deeper into the reaches of science fiction. I've long been influenced by classic sci-fi illustrations of the past, but I usually painted my astronaut into a landscape more closely resembling present day Earth. Or, at the very least, a future or past not too far off from our own. But I've been craving escapism lately, and who could blame me, right? And so, in this show I've left some of the present day concerns behind and let my astronaut wander a spacey and cyberpunk universe, filled with sprawling cities, neon signs, concrete forms, floating objects and, yes, suns and moons. It's a bright, electric world that might be some alternate universe from our own. It's a place I wanted to visit and spend some time, even if I didn't leave my house much to do so. Come join me on the rainbow of your imagination!

No? No one's up for the imagination rainbow? OK, I get it. Come join me on social media and the internet, then.

#556
NIGHT CITY [2021]

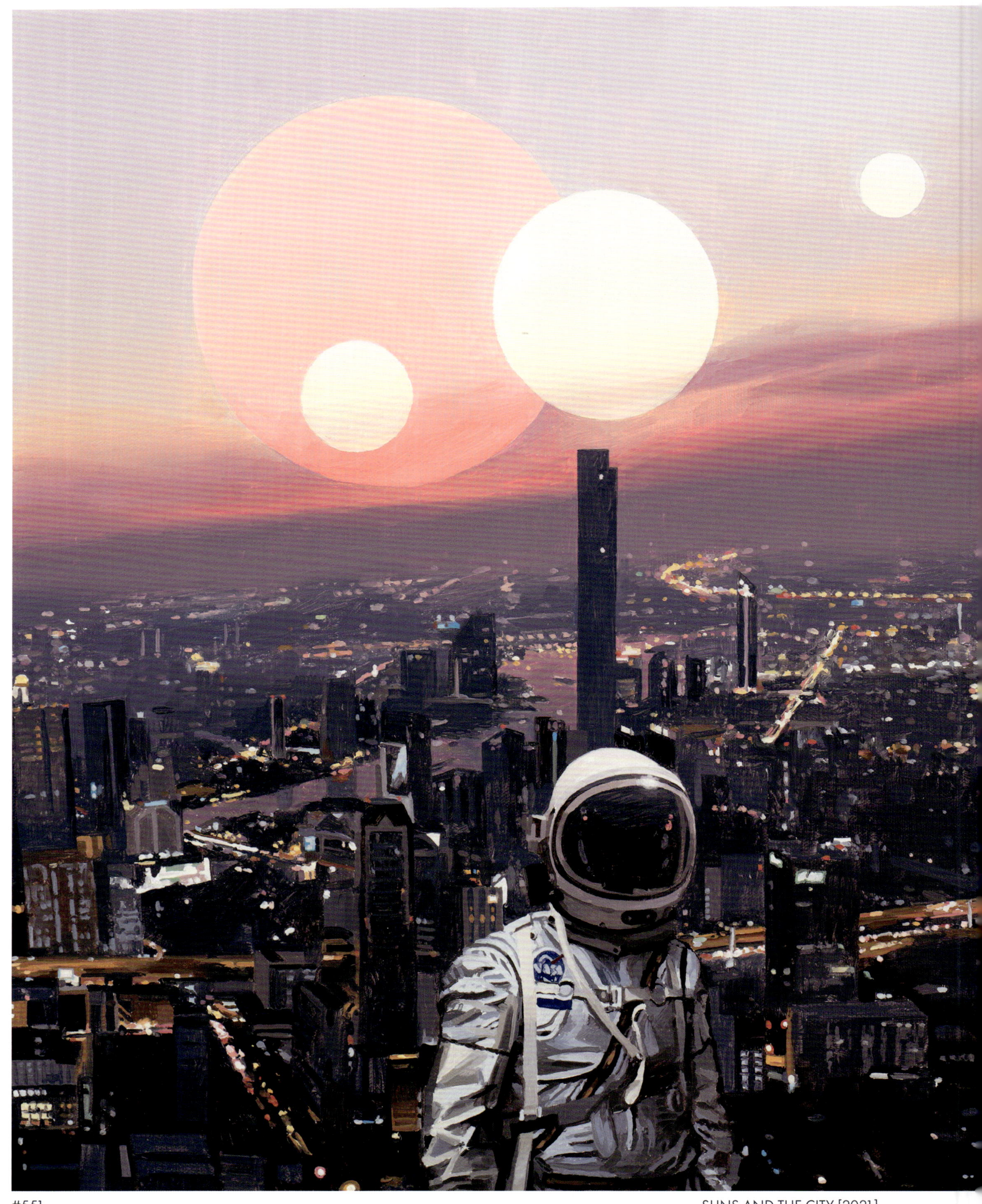

#551

SUNS AND THE CITY [2021]

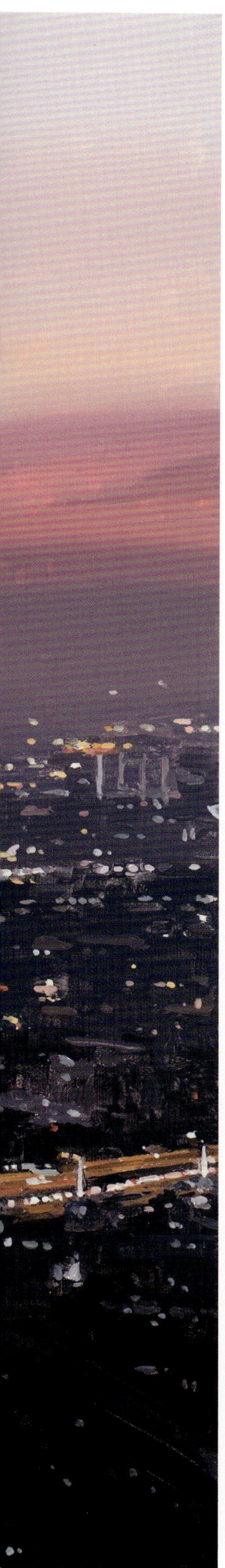

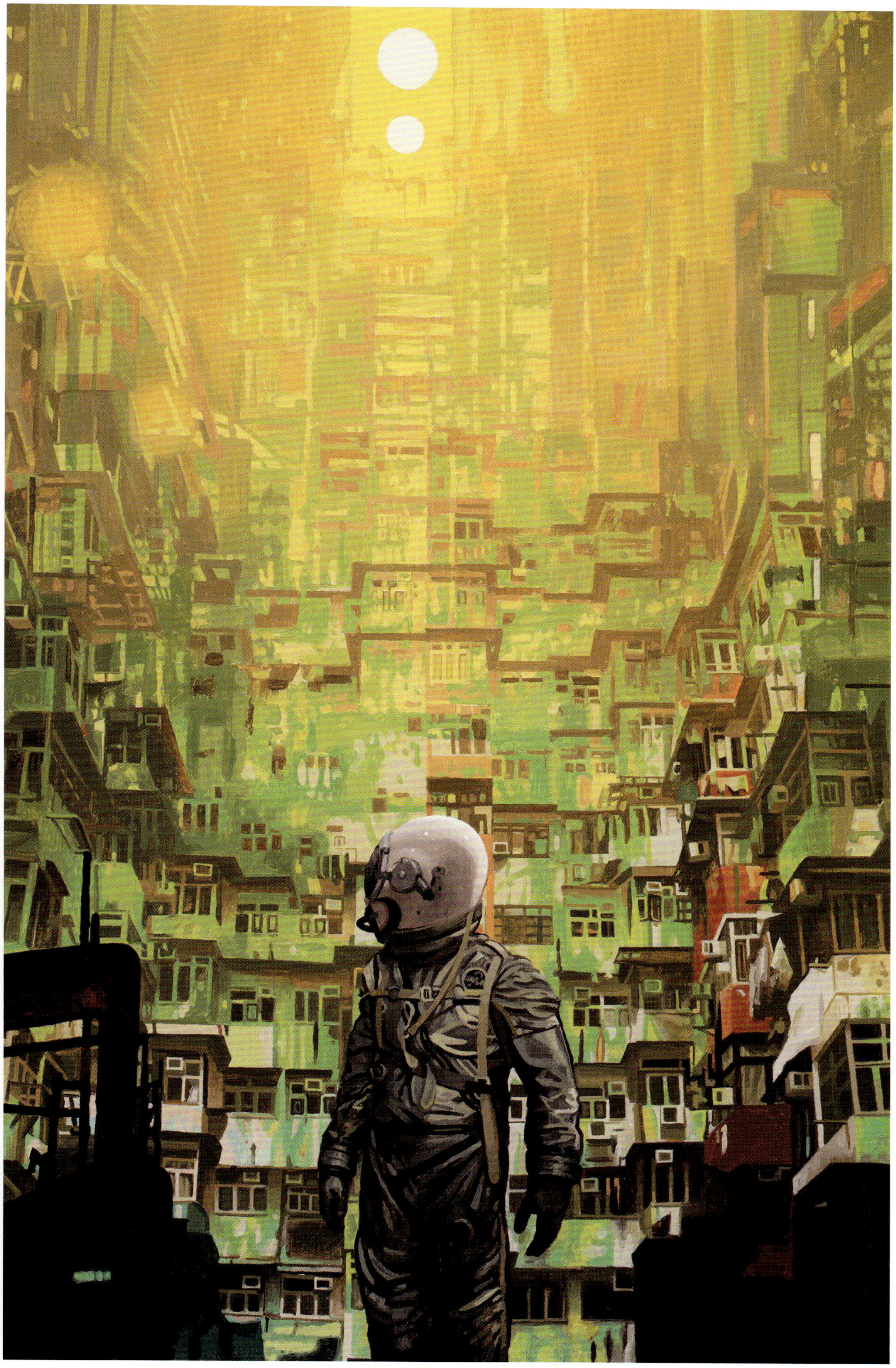

#553

DWELLING [2021]

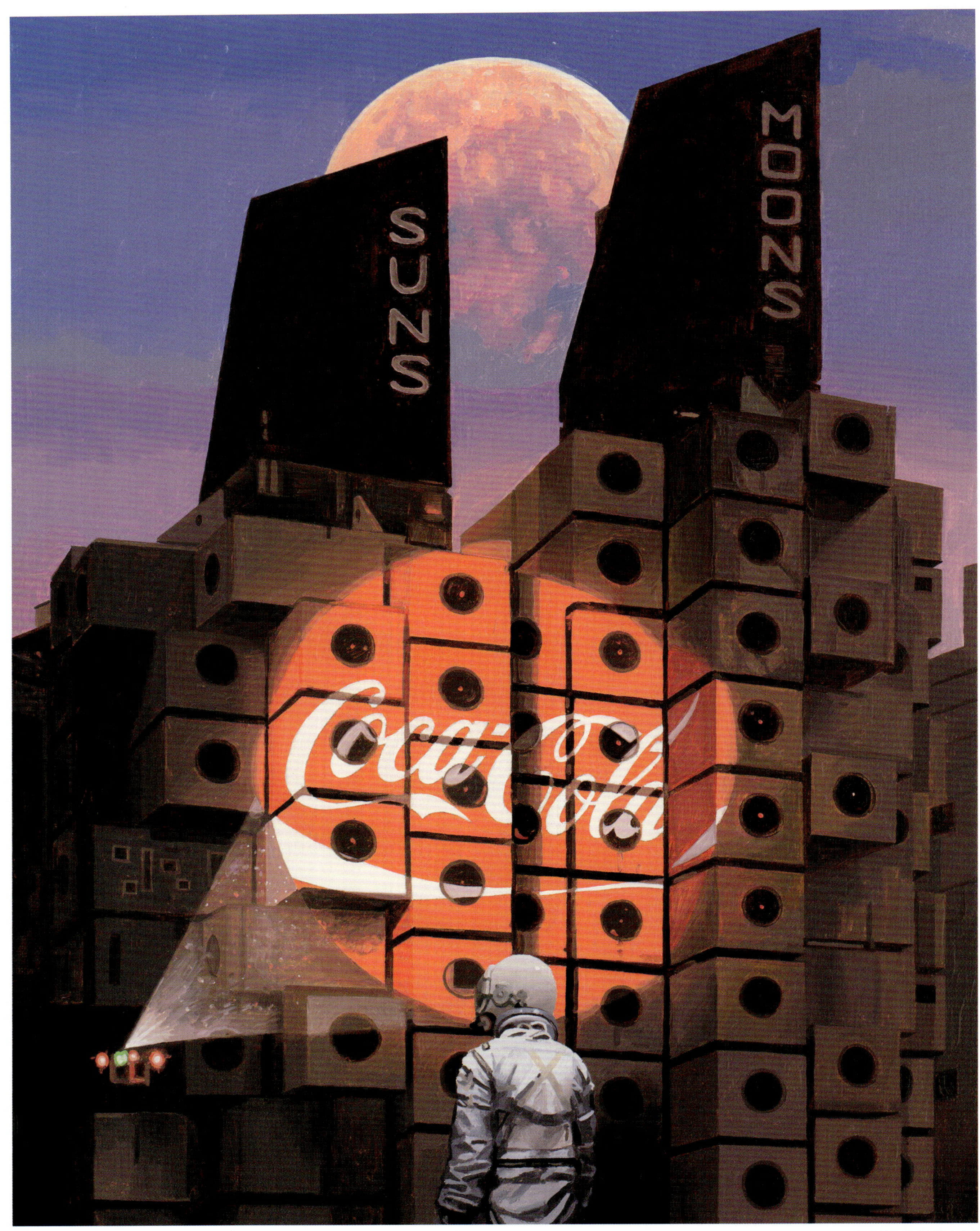

#554

COKE IS IT [2021]

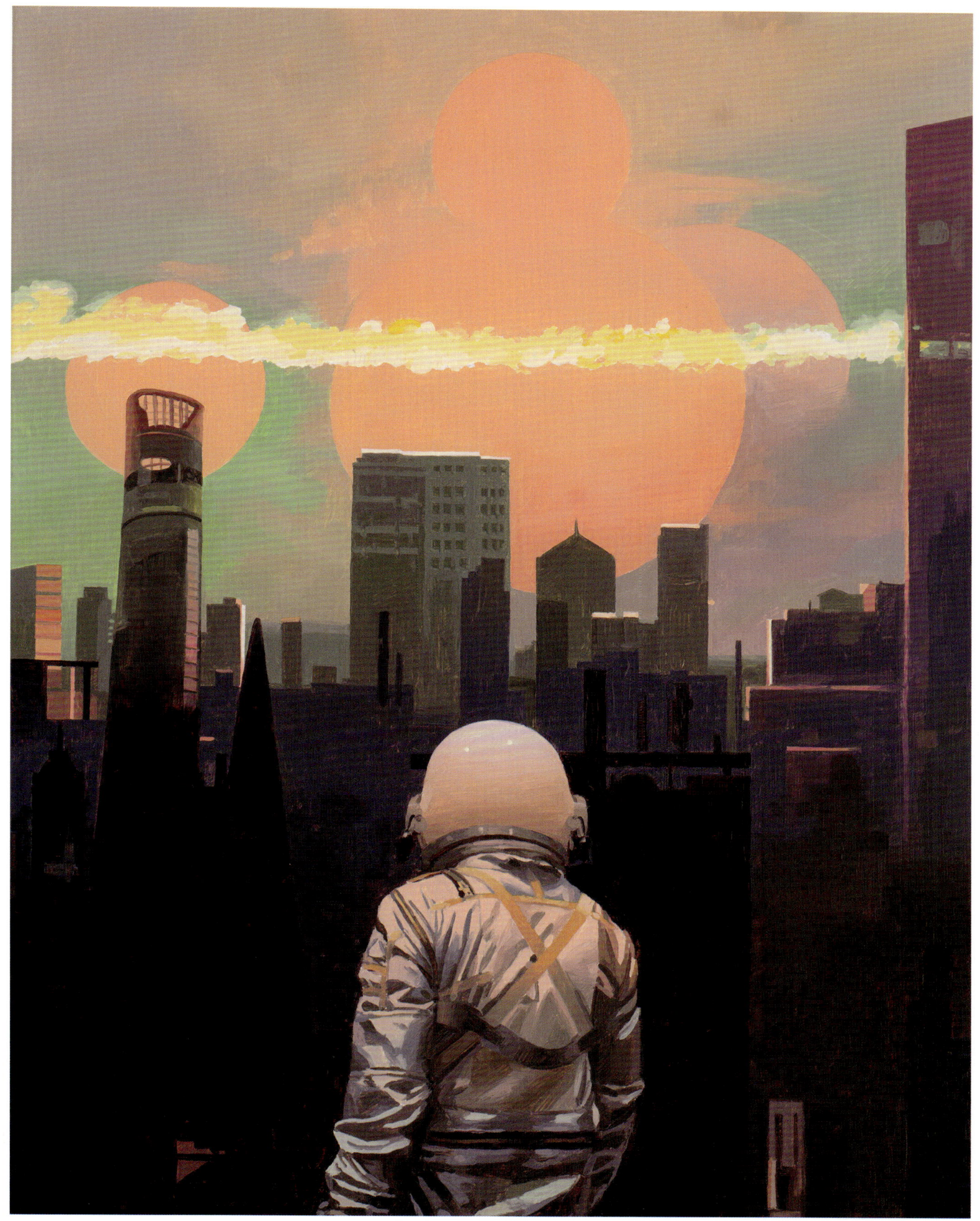

#548

SETTING SUNS [2021]

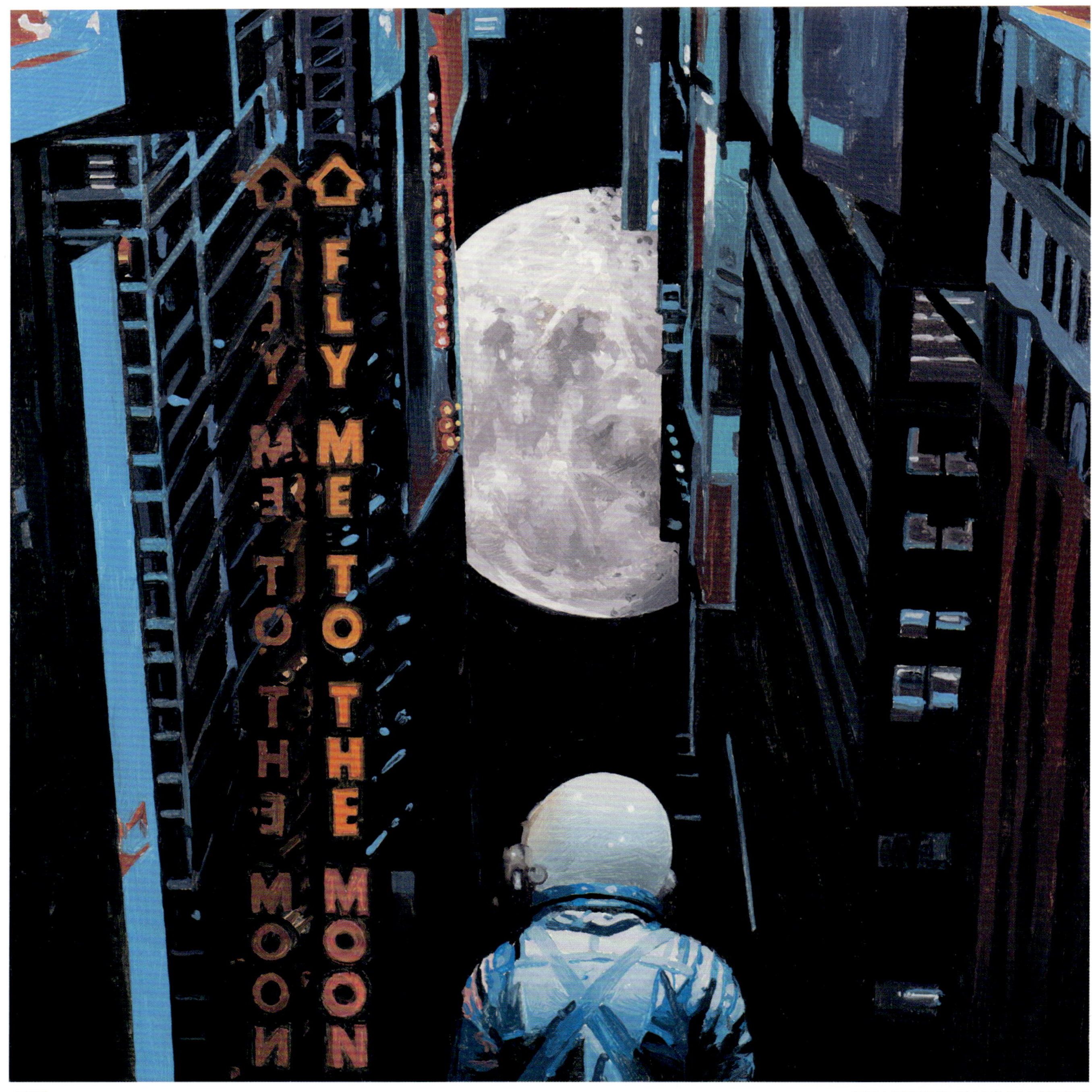

#552

FLY ME TO THE MOON [2021]

#558

URSA [2021]

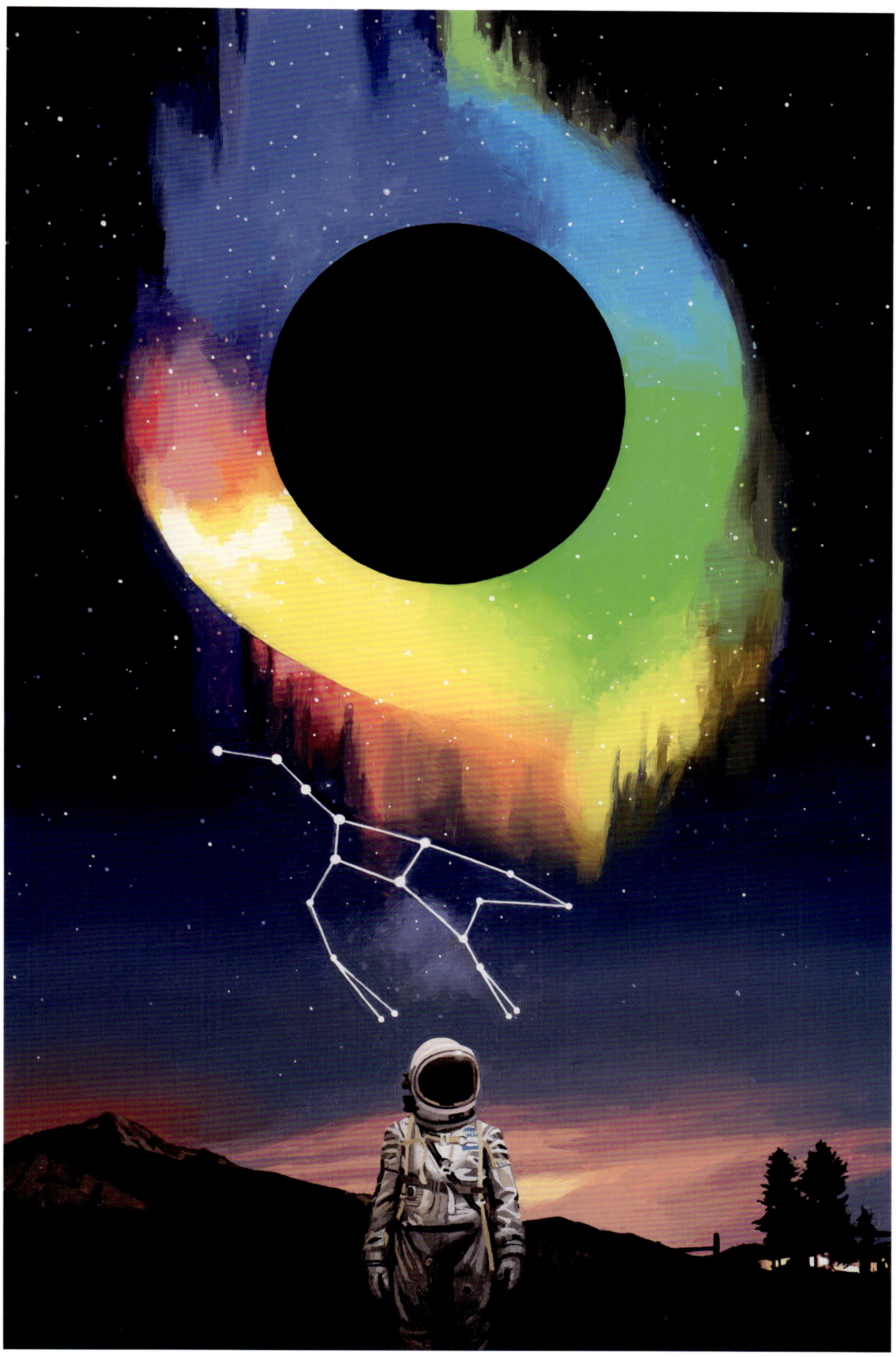

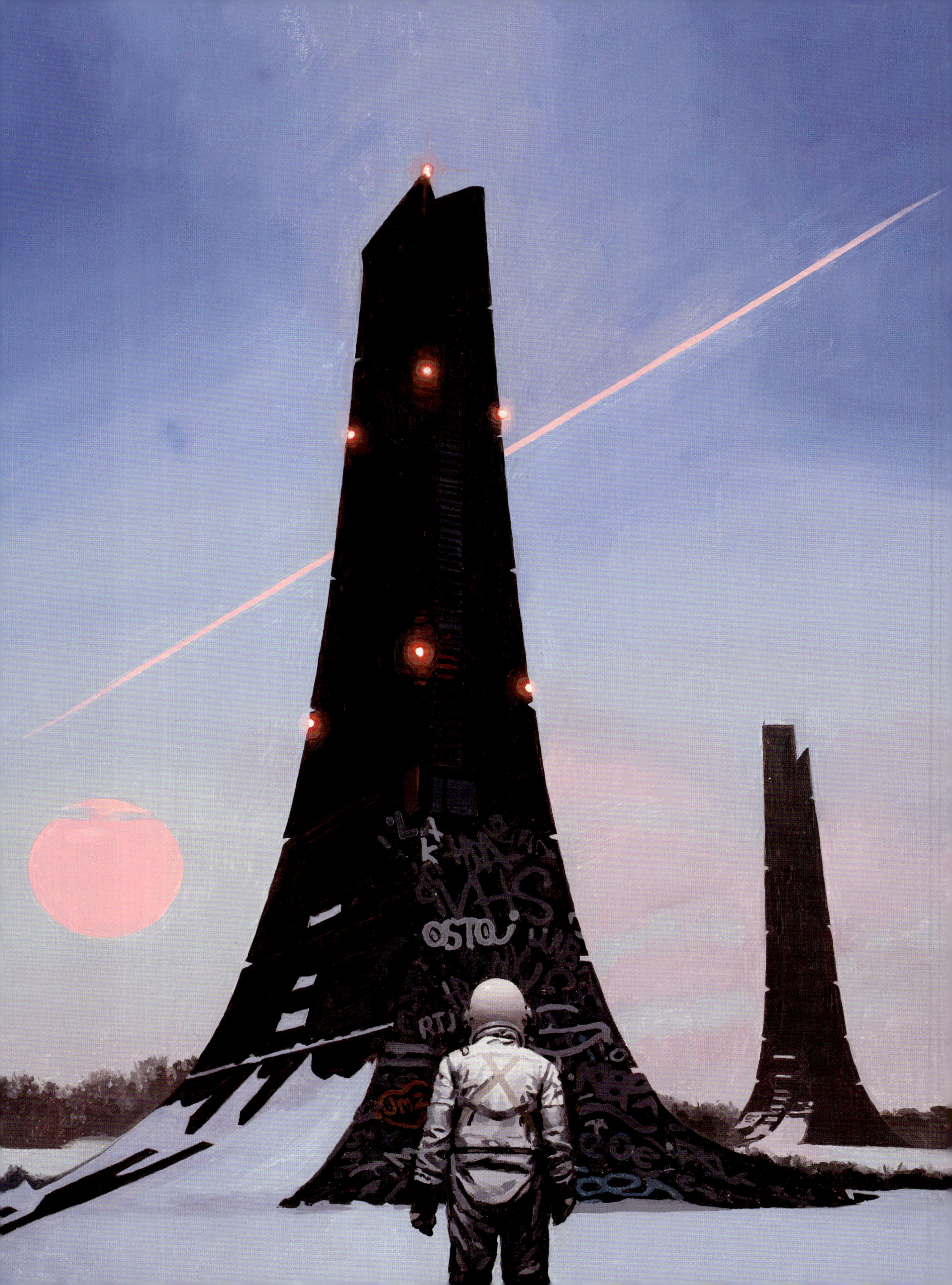
VHS
RTJ

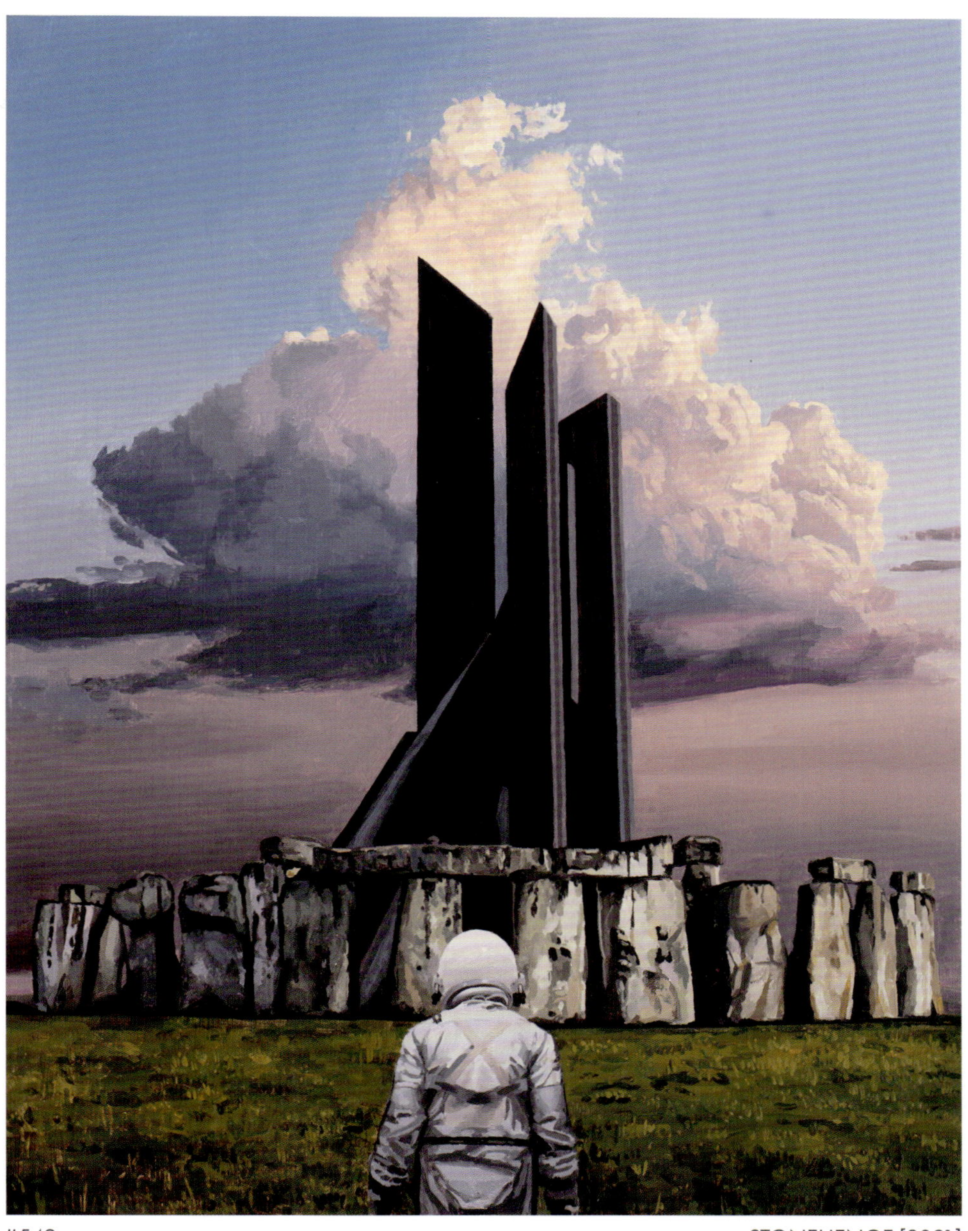

#549 STONEHENGE [2021]

#544
TWO TOWERS [2021]

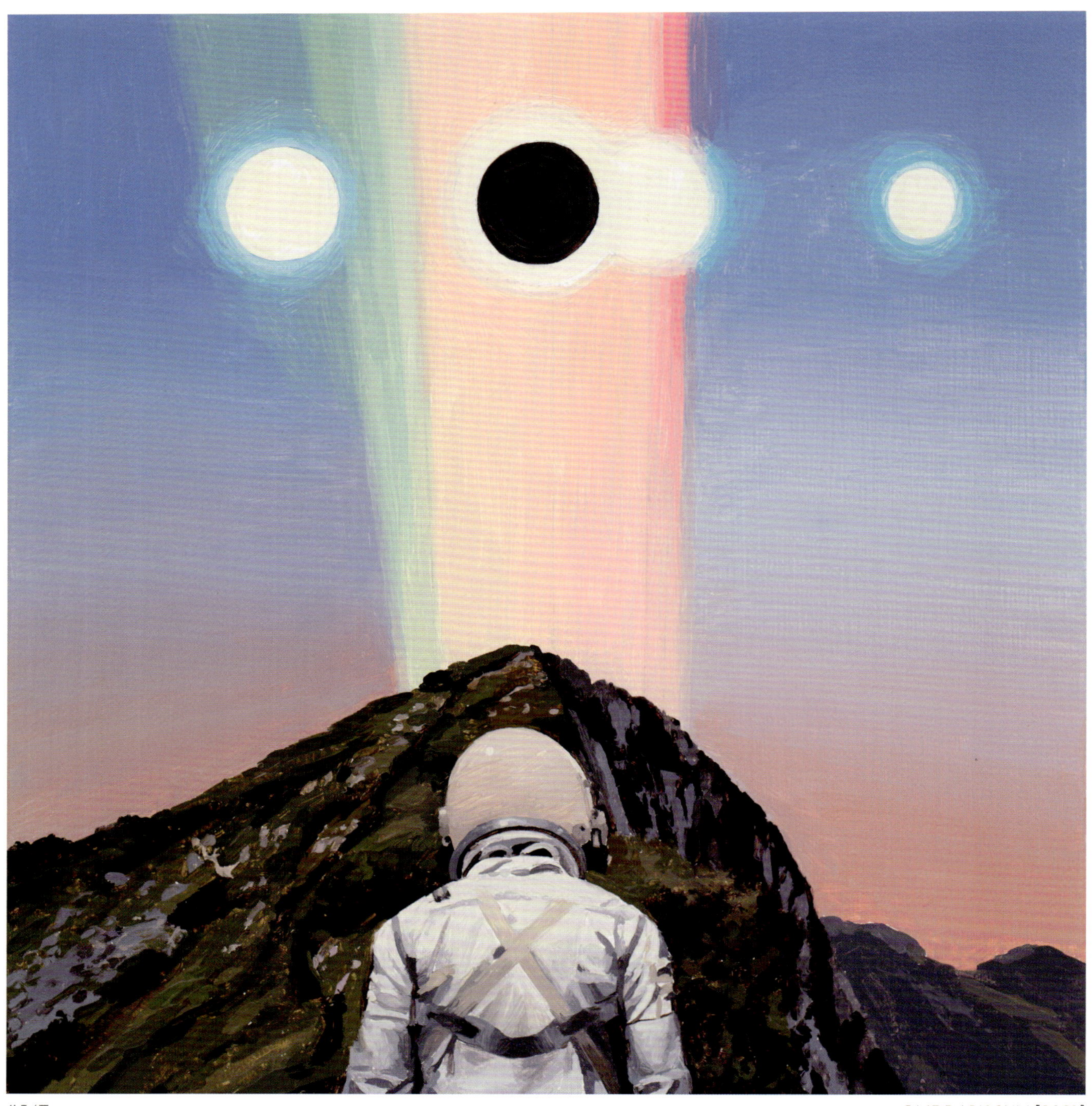

#547

ONE DARK SUN [2021]

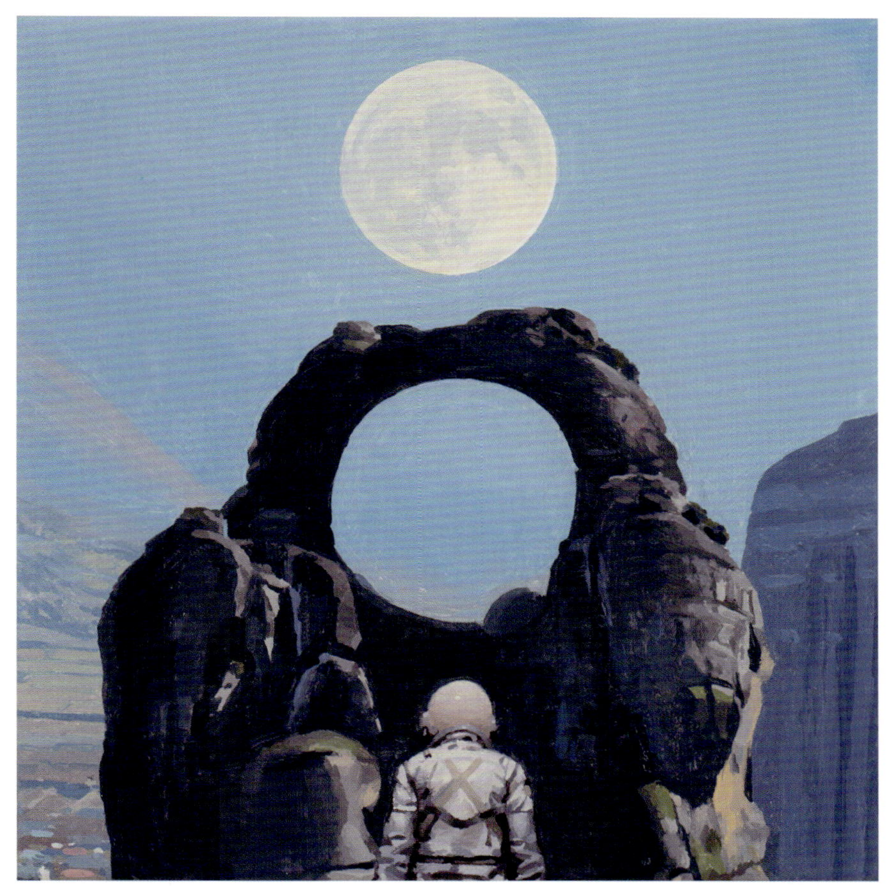

#545 WAITING [2021]

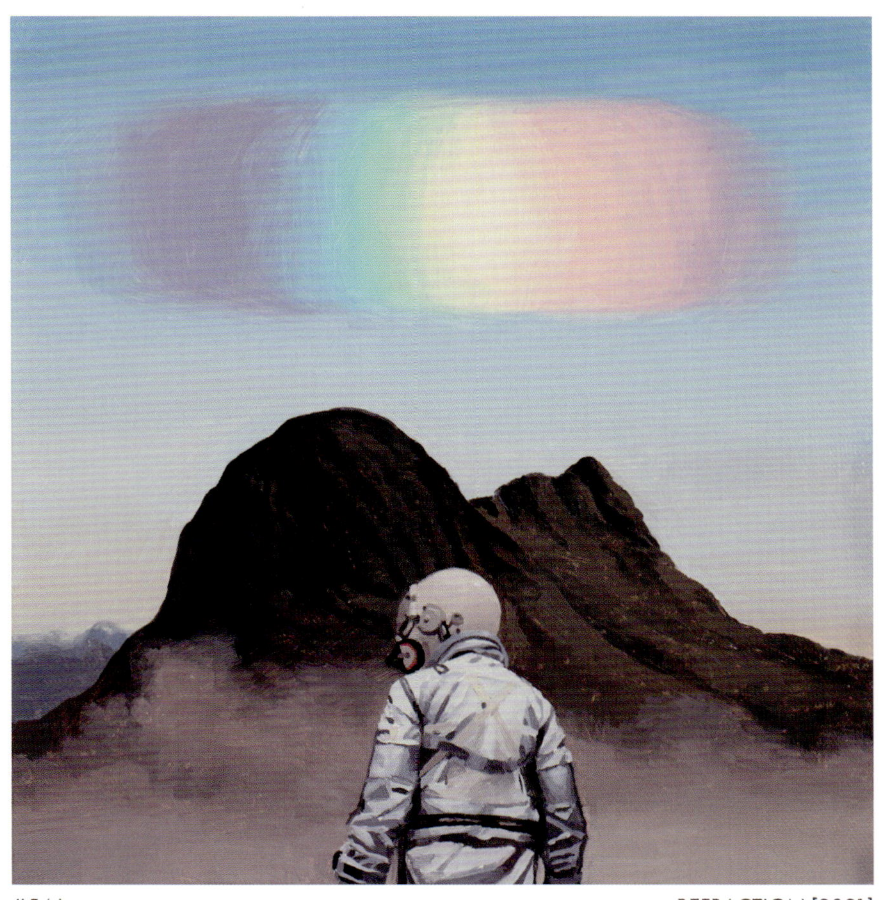

#546 REFRACTION [2021]

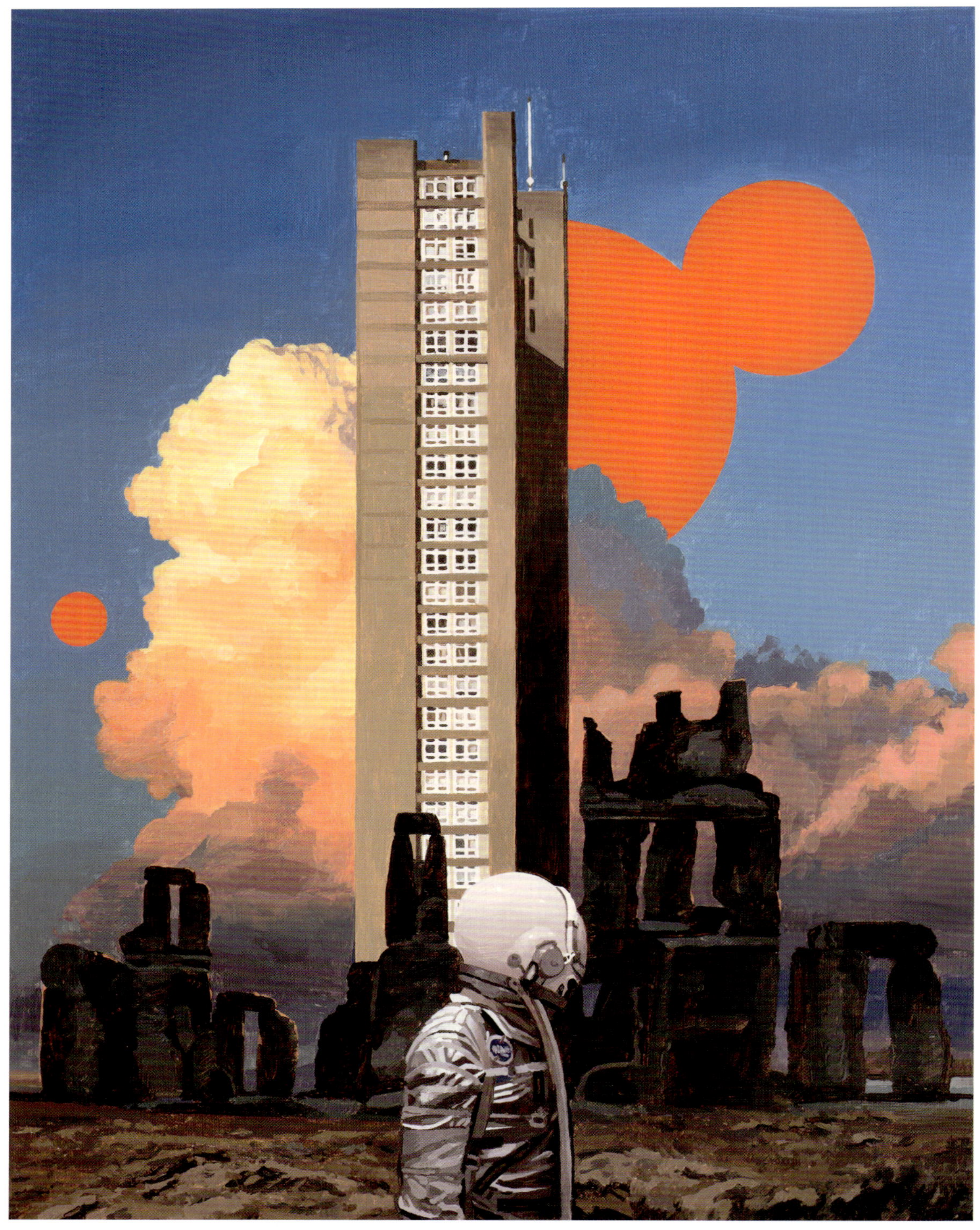

#550 REDEVELOPMENT [2021]

#543
ROCKS [2021]

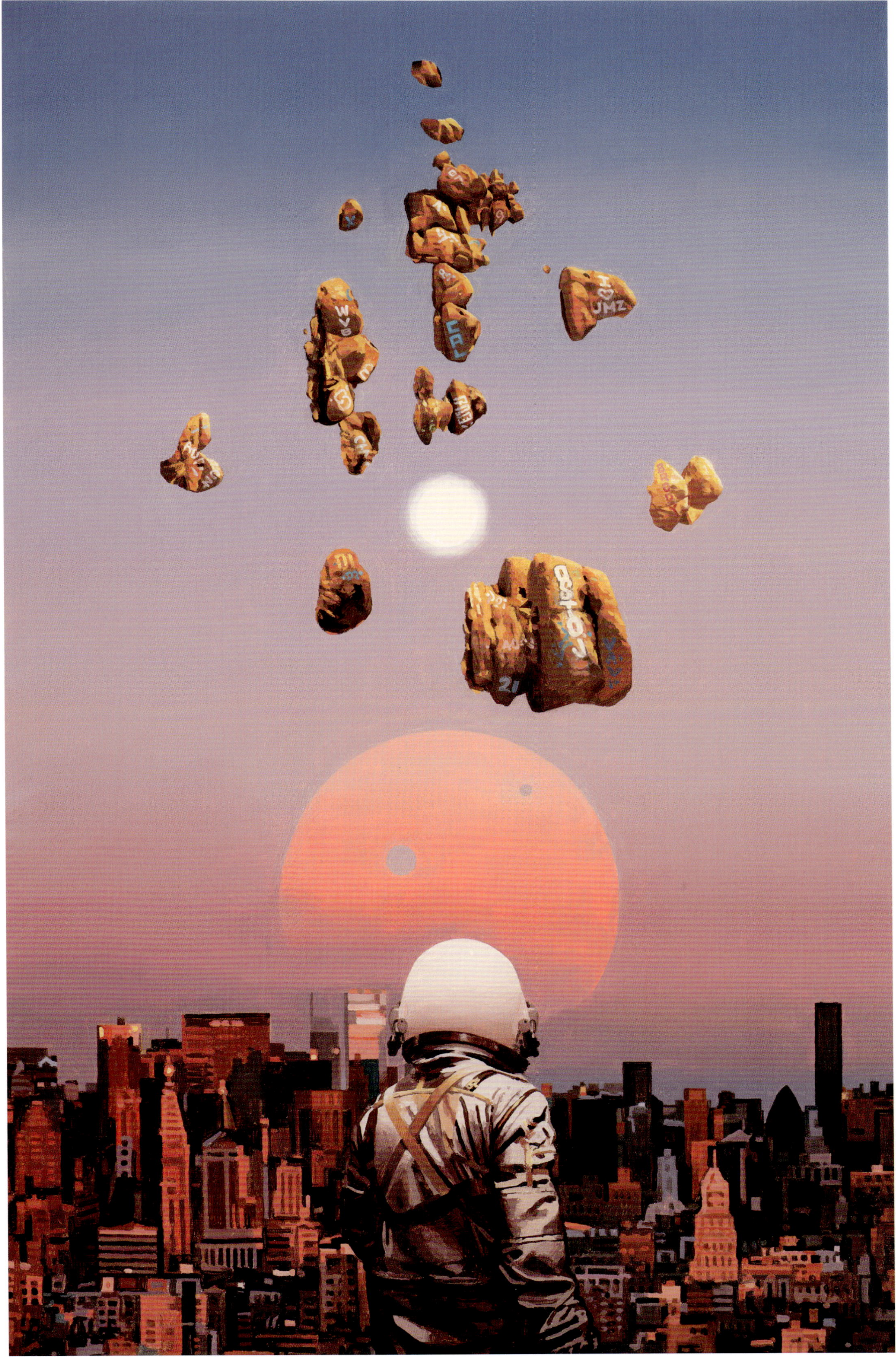

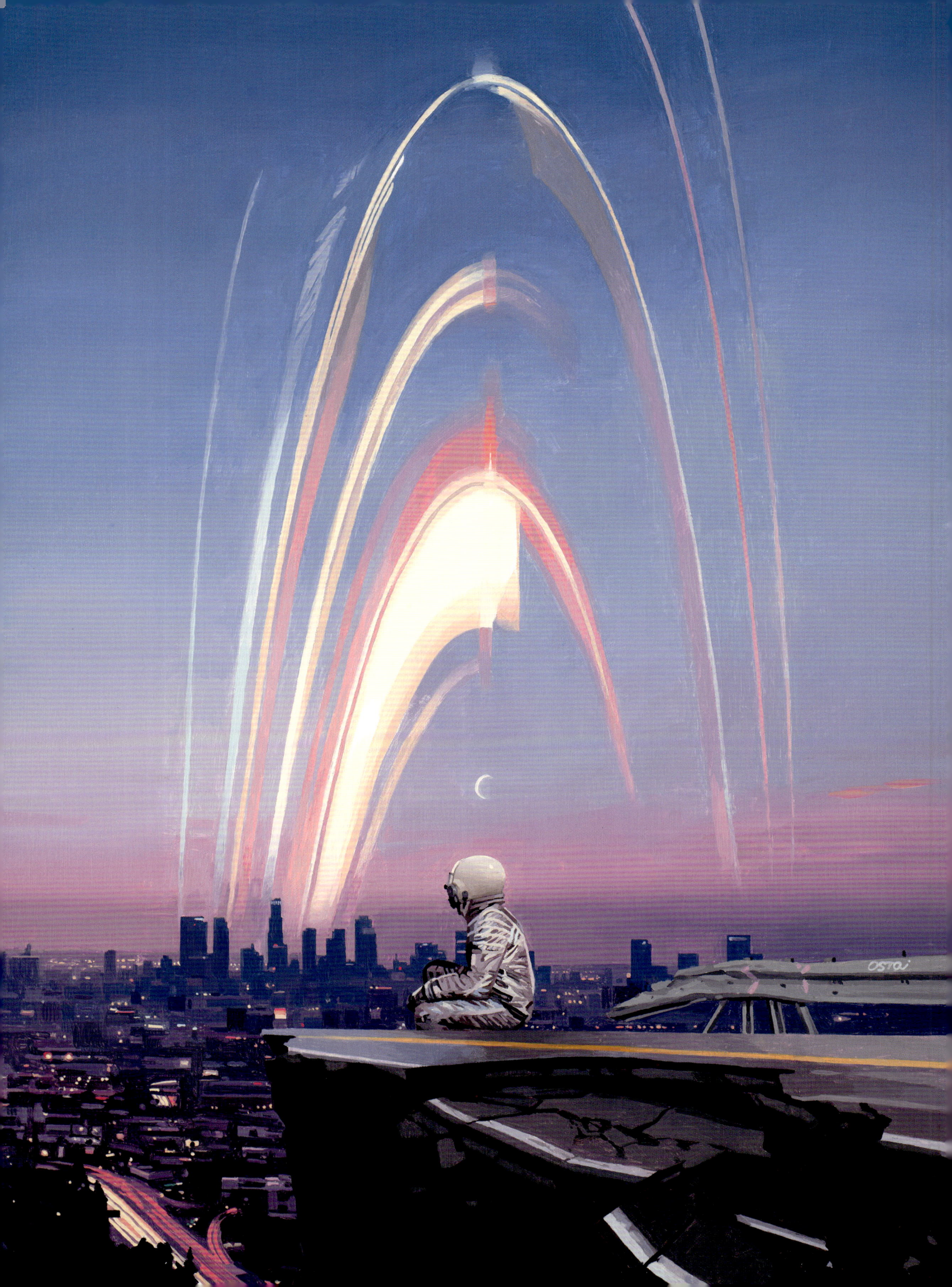
OSTOJ

THE

MULTIVERSE

///

Thinkspace Projects, Los Angeles, CA
June, 2022

I've been inside lately.

Inside my house, inside my studio, inside my own head. Outside, things closed down, then reopened. Then closed and reopened. Time stopped making sense. The sun went up and down and the moon came out. At night my mind, bored from being inside so much, would fold back in on itself. I dreamt of foreign places I visited once and then never again. I spent time with friends long gone and walked again in the steps of a younger version of me. I feel like a ghost sometimes, haunting my own life.

« **It's 2021** and I'm a ghost. I just found out my old friend Jason Chase has passed. Our relationship had fractured in recent years and I thought I would have time to maybe fix that someday. We were friends in a different city and a different time. « **It's 2011**, Jason and I are showing our paintings together in Boston, trying to kick start our art careers after the recession derailed everything. « **It's 2007**, before things fell apart. We're young and plucky and made a somewhat jokey playlist for our first show together. I'm listening to it now, only it's 2022. I'm in my studio, I'm painting, and I'm alone.

« **It's 2004** and I'm a ghost. I paint astronauts and I'm having my first gallery show. My friend Wes is there. He used to come over to my house, have three PBR's too many, put a large arm over my shoulder, and drunkenly

#583
LOST HIGHWAY 2 [2022]

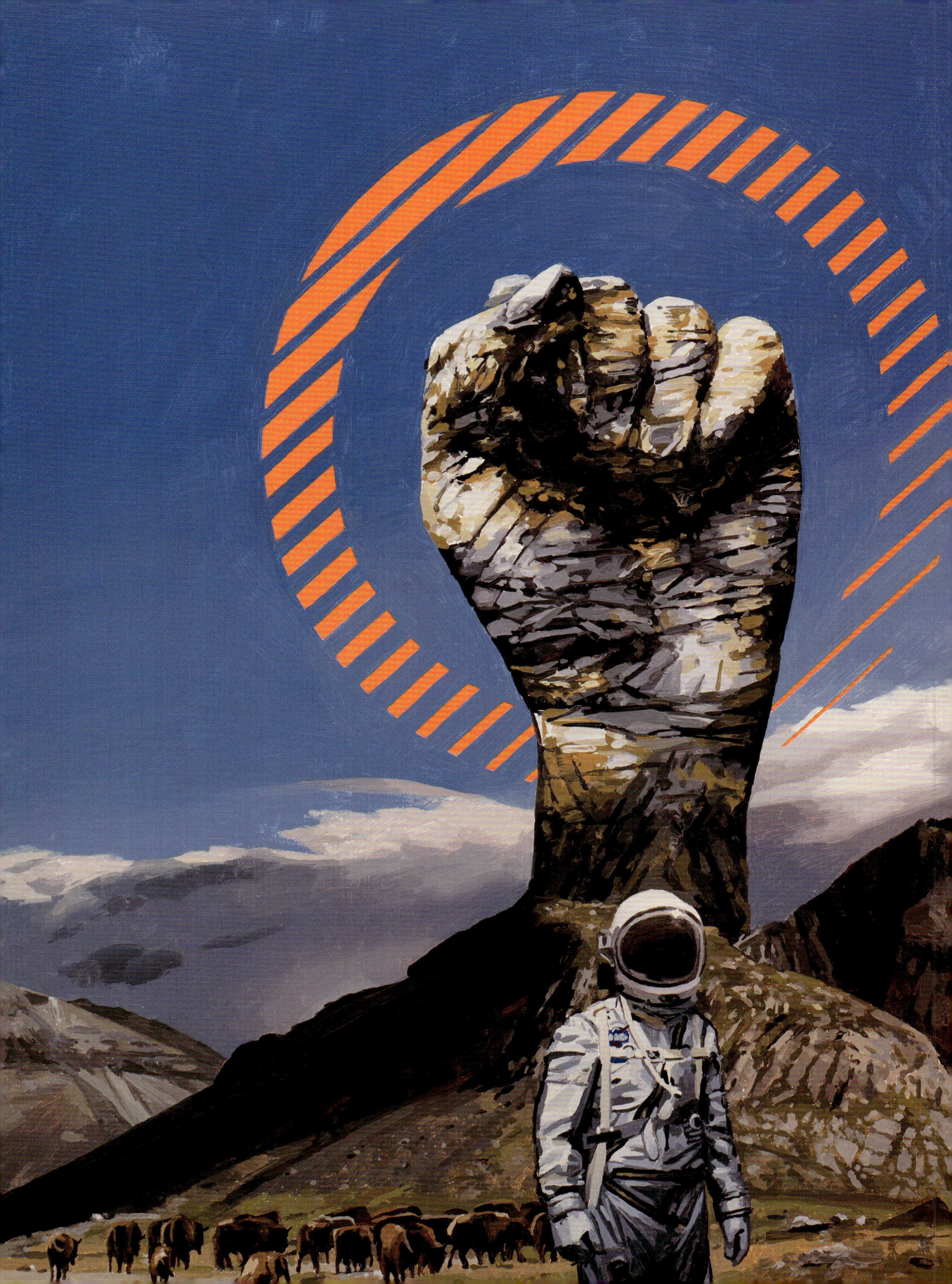

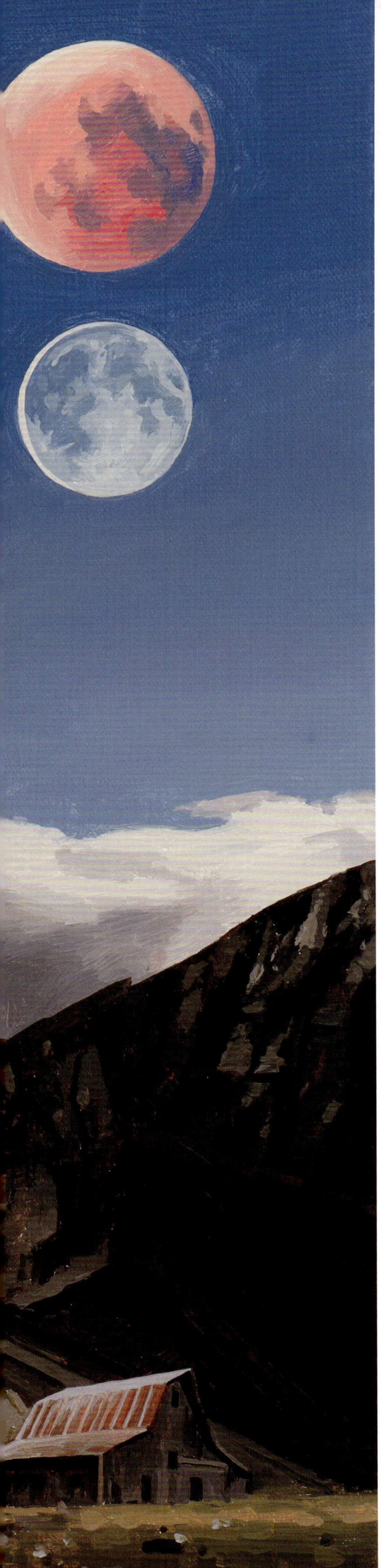

tell me I was better than Matisse. I wasn't. But Wes believed in me back then when almost no one else did. I was young and filled with self-doubt. I'm painting in a band T-shirt that Wes gave me in 2005. **» It's 2022**. The band hasn't existed since 2008.

« It's 1999 and I'm a ghost. I'm painting my first ever astronaut painting and I don't know that I'll be spending the next two decades doing the same thing. I have no idea what I'm doing. I tell my younger self to keep going.

« It's Christmas 1997 and I'm a ghost. I just returned from 3 months studying in Italy and I'm jet lagged, culture shocked, and crashing on my friend Chris Ostoj's couch. Only he's not here, so I'm alone, on Christmas, in Brooklyn. In Italy I listened to my friend Chris's band on a cheap Walkman that got stolen on a train outside of Amsterdam. I'm humming the same song now. **» It's 2022** and I'm in Los Angeles. My friend Chris grew up in Yucaipa, not far from here. He left it behind and didn't talk about it much. He spent his last days there, though.

» It's 2022 and my friends are ghosts, too. They're no longer around and so I do what I can. They live on in my paintings. I'm painting my different lives all at once. **It's 1999, it's 2004, it's 2007, it's 2010, it's 2018, it's 2022. It's**

THE MULTIVERSE

This is a show about escaping. Escaping back into my own life and finding it again. After almost 600 paintings, and a couple of tough years for all of us, I'm feeling reflective. This is the most personal show I've ever done: 23 new paintings where I step back in time and walk in the footsteps of younger versions of me. I revisit my oldest paintings and allow the astronaut to haunt familiar places. The centerpiece of this show are the three largest paintings I've ever made, each a literal monument to those I've lost along the way.

I've been inside lately, looking back. It's time to go outside again and look to the future.

#576
CLOSED HAND [2022]

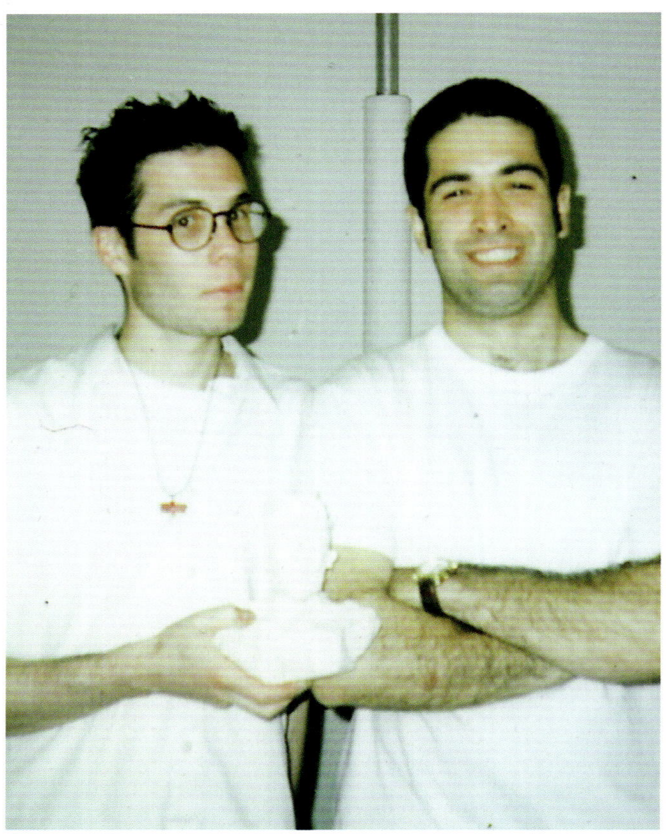

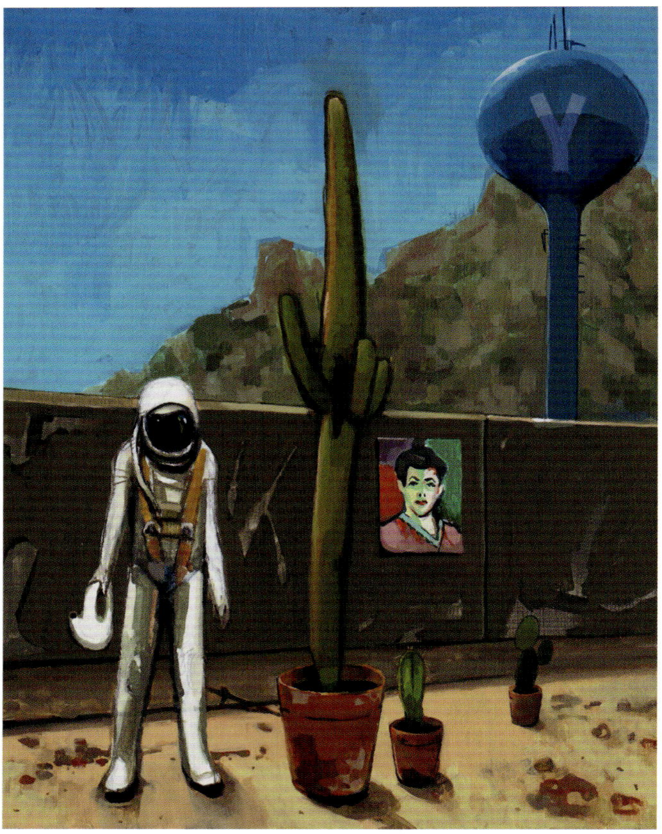

#015 YUCAIPA [2004]

« **It's June 1997,** my friend Chris Ostoj is about to graduate from college. We take an awkward photograph in his dorm room. Well, my part of it is awkward. He's got a wide grin on his face. I'm holding a self portrait I sculpted in clay, which always cracked him up, from a figure sculpture class we took together. So I gave it to him. All of his worldly belongings are in three boxes and a guitar case. He's leaving early the next morning for Brooklyn. One of those boxes (books, mostly) and the guitar case will go back with me to my parents house where they will sit in the basement for a while. The guitar I will eventually take to New York to give back to him. The box of books I'll eventually ship to his mother in Yucaipa after he's gone.

The photograph we took in his dorm room hangs in my studio now.

If you're familiar with my work, over the years, you've probably seen a bit of graffiti here or there that says "Ostoj." A lot of people over the years have asked me what it means. When we were in college together, up in a far corner of New Hampshire, Chris was something of a mentor to me. He might still be the smartest artist I have ever met. We were planning on taking the New York art world by storm. It didn't quite work out that way. When Chris passed away in 2002, it was a wake up call to me. I hadn't accomplished much of anything to that point, and was barely painting anymore. It was Chris's death that kickstarted my art career. Without him I wouldn't be here, doing this. I still think about him almost every day in my studio. My friend Chris lives on in my work.

This painting is set in the hills of New Hampshire, where Chris and I went to school together. It includes references to his college band, to Matisse, to the hundreds of times I've painted his name as graffiti into my work, and especially to the painting I made about his passing in 2004. At 60x40 inches, it's one of the largest paintings I've ever made.

#573
FIRST HAND [2022]

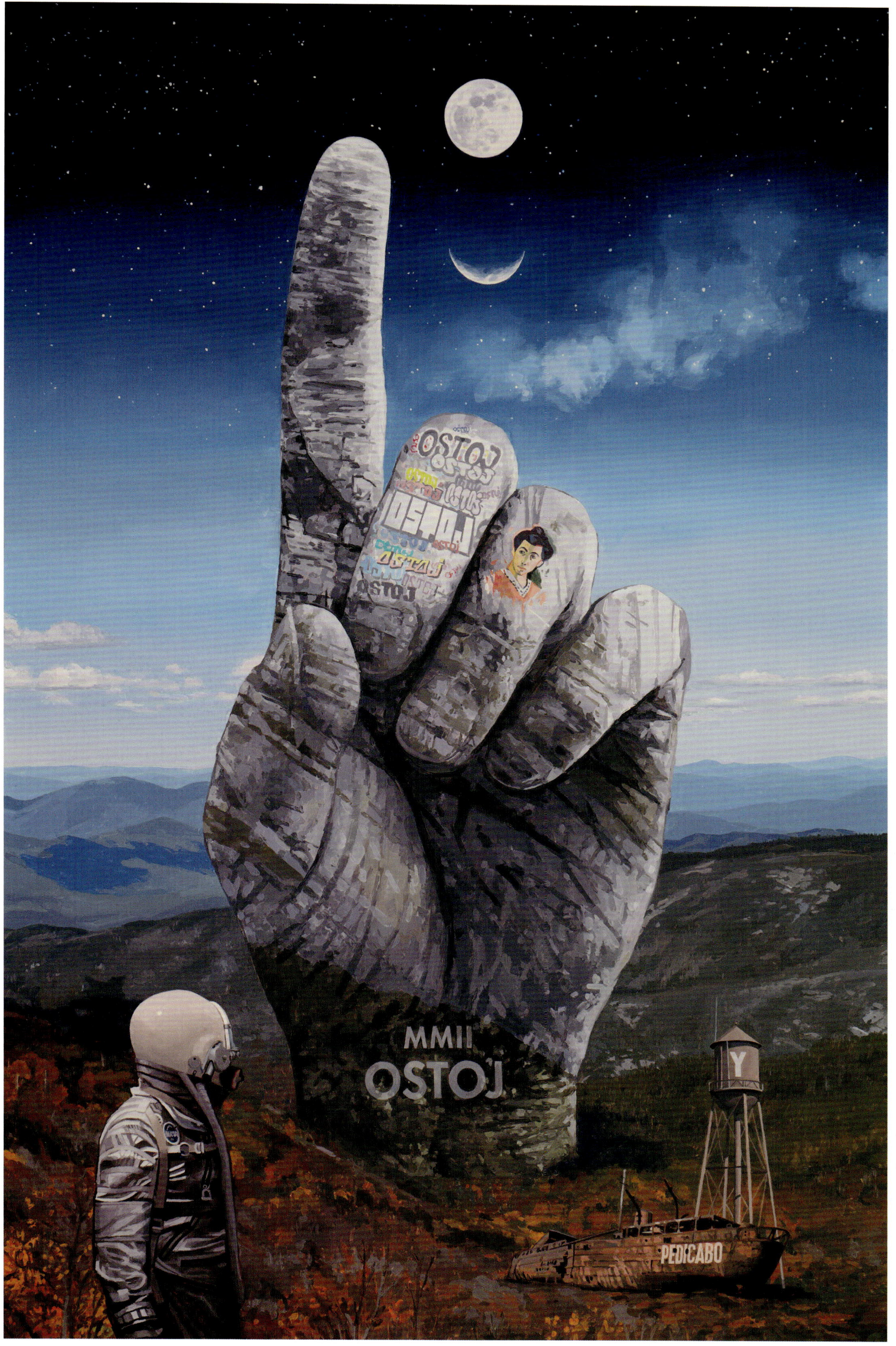
OSTOJ
OSTOJ
MMII
OSTOJ
Y
PEDICABO

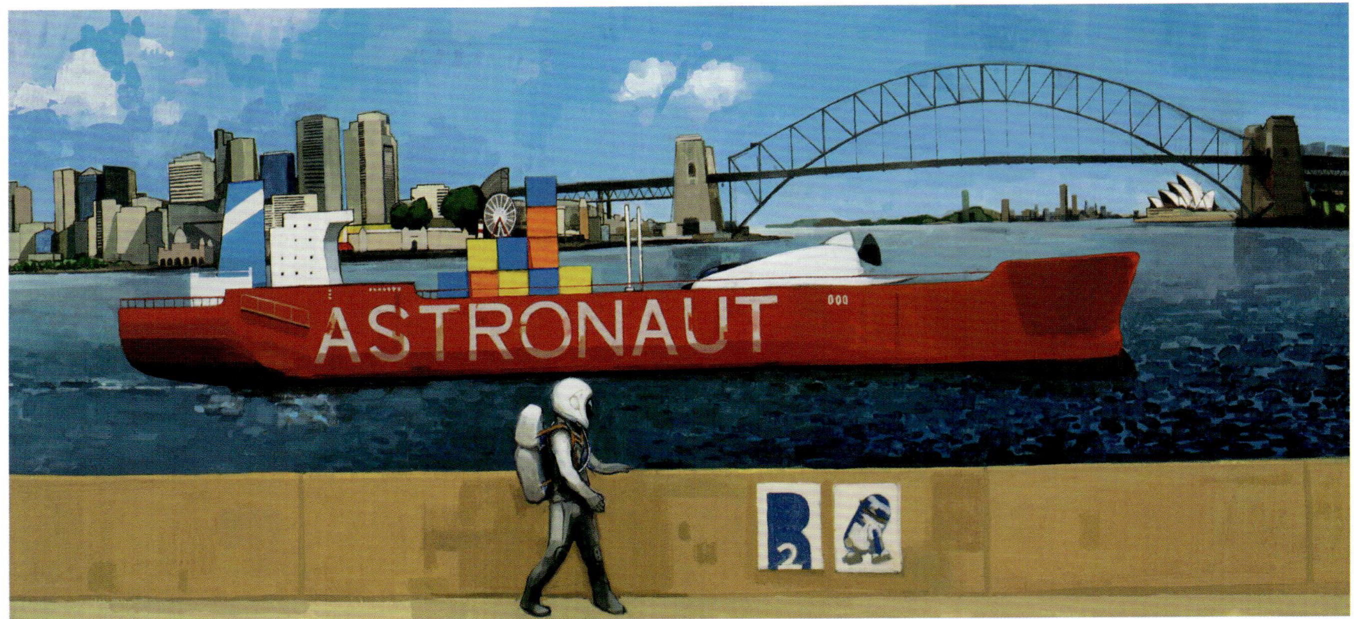

#017

BALMAIN EAST [2004]

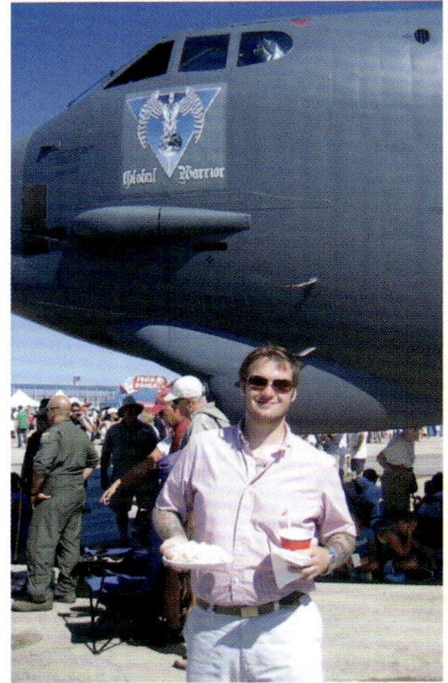

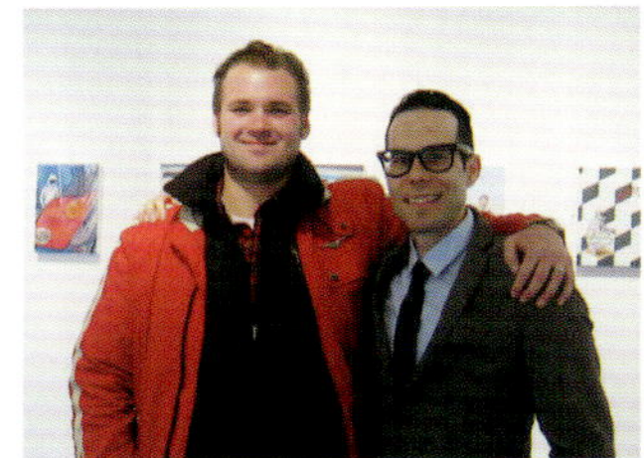

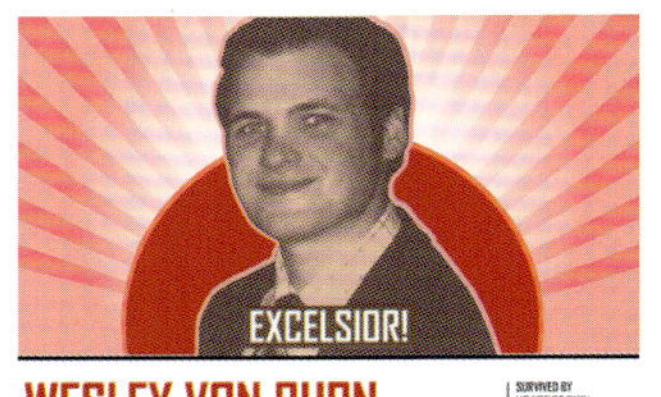

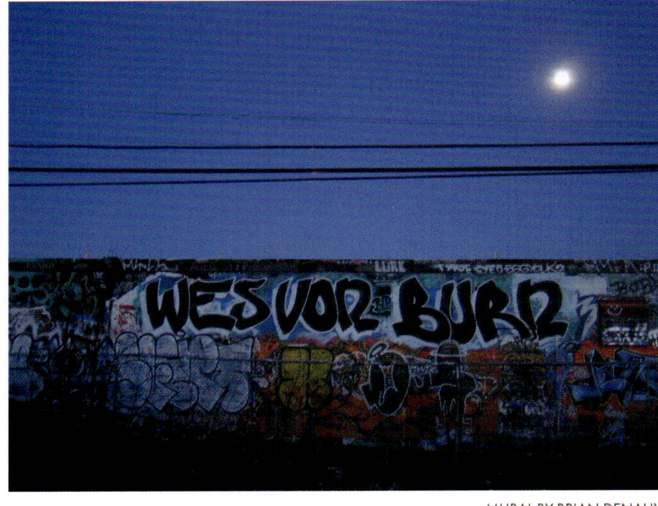

MURAL BY BRIAN DENAHY

» It's sometime in 2003 maybe? My memory on this one is hazy. My wife Joanna and I aren't yet married, but we go to a party at the house of an old college friend of hers. It's one of those parties that we had probably already outgrown, but we're there. We're not sure if we want to be there. We're kind of hiding out in the bedroom where all the coats get put on the bed. There's a guy there. A giant guy. Only he's dressed pretty much like me. I'm not a giant guy. We're both wearing corduroy blazers. We talk and he laughs and puts a giant hand on my shoulder. We're going to be friends, he says. He's there with Teegan, an old friend of my wife's from school. His name is Wes.

» It's 2004 and I'm having my first ever gallery show, in Boston. Wes is there. He used to come over to our apartment, get a little drunk and wander into my studio. He'd tell me how much he loved my paintings. Especially when he was a little drunk. Back then, not then many people had much interest in what I was doing. Wes did. Joanna did, too. Not too many other people cared whether I ever painted an astronaut again or not. Having that support from people in my life meant everything. **» It's 2011**, I'm having a small show at a university gallery. It's a nice show but my art career has seen more downs than ups. On the day of the opening, Wes drove all the way over from work, during his lunch break, on his motorcycle, just so he could see it.

« It's summer 2005 and Wes and Teegan get married on a boat. They both grew up near the ocean. **» It's 2012** and Joanna and I are awoken by a phone call.

This painting is set on a beautiful stretch of ocean, where Wes spent most of his life, and where his ashes reside now that he's gone. Bits and pieces of his life are here: a tattoo, a ship, and an old painting of mine, one that still hangs on my walls. My friend Wes lives on in my work.

#572

SECOND HAND [2022]

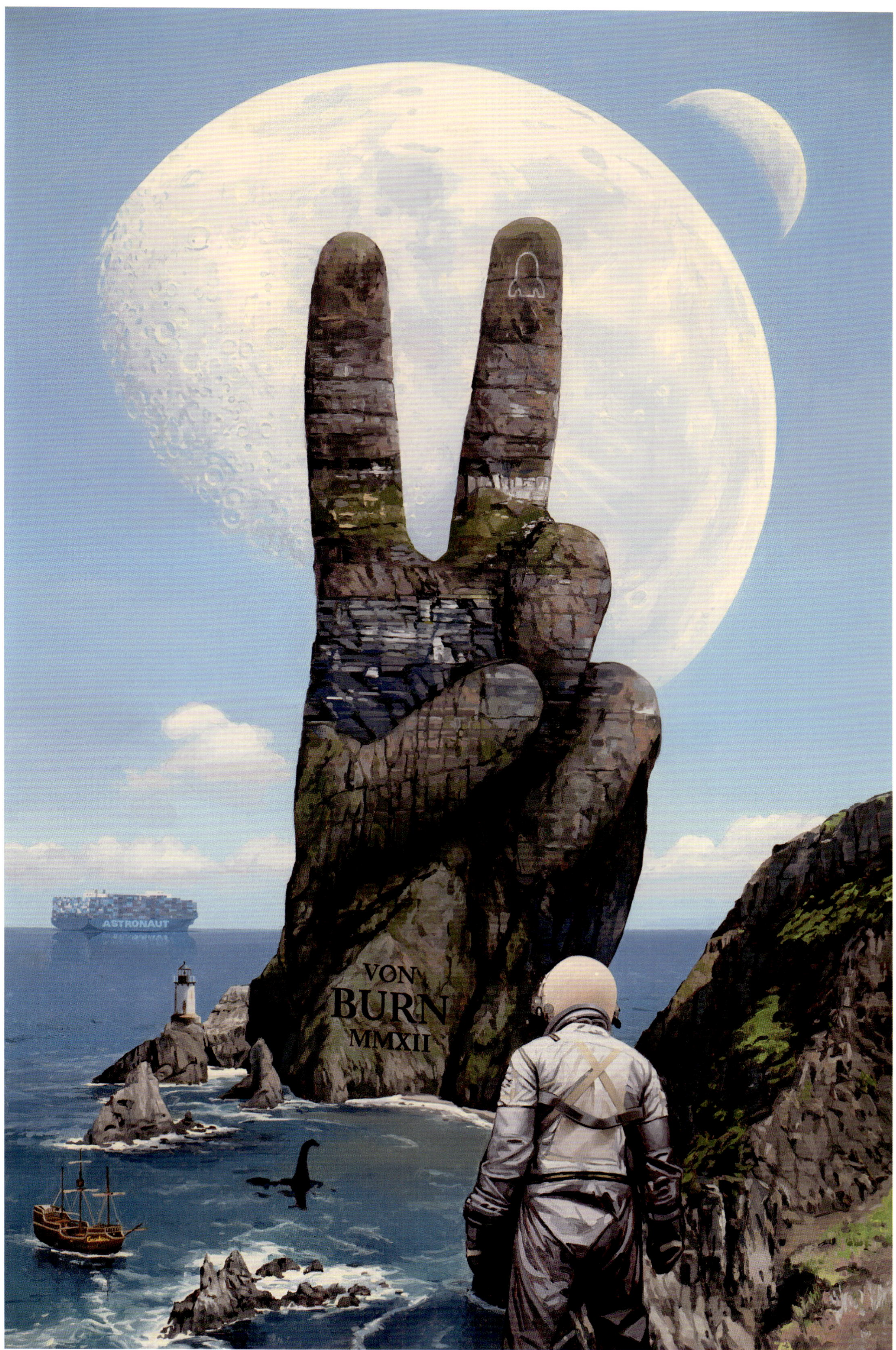
ASTRONAUT
VON
BURN
MMXII

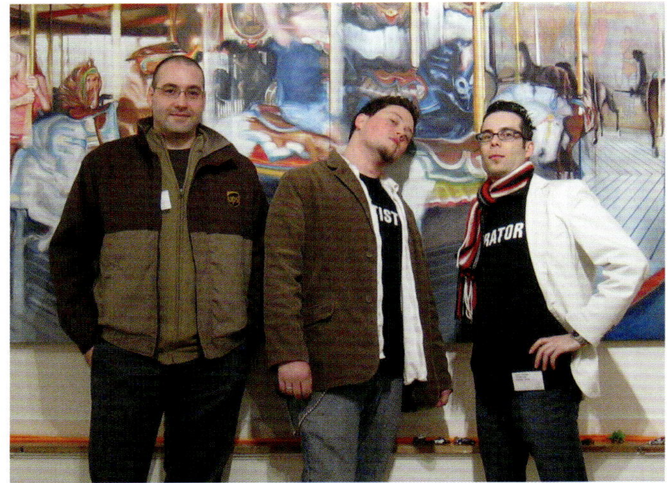

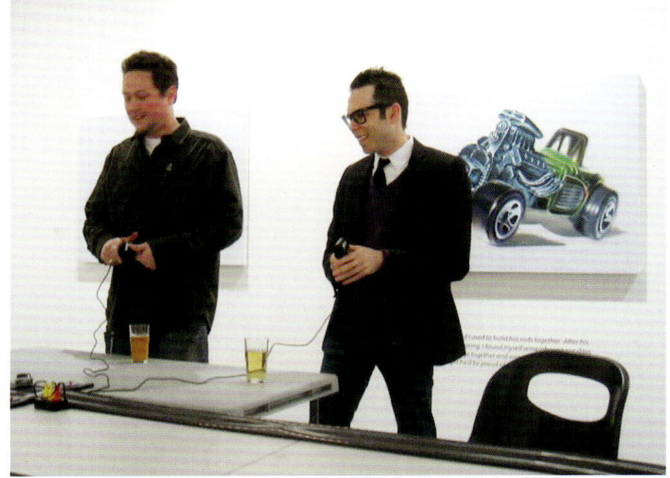

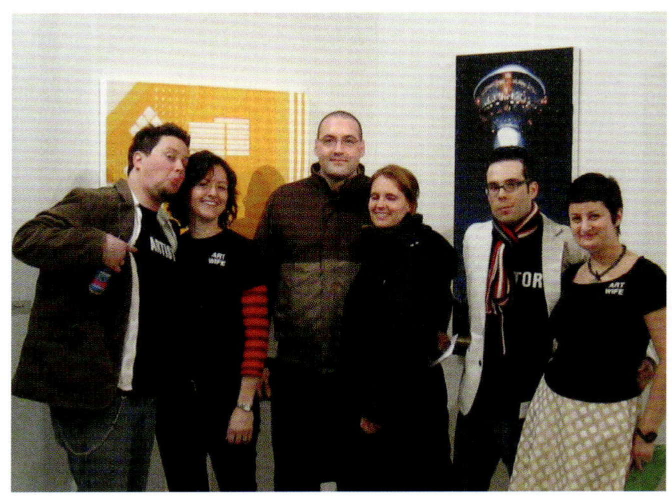

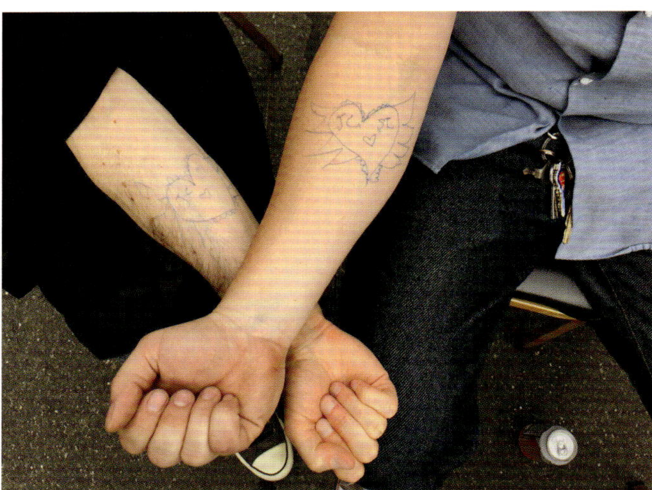

« It's fall 2006 and I'm about to have my second ever solo show at a gallery in Boston. I feel like my art career is on its way but I don't know that a coming recession will wipe most of it out. The previous spring I walked into Jason Chase's apartment during an open studios event and we instantly became friends. At that time, in Boston, there weren't many artists making large, bright, pop infused representational paintings. I was. So was Jason. Both of us, probably without realizing it, had been looking for an art community. We found each other.

» It's winter 2007 and I've curated a show in a gallery in what used to be an old church. It's me, it's Jason, and it's Will DiBello, another art pal with similar sensibilities. The show is about consumerism and cars and painting. We called it *Trans Am*. We made a soundtrack. We blew our modest budget on hot wheels cars. It's a fun show. The future seemed bright.

» It's winter 2010 and Jason and I are in another show together in Boston. Just us this time. Also car themed. Jason loved cars. He came from a long line of mechanics and hot rod racers. The intervening years had wiped out my art career, but after some long moments of self doubt, I was starting to bounce back. This show would end up being a turning point for me. I ended up selling a lot of the work in this show, and eventually caught the notice of galleries out on the west coast. But it might also be where my path diverged from Jason's.

» It's fall 2018 and I'm moving to LA. I'm leaving Boston behind. Jason was the nicest guy I ever met, sometimes, but he was complicated. He shed friendships like snake skins every few years. I lasted a while, until I didn't. We grew apart. I think my relative success in the art world had something to do with it, but I don't know. I saw him one last time before I left. It was the first time I'd seen him in a couple years. He seemed upbeat. I figured one day we'd talk it out, and everything would be ok. We never did.

» It's fall 2021 and I just found out my old friend Jason Chase is gone. An old Boston friend reached out to tell me. I'm listening to the *Trans Am* soundtrack we made together 14 years ago. This one still stings. I still think about him almost every day in my studio. My friend Jason lives on in my work.

Each of the three large paintings in this show represents a chapter in my life, and a friend I've lost along the way. Although I never managed to patch things up with Jason, I wish he could have come out to LA. I think he would have liked it here. People drive everywhere. He would have loved the lights at night, a million cars setting the city aglow. And so this painting is Los Angeles at night, where this chapter of my life has happened, with nods to the cars that Jason owned, painted, or both.

#586
THIRD HAND [2022]

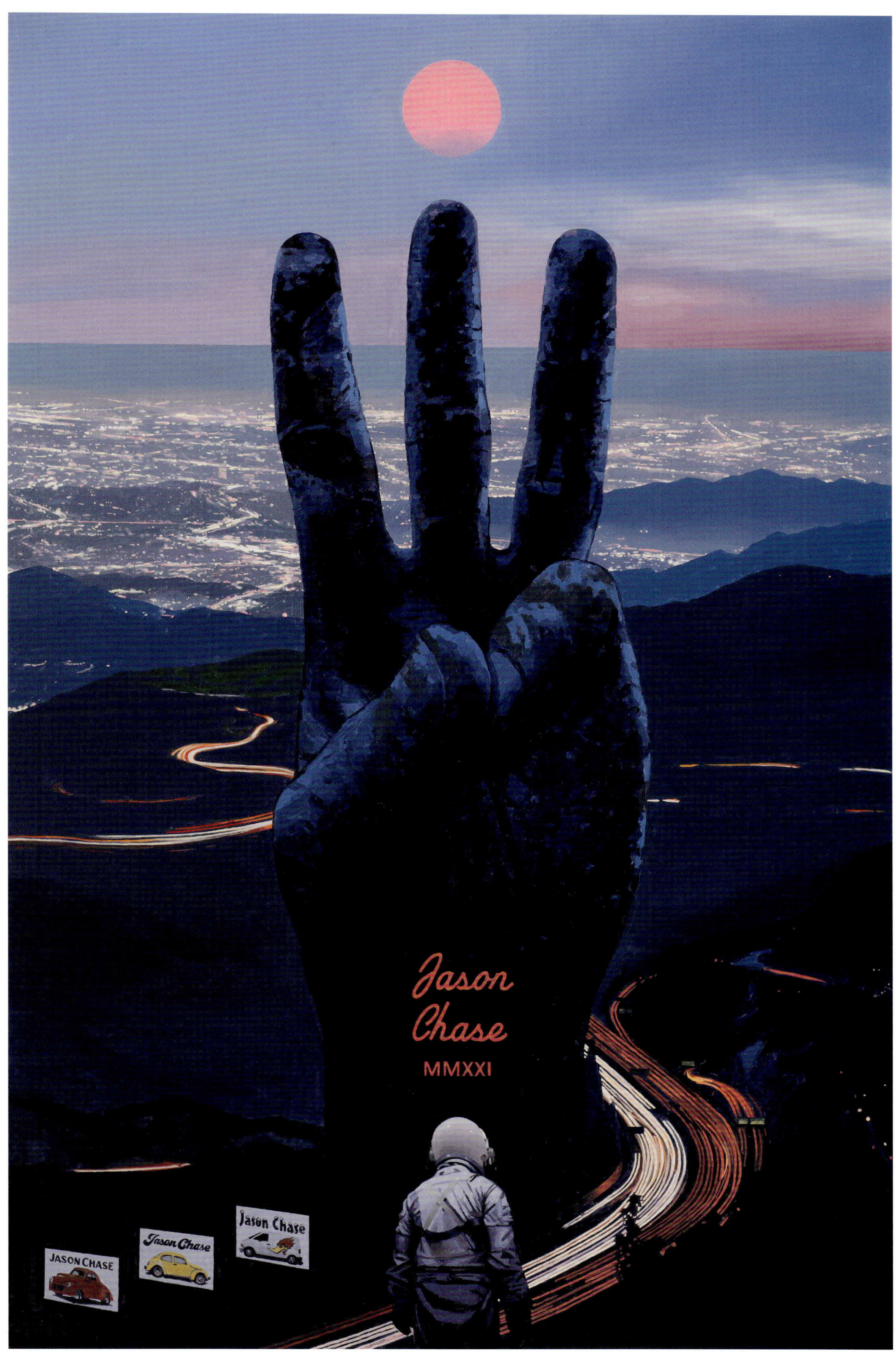
Jason
Chase
MMXXI
JASON CHASE
Jason Chase
Jason Chase

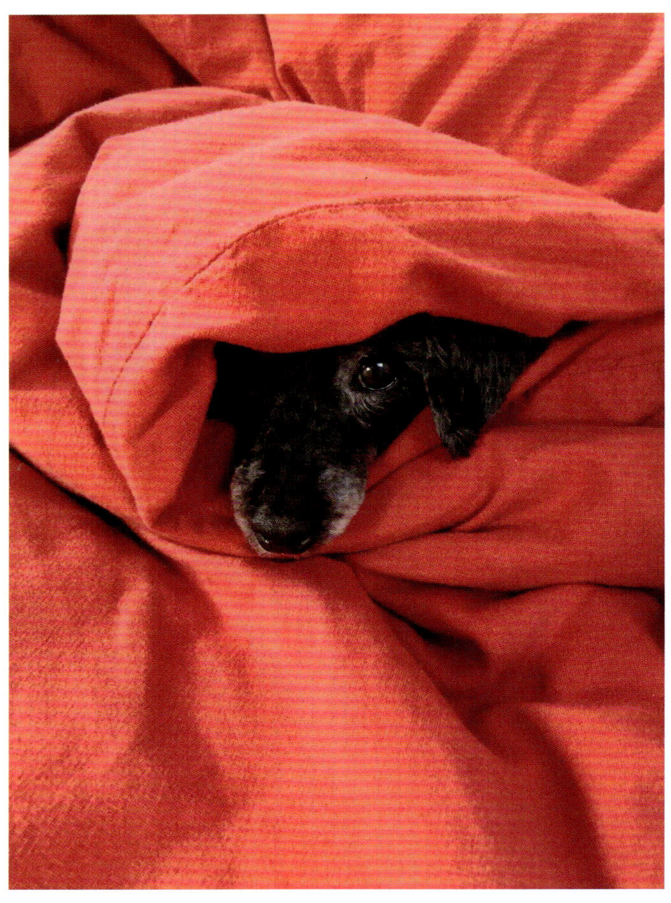

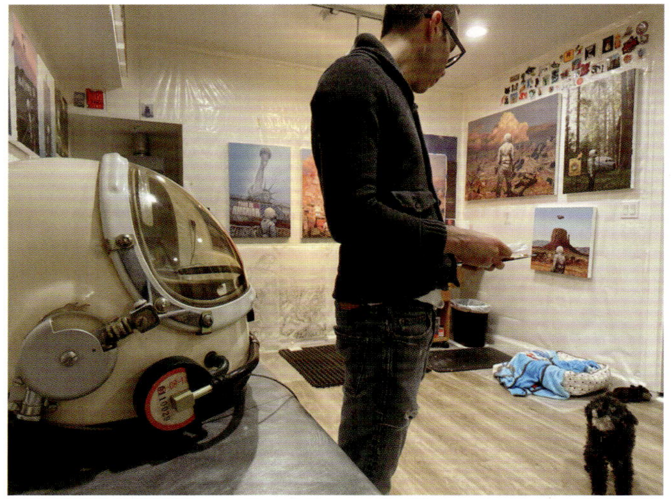

» **It's May 2022** and my bff and my best studio assistant passed away. She lived a good long life, peed on a lot of things, and ate a lot of people food. It was her time, but I still miss her lots. It's not the same without you in the studio, Brody. This show is dedicated to you.

#570
SIT & WATCH [2021]

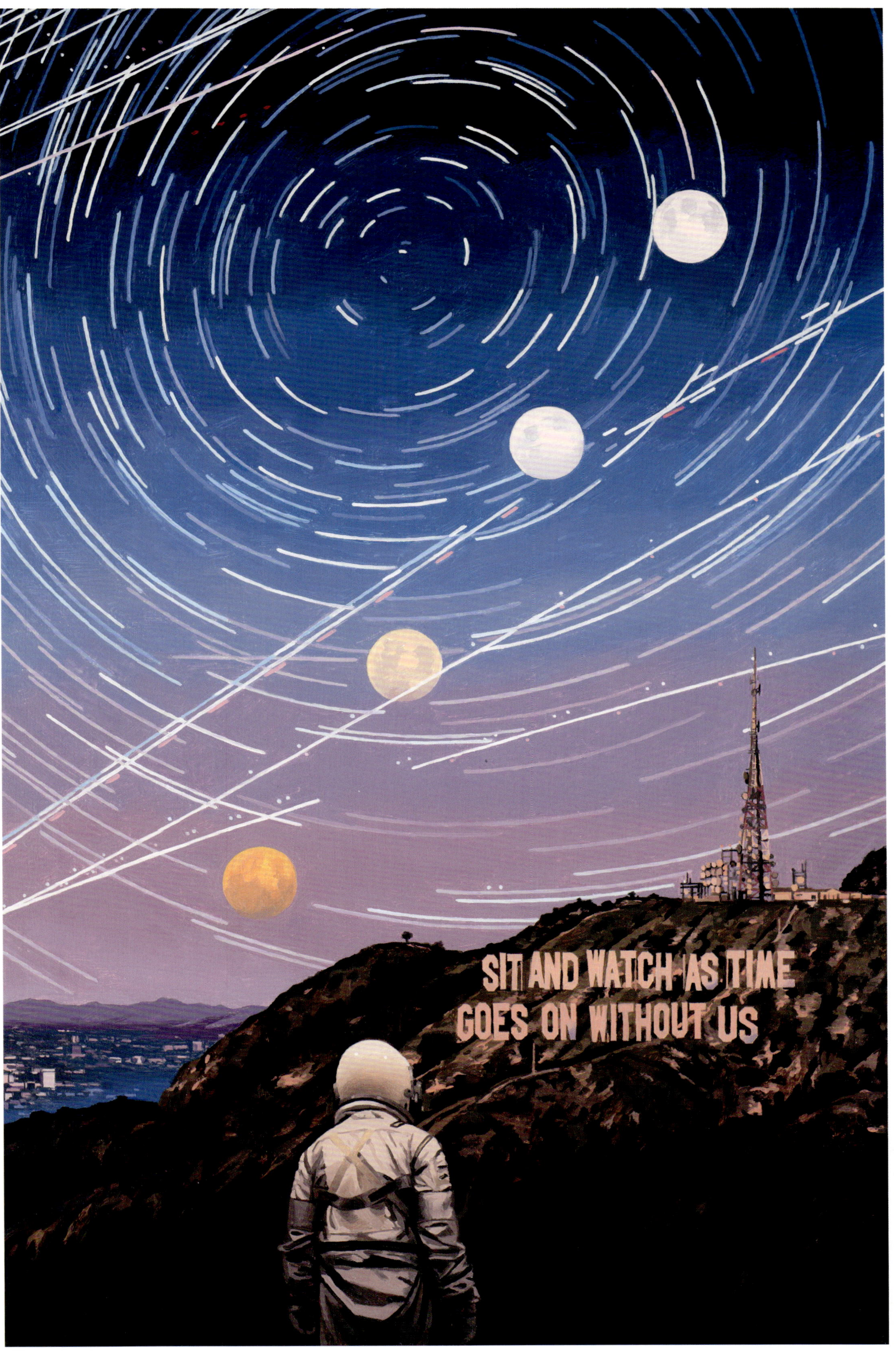
SIT AND WATCH AS TIME
GOES ON WITHOUT US

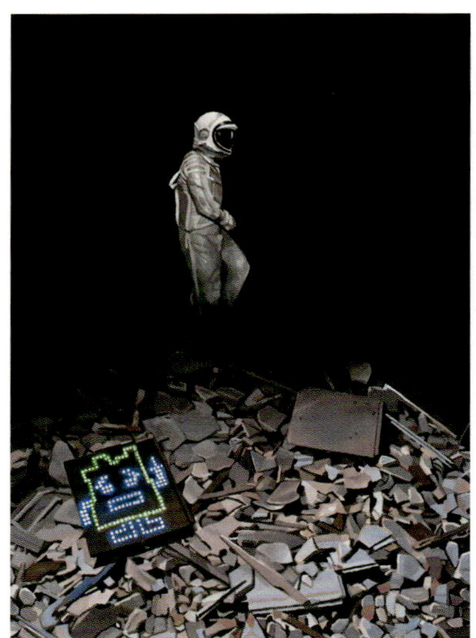

#089 MOONINITE [2011]

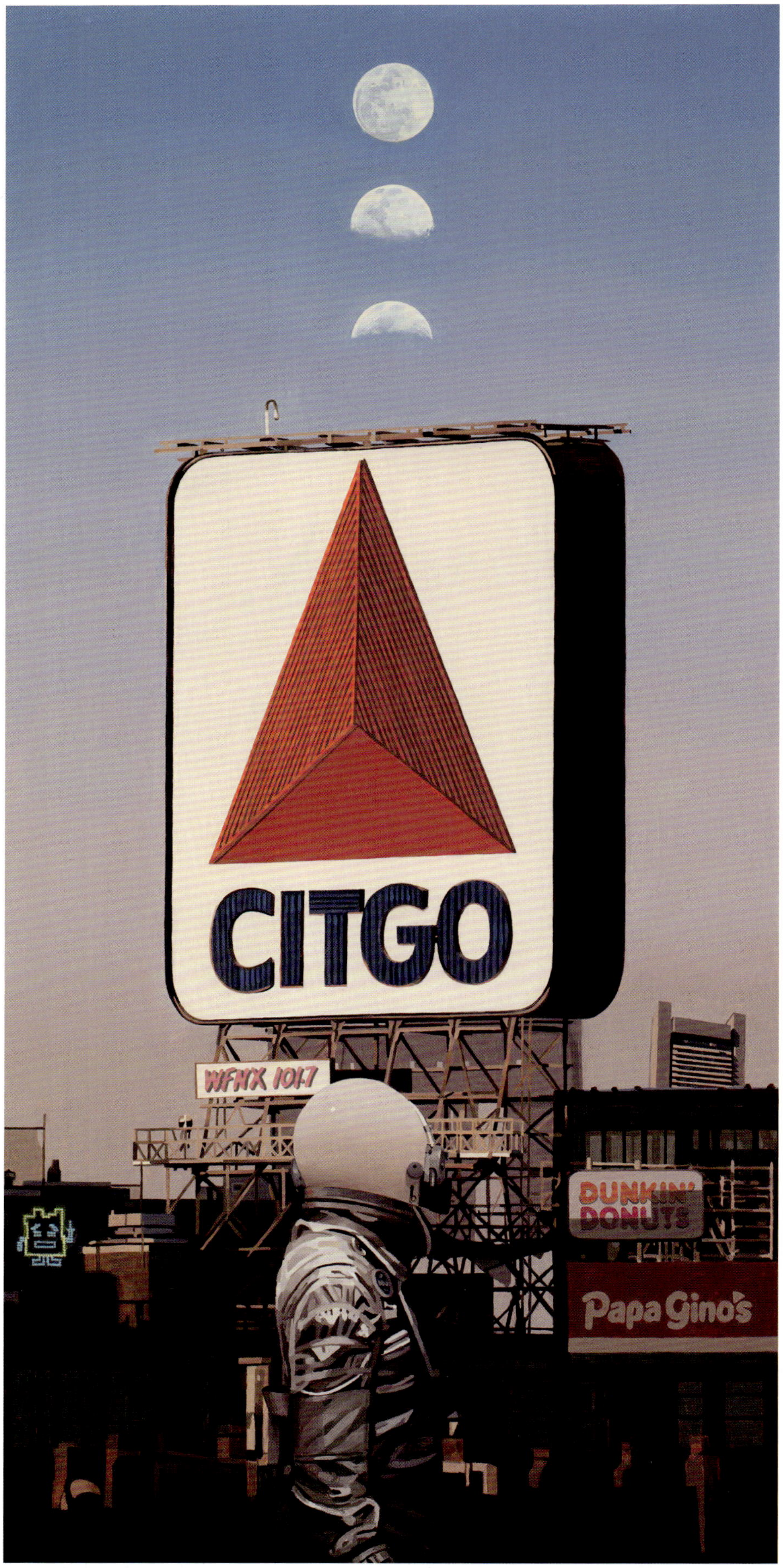

« **It's 2007** and *Adult Swim*, in an attempt at guerrilla marketing, put up a series of neon signs depicting a character from their *Aqua Teen Hunger Force* show around Boston. It did not go well. The police treated it like a bomb threat and shut down large swaths of the city. I lived in Boston at the time and I feel like this event is an adequate representation of why cool stuff doesn't happen there. Years later when I was invited to be in an official *Adult Swim* show, I created a nod to my home city, in all its absurdity.

Throughout most of my career I lived in Boston and almost never painted it. I was always looking for inspiration from places that seemed exotic, alien, or surreal to me, and my hometown inspired none of those feelings. But now? After living in Los Angeles these past few years and working on this show that is, in a lot of ways, about my own personal history? I had to make a Boston painting. I say this with love: Here you go, Massholes. This one's for you.

#579 KENMORE [2022]

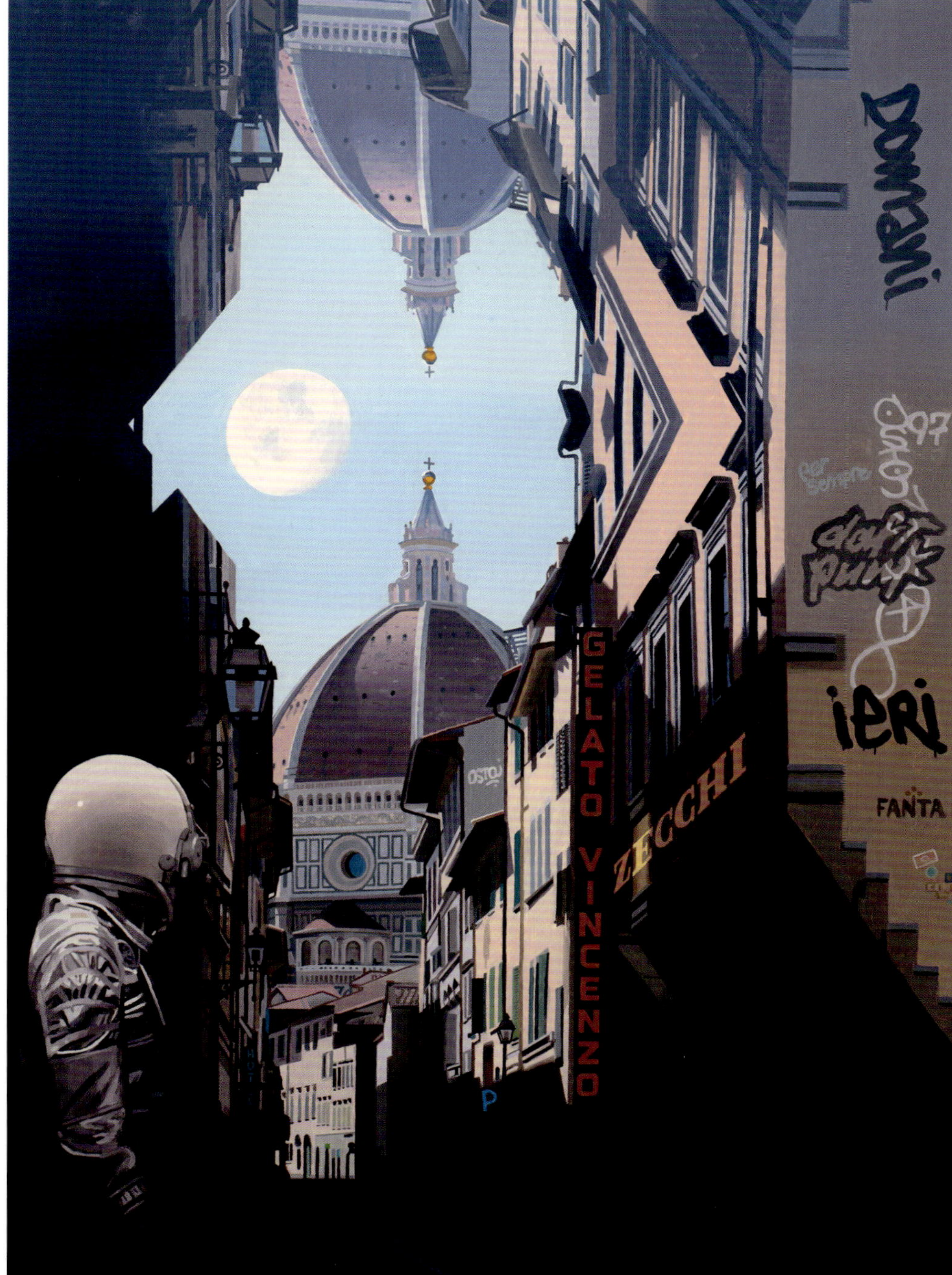

#582 DUOMO [2022]

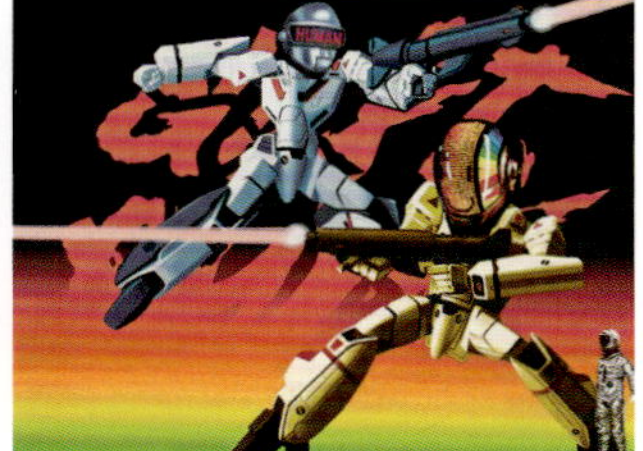

#116 ROBOT ROCK [2013]

« **It's 1997** and I'm living in Italy. I had never lived outside a small town before and found myself in Florence for a semester: a medieval city, a living museum, a claustrophobic maze filled with homicidal moped riders. I had a hard time adjusting to the language, the culture shock, and the expectations I placed on myself after seeing some of the world's greatest artwork. It was an inflection point in my life, opening myself up to traveling, often alone, and experiencing the world as an outsider. It undoubtedly laid the groundwork for my astronaut paintings, even if I didn't actually start painting them for another two years afterwards. I came back from this experience, attempted a couple of ambitious paintings about my time in Italy, then never made a painting about that country again. I'm not entirely sure why, but it seemed impossible to make a show about traveling the old roads of my own life without going back there.

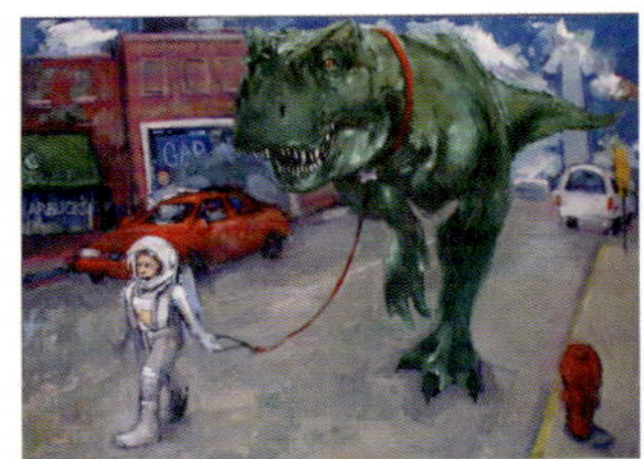

#002

ASTRONAUT & DINOSAUR [2000]

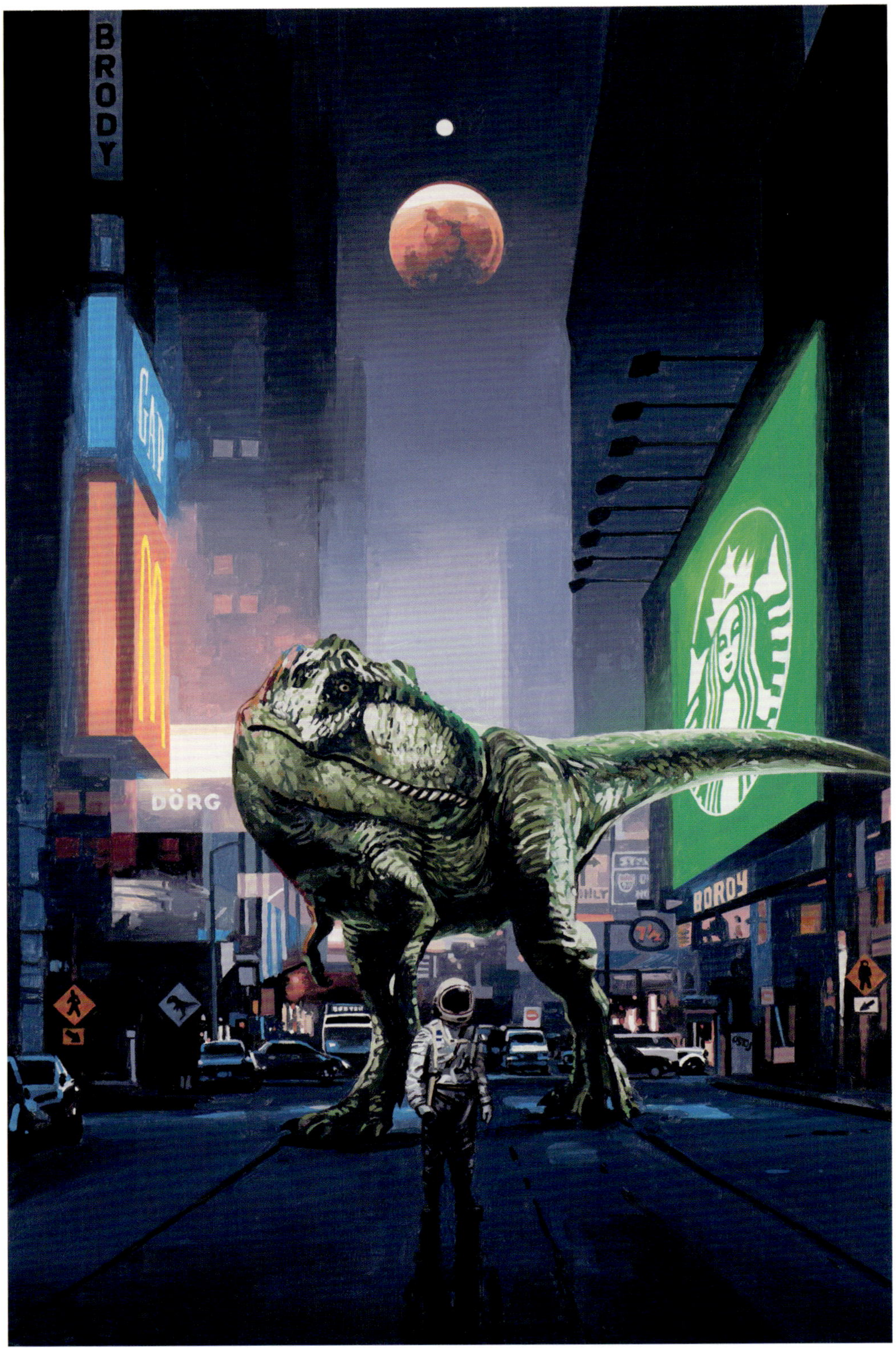

» It's 2000 and I'm painting my second ever astronaut and first ever dinosaur. At the time, I wasn't sure which I would go on to paint more of. It didn't take too long though for the astronaut to win out, but dinosaurs have continued to be an occasional presence in my work. For this show I revisited one of my earliest paintings, which maybe didn't totally feel like it fit in with my contemporary work, but it was fun to step back into those shoes and walk a dinosaur down the street.

#588

ASTRONAUT & DINOSAUR 2 [2022]

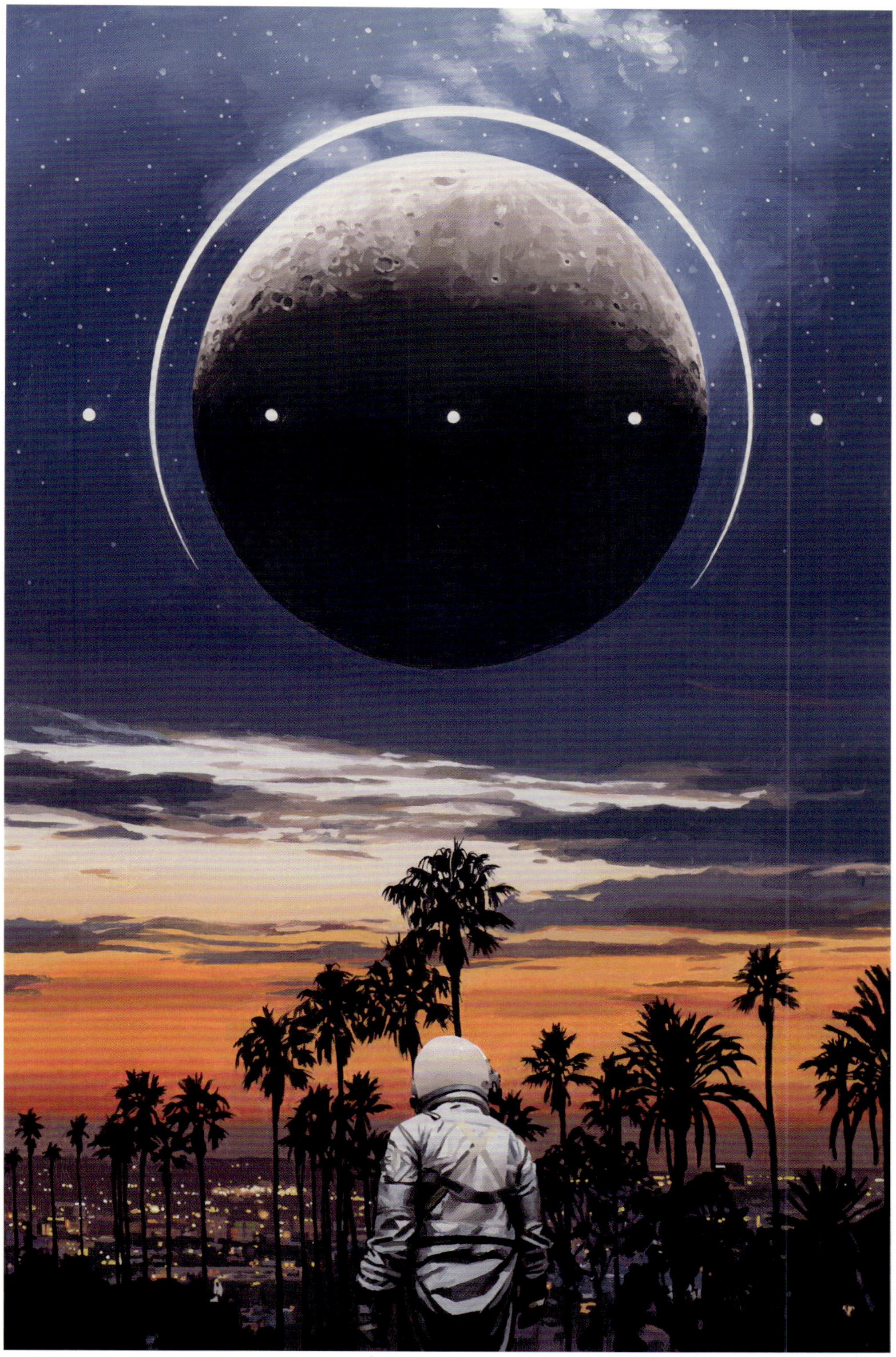

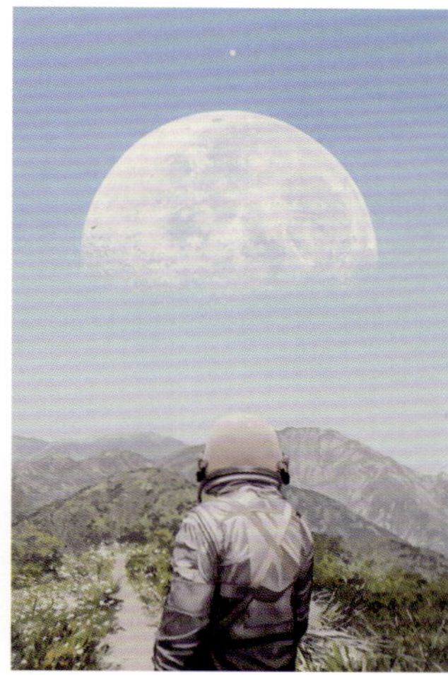

#380
WHITE MOON [2018]

» It's 2020 and I'm living in a pandemic. I had moved to Los Angeles just a year and a half before and found myself mostly stuck at home. I started taking increasingly long walks in the hills, parks, and neighborhoods around my house, getting semi-lost on an endless series of stairways up and down the hillside streets of LA. Although I was mostly locked away from friends and family during this time, I got to go out and explore and discover. It reminded me of my early days, inspired to paint astronauts by traveling a world I didn't know.

#569

ELYSIAN [2021]

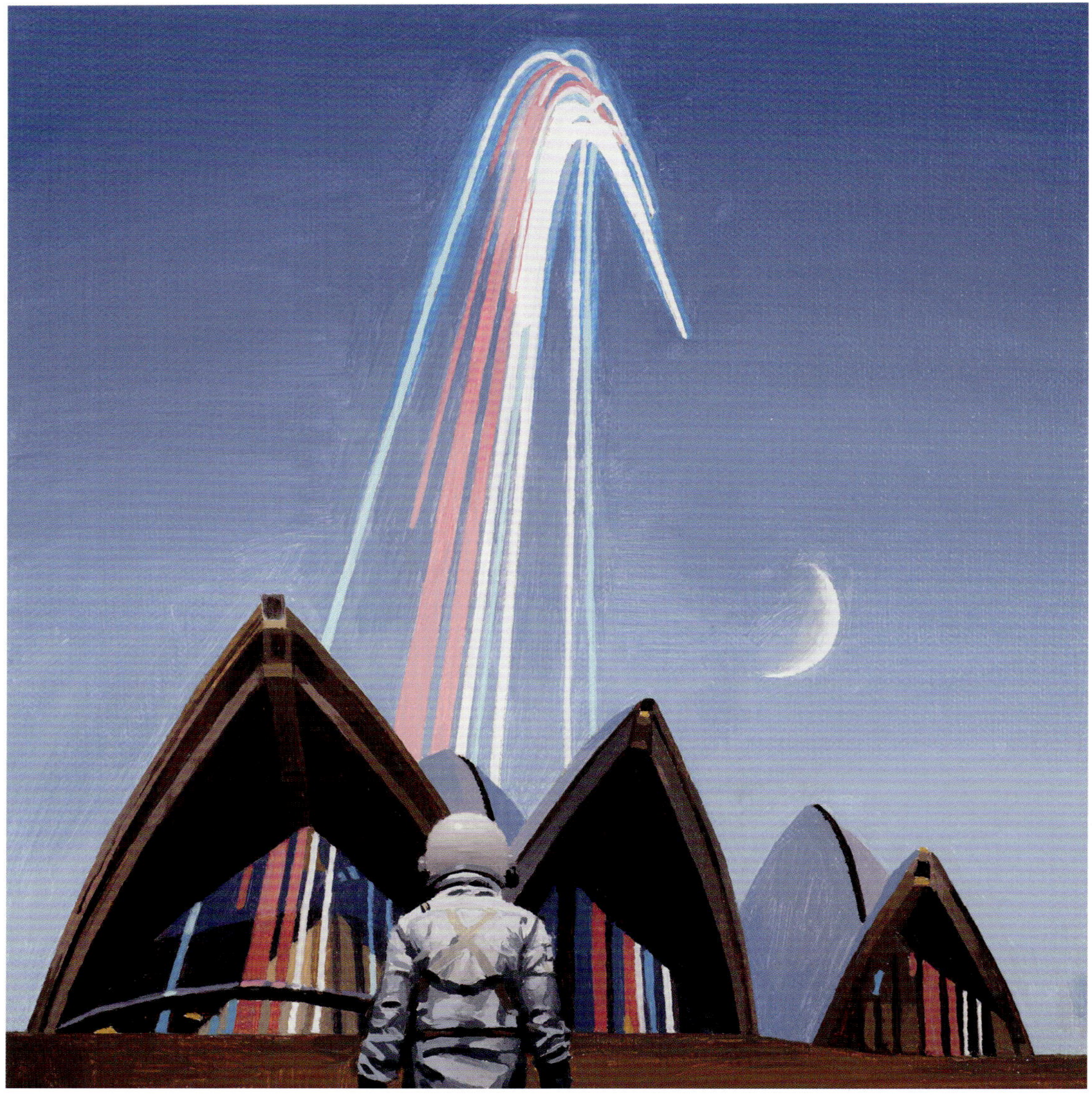

#590 SYDNEY [2022]

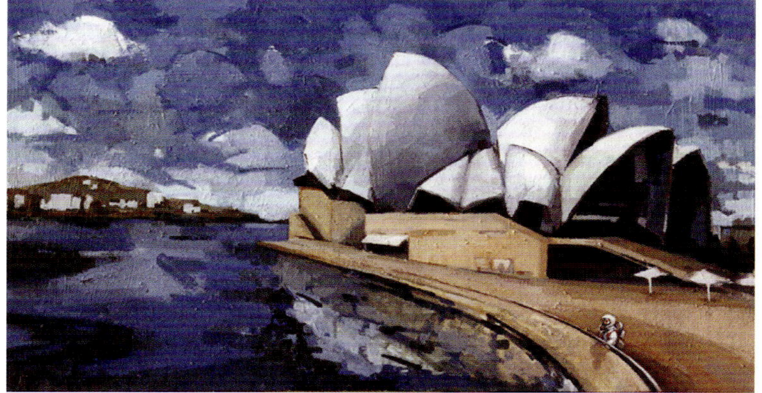

#004 SYDNEY OPERA HOUSE [2001]

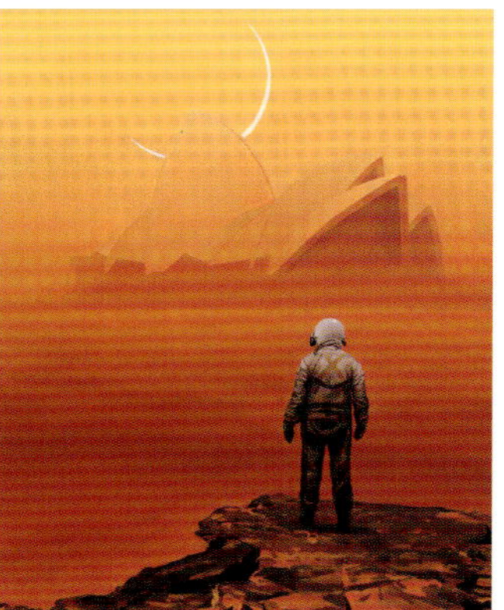

#425 DESERT OPERA [2019]

« **It's 1998** and I hopped a one way flight to Sydney two days after I graduated college. I had no idea what would happen next in my life. I ended up spending about 6 months in Australia. I wish it could have been more, but I needed to get a job and start my life, which I couldn't totally legally do down there. My time spent living in Australia, walking streets I'd never visit again, hopping trains or boats to places I didn't know, eating an endless string of fast food chicken sandwiches, living in a place that felt entirely foreign but also weirdly kind of familiar, all served as the original inspiration for two decades of astronaut paintings. I've often returned to Australia in my mind (and twice in real life), and painting the Sydney Opera House transports me right back to that time in my life. Stepping on a plane with no plan at all.

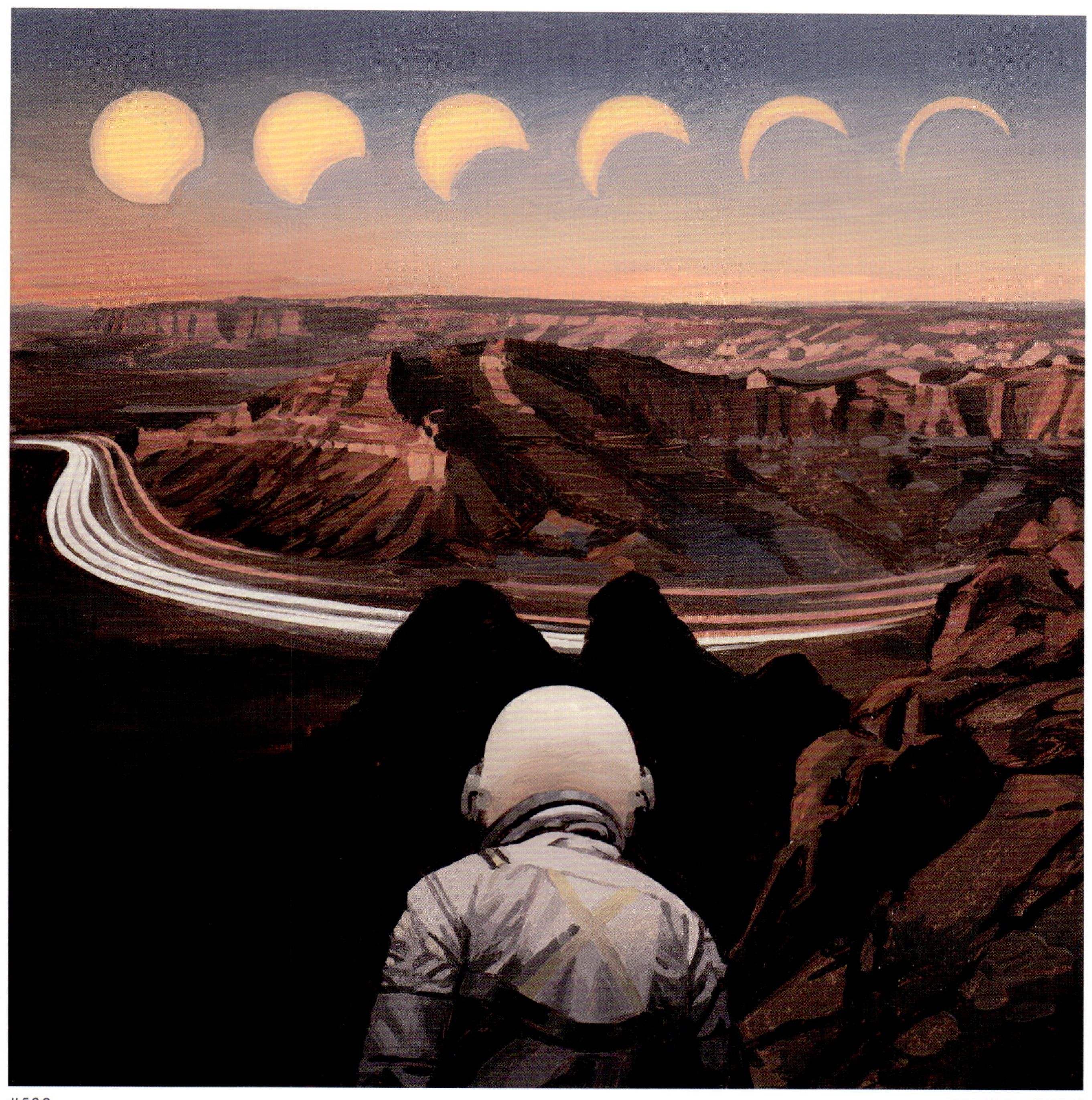

#580

CANYON [2022]

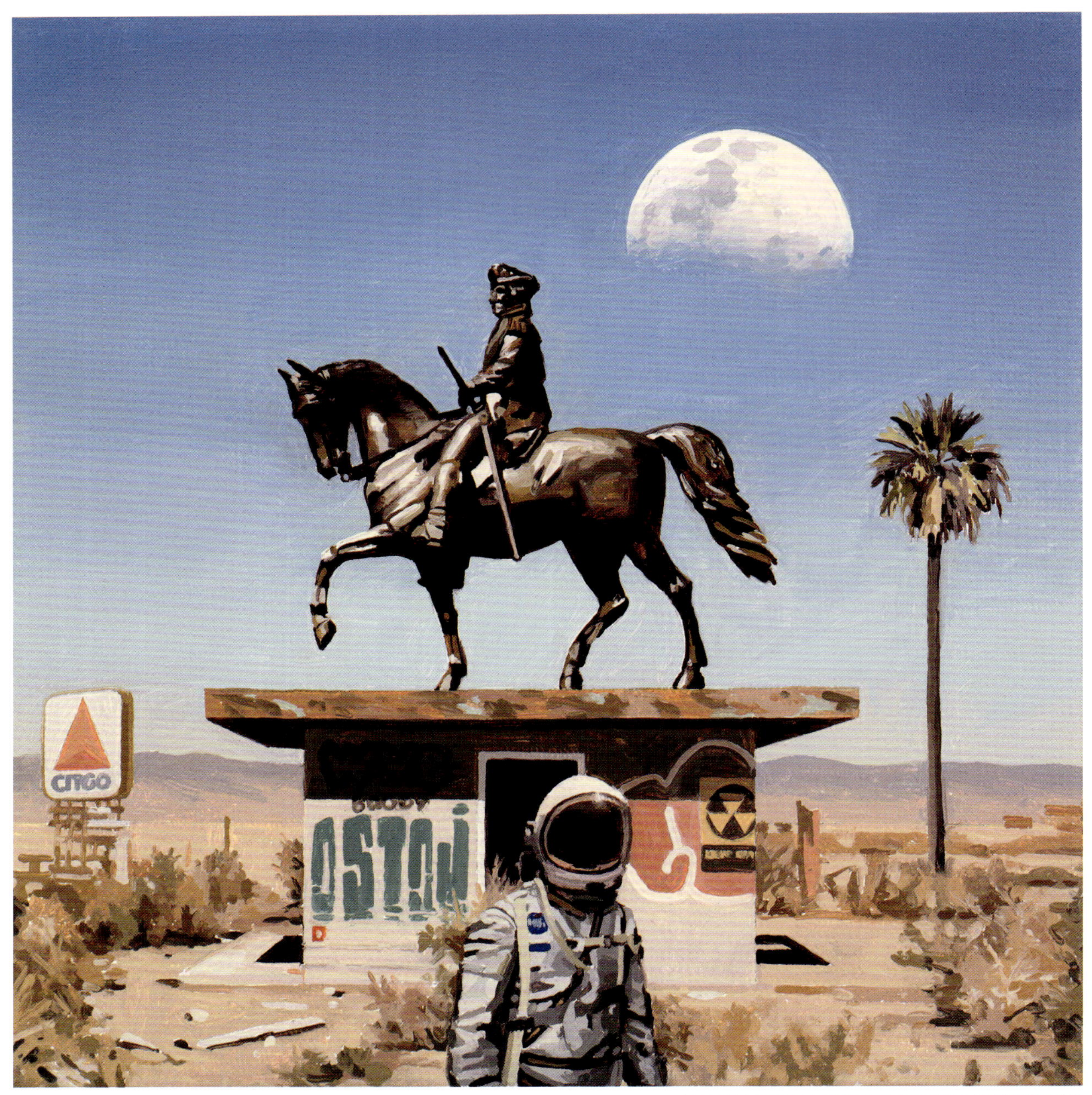

#581 WASHINGTON CROSSING THE DESERT [2022]

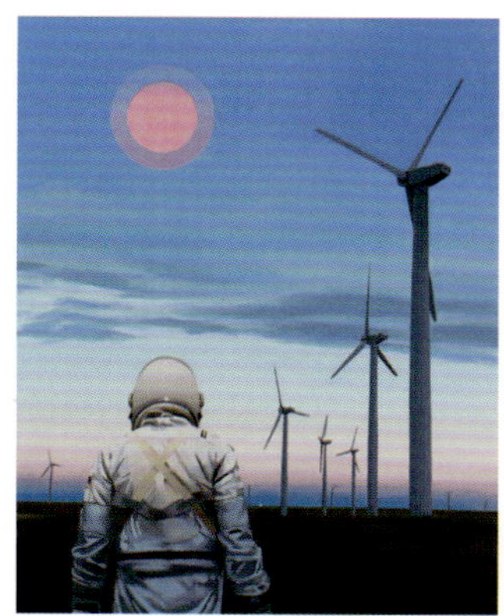

#279
TURBINES [2017]

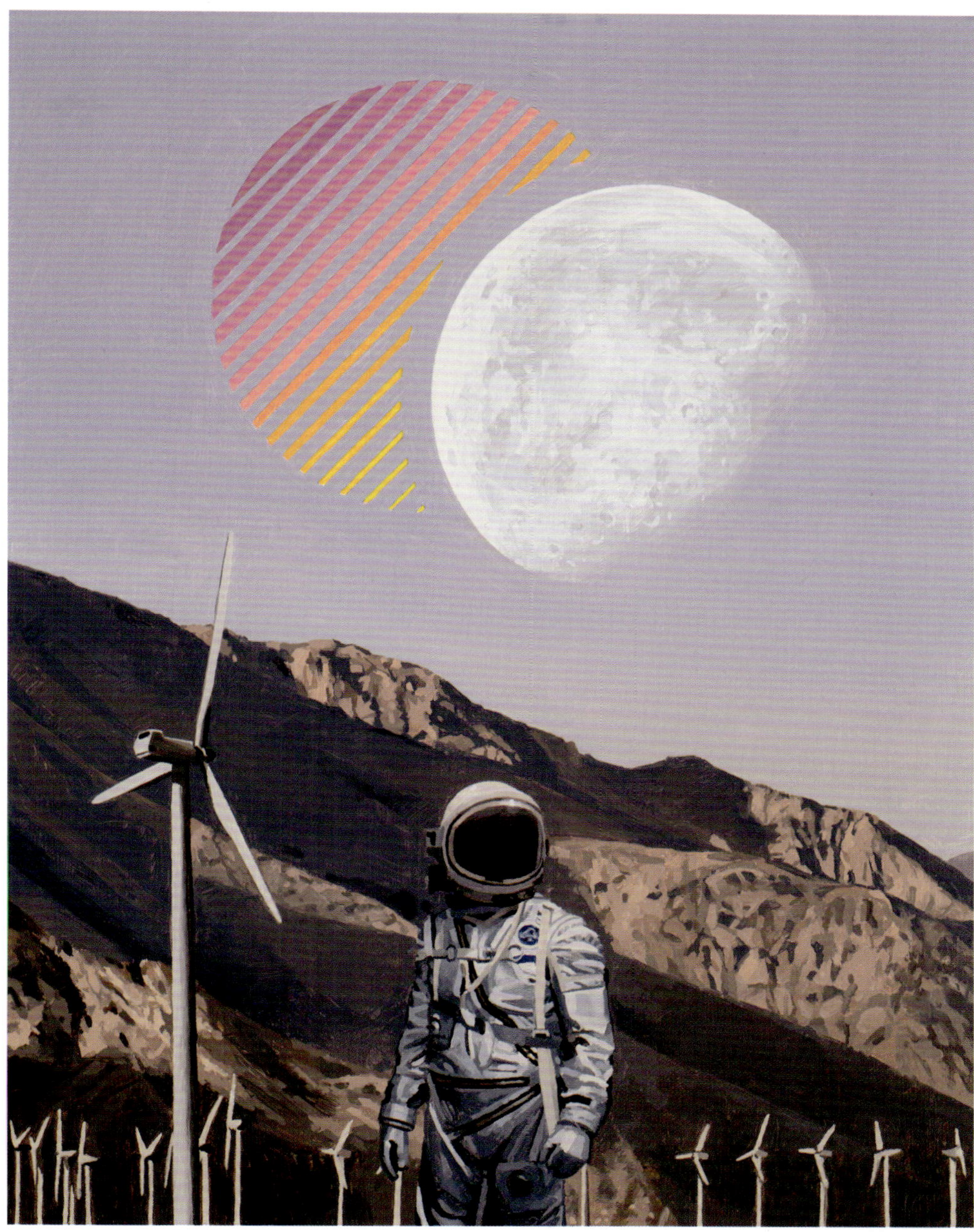

#589 WIND [2022]

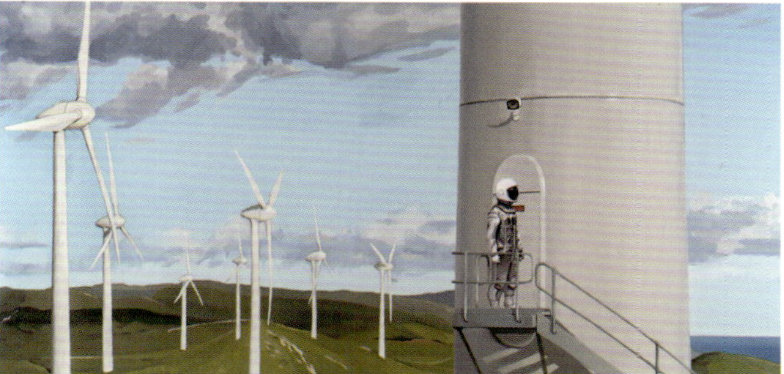

#039 MAN OF LA MANCHA [2006]

» **It's 2005** and I visited Los Angeles for the first time. At least as an adult. I came out for an art show, my first in LA, then drove out to Yucaipa to spend time with my friend Chris Ostoj's mom. We talked about his life and, sadly, his death. In the afternoon I drove out to Joshua Tree, past the Cabazon dinosaurs and the seemingly endless rows of windmills lining the desert and the mountains. I arrived near sunset, just enough time to hop out of my car and listen to a distant coyote. Then I drove back to the city, and flew home to Boston. I still think about that day often, and it's in turn inspired a few paintings over the years.

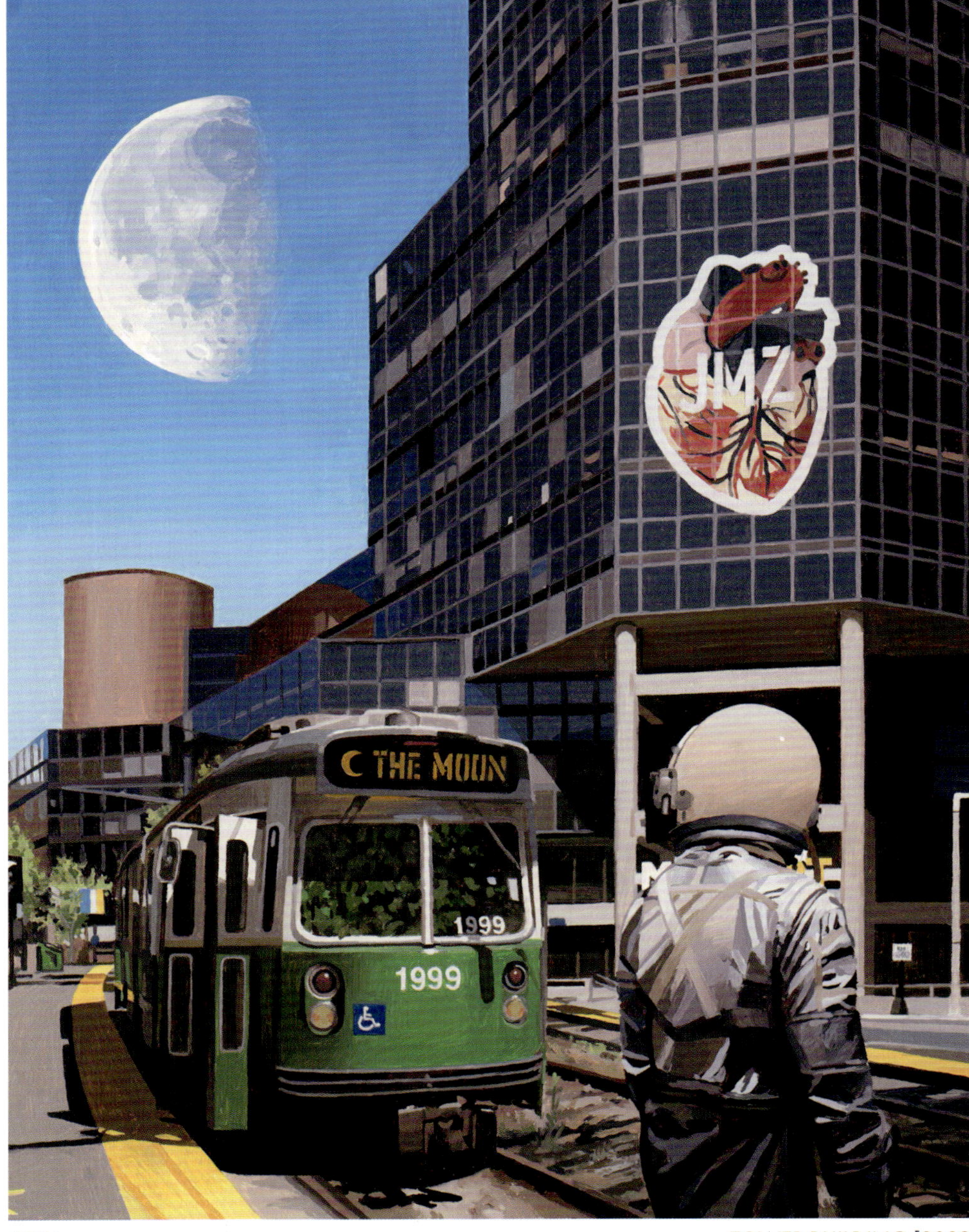

#584 TOWER BUILDING [2022]

#022
TO THE MOON [2004]

« **It's 1999** and I had just come back from living in Australia. I tried to move to New York and abjectly failed, and was living at my parent's house, outside of Boston, riding the train into the city every day to take classes at Massachusetts College of Art. After spending some time traveling the world, it felt like I had somehow gone backwards, living much of my life in my childhood bedroom. But on an early spring evening in the cafeteria of Tower Building of MassArt I noticed a girl and her friends all staring at me. Not subtly. Like, a "Who the hell are you?" kind of look. This happened a few more times over the ensuing weeks, and I wondered if I should leave and never come back. Eventually, standing in line to buy a turkey sandwich, that girl tapped me on the shoulder and said "Who the hell are you?" We're married now.

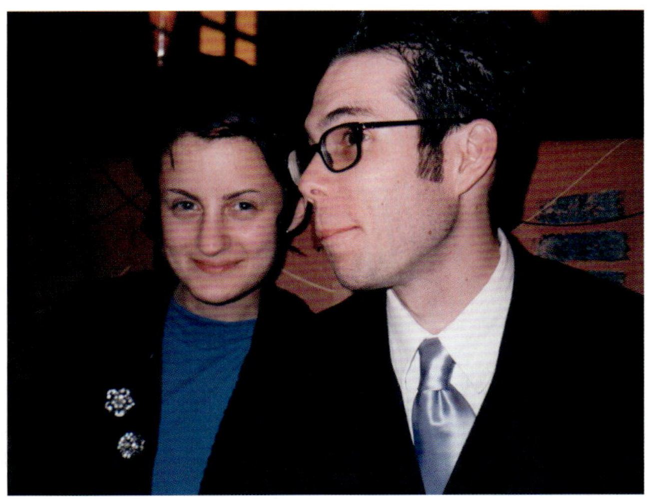

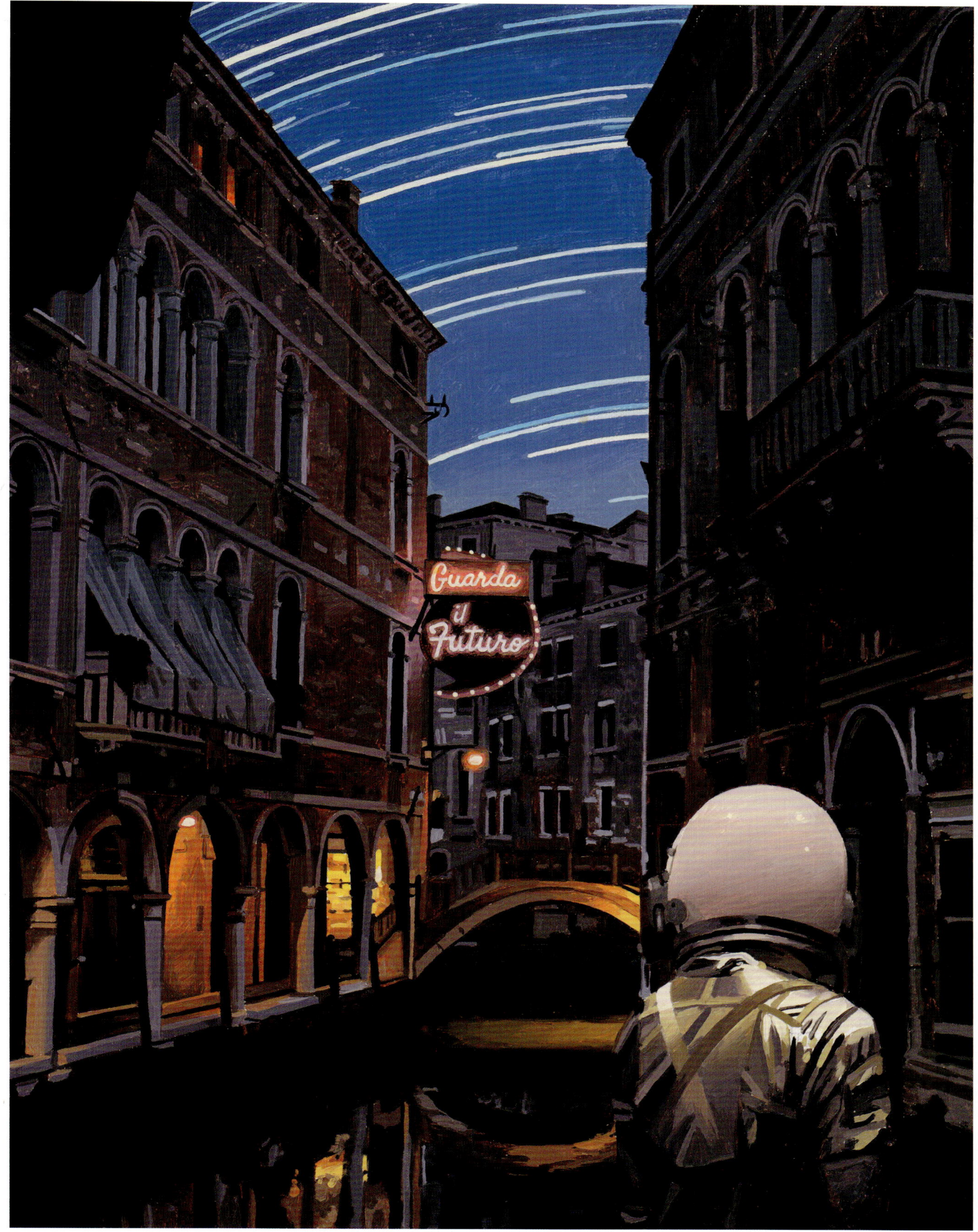

#578

CANAL [2022]

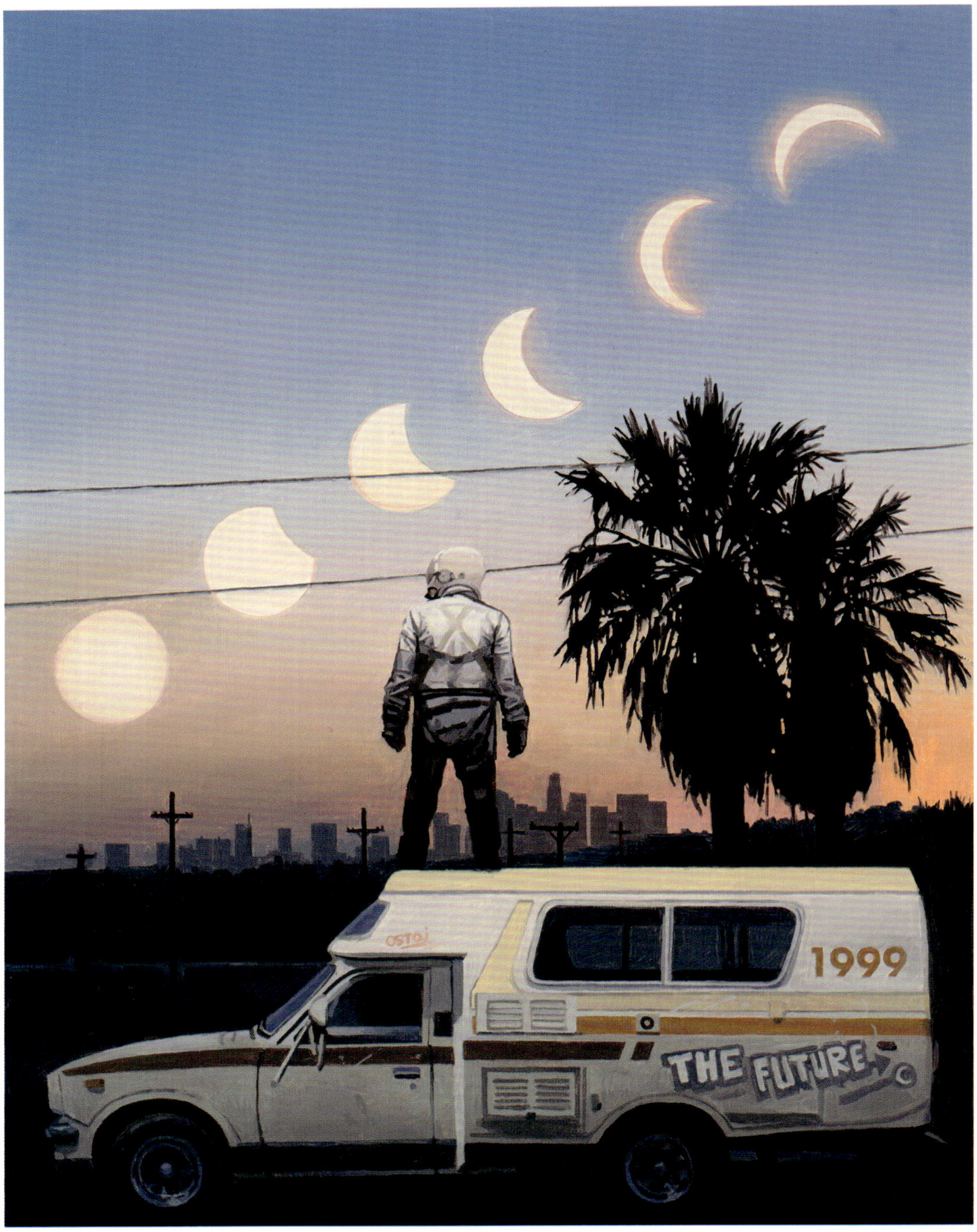

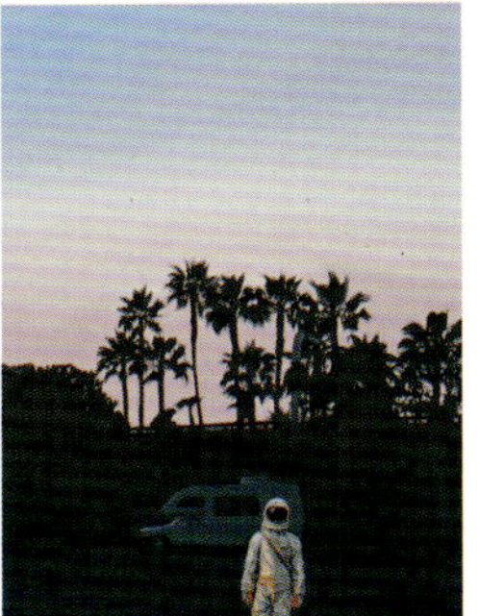

#083

RV DUSK [2011]

#577

RV DUSK 2 [2022]

» **It's 2012** and I showed with Thinkspace Gallery for the first time. It was a large group show called *Picks of the Harvest,* with a ton of artists I had admired for a long time. I made a painting called *RV Dusk,* based on a photograph I had taken in San Diego earlier that year. 10 years later, here we are.

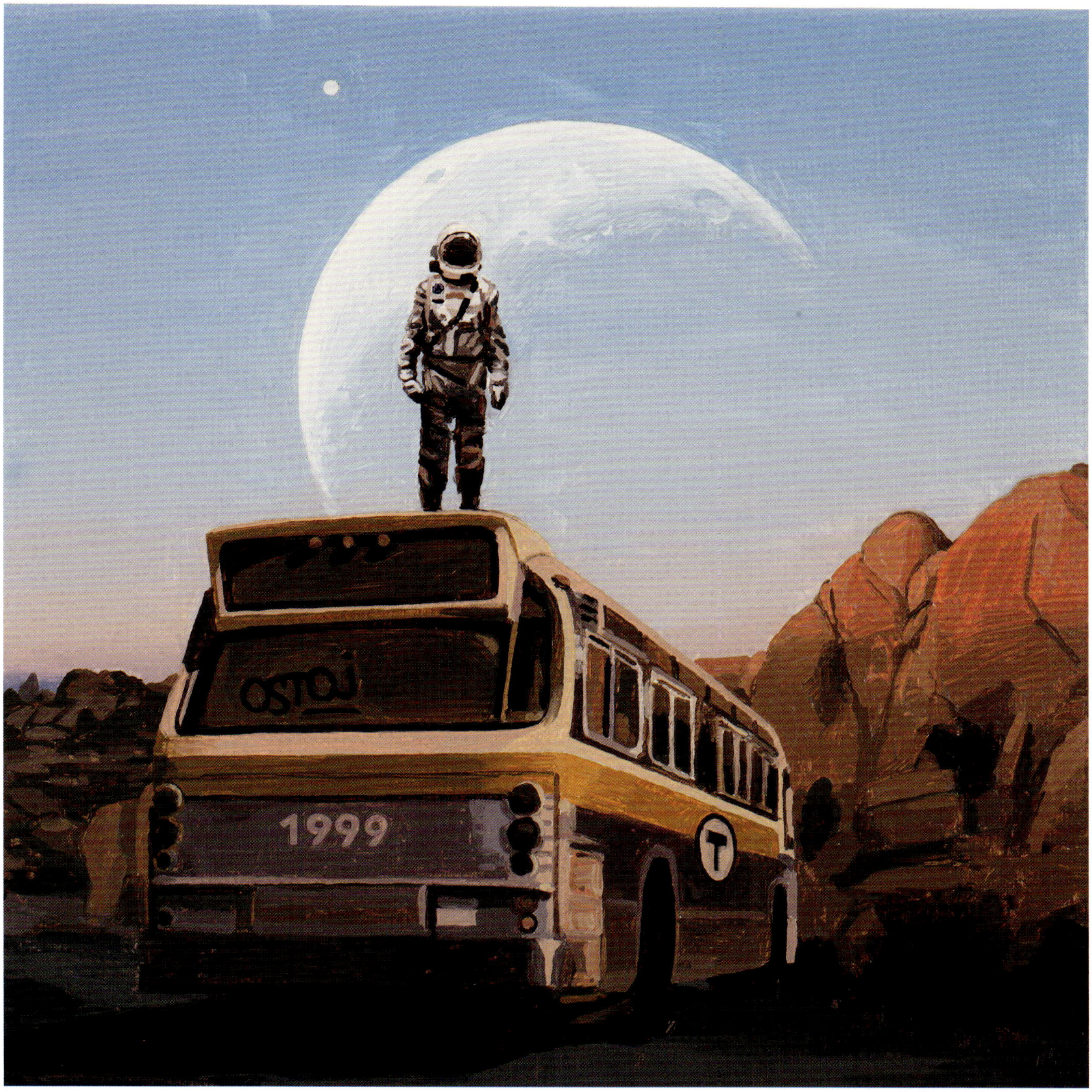

#587 ASTRONAUT ON THE BUS 2 [2022]

« It's 1999 and I'm painting my first ever astronaut. He has a face, which is weird, and he's sitting on a bus. There's not much more to it than that. An inauspicious start, but trust me, it led to bigger things.

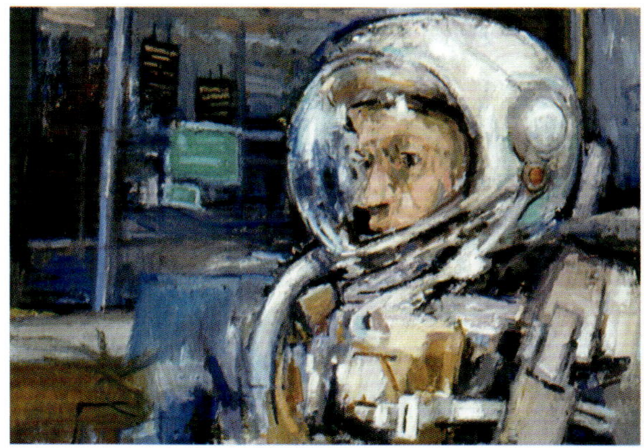

#001 ASTRONAUT ON THE BUS [1999]

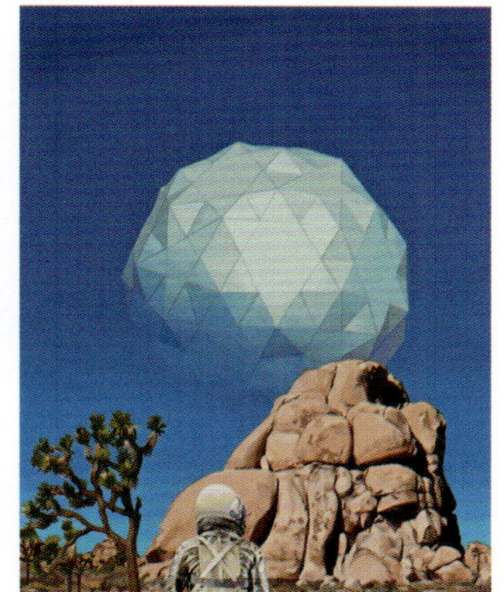

#130 NEW MOON [2013]

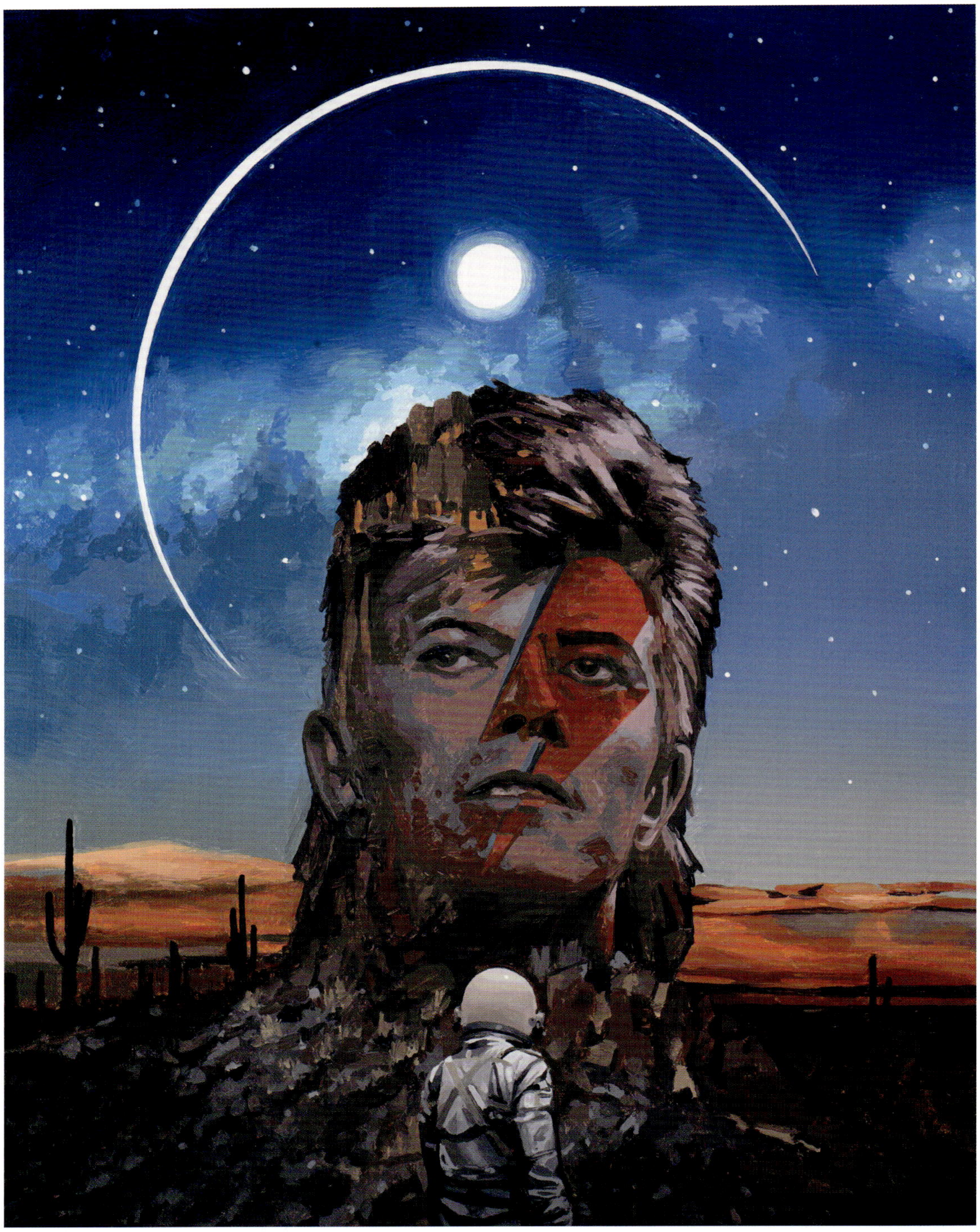

#585 DAVID [2022]

» **It's 2016** and David Bowie has just passed away. Not that I knew him personally, of course, but like so many other people, he left a huge imprint on my life. The world felt sadly less interesting without David Bowie in it. I had already painted his likeness once before, but over the ensuing years, references to him and many of his songs would wind their way into my work. If *2001: A Space Odyssey* was the initial source of inspiration for my astronaut paintings, David Bowie is what kept that inspiration going.

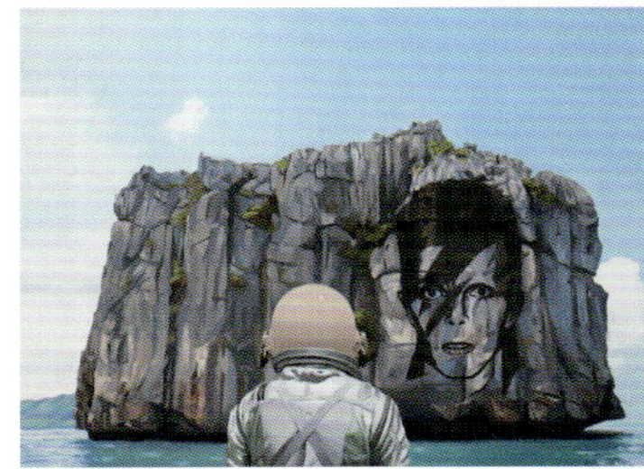

#206
ISLAND OF ALADDIN SANE [2016]

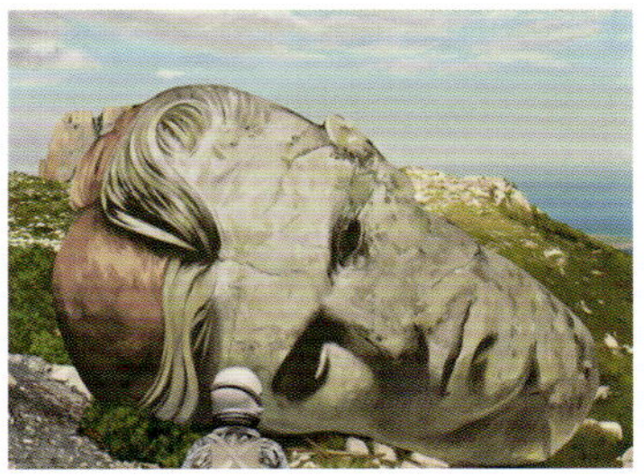

#129
THE MAN WHO FELL TO EARTH [2013]

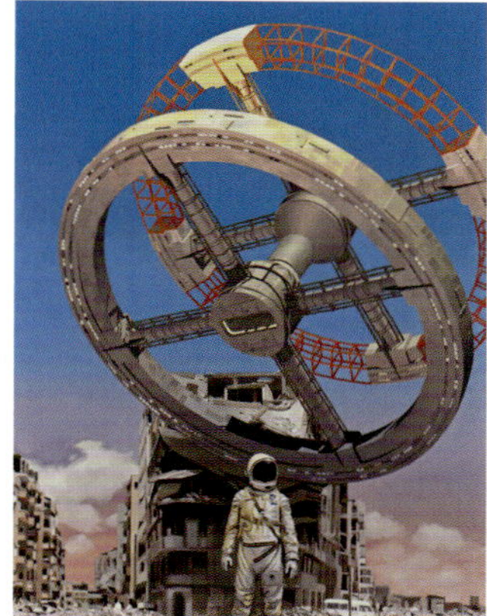

#147

MOONAGE DAYDREAM [2014]

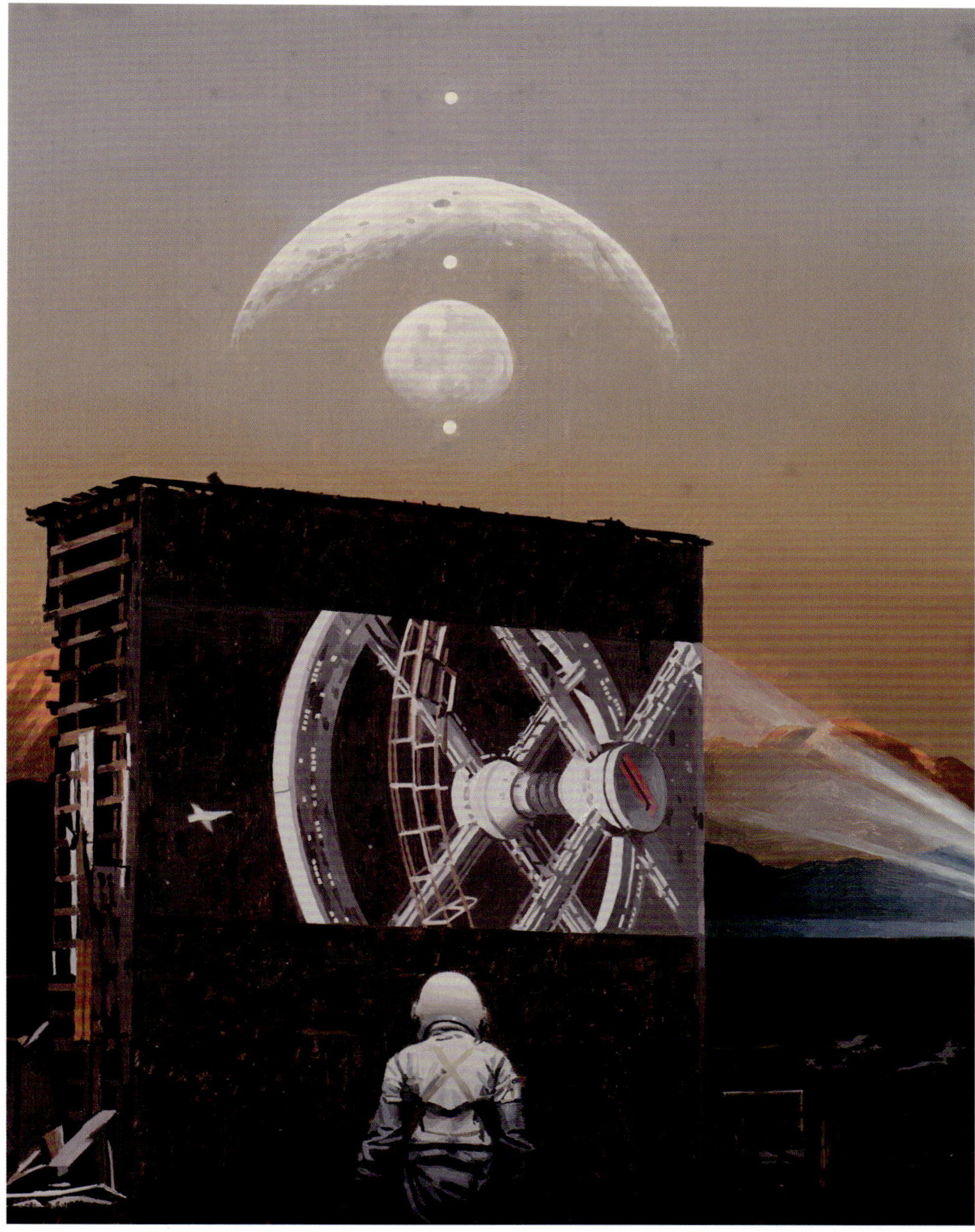

#574 MOVIE NIGHT [2022]

« **It's 1999** and I'm watching *2001: A Space Odyssey* for the first time. I was living on my own in the tiniest studio apartment in Boston, after having spent most the previous year traveling to very distant places. While abroad, I had always been very aware of the feeling like I was a stranger, an alien, walking along in someone else's streets. I thought, upon returning home, that feeling would fade. It didn't. And so I started on a series of paintings about how out of place I felt in the contemporary world, and was looking for a protagonist to appear in each one. In the middle of watching *2001*, I knew I had found that protagonist: the astronaut from the fictional *2001*. The one from my childhood that I thought I would grow up to be, living on the moon and hanging with my robot best friend. I had no idea, of course, at the time that I'd spend the next two decades painting astronauts.

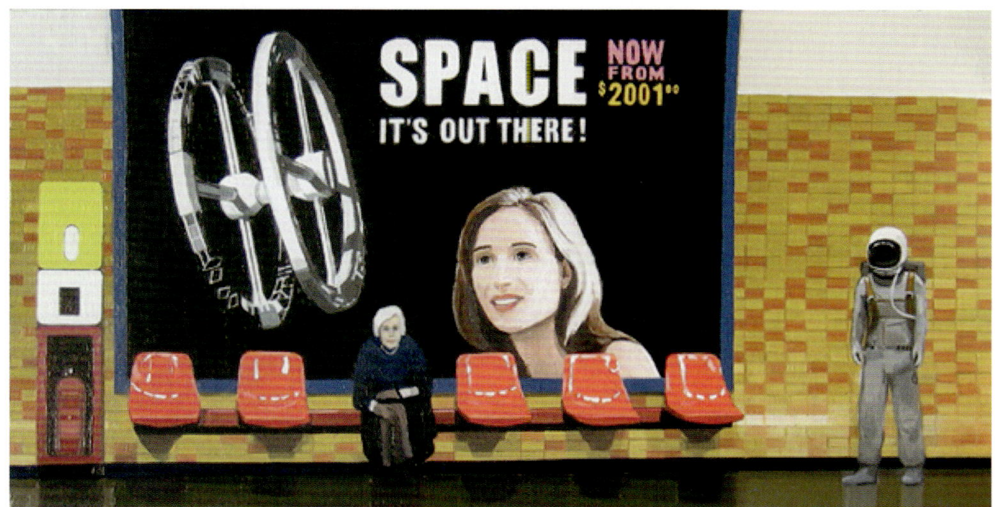

#033 TWO THOUSAND AND ONE [2006]

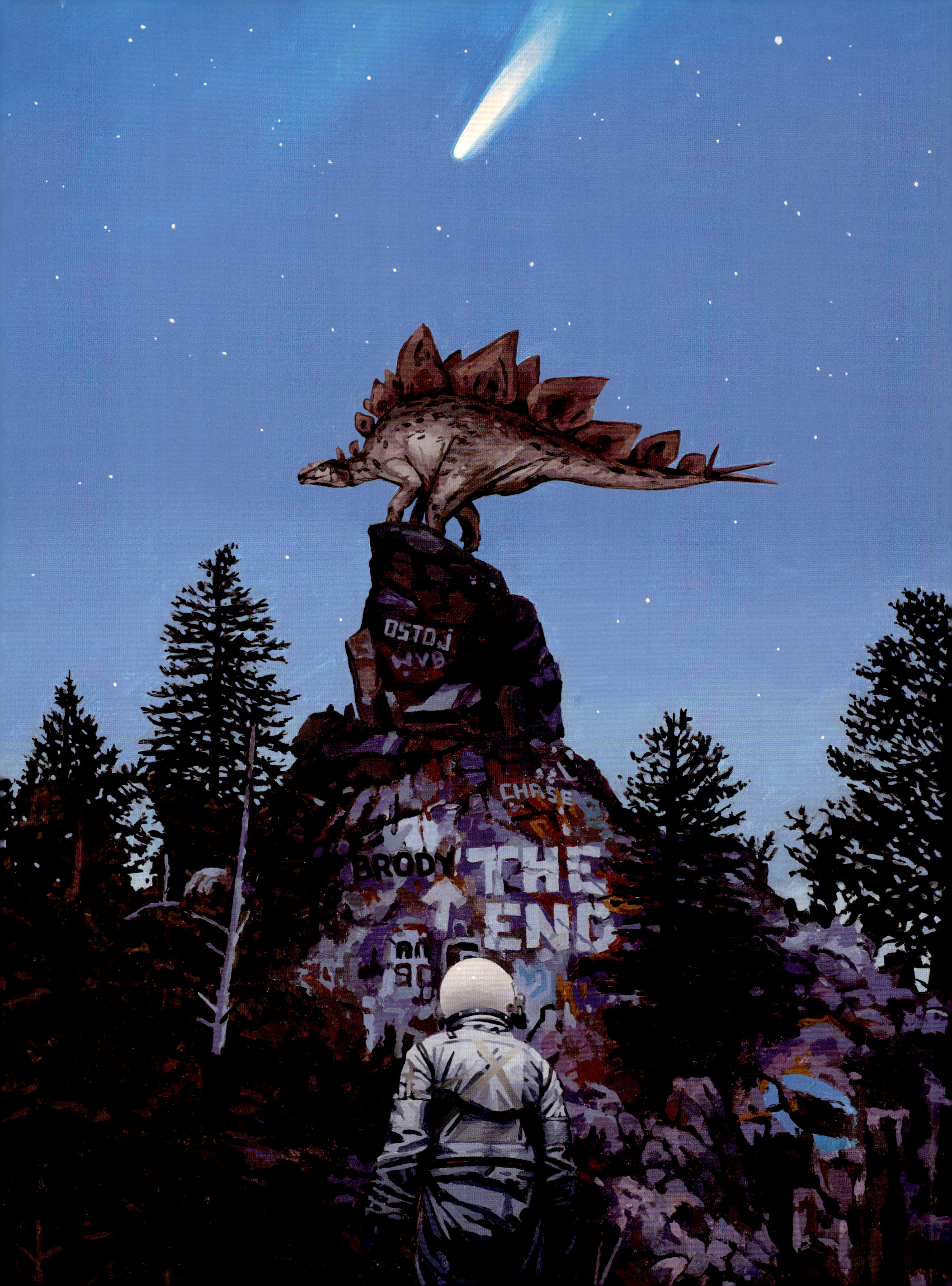
CHASE
BRODY
THE END

THE LOST WORLD

Antler Gallery, Portland, OR
September, 2022

"My name is Scott Listfield. I paint astronauts and, sometimes, dinosaurs." That's been the opening line of my artist statement since I first started painting astronauts, a very long time ago now. In more recent years, some internet person will occasionally pop up to comment "Hey! What ever happened to the 'sometimes dinosaurs'?" Well, random internet person, this show is for you.

I've found myself thinking about dinosaurs lately. I've been watching, over and over again, the incredible documentary series *Prehistoric Planet*, narrated by David Attenborough, on Apple TV. I've also been thinking, not for the first time, about dinosaurs as a metaphor, during a time when we seem increasingly driven to follow in their large footsteps towards extinction. And during a time when certain political factions seem intent on sending us back in time to the stone age. I want to remember a simpler time in my life, when I could sit and draw dinosaurs for hours and then go dig a large hole in my backyard because I thought maybe there might be a Stegosaurus down there somewhere (there wasn't). And so I made an entire show of dinosaur paintings.

The Lost World: A show of astronauts and dinosaurs.

#595
STEGOSAURUS 2 [2022]

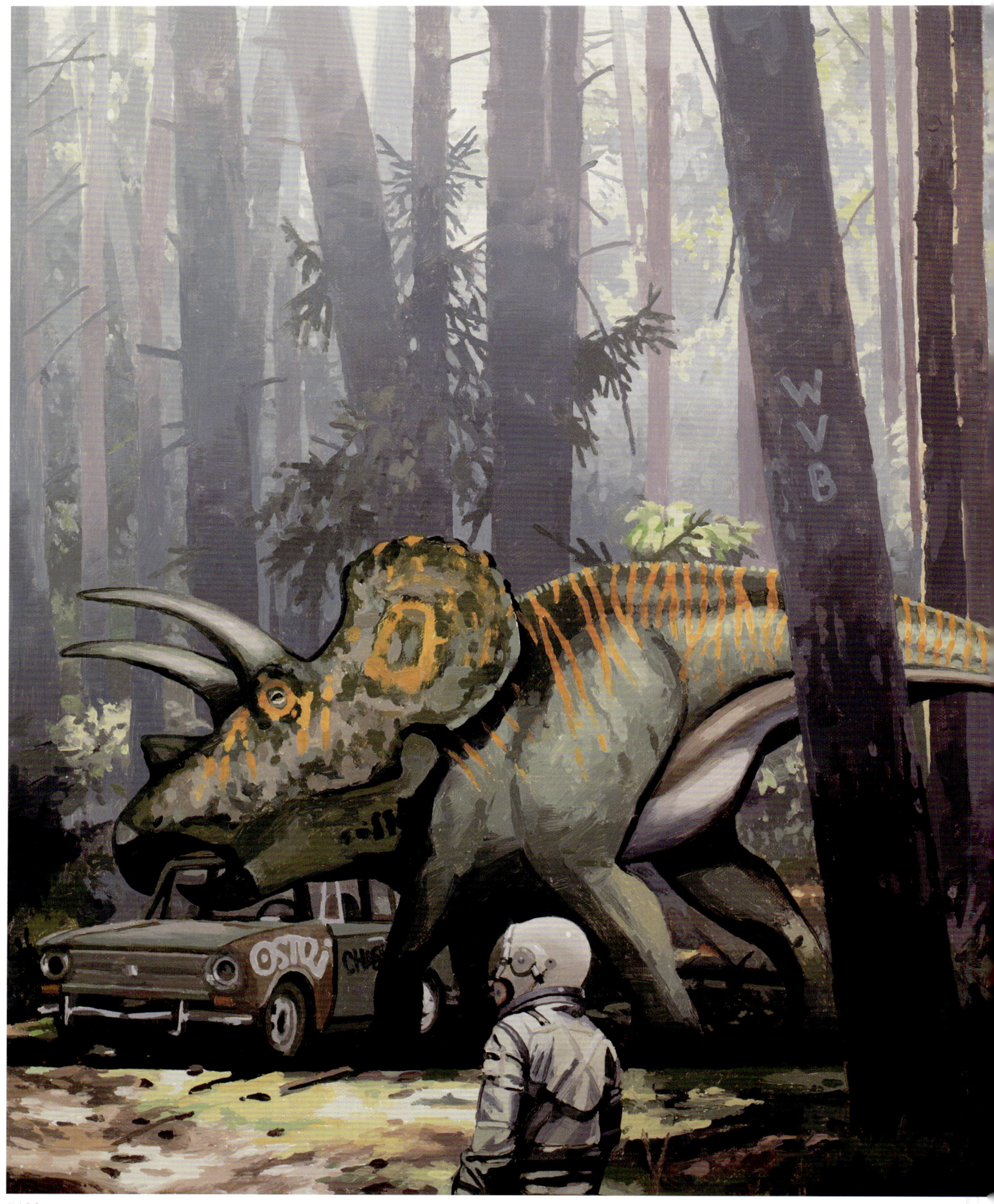

#603

TRICERATOPS [2022]

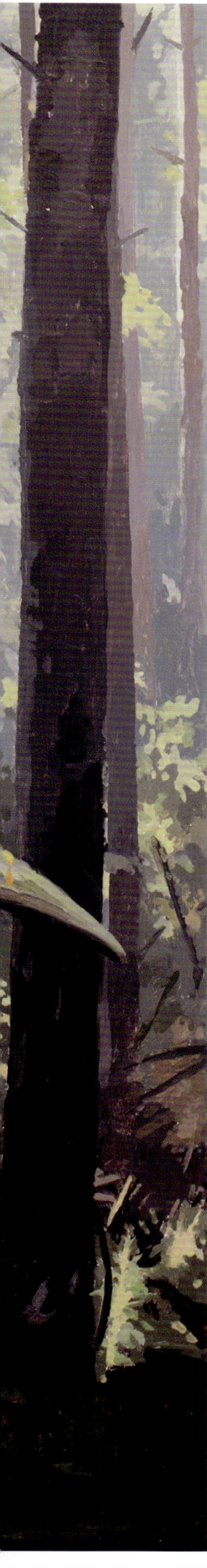

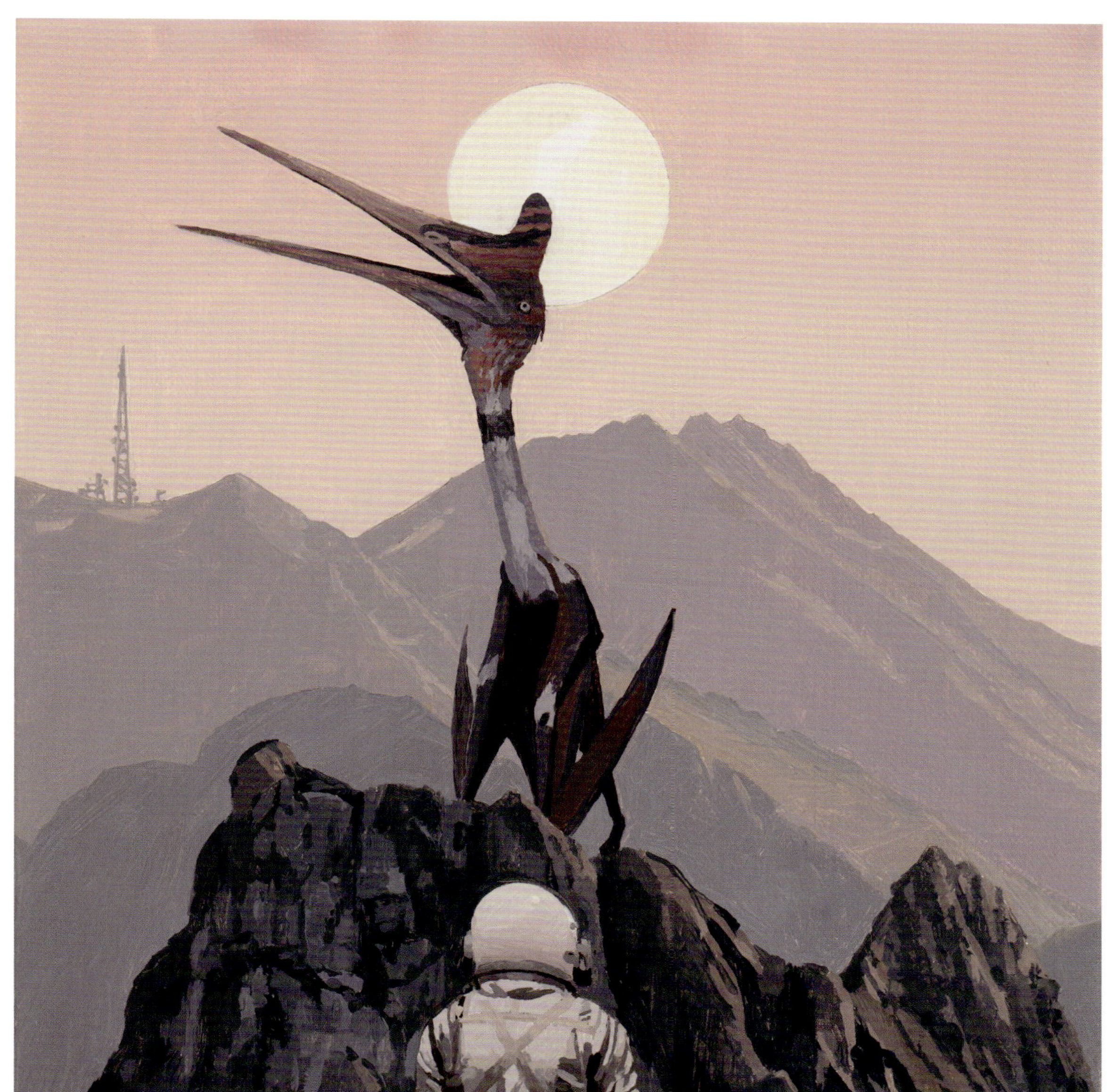

#598 QUETZALCOATLUS [2022]

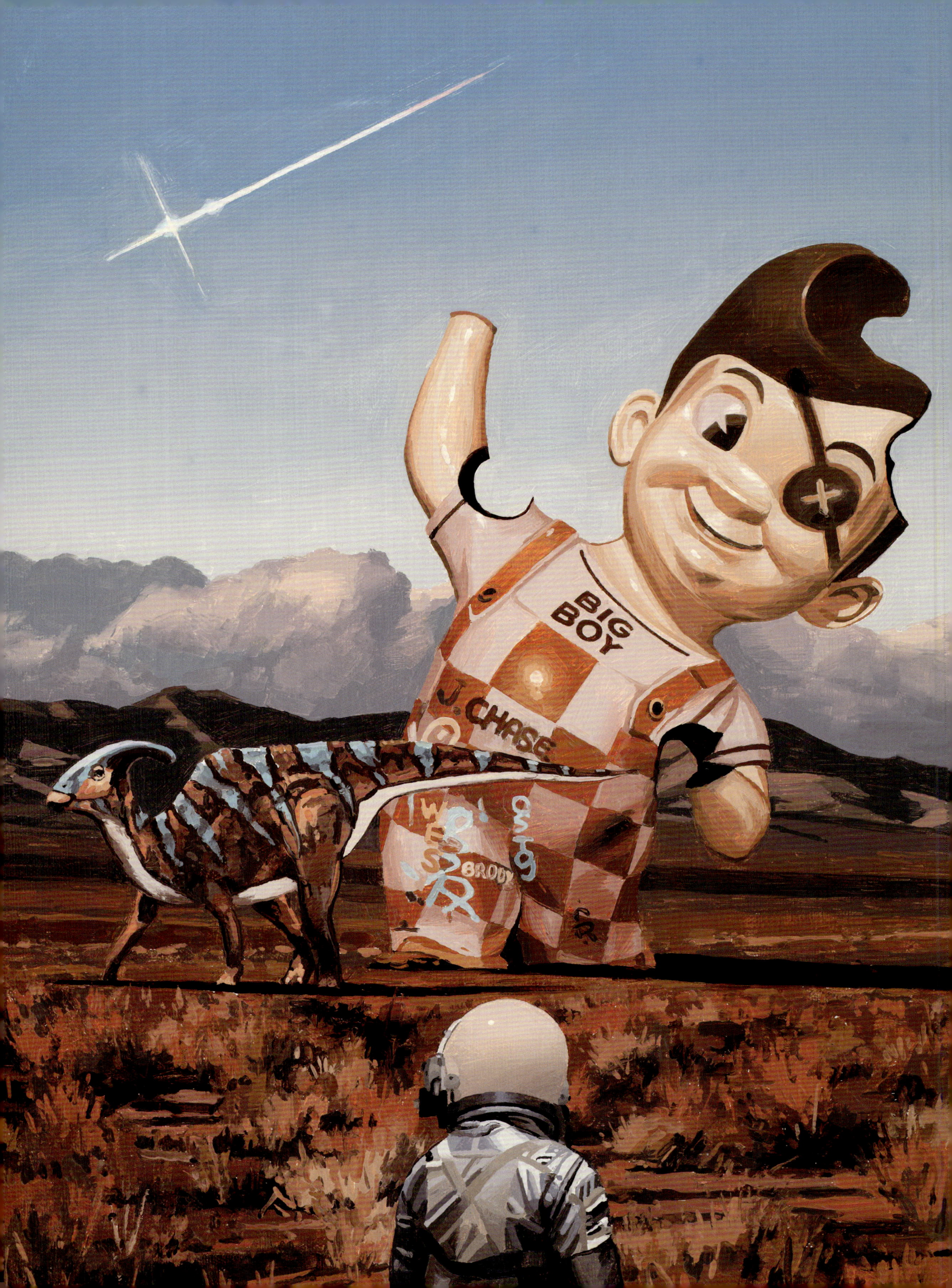
BIG
BOY
J. CHASE
BRODY

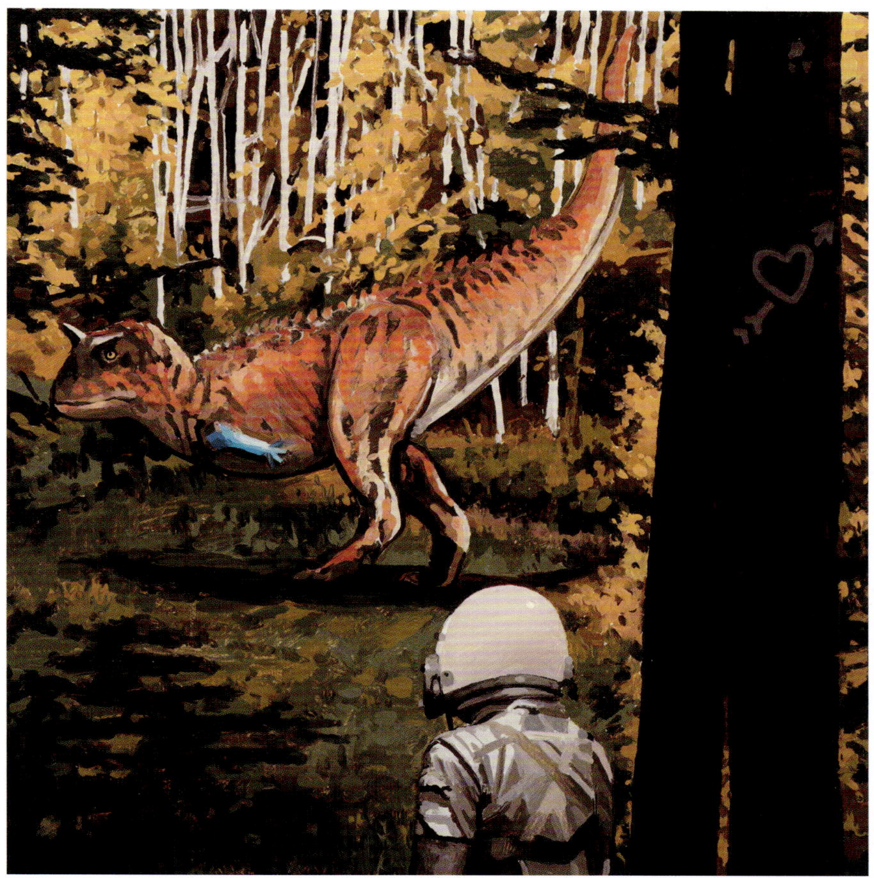

#600 CARNOTAURUS [2022]

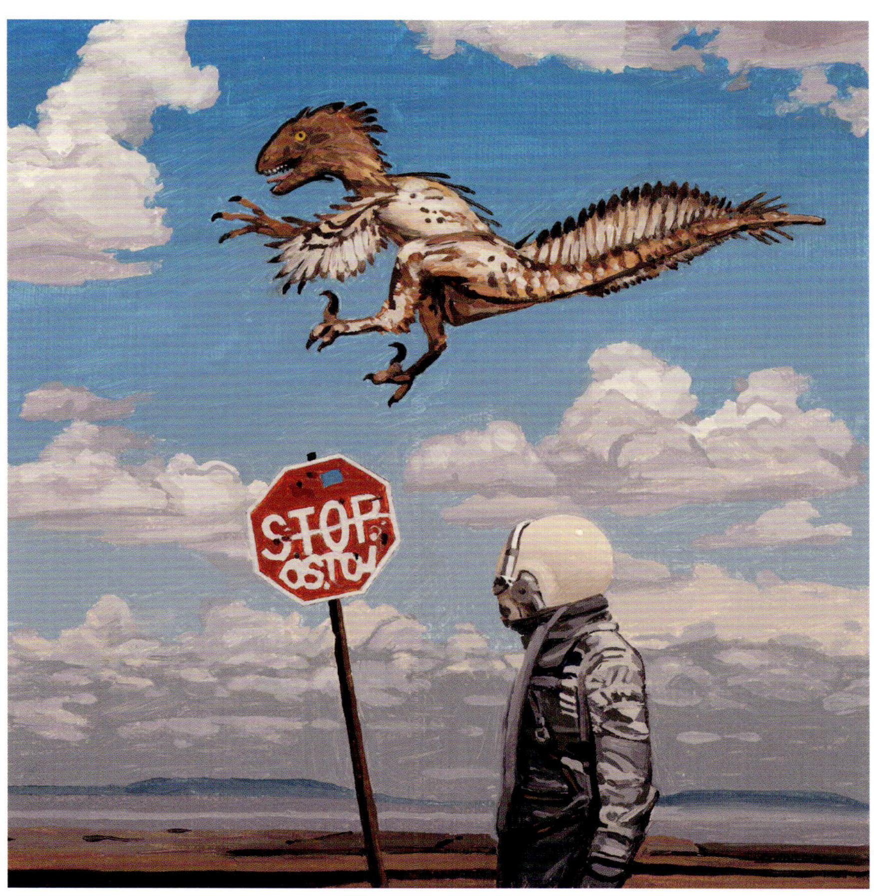

#597 DEINONYCHUS [2022]

#601
PARASAUROLOPHUS [2022]

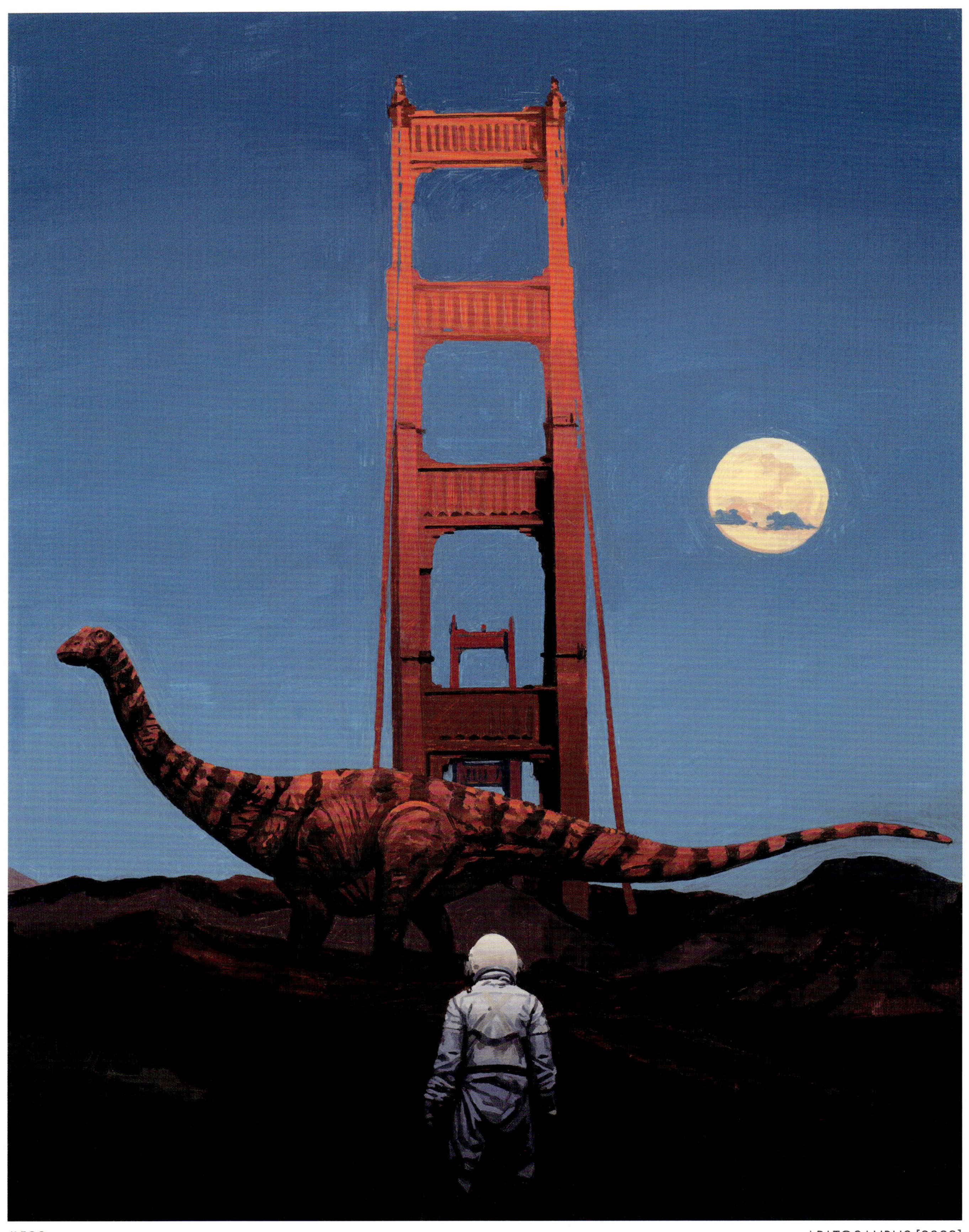

#599

APATOSAURUS [2022]

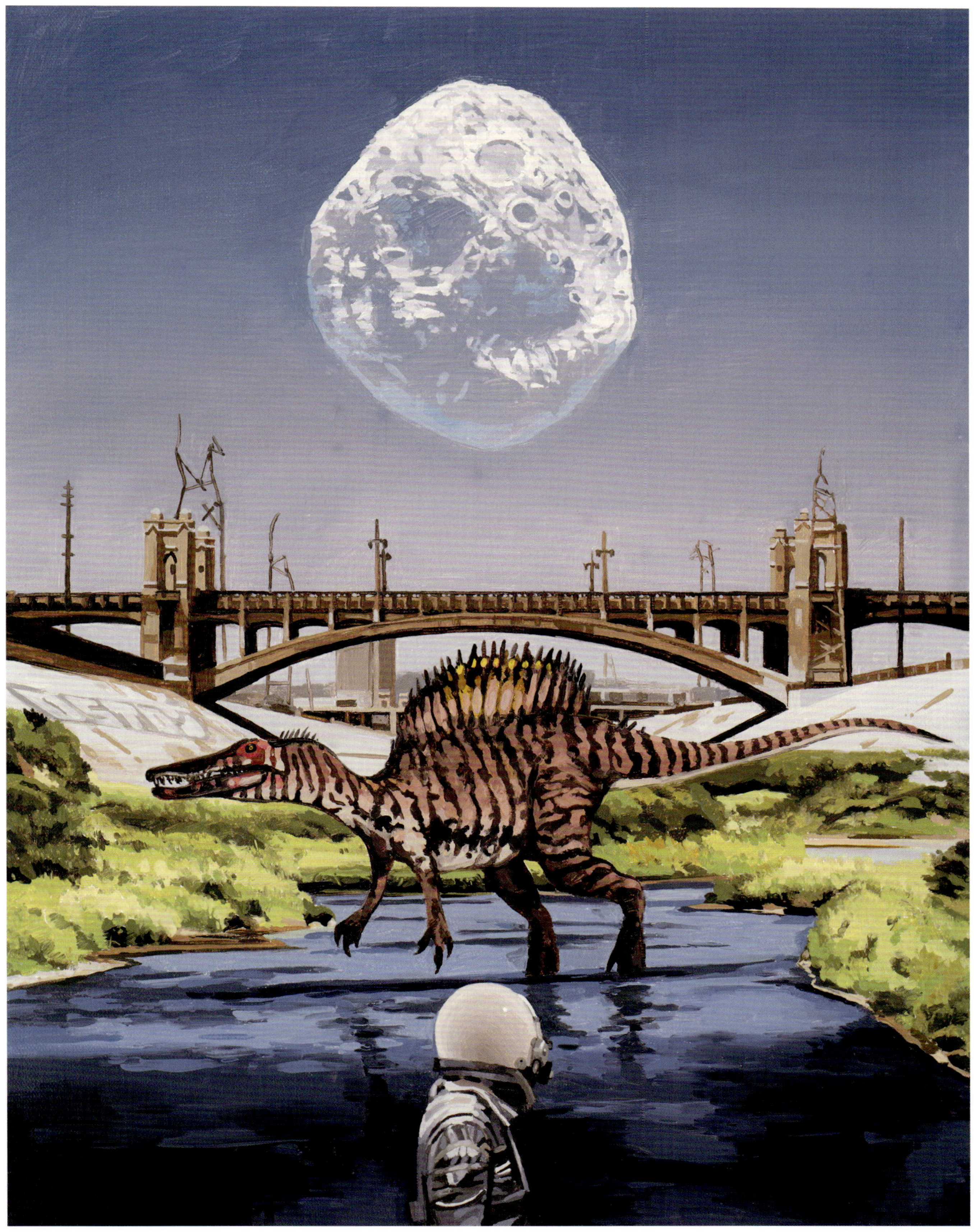

#602 SPINOSAURUS [2022]

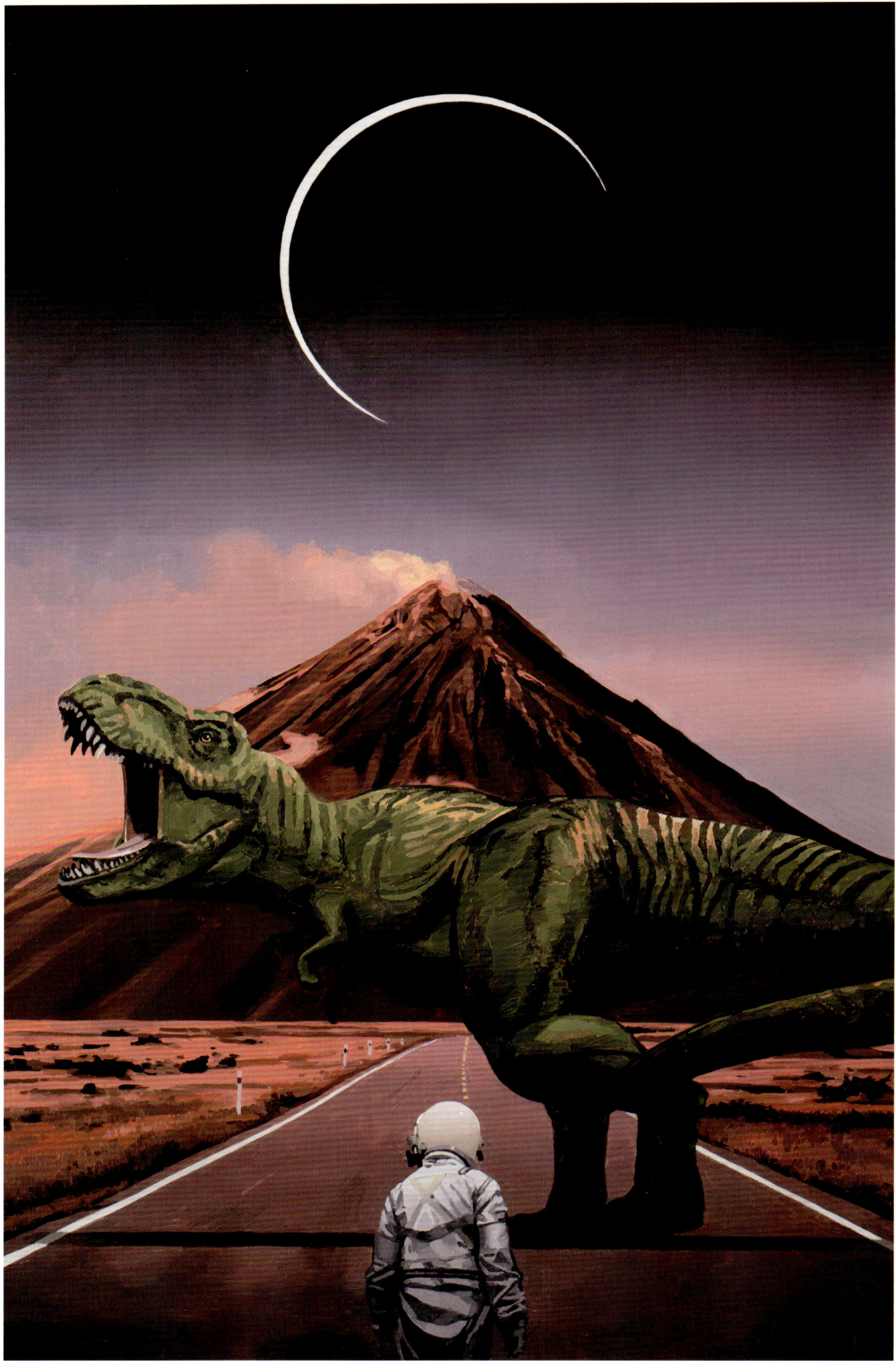

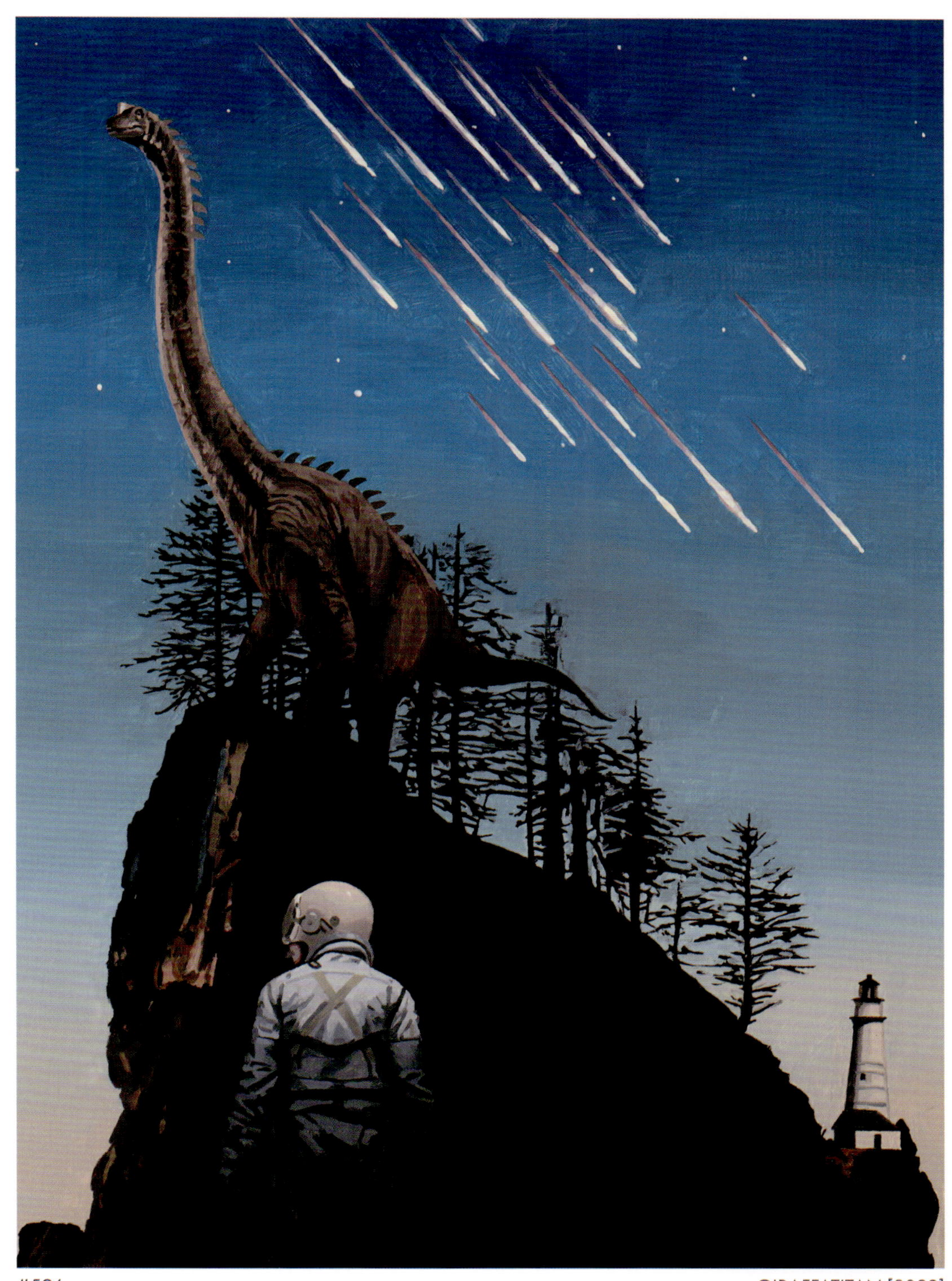

#596 GIRAFFATITAN [2022]

#605
TYRANOSAURUS REX [2022]

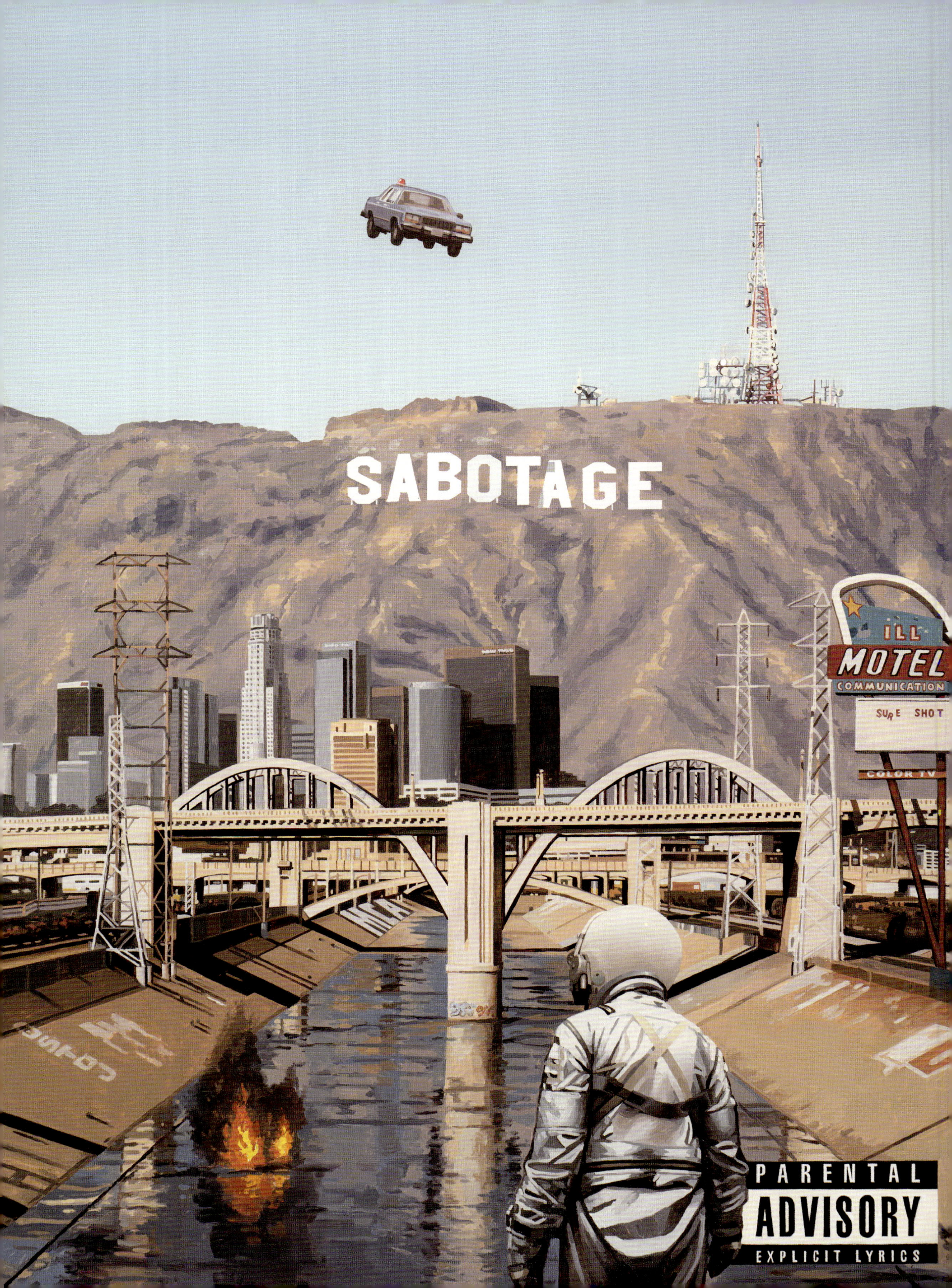
SABOTAGE
ILL
MOTEL
COMMUNICATION
SURE SHOT
COLOR TV
PARENTAL
ADVISORY
EXPLICIT LYRICS

AM GOLD

Harman Projects, New York City, NY
April, 2023

This is a show about music and time travel.

After spending most of my life making paintings about the future, I've recently started looking more backwards than forwards. Maybe I'm getting older (I'm definitely getting older). Or maybe it's because the last three years have been, to put it as eloquently as I can, massively f*cked up. But if I had to summarize the unifying theme of my work from this chapter of my life it would be traveling through time and visiting the past. I've revisited old paintings. Old lives. Old friends. Old places I used to live and old places I've traveled to. Old dinosaurs, even. These paintings have been much more about my own personal story, more autobiographical, than anything else I had previously done, and it's been nice to share more of my own self in the context of my lone, wandering astronaut.

Part of the process of looking back on my life has been listening to—and cataloging—music from all of my various stops along the way. The top 40 stuff I used to tape off the radio when I was in 6th grade. Hipster blog music from the mid 2000s. Semi-forgotten indie rock from the '90s. More distant '70s soft rock which I have only vague memories of, but which I often rediscovered much later through familiar sounding hip hop samples. Brit pop from that period when I thought I wanted to move to London. A brief Industrial phase. We're now what—a decade or more into the streaming era? And it's become increasingly easy to recreate playlists from all parts of my life, including piecing together songs I probably hadn't listened to since my yellow Sport Walkman ate the mixtape they were on, back in 1997.

#620
SABOTAGE [2022]

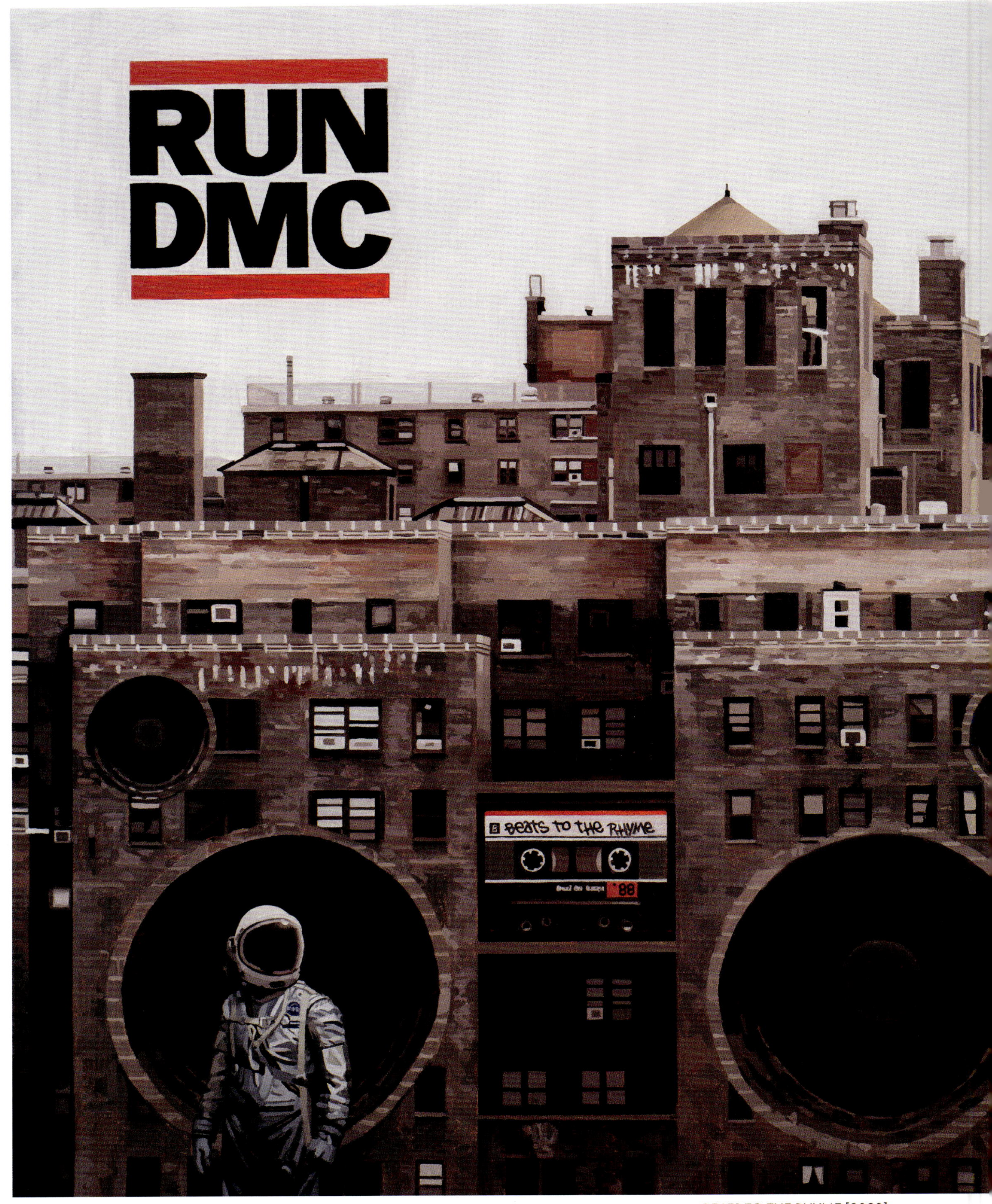

#630

BEATS TO THE RHYME [2023]

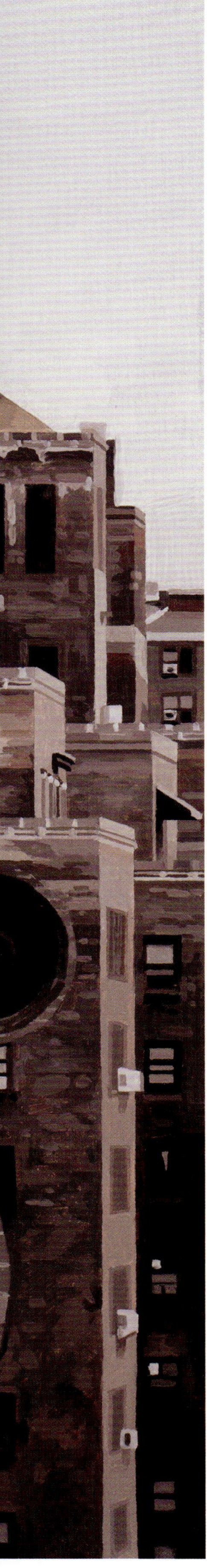

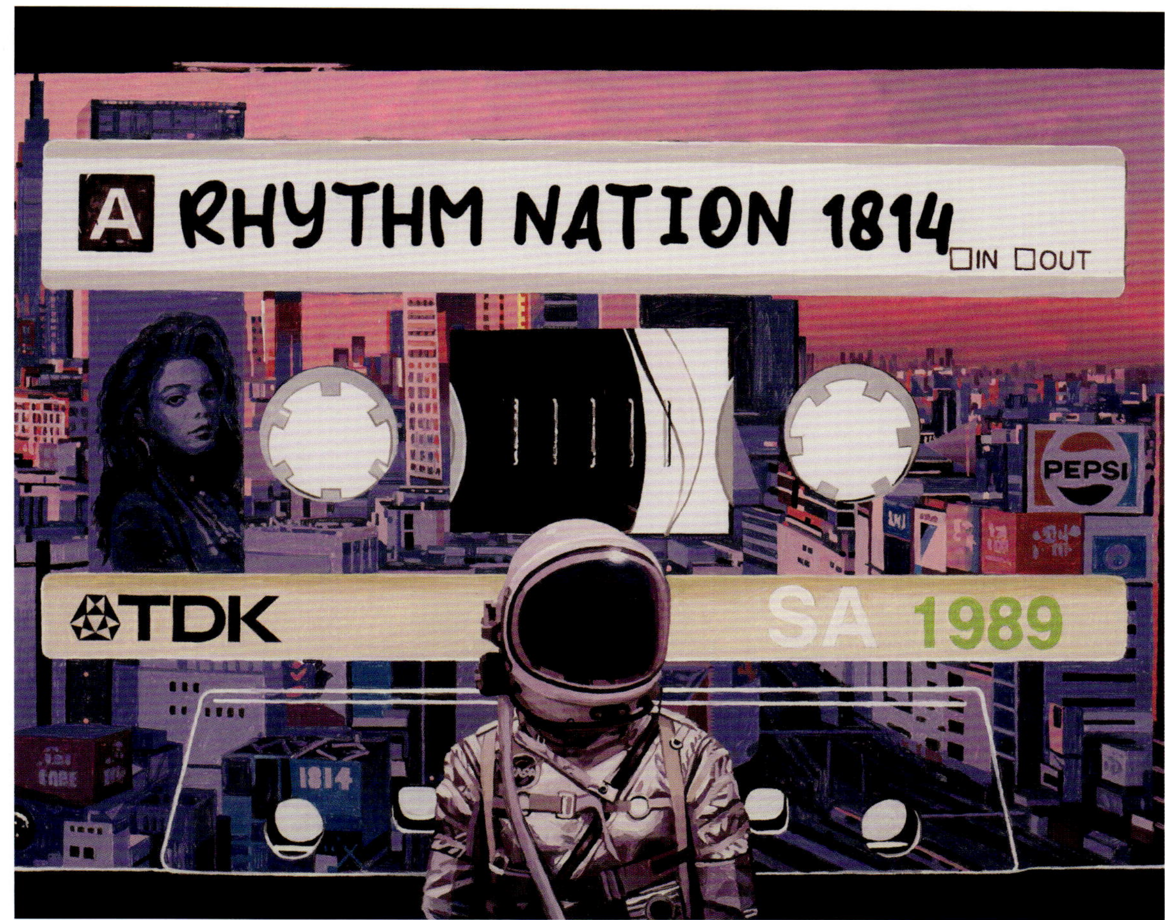

#635

JANET [2023]

As much as anything else, these songs define my life. They're the soundtrack to everything I've ever done. And although I began this journey making playlists to help me document my life, mostly in order to spur memories and nostalgia for those times, so that I could then paint about it, I realize that the songs themselves are as much the subject matter as the memories they inspire.

And so I made a show about music and time travel.

AM Gold is inspired by the music of my life. Although these 24 brand new paintings don't necessarily represent my 24 favorite songs, or my all time favorite bands, I tried to pick music which brought back the most tangible memories for me: riding in a friend's mom's wood paneled car on the way to nursery school with the radio on. Being on break from college and wandering around New York City with my walkman. Watching European MTV in a hotel room on the one night I spent in Amsterdam. Riding the subway home from work on a summer night with my first iPod. Going to Australia for 4 months with basically only *Enter the Wu-Tang (36 Chambers)* to listen to a trillion times over.

I was also inspired by the kind of physical media we mostly don't have, don't need, or don't care about anymore. Album covers, CD's, posters, cassette tapes, stereo equipment with actual knobs on them, zines, band flyers, photos cut and pasted from magazines onto your wall, mixtapes shared amongst friends, passed down from cooler older siblings, or made to impress crushes. Not just to be overly nostalgic about all of this, of course. There's much to be said for technical progress. Trust me, it's way easier to type a few letters into the Spotify search bar than it is to wait around all day hoping your

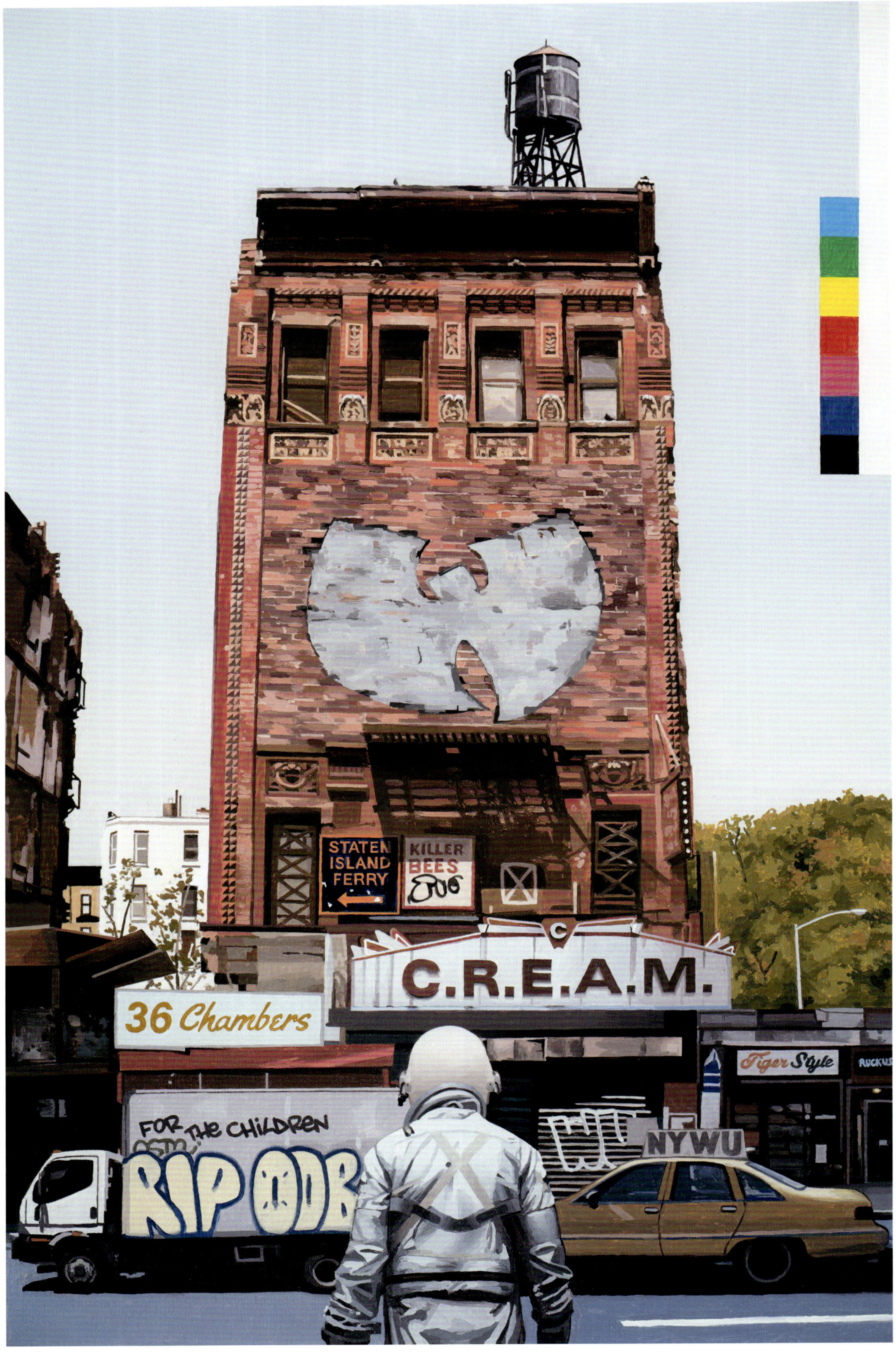

STATEN ISLAND FERRY
KILLER BEES
C.R.E.A.M.
36 Chambers
Tiger Style
FOR THE CHILDREN
RIP ODB
NYWU

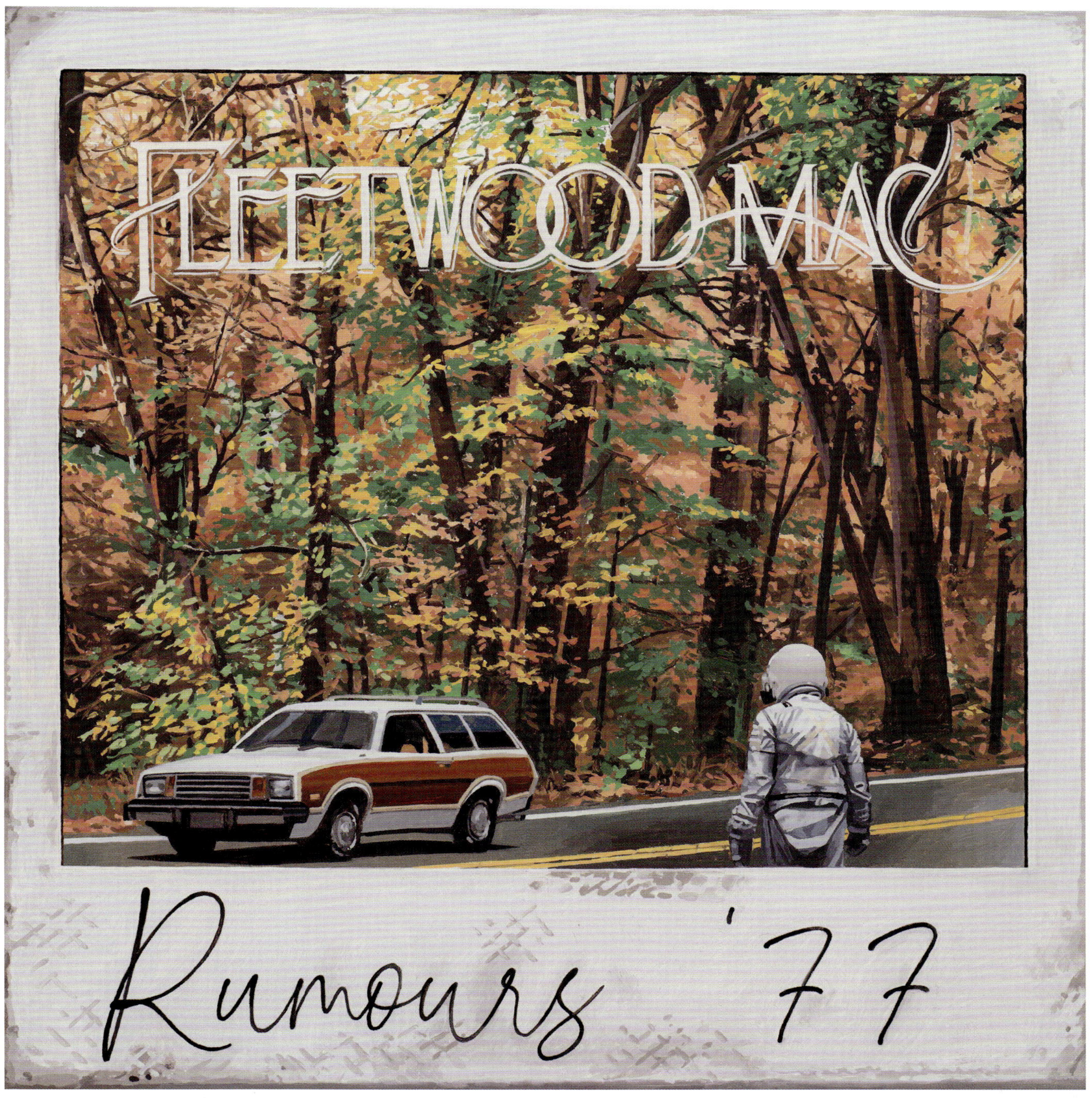

#629 RUMOURS [2023]

favorite radio station will play your favorite song, and that you'll be able to press the record button on your cassette deck in time. I wouldn't have been able to revisit all the hundreds of songs which make up the story of my life without living in the streaming era. For that I'm thankful. And yet, like all people getting older, I miss the things I loved in my younger days. I miss the feeling of unwrapping a CD and putting it into the stereo for the first time, not really knowing if you just wasted $17.99 of your hard earned money. I miss studying an album's booklet for hours, sitting on the carpeted floor of my childhood bedroom while the music plays on loop. I even miss rewinding that old mixtape by hand after my stupid walkman spat it out at me. OK, maybe not so much the last one.

This is what this show is about. My own story told through music. It's *AM Gold*. It's the songs from my past, in the present.

#616
WU TANG CLAN [2022]

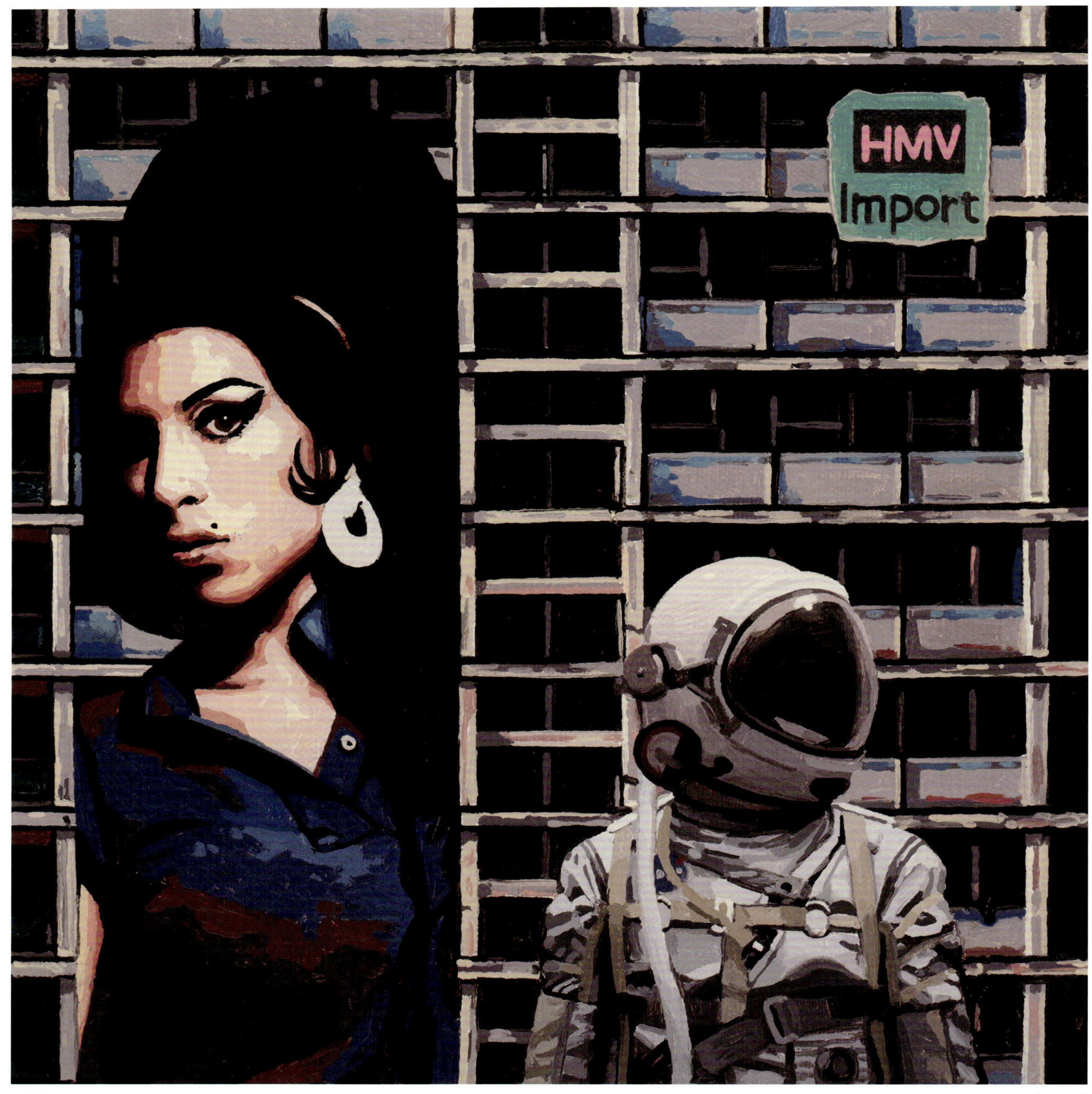

#621

BACK TO BLACK [2022]

#631

WHAT'S GOING ON [2023]

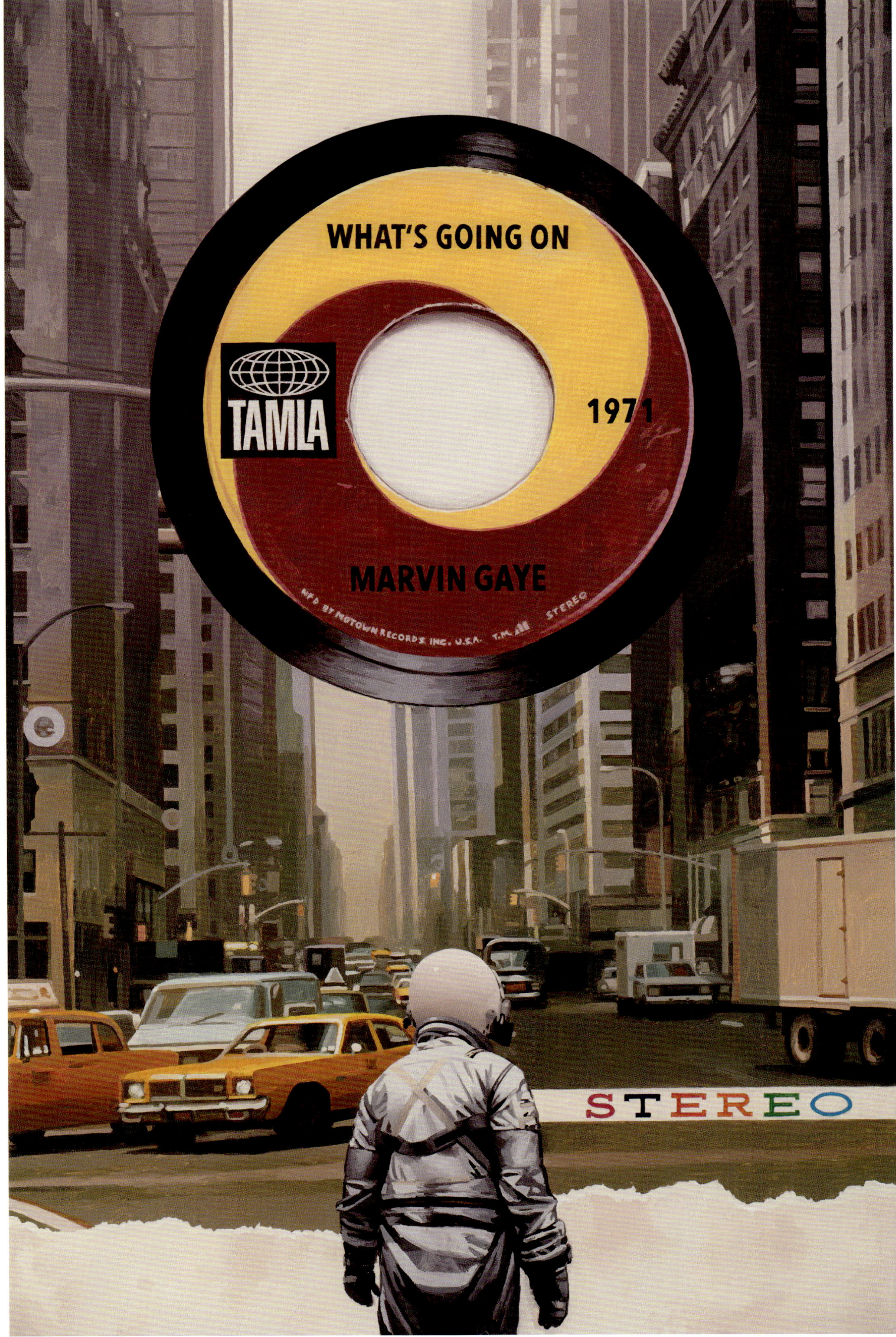
WHAT'S GOING ON
TAMLA
1971
MARVIN GAYE
MFD BY MOTOWN RECORDS INC. U.S.A. T.M.
STEREO
STEREO

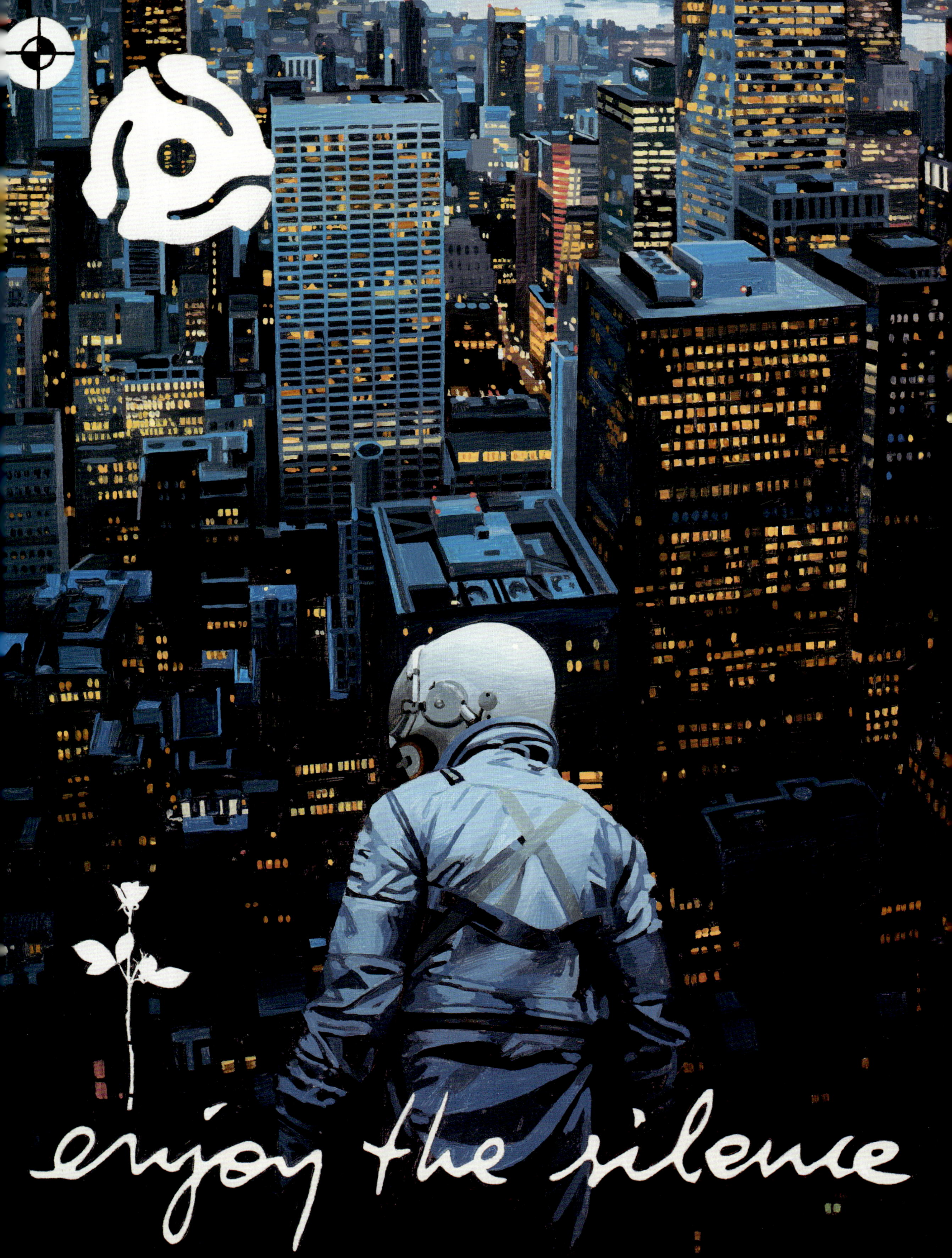
enjoy the silence

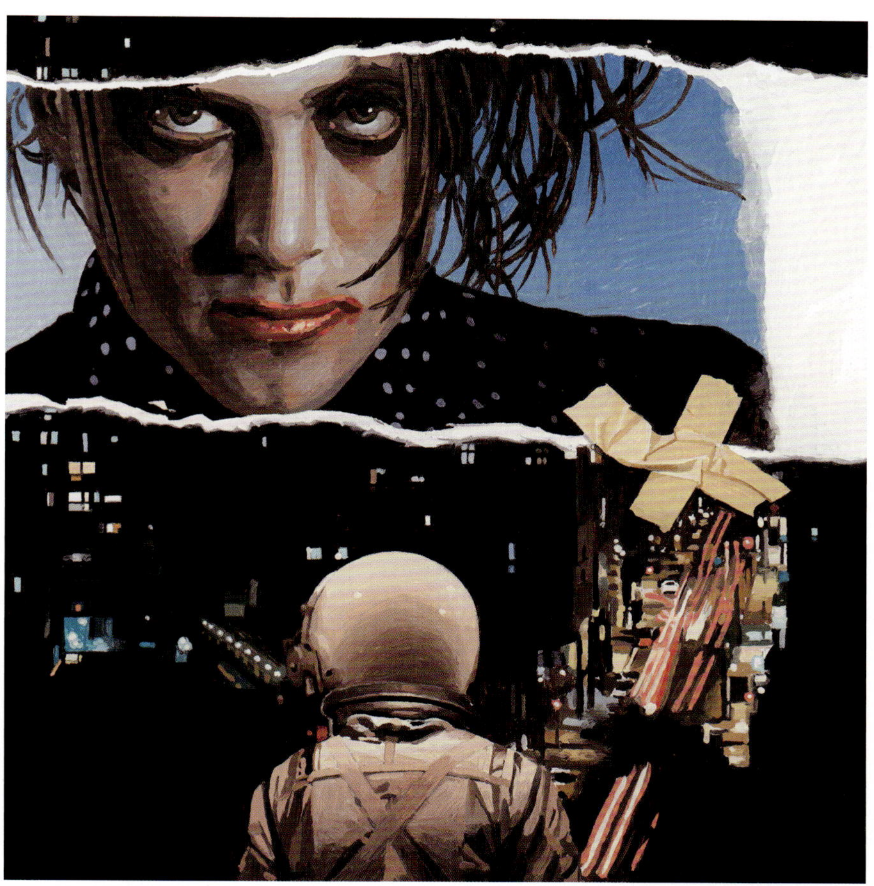

#624 DISINTEGRATION [2023]

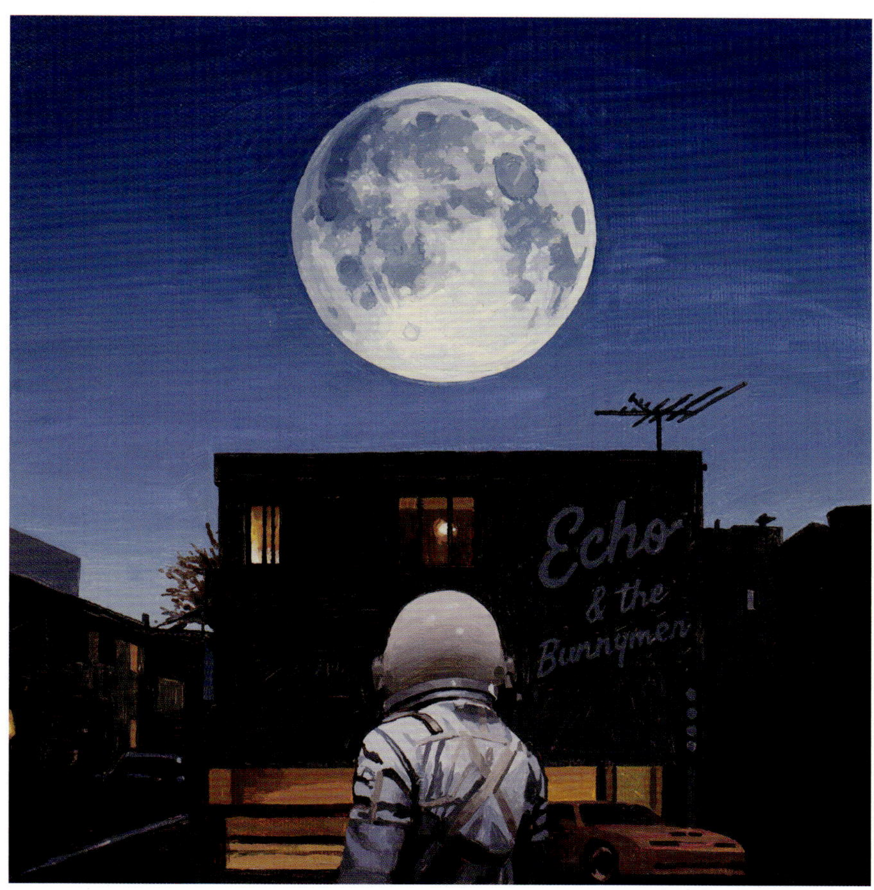

#619 KILLING MOON [2022]

#617
ENJOY THE SILENCE [2022]

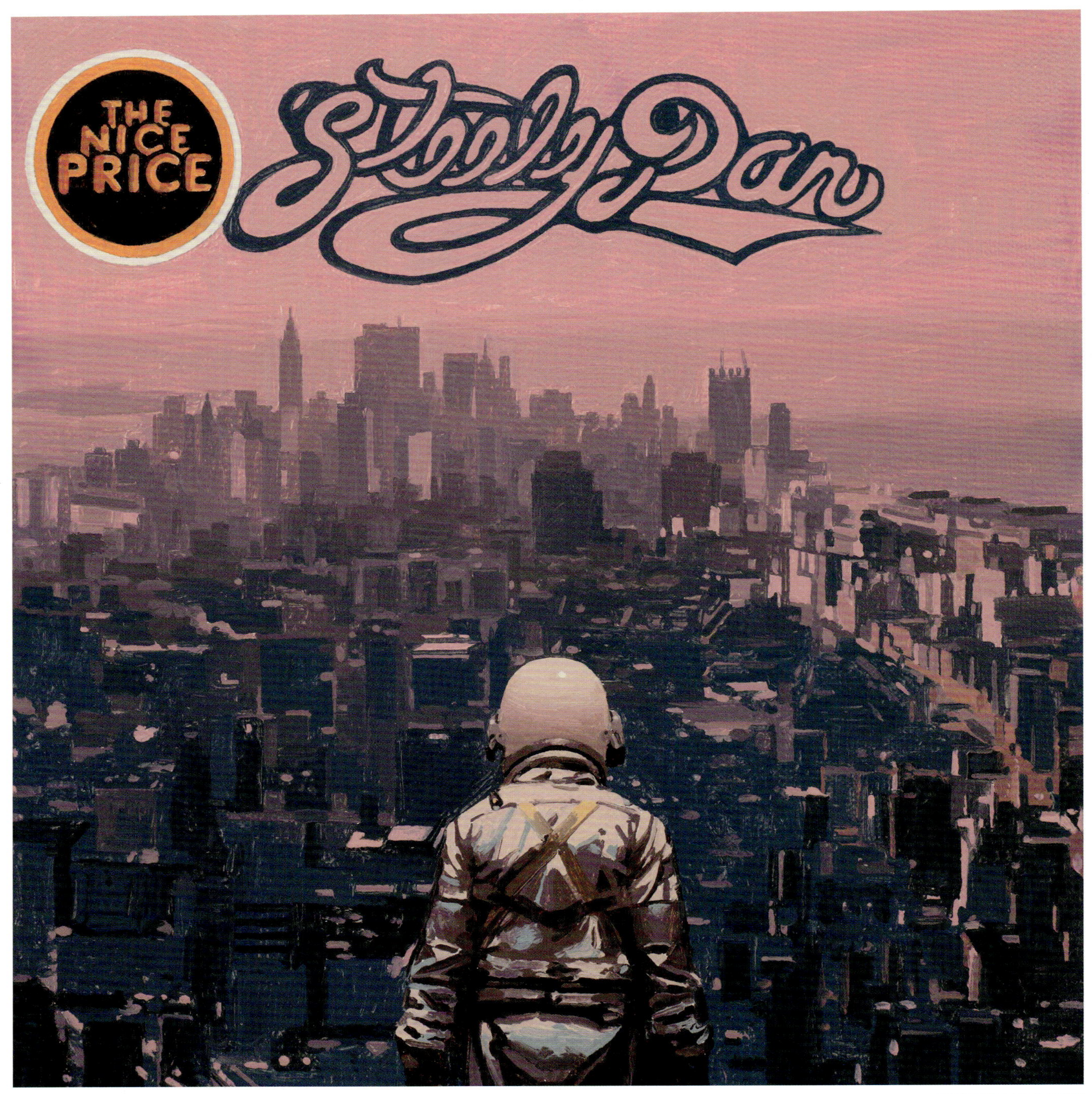

#632

STEELY DAN [2023]

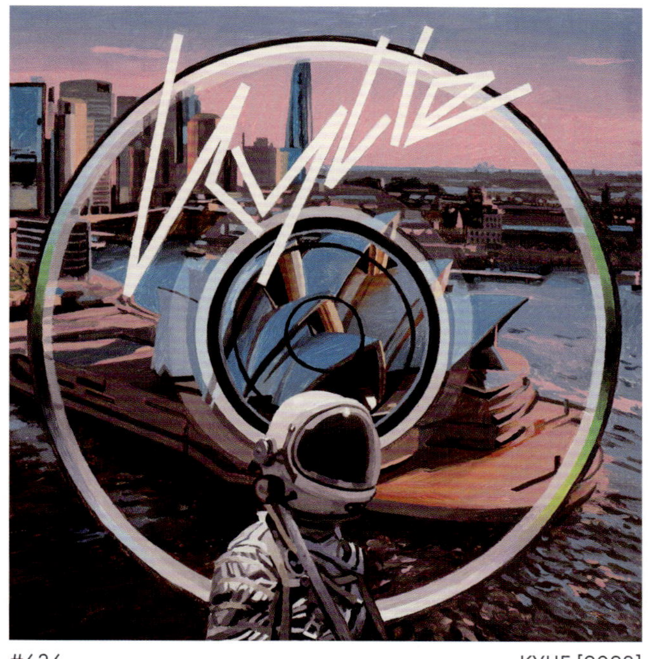

#636 KYLIE [2023]

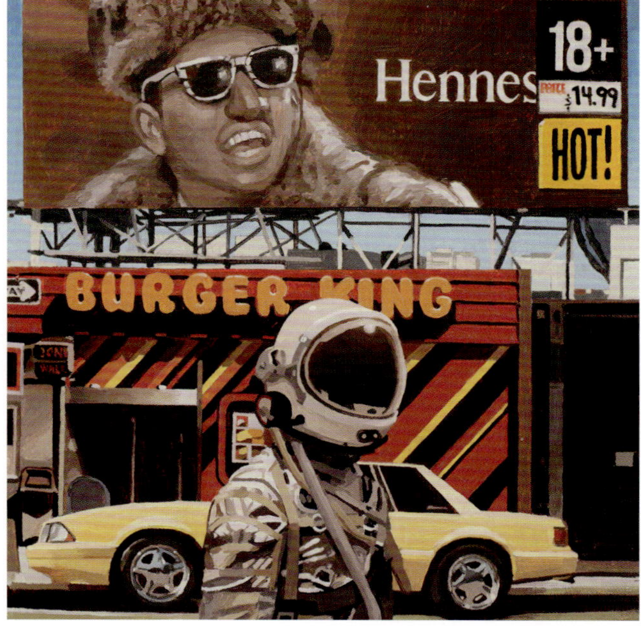

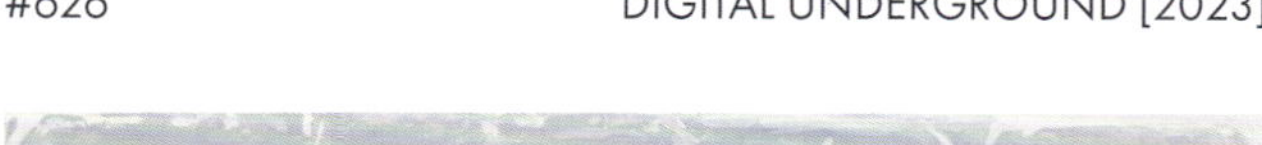
#626 DIGITAL UNDERGROUND [2023]

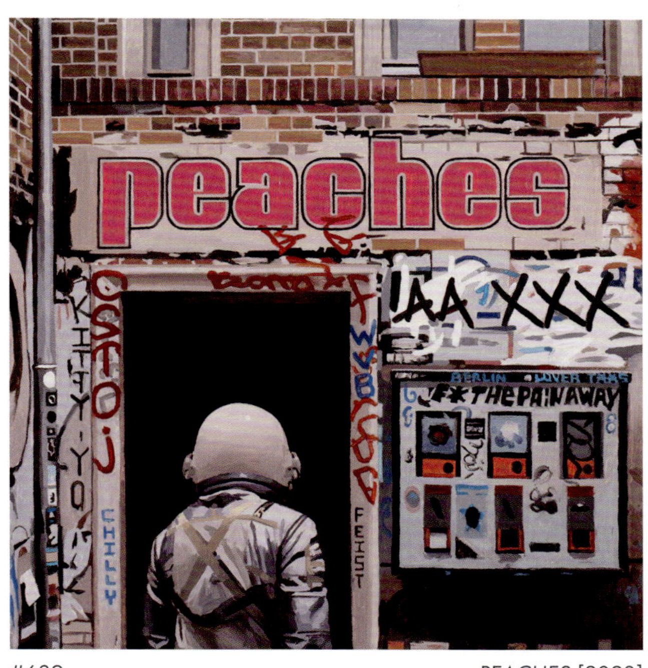

#639 PEACHES [2023]

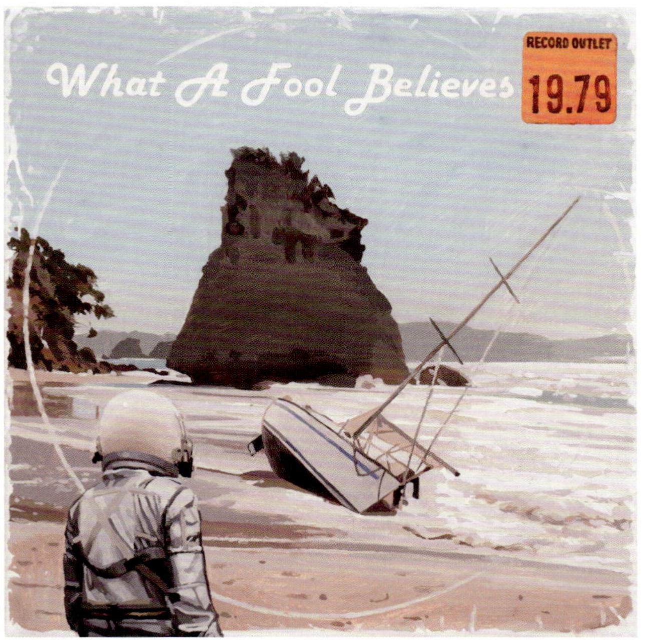

#628 WHAT A FOOL BELIEVES [2023]

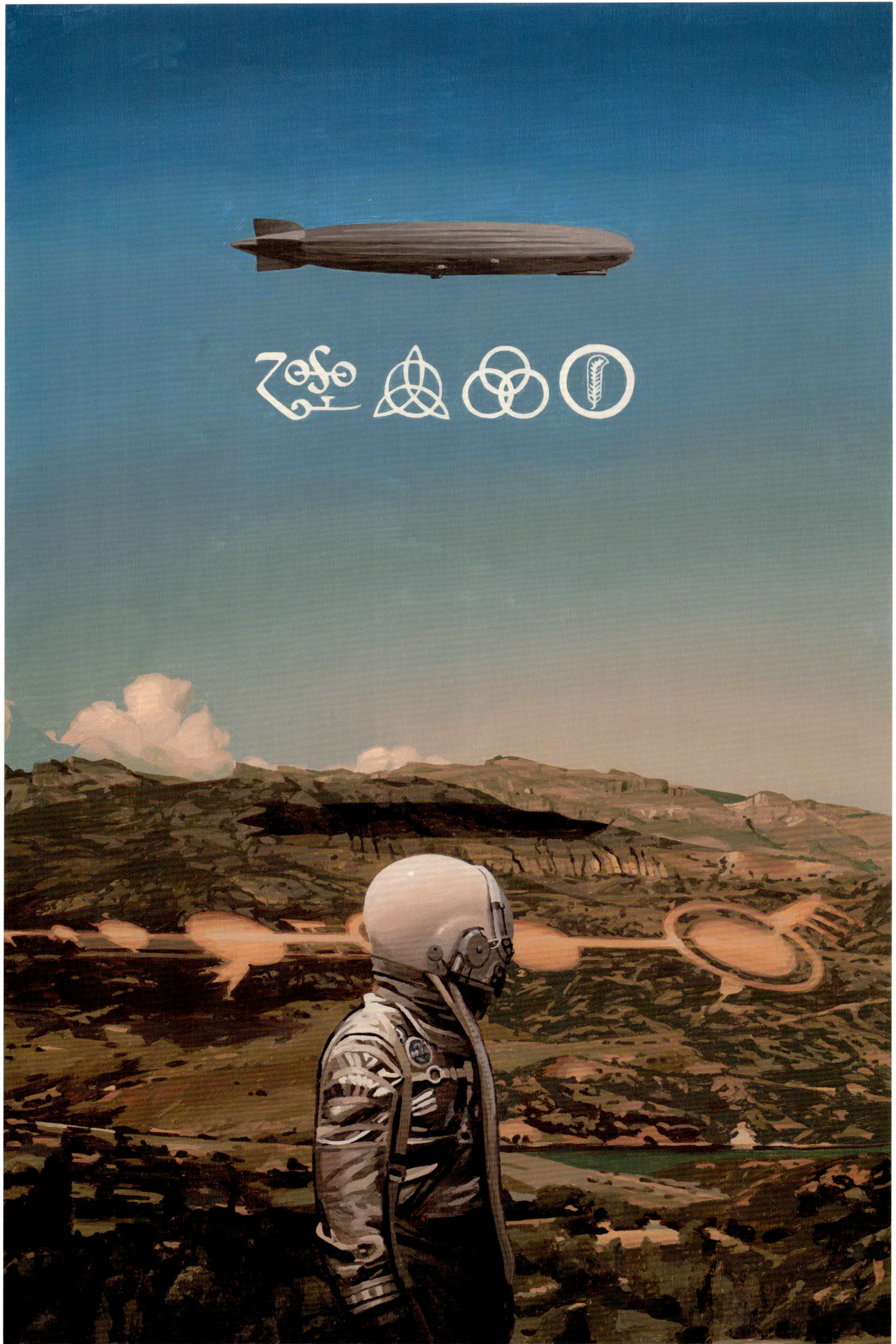

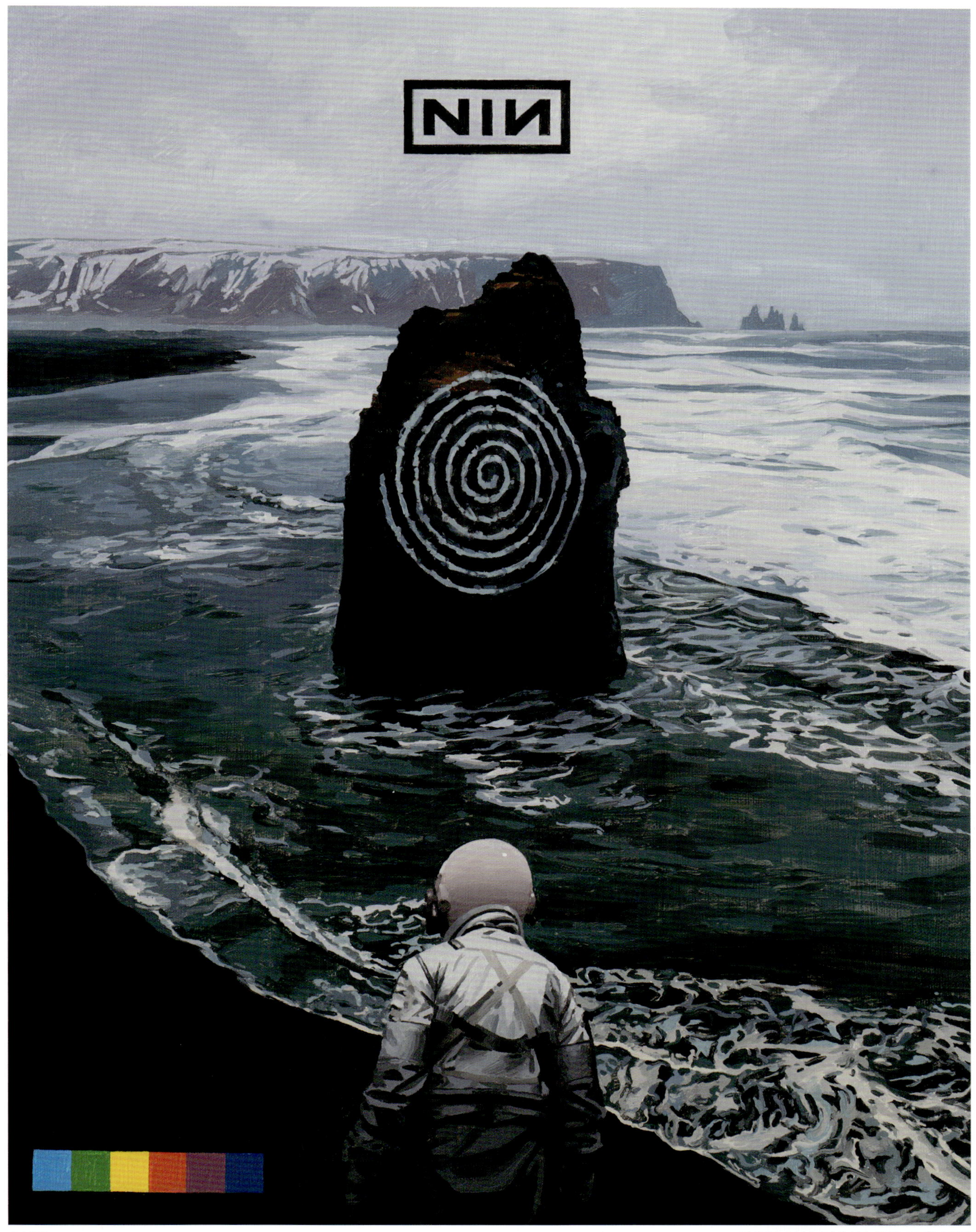

#625

THE DOWNWARD SPIRAL [2023]

#623

ZEPPELIN [2023]

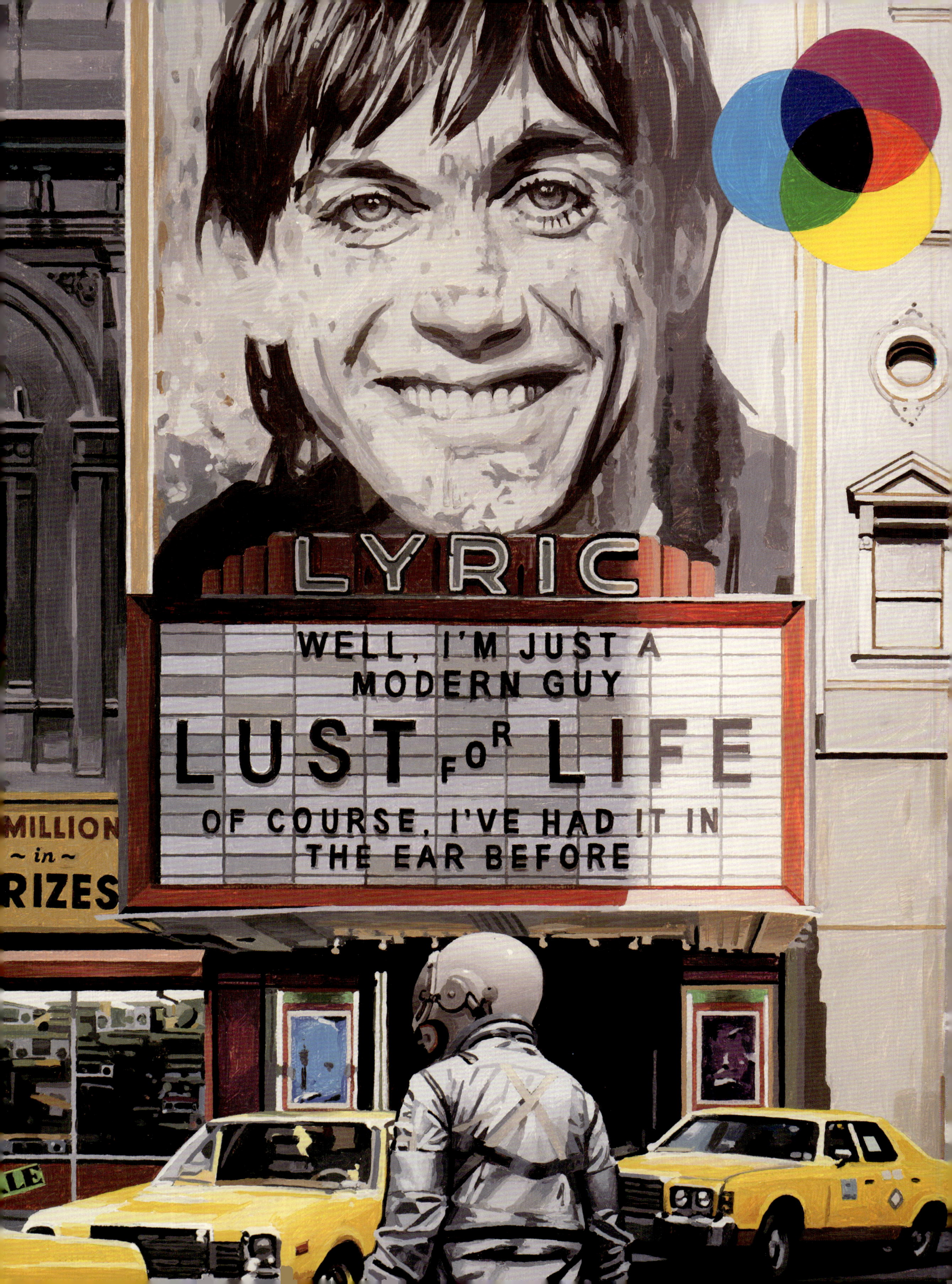
LYRIC
WELL, I'M JUST A
MODERN GUY
LUST FOR LIFE
OF COURSE, I'VE HAD IT IN
THE EAR BEFORE
MILLION
~ in ~
RIZES

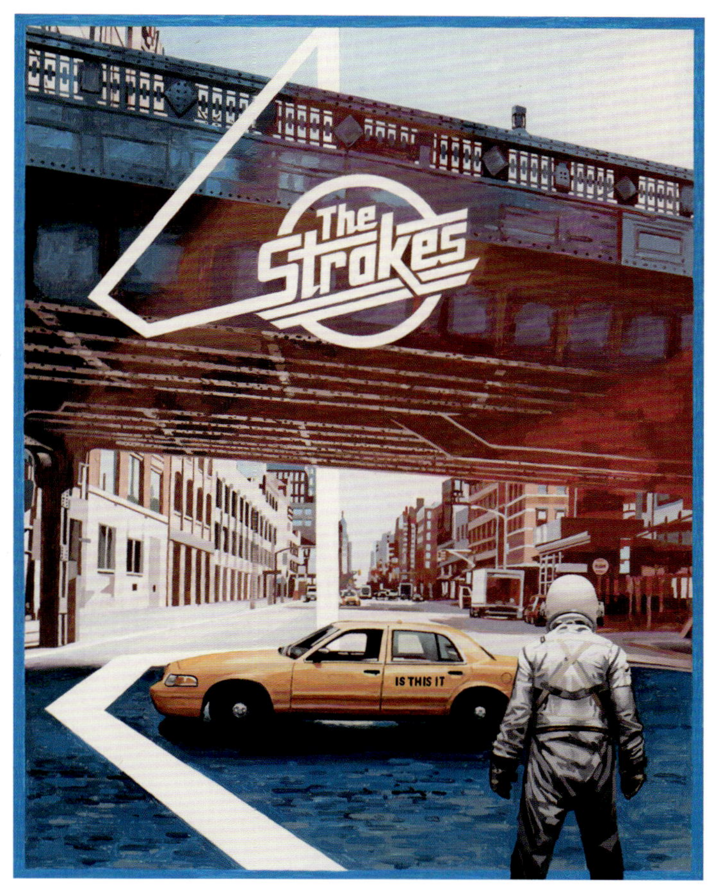

#627 IS THIS IT [2023]

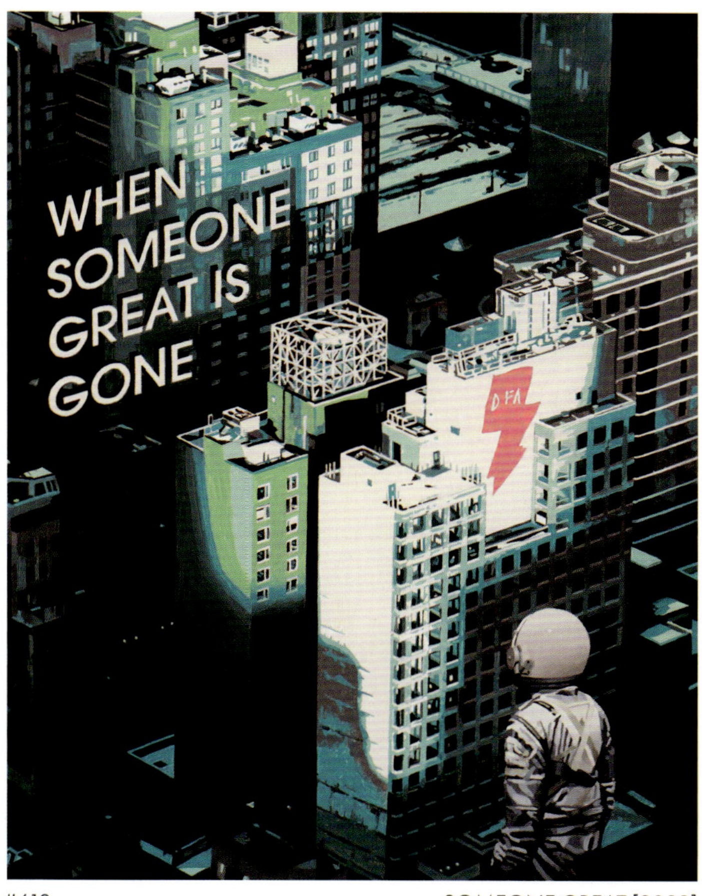

#618 SOMEONE GREAT [2022]

#622
LUST FOR LIFE [2022]

A PRINT ARRIVES IN THE MAIL

//////////////////////

April, 2023

I hadn't been to New York in years, for varied reasons, including there being a pandemic, and that I live out on the west coast now. But in the spring of 2023, I flew out there for the opening of my *AM Gold* show. While in town, I took the opportunity to revisit old friends, relatives, and memories.

And I spent a whole day bumming around New York with my old college pal (and very talented sculptor) Tom Beale. We grabbed bagels. We laughed and joked and reminisced about our old friend Chris Ostoj, now decades gone but still casting a shadow over our lives. We went to the Natural History Museum. We posed with dinosaurs. We wandered into stores in Chinatown and galleries in the Lower East Side. Mostly by chance, we found a show of paintings by Jake Berthot, a now deceased painter who 25 years previously had been the artist in residence at my college during the very first semester I took a painting class. I'm pretty sure I had a critique with him. I had been painting for maybe 3 months at the time. My entire portfolio was a couple of very bad self portraits, a still life, and a thoroughly mediocre copy of a Van Gogh. I can't imagine what he said to me. Probably something like "Keep at it."

It's 25 years later, and somehow I did.

The show of his work was a retrospective, and there were paintings there that I had actually seen in person at my college, two decades prior. It was so strange to see them again, after so much time, and with Tom, my college friend, there next to me. This experience brought back a lot of memories from my earliest days as an aspiring painter.

Not long after I returned home from this New York trip, I found a message on Instagram that had been sitting buried in an unread folder. Annika, a Swedish woman now living in Pennsylvania, had found some prints in a thrift store many years ago and had been meaning to reach out. One of them had my name written on the back, and she wanted to know if it was mine, and if I could maybe identify the other prints she had also purchased. Messages like this aren't entirely unsurprising to me. I have released tons of astronaut prints over the years, and some of them probably eventually end up in thrift stores. So I prepared myself to respond "Yup that's mine" and call it a day. But when I looked at the pictures of the prints she had sent, I found myself very surprised. These weren't prints of an astronaut.

I saw a younger version of myself staring back at me. It was a self portrait. An actual etching I had made in my junior year in college when I took a printmaking class

SELF PORTRAIT (RECTO)
[1997]

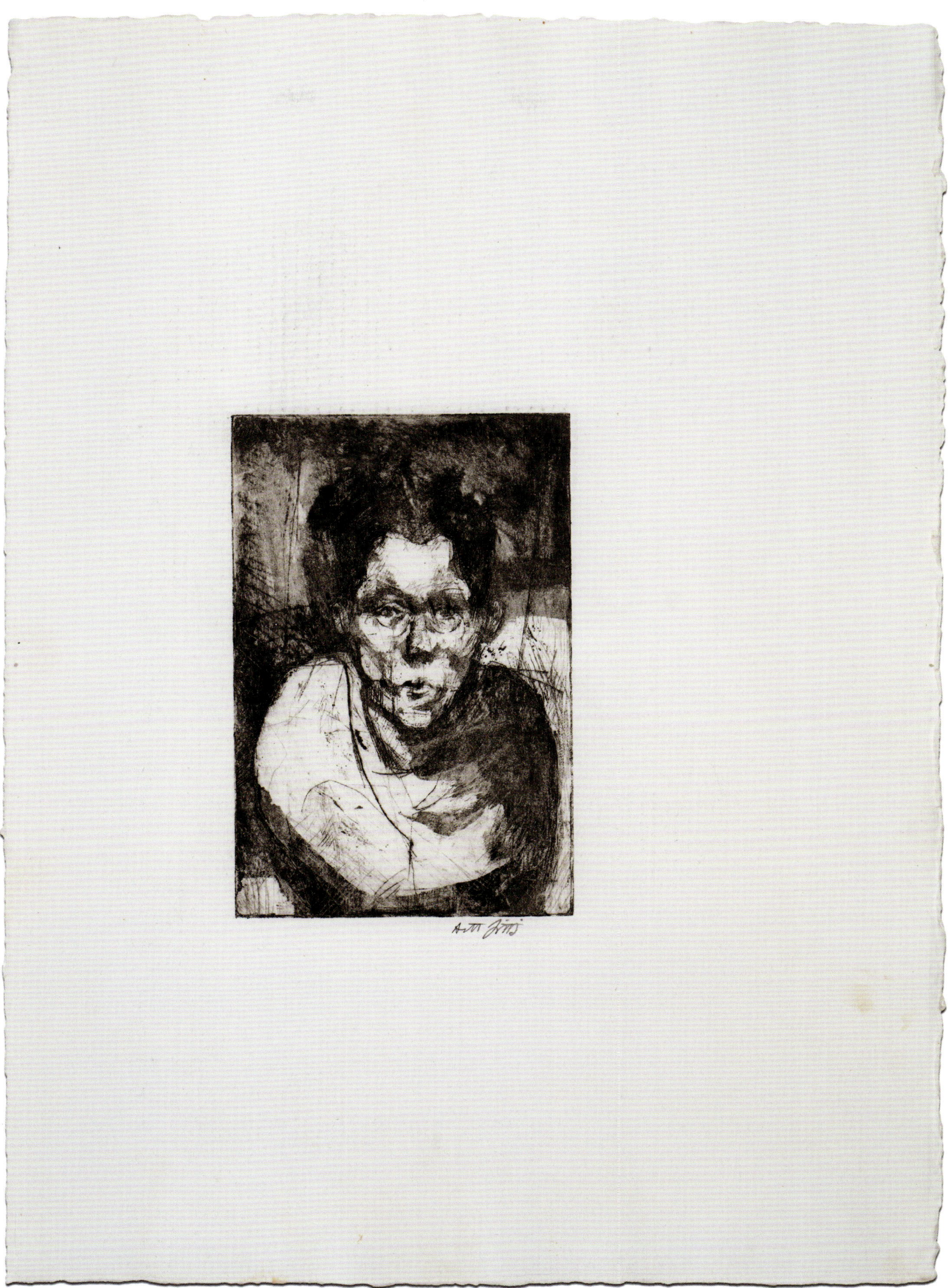

Scott Listfield
Spring '97
Scott Listfield
was here again Spring 2023

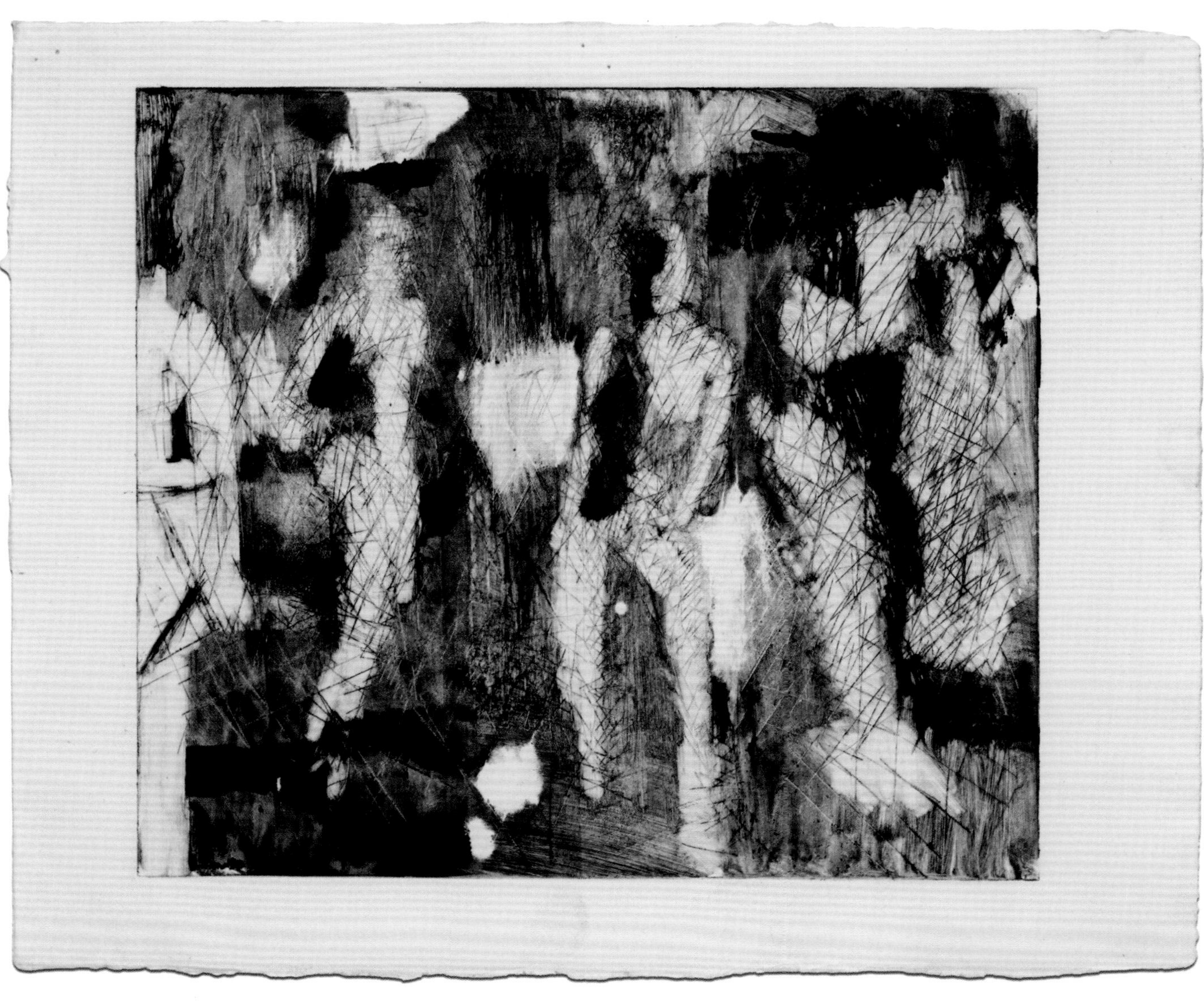

ETCHING BY CHRIS OSTOJ [C. 1997]

with my friend Chris Ostoj. Yes, that Chris Ostoj. The one who died young and prompted me to make a run at this whole artist thing. You might remember seeing his name, oh, hundreds of times in my work. And amongst the other prints in this group of prints that Annika had found? A blocky black and white print that looked kind of familiar. I stared at it for a while. A long while. And although it's unsigned, I'm fairly sure it was made by my friend Chris Ostoj. I sent it to my friend Tom in New York, and he agreed with me. It was probably an Ostoj.

How did these prints end up in a thrift store in Philadelphia? I have no idea.

After the surprise wore off of seeing a print of my much younger face, I responded to Annika, confused but happy to see these things again for the first time in decades, and confirmed that the self portrait was in fact mine. She asked if she might senc them my way to sign on the front, and I said sure, and she told me I could keep the one by Ostoj. And so I did.

Like the Jake Berthot paintings, but even more strange, I saw and held these prints for the first time in 25 years. I signed the self portrait on the front and was about to send it back to her, but then I looked at the back of it. In my handwriting it said "Scott Listfield Spring '97." And so I signed it again "Scott Listfield was here again Spring 2023."

Time loops back on itself. I framed the Ostoj print and now it hangs in my living room.

SELF PORTRAIT (VERSO)
[1997]

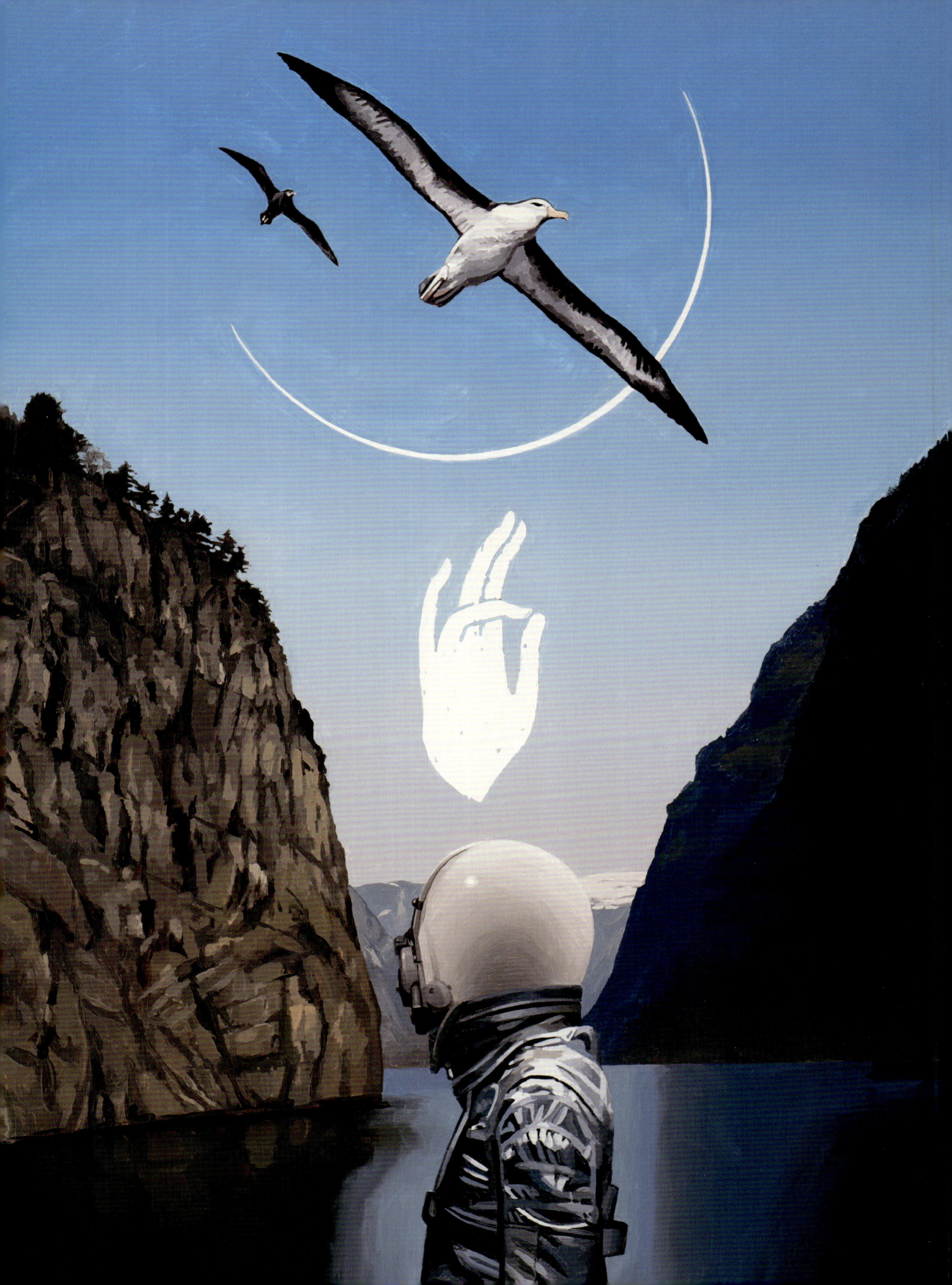

SYMBOLS

//

~~Galleri Ramfjord, Oslo, Norway~~
~~September, 2023~~

Antler Gallery, Portland, OR
October, 2023

All right. This one sucks. Let's just do this.

In the fall of 2022, I traveled to Portland, Oregon for my *Lost World* show with Antler Gallery, which is run by the universally beloved husband and wife team of Neil Perry and Susannah Kelly. This was something like my fifth or sixth show with them, but the first time I had made it up to Portland in person in about 4 years. Since before the pandemic. Since before a lot of things. While I was up there, I grabbed a coffee one morning with the two of them and they told me about a show they wanted to pitch to me. Would I be interested in having a small solo show of my work in Oslo, Norway in September of 2023? Would I also be interested in co-curating a group show with them there, to be shown alongside my work? Did I also want to go to Oslo? A city I've never been to? And hang out with Neil and Susannah, the nicest people I know? And also the lovely people from Galleri Ramfjord, the nicest people Neil and Susannah knew? Who they had met and befriended years before at the Scope Art Fair in Miami, because Neil and Susannah befriend everyone?

Of course I did.

I don't ask myself this often but why do I do all of this? I mean it might seem like fun to you, reader of this book, and I hope it does, but I spend a MASSIVE chunk of my time painting astronauts. It's a lot of work and I have to make a lot of sacrifices to make it all go. Why do I do it? I mean, there are many reasons, most prominently because I love doing it. But I also do it hoping that one day an opportunity like this comes my way somehow.

And so I left Portland in the fall of 2022 already counting the days until the fall of 2023 when we could do this show. Leading up to it, I made ten new paintings and I reached out to a number of artists and invited them to show with me. I coordinated with Neil and Susannah and I booked my trip to Oslo and then, just a few days before I left for Europe the bottom fell out of everything.

Susannah Kelly, one of the most vibrant, kind, and universally loved people I knew in the art world, or in any world, died. She was young and she was healthy, and then she was gone.

#649
ALBATROSS [2023]

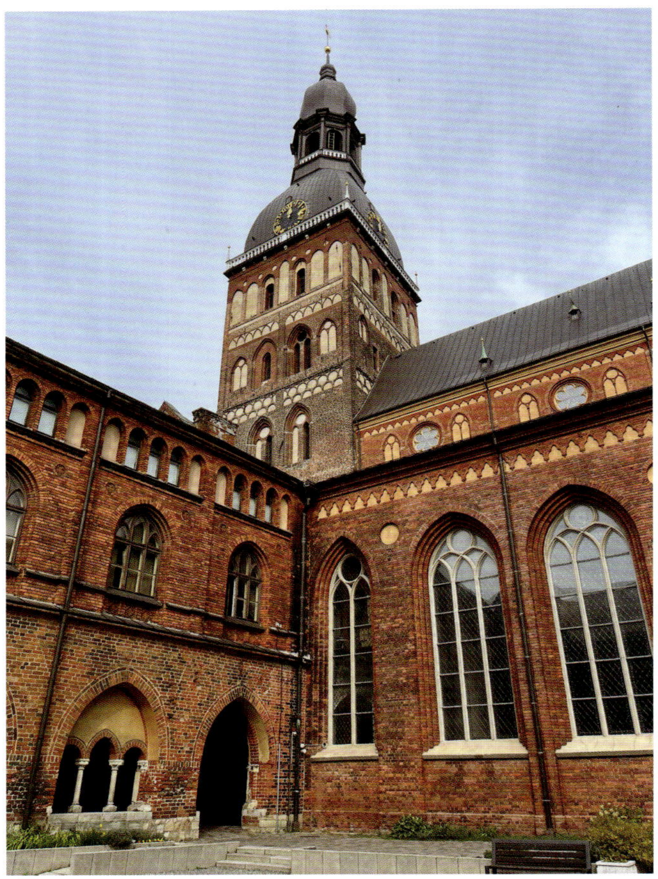

RIGA, LATVIA

The show was canceled, as it should be. And I went to Europe anyways, because it was too late to cancel. And life, it turns out, is short, so f*ck it.

Just days after hearing about Susannah, I flew to Copenhagen, and then spent a week traveling from Denmark to Sweden, and then on to Oslo, with what felt like a literal dark cloud chasing me all the way. In Oslo, it caught up with me. While there, I met up with the artist Elizabeth Livingston. She had been one of the people I had invited to be in the group show, and had, like me, booked her tickets to Europe before hearing the terrible news. I didn't know her beforehand, and she didn't know Susannah, so it was both sad and also a little weird, at first. But we made the best of it. We spent a couple days wandering the city and talking about Susannah. We met the lovely people from Galleri Ramfjord, who were equally as sad and confused as we were. We ate some Scandinavian baked goods. Elizabeth had the thoughtful idea to wander into one of the many churches around town and light a candle in honor of Susannah. Only it was late in the day and the churches were all closed.

So we parted company, and my trip continued on from there, to my next stops: Latvia and Lithuania, where I met up with my brother to visit the places where our ancestors came from. Which was heavy in a different way. That's a story for another chapter, but when I arrived in Riga, the lovely capital of Latvia, I did finally light that candle for Susannah, in a towering Catholic cathedral. I'm not Catholic and I don't know that Susannah was, either, but it seemed like a thing to do. It was what this trip needed. It's a memory I hope I'll hold onto for as long as I can.

When I returned from Europe, Neil decided—bravely in my opinion—to put on the show we had planned for Oslo in their gallery in Portland. And so, the show got a second life. Which is somehow fitting. I know Susannah would have wanted it that way.

I made all of the paintings for this show well before I left for Europe and well before I heard the terrible news about Susannah. And yet it somehow feels like I made it in response to all of this. The 10 paintings in this show were all inspired by northern landscapes and wildlife, with symbols pulled from tarot cards, vintage tattoos, and old manuscripts. I wanted to capture the feeling of entering a quiet snowy forest alone and seeing your breath. Of watching a solitary crow land nearby and give you a meaningful look. Of walking an old mountain path and feeling your own story being added to that of everyone else who had walked that way.

I don't often use words like "spiritual" or "mysticism" when it comes to my work. More often I'm thinking about science or music or Burger King. Things that are a bit more grounded in my day to day life. But this show incorporates ideas of myth, and darkness, of animal spirits and hands outside of our own that control our fates in mysterious ways. When I made these paintings, I knew I'd be traveling through Europe alone for the first time in decades, visiting northern towns I'd never seen before, and then also places where my ancestors once lived and died. Where people I don't know experienced all of the love, hope, fear, and despair that they ever will. Where no more of my people now live. Looking back on it now, the paintings I made then feel something like an omen. Perhaps very much like a tarot card: a symbol of things to come, but left open to interpretation.

A CANDLE FOR SUSANNAH
RIGA, LATVIA

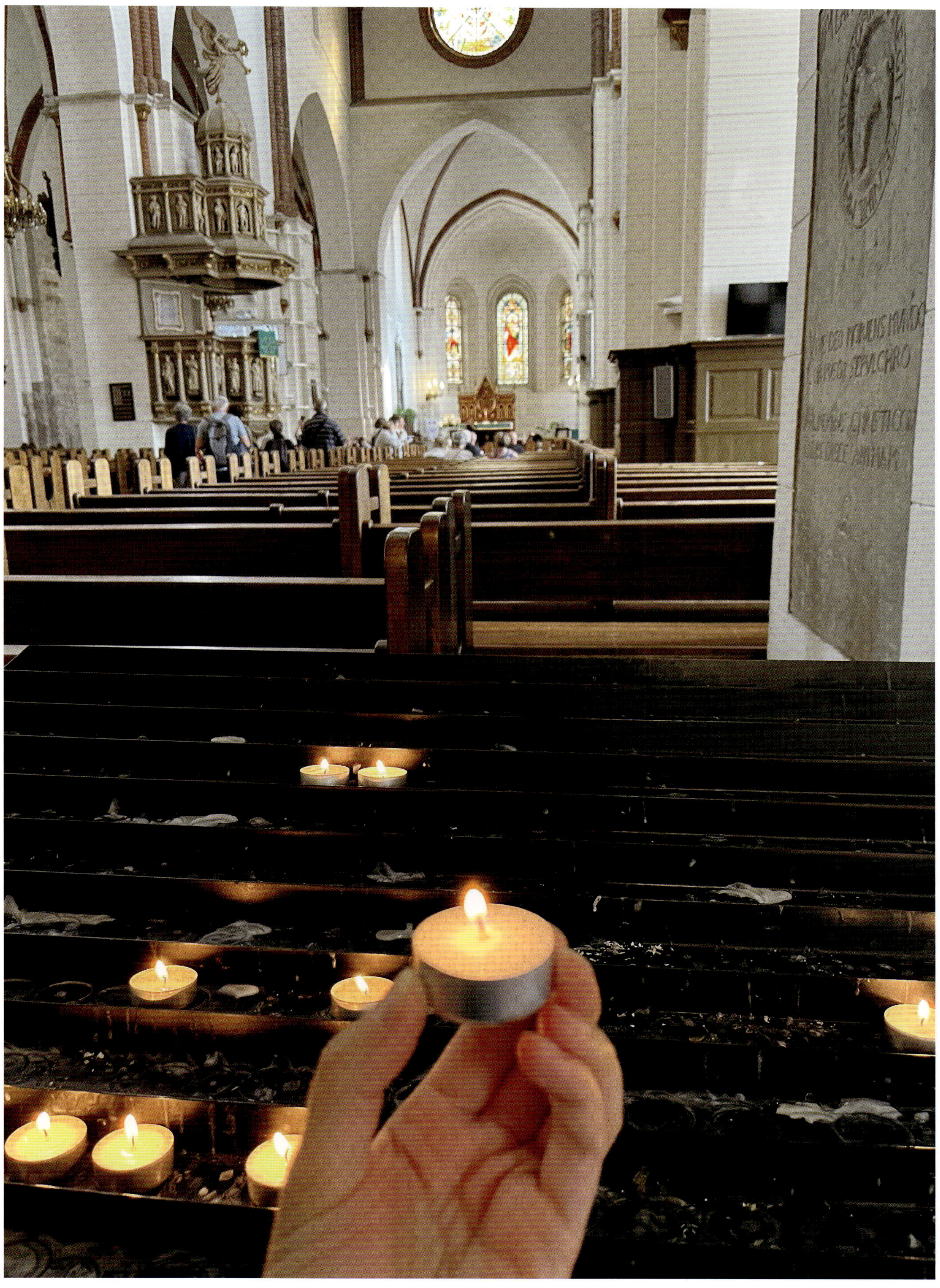

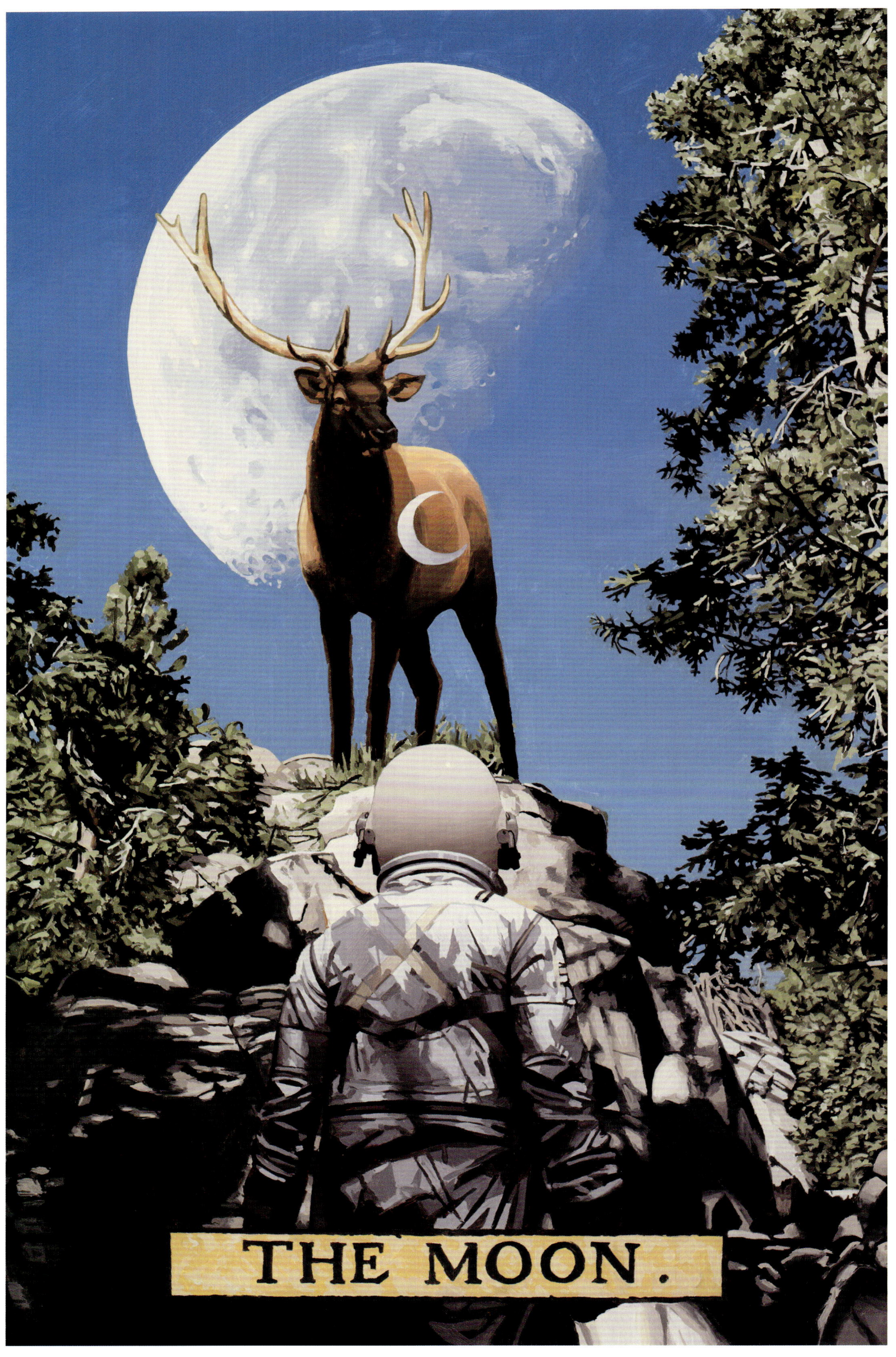
THE MOON.

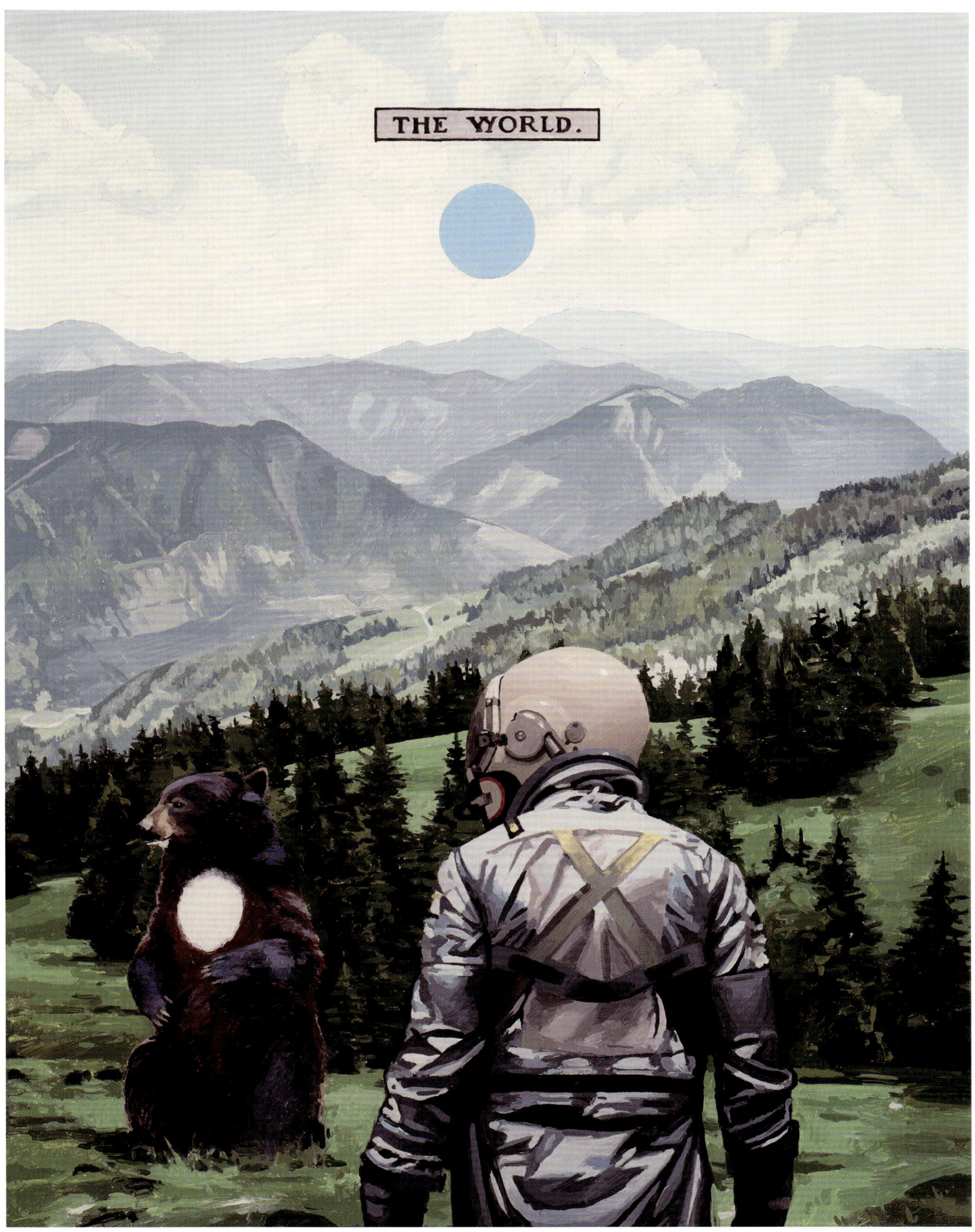

#648

THE WORLD [2023]

#645

THE MOON [2023]

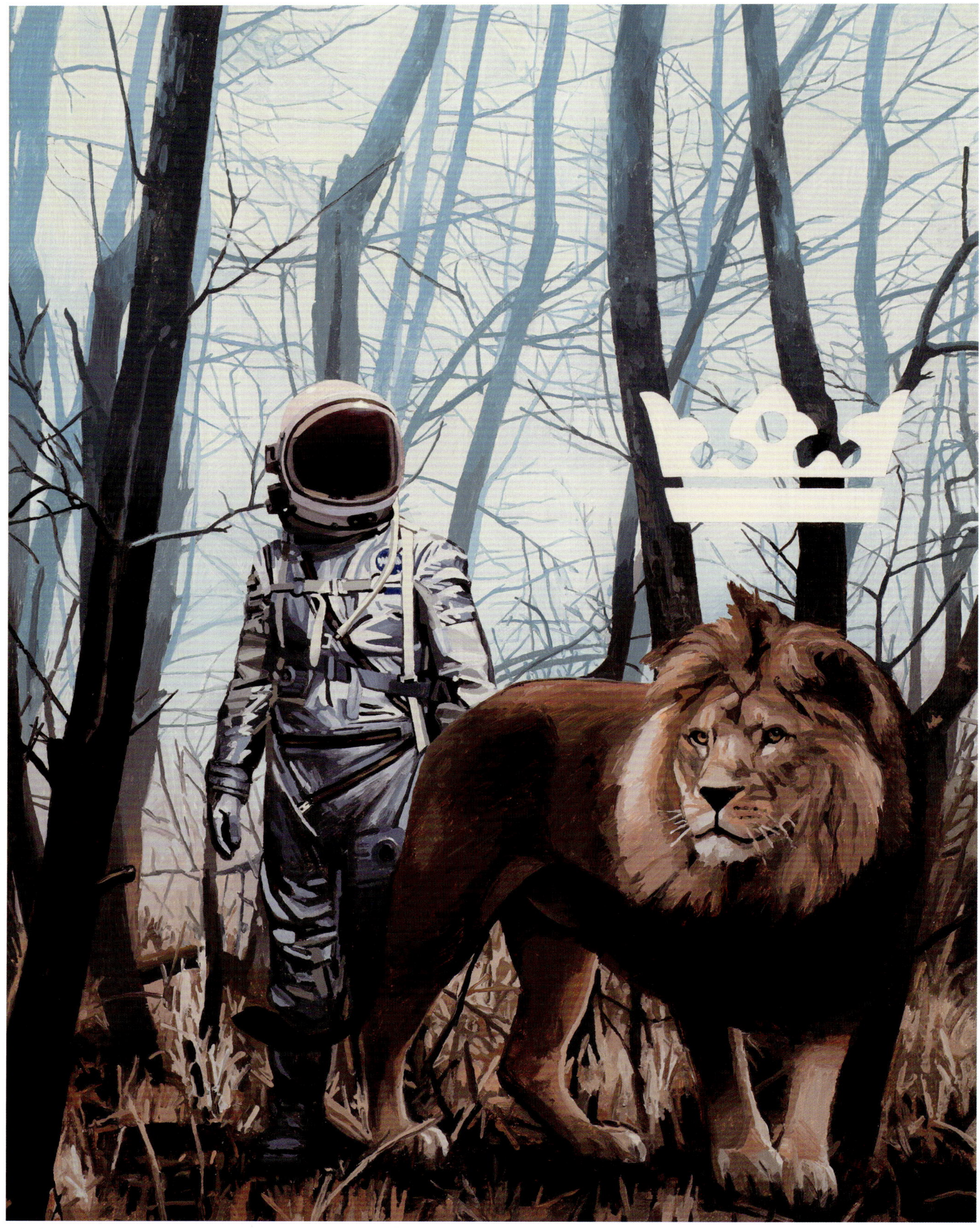

#650

LEO [2023]

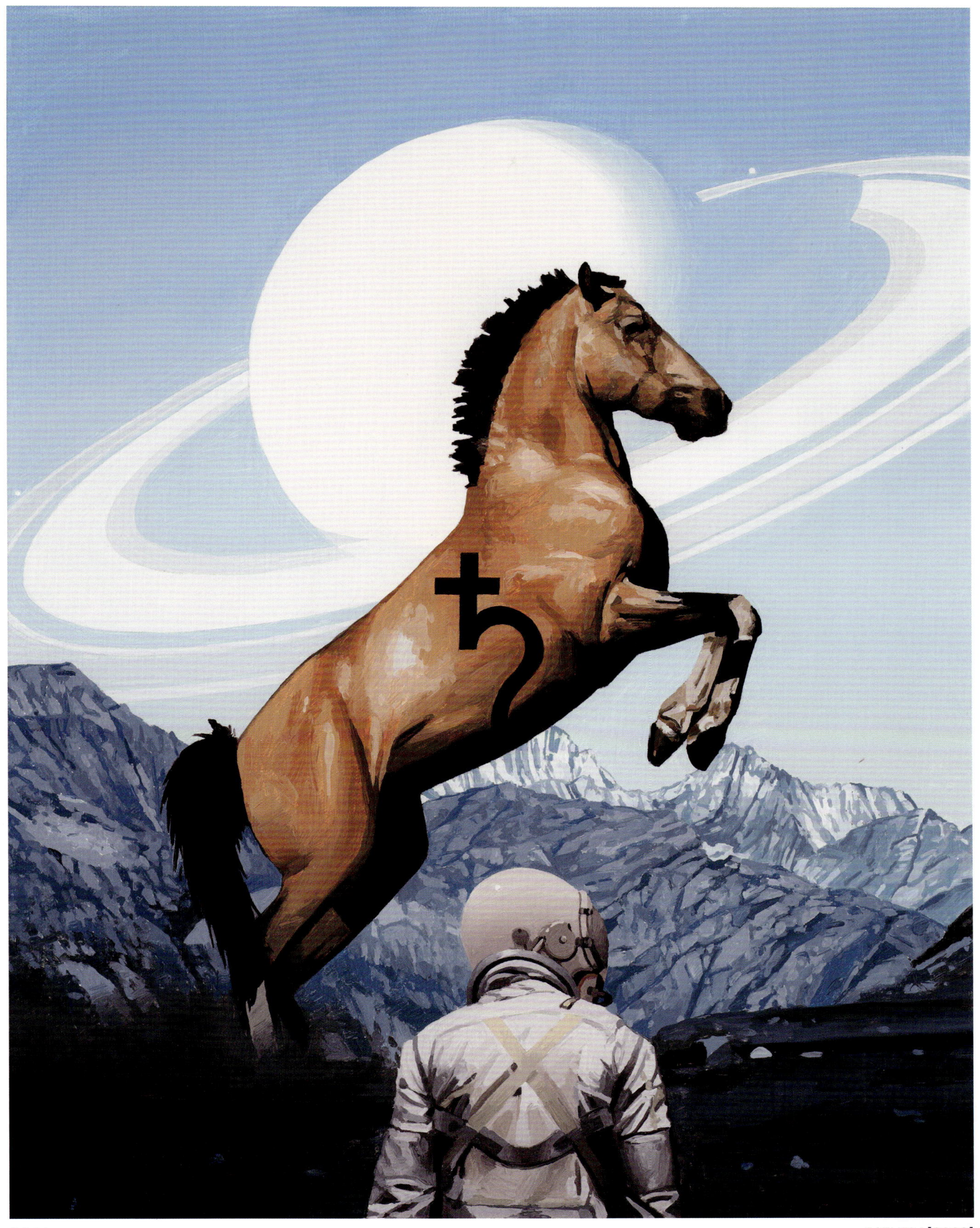

#644

SATURN [2023]

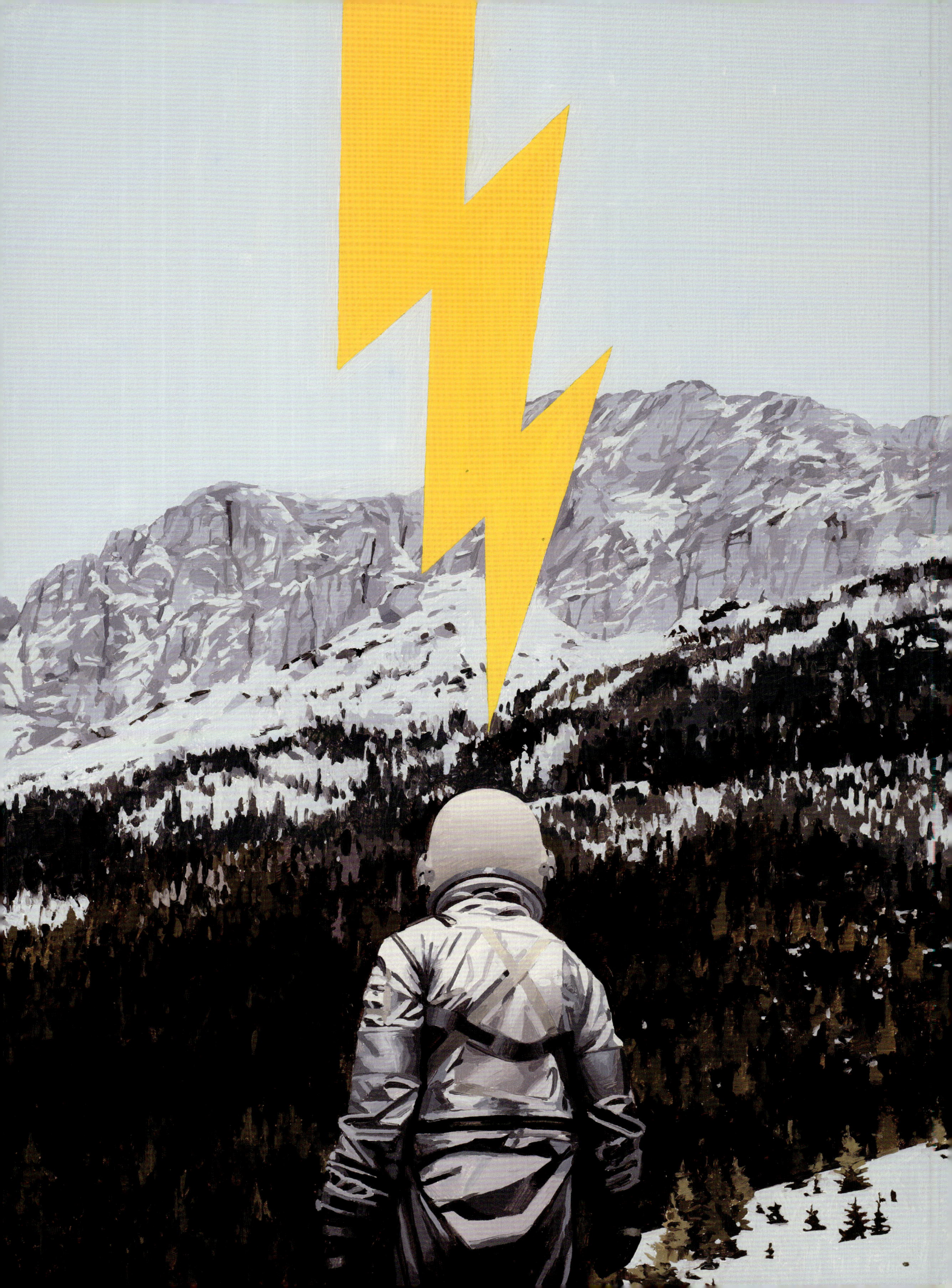

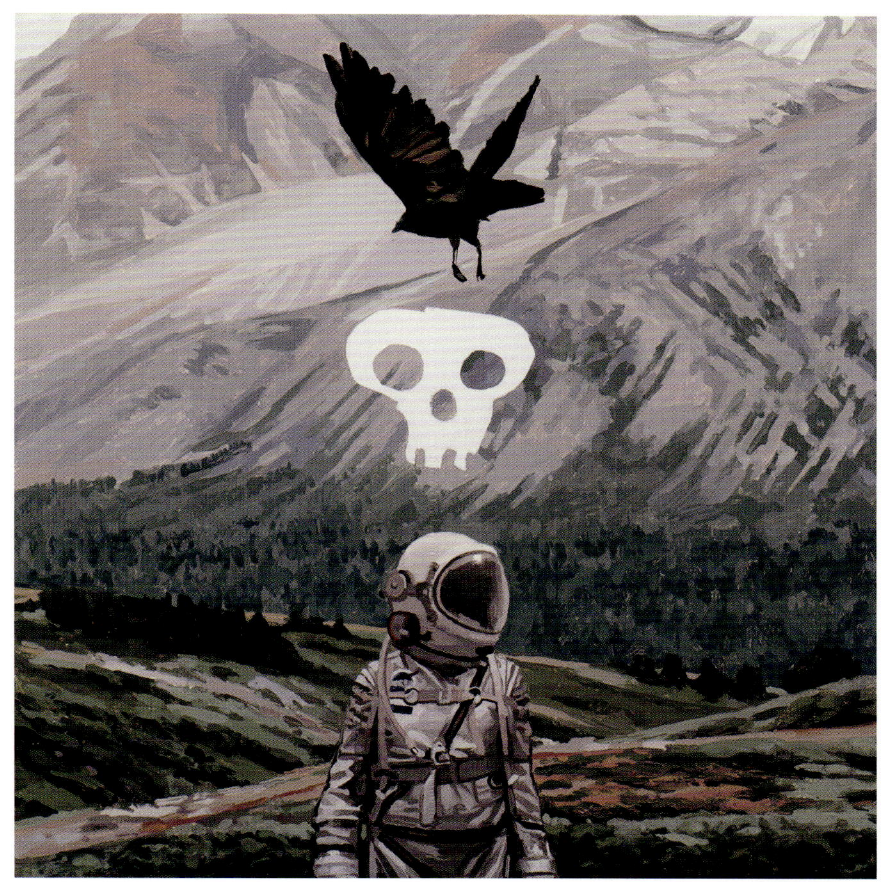
#647 SKULL [2023]

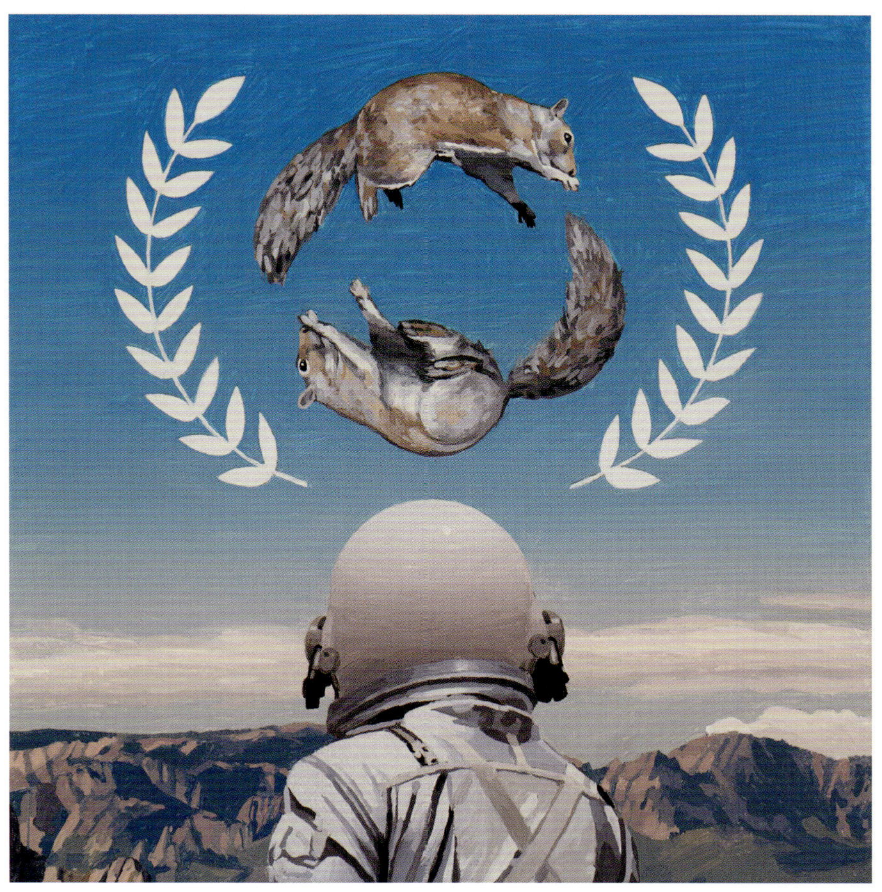
#646 SQUIRRELS [2023]

#642
LIGHTNING STRIKE [2023]

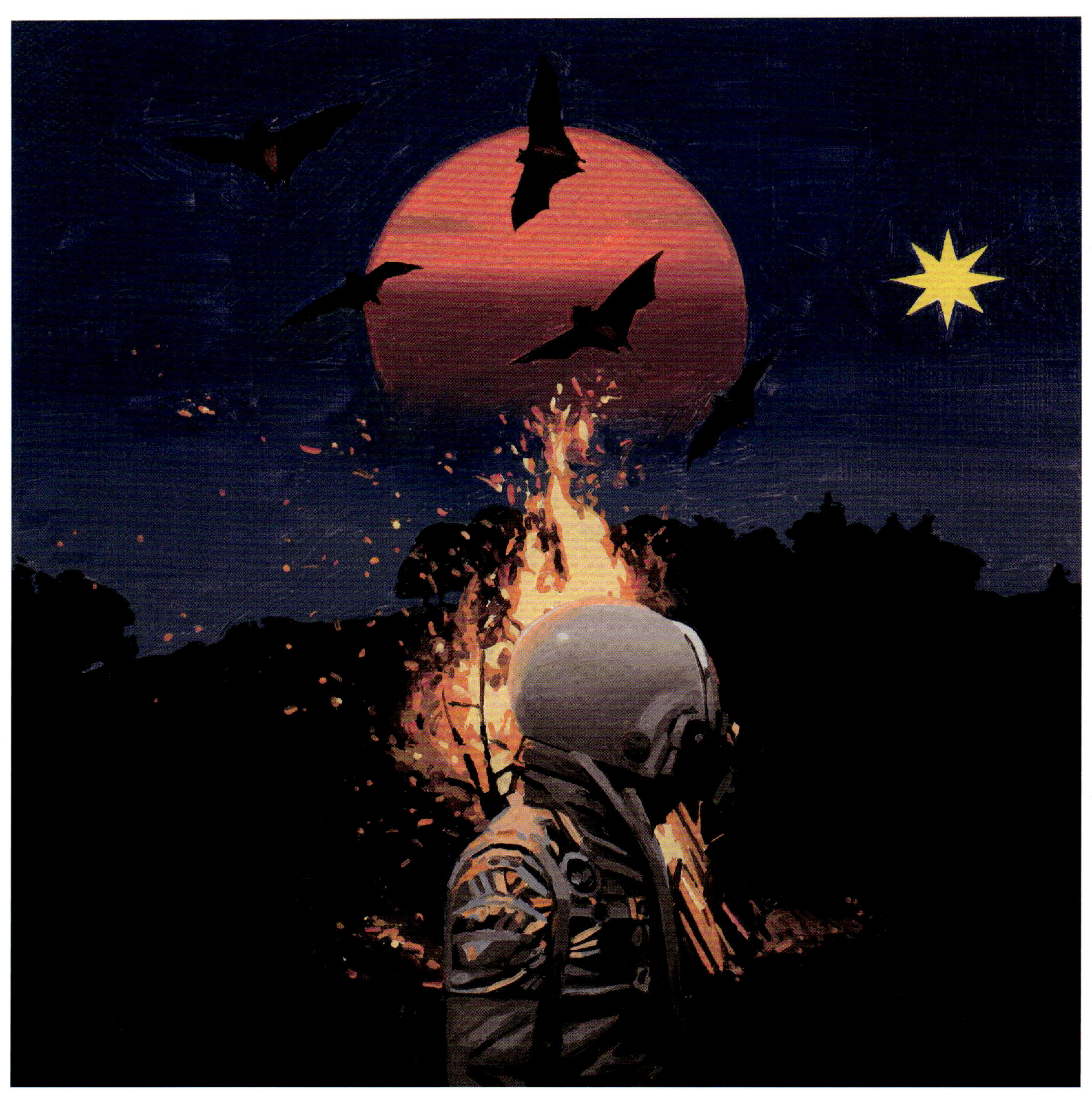

#651 BATS [2023]

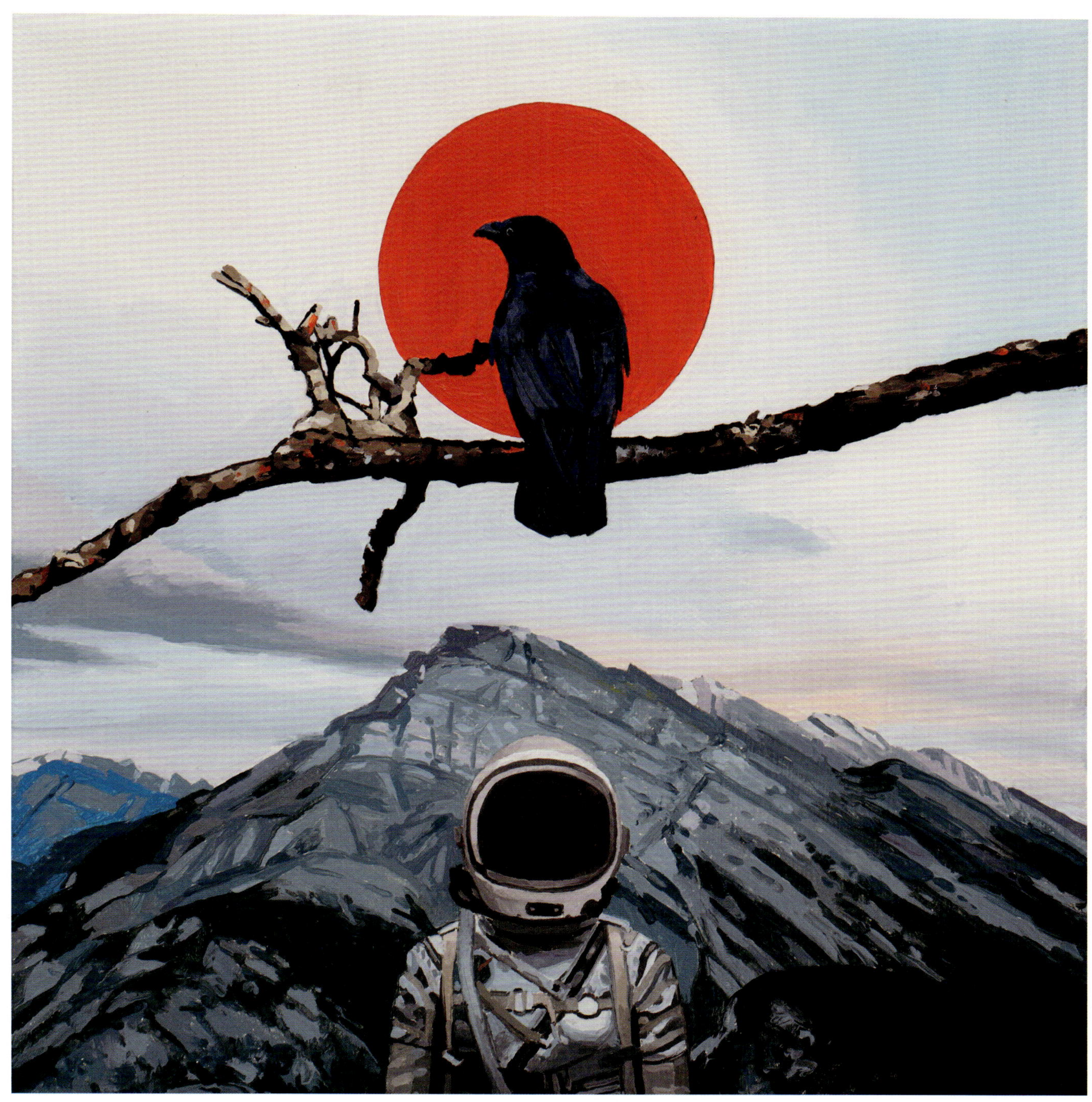

#643

CROW [2023]

I FIND MYSELF IN COPENHAGEN

//////////////////////////////

September, 2023

The name Ostoj appears frequently in my work, usually as a bit of graffiti somewhere, although occasionally in other formats. Many people have noticed this and asked me about it, and many times I have answered, but I never mind doing it again.

I've talked about him already in this book, but in case you're skipping around, I'll give you a brief recap. Chris Ostoj was a friend of mine from college. More of a mentor, really, as he was two years older than me and far more worldly. Sadly, he passed away young, at a time when the idea of a friend dying was an entirely foreign concept to me. Unsurprisingly, I took it hard. As one does. But his loss is what inspired me to get serious about my art career. It was a major turning point in my life. And so I continue to paint him into my work. In a small way, he lives on in my paintings.

In 2004, not long after his death, I made a painting of my astronaut tending a small cactus farm in Yucaipa, California, which is how Chris spent his last days. In the painting, I pinned a copy of Matisse's *The Green Line (portrait of Madame Matisse)* to the wall. Chris loved Matisse and we had many conversations about this particular painting. For him it personified the absolute mystery of how paint can work in the hand of a great artist.

Many years later, in my 2022 show *Multiverse*, I revisited this idea again, painting *The Green Line* one more time into a painting that was explicitly about loss and grief and the memory of my friend Chris.

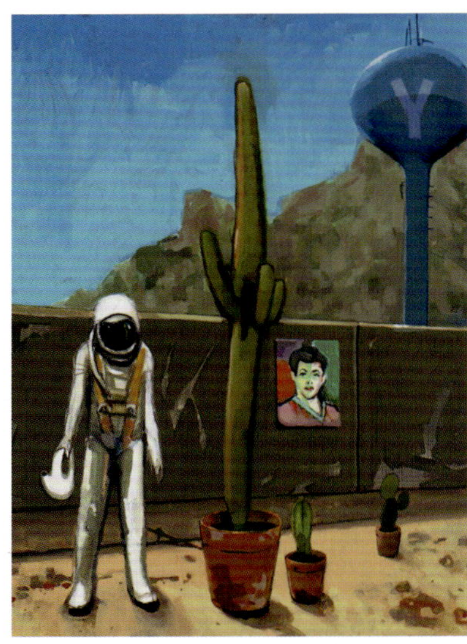

#015 YUCAIPA [2004]

As mentioned in the previous chapter, in the fall of 2023 I found myself traveling in Scandinavia. I was supposed to be making my way towards Oslo for a big show that had just been canceled, for very sad reasons. I was trying to enjoy the trip despite that, with mixed results. This trip reminded me of a time when I was much younger. When I studied in Italy for a semester in college, and would hop a train on the weekend to places I'd never been

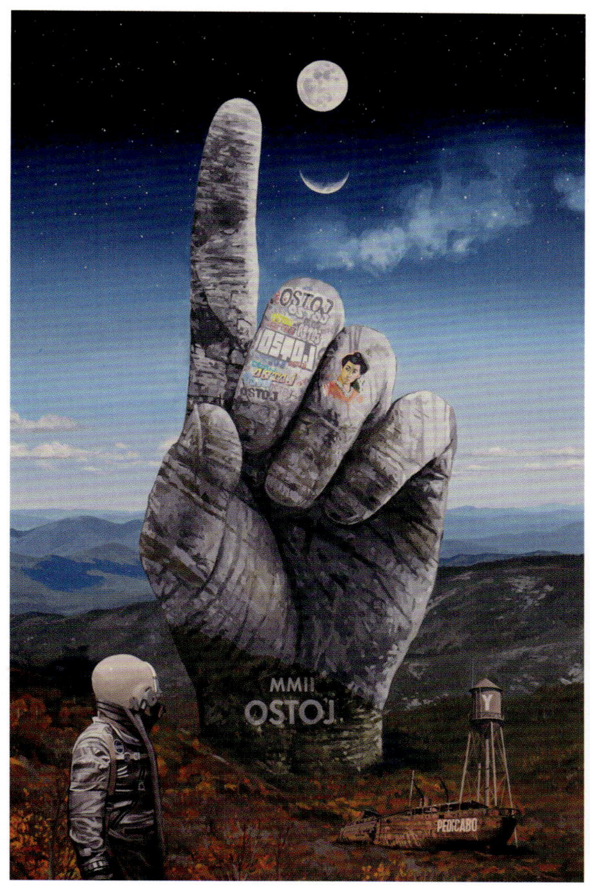

#573

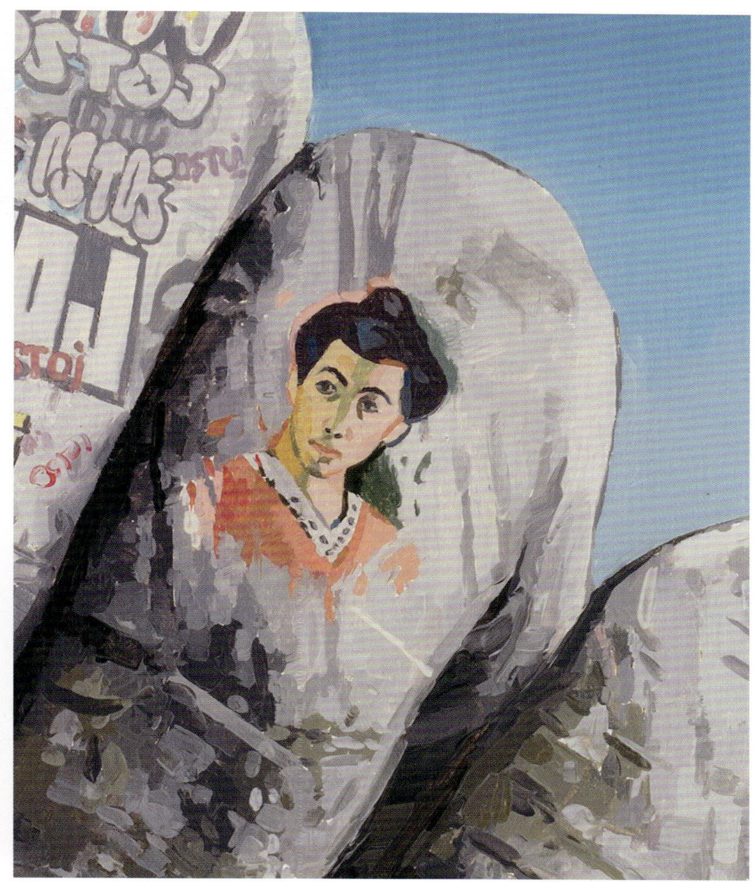

FIRST HAND [2022] W/DETAIL

before and might never visit again. And so nostalgia mixed awkwardly with sadness as I set out across northern Europe.

My journey began in Copenhagen, where I went to the museum of art. As one does. Who do I find there?

Madame Matisse. The Green Line. I stood in front of her and I thought of my friend Chris. I thought of my friend Susannah. I thought of times in my youth where I would travel for days just to see a single painting. Not for the last time on this trip, I wonder if I'm meant to be in exactly this spot at exactly this time. I feel dots start to connect across space and time, and I wonder if it's just my imagination.

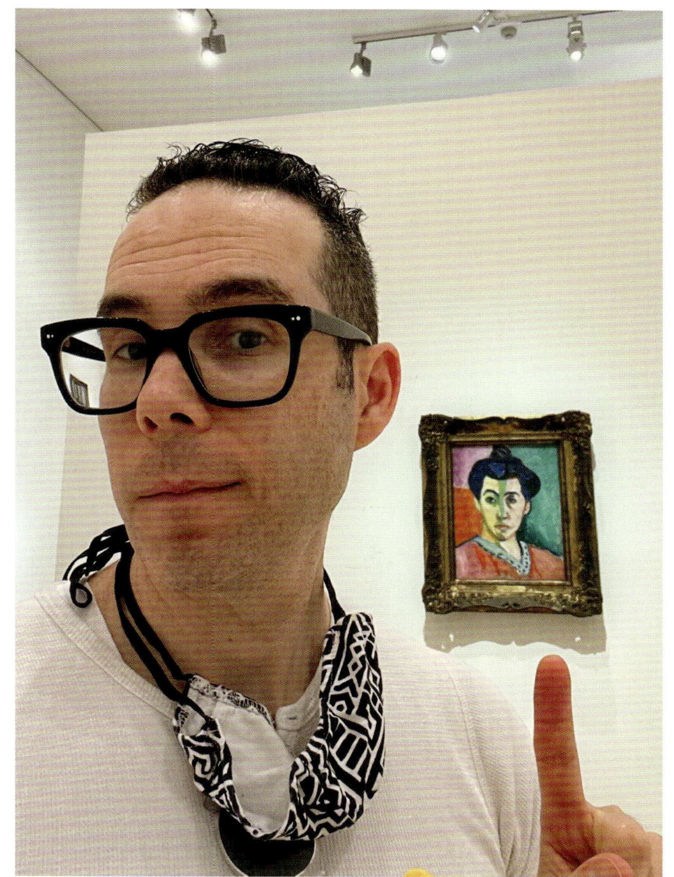

SCOTT LISTFIELD W/
MATISSE'S *THE GREEN LINE*

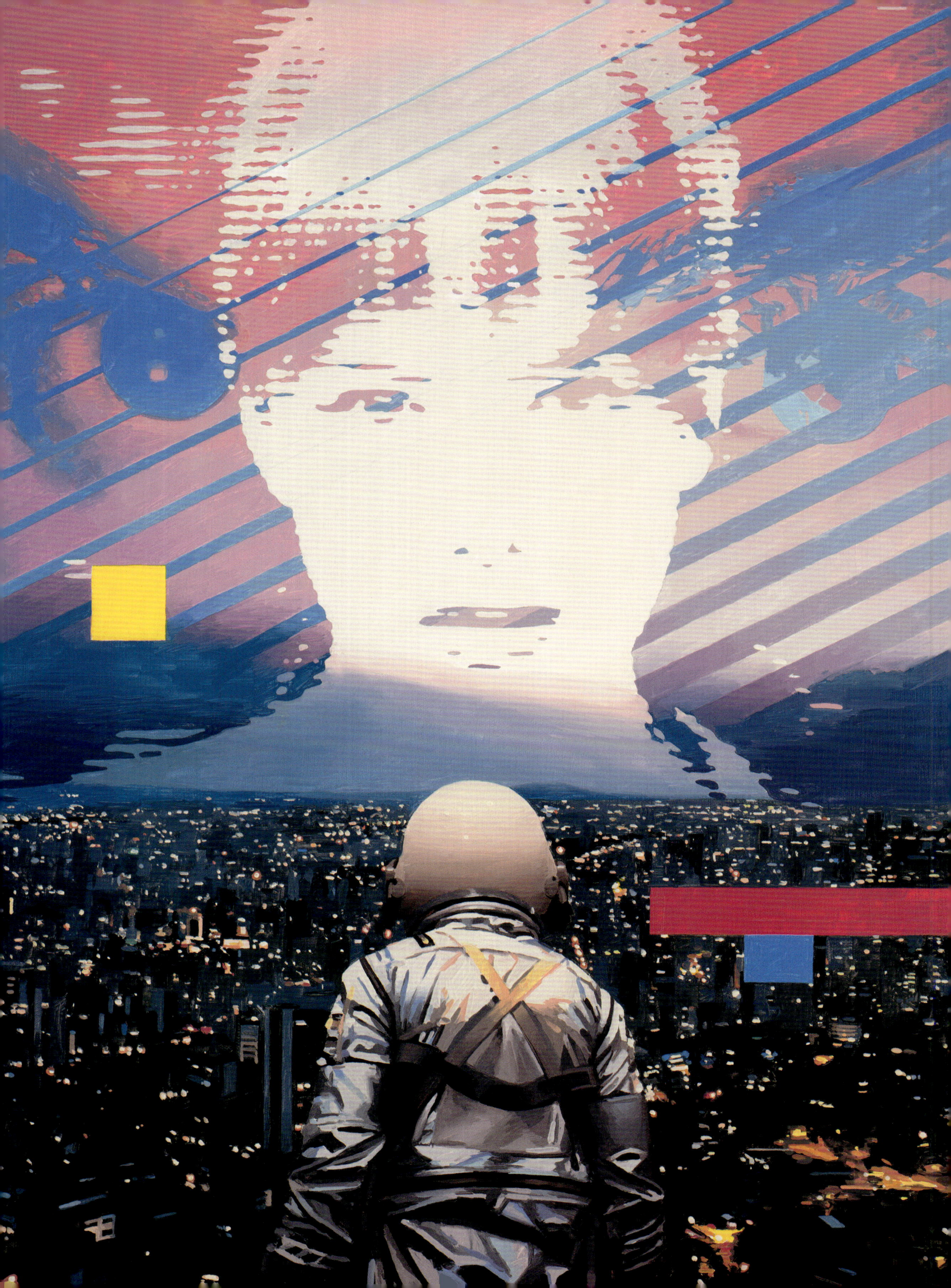

UNREAL

//

Beinart Gallery, Melbourne, Australia
October, 2023

As usual, I've been thinking about the future.

It feels like we're on the cusp of something uncertain, as AI looms and our lives might soon change in unforeseen ways. It felt like the right moment to make a show of paintings about how the lines between our digital lives and our real lives are starting to blur beyond recognition.

Are we living in the last days of human creativity? Will our movies be written by machines and our art created by robots? Will we ever again be able to trust that a photograph is real? That the Wes Anderson movie we are watching was made by Wes Anderson and not a Wes Anderson algorithm? Will I need to make small talk with my smart appliances in order to get them to vacuum the carpets, to wash the dishes, to not send a nuclear strike against Omaha, Nebraska?

I don't have the answer to any of these questions, and I'm not sure anyone else does, either. But it sure does feel right now like we're at the end of something, and the beginning of something else, doesn't it?

#652
THE CITY HAS EYES [2023]

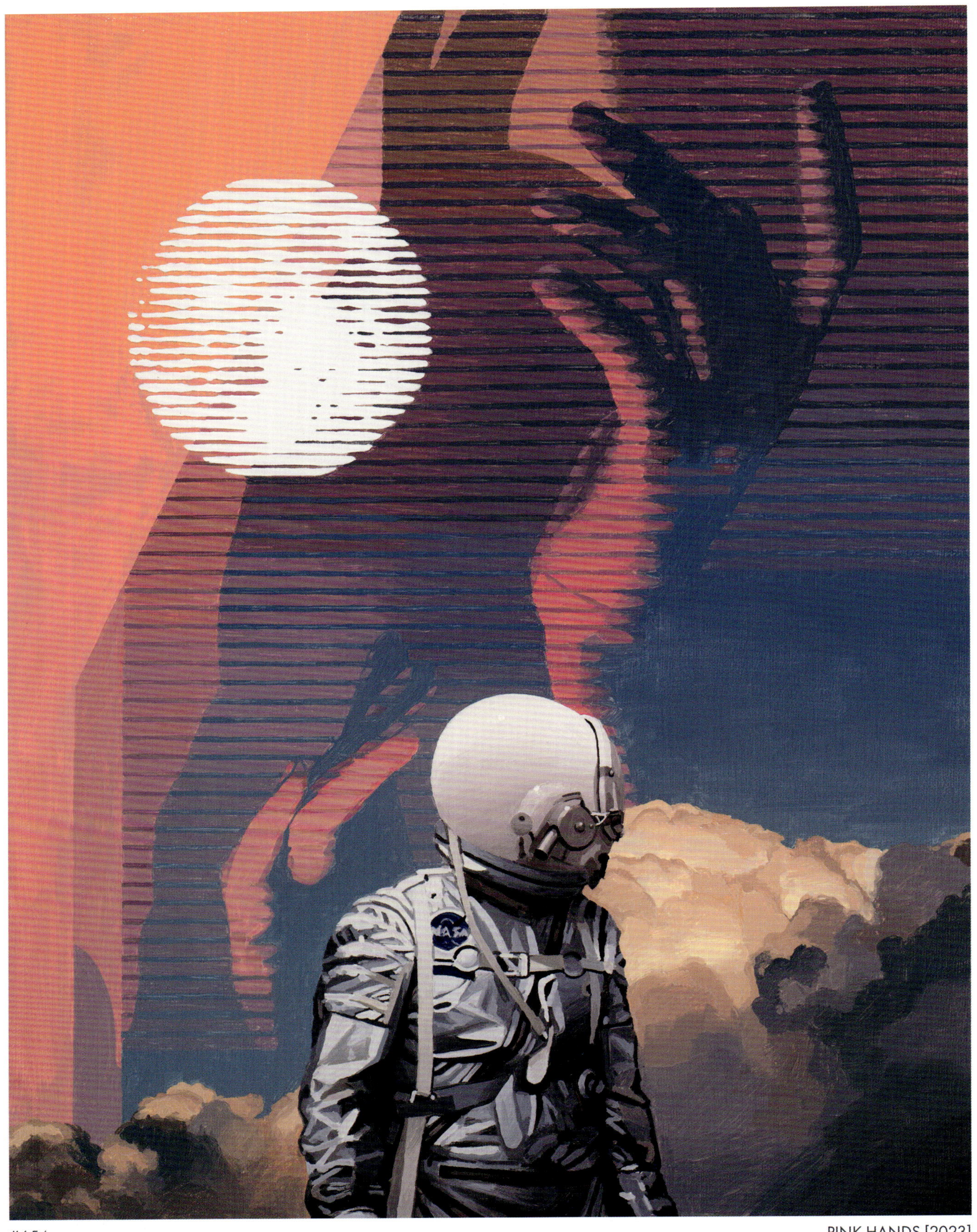

#654

PINK HANDS [2023]

#664

HEAD IN THE CLOUDS [2023]

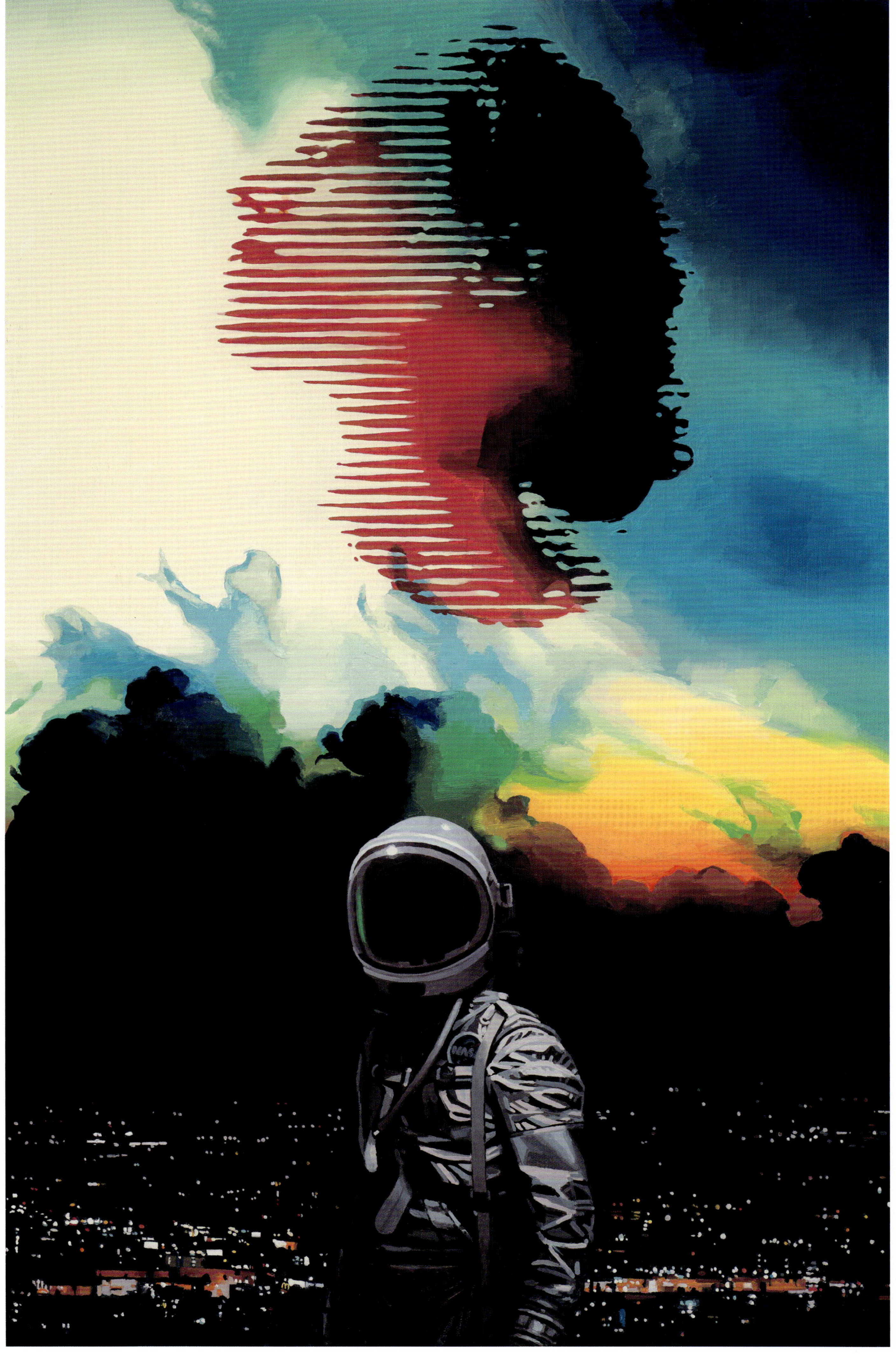

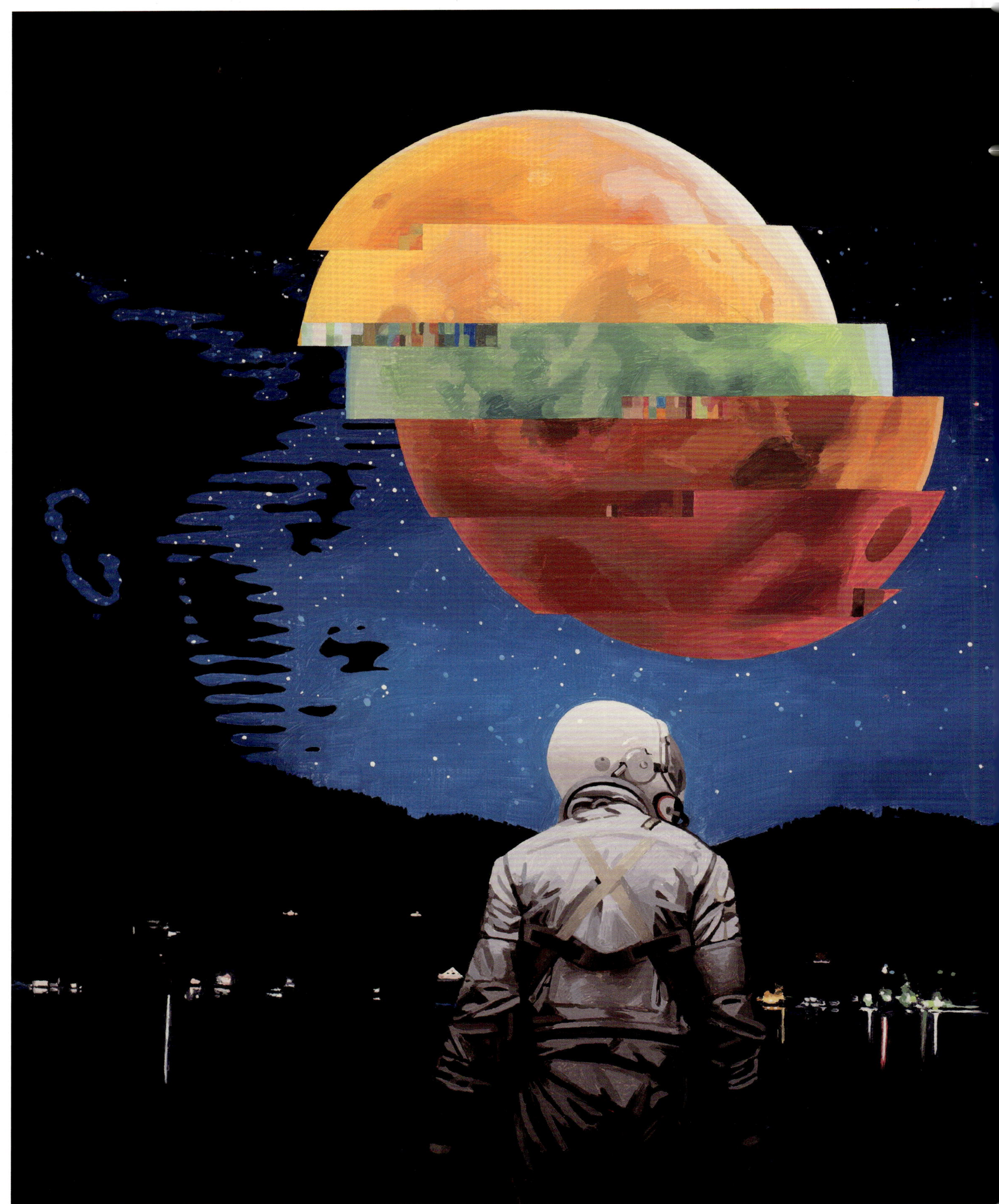

#653 SPLIT MOON [2023]

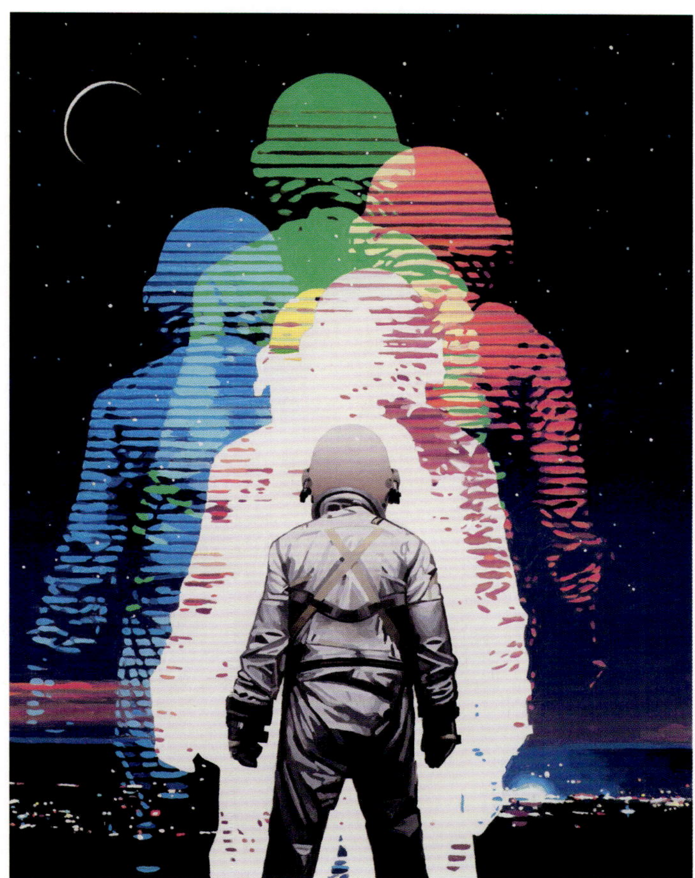

#659 MULTIPLICATION [2023]

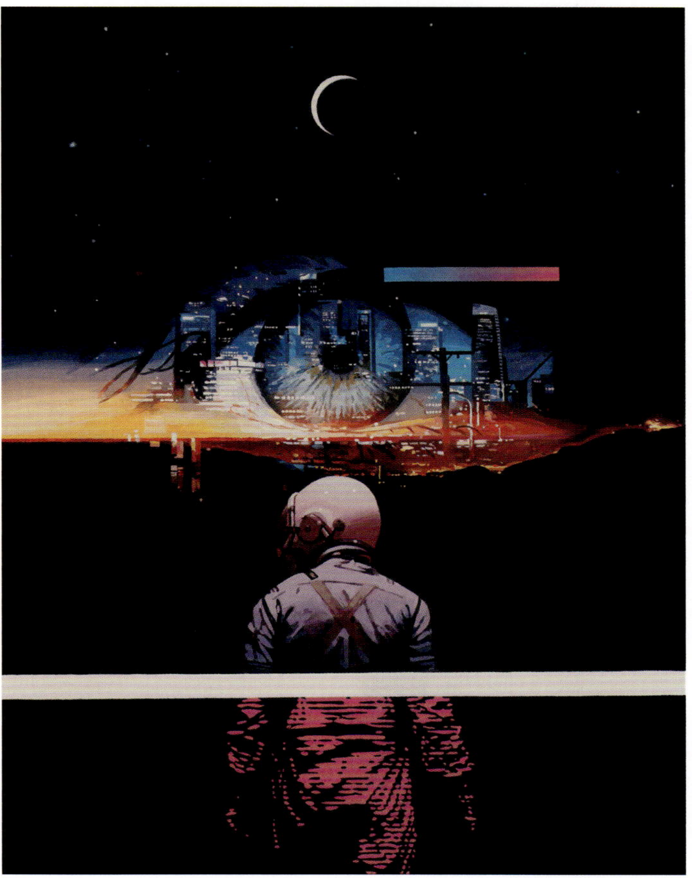

#662 GOODNIGHT [2023]

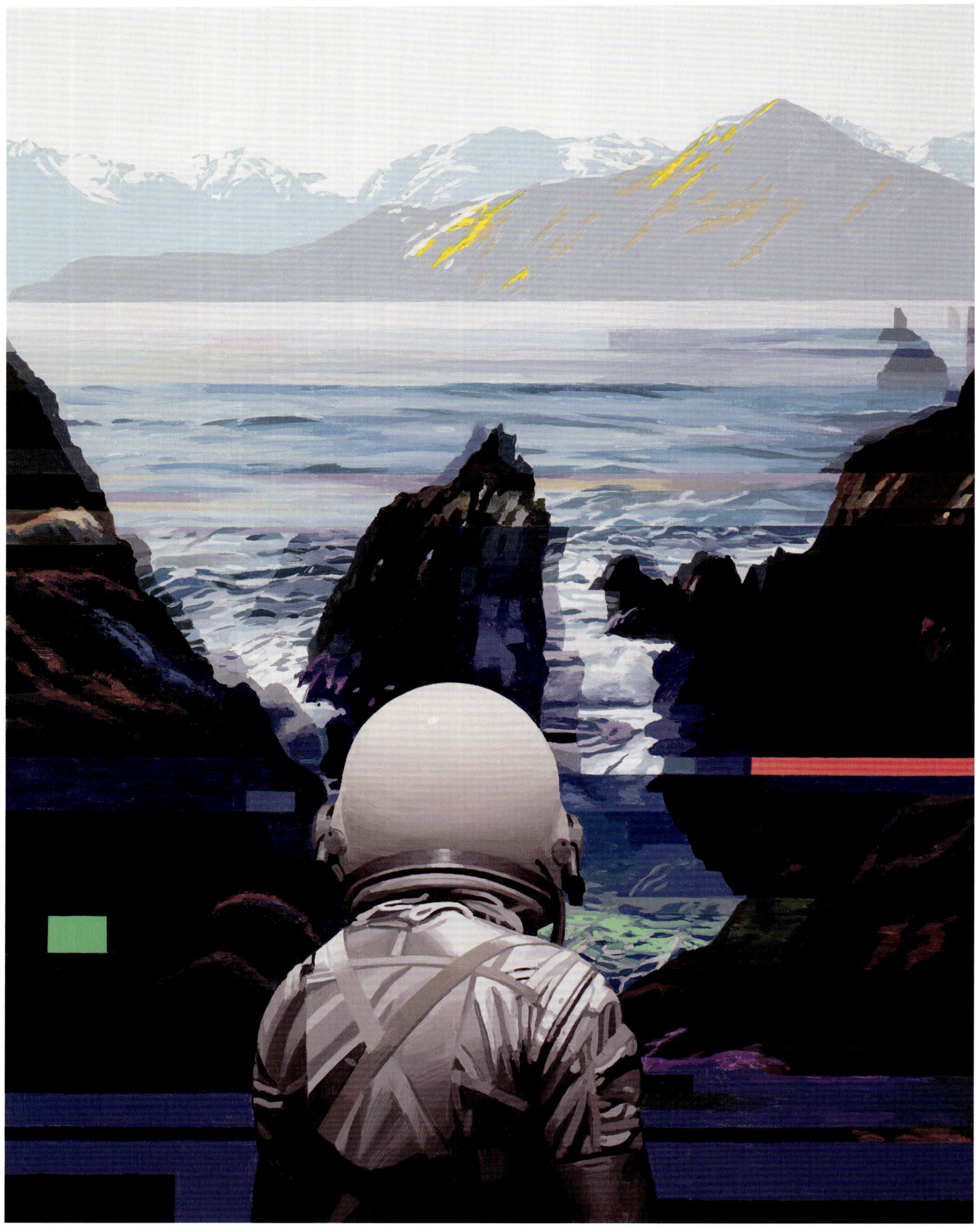

#661 CRASHING WAVES [2023]

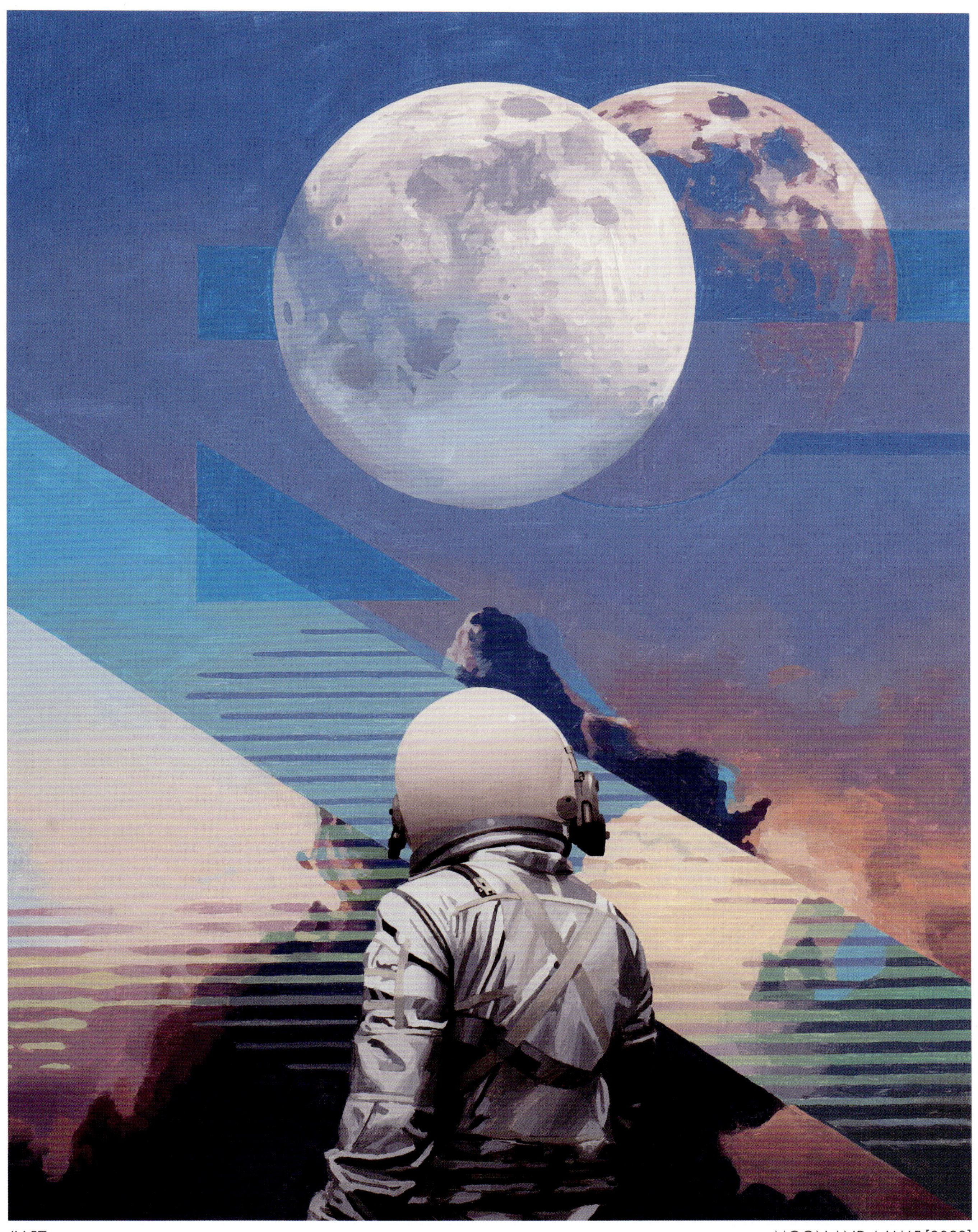

#657

MOON AND A HALF [2023]

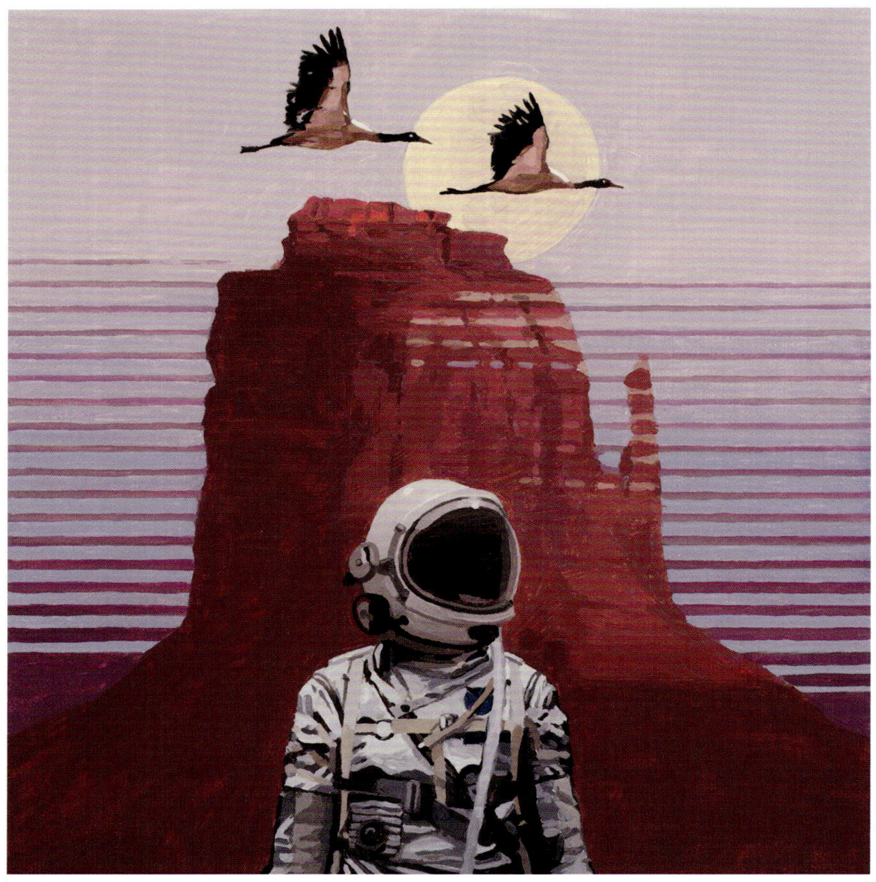

#656 TWO BIRDS [2023]

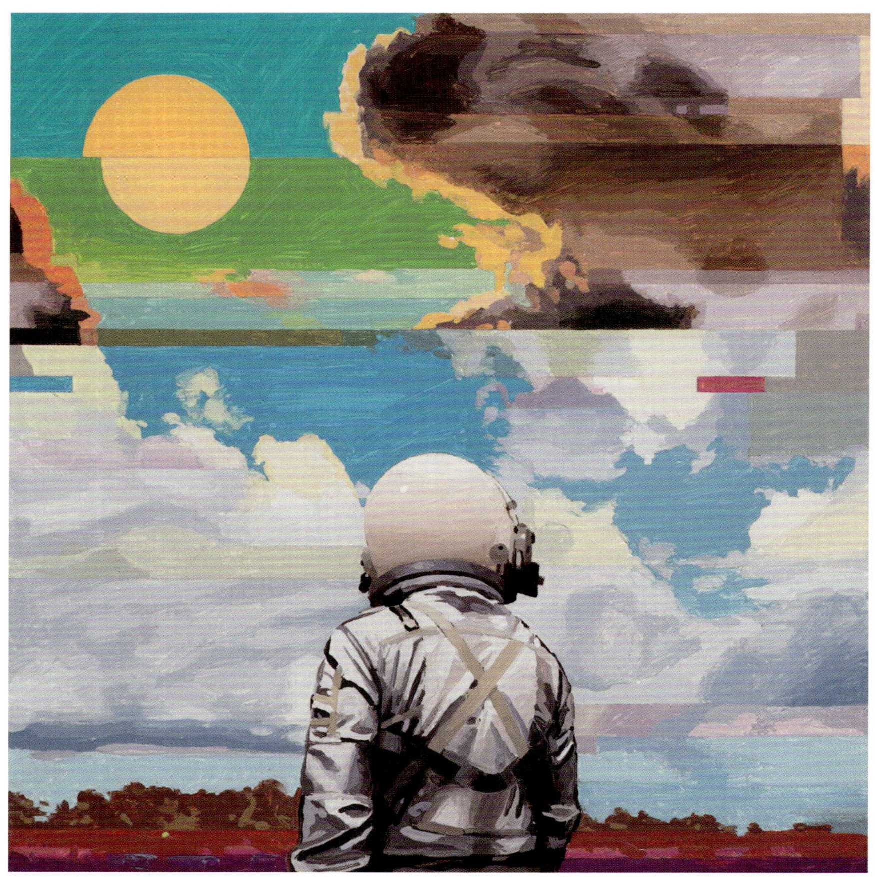

#658 GREEN & ORANGE MORNING [2023]

#655
KABOOM [2023]

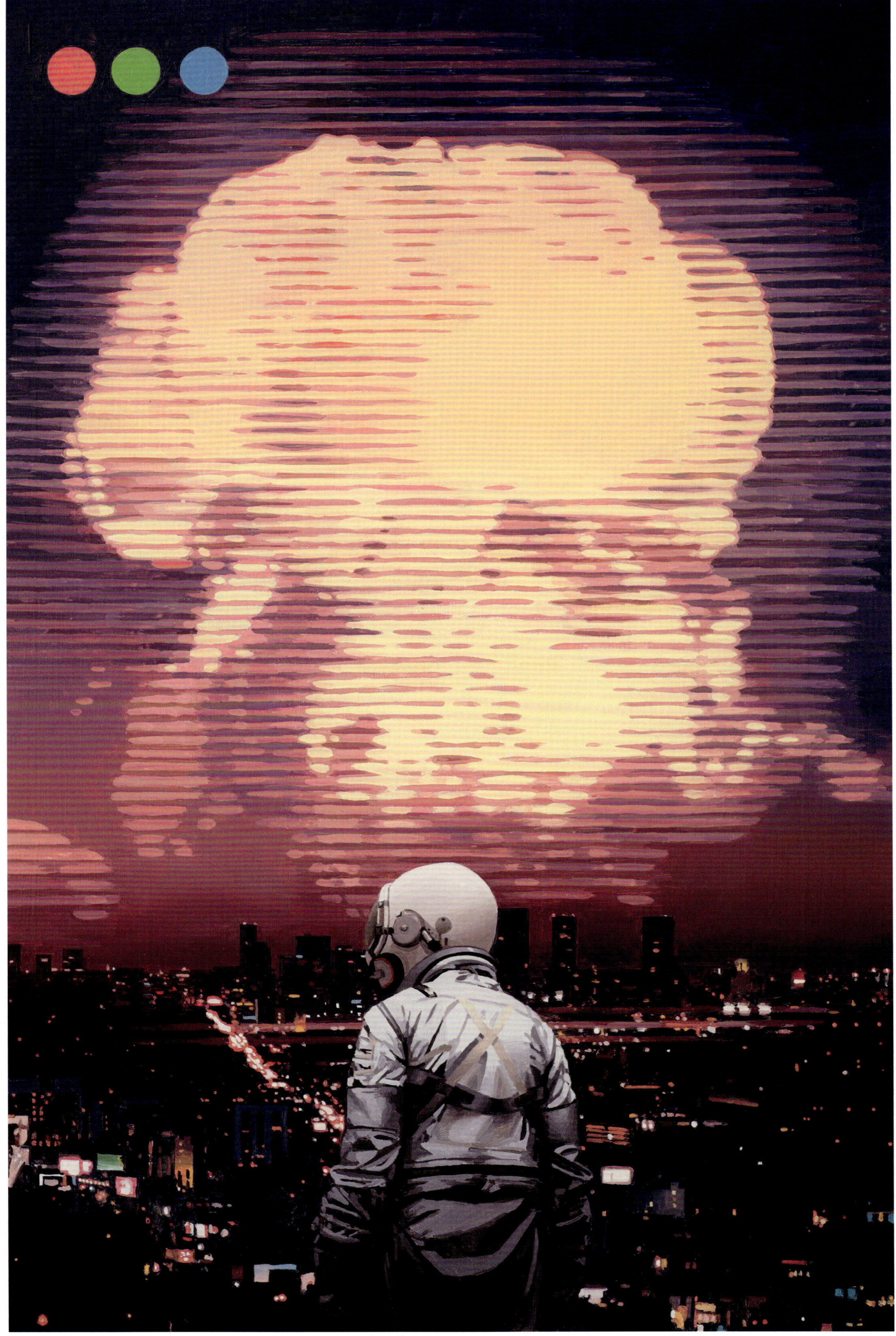

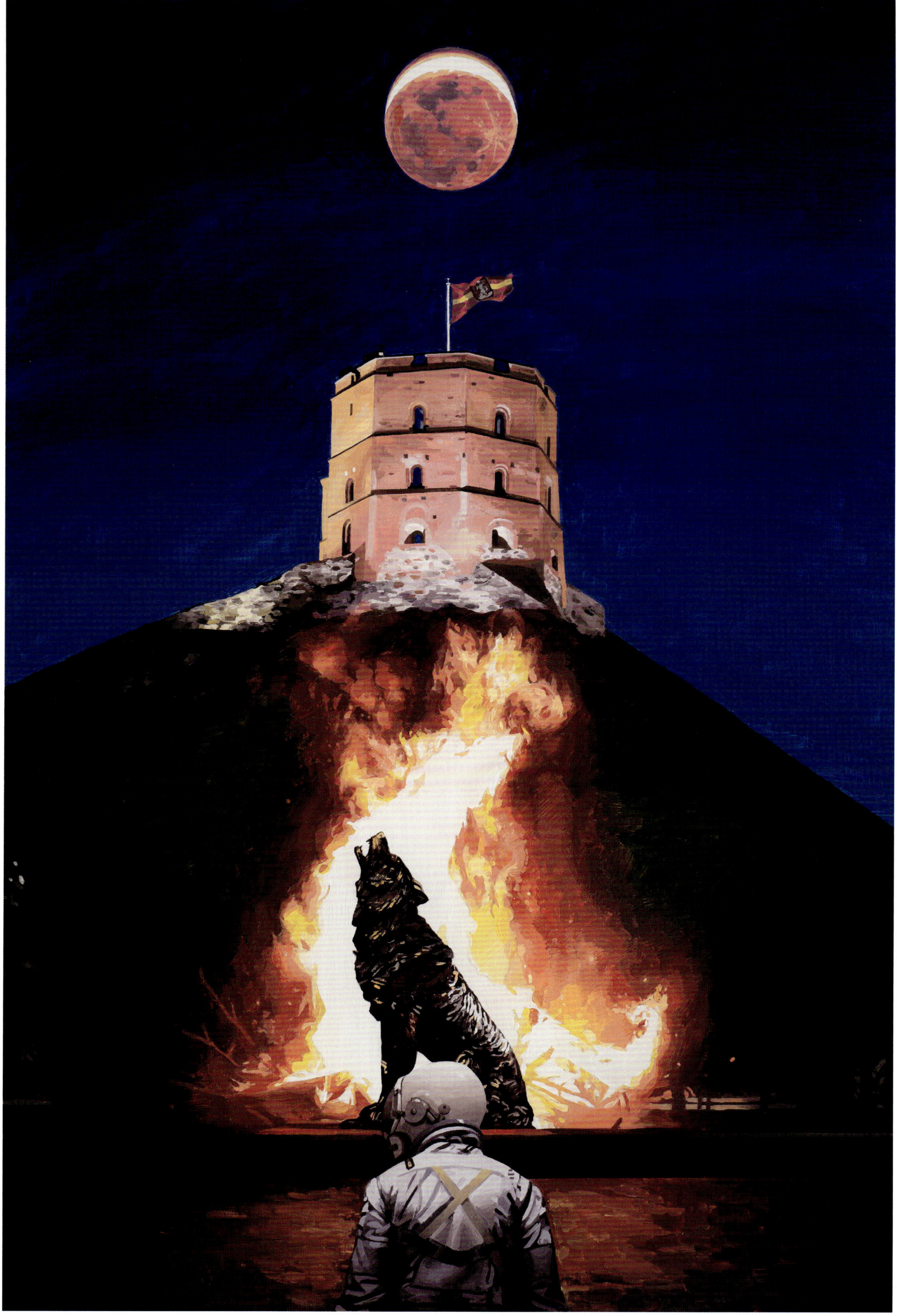

THE EQUINOX

StolenSpace Gallery, London, UK
April, 2024

Here's a story about a wolf.

It begins a long time ago when a much younger version of me went off to Europe for the first time. I studied in Italy. I walked cobblestone streets. So many cobblestone streets. I rode trains and saw places I might never see again. I came home and those journeys eventually inspired me to paint astronauts.

Last fall I traveled to Europe again. I began in Copenhagen, and spent the next 10 days heading north, first to Malmö and Gothenburg, in Sweden, and then on to Oslo, Norway for a gallery show I was supposed to be having. A show which I found out just a few days before I was supposed to leave, had been canceled. Well, delayed. To a time and place that wasn't Oslo. This all happened for a very sad and extremely valid reason but it left me traveling Europe, alone, on a trip that suddenly had no real purpose. But it was about to find one.

From Oslo I flew to Riga, Latvia and met up with my brother Jeff at the airport, who had arrived just before me from Boston. We spent the next week traveling through Latvia and Lithuania to the places where our ancestors once lived. Through smallish towns and bigger cities. I didn't really have any preconceived notions as to how this part of the trip would go. There would probably be no long lost Listfield cousins to find. No one in my family is left in this part of the world. I guess I wanted to see where I come from. I wanted to walk the same cobblestone streets my ancestors once did. I didn't necessarily expect anything profound to happen. It did though.

Our trip ended in Vilnius, Lithuania's very charming capital city. Arriving late, and tired from the road, we wound up by chance walking along the river that winds its way through the center of town. The sun was setting, and it was a mild September night. People were about. Lots of people. So very many people. My brother noticed it first: something was happening. We found ourselves amongst a large crowd. That's when we saw the wolf.

On the riverbank just ahead of us was a large statue of a wolf. Looming over it was an ancient castle tower, lit dramatically from below and perched precariously on a hill. As the last bit of sunlight faded, the wolf spoke.

I don't speak Lithuanian, but some quick googling revealed that the wolf was sharing the story of the

#676
THE EQUINOX [2023]

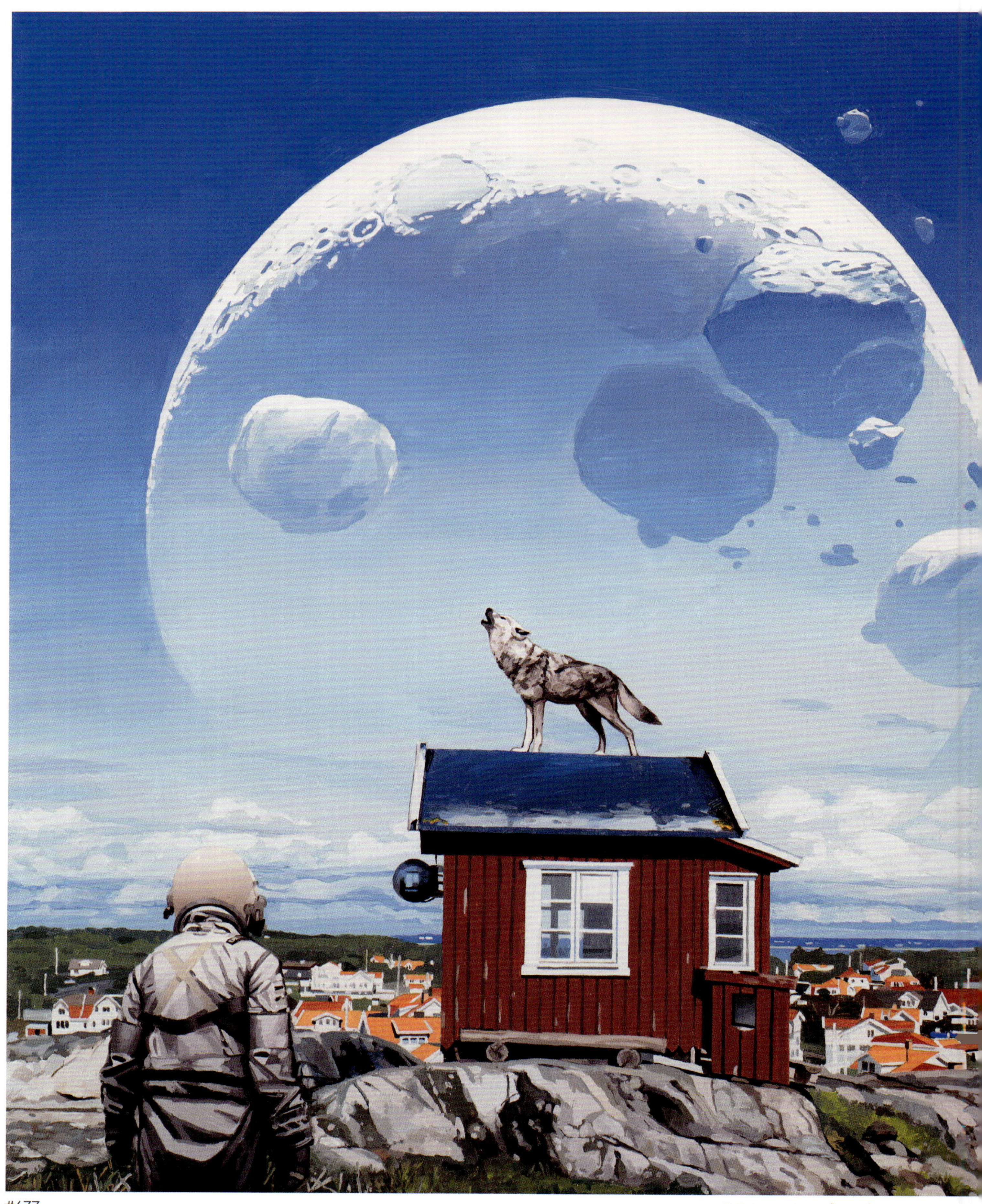

#677

THE RED HOUSE [2024]

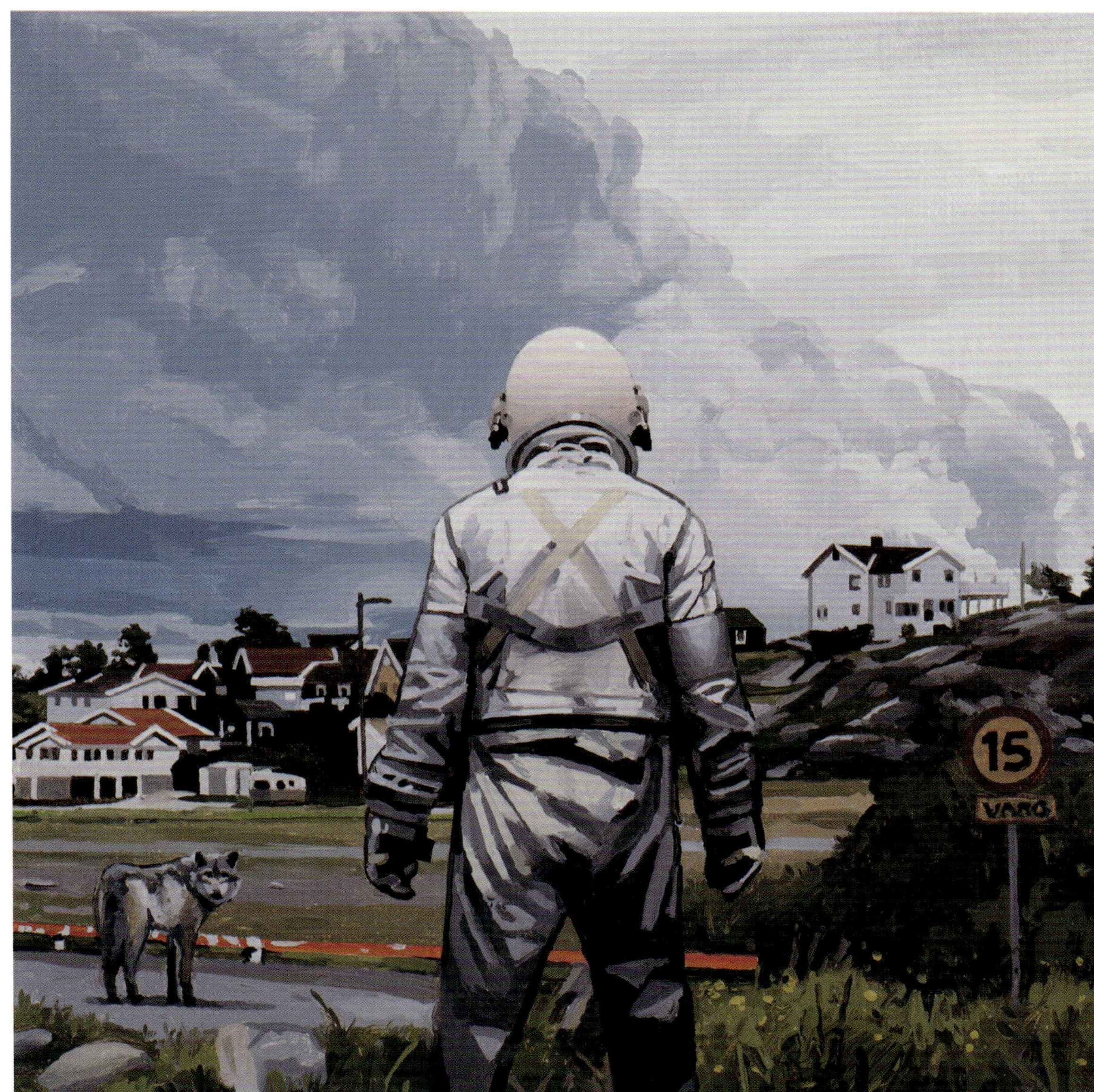

#680 ON THE ISLAND [2024]

founding of Vilnius. It spoke in a booming voice, with occasional pauses as music swelled. Fire from an unknown source danced around the bottom of the wolf and eventually, as the night wore on, it was engulfed in flames. Smoke and hot ash fell on our faces. I wondered if we were a safe enough distance away.

As the fire subsumed, we wandered off, dazed, along the river bank with hundreds of Vilnius residents. We had just celebrated the fall equinox and the 700th anniversary of the founding of Vilnius. It felt like we had just been part of something very primeval. I felt Lithuanian. I felt pagan. I felt wolf. I returned to my hotel room, ash still on my face.

THE EQUINOX features 9 paintings of an astronaut traveling to some of the places I visited on this trip, accompanied by a wolf who appears in one form or another in each of them. Sometimes as a companion, sometimes as a statue, a relic, a mural, a ghost, or a metaphor.

Epilogue: My third great grandfather was born in the small town of Šėta, Lithuania, sometime around the year 1837. His name was Wolfe.

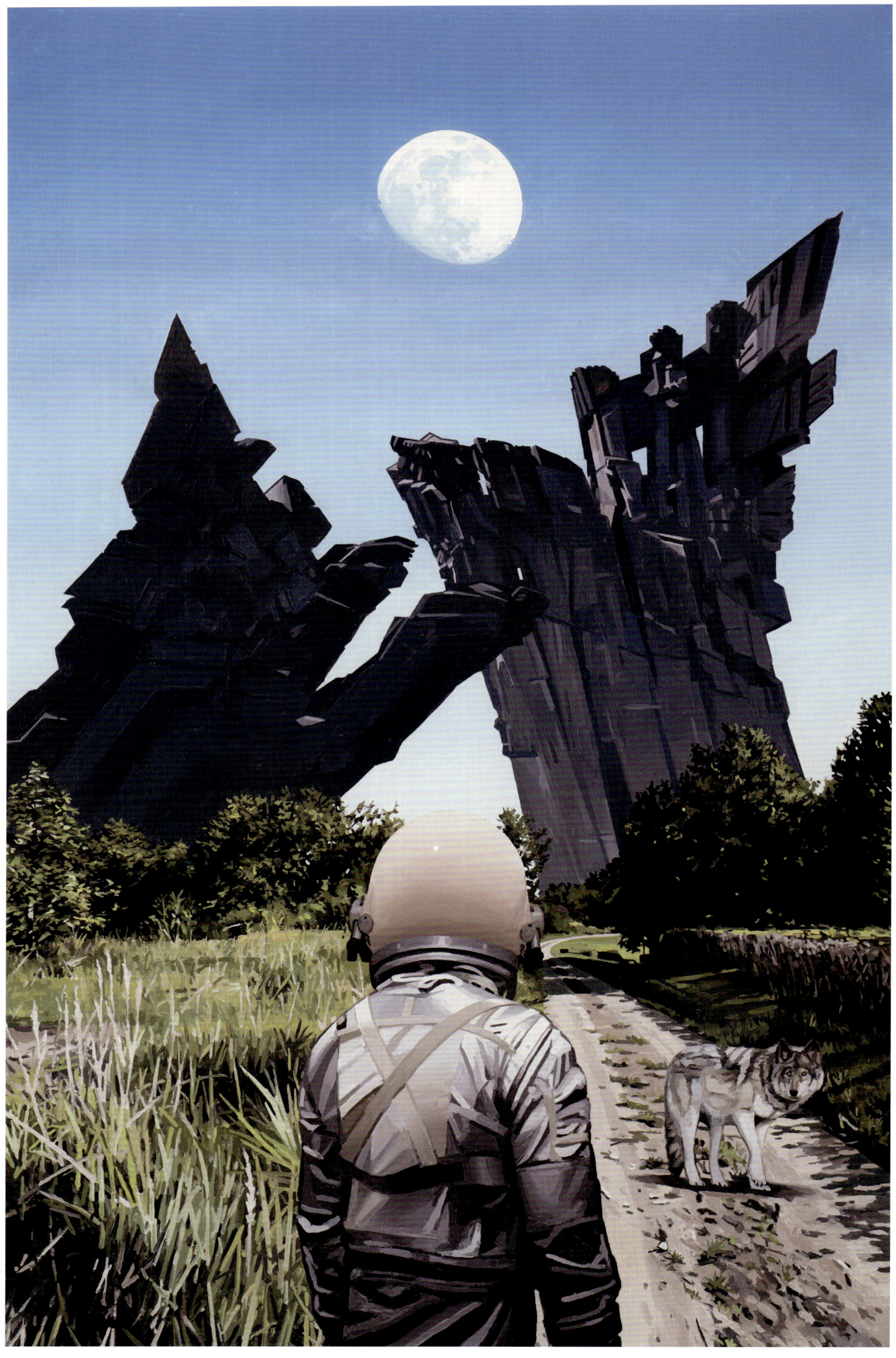

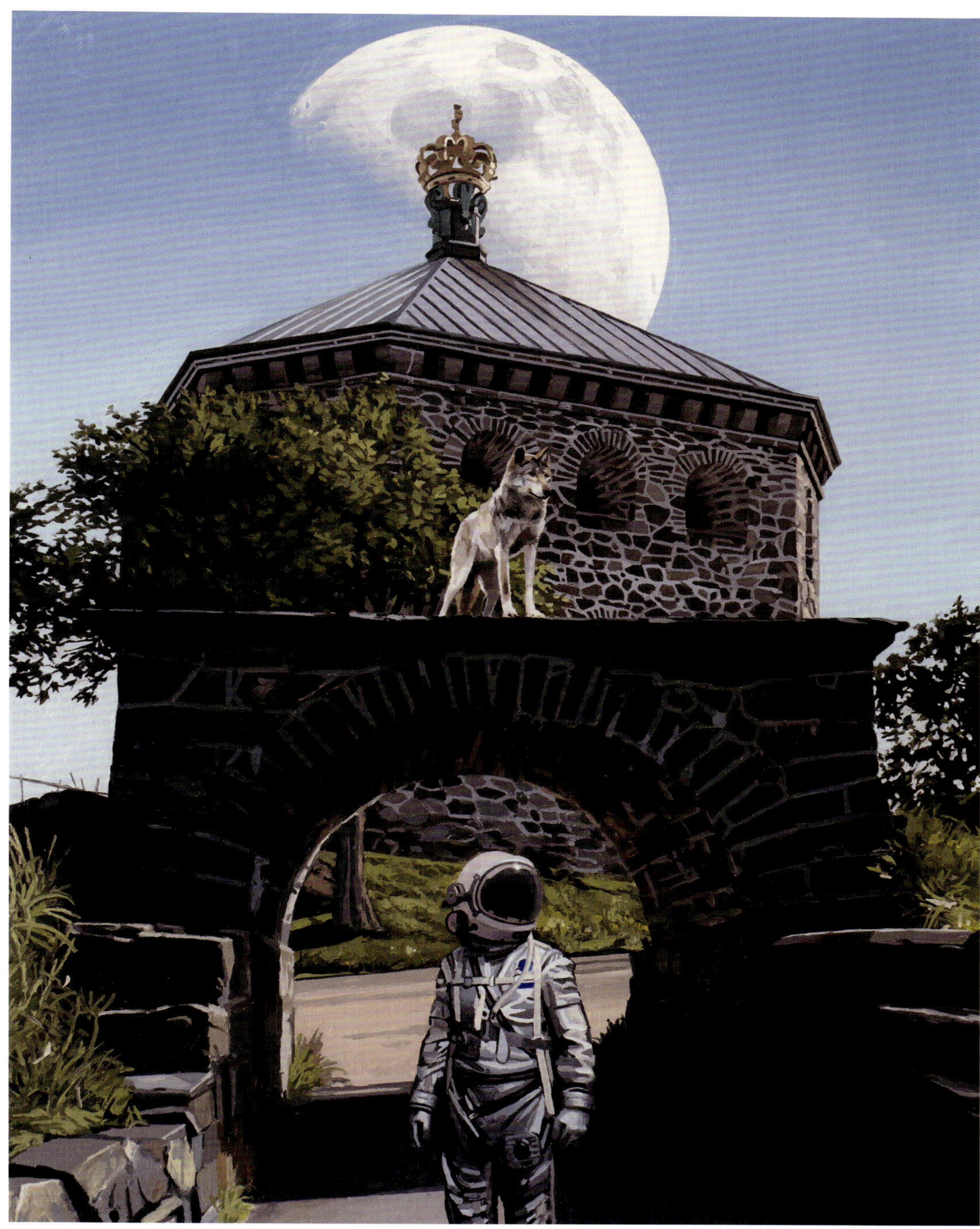

#684 THE ARCHWAY [2024]

Perched high on a hill overlooking the old town in Gothenburg is a fortress. My first day there I climbed the hill, looking for the high ground to get views of the entire city. Gothenburg has countless hills and, to my delight, countless stairways leading up those hills. I spent the day climbing up and down, visiting stone forts and wooden chapels, going over bridges, over canals and streams, and wandering through forested parks. This was still early in my trip and only in hindsight did I feel the presence of a wolf companion. I hadn't yet visited the places where my ancestors were from. But I felt like I was, in a way, retracing the steps of a much younger version of myself. Although I had never been to this part of the world before, I spent a formative part of my life traveling through Europe, largely on my own, and those travels shaped who I am and inspired me to make my very first paintings of astronauts. A lone traveler, lost in a world that is recognizable but not his own. History hangs over this place. It wasn't my history. But now that I've been there and seen it in person, it is.

#682
THE ROAD [2024]

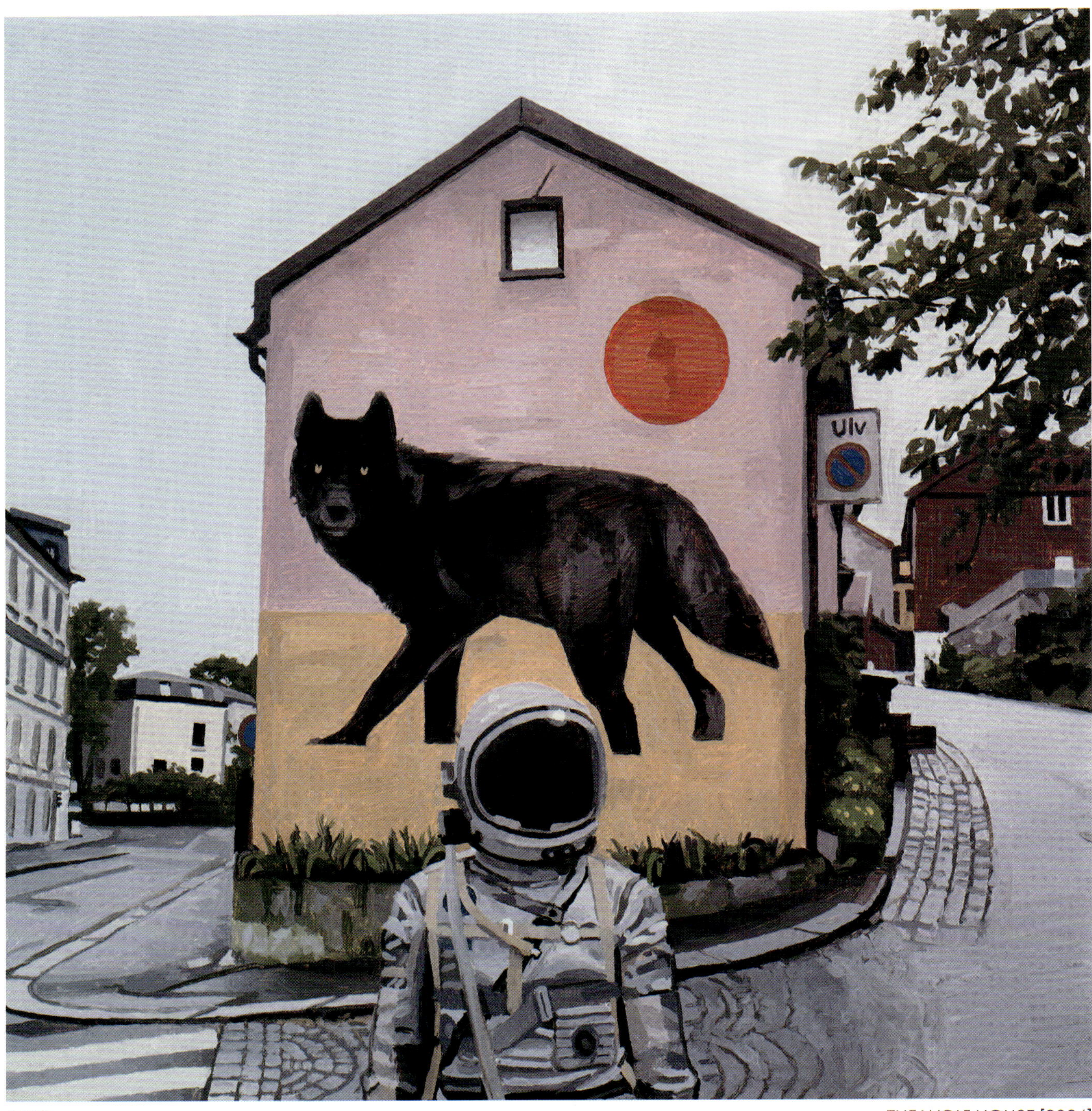

#679

THE WOLF HOUSE [2024]

I arrived in Oslo knowing that the show I was to be having there had already been canceled. Tragedy struck just a few days before I left for Scandinavia. It was too late to cancel my trip, and so I went anyways, trying not to let the sadness and suddenness of that loss hang over me while I traveled. But once I arrived in Oslo, the dark clouds and rain felt like a reminder. It was hard to shake the feeling of sadness hanging over me and the city. But after a day in Oslo, I was joined by Elizabeth Livingston, another artist who was supposed to be in the show. She, too, had bought a plane ticket not knowing the whole thing would be called off, and so both of us, in town for no real purpose, wandered Oslo in the rain. We tentatively talked of the tragedy. She suggested we light a candle in one of the towering cathedrals in town. Despite neither of us being particularly religious, I liked this idea.

We stopped at a local bakery for a light lunch, and then rounded the next corner and found ourselves facing up towards a cobblestone street and a small, brightly painted house. I felt my spirits begin to lift and later that day the clouds began to break and we spotted the sun over Norway for the first time.

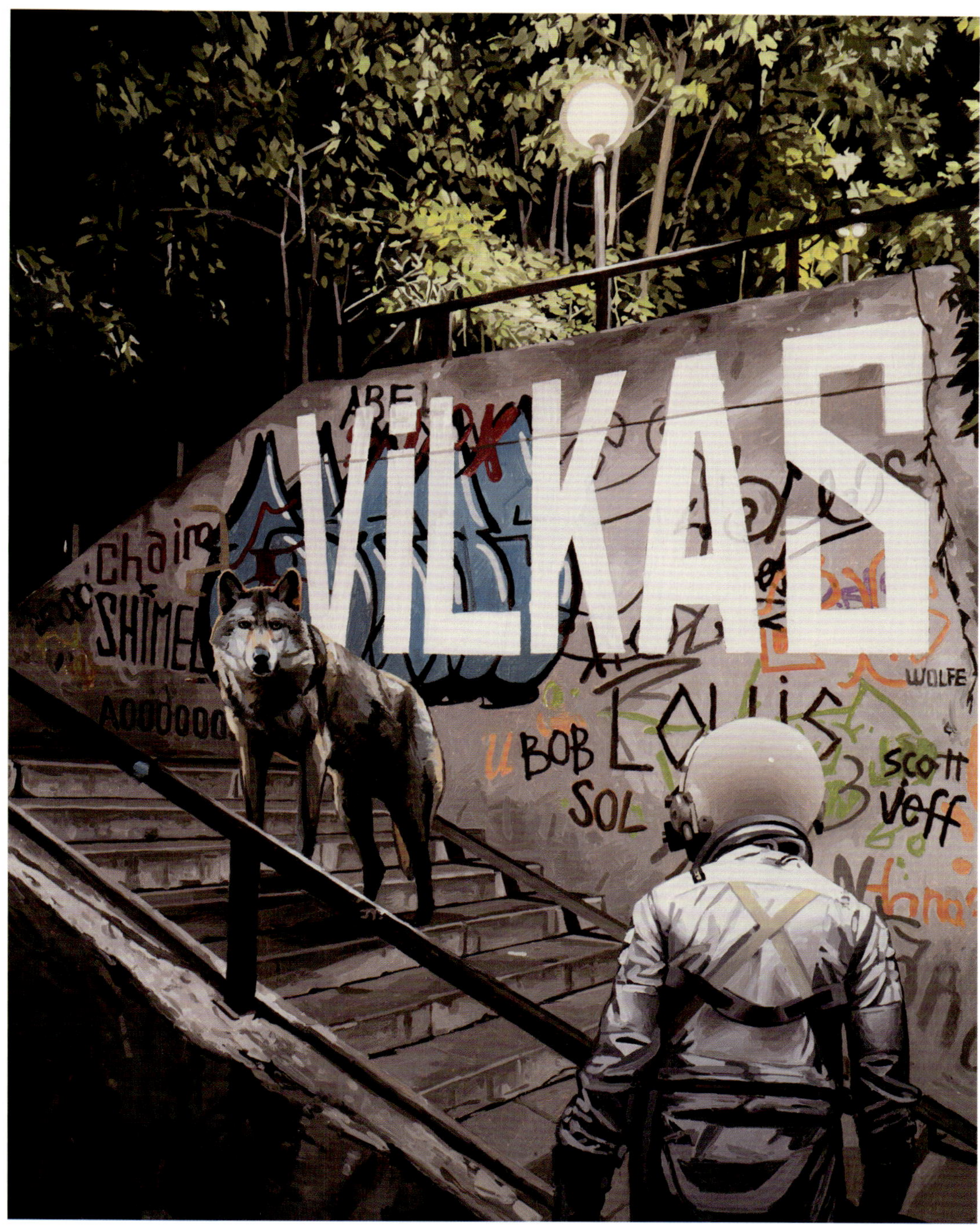

#681

THE STAIRWAY [2024]

People who know me well know that my unusual pastime of choice is to walk stairs. I moved to Los Angeles from Boston in late 2018. When the pandemic hit, and I found myself locked in and bored, I began walking the numerous stairs cut into the hills and mountains near my new home. When I arrived in Kaunas, Lithuania with my brother, after spending the previous days visiting smaller towns where our ancestors once lived, I was excited to find that Kaunas had hills and stairs of its own. I spent our first night there tentatively exploring the ones nearest where we were staying, then my brother joined in the following morning as we explored the city from its highest points, climbing up hills to churches, monuments, statues, and overlooks, occasionally hopping an old funicular along the way.

This particular stairway, captured that first night in town, was covered in graffiti, and bright lights lit up the forest hanging above it. The wolf who appears in each painting in this show represents a few different things, but I think of it primarily as a ghost of my ancestors accompanying me on this trip, where I visited the places they once lived. Vilkas means wolf in Lithuanian. And the names written on the wall are my direct patriarchal line. Listfields, all, beginning with me and my brother, and going backwards—my father, my grandfather, my great-grandfather—all the way back in time, as far as I can trace. The ancestors who lived in this part of the world, then those of us who had never been there, and then me and my brother, visiting for the first and maybe only time, to see the places where we come from. Leaving our mark on a wall, without knowing how long it might last.

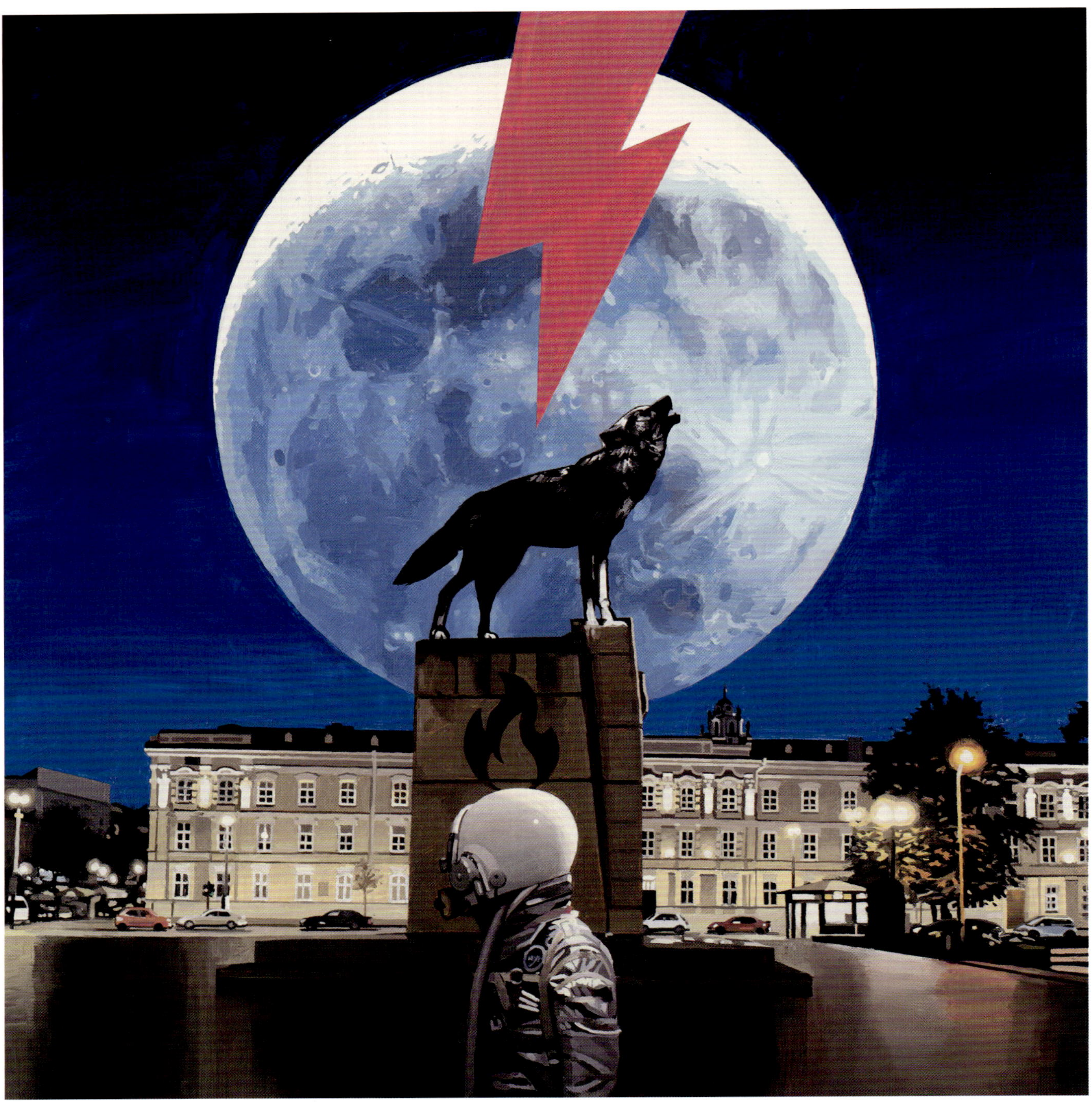

#678 THE PLAZA [2024]

My trip wrapped up in Vilnius, Lithuania's state y capital city. Filled with towers and churches, monuments and plazas, my brother and I spent three days walking the city, coming to grips with the places we had seen on this trip. We had spent the previous week visiting smaller towns where ou- ancestors came from. In some of those p aces I felt the memory of that ancestral history, still alive and vibrant, despite there being no living members of my family still there. In other places, the history had been literally bulldozed. Empty fields and abandoned roads where people once lived and where people once died, overgrown cemeteries that in another generation or two will be lost forever. I felt caught between my own family history, the lives they lived, largely uncelebrated but key to my own existence, and the grandeur of monuments to kings, saints, and empires. The two began to blend in my mind. This trip had been like me creating a monument of my own, to my past, my ancestry, to those who came from the small towns, to those who lived and died, those who fled, and those who didn't make it out in time.

#683
THE WALL [2024]

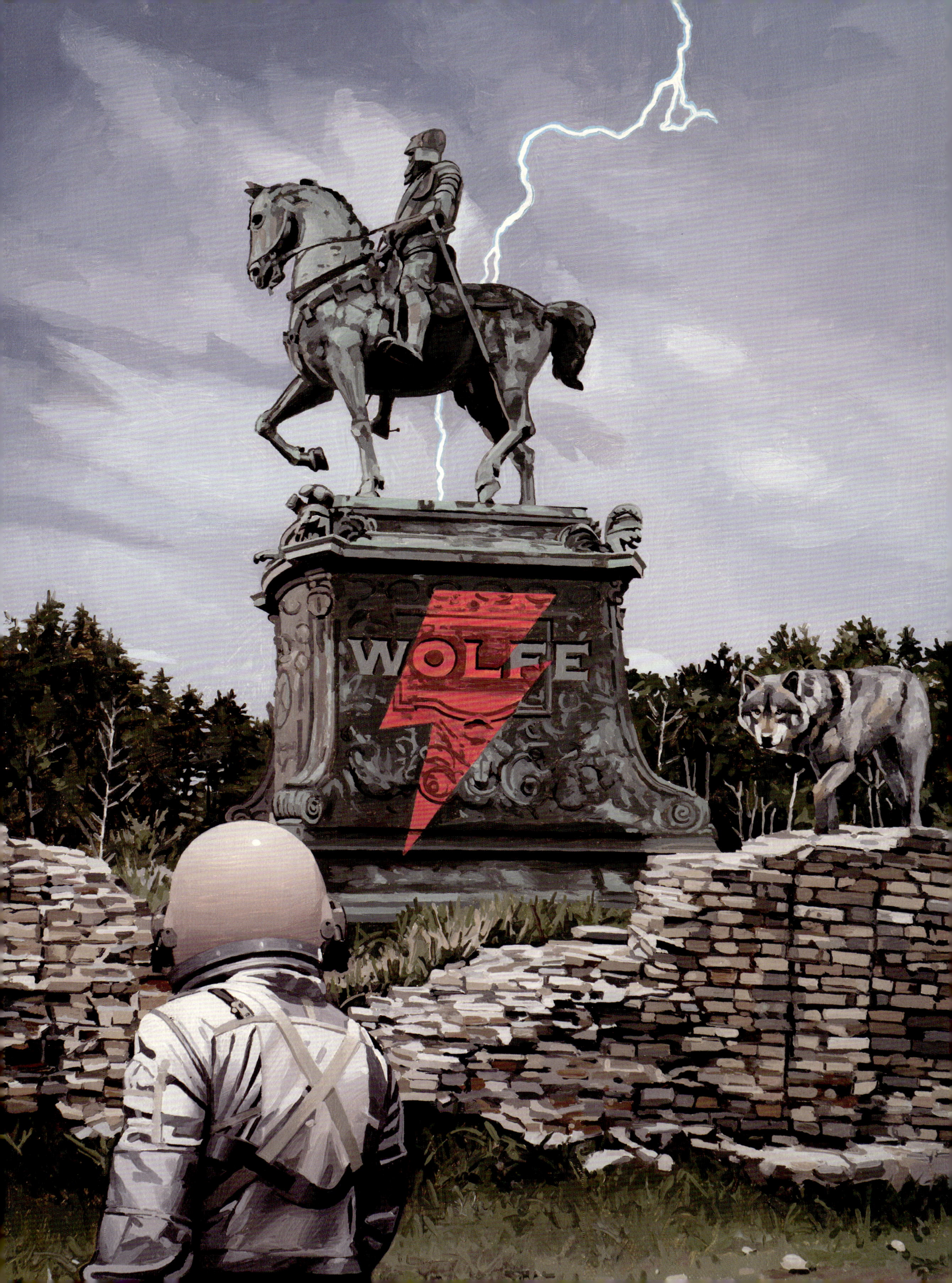
WOLFE

IN MEMORY OF

SHAWN VEZINAW HOSNER

///////////////////////////////////

February 15, 2024

Exactly 12 years ago this week I was working on a painting for my very first group show with Thinkspace.

12 years feels like a lifetime, and I have no idea what got me on Shawn and Andrew Hosner's radar in the first place. At the time, I was just a guy, living in Boston, making paintings of astronauts, hoping someone would notice. I eventually ended up moving out to LA, in part because I knew I had people here who would treat me like family, and by that I mean Shawn. Shawn made me feel like family. Shawn made a lot of people feel like family.

Los Angeles is a big place and it can often feel lonely, but the art scene here was so warm and kind to me. And though it's huge and sprawling, just like LA itself, pockets of it are still small enough that one or two forceful people can really shape it. LC doing Cannibal Flower. Andrew and Shawn and LC, again, doing Thinkspace. But that's the art side of things. The kindness, the welcoming sensibility, the warmth? I think that's Shawn. People looked to Shawn, saw how she treated people, and followed suit.

This week has been hard. Losing beloved people hurts. My wife Joanna and I went to visit Shawn in the hospital, along with—as far as I can tell—all of greater Los Angeles. I think traffic in LA was extra bad on the west side for a few days just because of all the people going to visit Shawn. So this sucks. Shawn has left a hole that is going to be hard to fill.

My last show at Thinkspace was about time and memory. I revisited key moments, and paintings, from my life. The centerpiece of that show was three large paintings made in remembrance of close friends who I lost along the way. It taught me a lot about my own grief, making those paintings, forcing myself to look back and inhabit the younger version of myself, remembering the loss I felt, both at the time, and now. But it also taught me that those friends of mine, in a small but very real way, they live on. In my paintings, in my memories, in my heart. They live on when I think about them every day, when they inspire me to keep painting, to keep telling my story—and theirs—through my work. It's maybe small comfort, especially right now when the sadness of Shawn's passing is so near. I really wish my friends were still here. I really wish Shawn were still here. But those aren't things I can change, unfortunately. But her memory? That's Shawn's legacy, and it's ours now. So think of Shawn while you paint. Think of Shawn when you go to a gallery, or to your next concert. Think of Shawn while you follow the Dead on tour for an unfathomably long time. Think of Shawn when you go to a food festival, or when you volunteer to help people, or cats, or goats. Live your life like she did, treasuring all of the moments.

I'm remembering Shawn's laugh right now. A sharp *HA* that I hope will stay with me a really long time.

#685
FOREVER [2024]

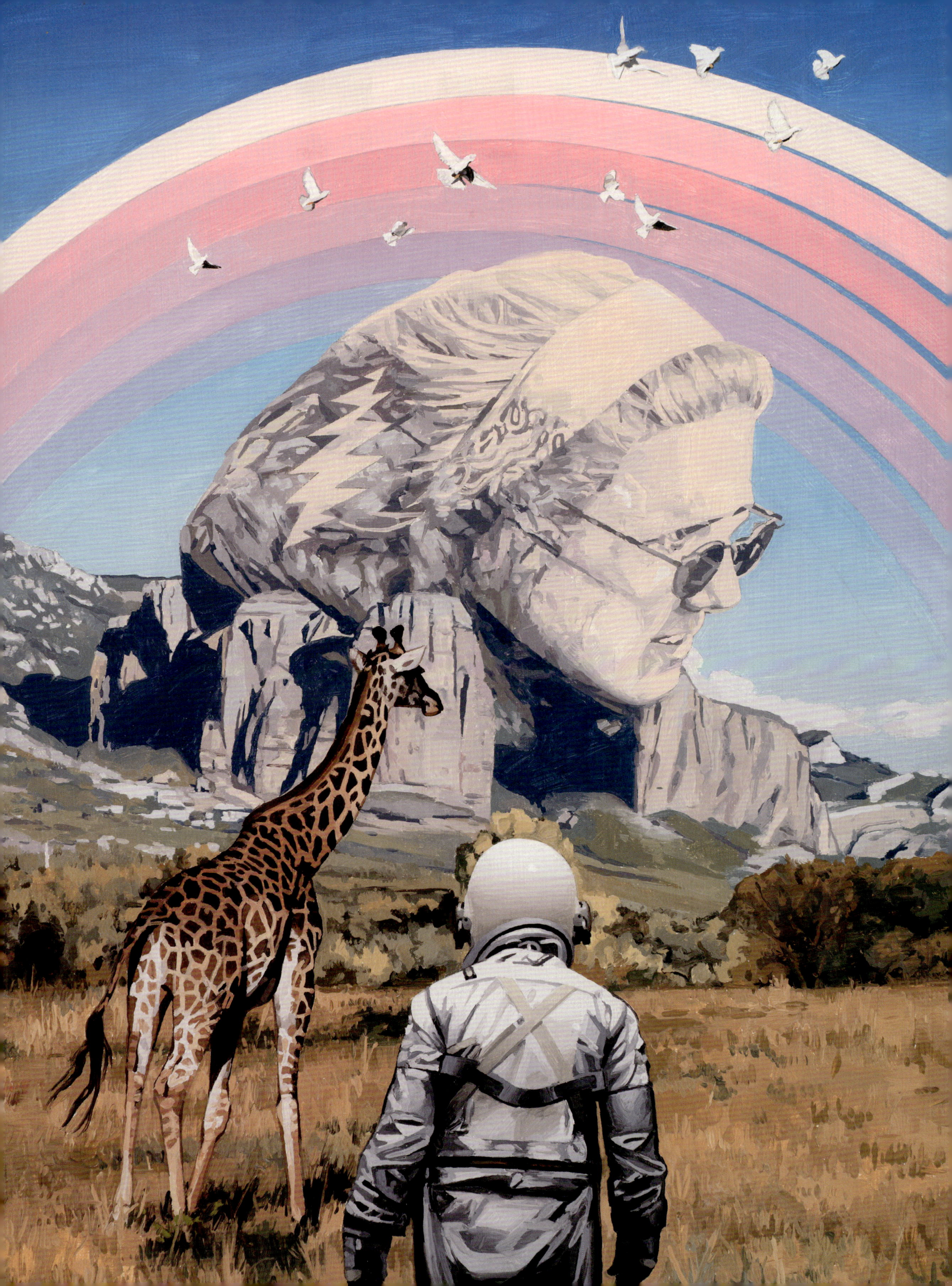

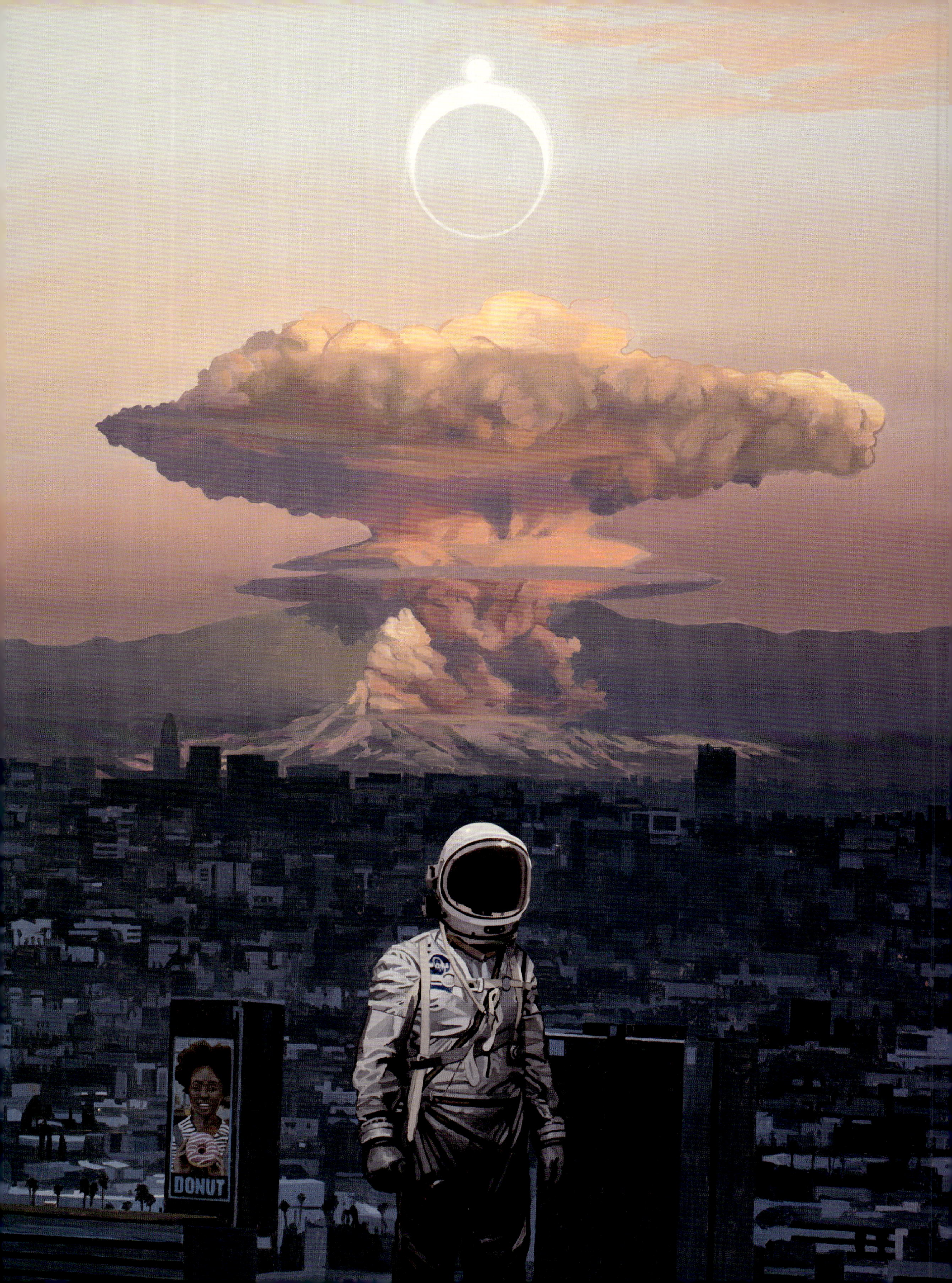
DONUT

OH, DYSTOPIA

//

Thinkspace Projects, Los Angeles, CA
August, 2024

Are you feeling stressed or anxious? Has the erosion of democracy and the feeling of impending societal collapse got you down? Are you tired of technological solutions no one asked for? Worn out by end stage capitalism? Sick of social media? Billionaires? Traffic? War? The Supreme Court? Well then, have I got just the thing for you!

Oh, Dystopia is a show about finding beauty in the end of things.

Friends, let's go off into the end times together. We'll frolic amongst the leftover bits of our civilization: Crumbling skyscrapers! Partially destroyed machines! Piles of trash! A giant donut! Sad robots! The remains of a sunburnt Earth! We'll leave our names on a broken building and hope that our distant ancestors find it one day and remember us.

It's the end of the world as we know it, and I feel fine.

Scenes from a semi-dystopian future have long been a big part of my work, and I wanted to lean into it with this show, but in a way that felt.. kind of fun? It just feels like everything has been doom and gloom for so long and I'm tired of it. I wanted to celebrate the possibility that we could send messages out to those who come long after us. Maybe intentional, or maybe just whatever pieces of our weird society remain for someone (or something) to find.

#694
CITY OF ANGELS [2024]

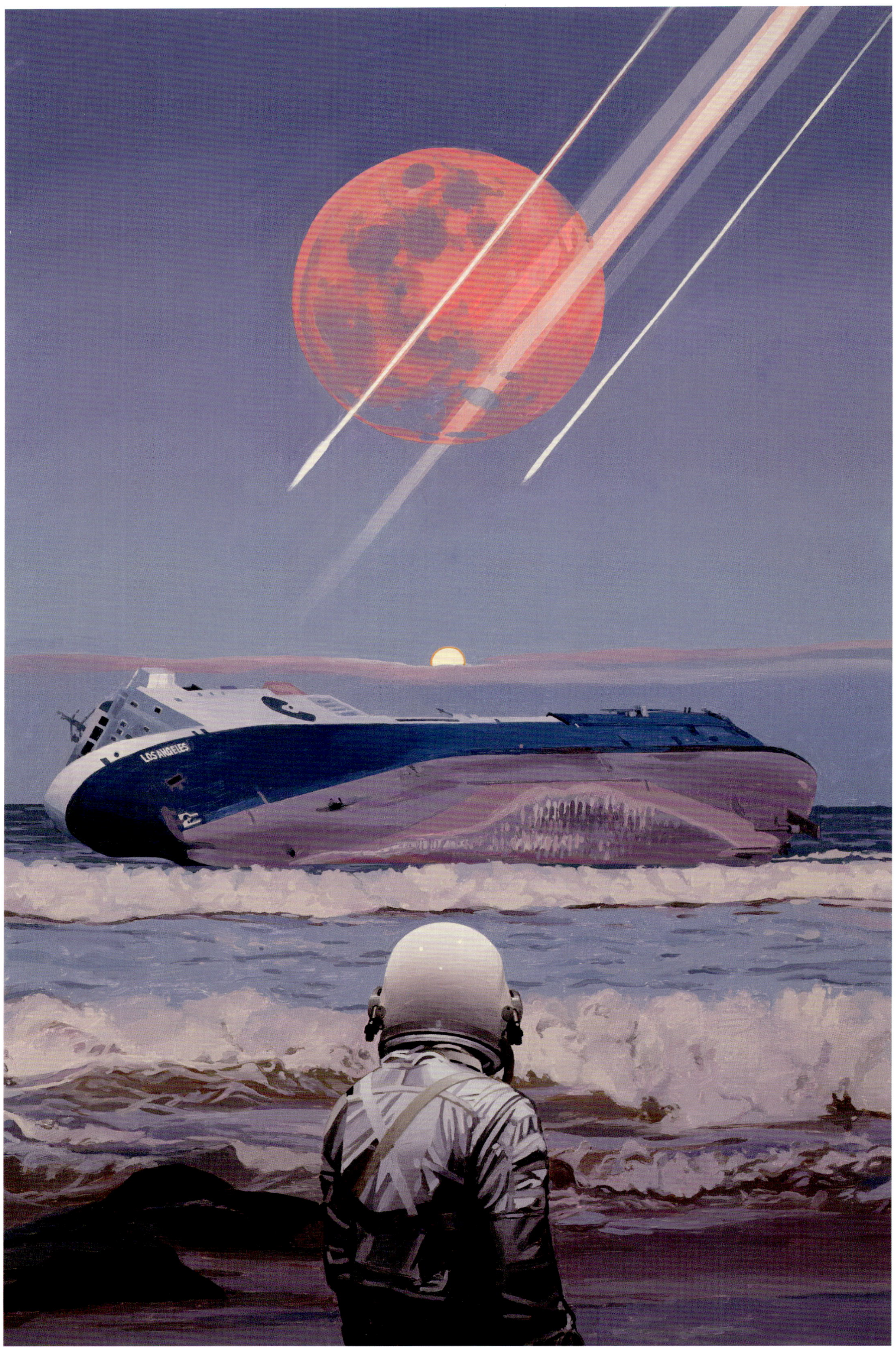
LOS ANGELES

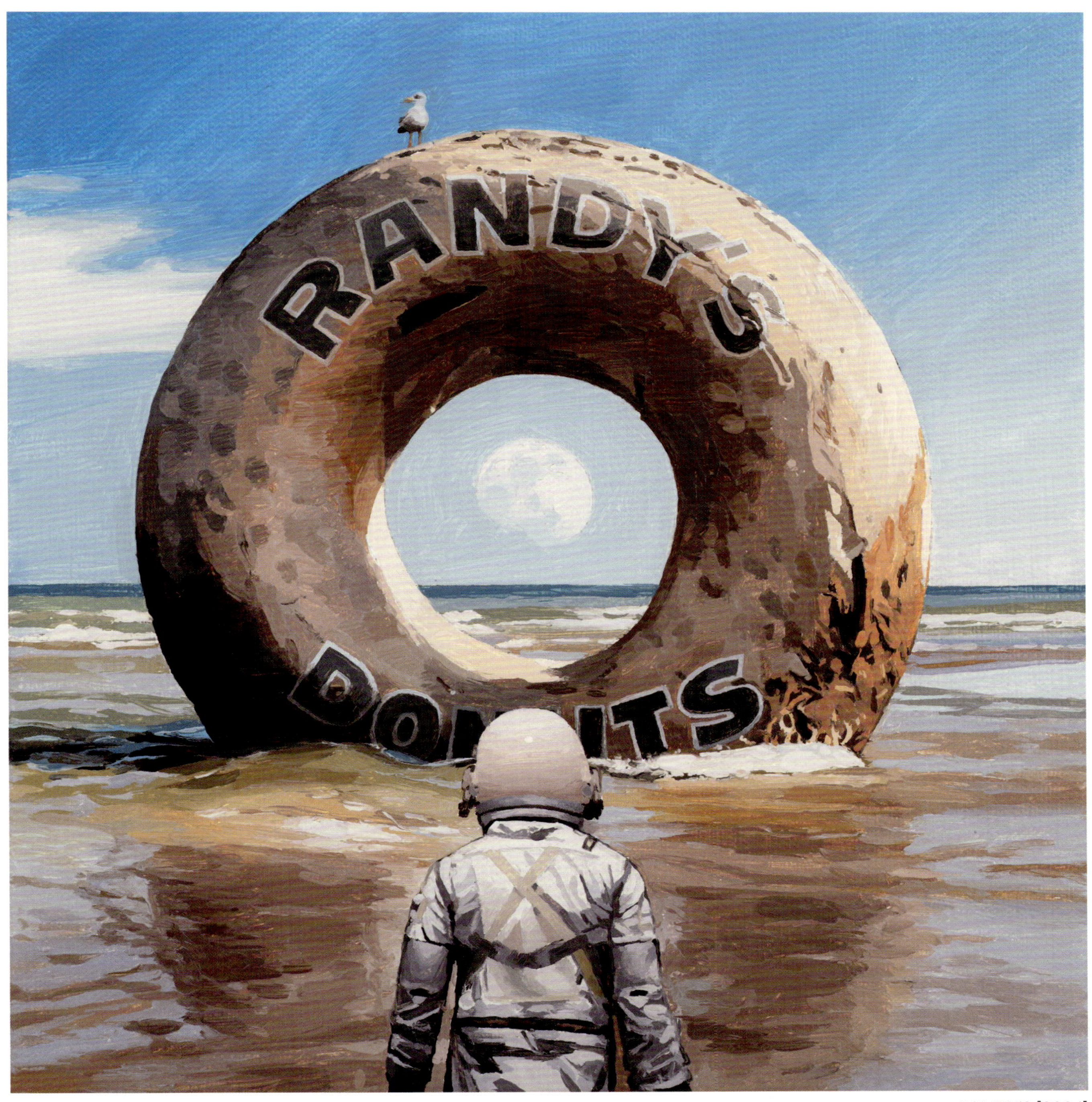

#689

RANDY'S [2024]

#697

WASHED ASHORE [2024]

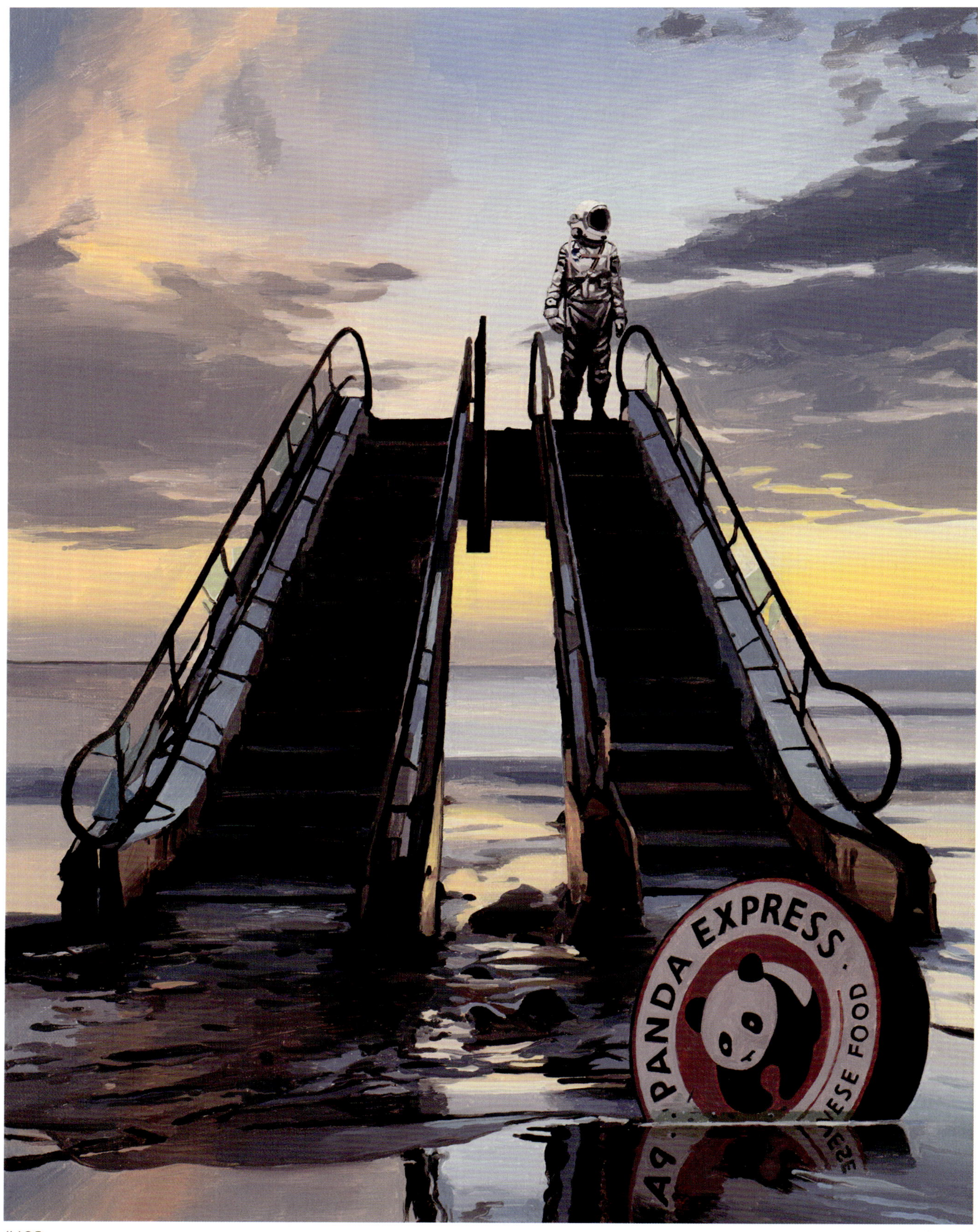

#695

THE ESCALATOR [2024]

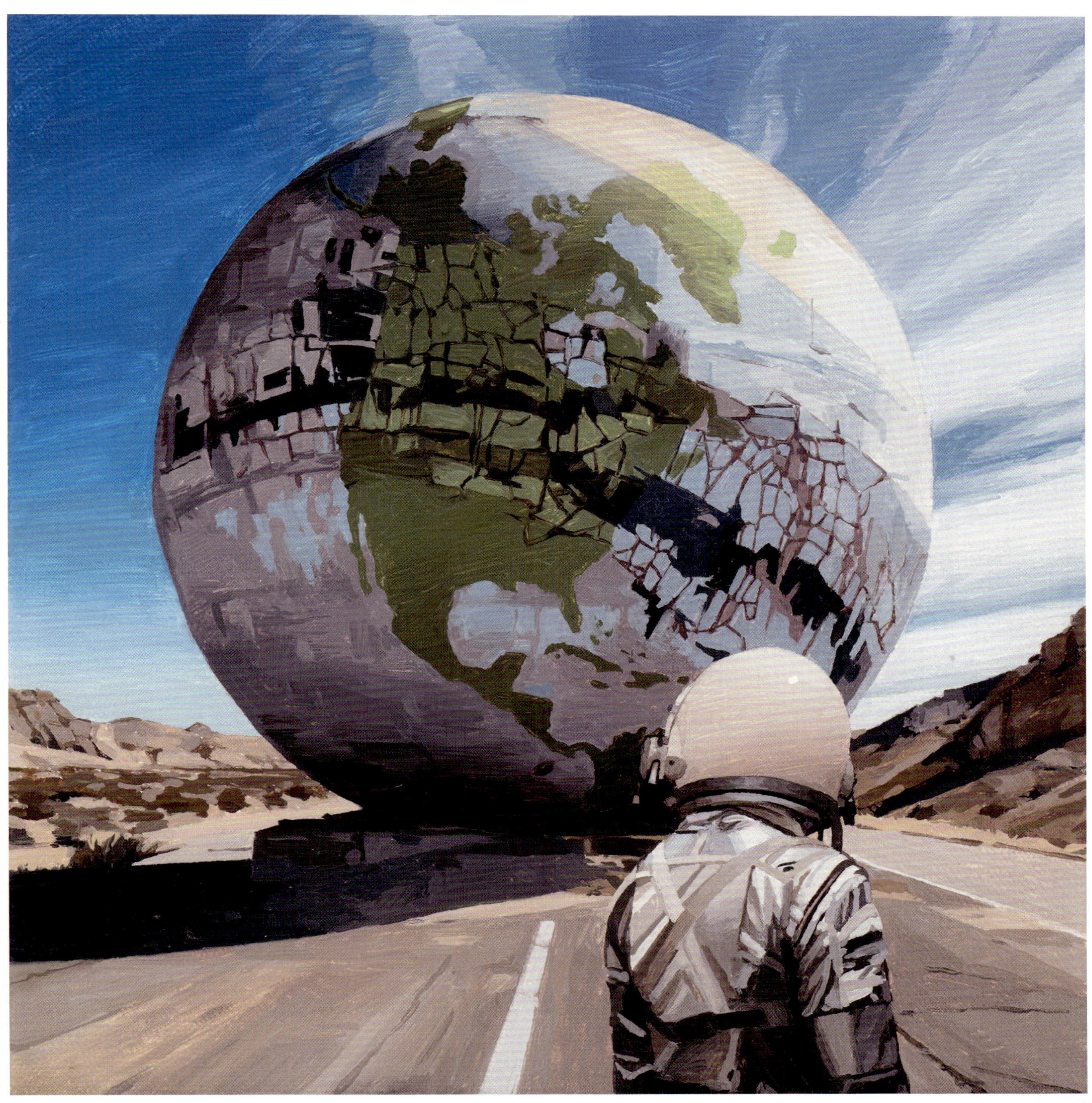

#690 GLOBE [2024]

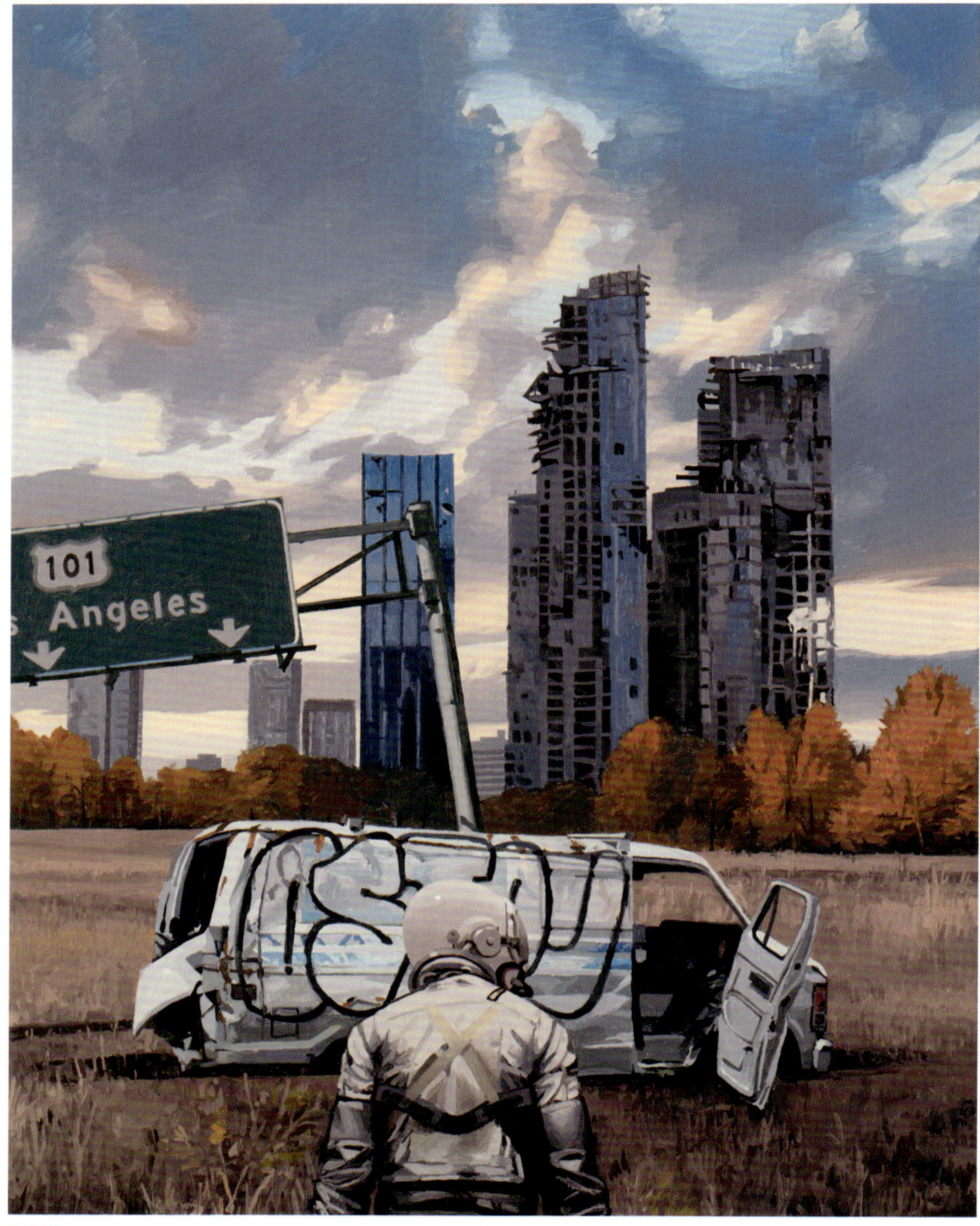

#699 THE ONE OH ONE [2024]

***We Who Remain* (ACROSS),** arguably the most ambitious thing I've ever done, was inspired by the giant graffiti tower that sprung up here in LA on an unfinished high rise building in early 2024. I loved the idea of turning this enormous slab of forgotten concrete and glass into a monument to those people bold enough to climb it and leave their mark.

In my version, the vertical names across the top are close friends who I have lost along the way. I have written about each of them in this book. The many names written along the side compose most of my family tree, going back as far as I can trace it. Inspired by my trip to Europe the previous year, and from some amateur sleuthing I've done into my own ancestry.

This painting is about leaving some kind of legacy. About what of us remains long after we're gone. About having the courage to carve our own names into something and hope that in some way they last the test of time. Even if—or when—the world around us crumbles.

#693
WE WHO REMAIN [2024]

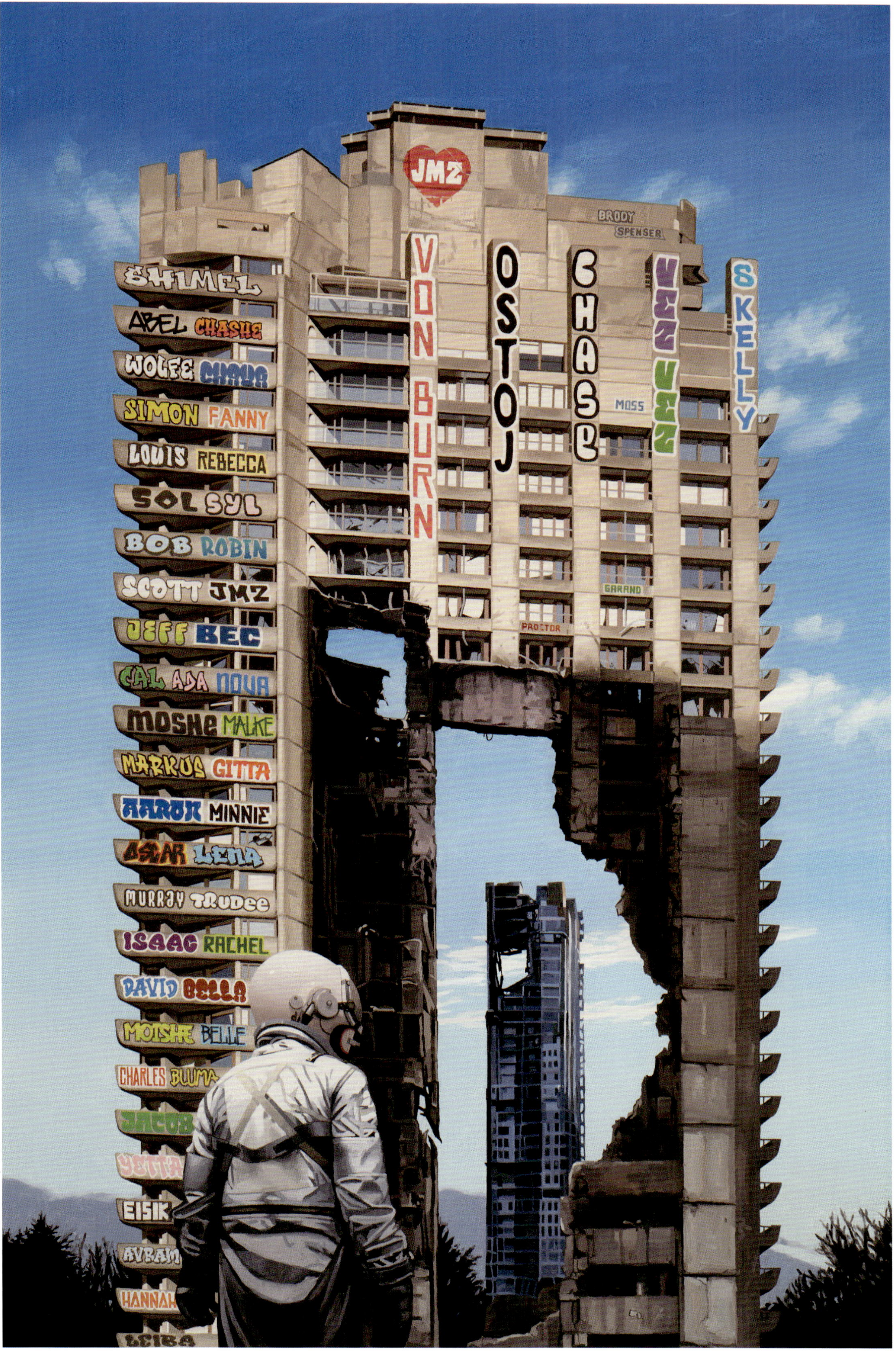
JMZ
BRODY
SPENSER
VON BURN
OSTOJ
CHASE
VEZ VEZ
SKELLY
MOSS
GARAND
PROCTOR
SHIMEL
ABEL CHASHE
WOLFE
SIMON FANNY
LOUIS REBECCA
SOL SYL
BOB ROBIN
SCOTT JMZ
JEFF BEC
CAL ADA NOVA
MOSHE MALKE
MARKUS GITTA
AARON MINNIE
OSCAR LENA
MURRAY TRUDEE
ISAAC RACHEL
DAVID BELLA
MOISHE BELLE
CHARLES BLUMA
JACOB
YETTA
EISIK
AVRAM
HANNAH
LEIBA

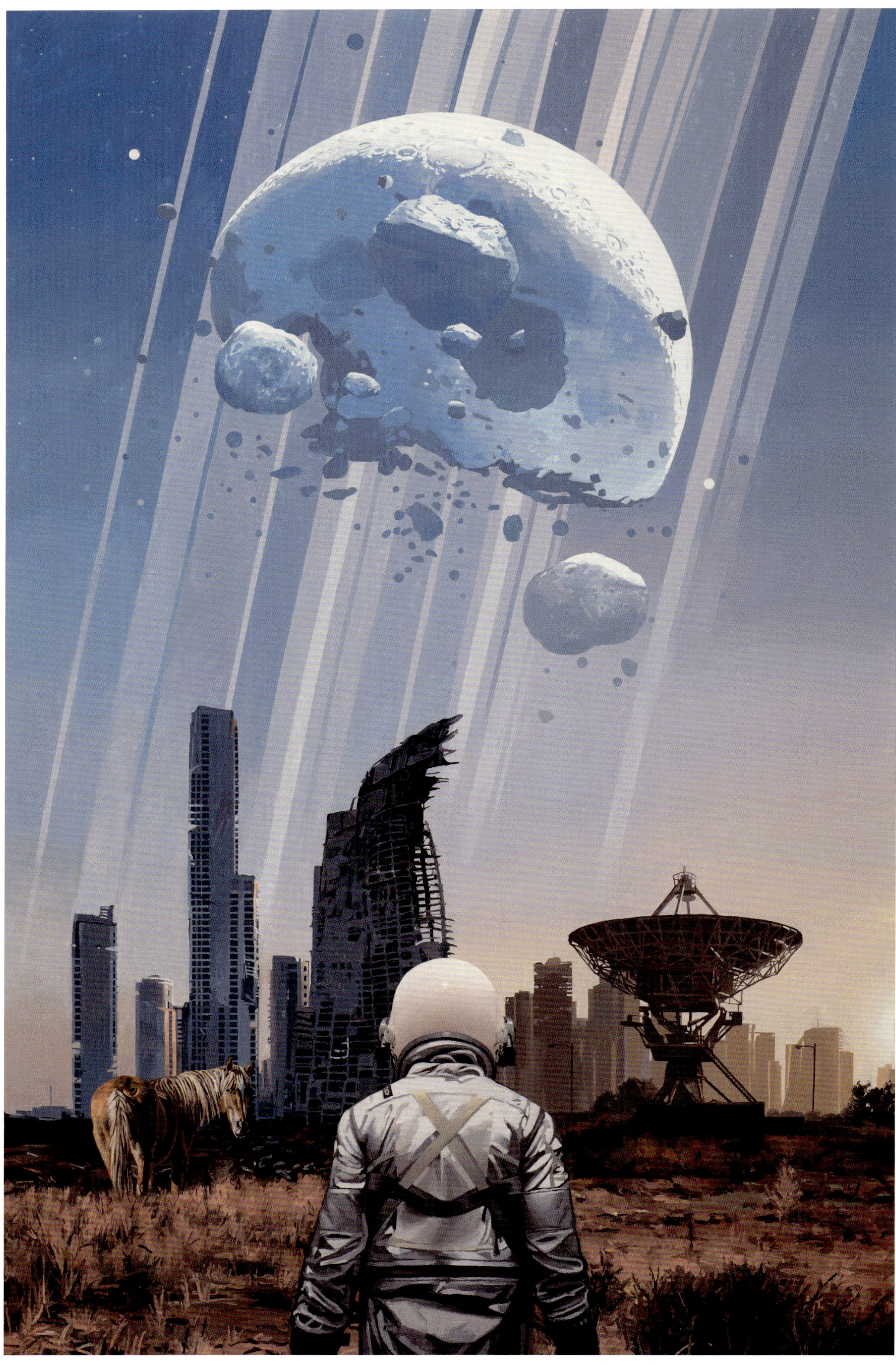

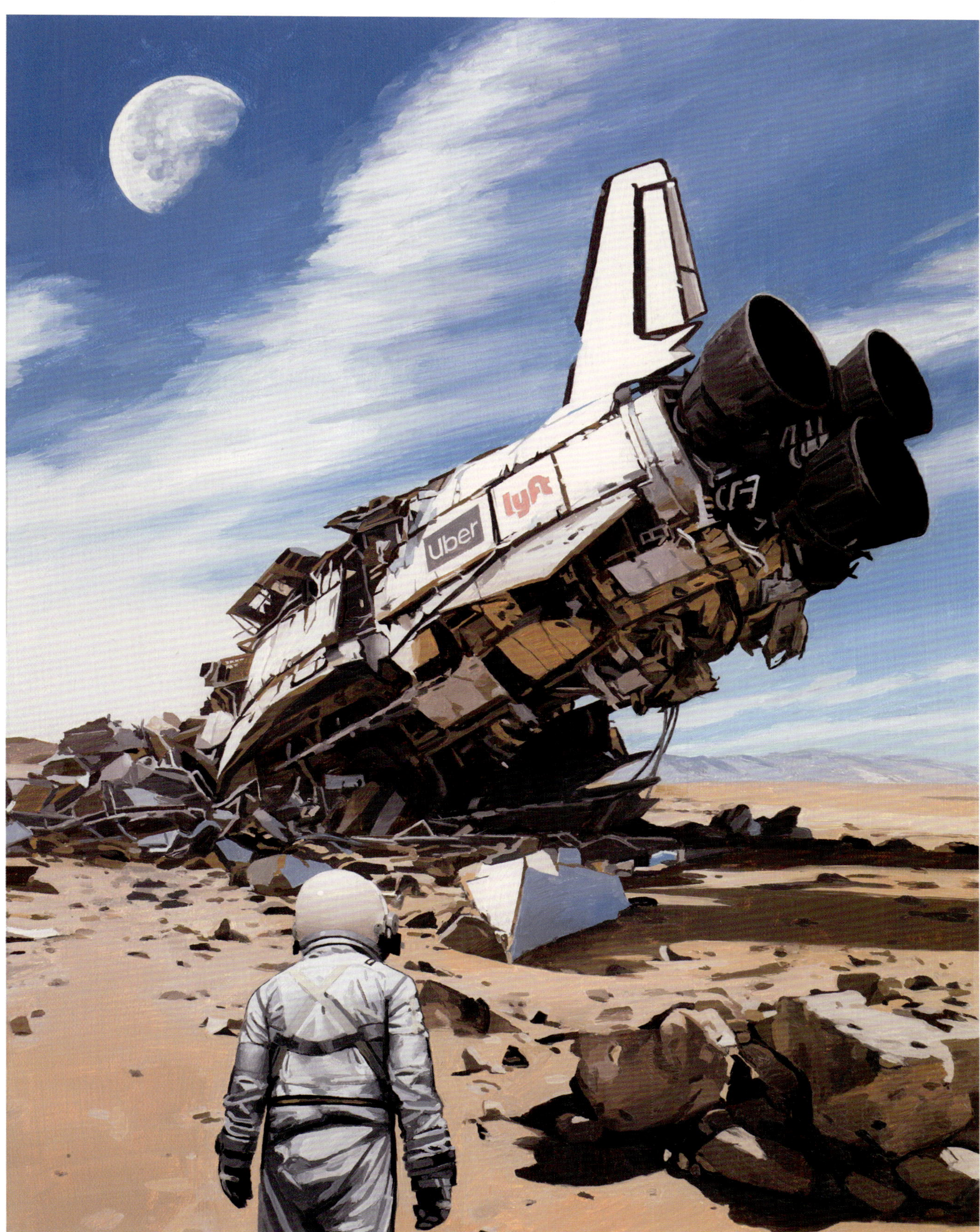

#688

CRASH SITE [2024]

#705

HALF MOON RISING [2024]

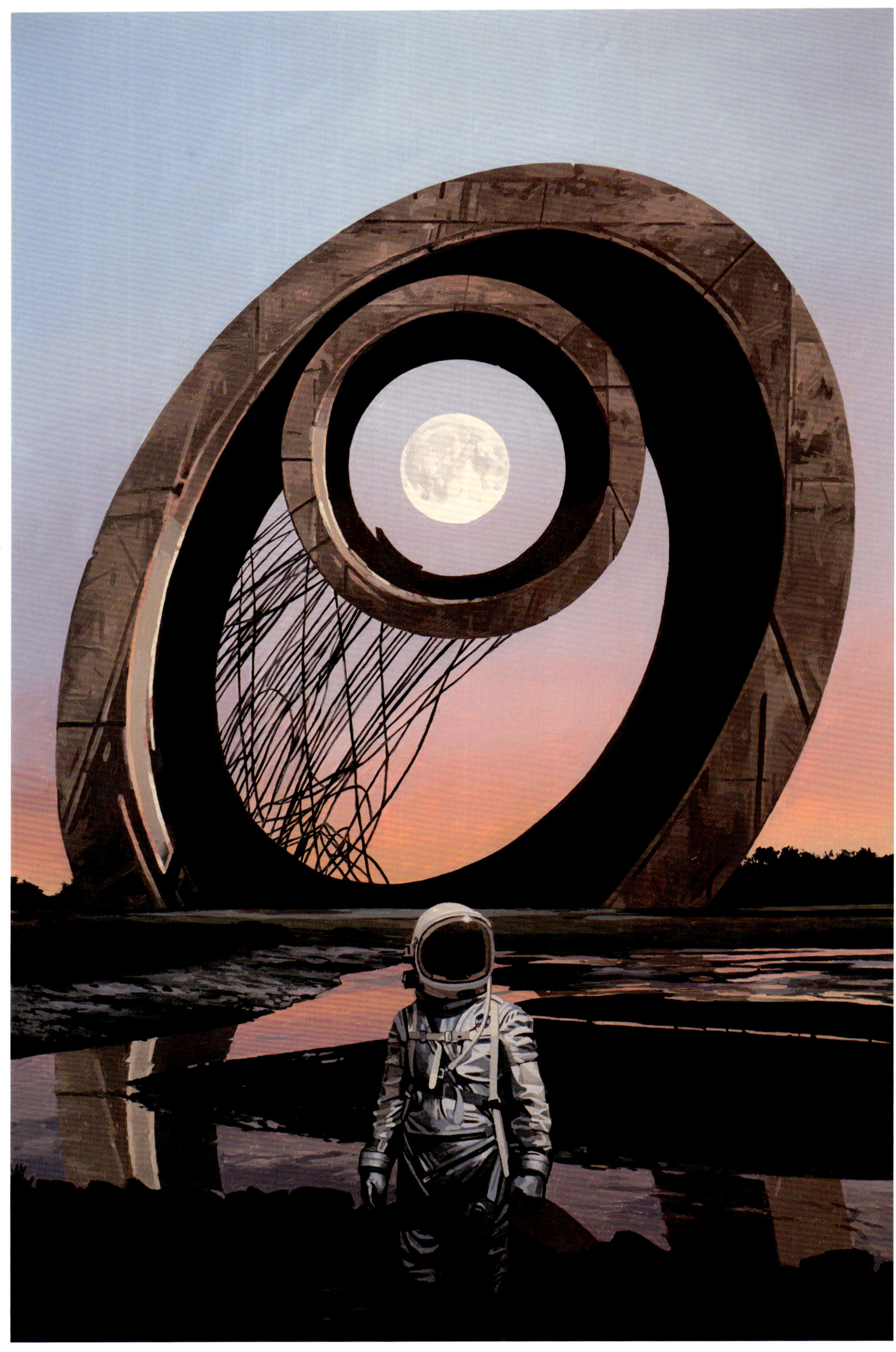

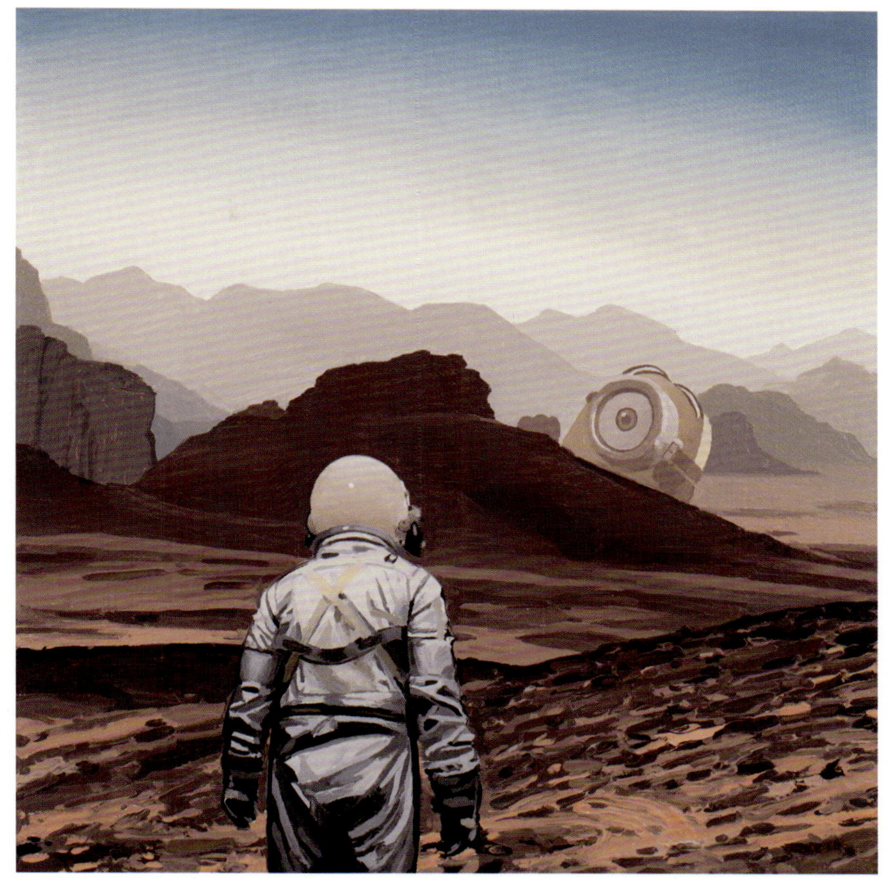

#707 MINIONPOCALYPSE [2024]

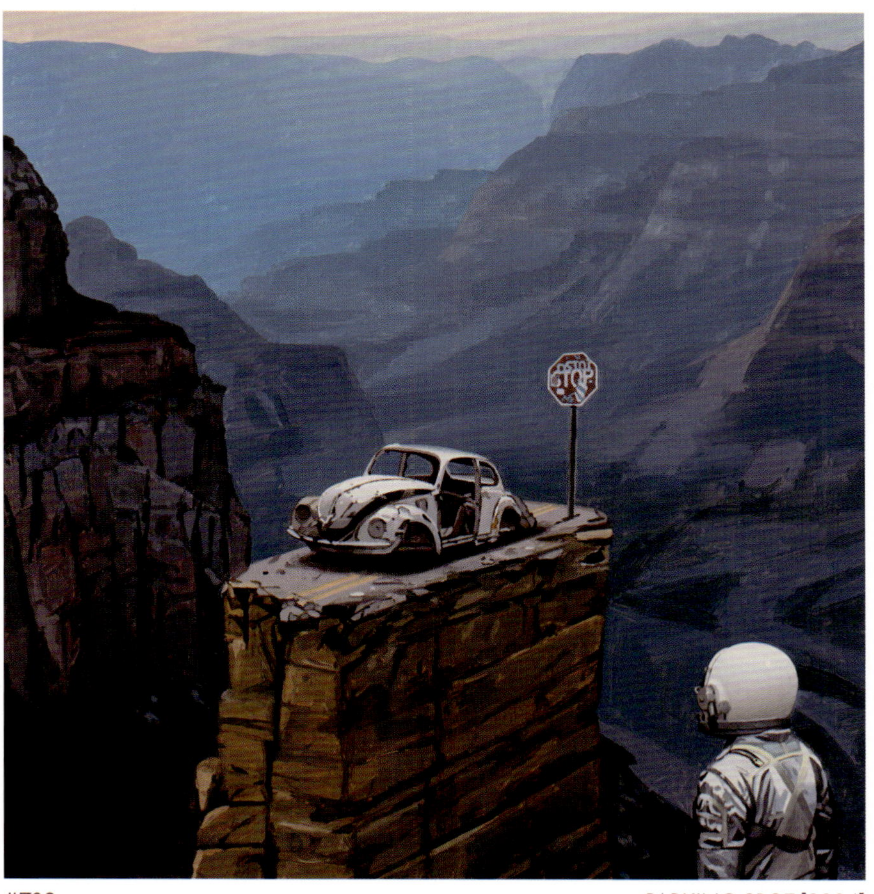

#703 PARKING SPOT [2024]

#687
OCULUS [2024]

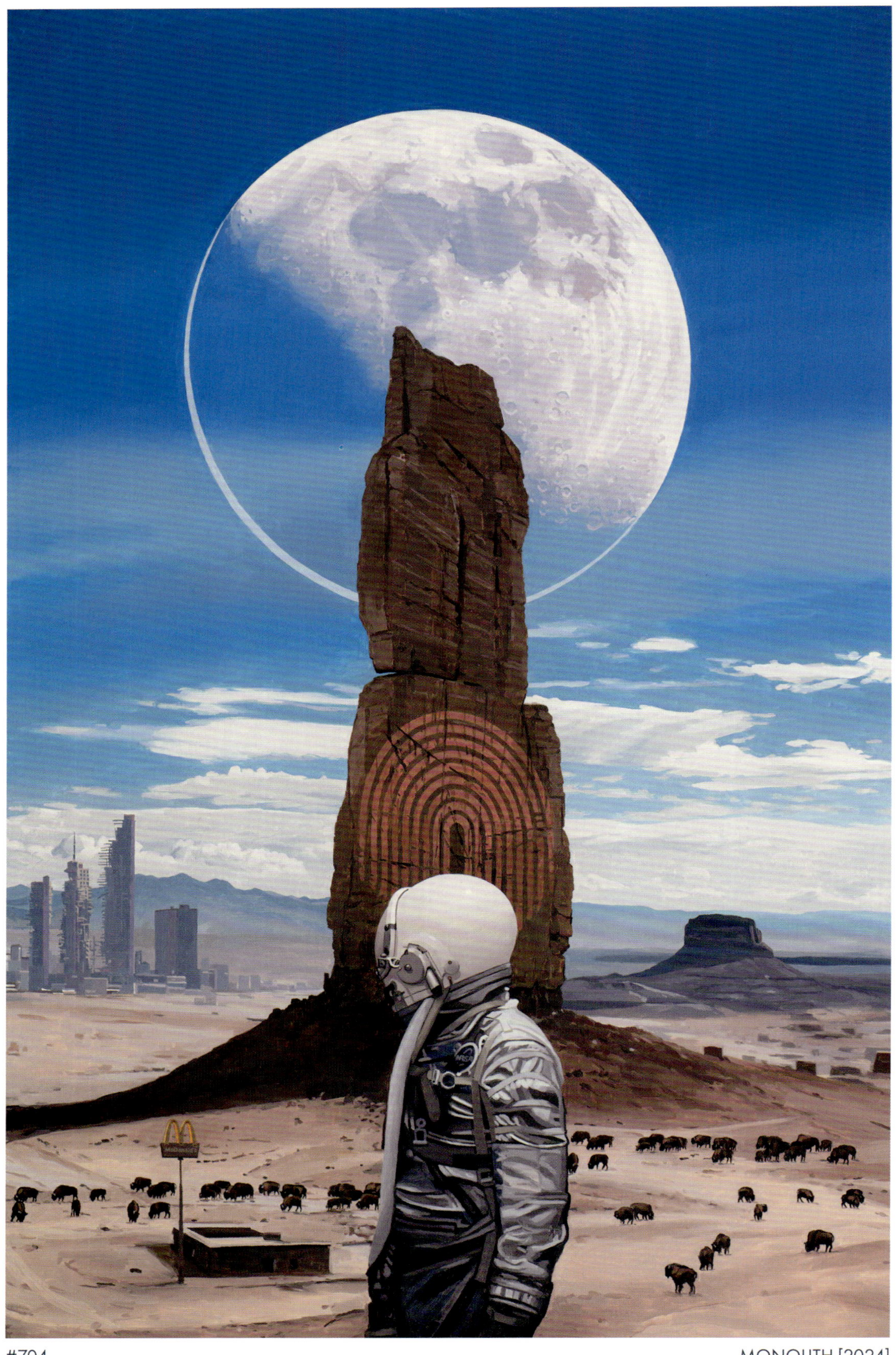

#704 MONOLITH [2024]

#706

THE FALLS [2024]

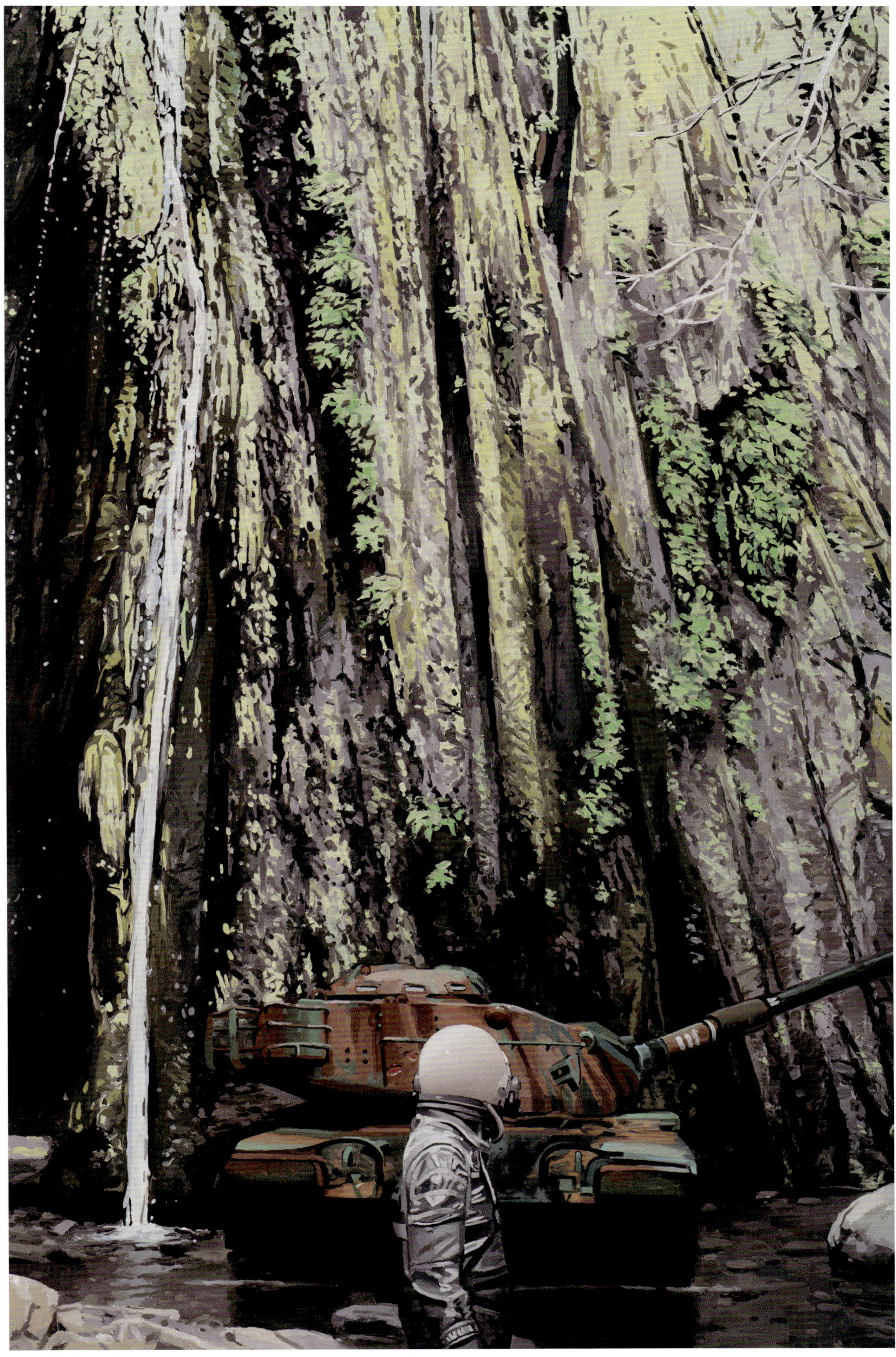

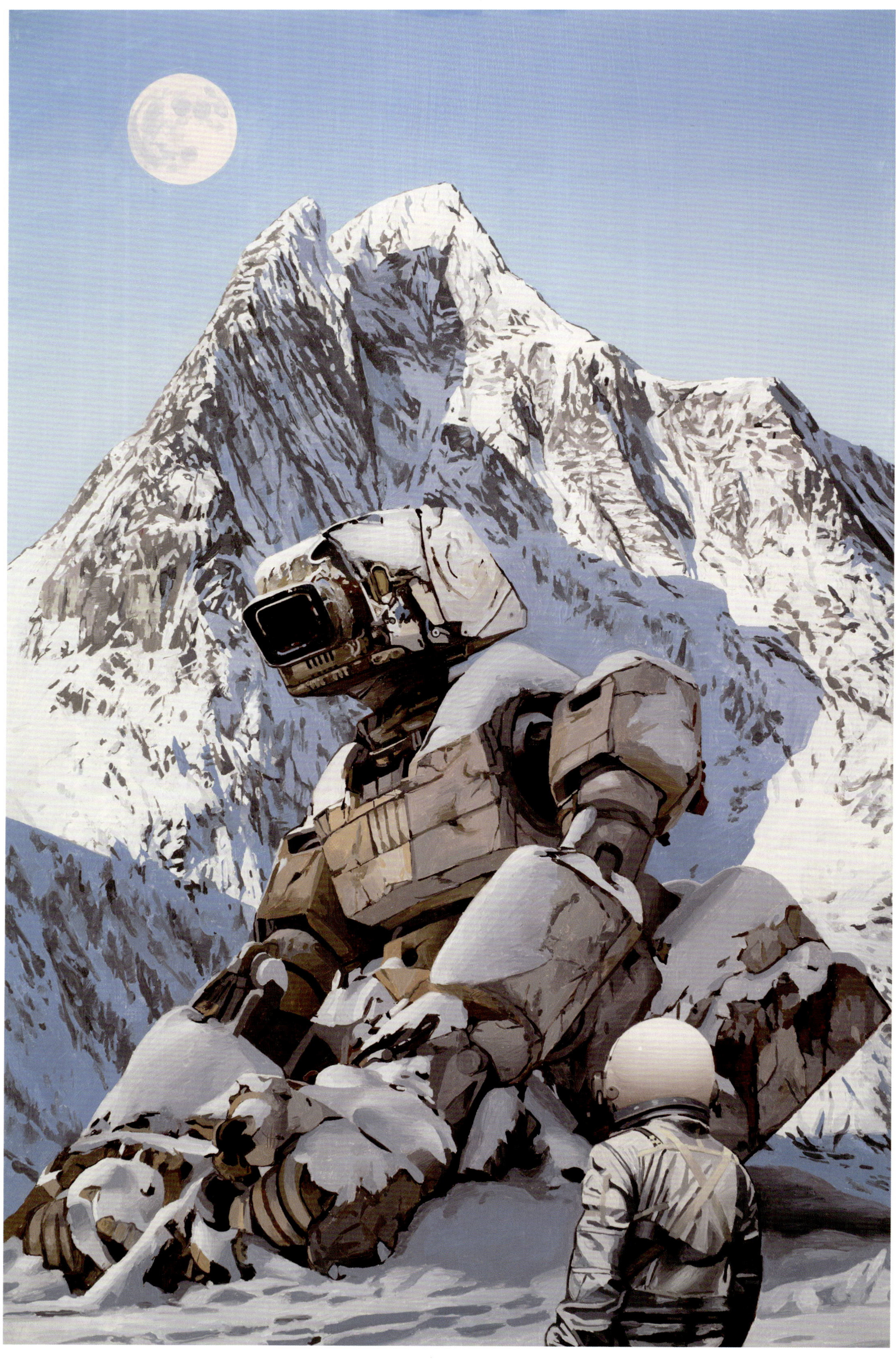

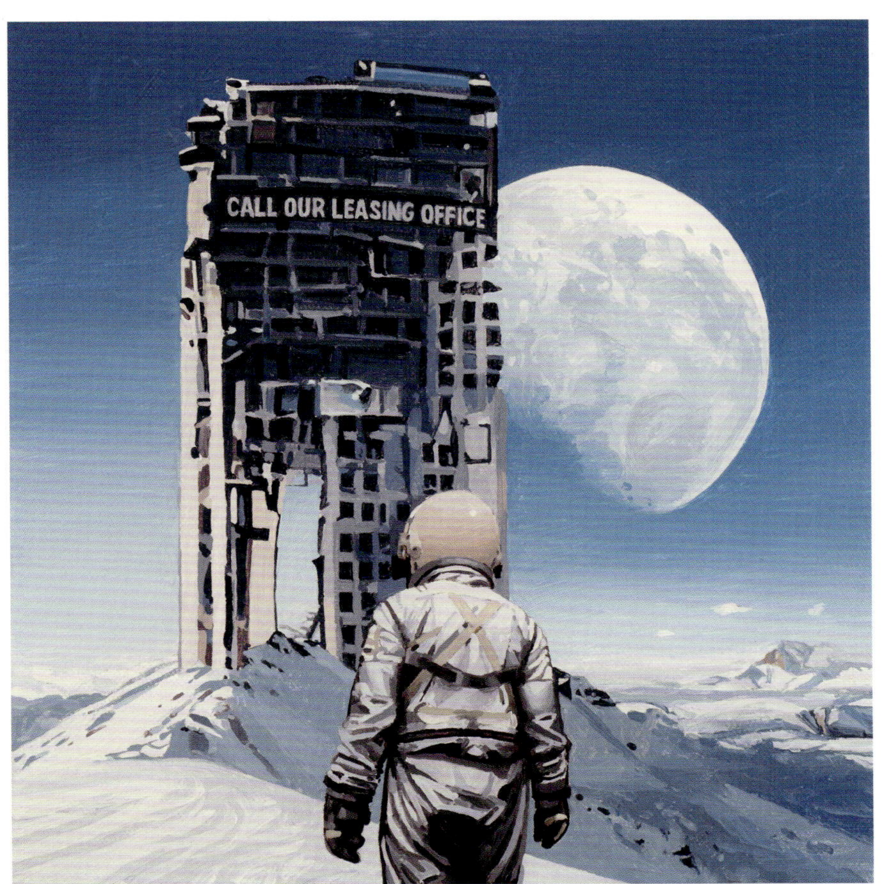

#701 CALL OUR LEASING OFFICE [2024]

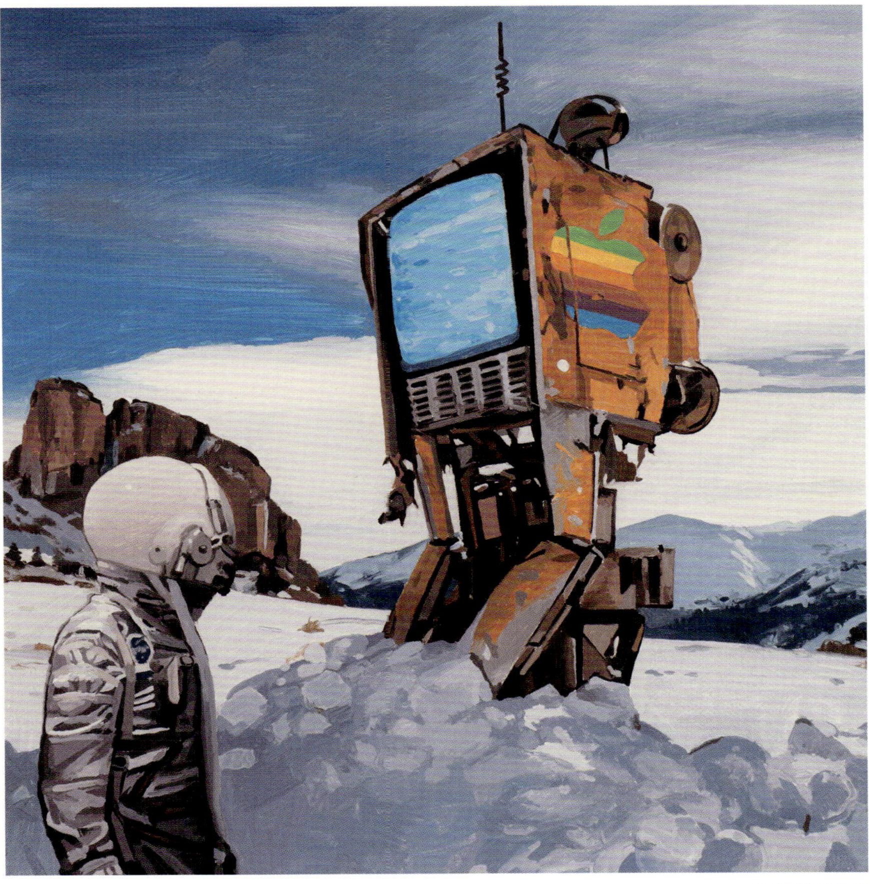

#698 IBOT [2024]

#691
SNOWBOT [2024]

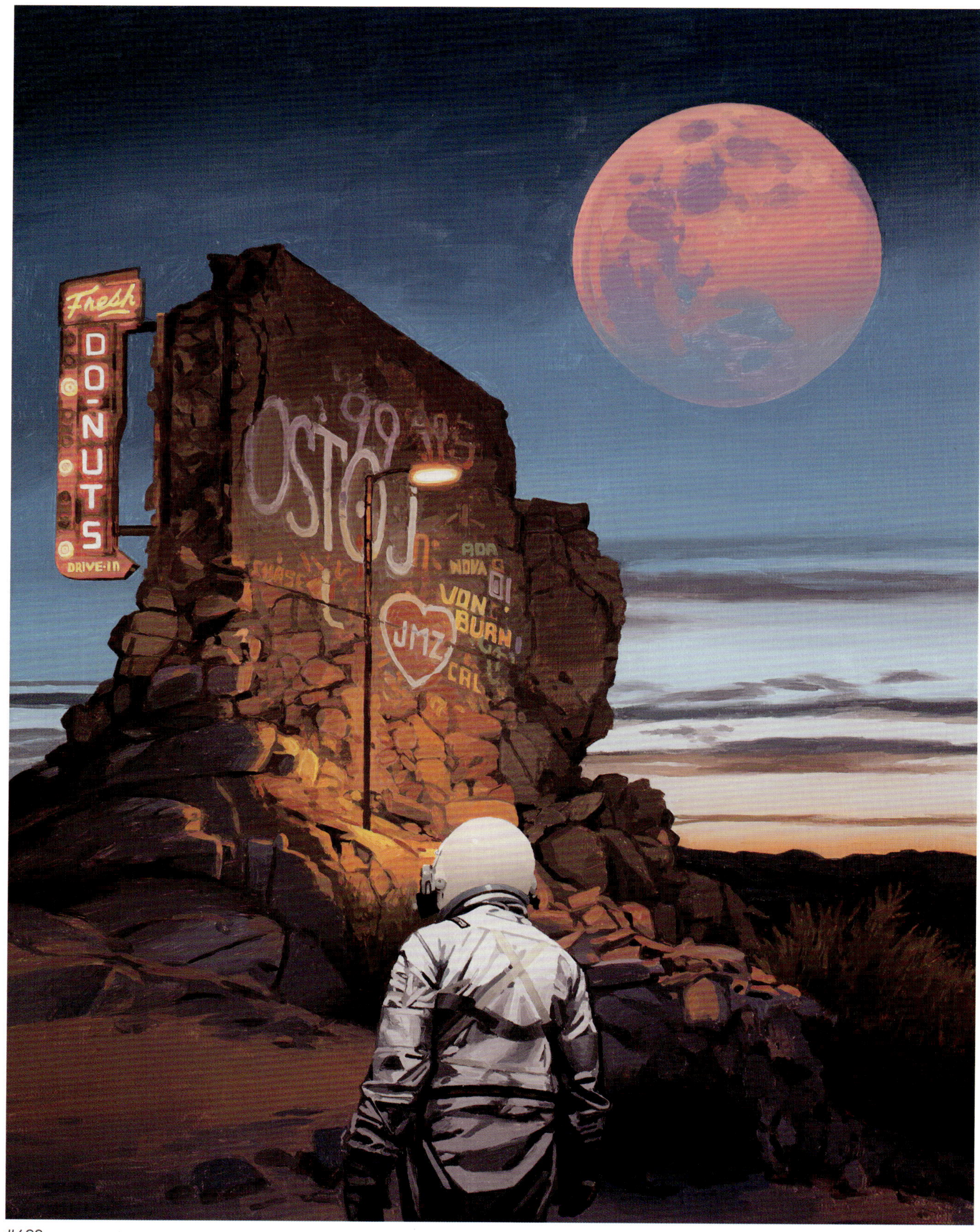

#692

FRESH DONUTS [2024]

CITIZENS OF TOMORROW

//

Beinart, Melbourne, Australia
February, 2025

What does the future look like? I've asked myself that question regularly for the last 25 years, and I try my best to answer it in my paintings. Sometimes my answer is "like the present, only worse" and sometimes it's "like the present, only weirder" and sometimes it's "actually not like the present at all." Sometimes I feel optimistic about the future and sometimes I don't. Often I make paintings about the future that are really more about the present. Often enough, too, I paint the future as a way to talk about the past.

For this, my fourth show at Beinart Gallery in Melbourne, Australia, I have grown weary of the present. I have been looking increasingly further ahead, so far that time begins to feel like a long tunnel looping back on itself. What remains of us when our monuments have crumbled to sand and dust? What will future generations leave behind when they, too, are gone, and would the remains of their civilizations make any sense to us at all? Will they too battle the climate, try to invoke their will upon higher tides and higher temperatures? Will objects crafted by machine instead of by human hand eventually take on some form unknowable to us? What will our legacy be on this planet, so many distant years out, and will our footprints still remain?

That's a lot of questions. Did I answer any of them in these paintings? I guess you'll have to wait until the future to find out.

#718
THE FACE WITH ONE EYE [2024]

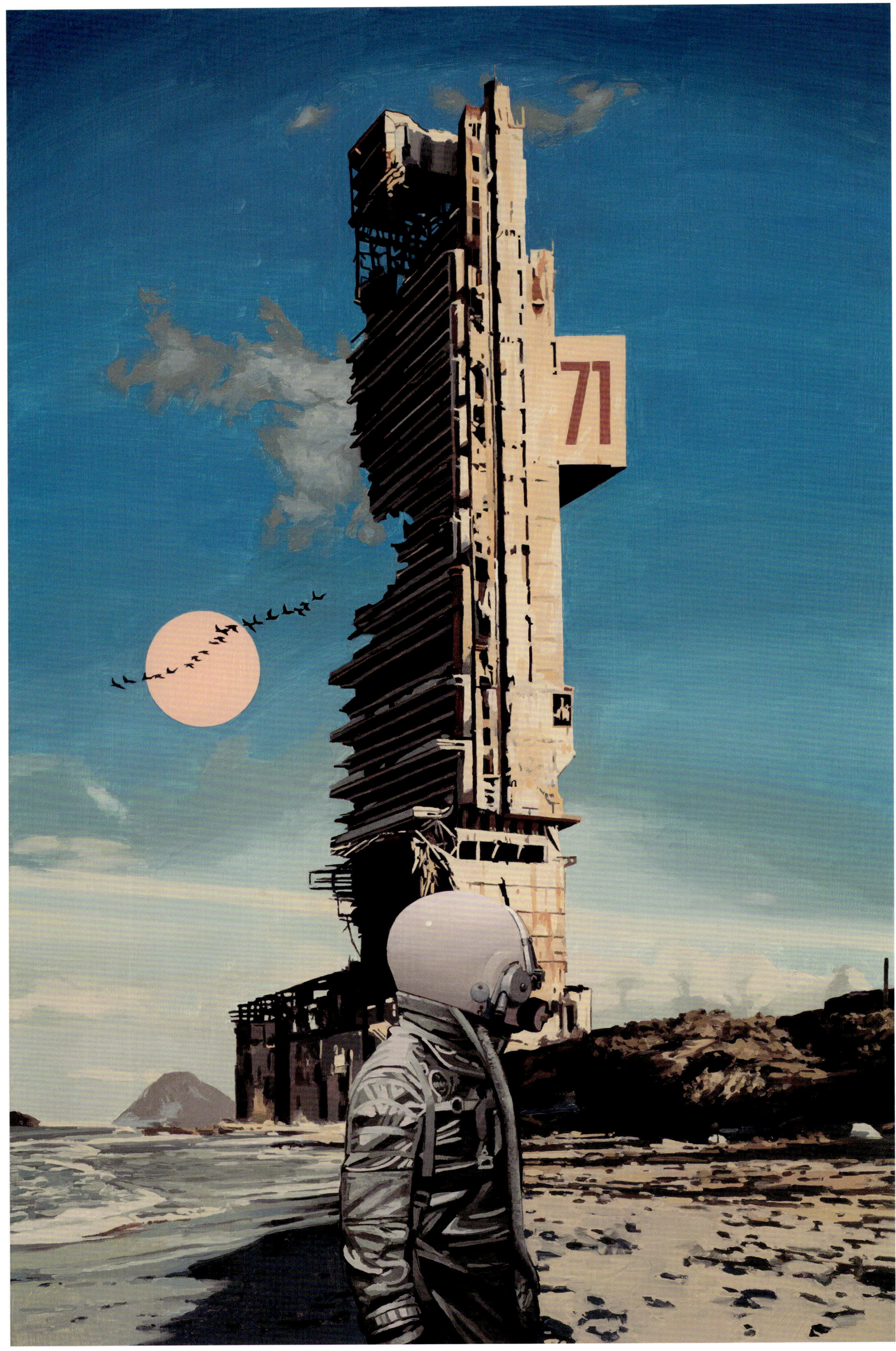
71

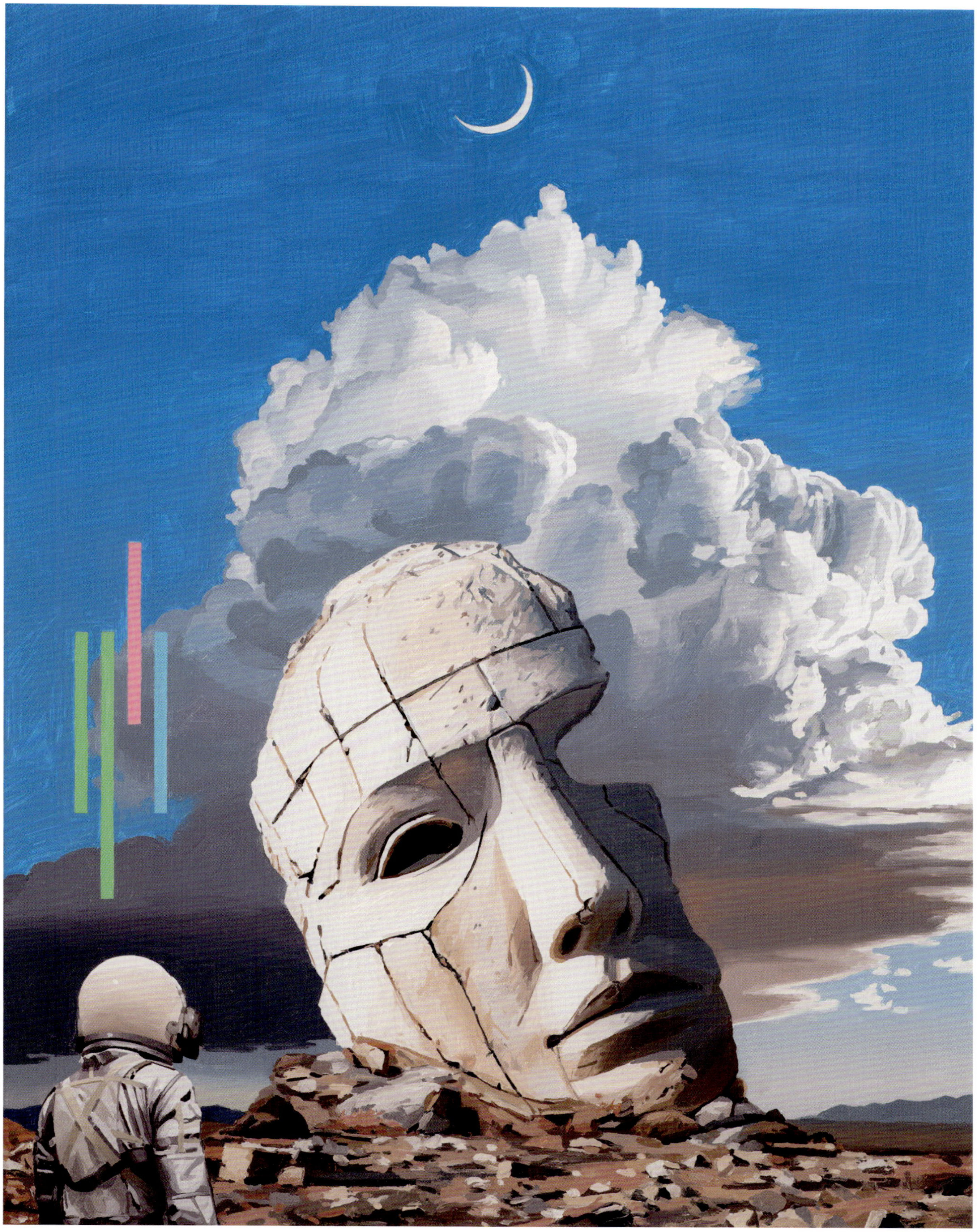

#720

ULTRAVIOLET SPECTRUM [2024]

#722

BUILDING 71 [2024]

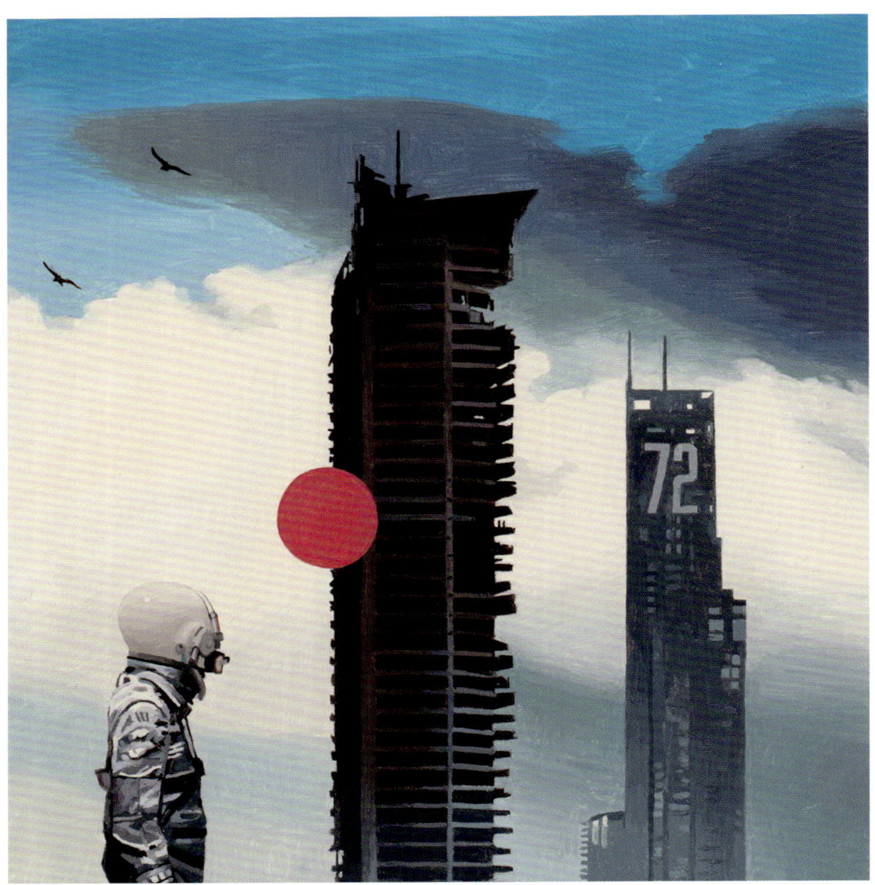

#723

BUILDING 72 [2024]

#727

BUILDING 25 [2024]

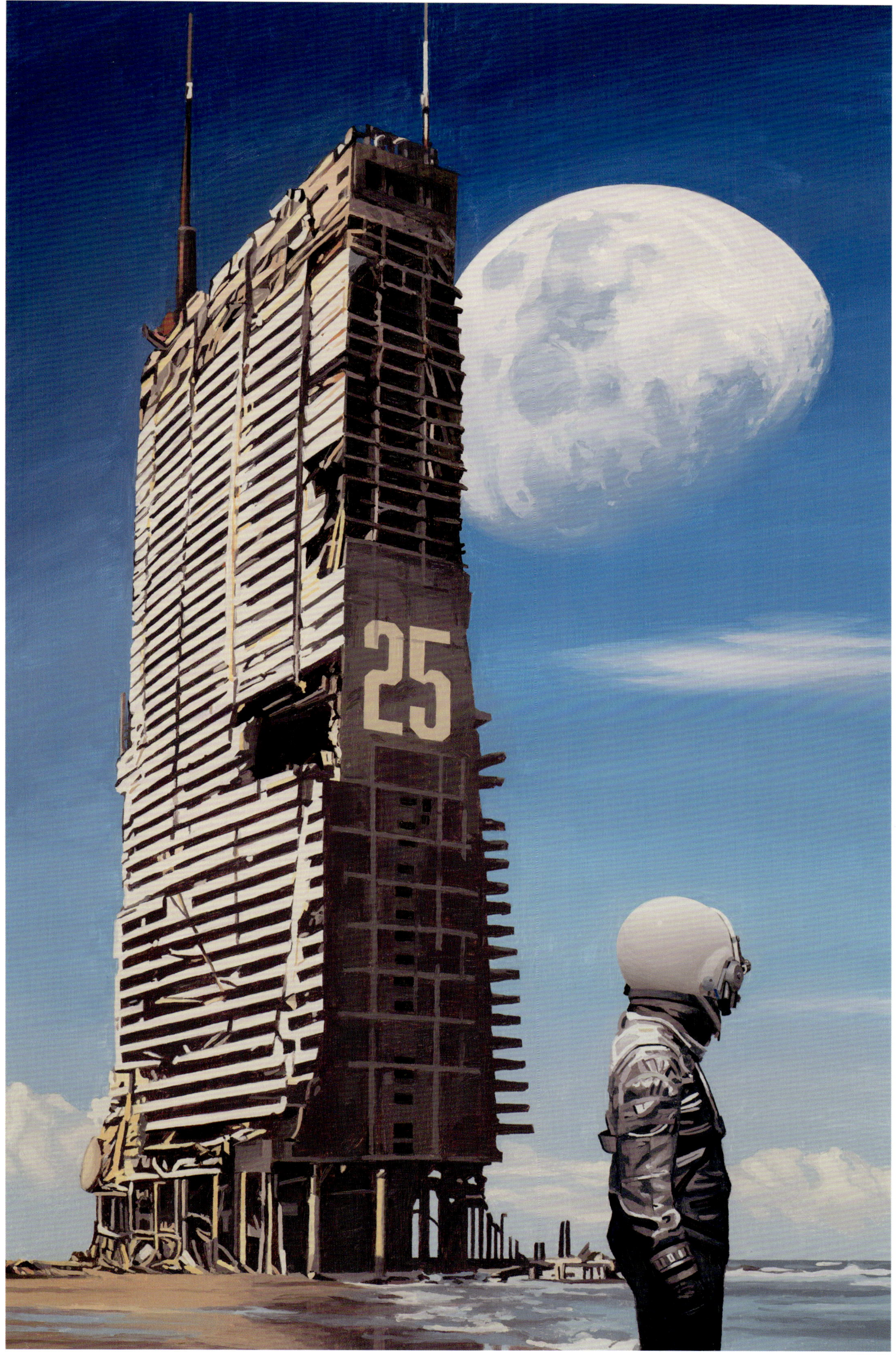
25

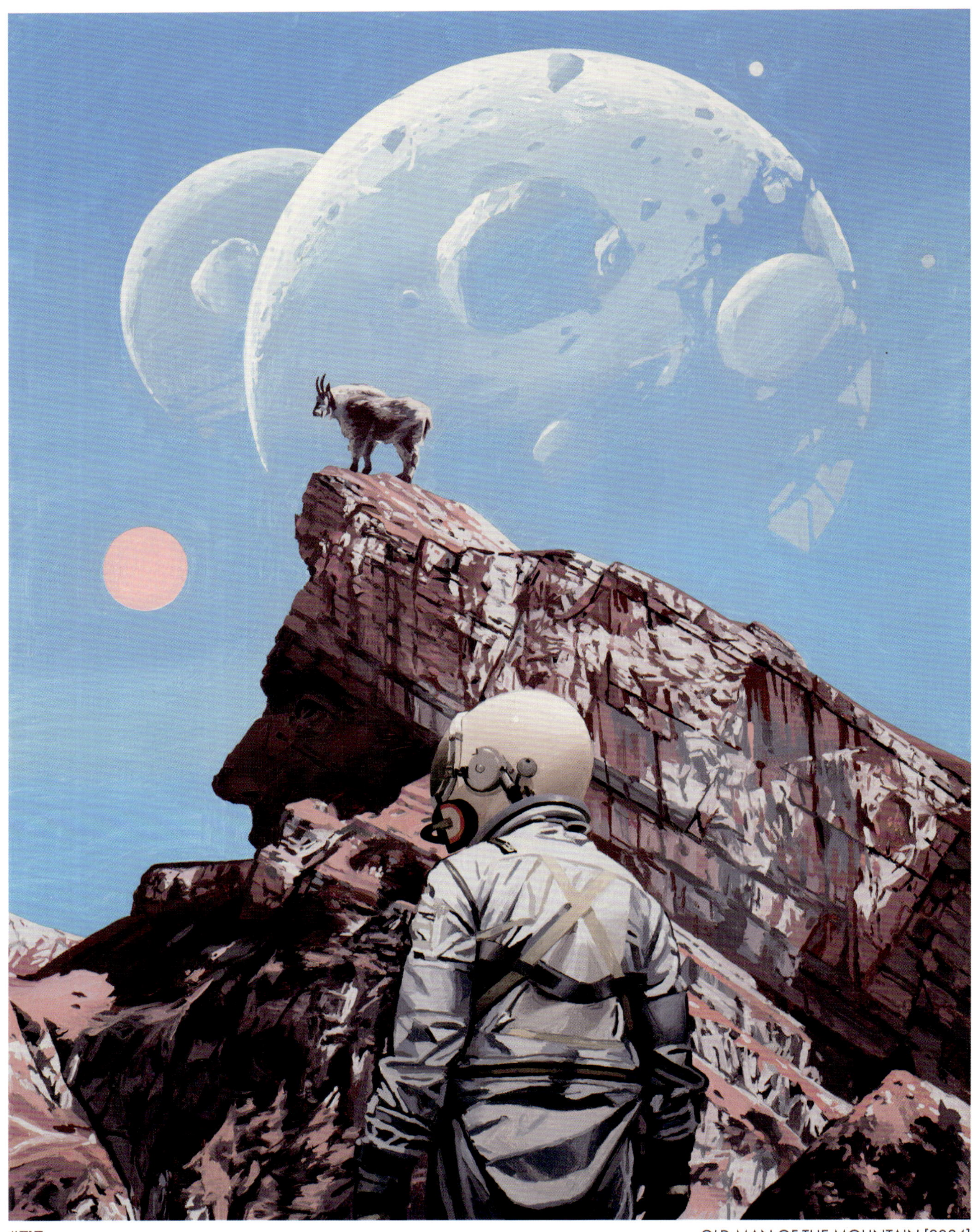

#717 OLD MAN OF THE MOUNTAIN [2024]

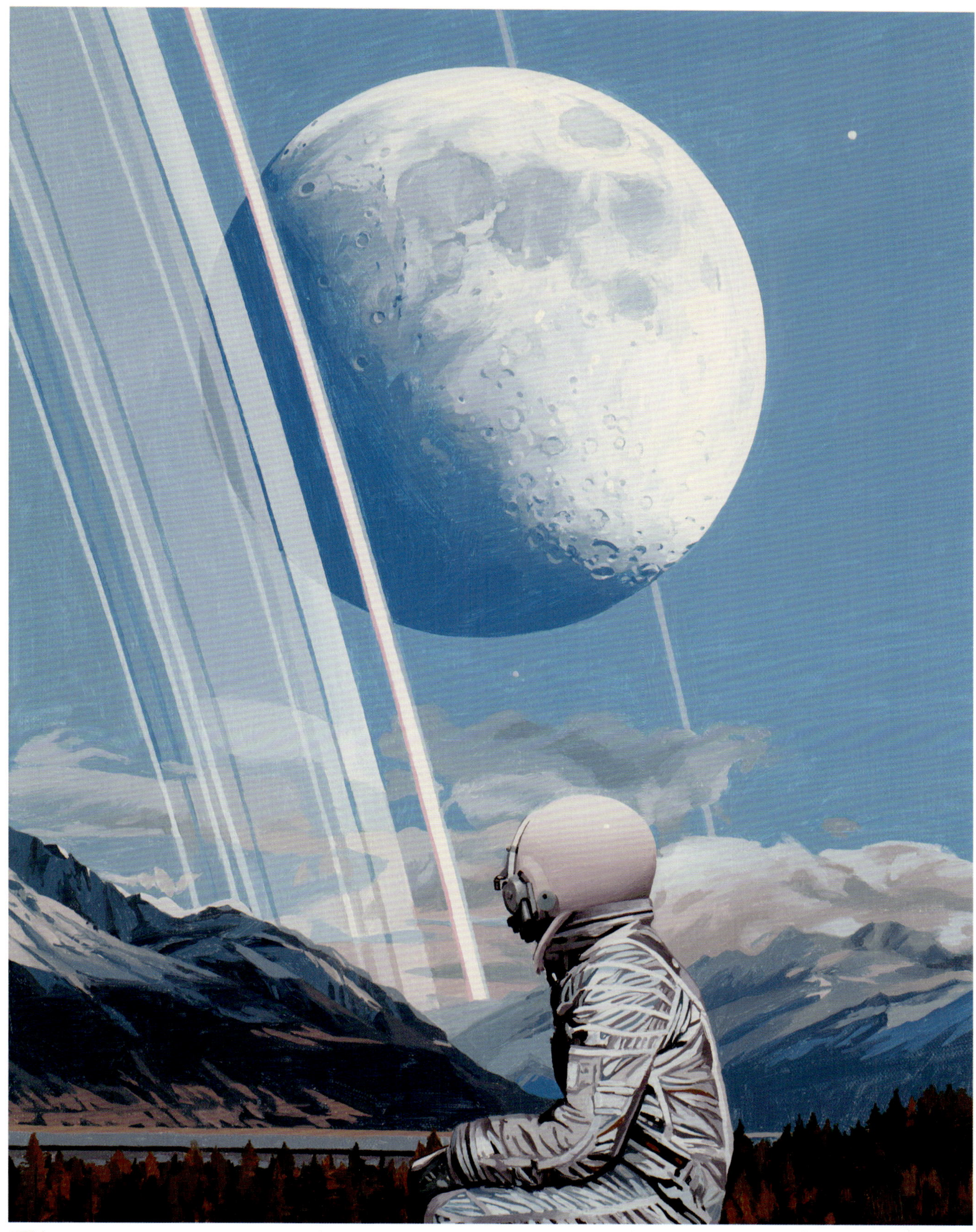

#724

MOONFALL [2024]

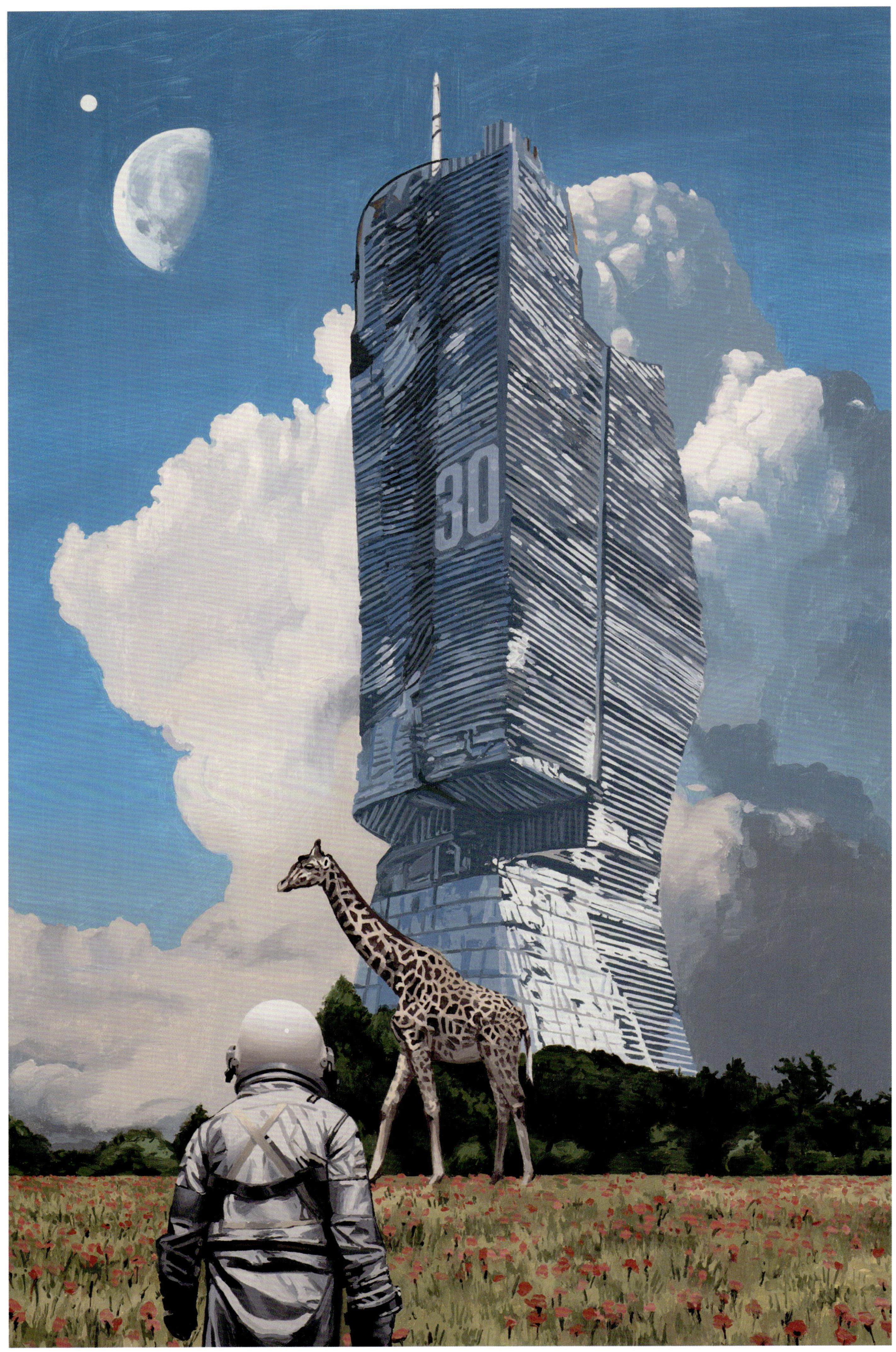
30

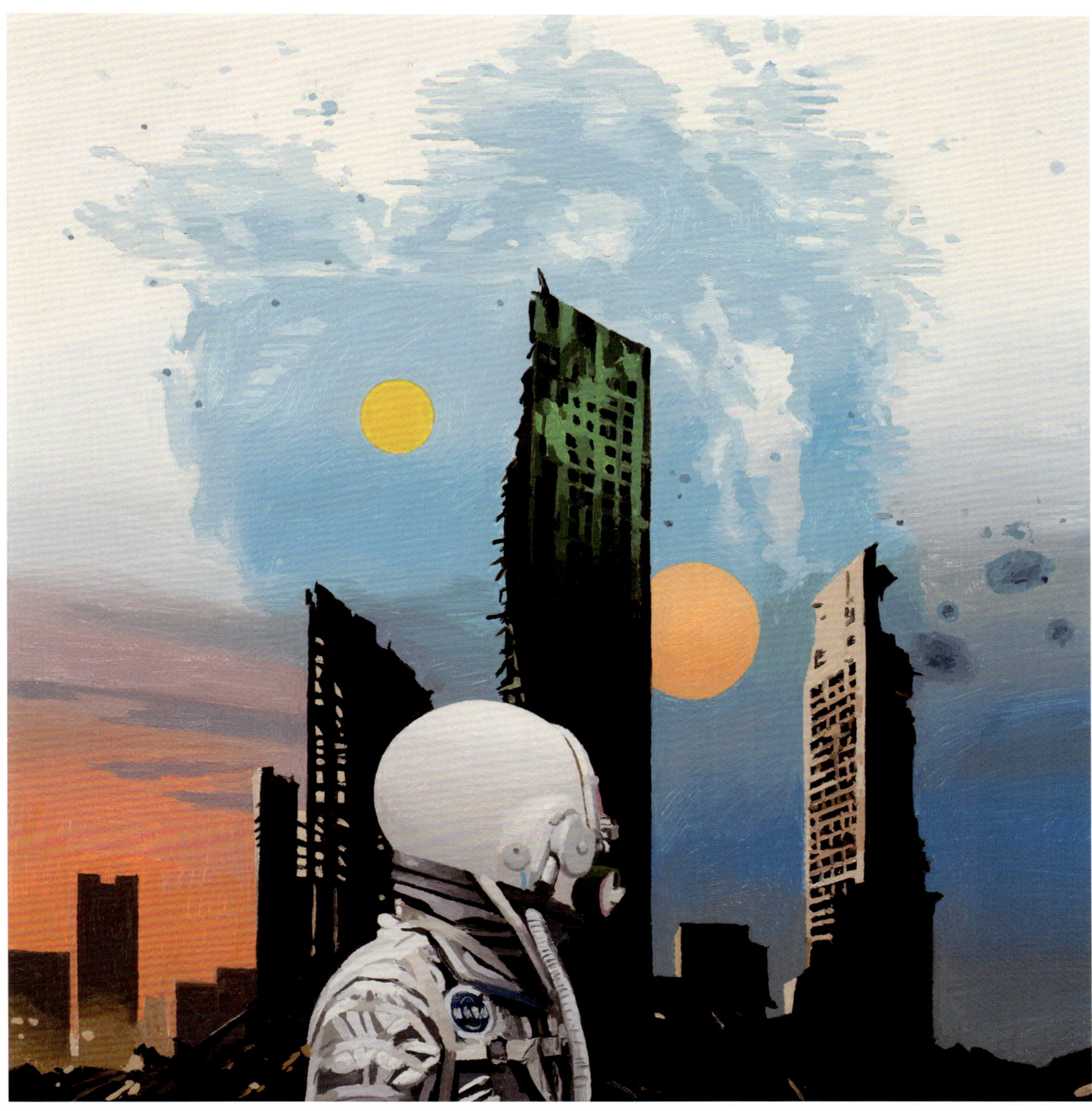

#726

CHEMICAL SKY [2024]

#730

BUILDING 30 [2024]

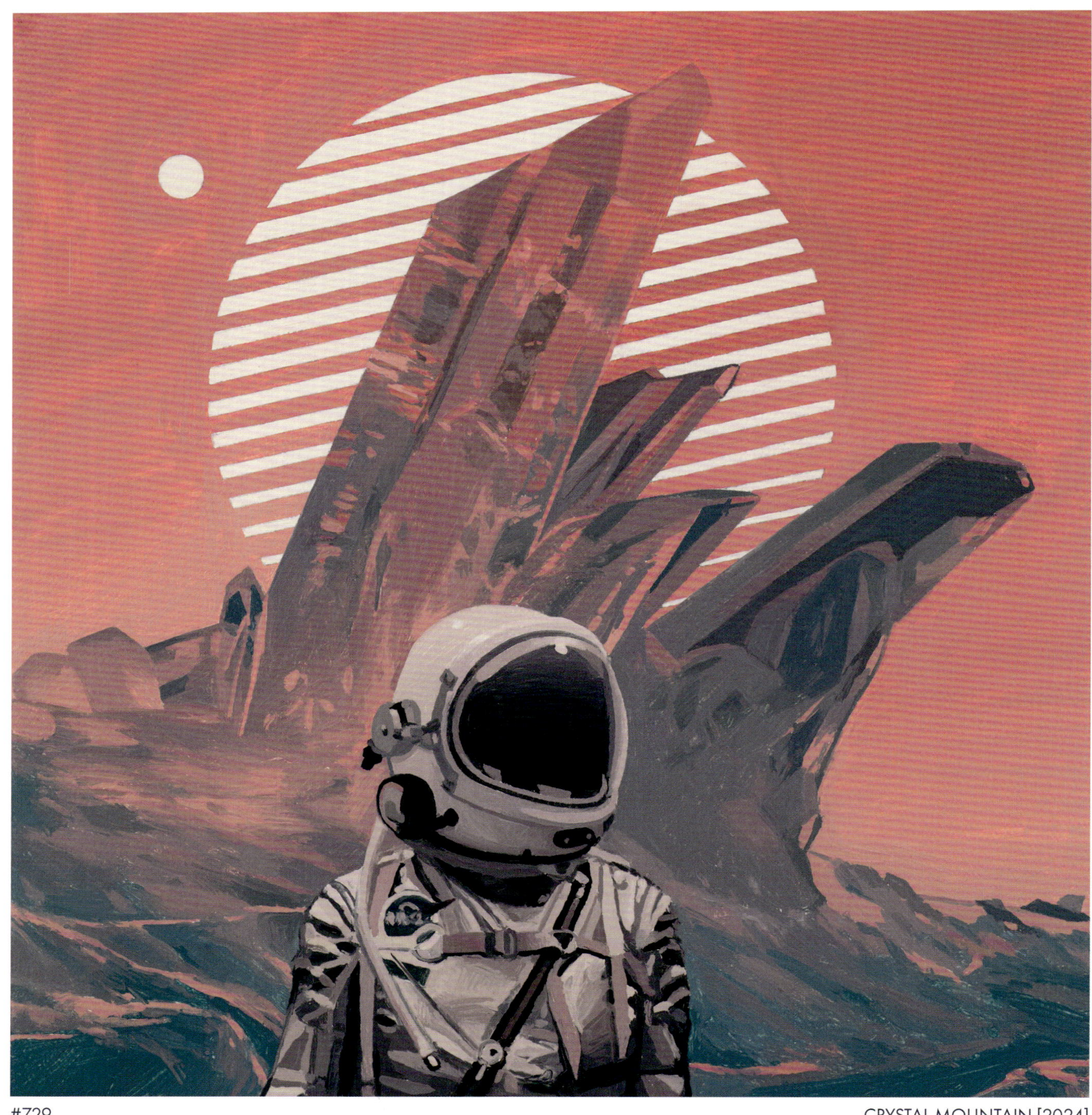

#729

CRYSTAL MOUNTAIN [2024]

#731

THE REMAINS OF BUILDING 66 [2024]

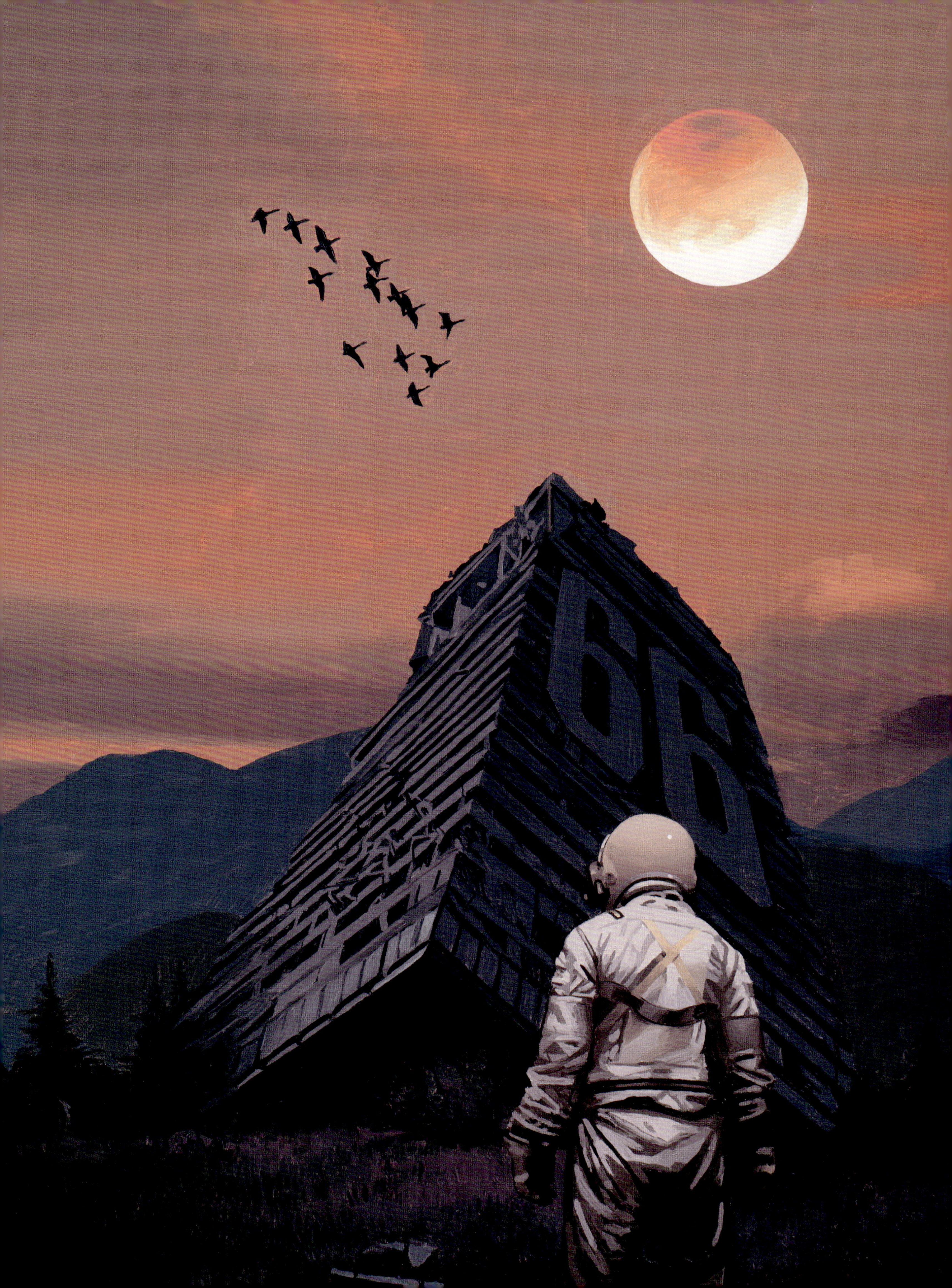

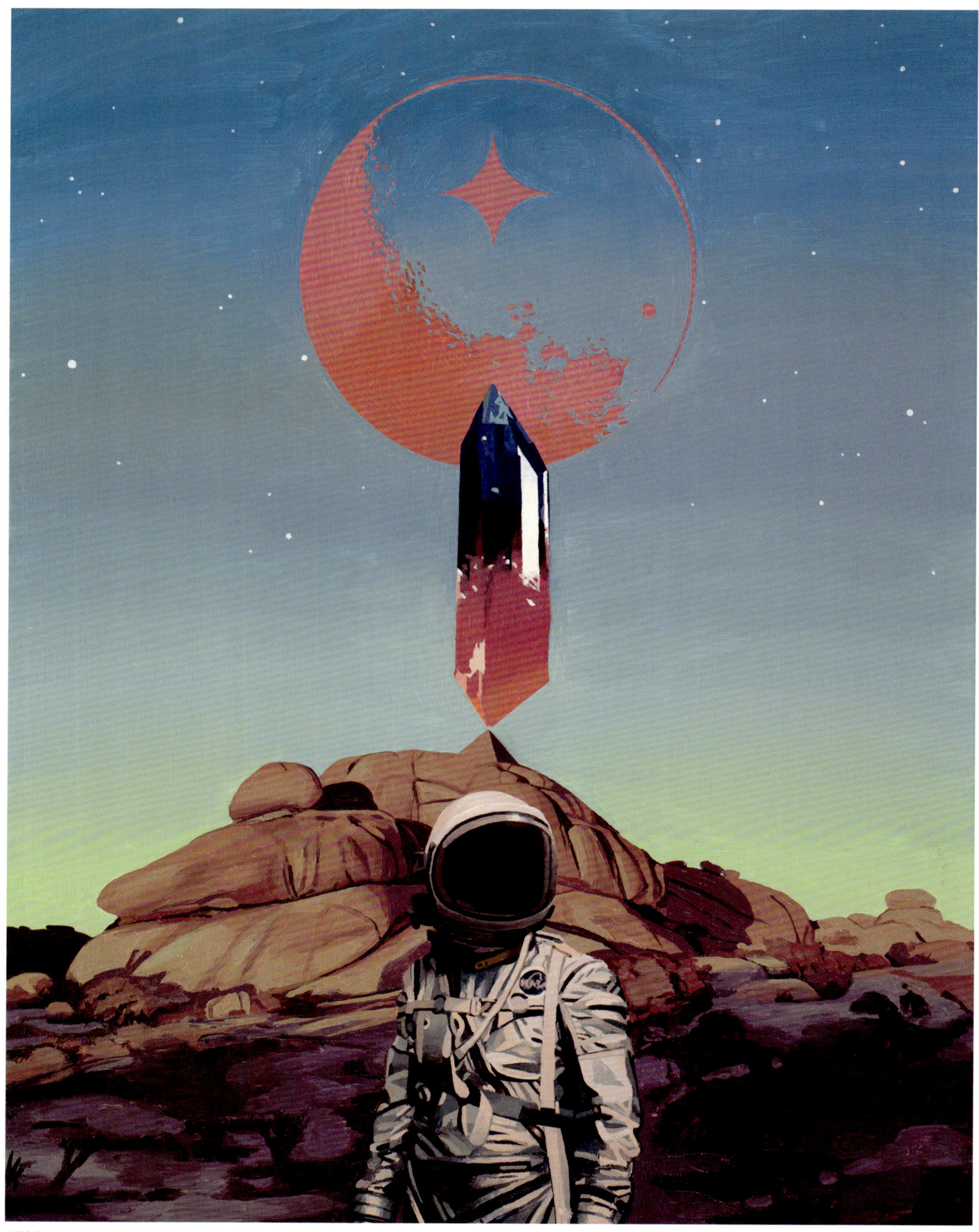

#725

CRYSTAL ORACLE [2024]

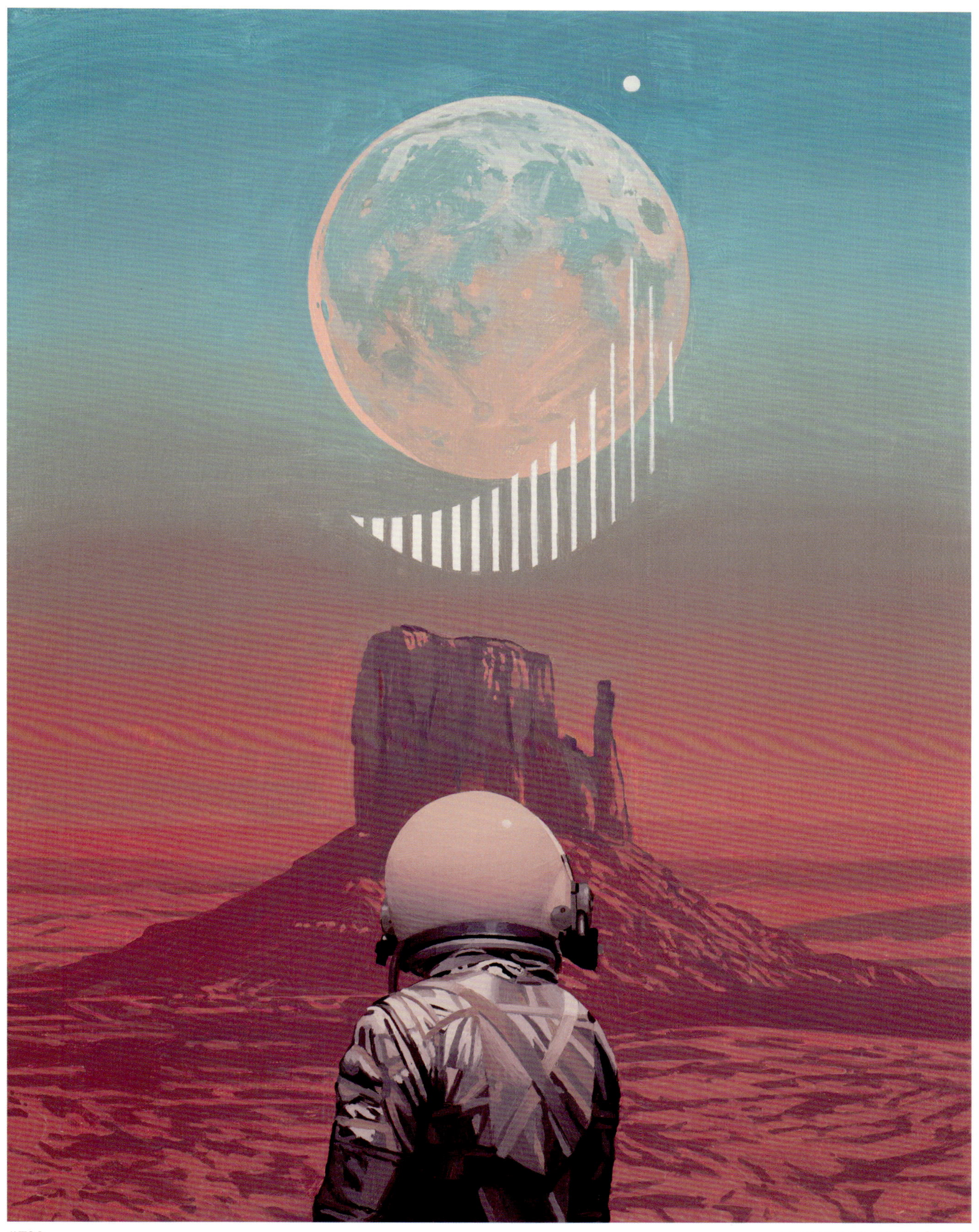

#728

PINK MOONSCAPE [2024]

CATALOG 2018–2025

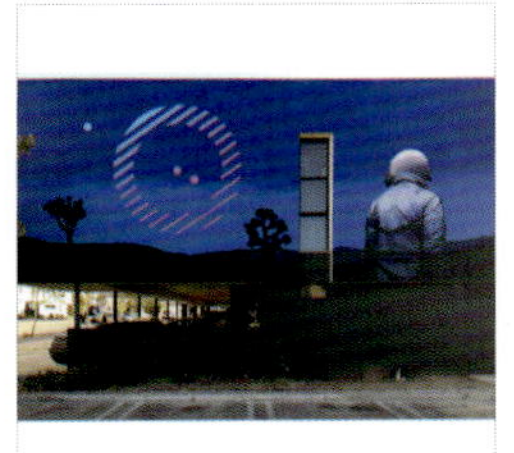

378
LANCASTER ASTRONAUT

2018
mural
17 x 41 ft.

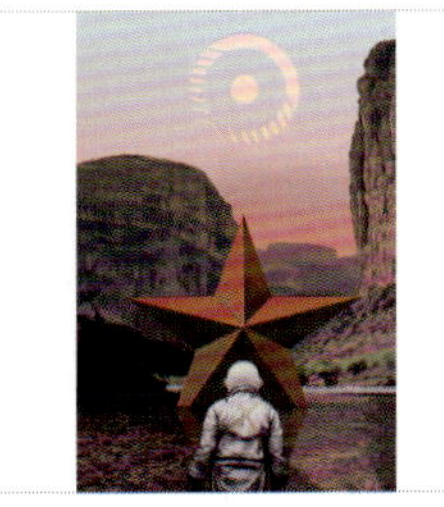

379
RED STAR

2018
oil on canvas
30 x 20 in.

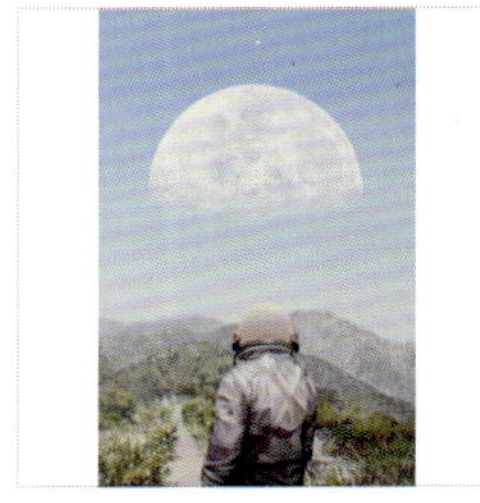

380
WHITE MOON

2018
oil on canvas
30 x 20 in.

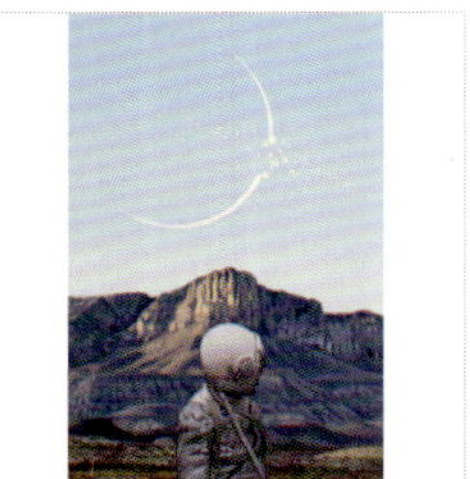

381
SHATTERED MOON

2018
oil on canvas
30 x 20 in.

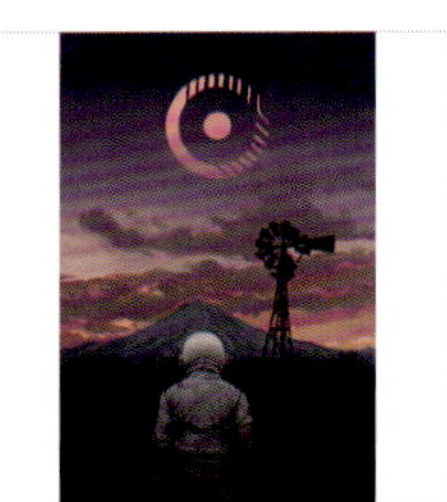

382
WINDMILL

2018
oil on canvas
30 x 20 in.

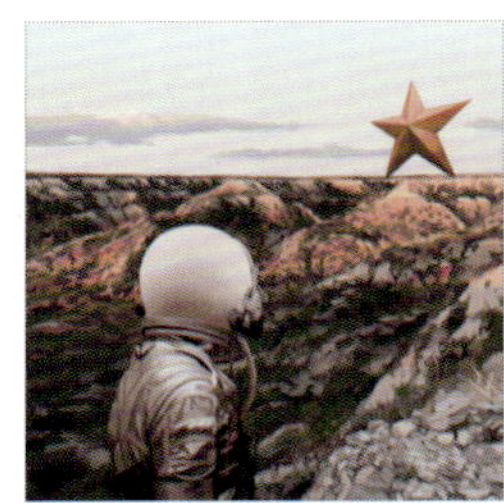

383
SUNSET STAR

2018
oil on canvas
20 x 20 in.

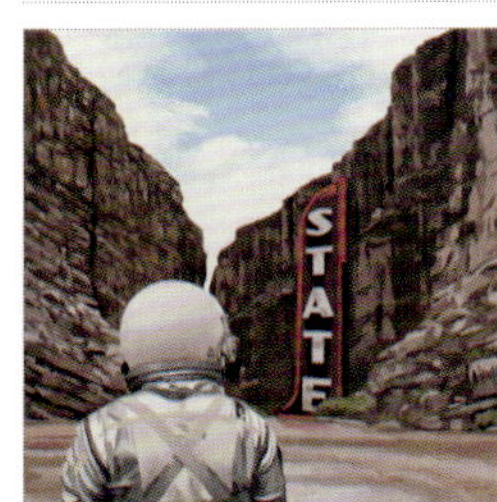

384
STATE

2018
oil on canvas
10 x 10 in.

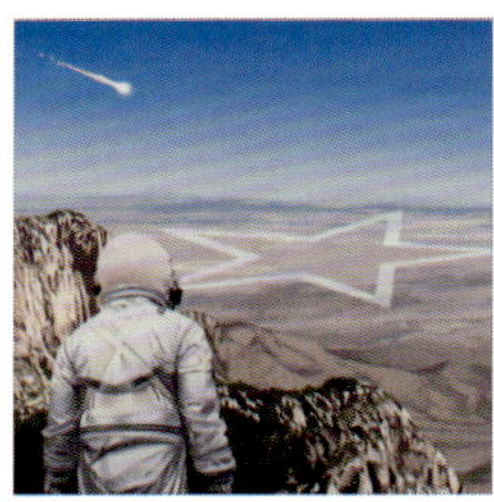

385
SHOOTING STAR

2019
oil on canvas
20 x 20 in.

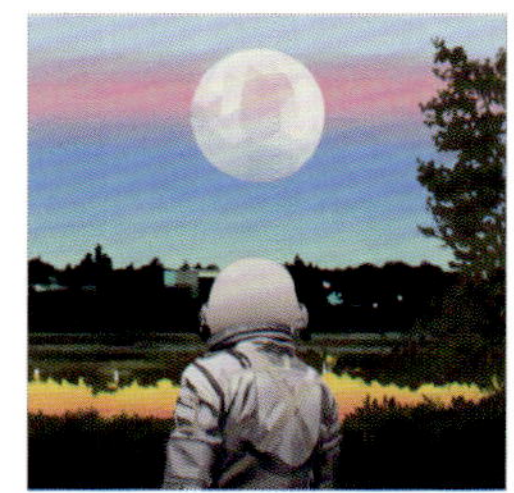

386
CRYSTAL MOON

2019
oil on canvas
10 x 10 in.

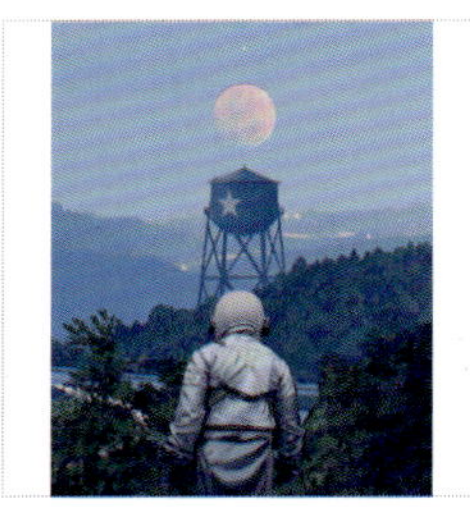

387
PINK MOON

2019
oil on canvas
20 x 16 in.

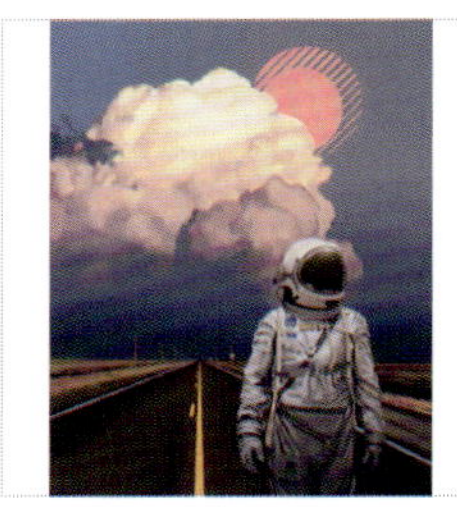

388
ORANGE CLOUD

2019
oil on canvas
20 x 16 in.

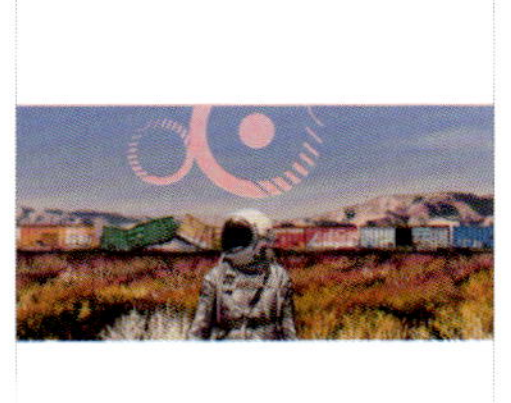

389
THE RAILROAD

2019
oil on canvas
20 x 40 in.

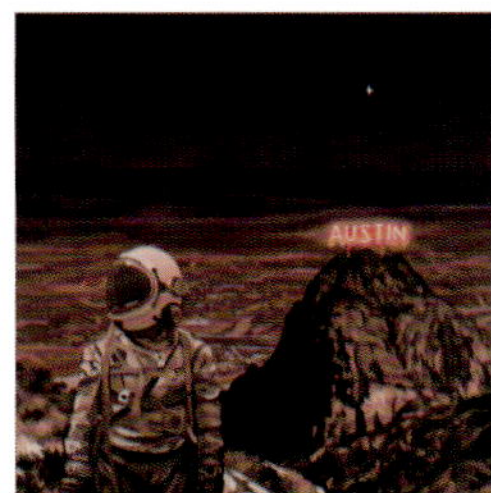

390
AUSTIN

2019
oil on canvas
10 x 10 in.

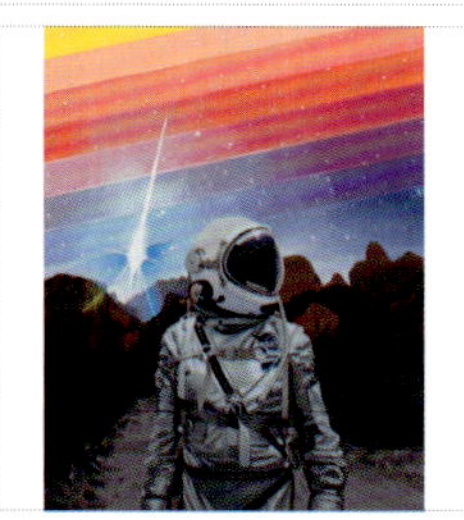

391
RAINBOW ONE

2019
oil on canvas
20 x 16 in.

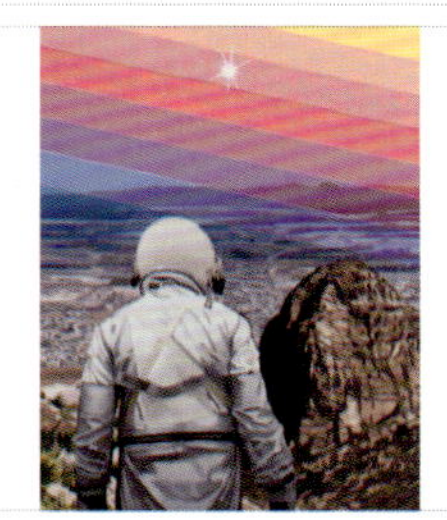

392
RAINBOW TWO

2019
oil on canvas
20 x 16 in.

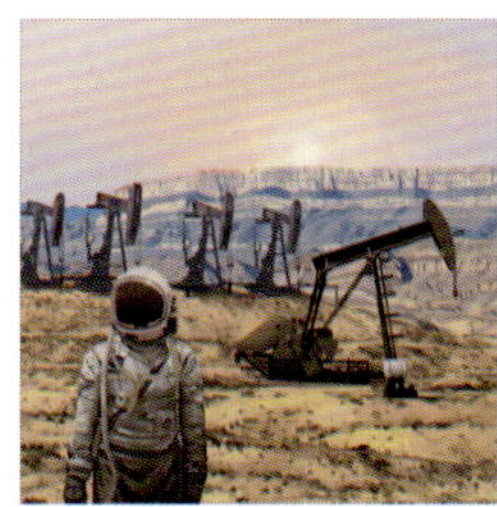

393
OIL WELLS

2019
oil on canvas
20 x 20 in.

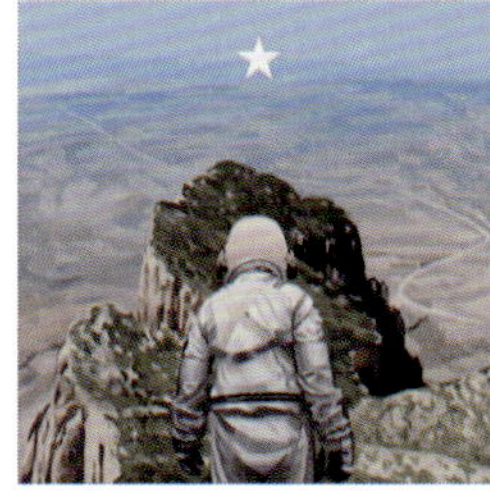

394
CLIFF STAR

2019
oil on canvas
10 x 10 in.

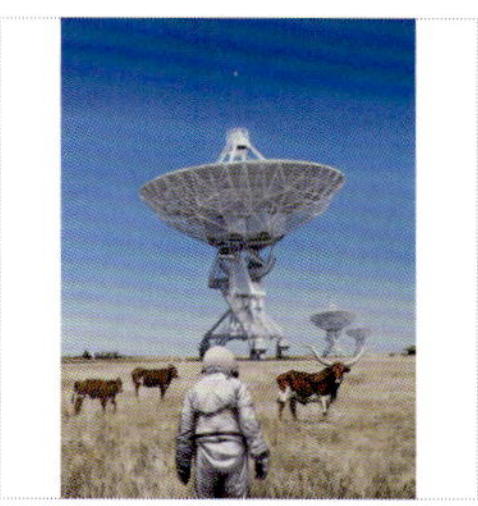

395
LONGHORNS

2019
oil on canvas
40 x 30 in.

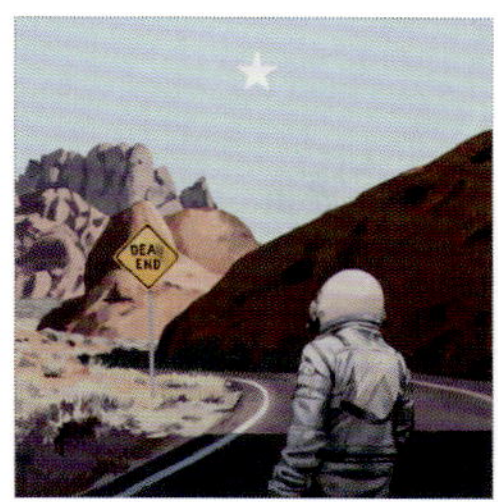

398
DEAD END

2019
oil on canvas
10 x 10 in.

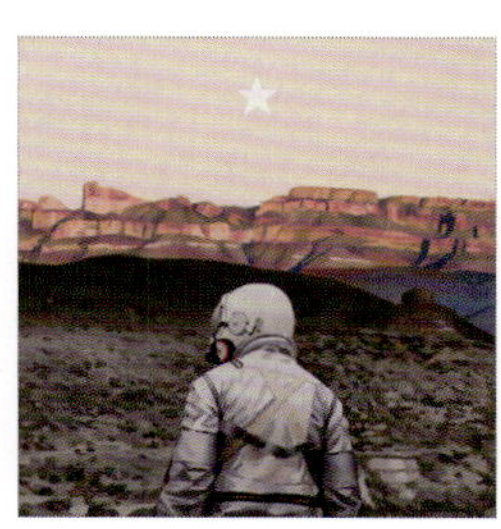

397
PINK CANYON

2019
oil on canvas
10 x 10 in.

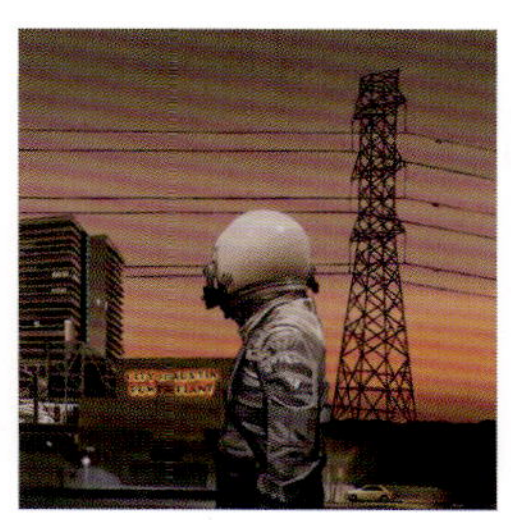

398
POWER PLANT

2019
oil on canvas
20 x 20 in.

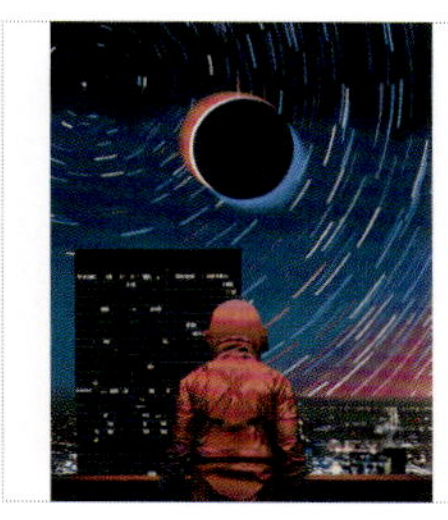

399
ECLIPSE

2019
oil on canvas
20 x 16 in.

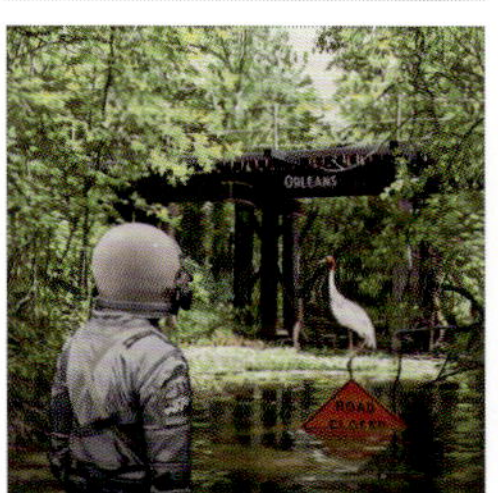

400
ORLEANS

2019
oil on canvas
20 x 20 in.

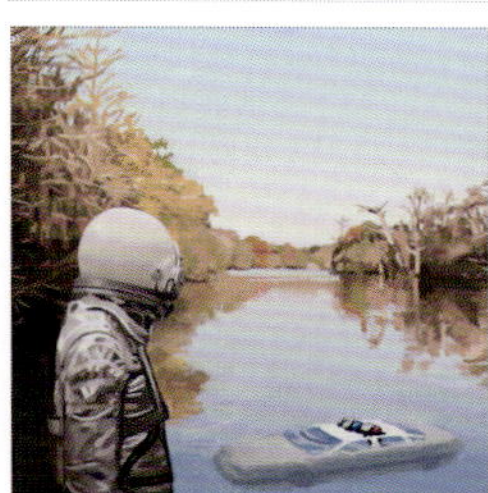

401
SUNKEN CAR

2019
oil on canvas
10 x 10 in.

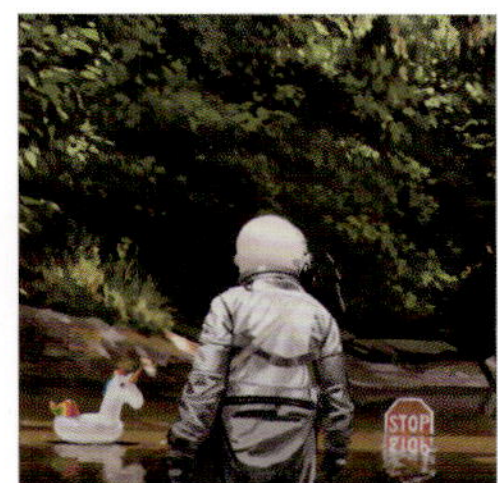

402
UNICORN

2019
oil on canvas
10 x 10 in.

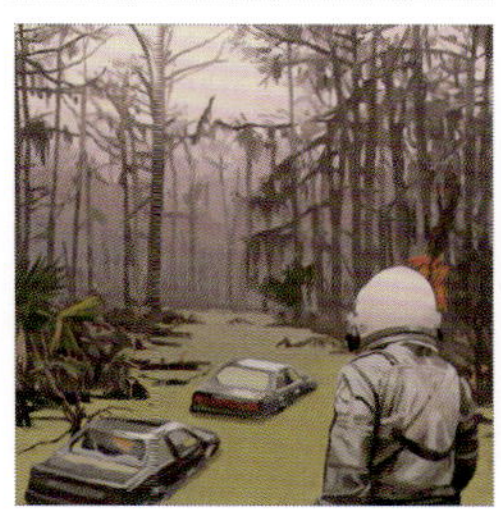

403
BAYOU PARKING LOT

2019
oil on canvas
10 x 10 in.

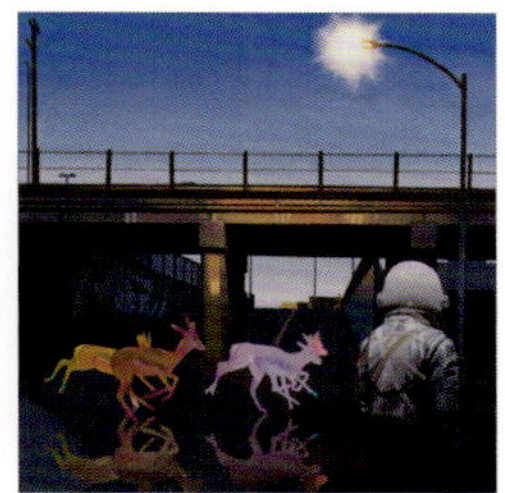

404
DEER

2019
oil on canvas
20 x 20 in.

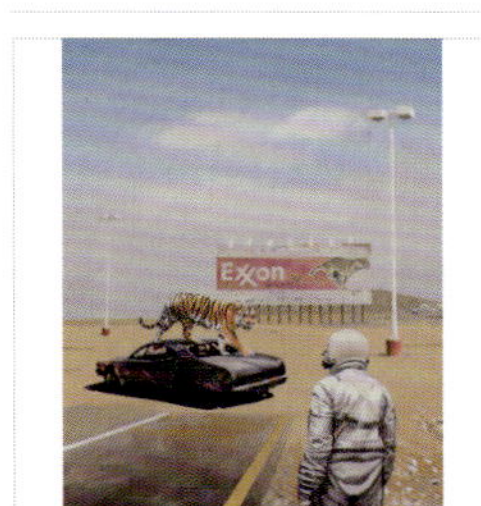

405
TIGER

2019
oil on canvas
20 x 16 in.

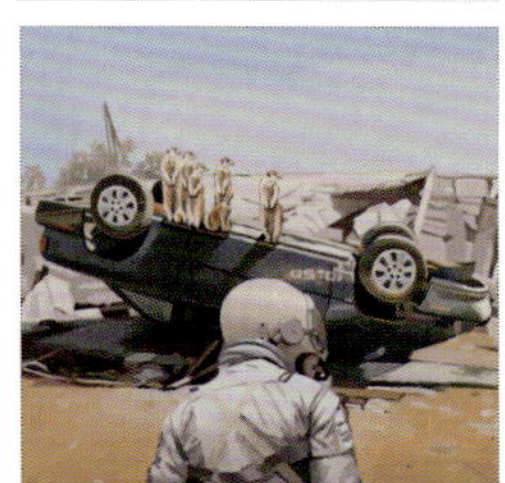

406
MEERKATS

2019
oil on canvas
10 x 10 in.

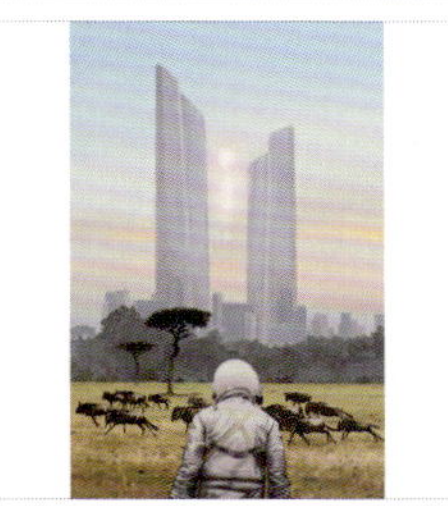

407
WILDEBEEST

2019
oil on canvas
30 x 20 in.

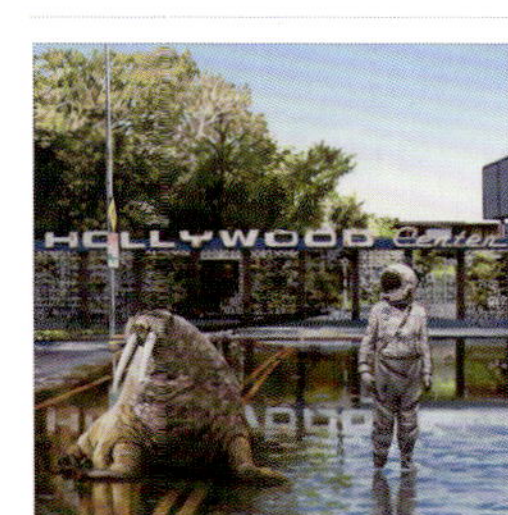

408
WALRUS

2019
oil on canvas
20 x 20 in.

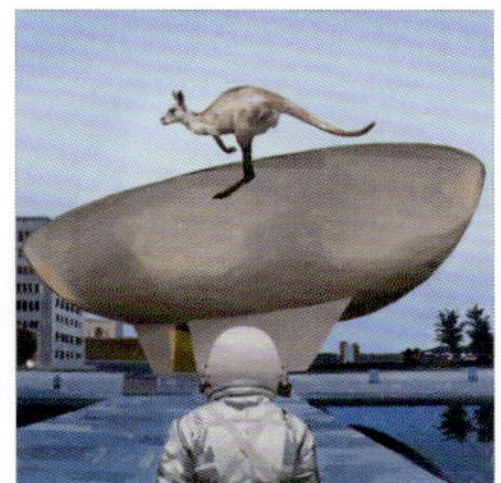

409
KANGAROO

2019
oil on canvas
10 x 10 in.

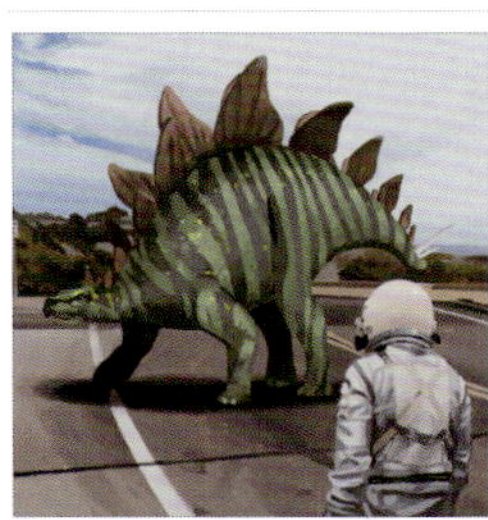

410
STEGOSAURUS

2019
oil on canvas
10 x 10 in.

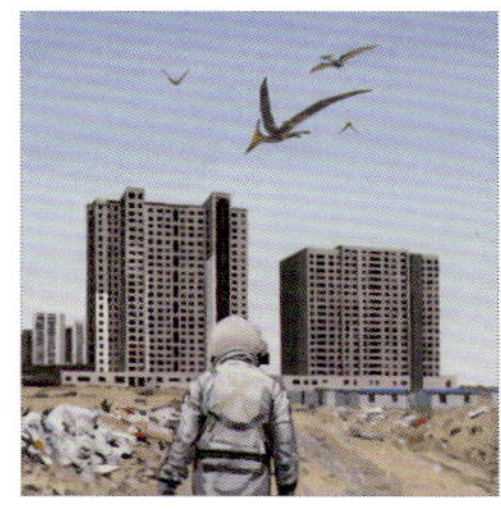

411
PTERODACTYL

2019
oil on canvas
10 x 10 in.

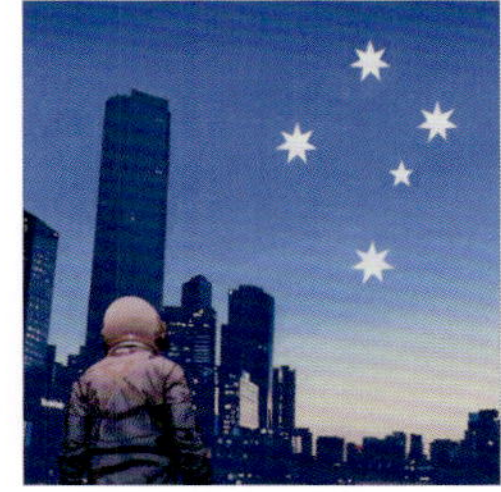

412
SOUTHERN CROSS

2019
oil on canvas
10 x 10 in.

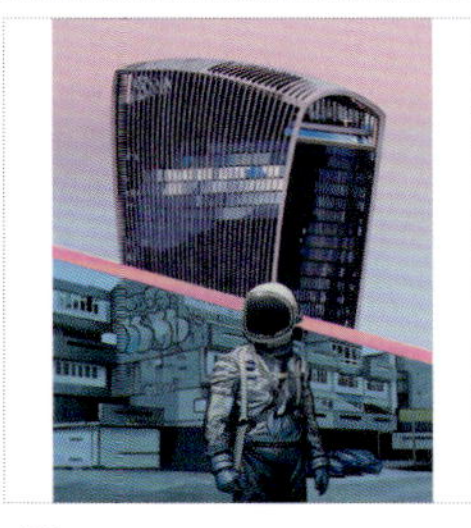

413
WALKIE-TALKIE

2019
oil on canvas
20 x 16 in.

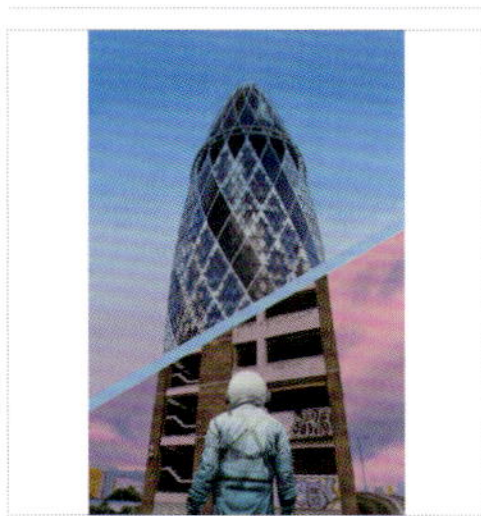

414
GHERKIN

2019
oil on canvas
30 x 20 in.

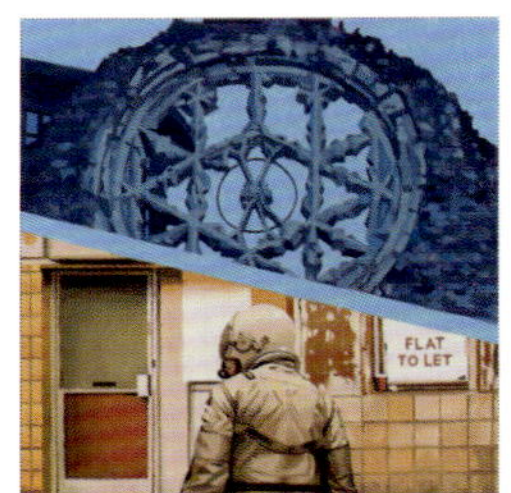

415
WINCHESTER PALACE

2019
oil on canvas
10 x 10 in.

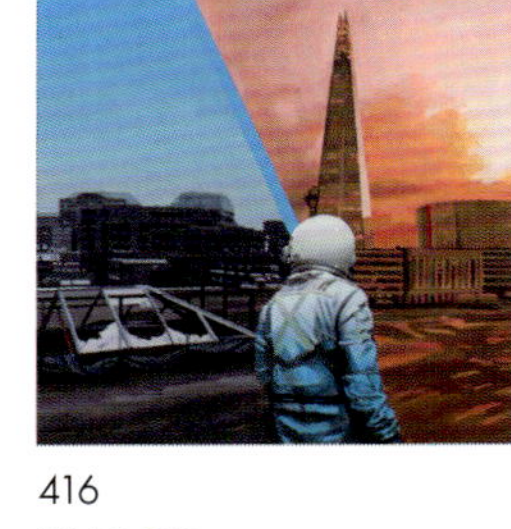

416
SHARD

2019
oil on canvas
20 x 20 in.

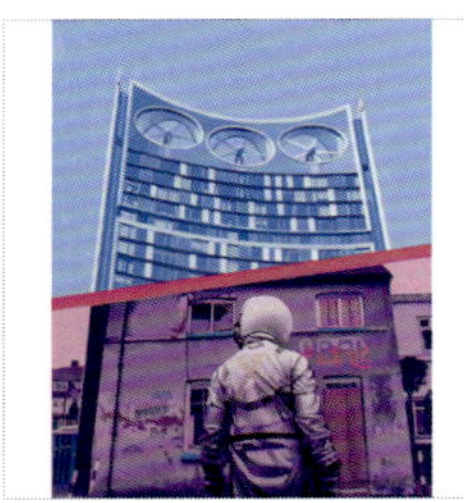

417
RAZOR

2019
oil on canvas
20 x 16 in.

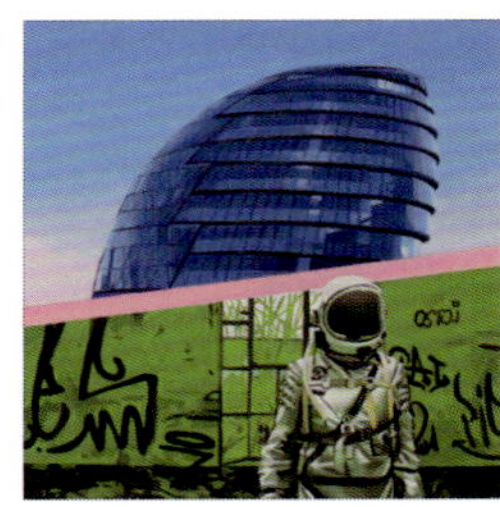

418
THE SNAIL

2019
oil on canvas
10 x 10 in.

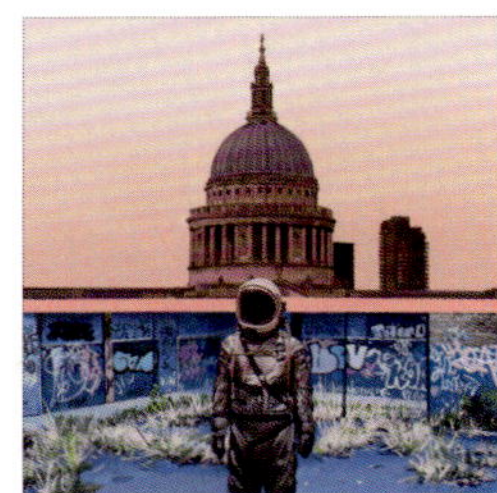

419
ST. PAUL'S

2019
oil on canvas
20 x 20 in.

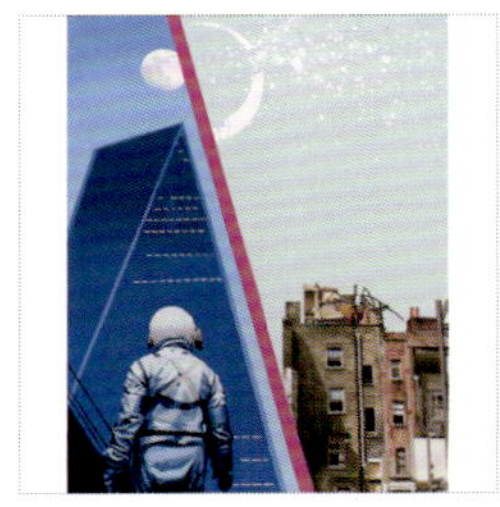

420
THE SCALPEL

2019
oil on canvas
20 x 16 in.

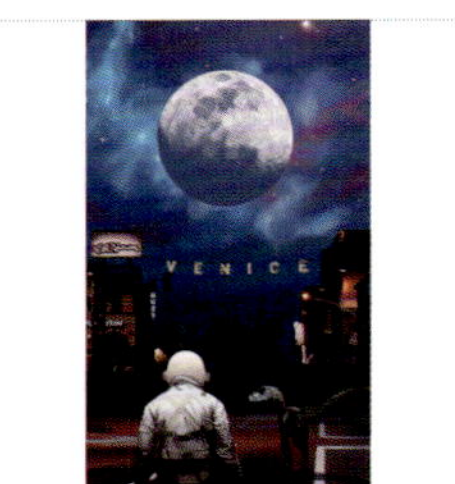

421
VENICE

2019
oil on canvas
60 x 36 in.

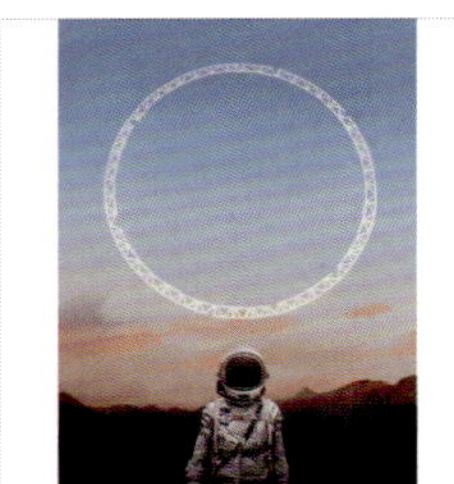

422
THE GATE

2019
oil on canvas
24 x 18 in.

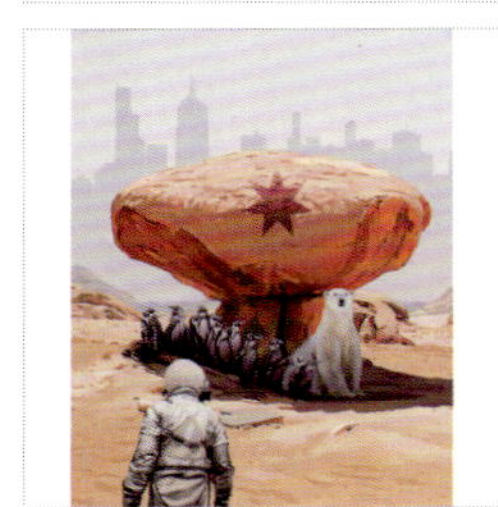

423
SHELTER

2019
oil on canvas
20 x 16 in.

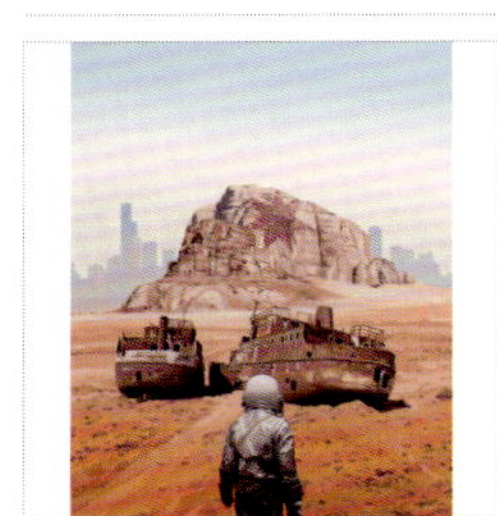

424
THE SEA

2019
oil on canvas
20 x 16 in.

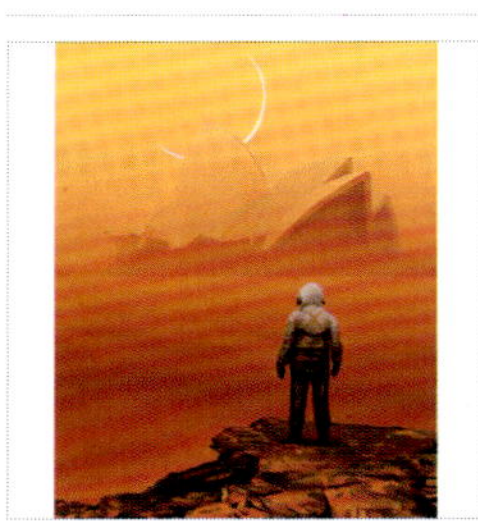

425
DESERT OPERA

2019
oil on canvas
20 x 16 in.

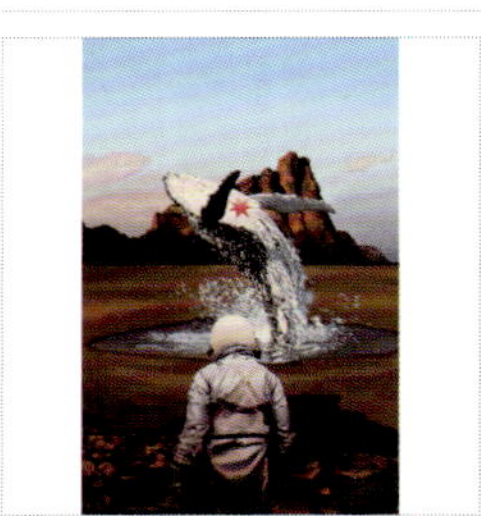

426
HUMPBACK

2019
oil on canvas
30 x 20 in.

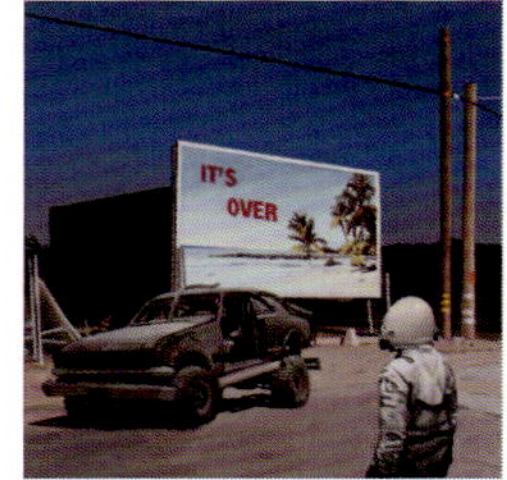

427
IT'S OVER

2019
oil on canvas
10 x 10 in.

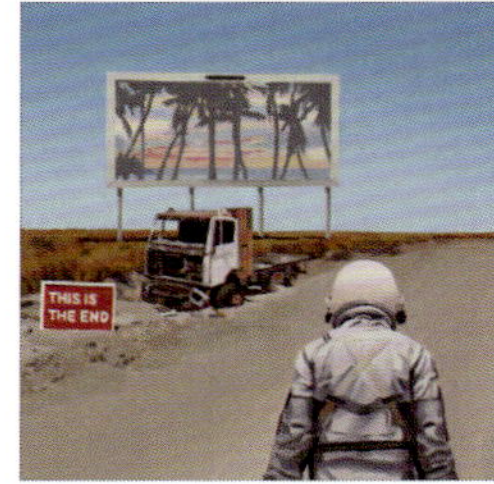

428
THIS IS THE END

2019
oil on canvas
10 x 10 in.

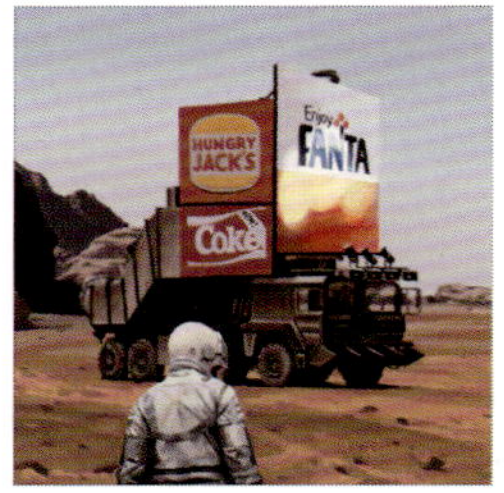

429
DOOF WAGON

2019
oil on canvas
10 x 10 in.

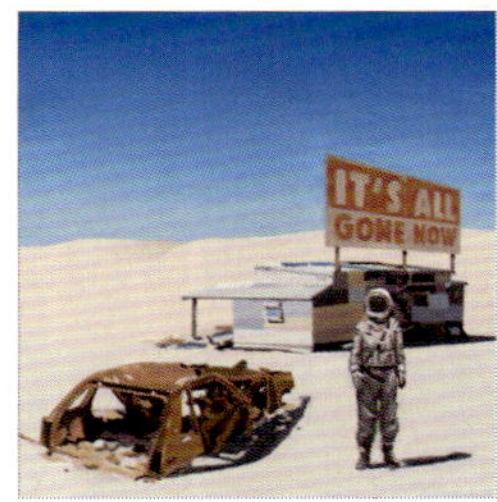

430
IT'S ALL GONE NOW

2019
oil on canvas
10 x 10 in.

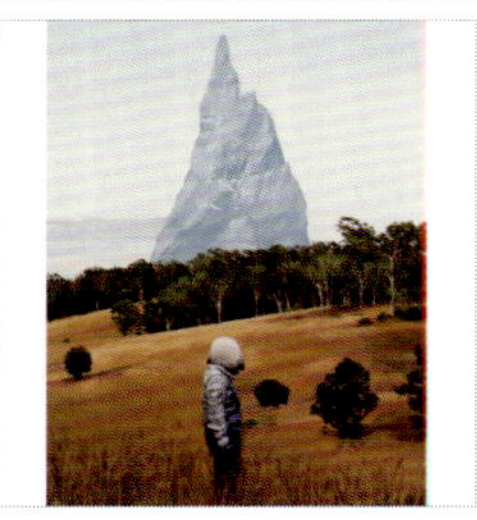

431
BALL'S PYRAMID

2019
oil on canvas
20 x 16 in.

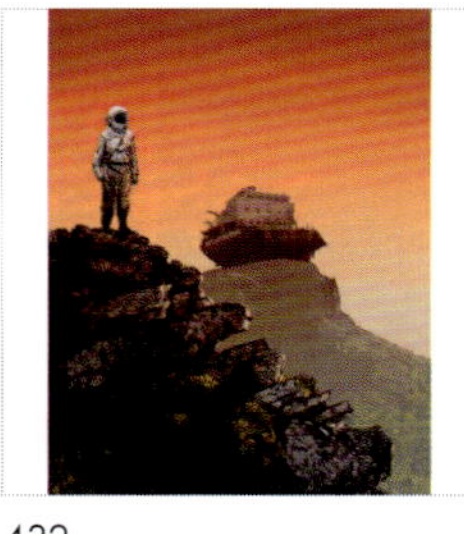

432
WRECK OF THE MELBOURNE

2019
oil on canvas
20 x 16 in.

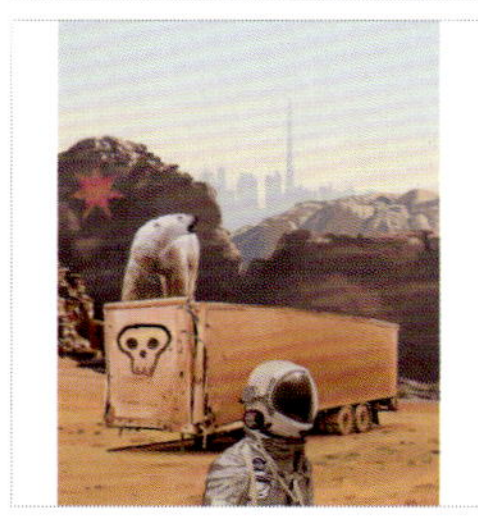

433
DESERTED TRUCK

2019
oil on canvas
20 x 16 in.

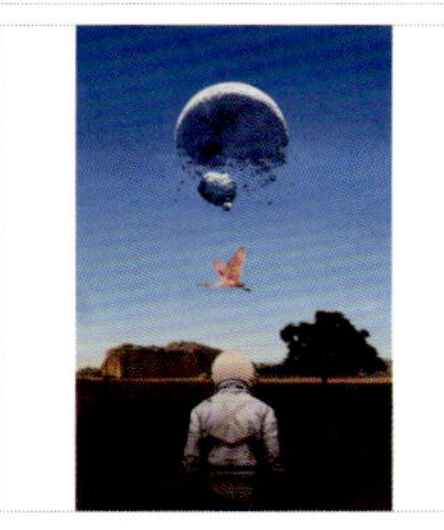

434
SPOONBILL

2019
oil on canvas
30 x 20 in.

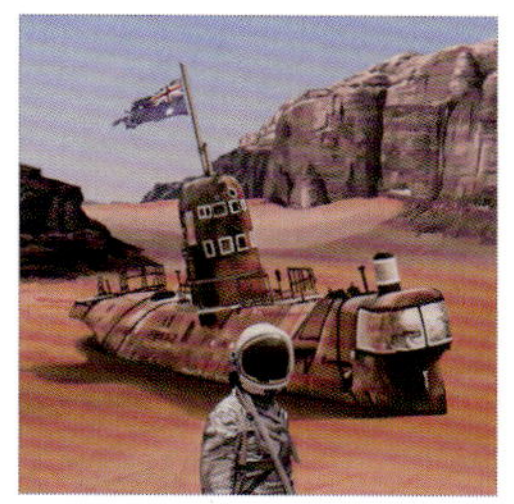

435
SUBMARINE

2019
oil on canvas
20 x 20 in.

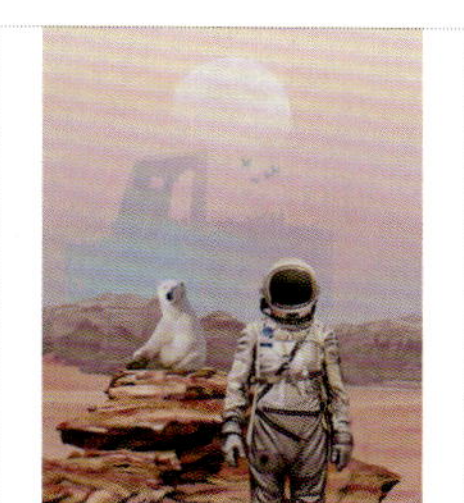

436
SHIP ON THE HORIZON

2019
oil on canvas
20 x 16 in.

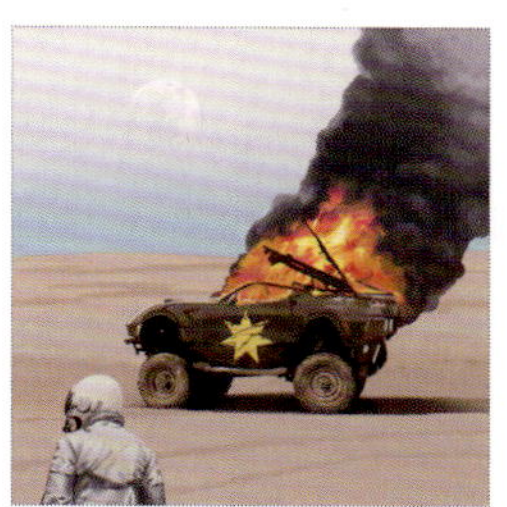

437
BURNING

2019
oil on canvas
20 x 20 in.

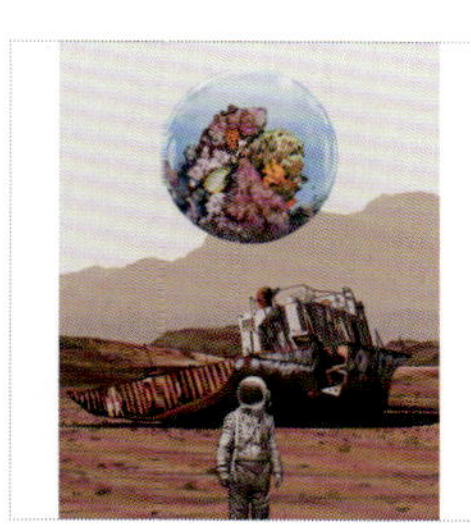

438
CORAL REEF

2019
oil on canvas
20 x 16 in.

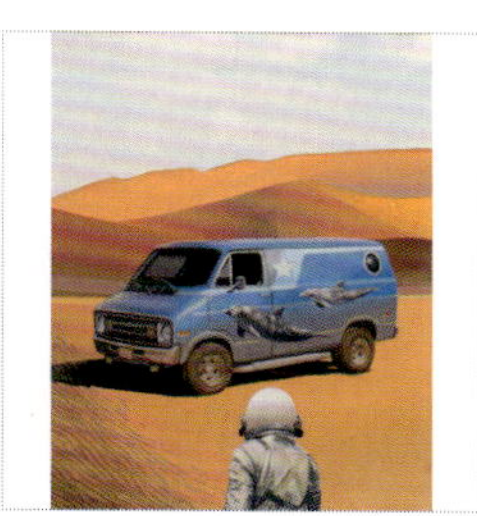

439
BITCHIN' VAN

2019
oil on canvas
20 x 16 in.

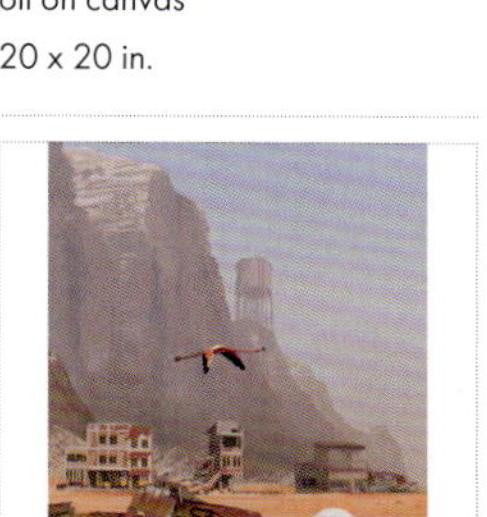

440
FLAMINGO

2019
oil on canvas
20 x 16 in.

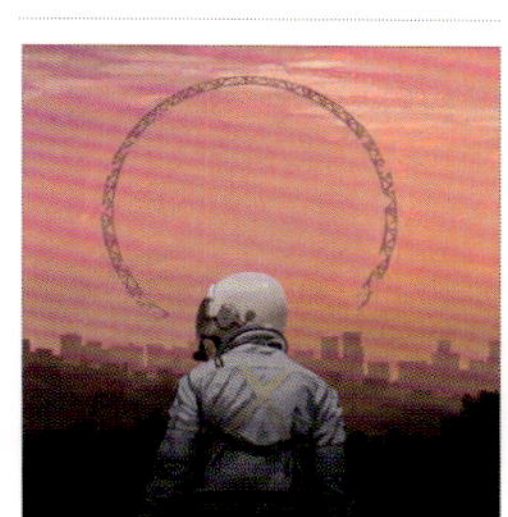

441
PINK RING

2019
oil on canvas
12 x 12 in.

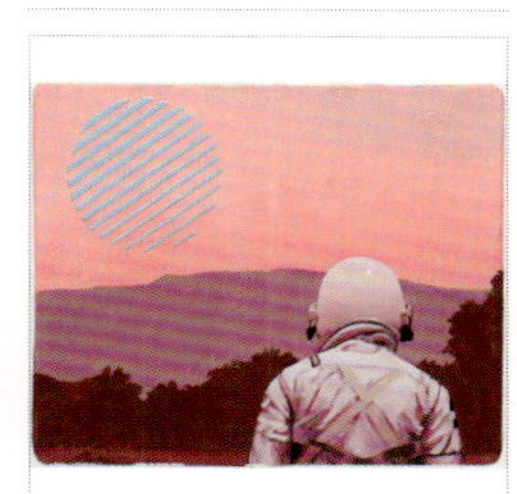

442
PINK MOUNTAINS

2019
oil on moleskine
8.25 x 10.25 in.

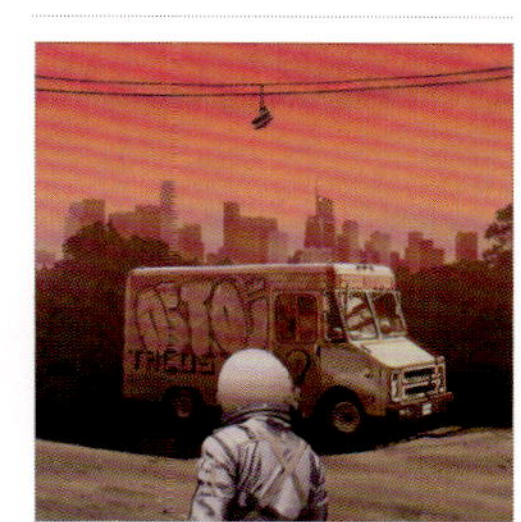

443
ON THE WIRE

2019
oil on canvas
15 x 15 in.

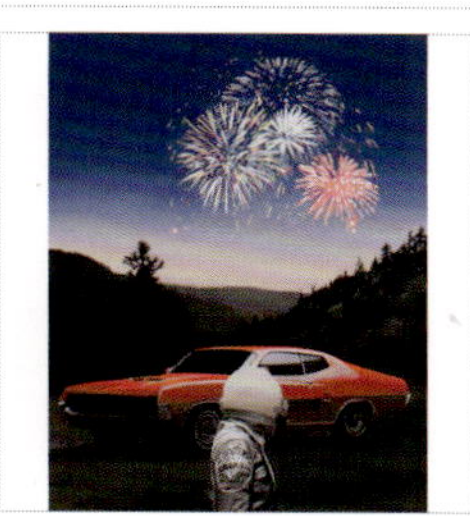

444
TORINO

2019
oil on canvas
20 x 16 in.

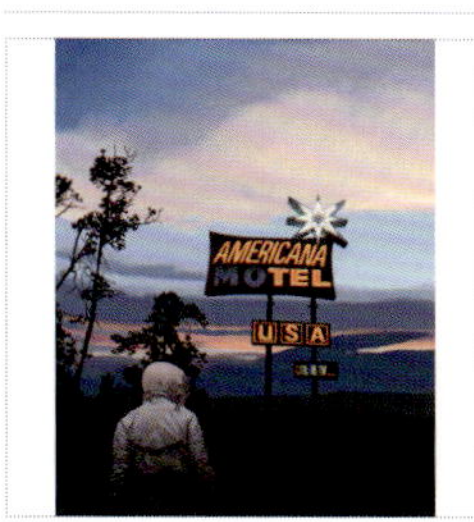

445
AMERICANA MOTEL

2019
oil on canvas
20 x 16 in.

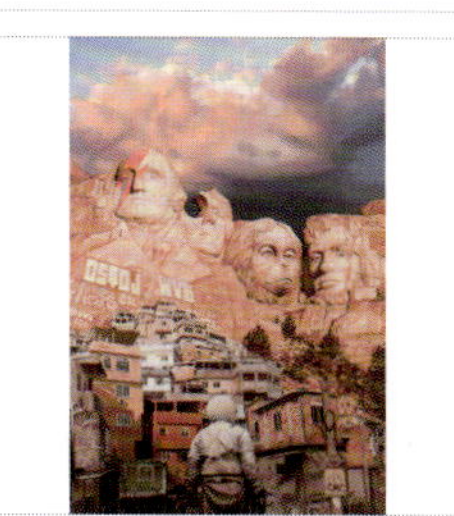

446
MOUNT RUSHMORE

2019
oil on canvas
30 x 20 in.

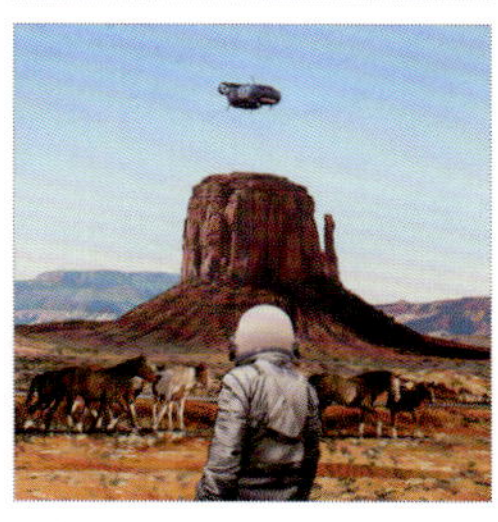

447
MONUMENT VALLEY

2019
oil on canvas
20 x 20 in.

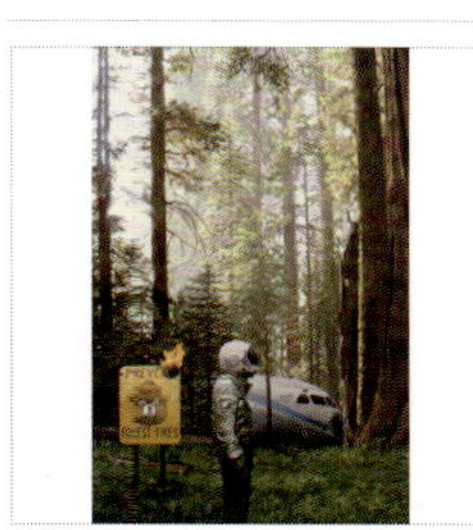

448
SMOKEY

2019
oil on canvas
30 x 20 in.

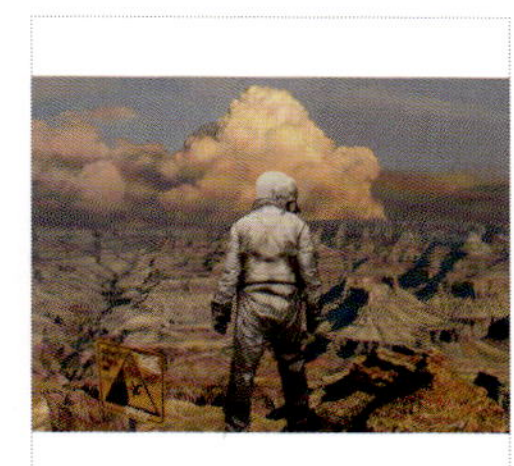

449
GRAND CANYON II

2019
oil on canvas
30 x 40 in.

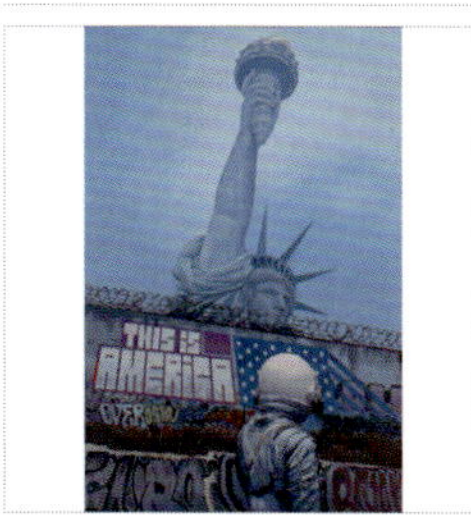

450
STATUE OF LIBERTY

2019
oil on canvas
30 x 20 in.

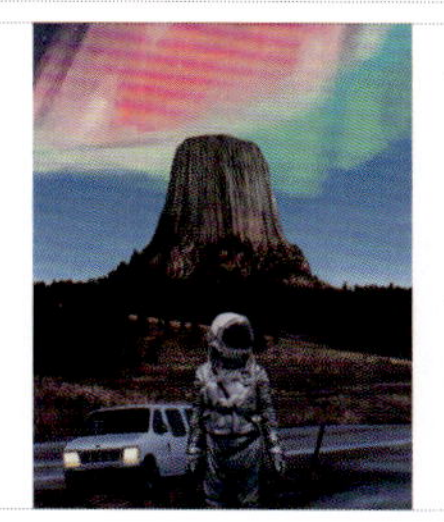

451
DEVIL'S TOWER

2020
oil on canvas
20 x 16 in.

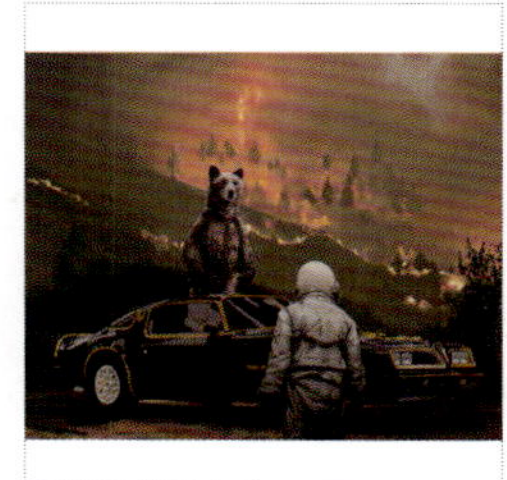

452
THE BANDIT

2020
oil on canvas
16 x 20 in.

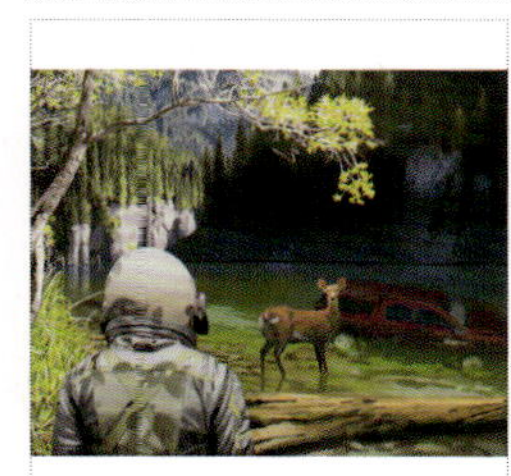

453
SUBMERGED

2020
oil on canvas
16 x 20 in.

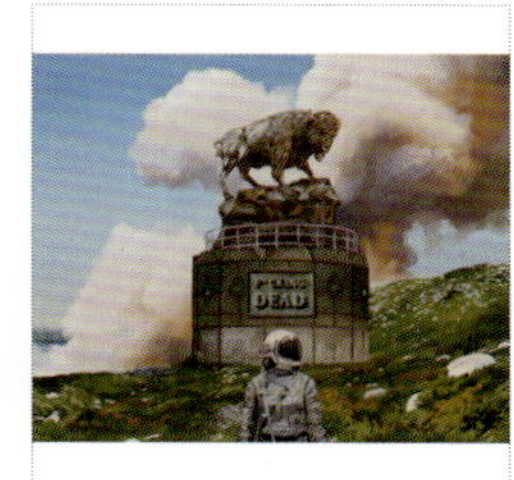

454
MEMORIAL

2020
oil on canvas
16 x 20 in.

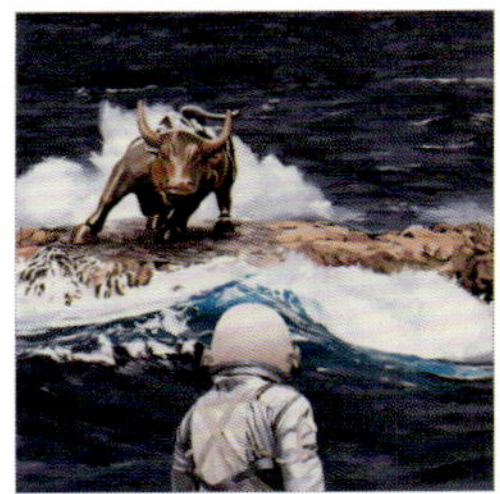

455
BULL

2020
oil on canvas
10 x 10 in.

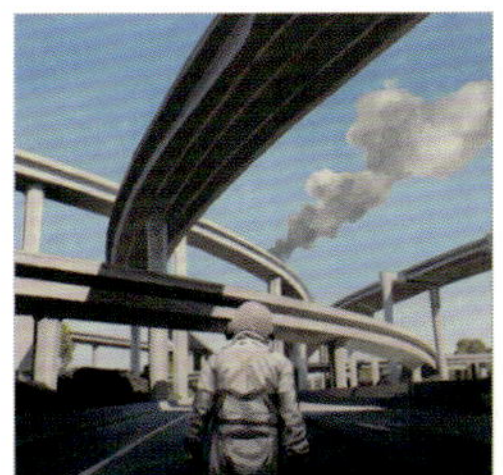

456
SMOKE ON THE ON RAMP

2020
oil on canvas
10 x 10 in.

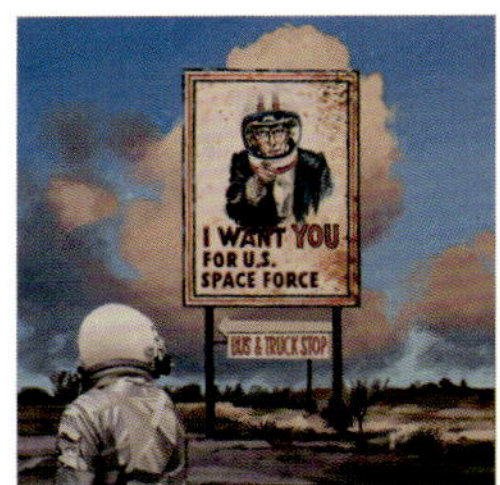

457
JOIN THE SPACE FORCE

2020
oil on canvas
10 x 10 in.

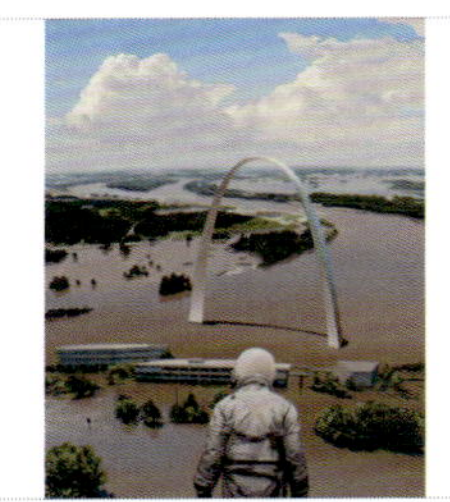

458
FLOODED ARCH

2020
oil on canvas
20 x 16 in.

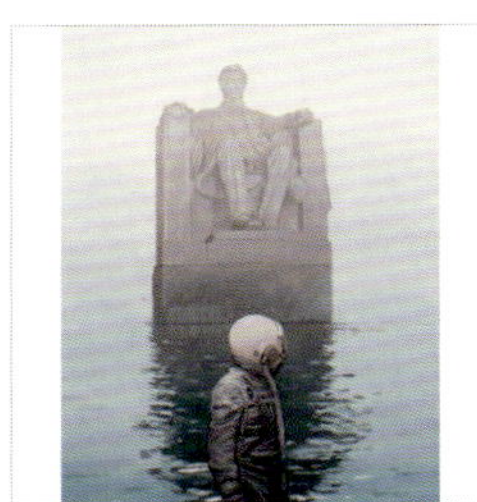

459
ABE

2020
oil on canvas
20 x 16 in.

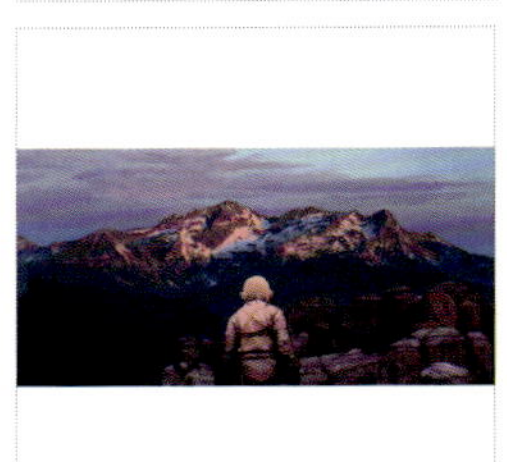

460
PURPLE MOUNTAINS

2020
oil on canvas
24 x 48 in.

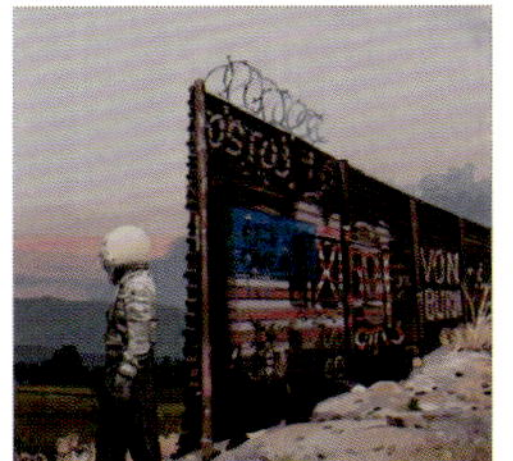

461
WHERE THE WALL ENDS

2020
oil on canvas
10 x 10 in.

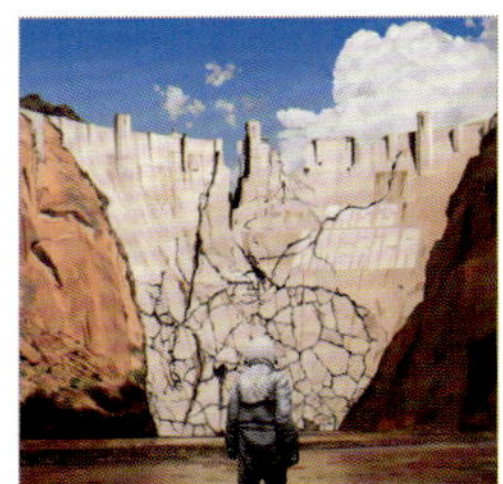

462
HOOVER DAM

2020
oil on canvas
20 x 20 in.

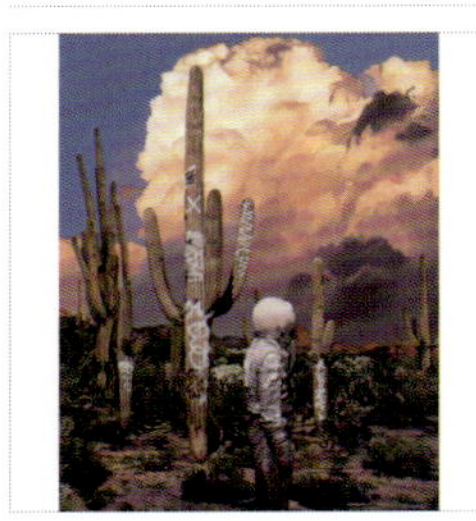

463
SAGUARO

2020
oil on canvas
20 x 16 in.

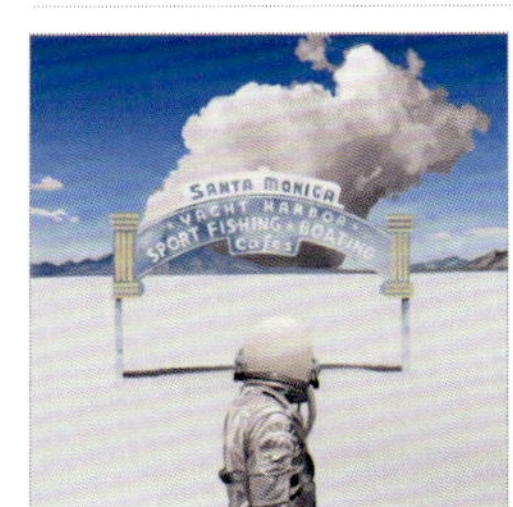

464
SALT FLATS

2020
oil on canvas
10 x 10 in.

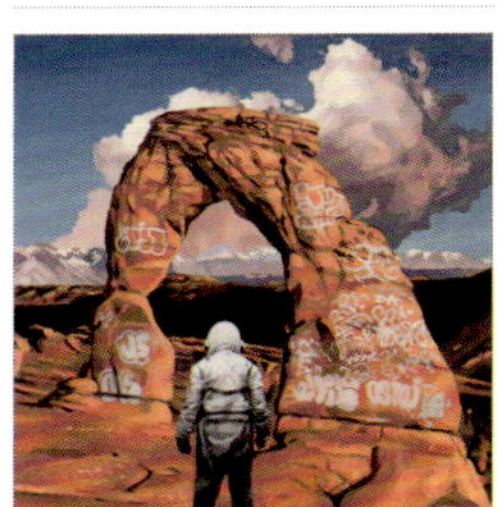

465
ARCH

2020
oil on canvas
10 x 10 in.

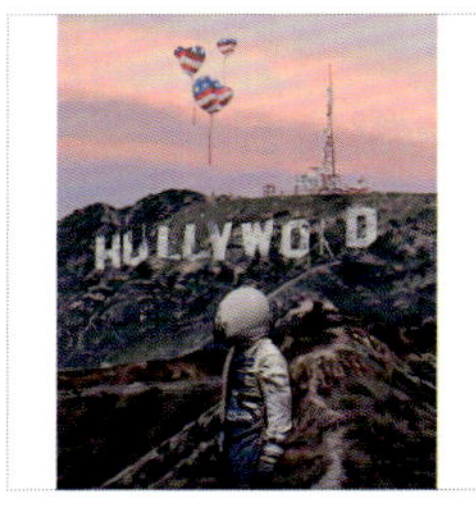

466
HOLLYWOOD FOREVER

2020
oil on canvas
20 x 16 in.

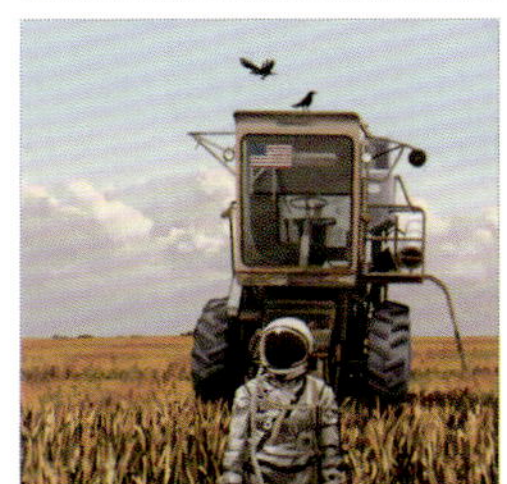

467
CORNFIELD

2020
oil on canvas
10 x 10 in.

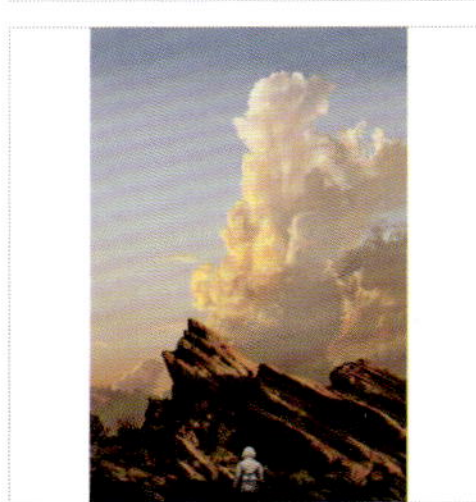

468
VASQUEZ

2020
oil on canvas
30 x 20 in.

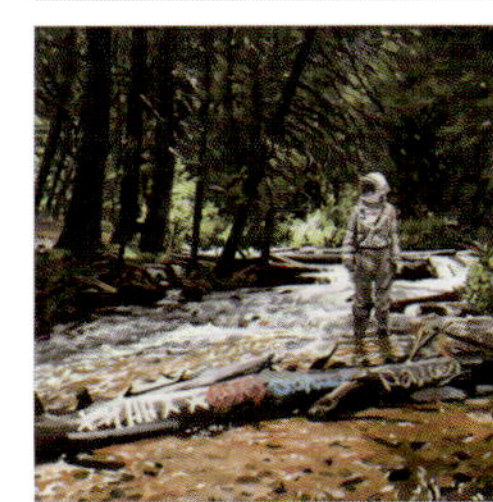

469
THE STREAM

2020
oil on canvas
10 x 10 in.

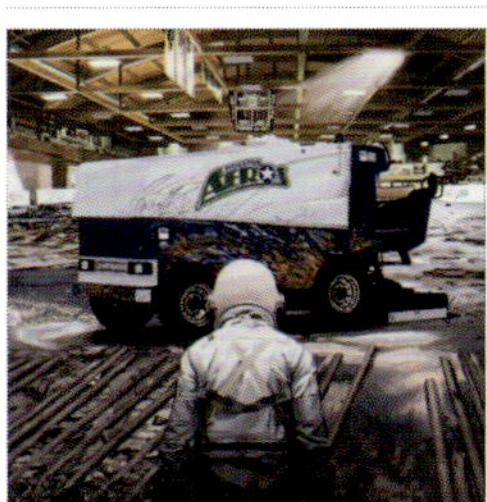

470
ZAMBONI

2020
oil on canvas
20 x 20 in.

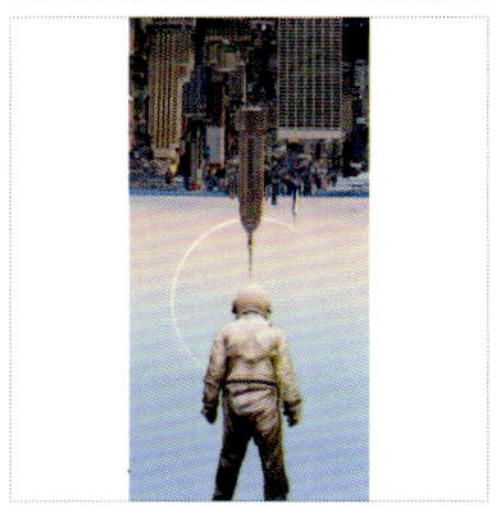

471
THE WRONG WAY UP

2020
oil on canvas
40 x 20 in.

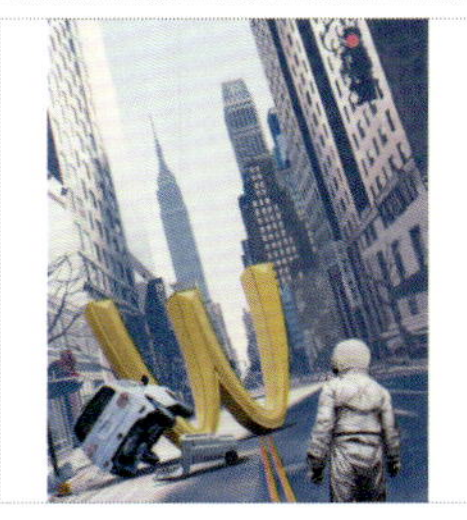

472
M IN THE STREET

2020
oil on canvas
20 x 16 in.

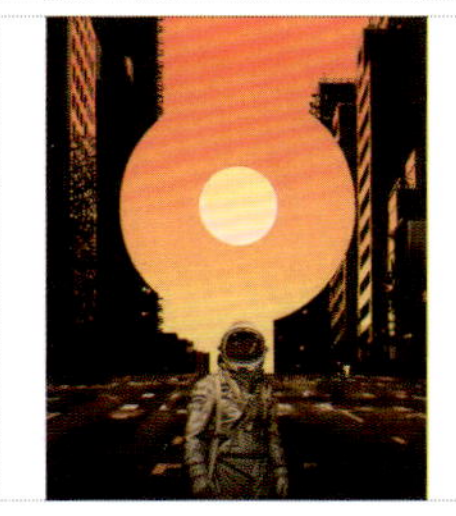

473
HOLE

2020
oil on canvas
20 x 16 in.

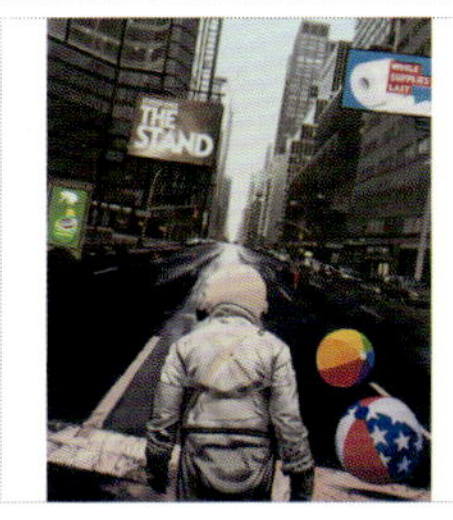

474
THE STAND

2020
oil on canvas
20 x 16 in.

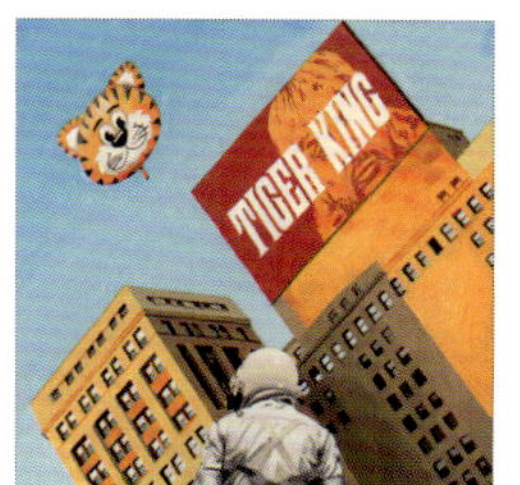

475
TIGER KING

2020
oil on canvas
10 x 10 in.

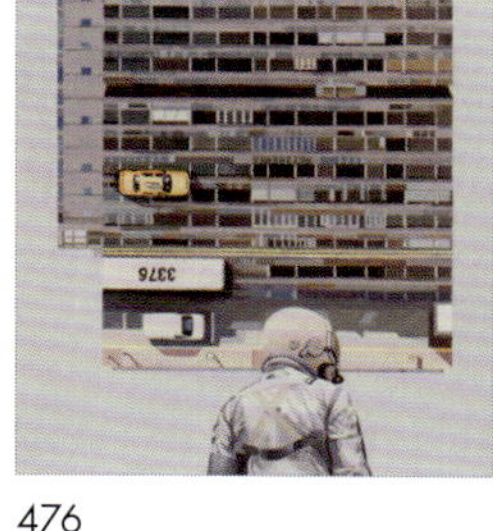

476
RIGHT OF WAY

2020
oil on canvas
10 x 10 in.

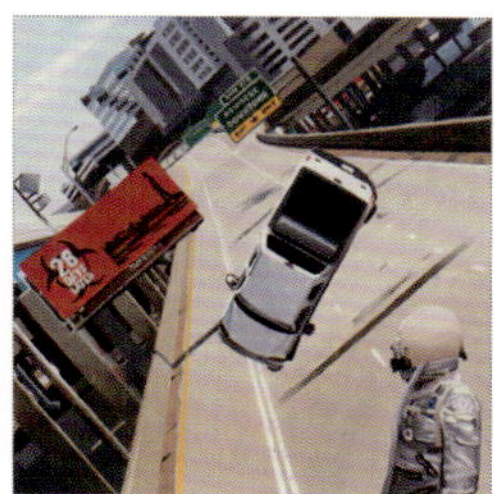

477
28 DAYS LATER

2020
oil on canvas
10 x 10 in.

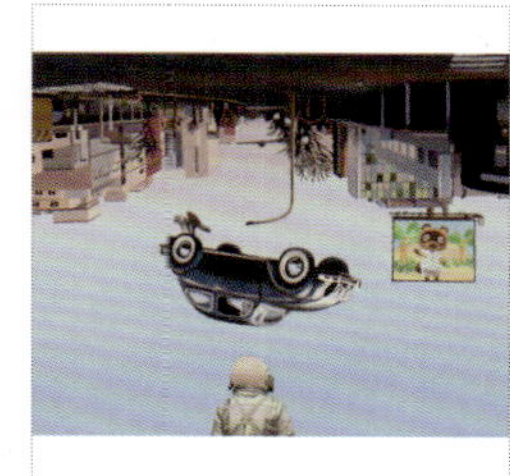

478
ANIMAL CROSSING

2020
oil on canvas
16 x 20 in.

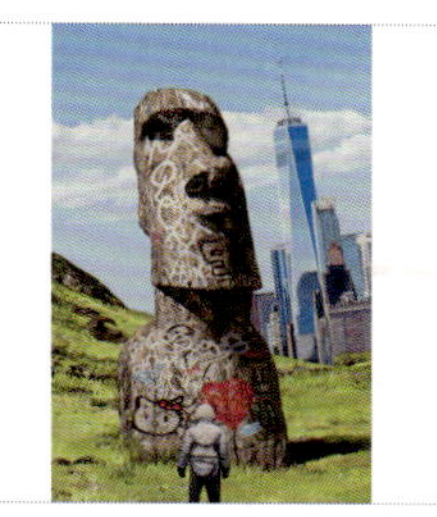

479
EASTER ISLAND

2020
oil on canvas
30 x 20 in.

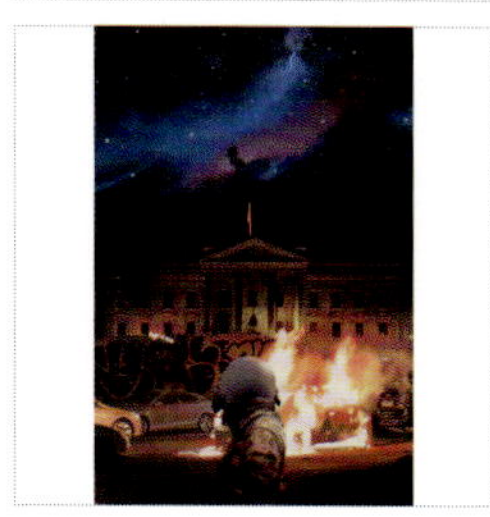

480
WHITE HOUSE

2020
oil on canvas
30 x 20 in.

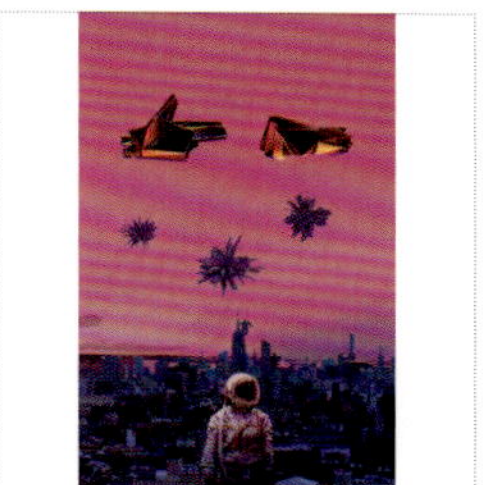

481
RTJ

2020
oil on canvas
30 x 20 in.

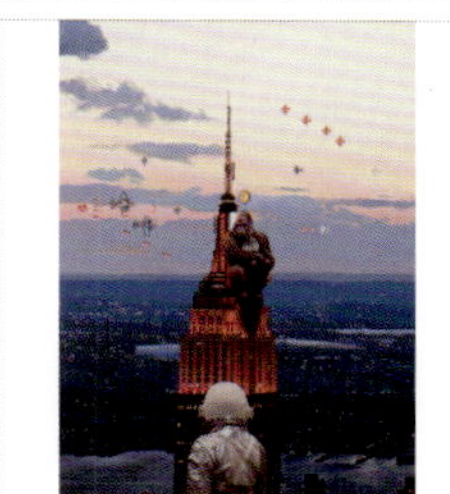

482
KONG

2020
oil on canvas
40 x 30 in.

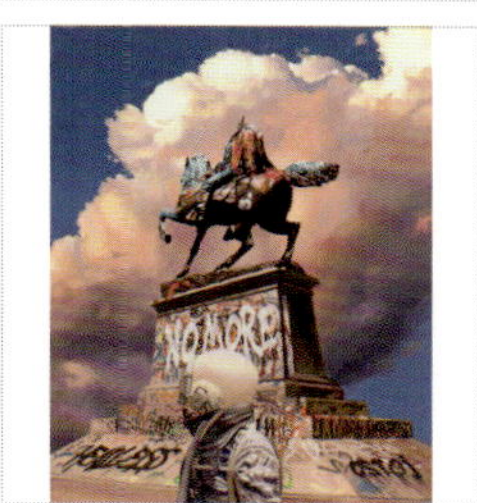

483
HEADLESS HORSEMAN

2020
oil on canvas
20 x 16 in.

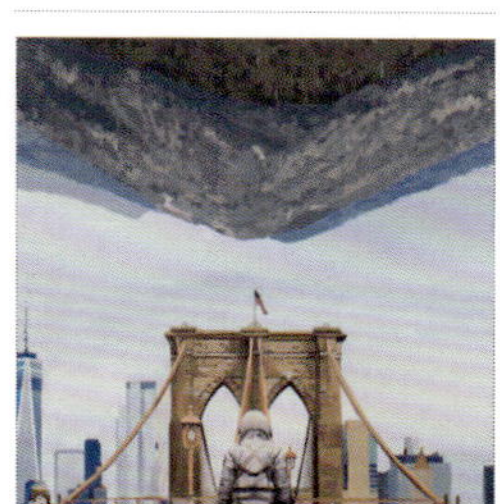

484
BROOKLYN

2020
oil on canvas
10 x 10 in.

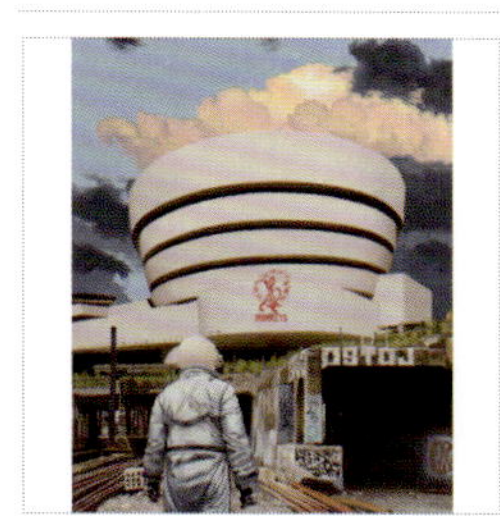

485
12 MONKEYS

2020
oil on canvas
20 x 16 in.

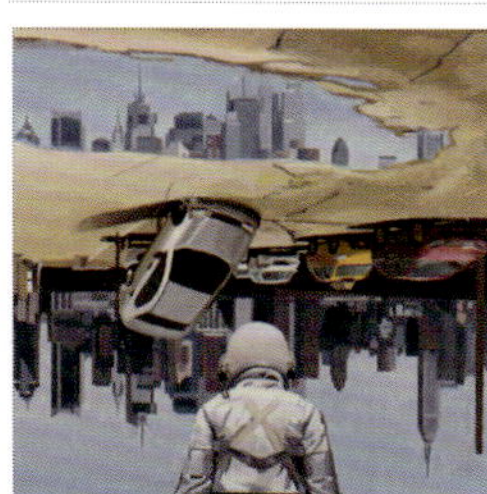

486
PUDDLE

2020
oil on canvas
10 x 10 in.

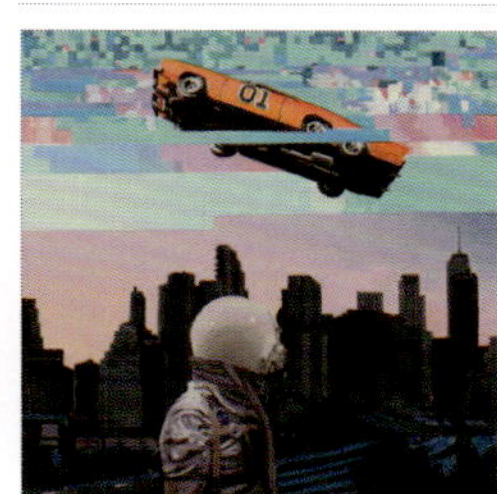

487
GLITCH

2020
oil on canvas
10 x 10 in.

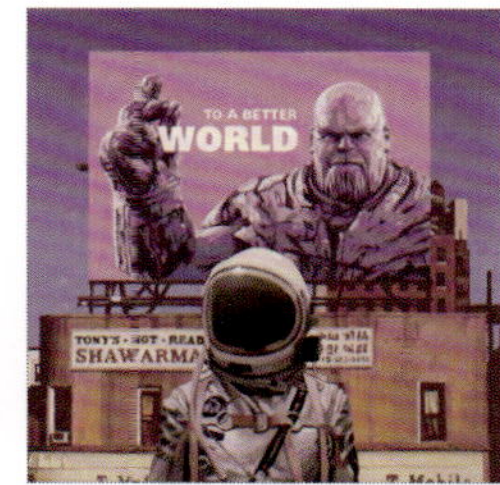

488
TO A BETTER WORLD

2020
oil on canvas
10 x 10 in.

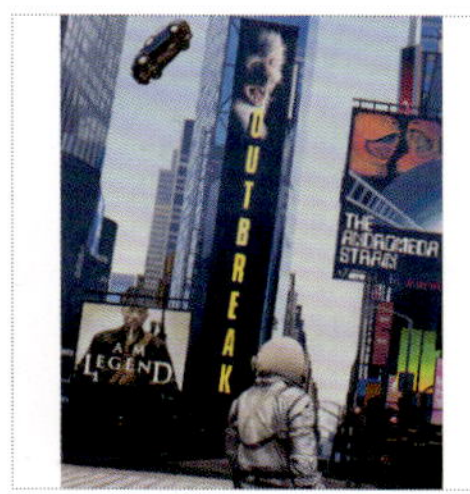

489
TIMES SQUARE

2020
oil on canvas
20 x 16 in.

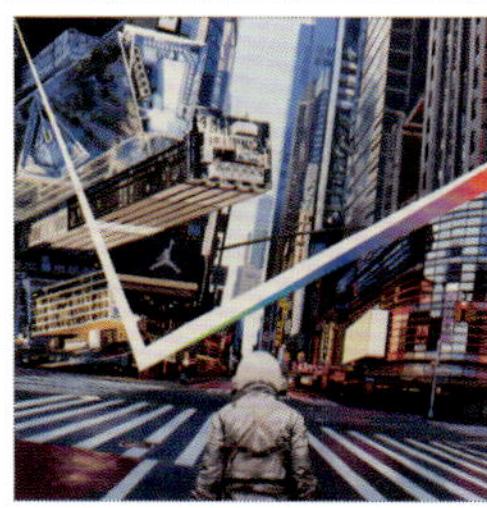

490
EMPTY CITY

2020
oil on canvas
20 x 20 in.

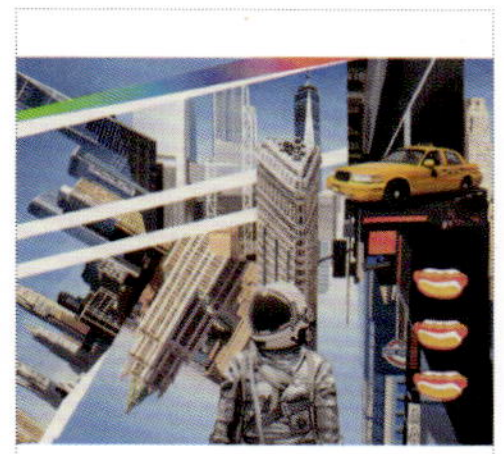

491
TAXI

2020
oil on canvas
16 x 20 in.

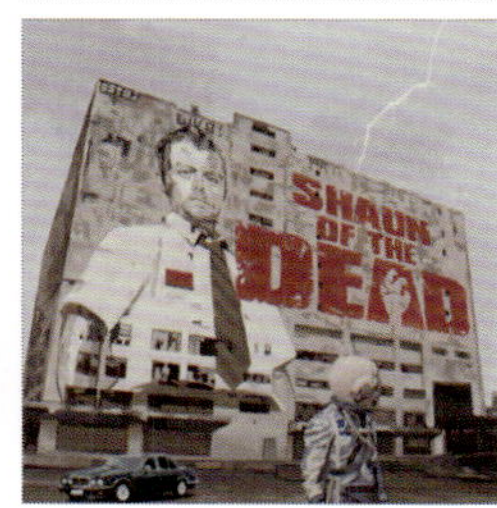

492
SHAUN

2020
oil on canvas
10 x 10 in.

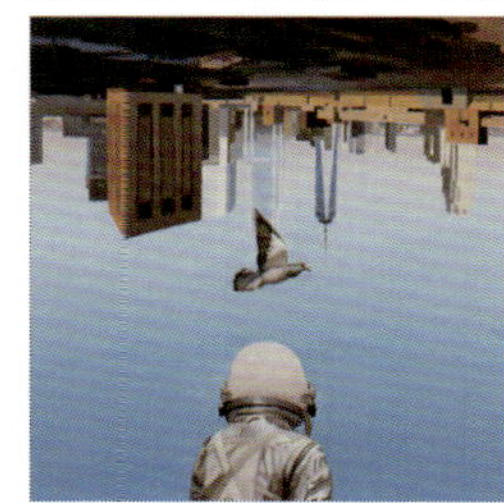

493
PIGEON

2020
oil on canvas
10 x 10 in.

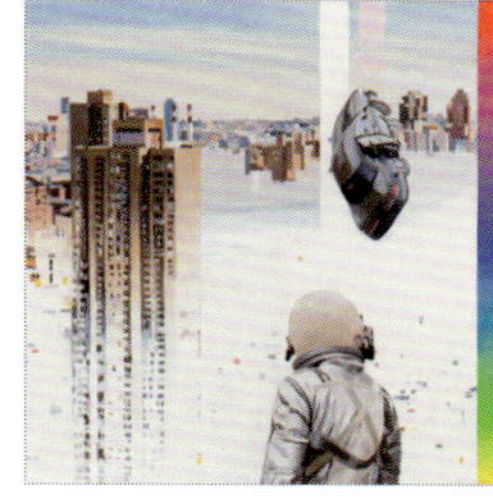

494
FADE OUT

2020
oil on canvas
10 x 10 in.

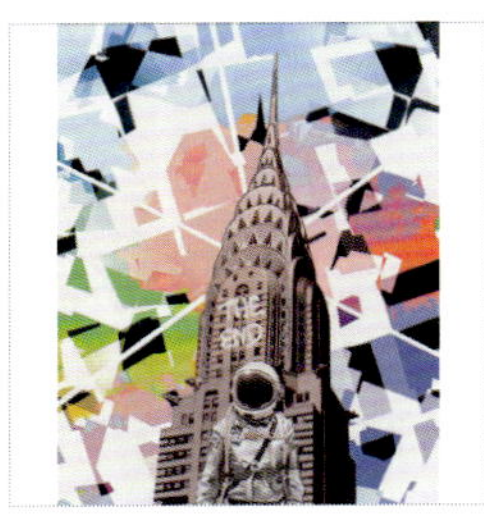

495
CHRYSLER BUILDING

2020
oil on canvas
20 x 16 in.

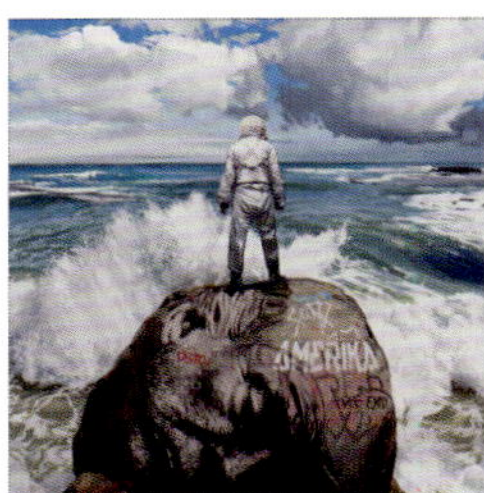

496
OZYMANDIAS

2020
oil on canvas
20 x 20 in.

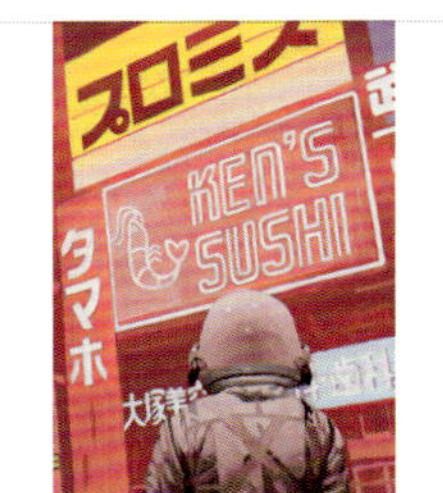

497
SUSHI

2020
oil on canvas
7 x 5 in.

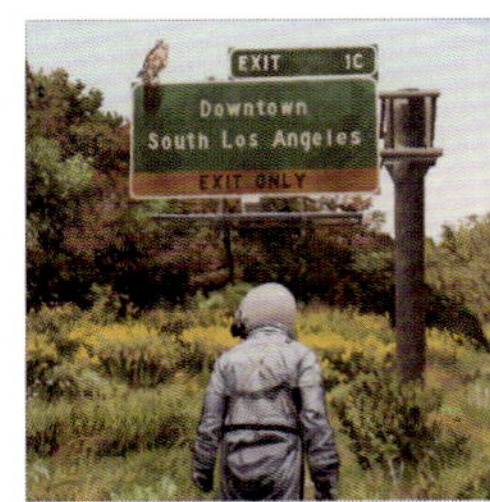

498
EXIT 1C

2020
oil on canvas
12 x 12 in.

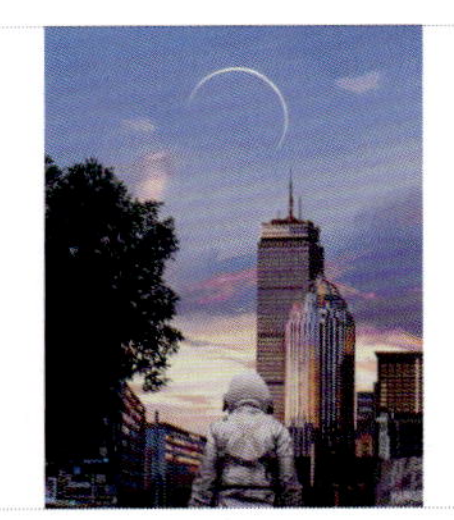

499
CRESCENT

2020
oil on canvas
20 x 16 in.

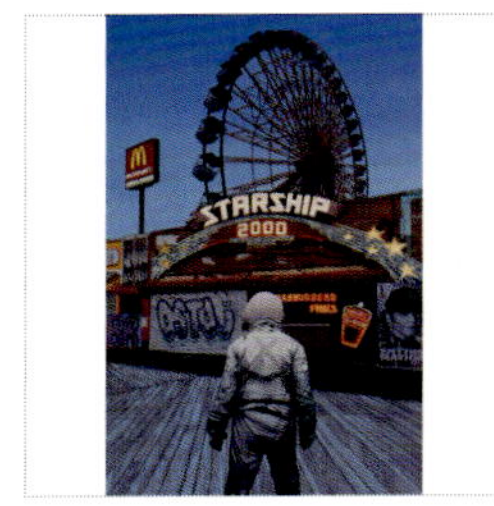

500
STARSHIP 2000

2020
oil on canvas
30 x 20 in.

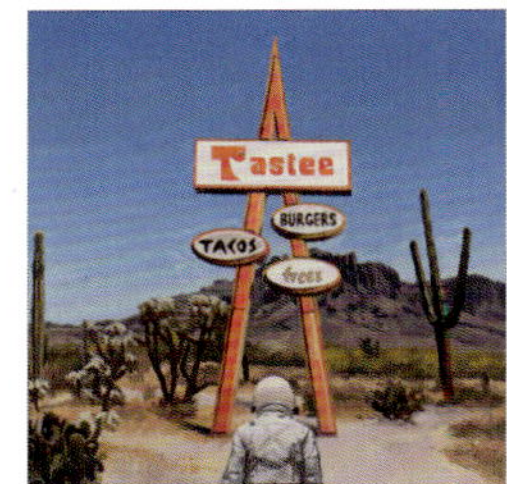

501
TASTEE

2020
oil on canvas
10 x 10 in.

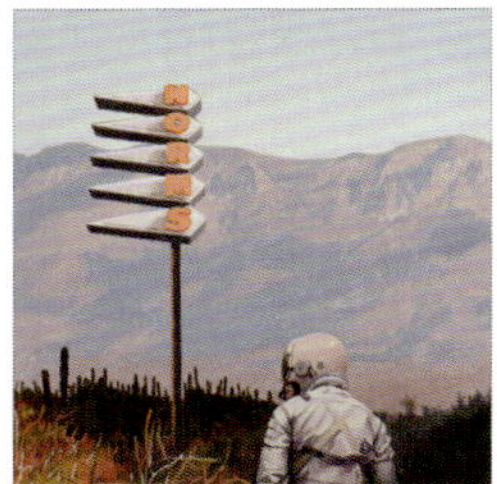

502
NORMS

2020
oil on canvas
10 x 10 in.

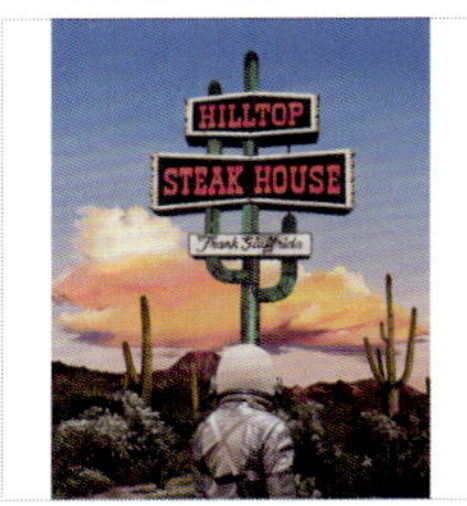

503
HILLTOP

2020
oil on canvas
20 x 16 in.

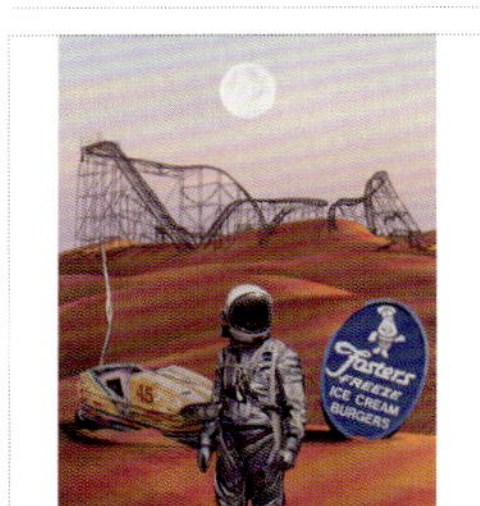

504
ROLLERCOASTER

2020
oil on canvas
20 x 16 in.

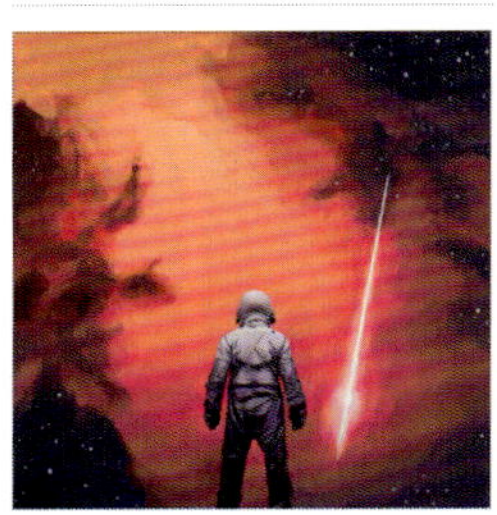

505
STARFALL

2020
oil on canvas
12 x 12 in.

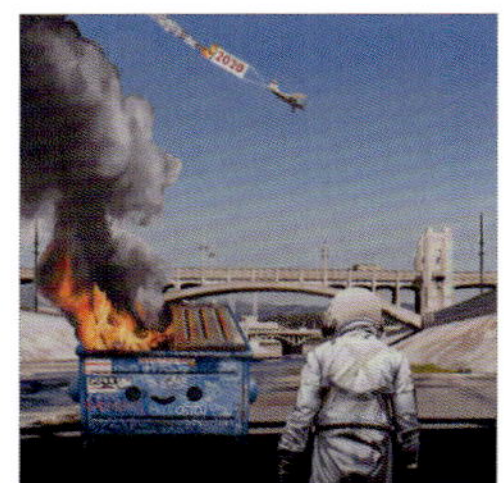

506
DUMPSTER FIRE

2020
oil on canvas
20 x 20 in.

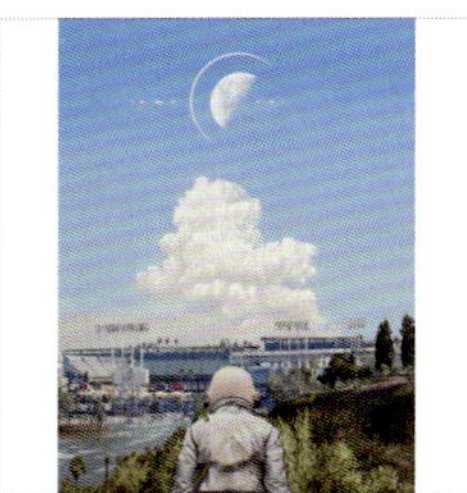

507
DODGER STADIUM

2020
oil on canvas
40 x 30 in.

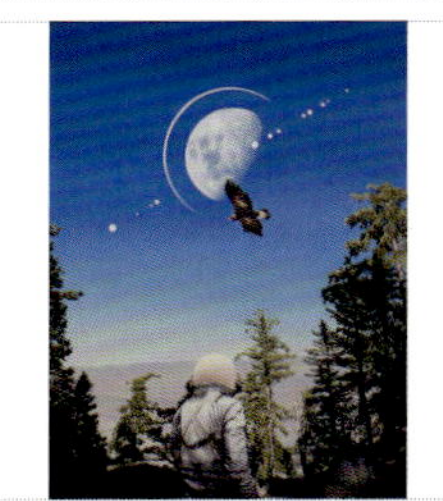

508
SAN JACINTO

2020
oil on canvas
40 x 30 in.

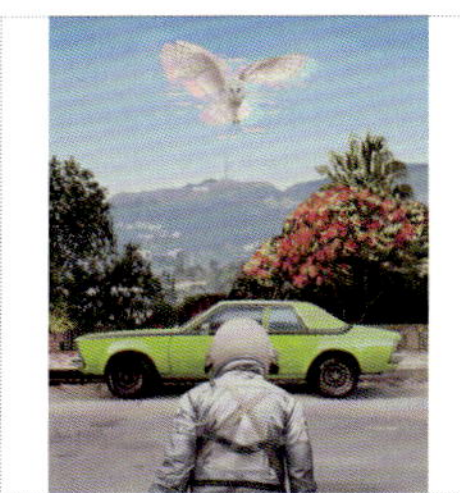

509
OWL

2020
oil on canvas
20 x 16 in.

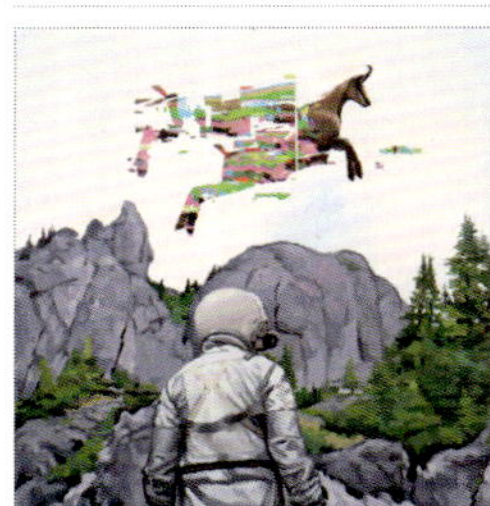

510
MID-JUMP GLITCH

2020
oil on canvas
10 x 10 in.

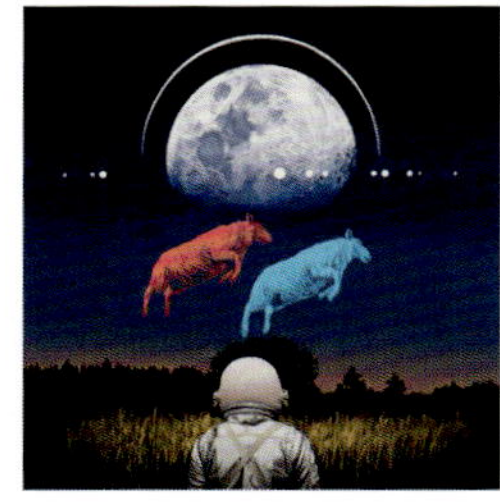

511
DREAM OF ELECTRIC SHEEP

2021
oil on canvas
20 x 20 in.

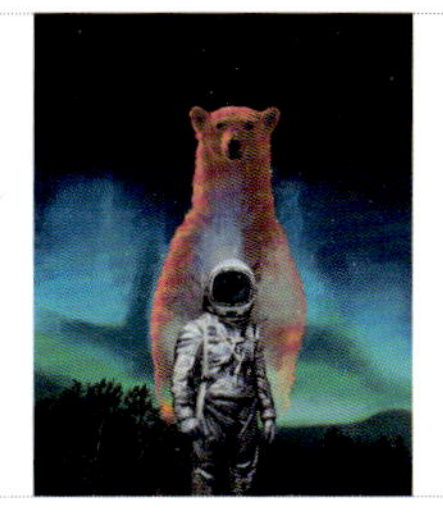

512
NIGHT BEAR

2021
oil on canvas
20 x 16 in.

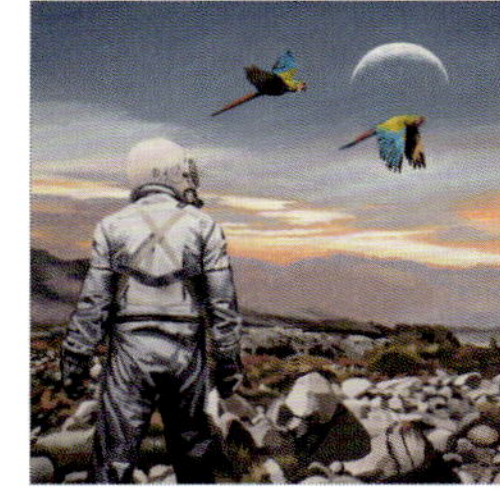

513
PARROTS

2021
oil on canvas
10 x 10 in.

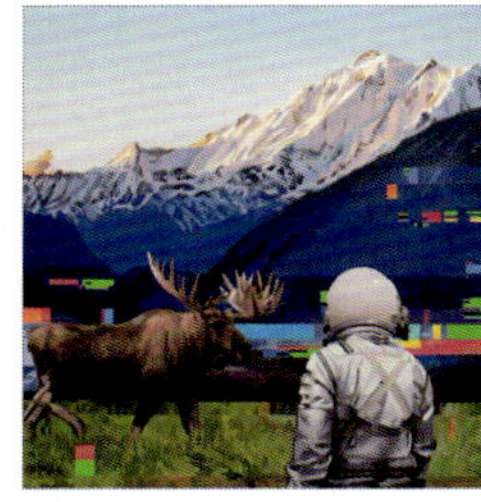

514
MOOSE

2021
oil on canvas
10 x 10 in.

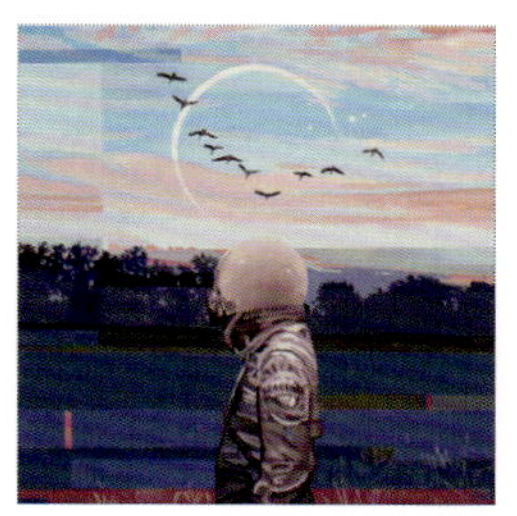

515
FLOCK

2021
oil on canvas
10 x 10 in.

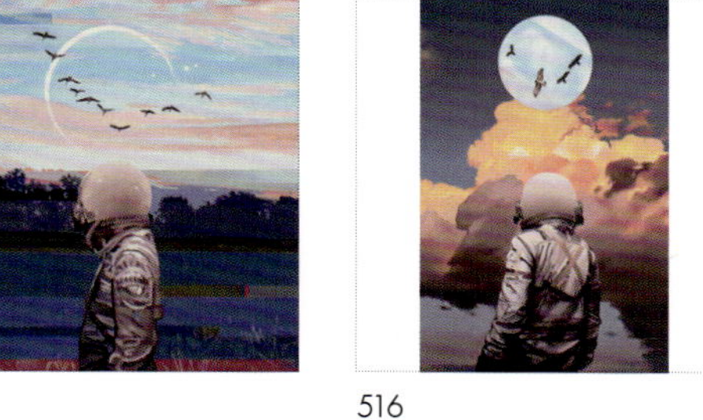

516
CIRCLE IN THE SKY

2021
oil on canvas
30 x 20 in.

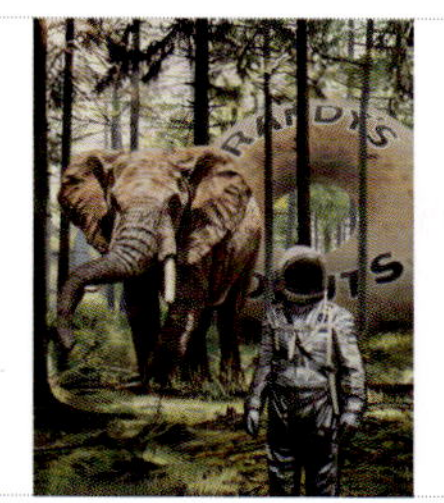

517
ELEPHANT

2021
oil on canvas
20 x 16 in.

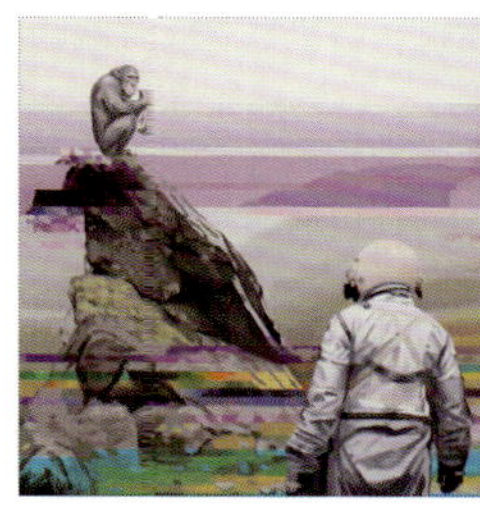

518
CHIMP

2021
oil on canvas
10 x 10 in.

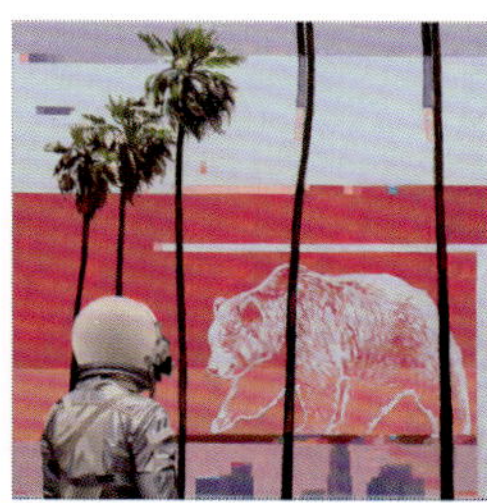

519
RED BEAR

2021
oil on canvas
10 x 10 in.

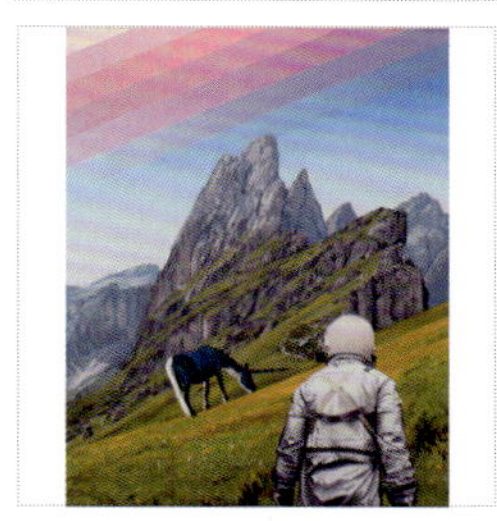

520
HIGHLANDS

2021
oil on canvas
20 x 16 in.

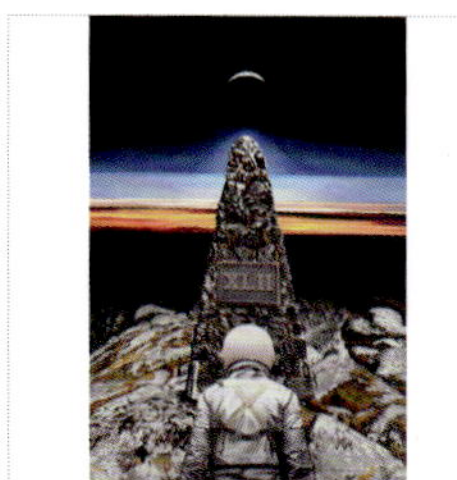

521
XLII

2021
oil on canvas
30 x 20 in.

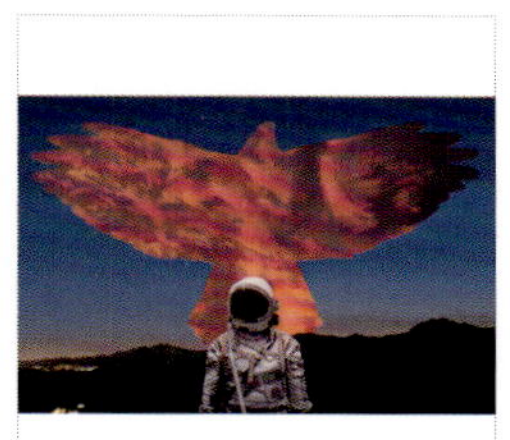

522
PHOENIX

2021
oil on canvas
20 x 30 in.

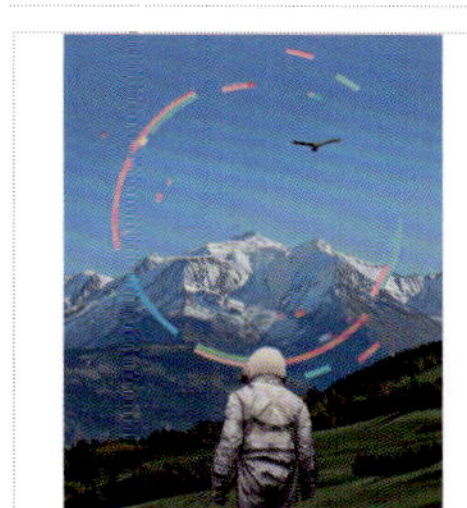

523
THE AIR'S THIN

2021
oil on canvas
20 x 16 in.

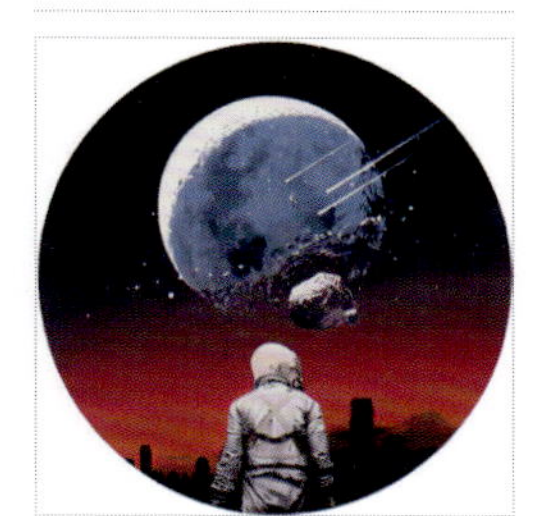

524
MOON TONDO

2021
oil on canvas
16 x 16 in.

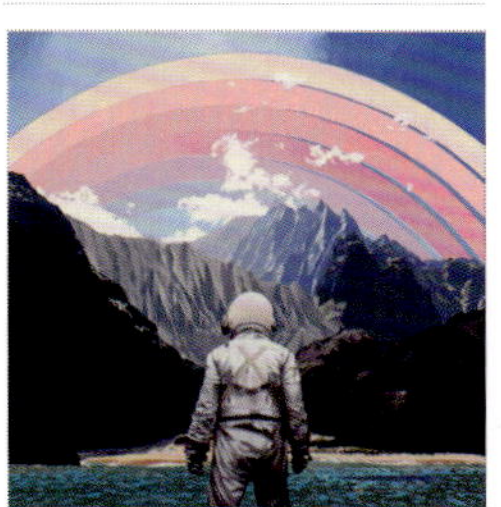

525
COVE

2021
oil on canvas
24 x 24 in.

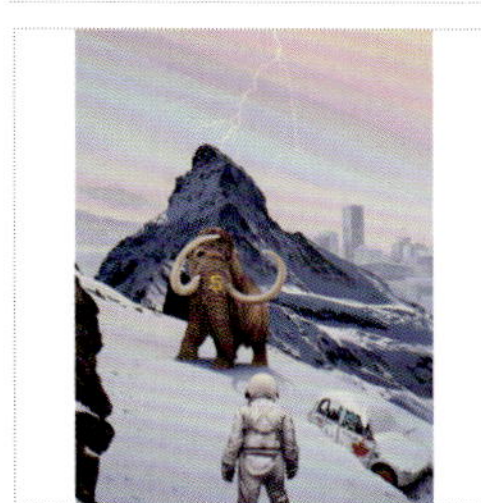

526
MAMMOTH

2021
oil on canvas
40 x 30 in.

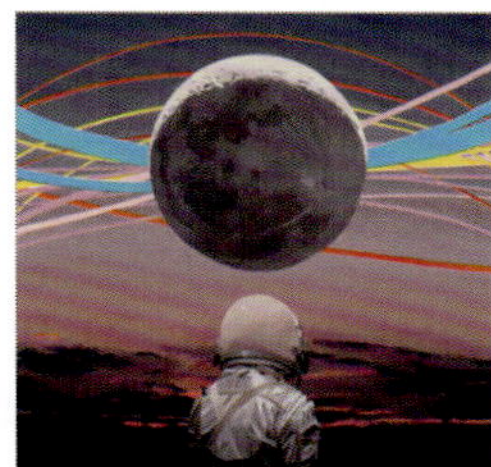

527
ARCS

2021
oil on canvas
10 x 10 in.

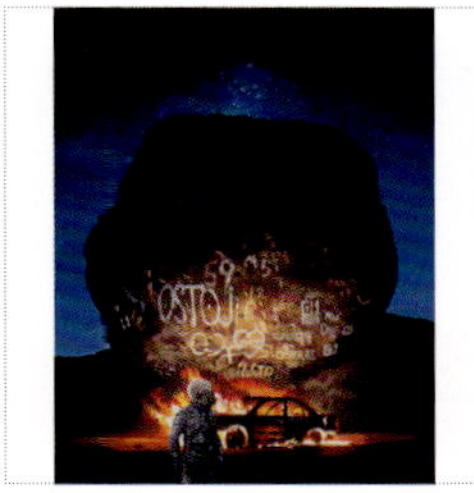

528
BIG ROCK

2021
oil on canvas
20 x 16 in.

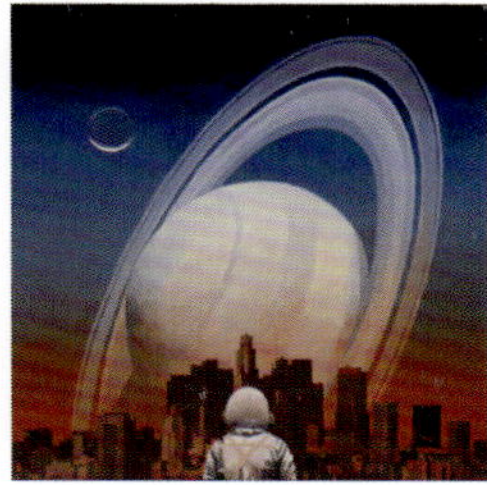

529
SATURN RISES

2021
oil on canvas
10 x 10 in.

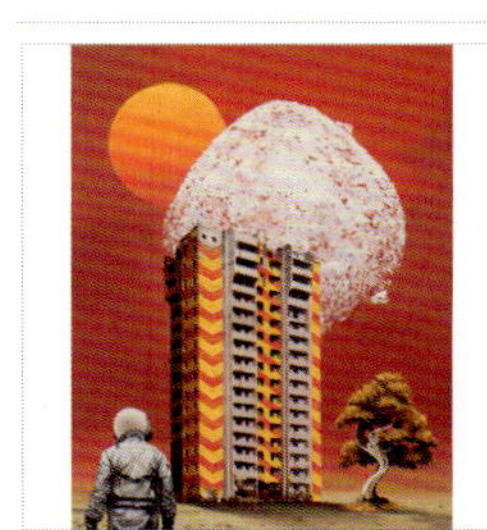

530
ASTEROID

2021
oil on canvas
20 x 16 in.

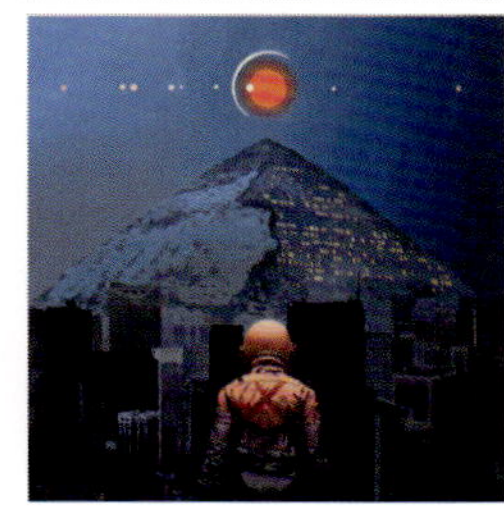

531
PYRAMID

2021
oil on canvas
20 x 20 in.

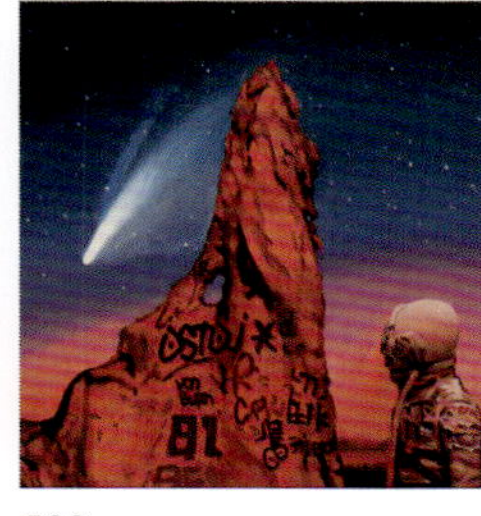

532
OUTCROP

2021
oil on canvas
10 x 10 in.

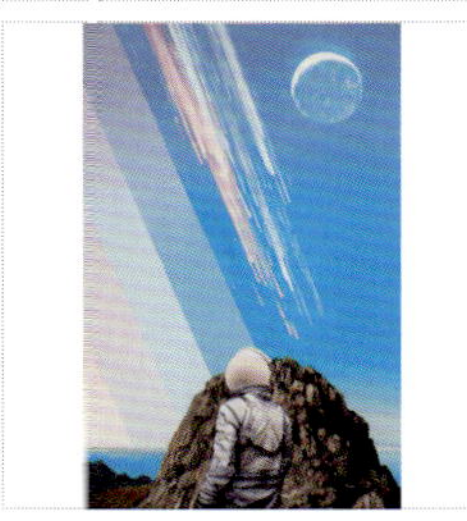

533
STAR FALL

2021
oil on canvas
30 x 20 in.

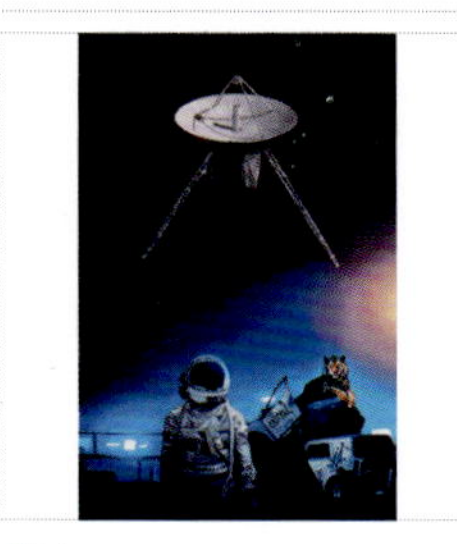

534
LOW ORBIT

2021
oil on canvas
30 x 20 in.

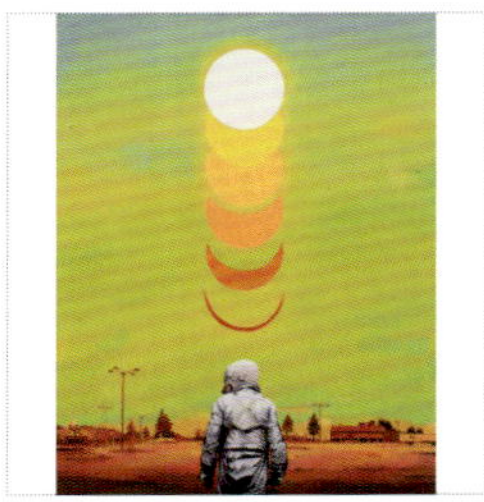

535
SUNSTAGES

2021
oil on canvas
20 x 16 in.

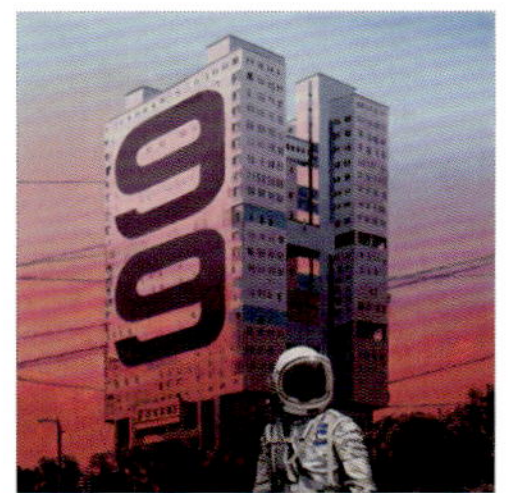

536
NINETY-NINE

2021
oil on canvas
10 x 10 in.

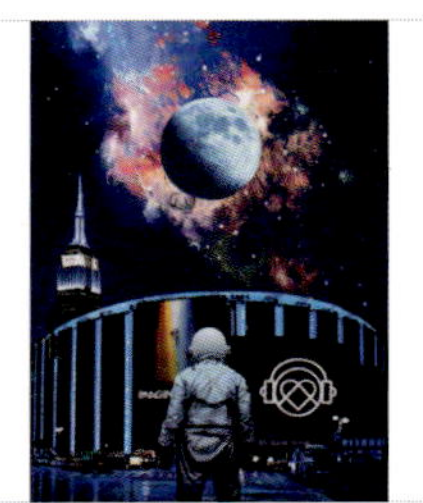

537
MADISON SQUARE GARDEN

2021
oil on canvas
40 x 30 in.

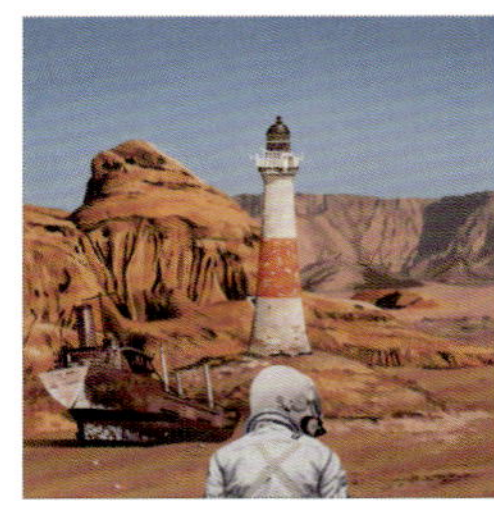

538
LIGHTHOUSE

2021
oil on canvas
12 x 12 in.

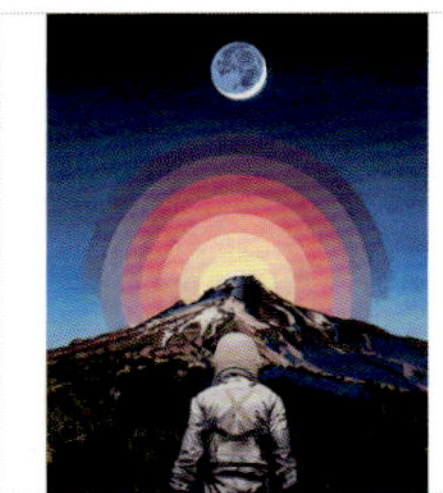

539
THE SUN & THE MOON

2021
oil on canvas
20 x 16 in.

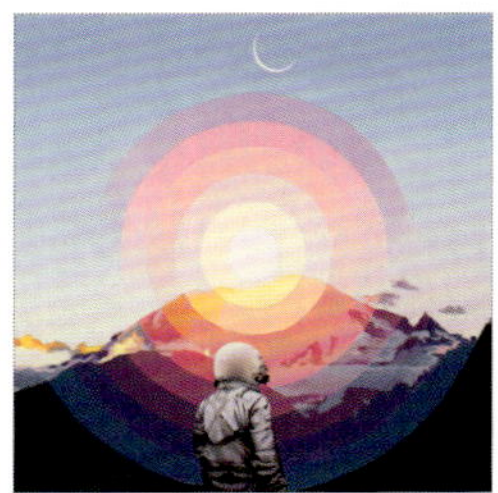

540
THE SUN & THE MOON II

2021
oil on canvas
10 x 10 in.

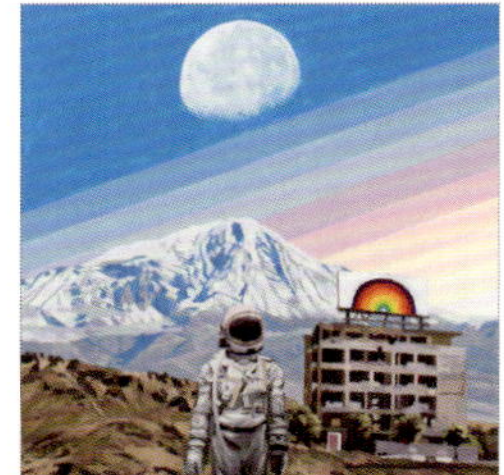

541
RAINBOW MOON

2021
oil on canvas
10 x 10 in.

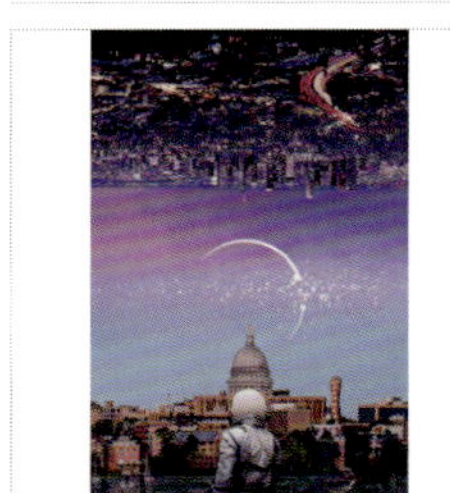

542
TWO CITIES

2021
oil on canvas
30 x 20 in.

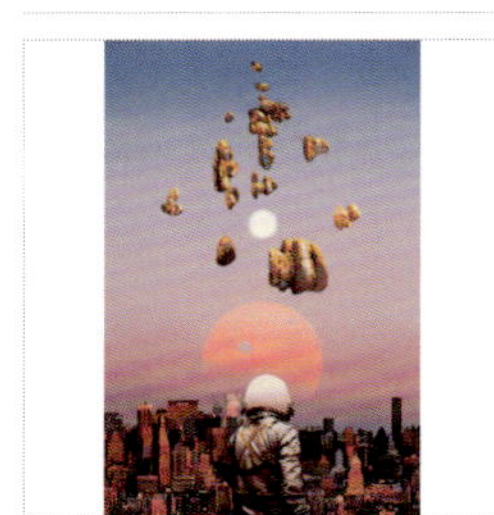

543
ROCKS

2021
oil on canvas
30 x 20 in.

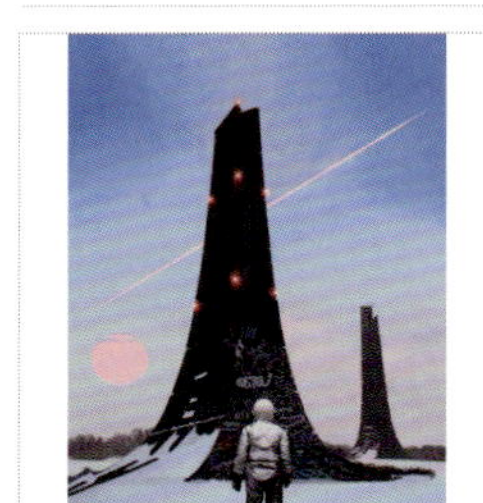

544
TWO TOWERS

2021
oil on canvas
20 x 16 in.

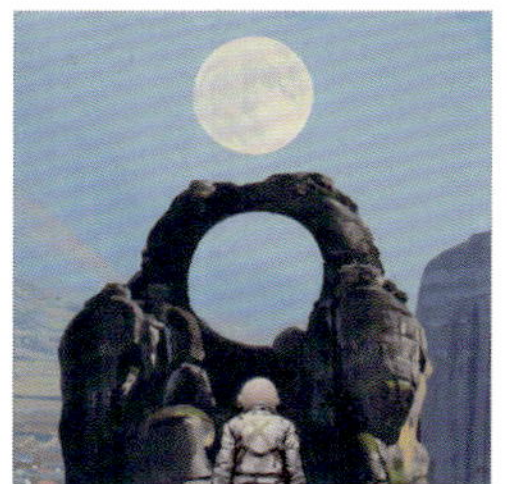

545
WAITING

2021
oil on canvas
10 x 10 in.

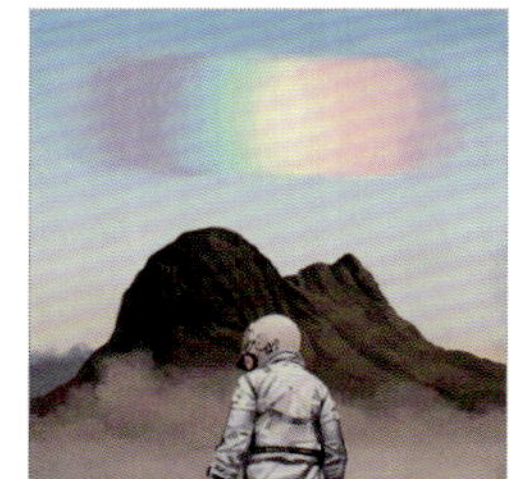

546
REFRACTION

2021
oil on canvas
10 x 10 in.

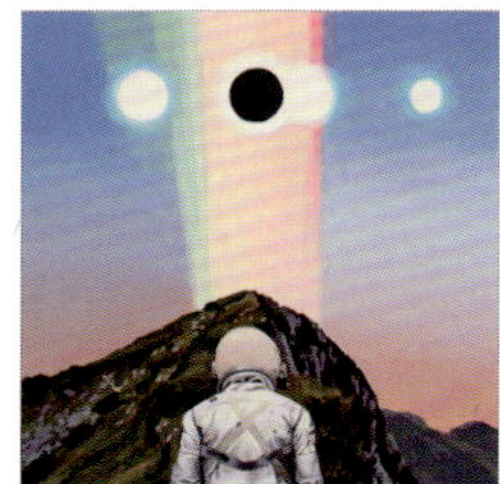

547
ONE DARK SUN

2021
oil on canvas
10 x 10 in.

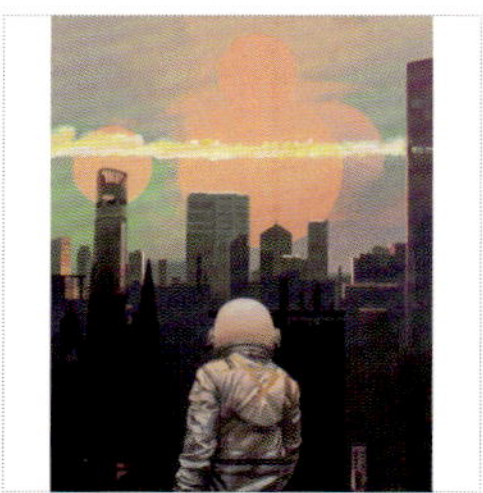

548
SETTING SUNS

2021
oil on canvas
20 x 16 in.

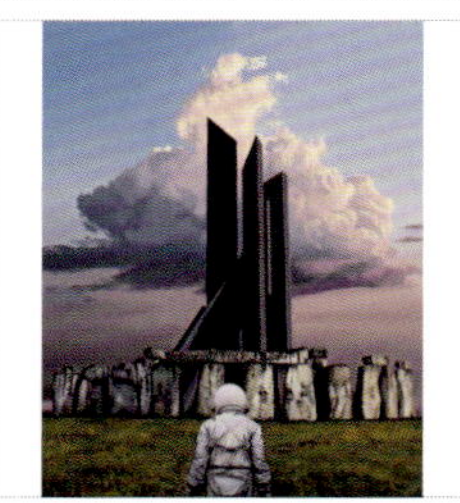

549
STONEHENGE

2021
oil on canvas
20 x 16 in.

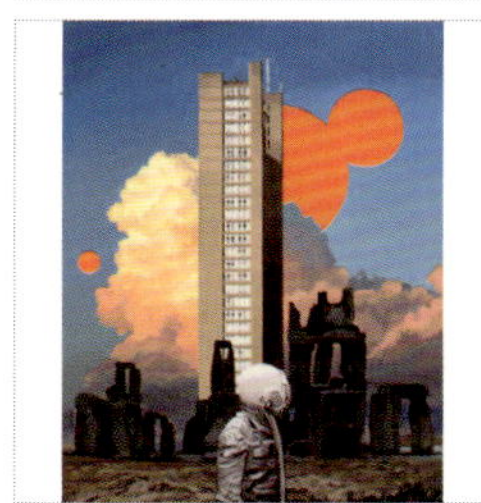

550
REDEVELOPMENT

2021
oil on canvas
20 x 16 in.

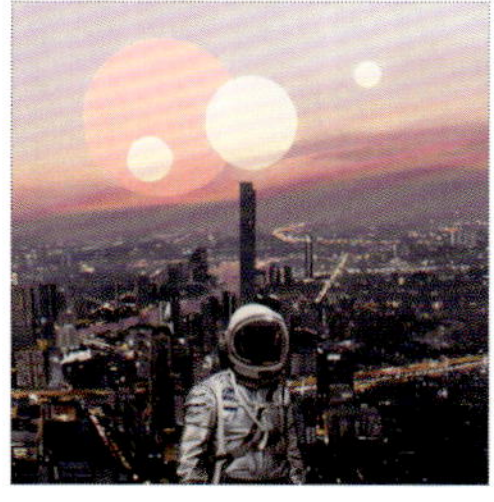

551
SUNS & THE CITY

2021
oil on canvas
20 x 20 in.

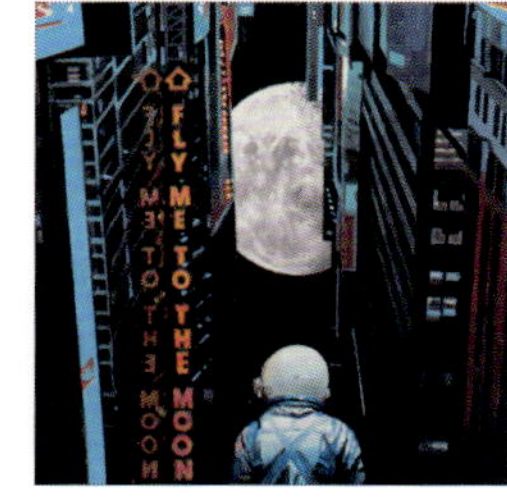

552
FLY ME TO THE MOON

2021
oil on canvas
10 x 10 in.

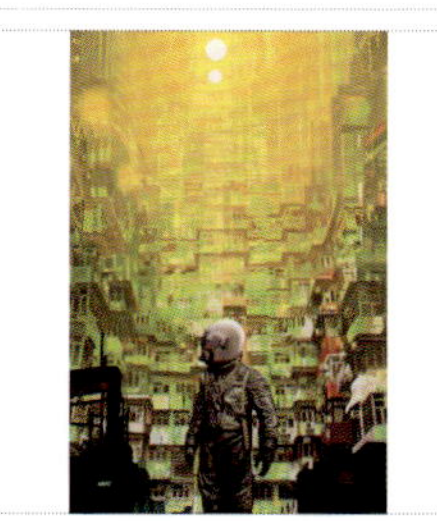

553
DWELLING

2021
oil on canvas
30 x 20 in.

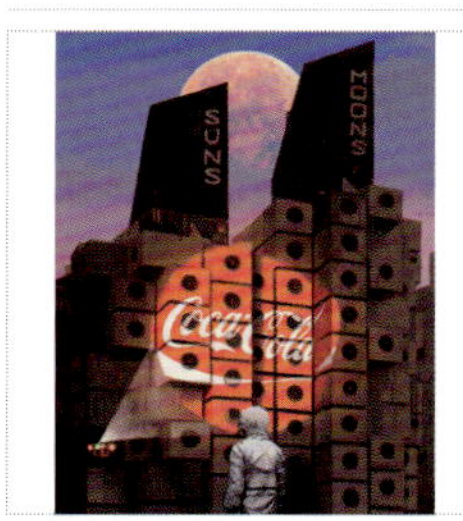

554
COKE IS IT

2021
oil on canvas
20 x 16 in.

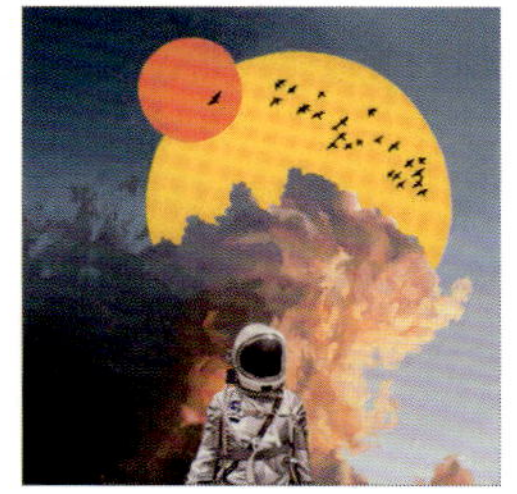

555
MORNING

2021
oil on canvas
10 x 10 in.

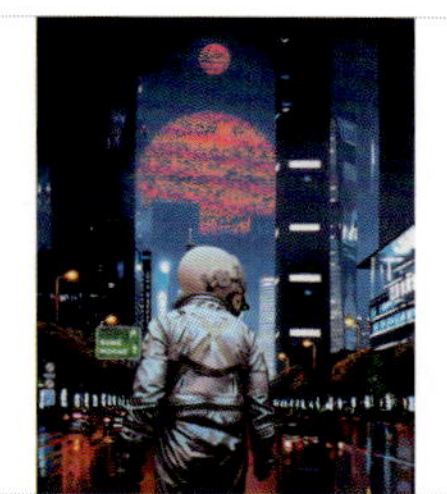

556
NIGHT CITY

2021
oil on canvas
20 x 16 in.

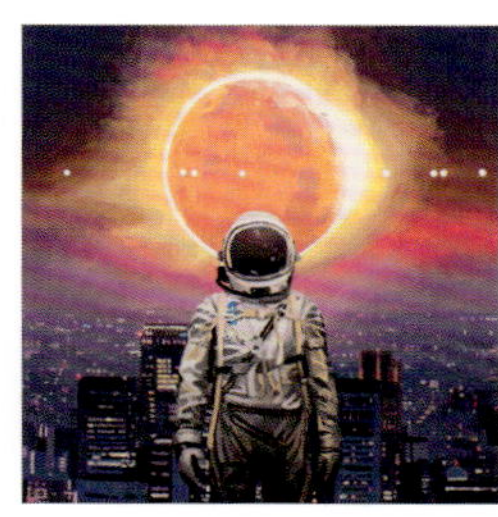

557
RED SUN

2021
oil on canvas
10 x 10 in.

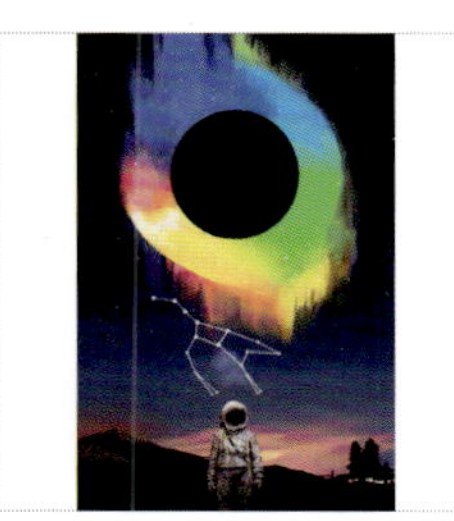

558
URSA

2021
oil & acrylic on canvas
30 x 20 in.

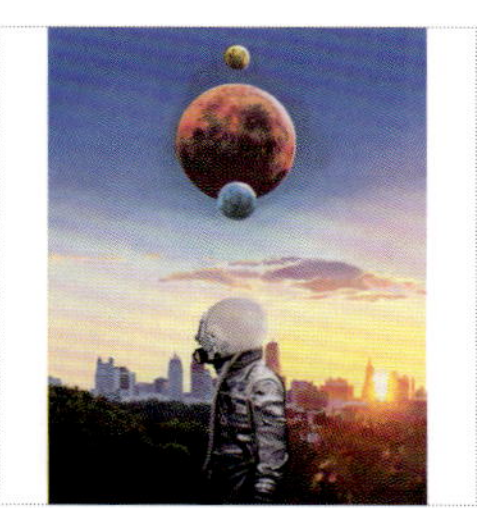

559
THREE MOONS

2021
oil on canvas
20 x 16 in.

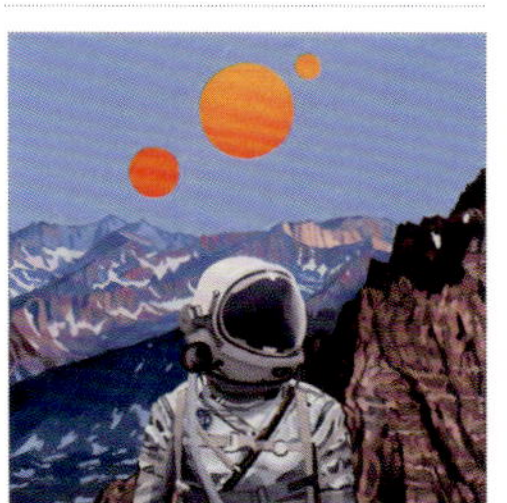

560
BLUE MOUNTAINS

2021
oil on canvas
10 x 10 in.

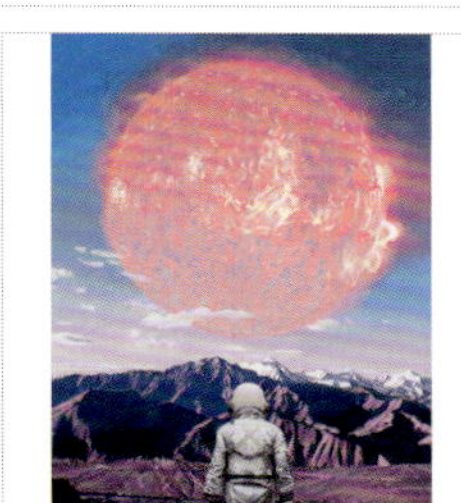

561
SHINE

2021
oil on canvas
20 x 16 in.

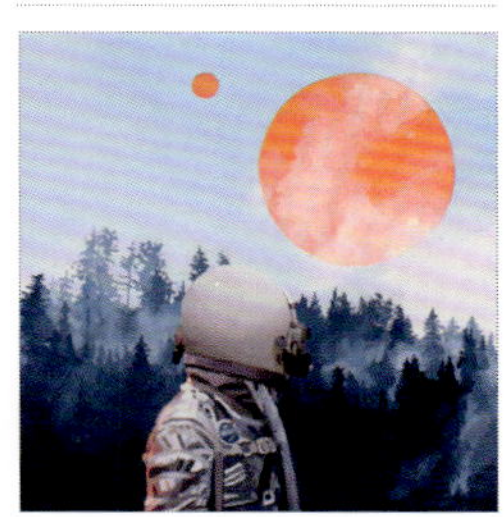

562
FOREST

2021
oil on canvas
10 x 10 in.

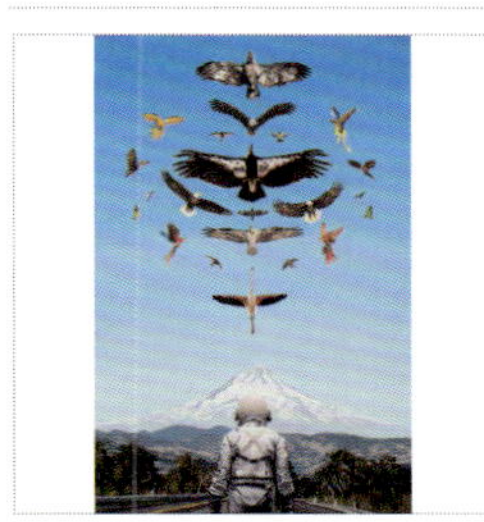

563
ORNITHOLOGY

2021
oil on canvas
30 x 20 in.

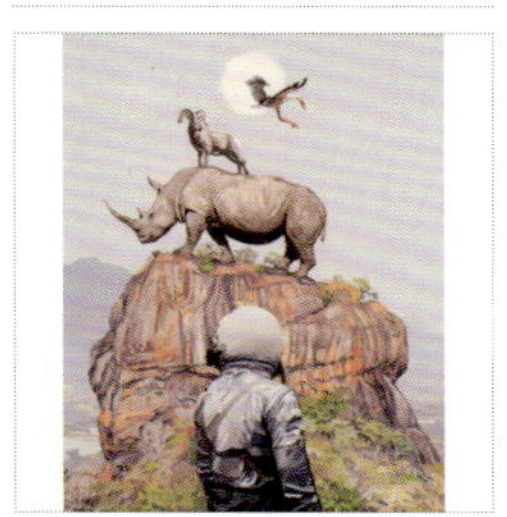

564
LOOKOUT SPOT

2021
oil on canvas
20 x 16 in.

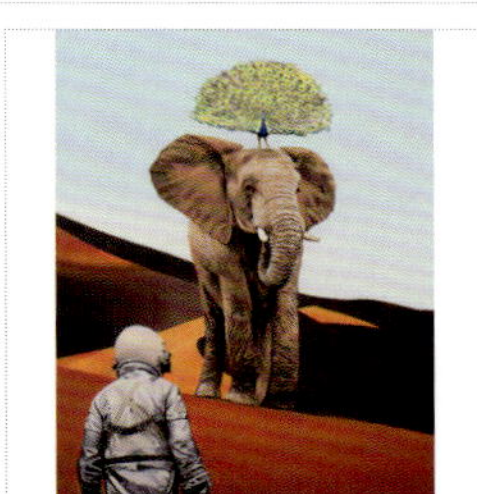

565
CROWN

2021
oil on canvas
20 x 16 in.

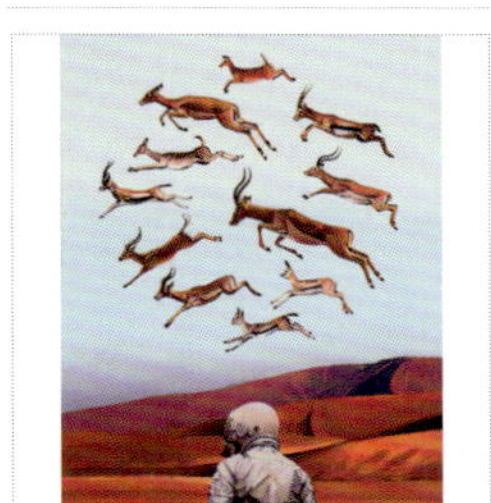

566
LEAP

2021
oil on canvas
20 x 16 in.

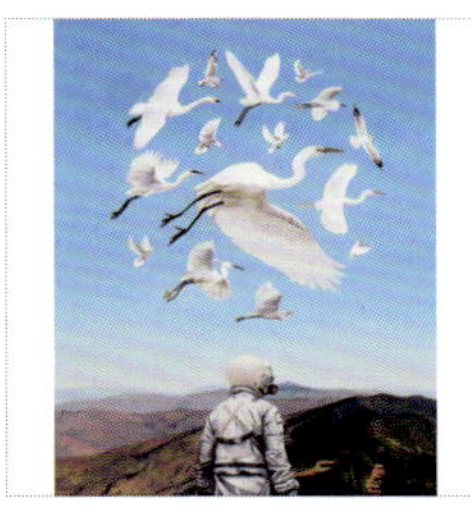

567
CONTINUED ORNITHOLOGY

2021
oil on canvas
20 x 16 in.

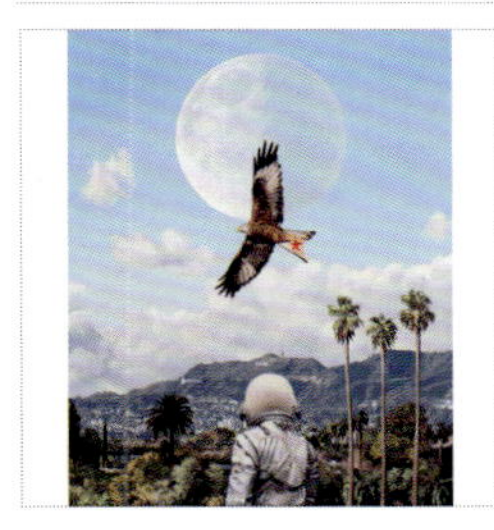

568
ALL STAR

2021
oil on canvas
20 x 16 in.

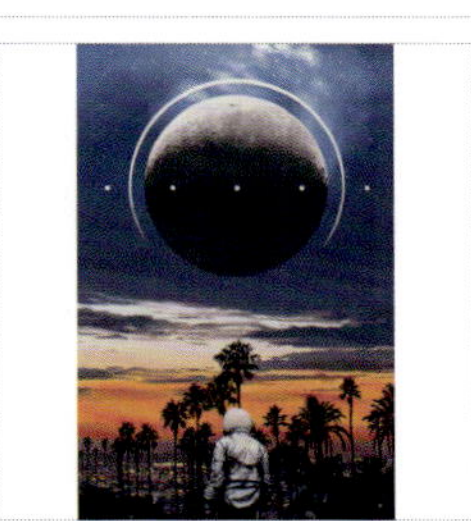

569
ELYSIAN

2021
oil on canvas
30 x 20 in.

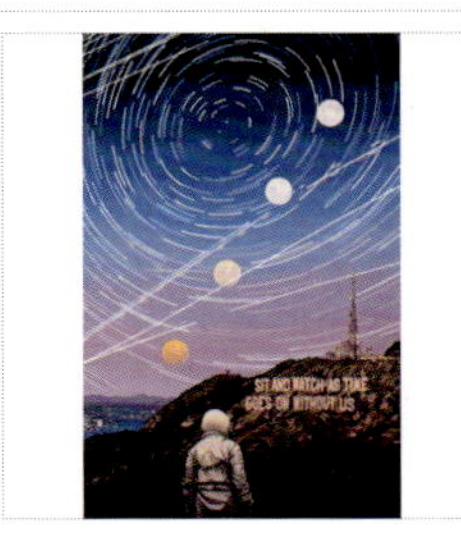

570
SIT & WATCH

2021
oil on canvas
30 x 20 in.

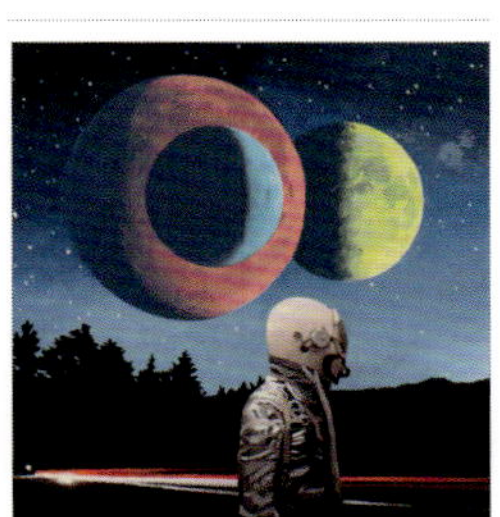

571
BY THE LIGHT OF THE MOONS

2022
oil on canvas
10 x 10 in.

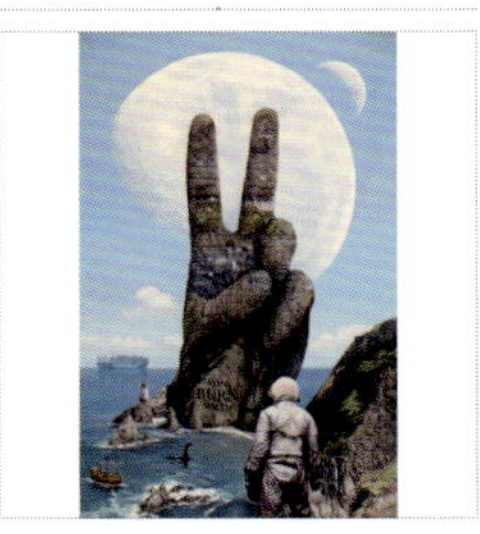

572
SECOND HAND

2022
oil on canvas
60 x 40 in.

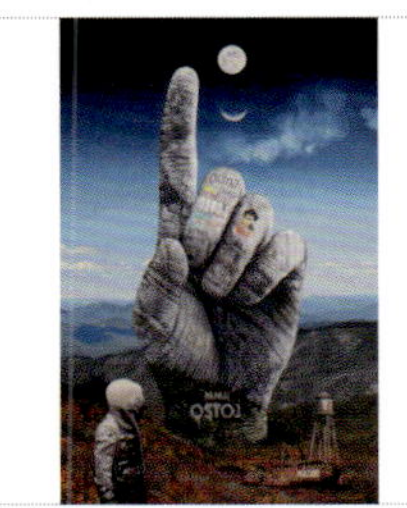

573
FIRST HAND

2022
oil on canvas
60 x 40 in.

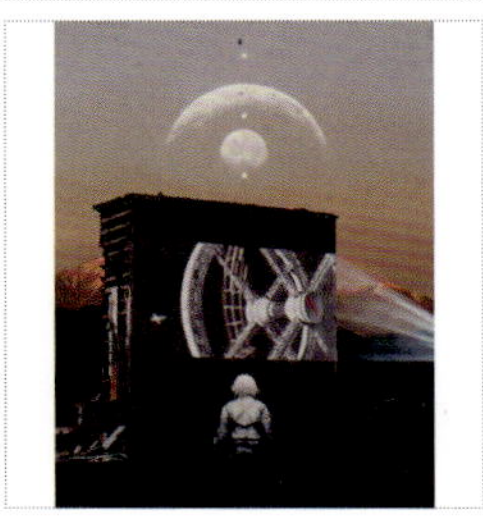

574
MOVIE NIGHT

2022
oil on canvas
20 x 16 in.

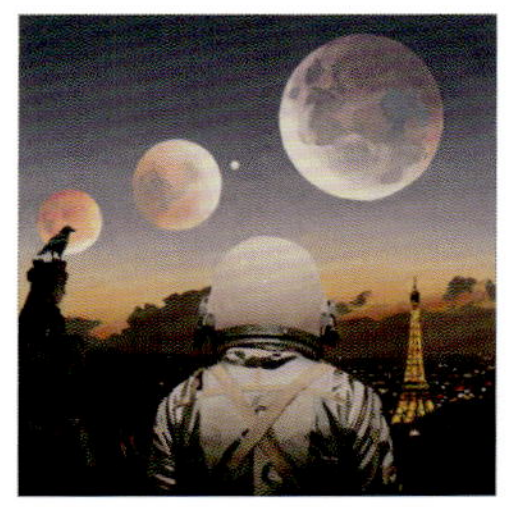

575
LES LUNES

2022
oil on canvas
10 x 10 in.

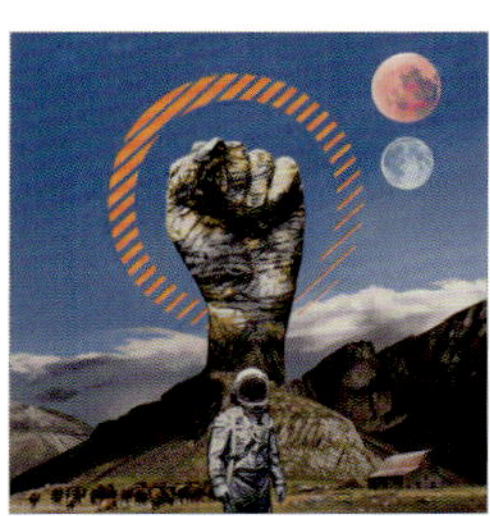

576
CLOSED HAND

2022
oil on canvas
20 x 20 in.

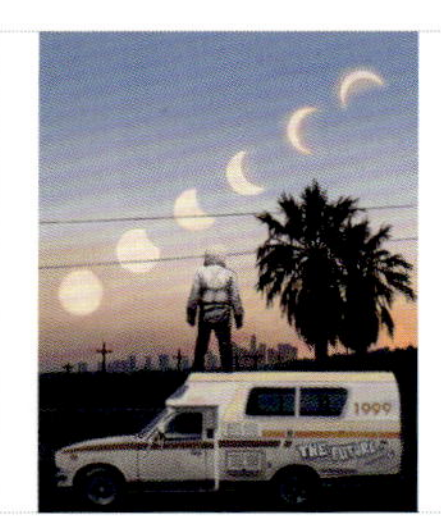

577
RV DUSK 2

2022
oil on canvas
20 x 16 in.

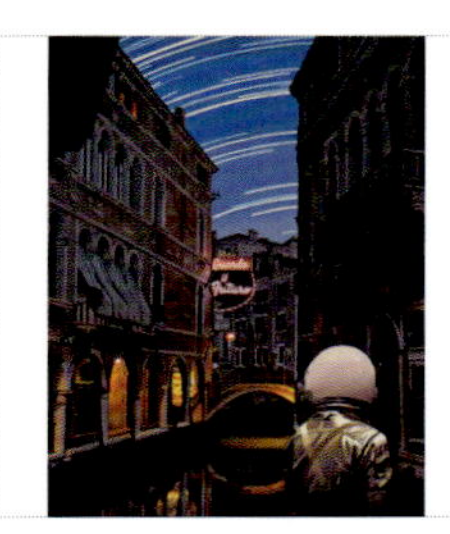

578
CANAL

2022
oil on canvas
20 x 16 in.

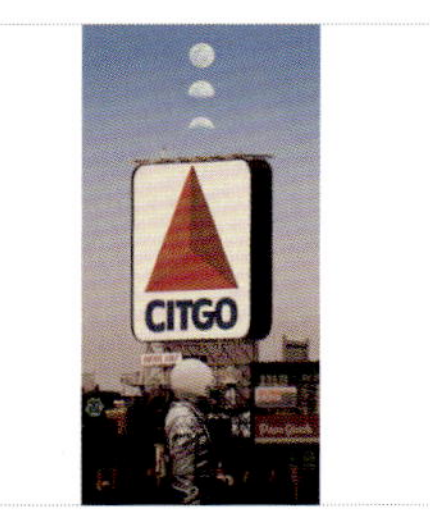

579
KENMORE

2022
oil on canvas
40 x 20 in.

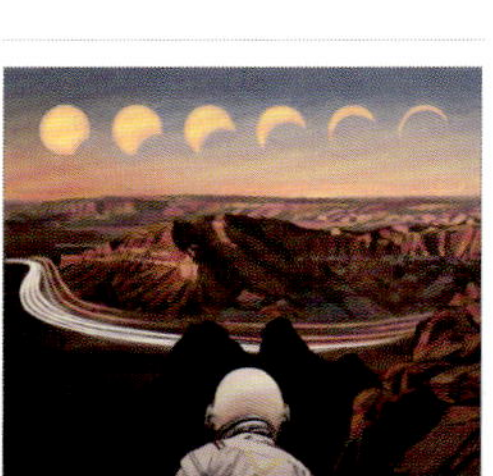

580
CANYON

2022
oil on canvas
10 x 10 in.

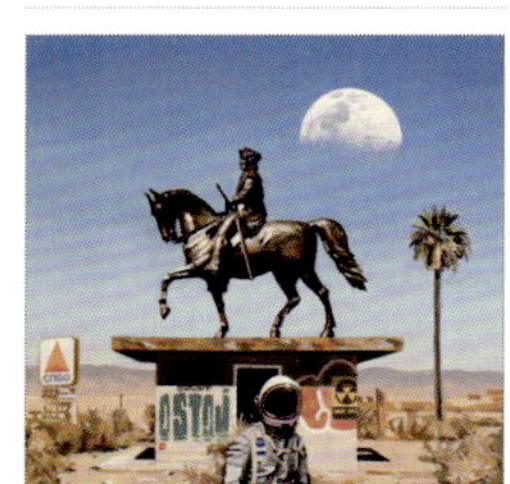

581
WASHINGTON CROSSING THE DESERT

2022
oil on canvas
10 x 10 in.

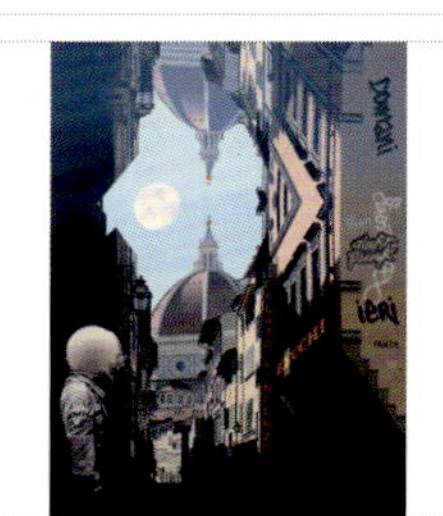

582
DUOMO

2022
oil on canvas
40 x 30 in.

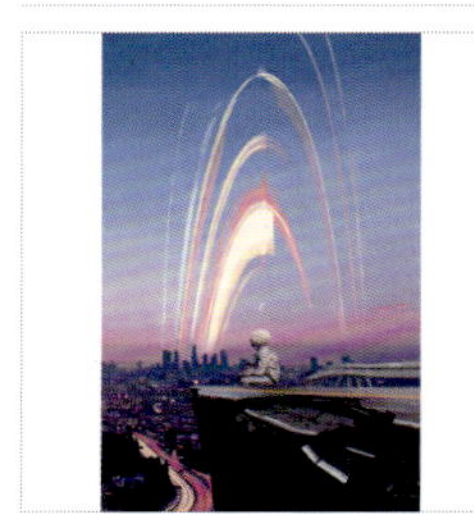

583
LOST HIGHWAY 2

2022
oil on canvas
30 x 20 in.

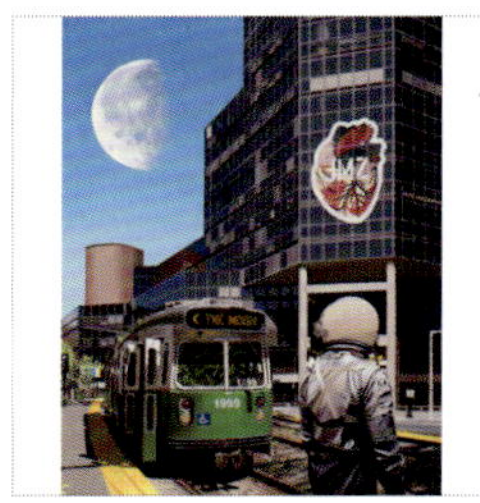

584
TOWER BUILDING

2022
oil on canvas
20 x 16 in.

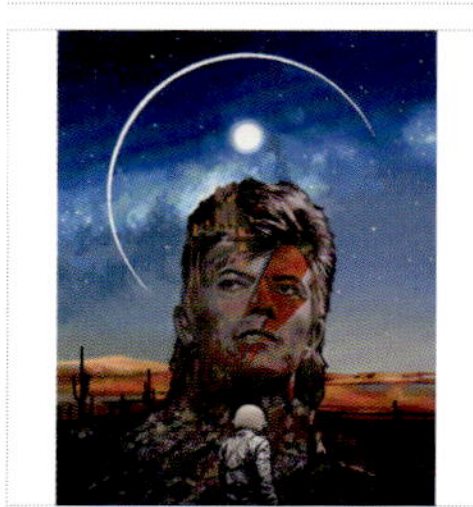

585
DAVID

2022
oil on canvas
20 x 16 in.

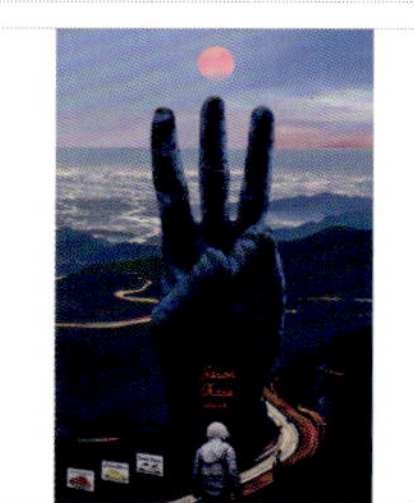

586
THIRD HAND

2022
oil on canvas
60 x 40 in.

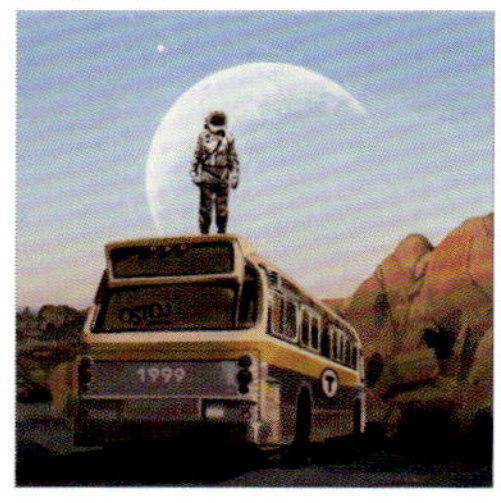

587
ASTRONAUT ON THE BUS 2

2022
oil on canvas
10 x 10 in.

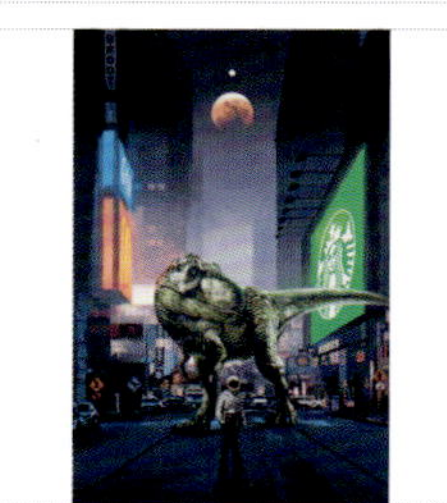

588
ASTRONAUT & DINOSAUR 2

2022
oil on canvas
30 x 20 in.

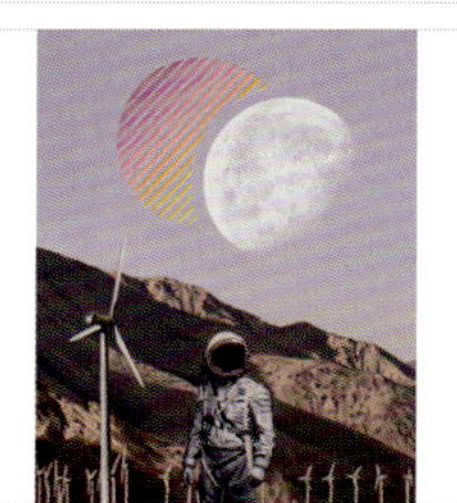

589
WIND

2022
oil on canvas
20 x 16 in.

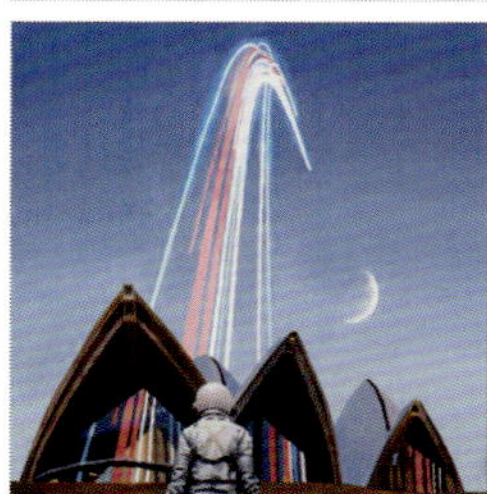

590
SYDNEY

2022
oil on canvas
10 x 10 in.

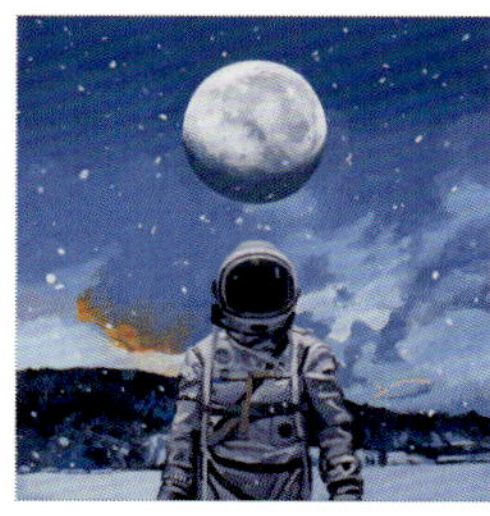

591
SNOWFALL

2022
oil on canvas
10 x 10 in.

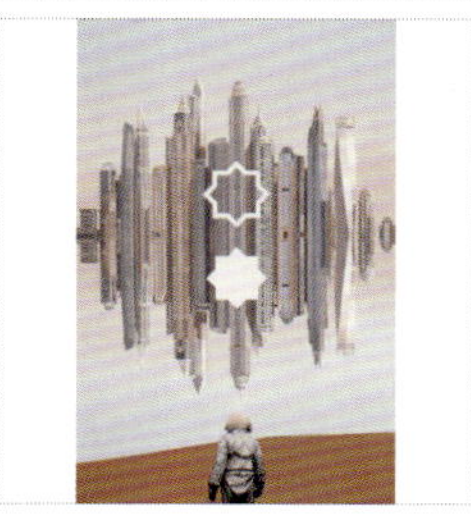

592
OASIS

2022
oil on canvas
36 x 24 in.

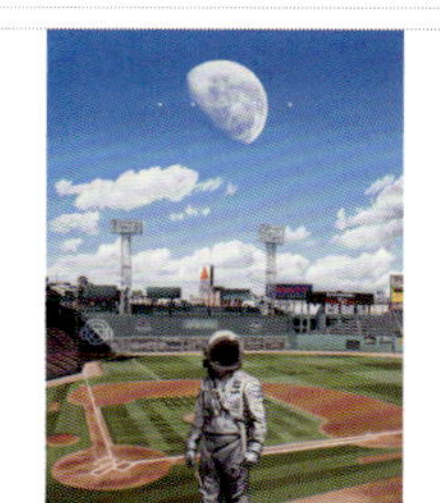

593
FENWAY

2022
oil on canvas
40 x 30 in.

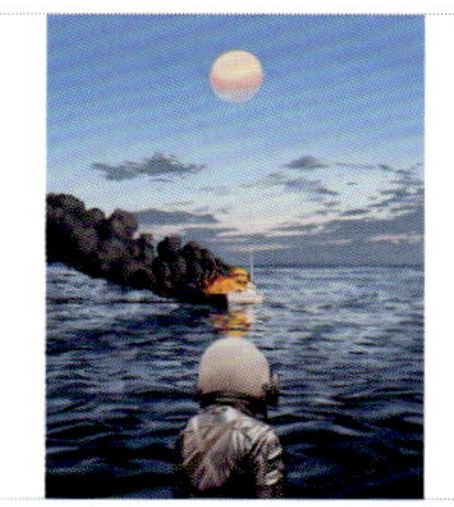

594
RAFT

2022
oil on canvas
20 x 16 in.

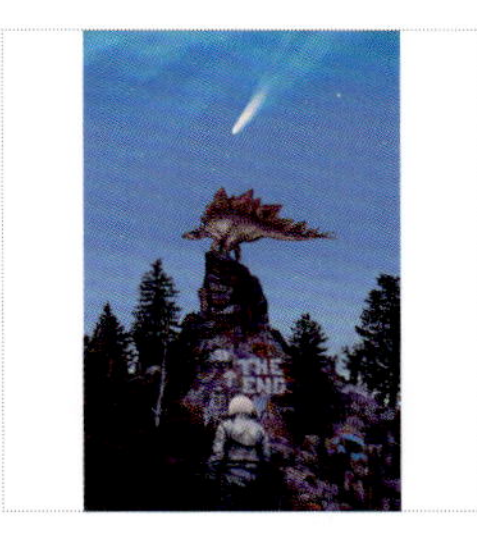

595
STEGOSAURUS 2

2022
oil on canvas
30 x 20 in.

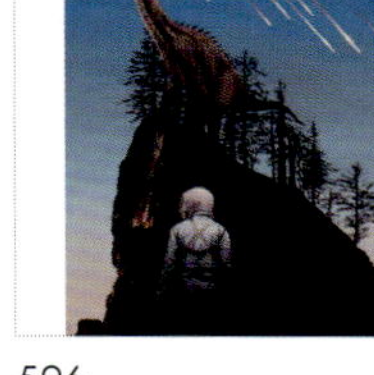

596
GIRAFFATITAN

2022
oil on canvas
20 x 16 in.

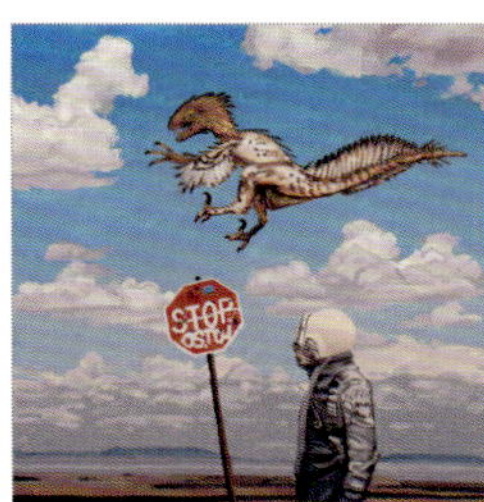

597
DEINONYCHUS

2022
oil on canvas
10 x 10 in.

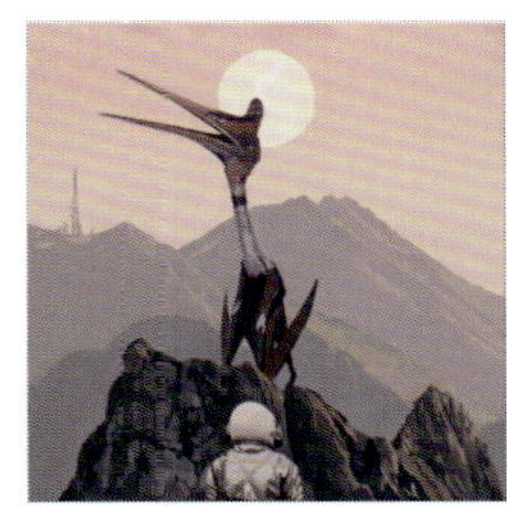

598
QUETZALCOATLUS

2022
oil on canvas
10 x 10 in.

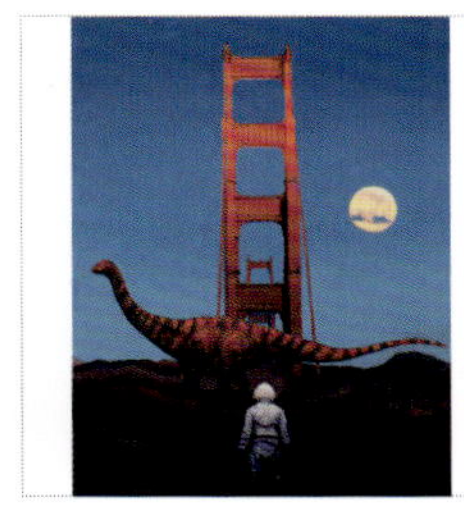

599
APATOSAURUS

2022
oil on canvas
20 x 16 in.

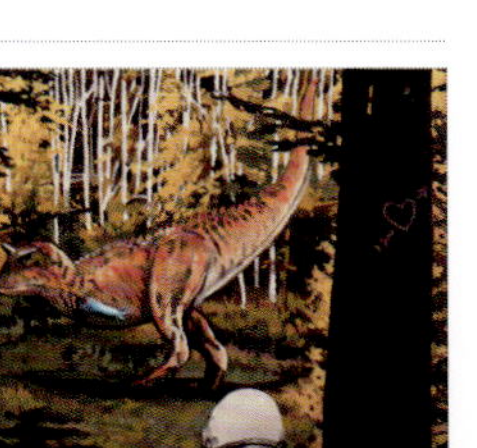

600
CARNOTAURUS

2022
oil on canvas
10 x 10 in.

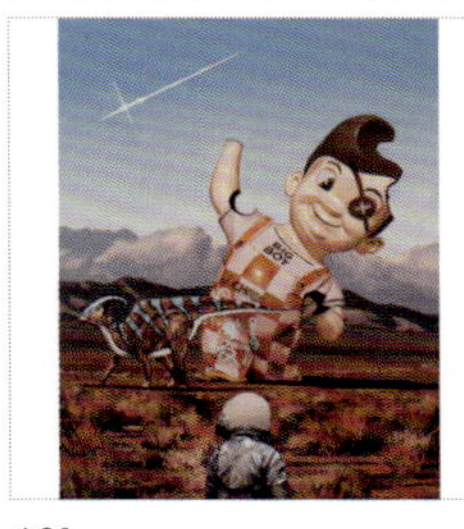

601
PARASAURO-LOPHUS

2022
oil on canvas
20 x 16 in.

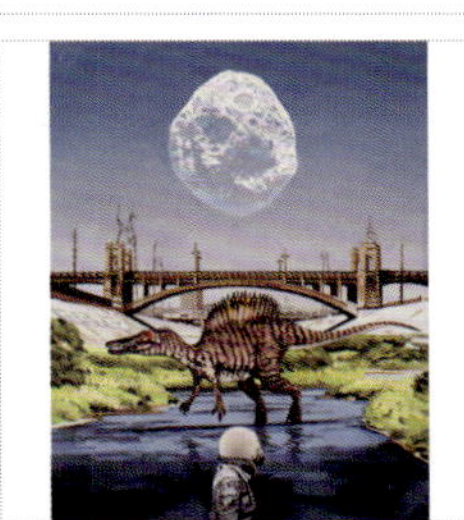

602
SPINOSAURUS

2022
oil on canvas
20 x 16 in.

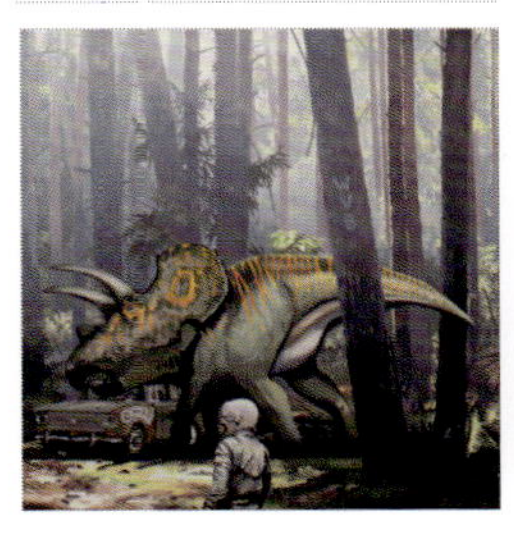

603
TRICERATOPS

2022
oil on canvas
20 x 20 in.

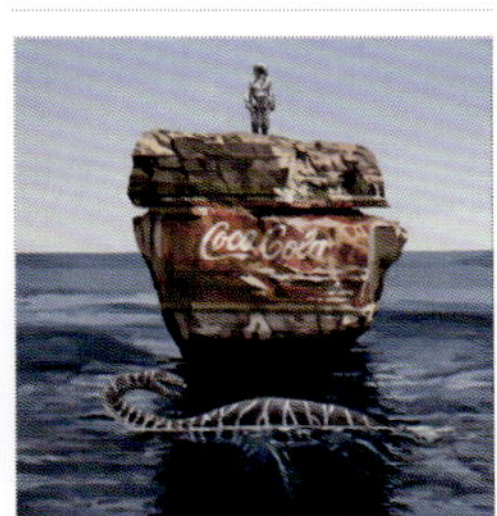

604
PLESIOSAUR

2022
oil on canvas
10 x 10 in.

605
TYRANOSAURUS REX

2022
oil on canvas
30 x 20 in.

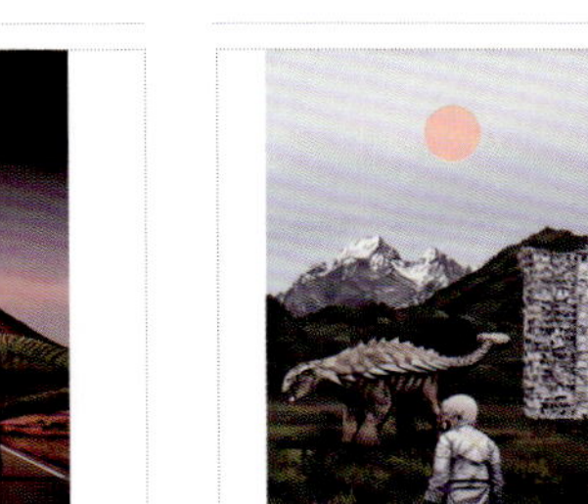

606
ANKYLOSAURUS

2022
oil on canvas
20 x 16 in.

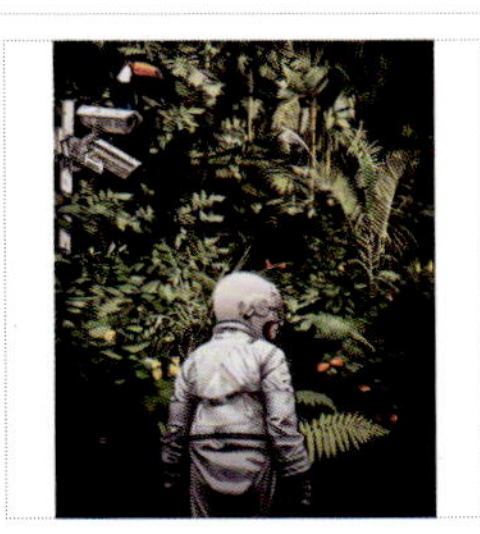

607
JUNGLE

2022
oil on canvas
20 x 16 in.

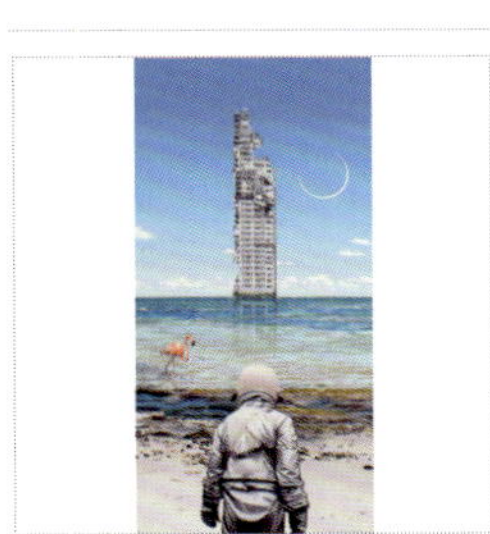

608
MIAMI

2022
oil on canvas
40 x 20 in.

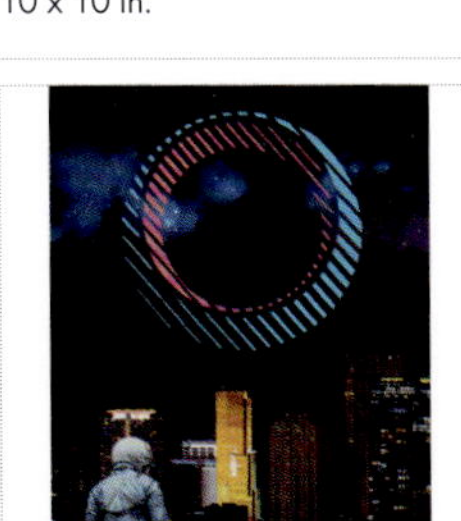

609
MIAMI NIGHT

2022
oil on canvas
20 x 16 in.

610
PURPLE & YELLOW

2022
oil on canvas
10 x 10 in.

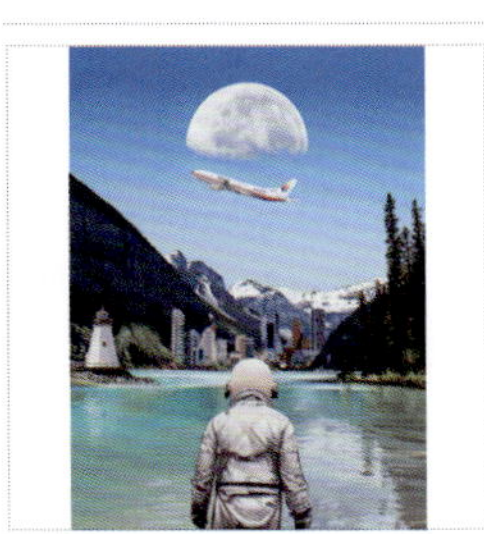

611
LAKE LOUISE

2022
oil on canvas
40 x 30 in.

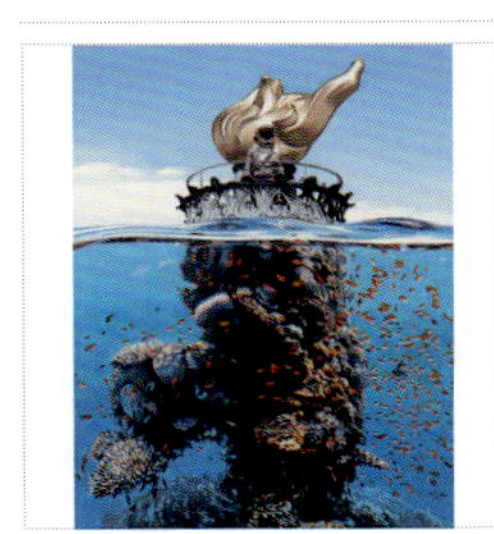

612
THE REEF

2022
oil on canvas
20 x 16 in.

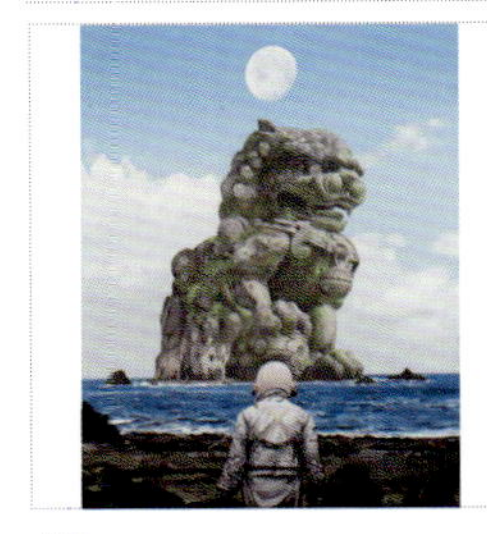

613
LION

2022
oil on canvas
20 x 16 in.

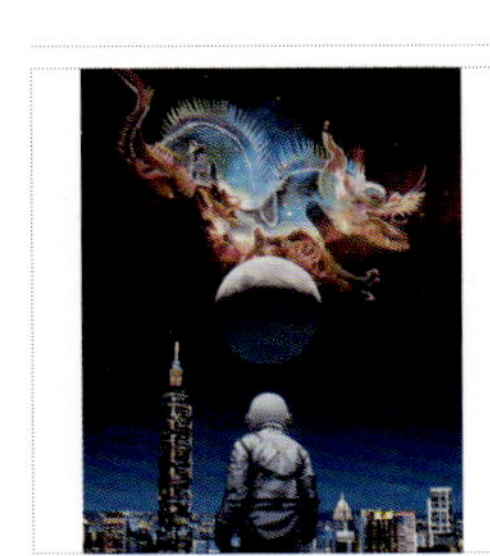

614
DRAGON

2022
oil on canvas
20 x 16 in.

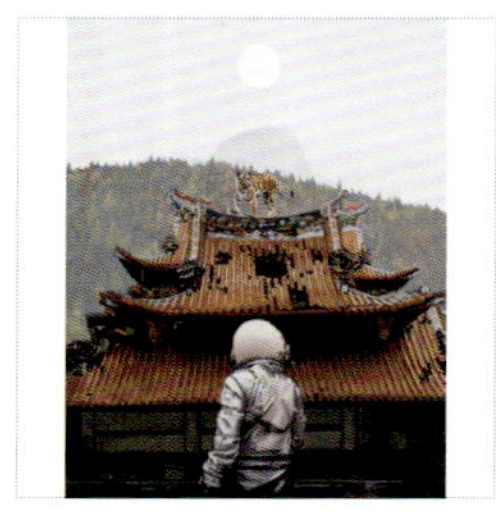

615
TIGER 2

2022
oil on canvas
20 x 16 in.

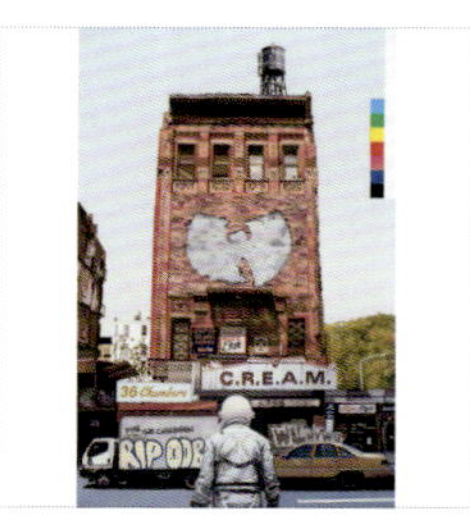

616
WU TANG CLAN

2022
oil on canvas
30 x 20 in.

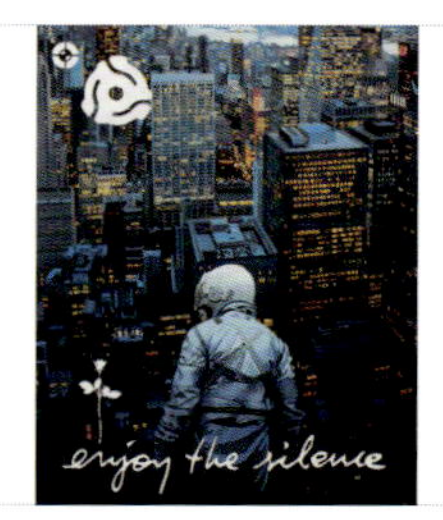

617
ENJOY THE SILENCE

2022
oil on canvas
20 x 16 in.

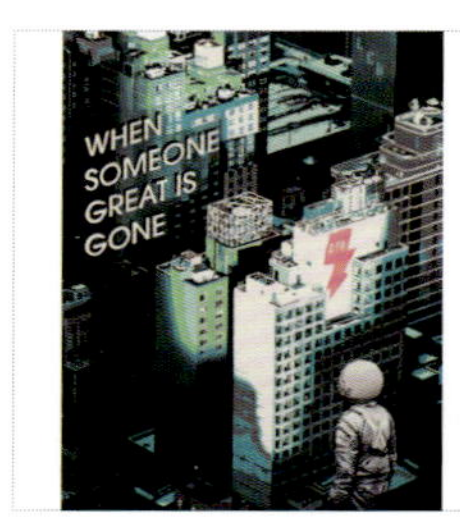

618
SOMEONE GREAT

2022
oil on canvas
20 x 16 in.

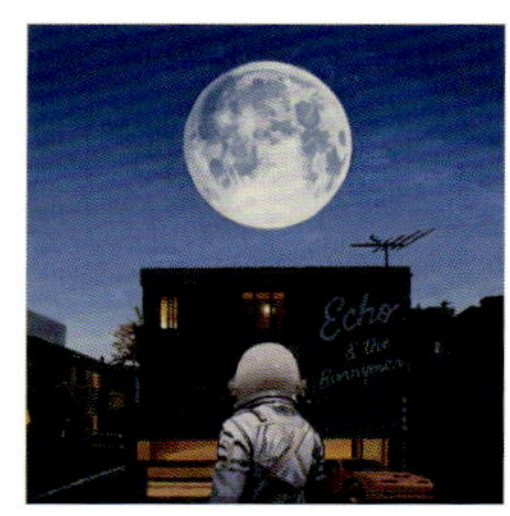

619
KILLING MOON

2022
oil on canvas
10 x 10 in.

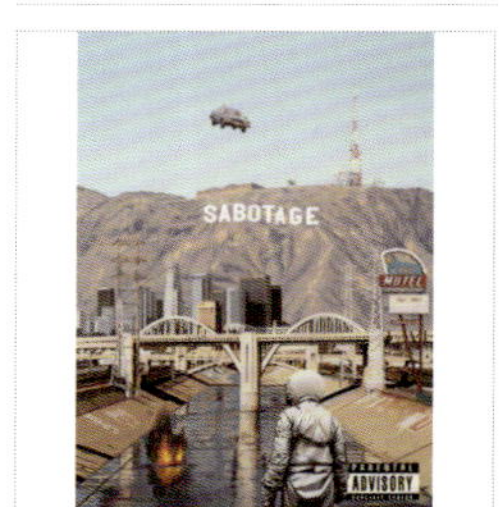

620
SABOTAGE

2022
oil on canvas
40 x 30 in.

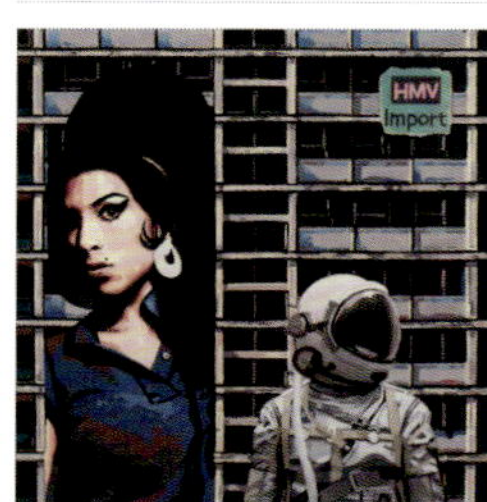

621
BACK TO BLACK

2022
oil on canvas
10 x 10 in.

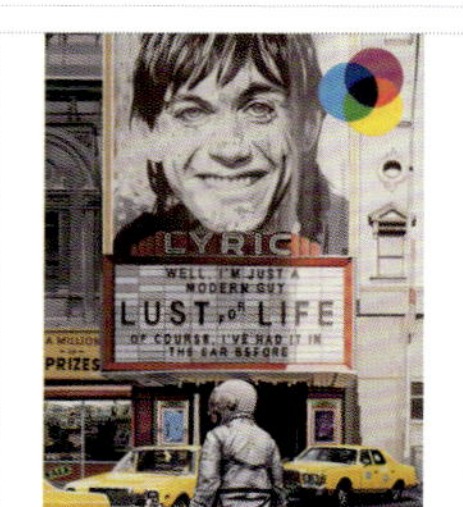

622
LUST FOR LIFE

2022
oil on canvas
20 x 16 in.

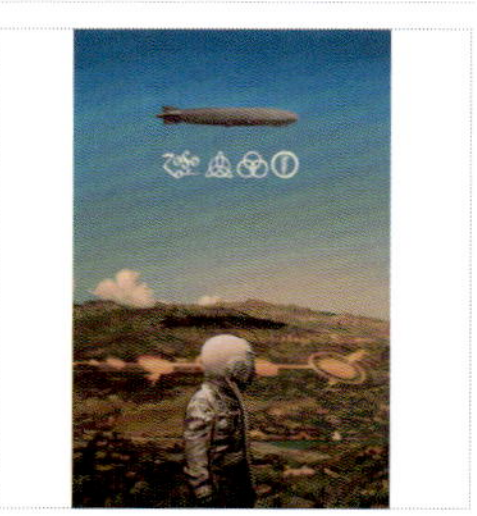

623
ZEPPELIN

2023
oil on canvas
30 x 20 in.

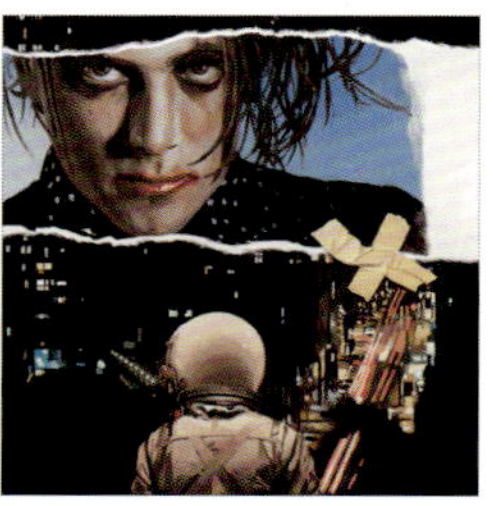

624
DISINTEGRATION

2023
oil on canvas
10 x 10 in.

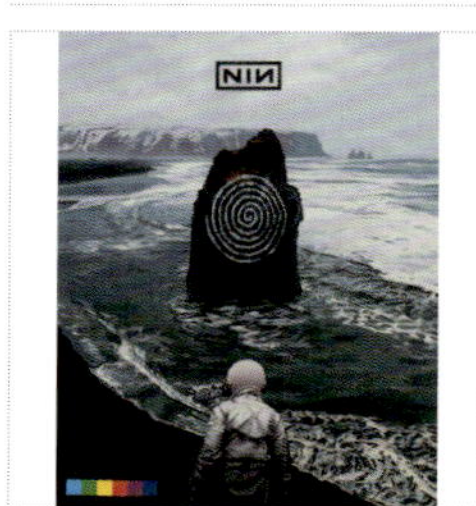

625
THE DOWNWARD SPIRAL
2023
oil on canvas
20 x 16 in.

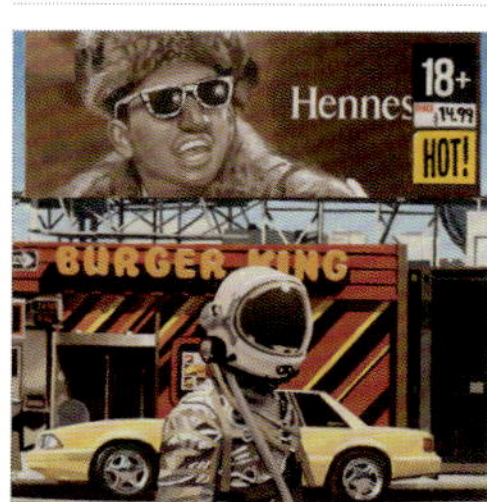

626
DIGITAL UNDERGROUND

2023
oil on canvas
10 x 10 in.

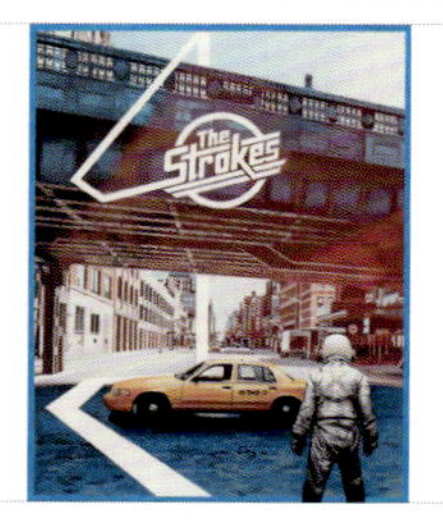

627
IS THIS IT

2023
oil on canvas
20 x 16 in.

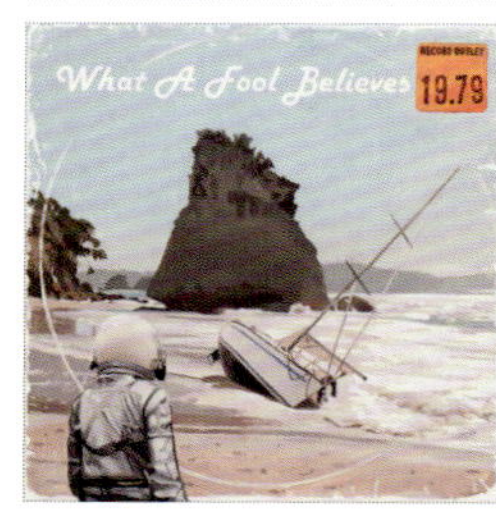

628
WHAT A FOOL BELIEVES

2023
oil on canvas
10 x 10 in.

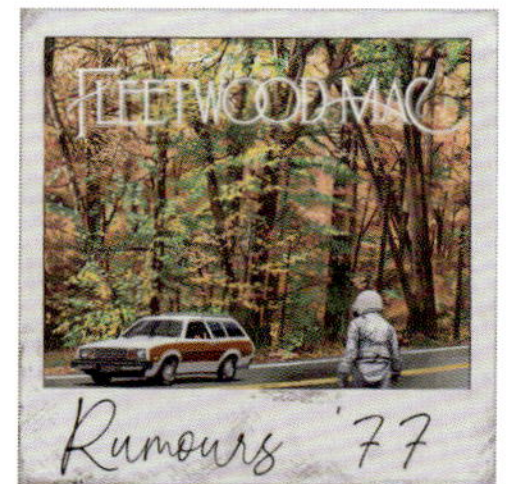

629
RUMOURS

2023
oil on canvas
20 x 20 in.

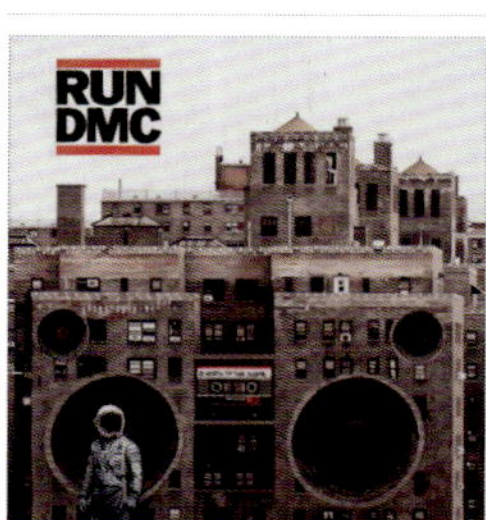

630
BEATS TO THE RHYME

2023
oil on canvas
20 x 20 in.

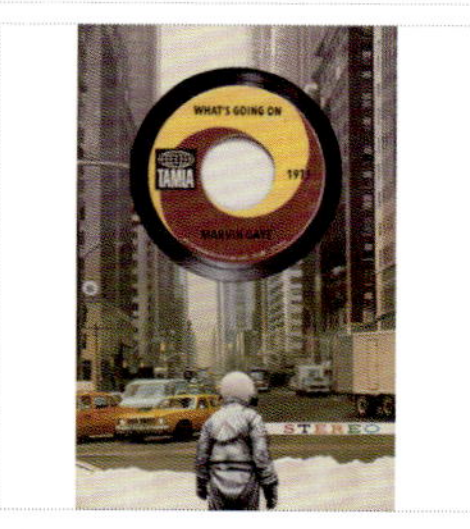

631
WHAT'S GOING ON

2023
oil on canvas
30 x 20 in.

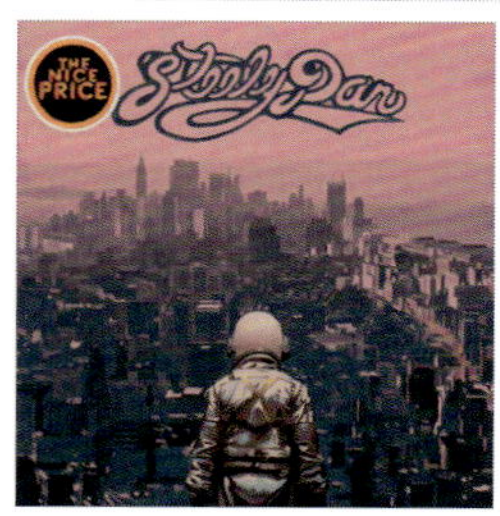

632
STEELY DAN

2023
oil on canvas
10 x 10 in.

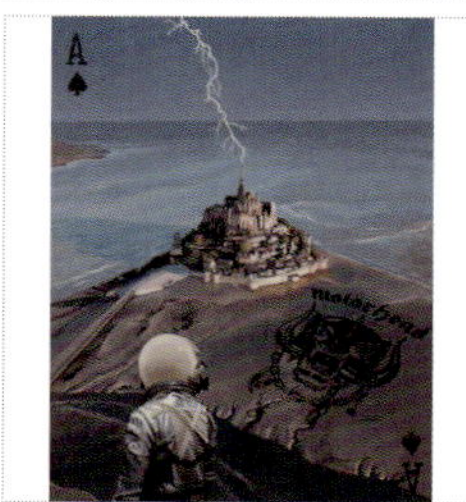

633
ACE OF SPADES

2023
oil on canvas
20 x 16 in.

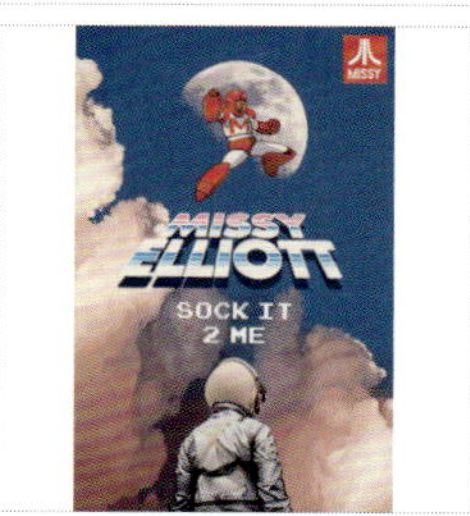

634
SOCK IT 2 ME

2023
oil on canvas
30 x 20 in.

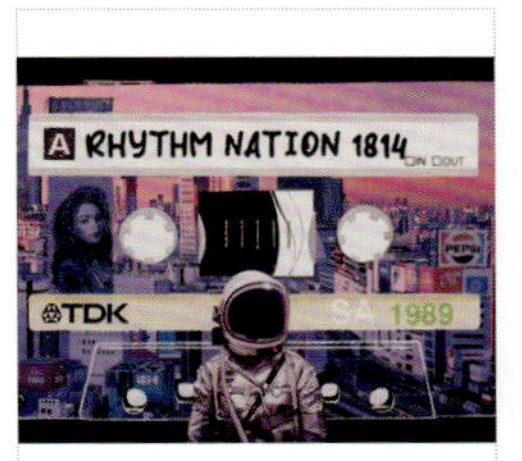

635
JANET

2023
oil on canvas
16 x 20 in.

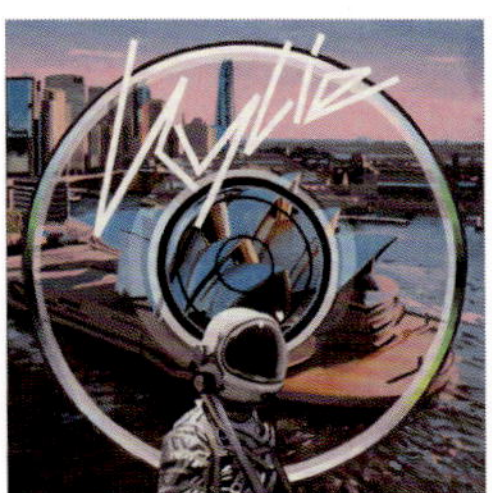

636
KYLIE

2023
oil on canvas
10 x 10 in.

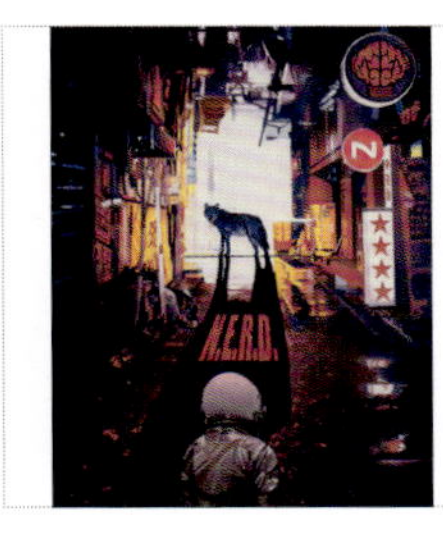

637
N.E.R.D.

2023
oil on canvas
20 x 16 in.

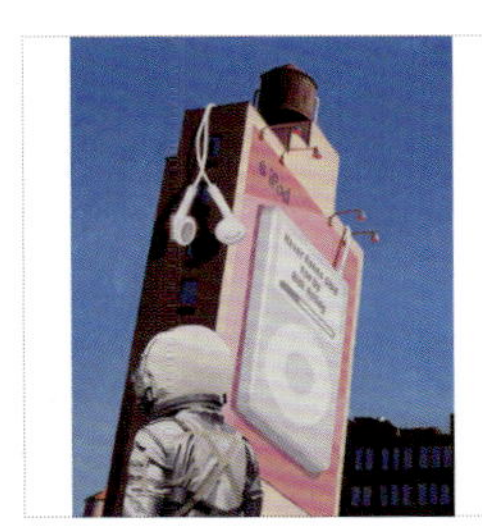

638
RICK

2023
oil on canvas
10 x 8 in.

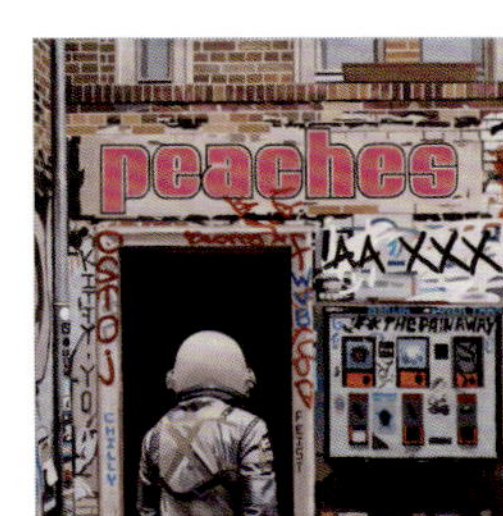

639
PEACHES

2023
oil on canvas
10 x 10 in.

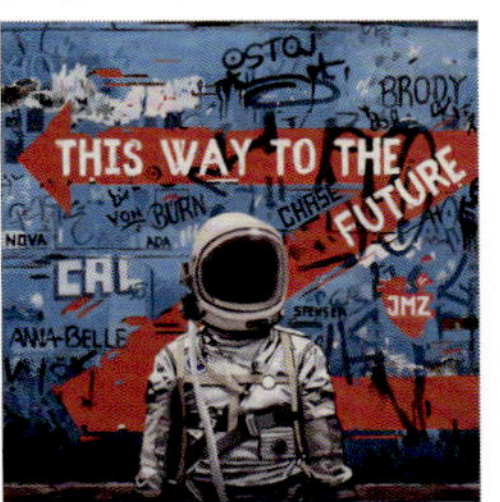

640
THIS WAY TO THE FUTURE

2023
oil on canvas
12 x 12 in.

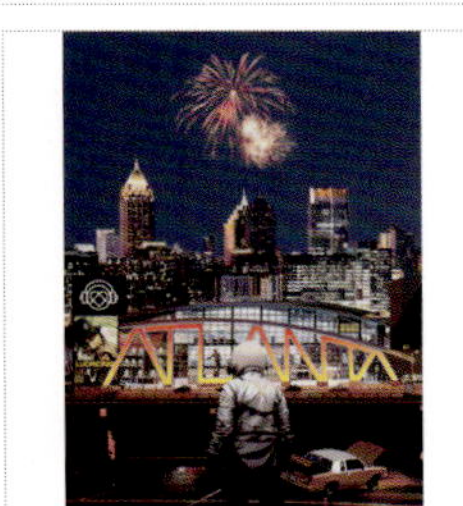

641
ATLANTA

2023
oil on canvas
40 x 30 in.

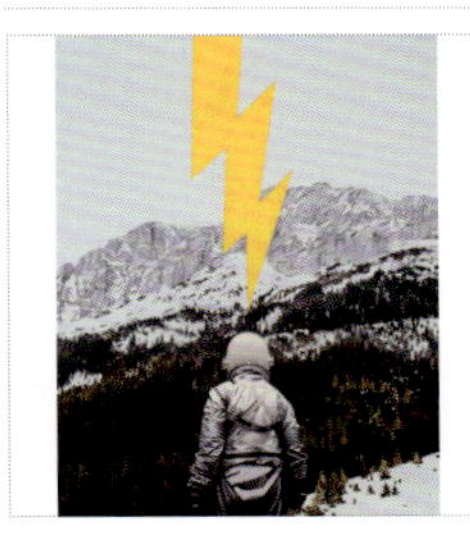

642
LIGHTNING STRIKE

2023
oil on canvas
20 x 16 in.

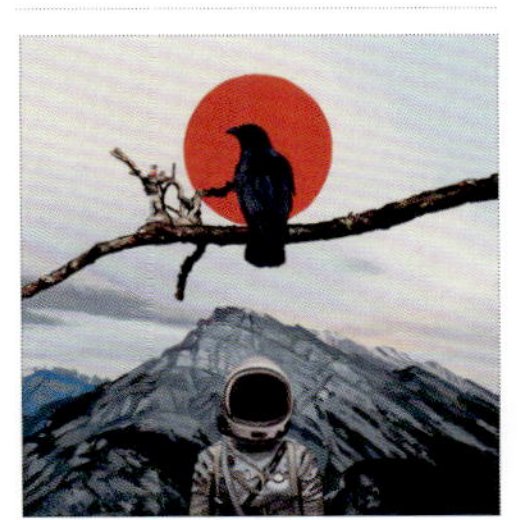

643
CROW

2023
oil on canvas
10 x 10 in.

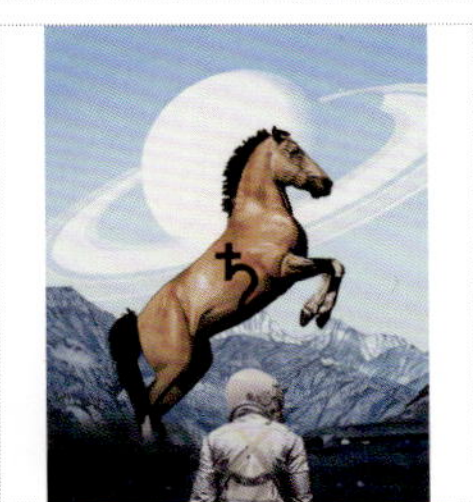

644
SATURN

2023
oil on canvas
20 x 16 in.

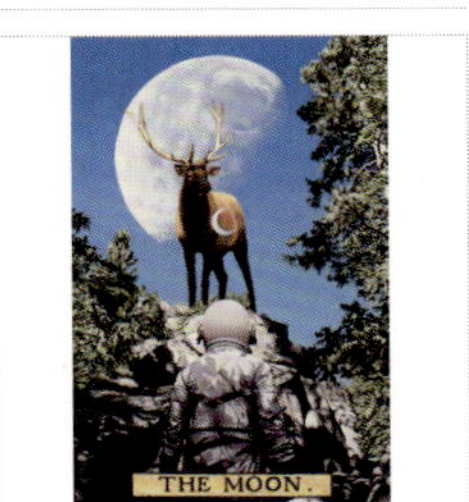

645
THE MOON

2023
oil on canvas
30 x 20 in.

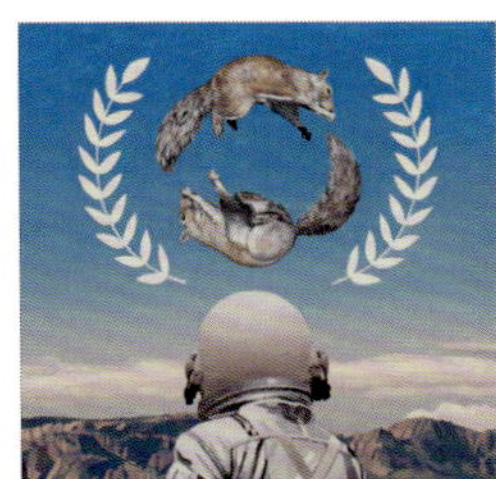

646
SQUIRRELS

2023
oil on canvas
10 x 10 in.

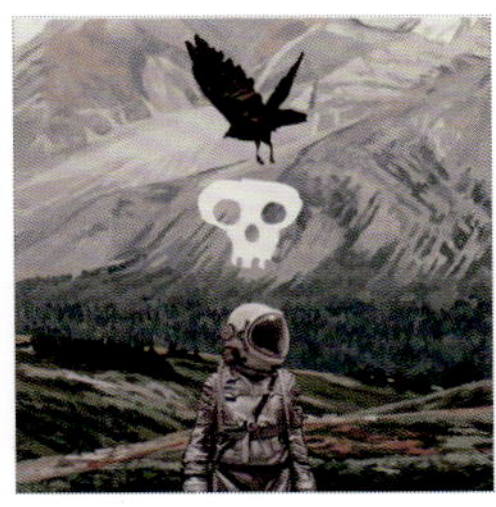

647
SKULL

2023
oil on canvas
10 x 10 in.

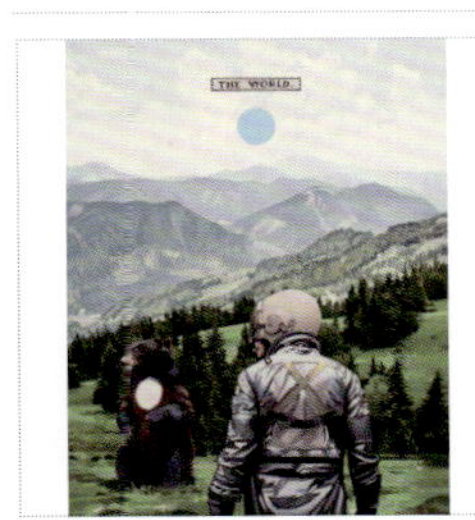

648
THE WORLD

2023
oil on canvas
20 x 15 in.

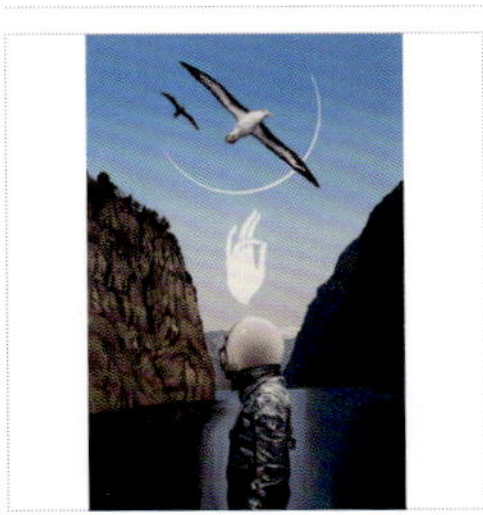

649
ALBATROSS

2023
oil on canvas
30 x 20 in.

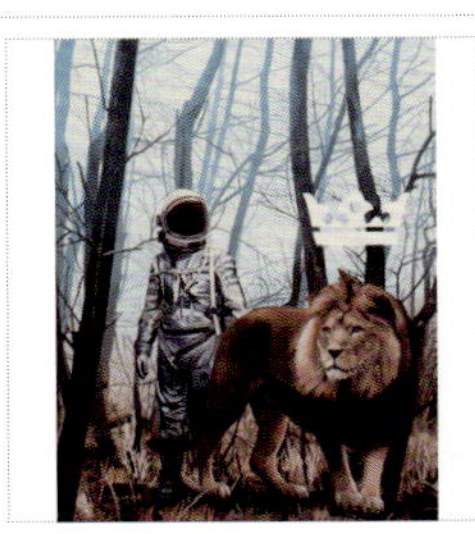

650
LEO

2023
oil on canvas
20 x 16 in.

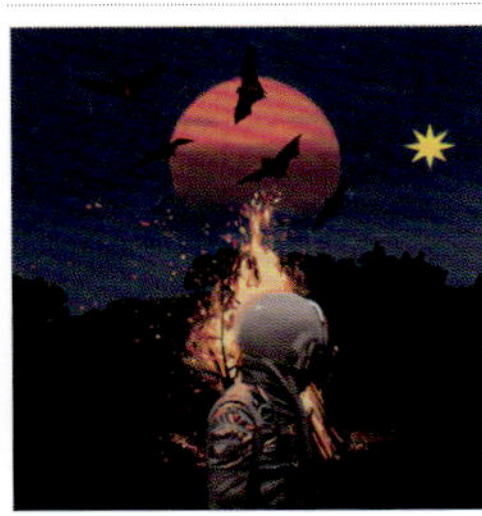

651
BATS

2023
oil on canvas
10 x 10 in.

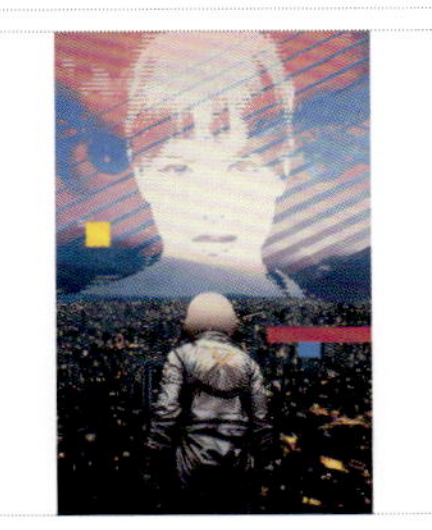

652
THE CITY HAS EYES

2023
oil on canvas
30 x 20 in.

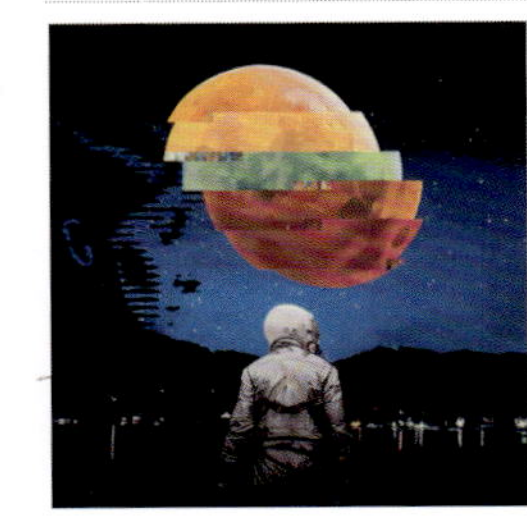

653
SPLIT MOON

2023
oil on canvas
20 x 20 in.

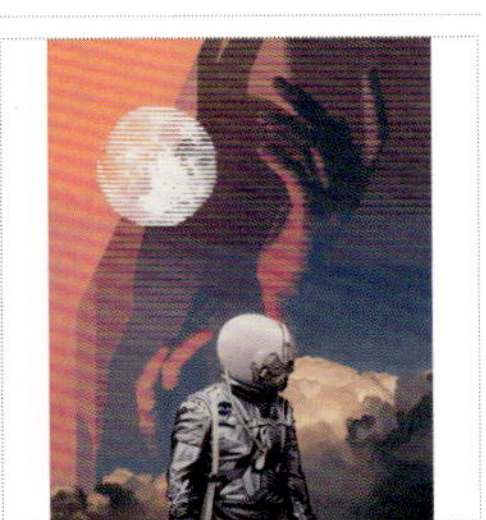

654
PINK HANDS

2023
oil on canvas
20 x 16 in.

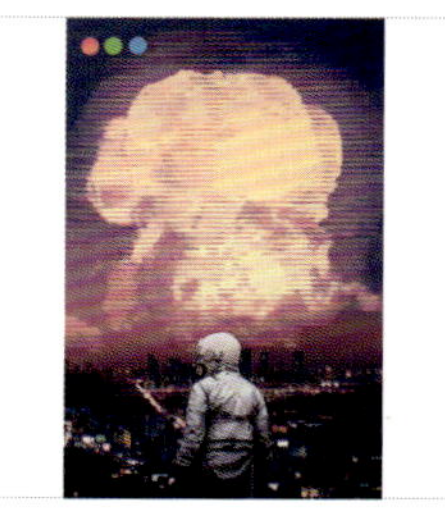

655
KABOOM

2023
oil on canvas
30 x 20 in.

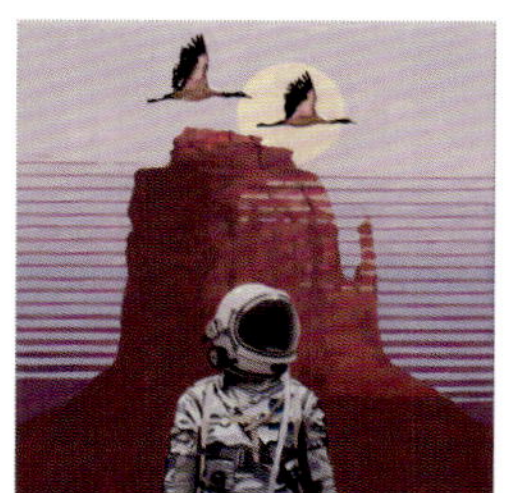

656
TWO BIRDS

2023
oil on canvas
10 x 10 in.

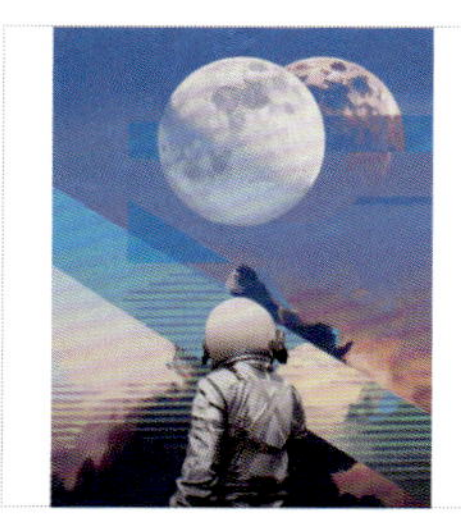

657
MOON & A HALF

2023
oil on canvas
20 x 16 in.

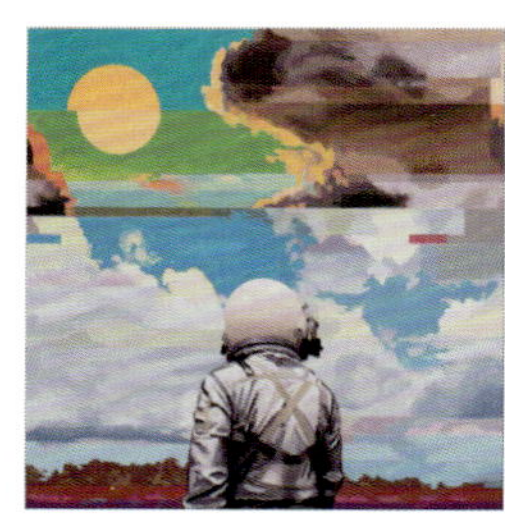

658
GREEN & ORANGE MORNING

2023
oil on canvas
10 x 10 in.

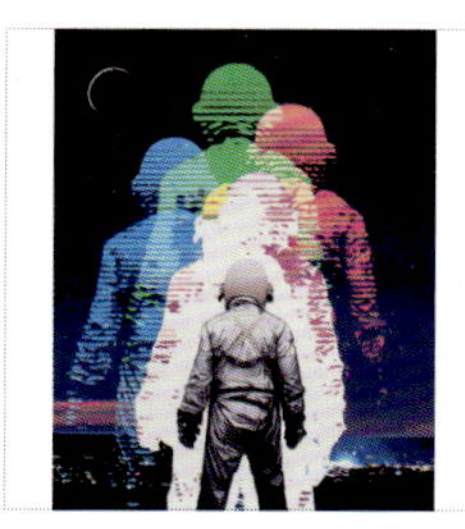

659
MULTIPLICATION

2023
oil on canvas
20 x 16 in.

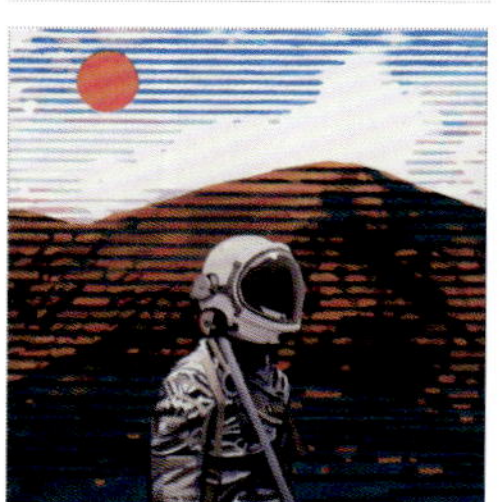

660
FOOTHILLS

2023
oil on canvas
10 x 10 in.

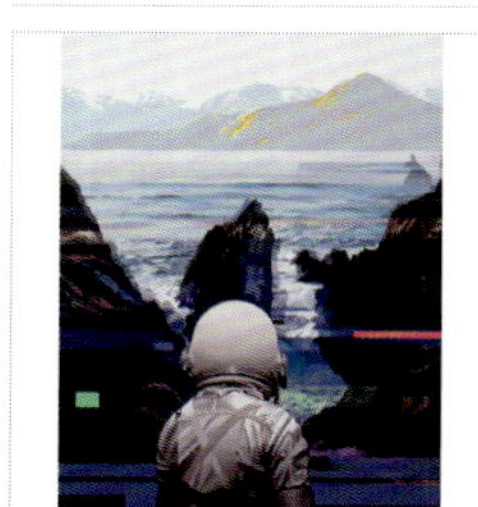

661
CRASHING WAVES

2023
oil on canvas
20 x 16 in.

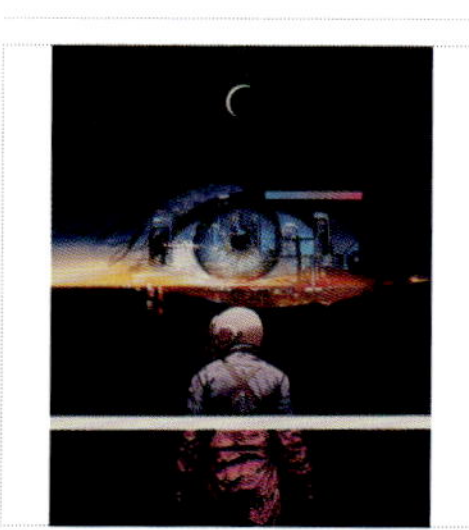

662
GOODNIGHT

2023
oil on canvas
20 x 16 in.

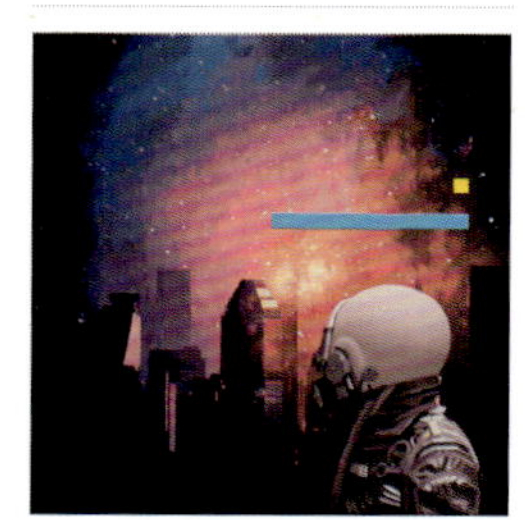

663
AT THE CENTER OF THE CITY

2023
oil on canvas
10 x 10 in.

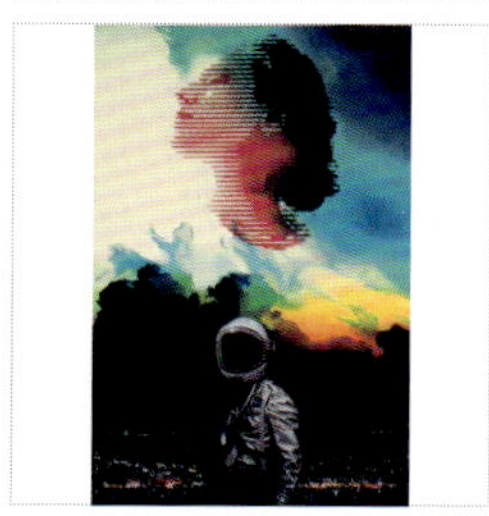

664
HEAD IN THE CLOUDS

2023
oil on canvas
30 x 20 in.

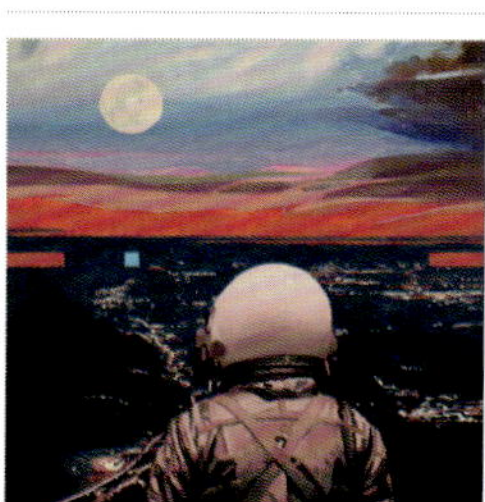

665
RED HORIZON

2023
oil on canvas
10 x 10 in.

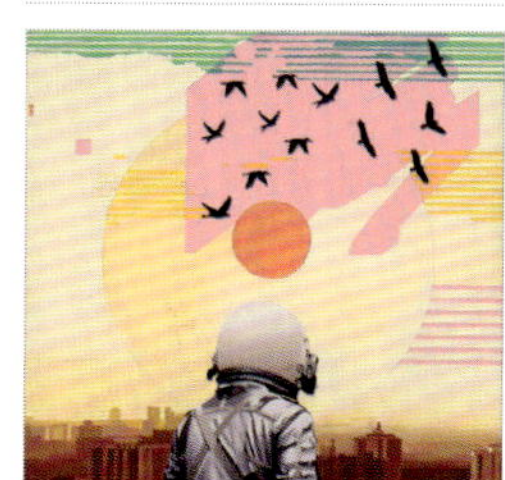

666
PINK FLOCK

2023
oil on canvas
10 x 10 in.

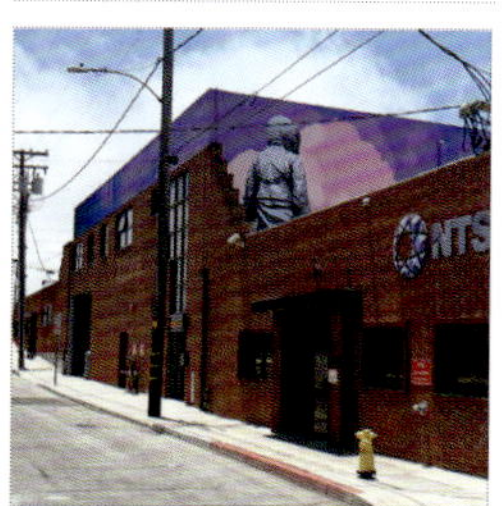

667
EL SEGUNDO ORBITS

2023
mural
15 x 100 ft.

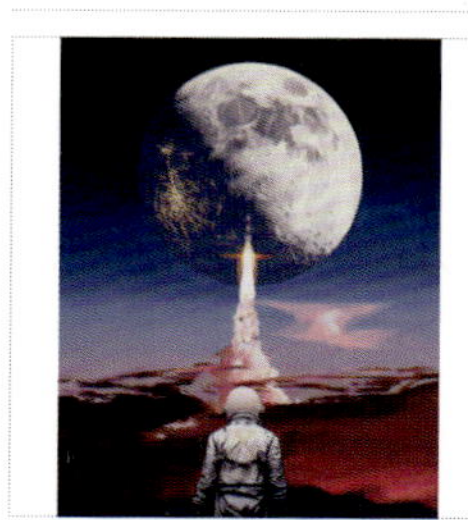

668
ROCKET

2023
oil on canvas
20 x 16 in.

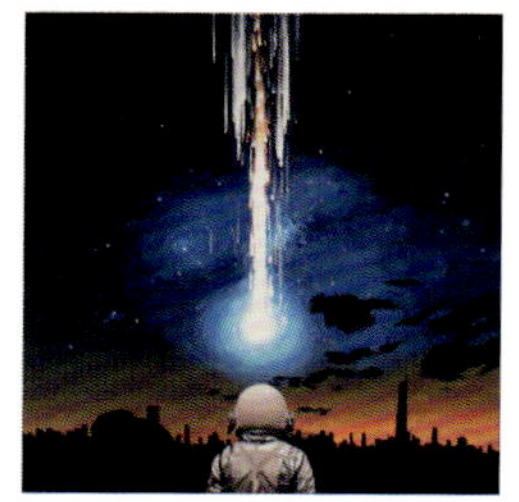

669
RAINING DOWN

2023
oil on canvas
10 x 10 in.

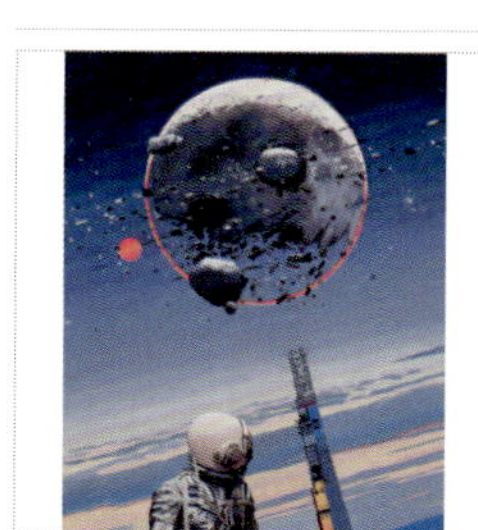

670
SPACE ELEVATOR

2023
oil on canvas
20 x 16 in.

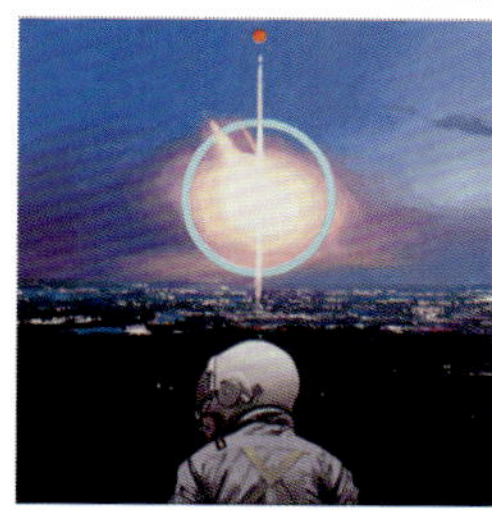

671
RED PLANET

2023
oil on canvas
10 x 10 in.

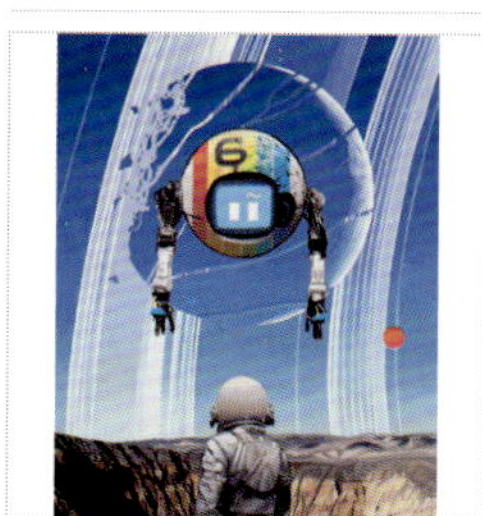

672
NUMBER 6

2023
oil on canvas
20 x 16 in.

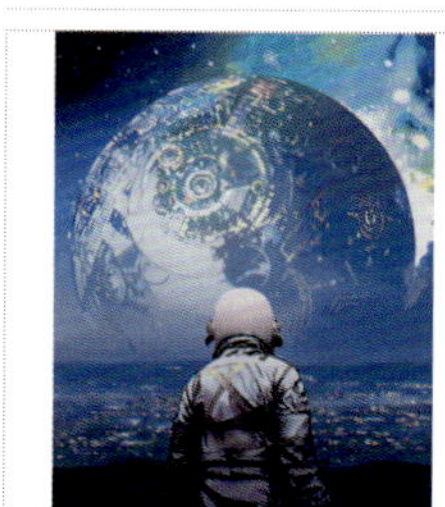

673
CYBERTRON

2023
oil on canvas
20 x 16 in.

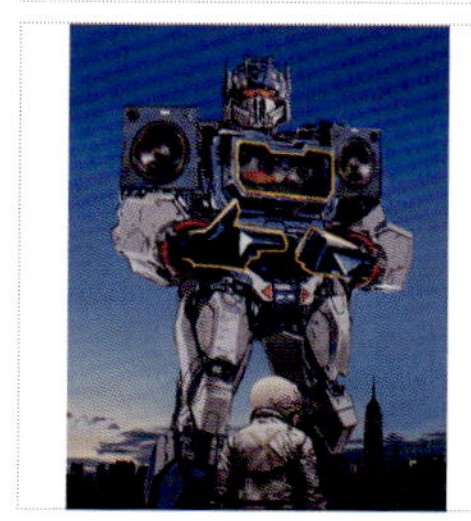

674
SOUNDWAVE

2023
oil on canvas
20 x 16 in.

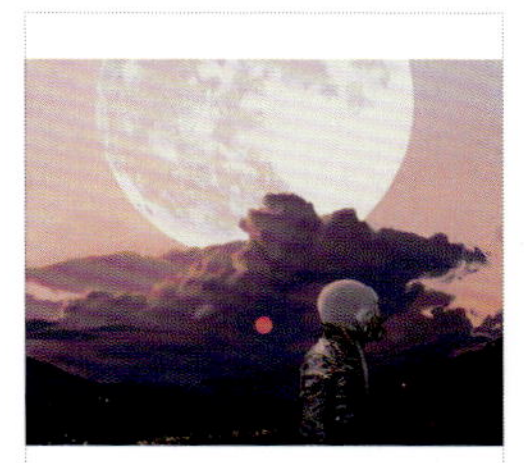

675
PINK & PURPLE EVENING

2023
oil on canvas
16 x 20 in.

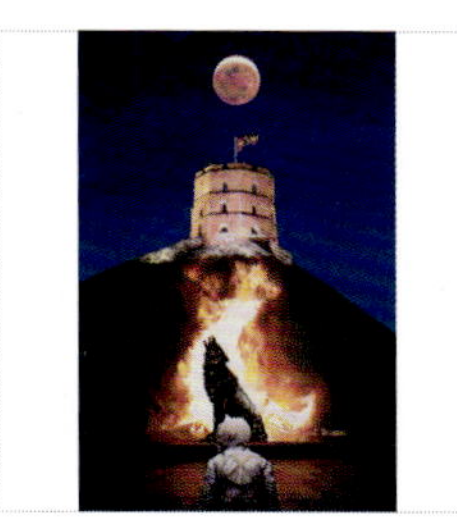

676
THE EQUINOX

2023
oil on canvas
30 x 20 in.

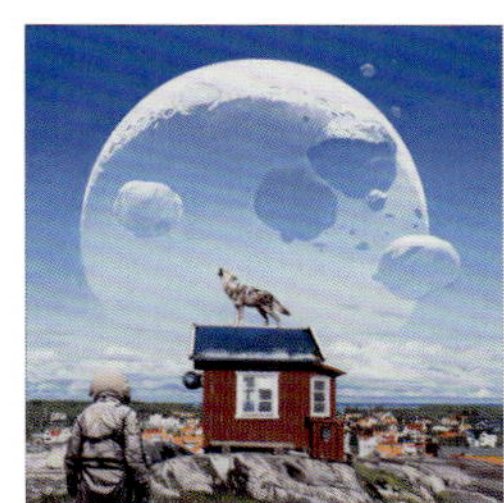

677
THE RED HOUSE

2024
oil on canvas
20 x 20 in.

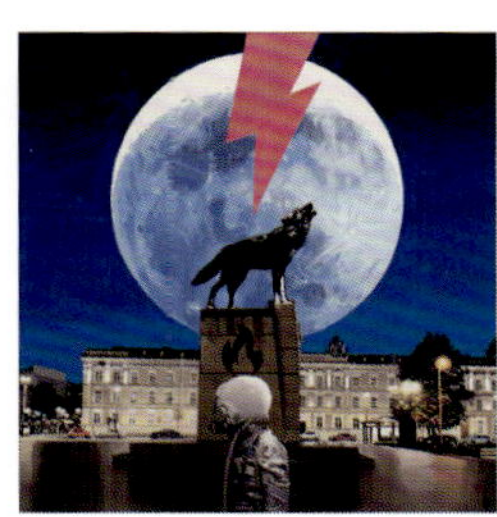

678
THE PLAZA

2024
oil on canvas
20 x 20 in.

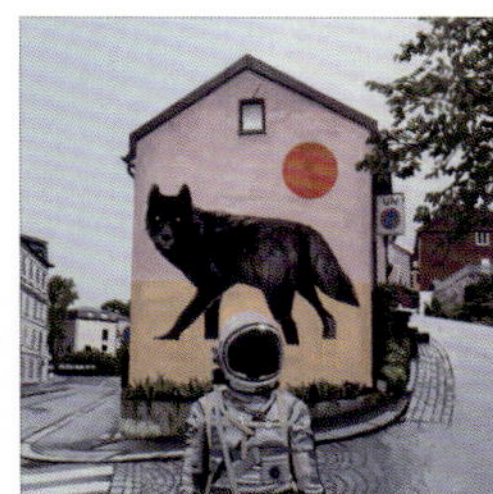

679
THE WOLF HOUSE

2024
oil on canvas
10 x 10 in.

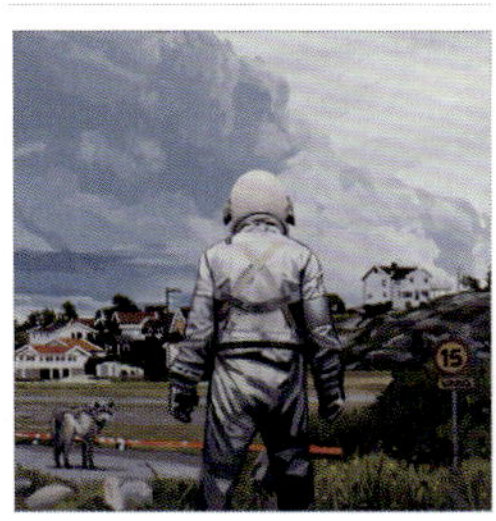

680
ON THE ISLAND

2024
oil on canvas
10 x 10 in.

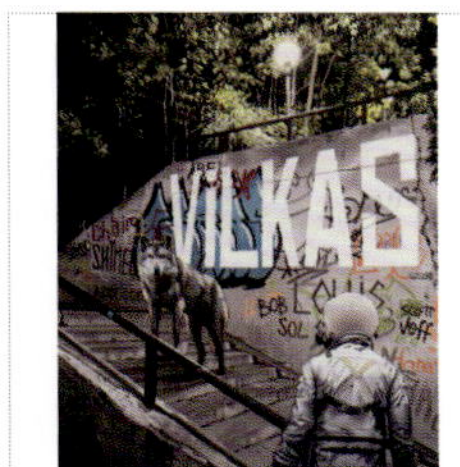

681
THE STAIRWAY

2024
oil on canvas
20 x 16 in.

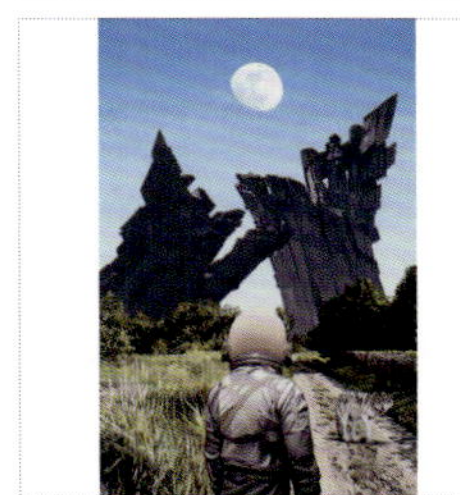

682
THE ROAD

2024
oil on canvas
30 x 20 in.

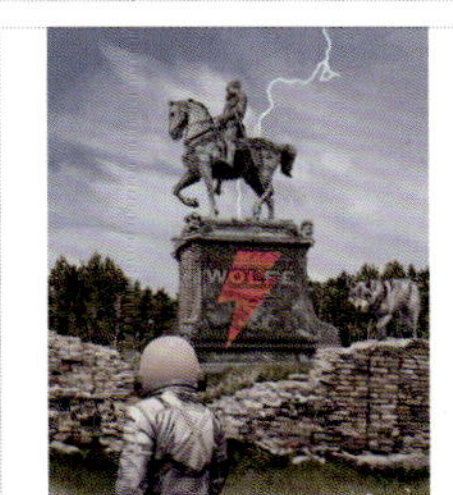

683
THE WALL

2024
oil on canvas
20 x 16 in.

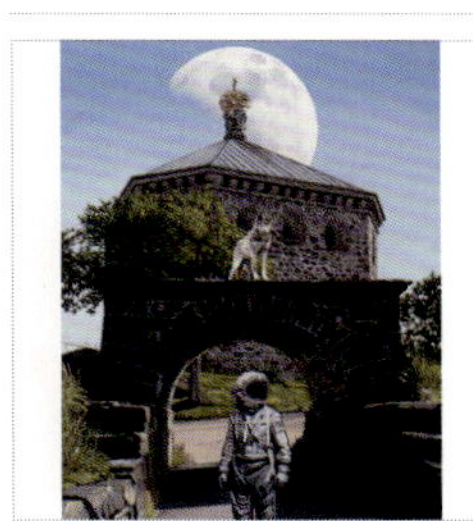

684
THE ARCHWAY

2024
oil on canvas
20 x 16 in.

685
FOREVER

2024
oil on canvas
20 x 16 in.

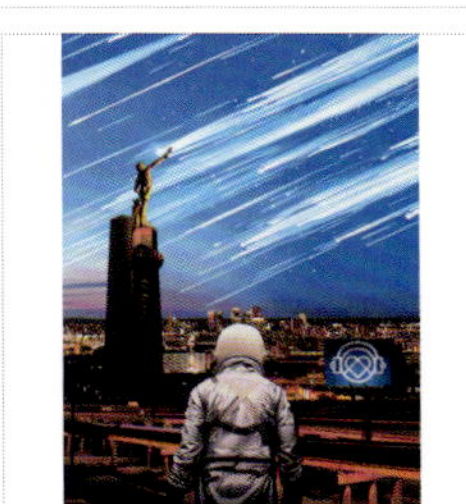

686
VULCAN

2024
oil on canvas
40 x 30 in.

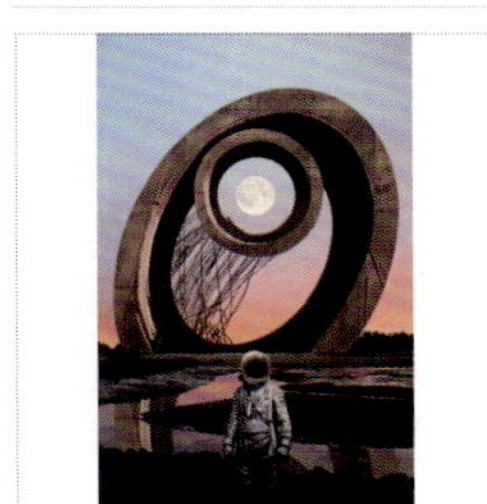

687
OCULUS

2024
oil on canvas
30 x 20 in.

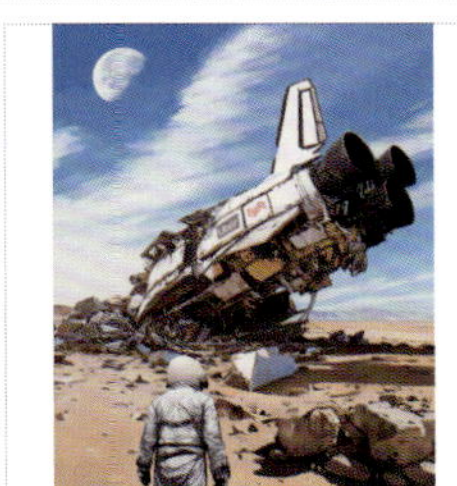

688
CRASH SITE

2024
oil on canvas
20 x 16 in.

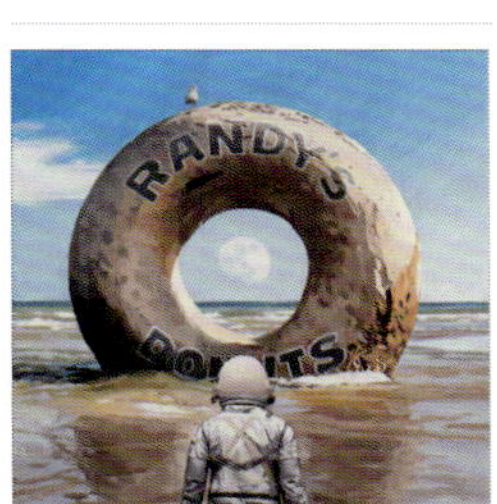

689
RANDY'S

2024
oil on canvas
10 x 10 in.

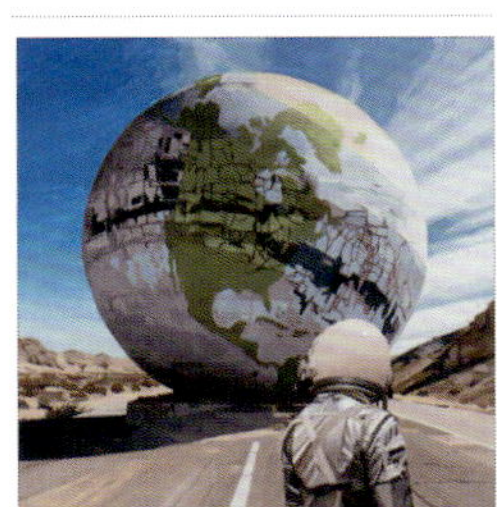

690
GLOBE

2024
oil on canvas
10 x 10 in.

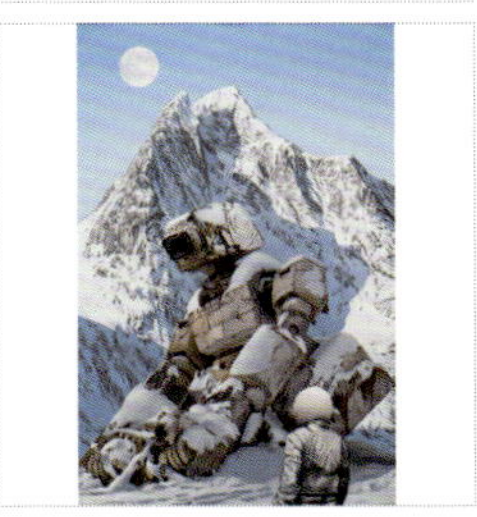

691
SNOWBOT

2024
oil on canvas
30 x 20 in.

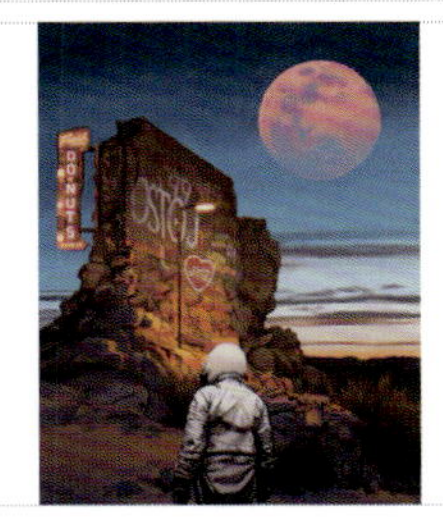

692
FRESH DONUTS

2024
oil on canvas
20 x 16 in.

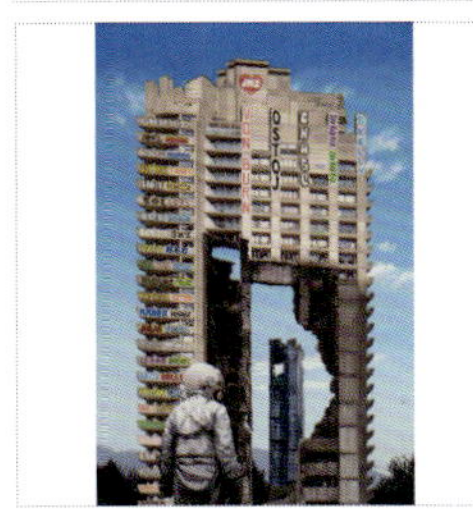

693
WE WHO REMAIN

2024
oil on canvas
60 x 40 in.

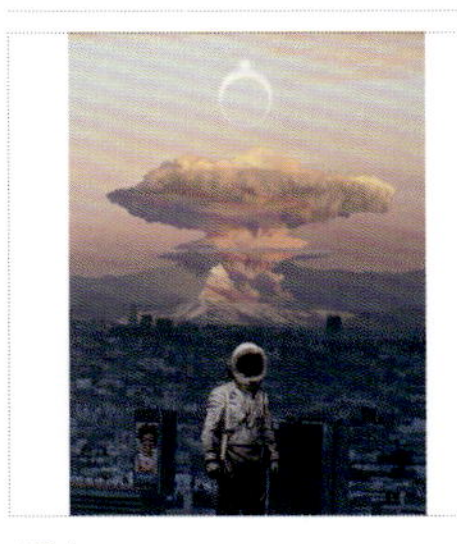

694
CITY OF ANGELS

2024
oil on canvas
40 x 30 in.

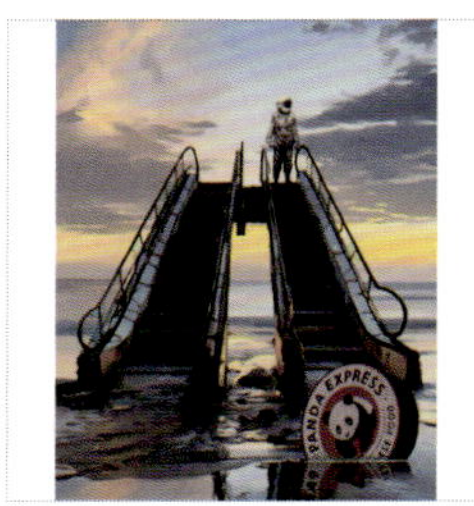

695
THE ESCALATOR

2024
oil on canvas
20 x 16 in.

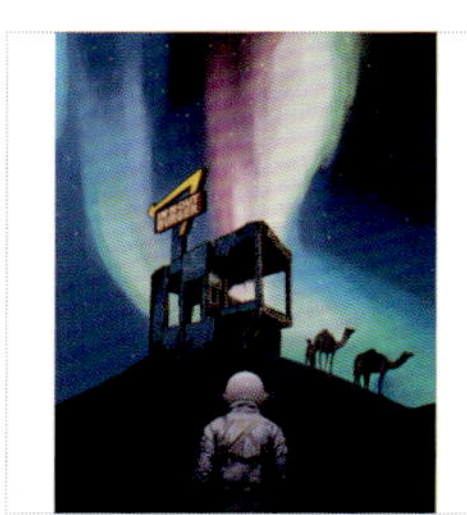

696
ON THE DUNES

2024
oil on canvas
20 x 16 in.

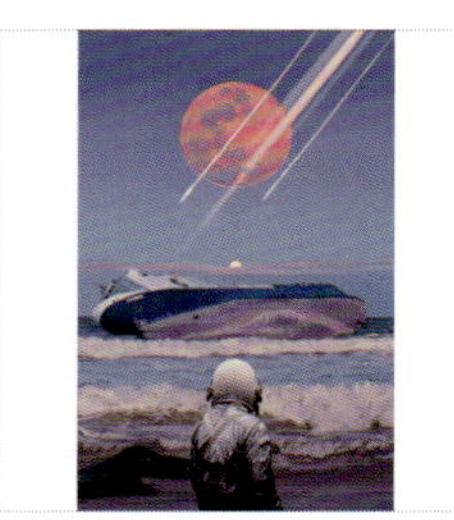

697
WASHED ASHORE

2024
oil on canvas
30 x 20 in.

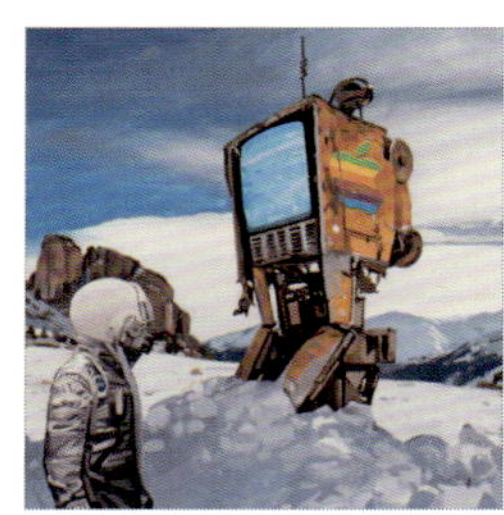

698
iBOT

2024
oil on canvas
10 x 10 in.

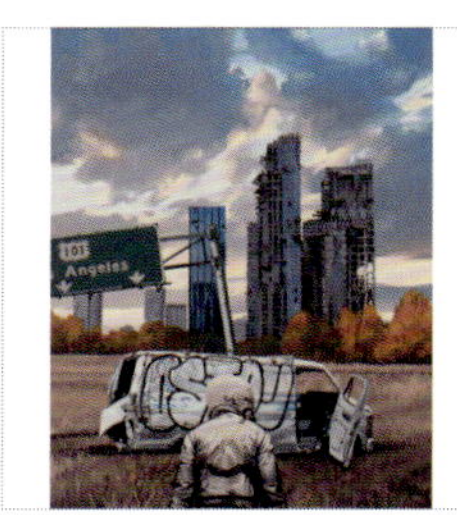

699
THE ONE OH ONE

2024
oil on canvas
20 x 16 in.

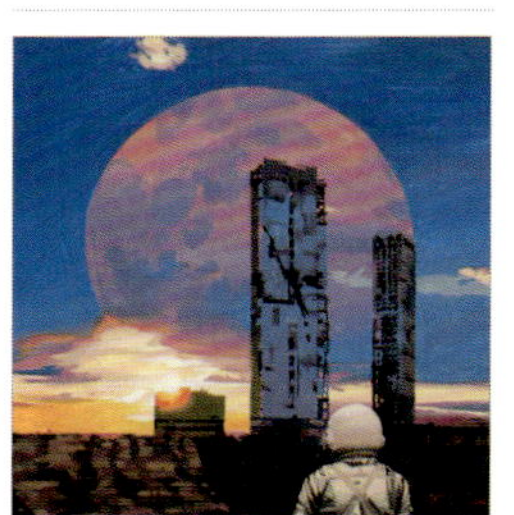

700
DOWNTOWN

2024
oil on canvas
10 x 10 in.

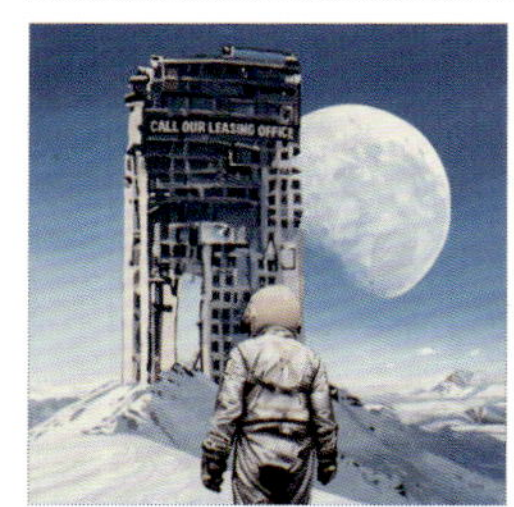

701
CALL OUR LEASING OFFICE

2024
oil on canvas
10 x 10 in.

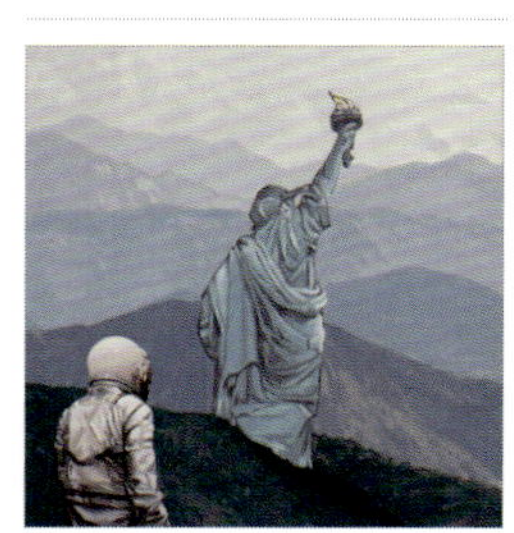

702
LIBERTY

2024
oil on canvas
10 x 10 in.

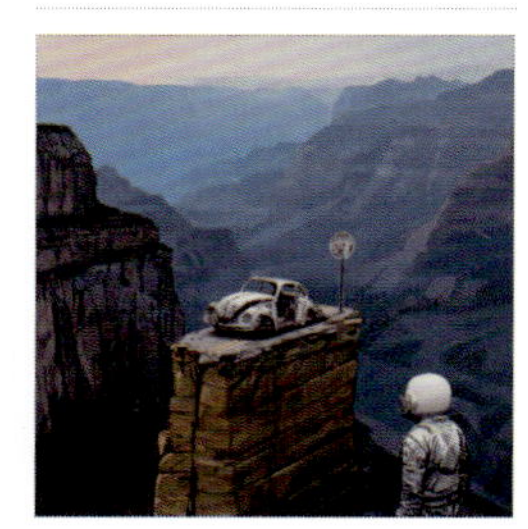

703
PARKING SPOT

2024
oil on canvas
20 x 20 in.

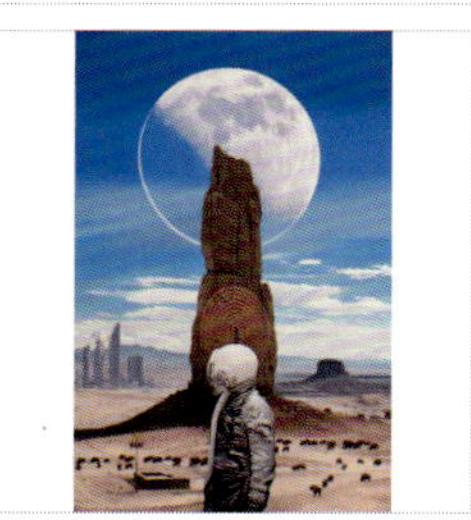

704
MONOLITH

2024
oil on canvas
60 x 40 in.

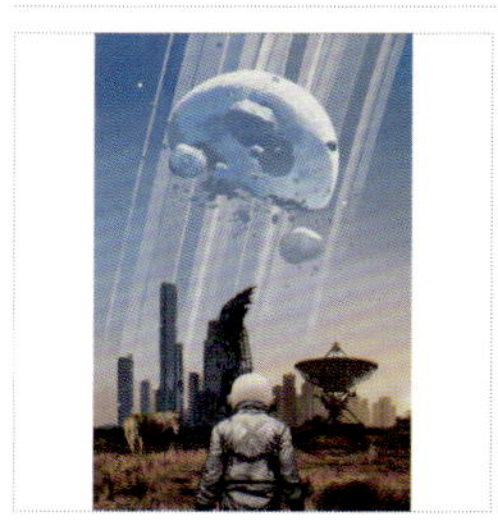

705
HALF MOON RISING

2024
oil on canvas
60 x 40 in.

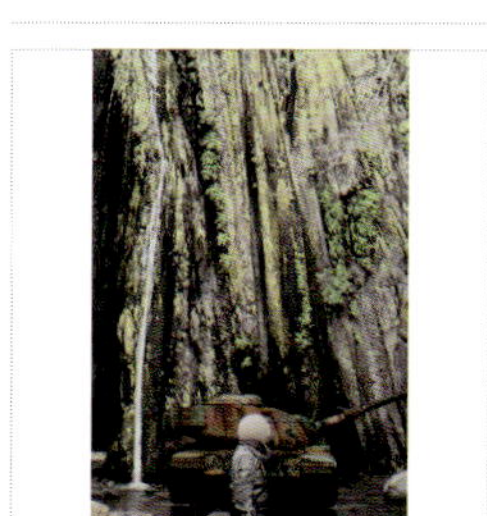

706
THE FALLS

2024
oil on canvas
30 x 20 in.

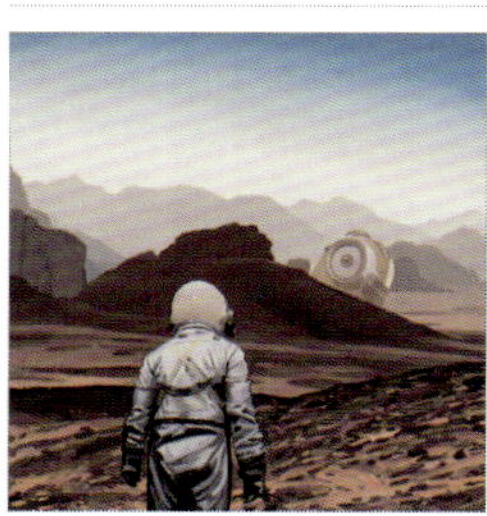

707
MINIONPOCALYPSE

2024
oil on canvas
10 x 10 in.

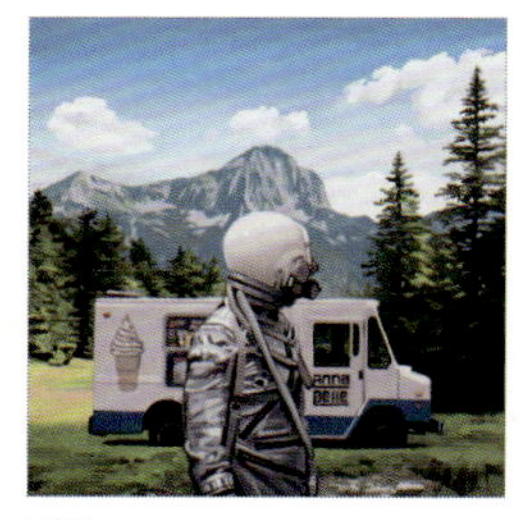

708
ICE CREAM TRUCK

2024
oil on canvas
10 x 10 in.

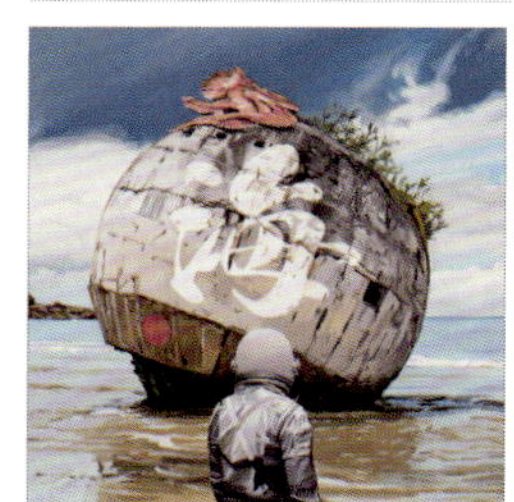

709
UMI

2024
oil on canvas
12 x 12 in.

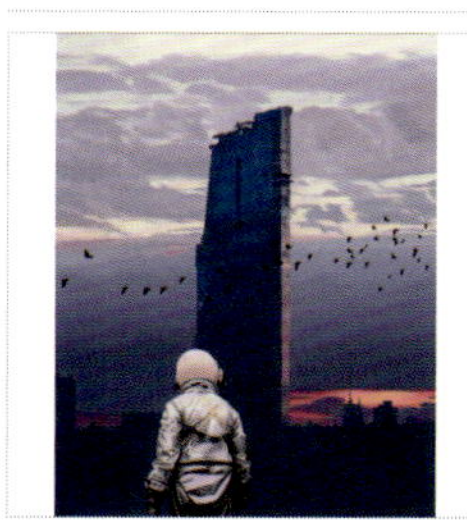

710
THE LAST TOWER

2024
oil on canvas
20 x 16 in.

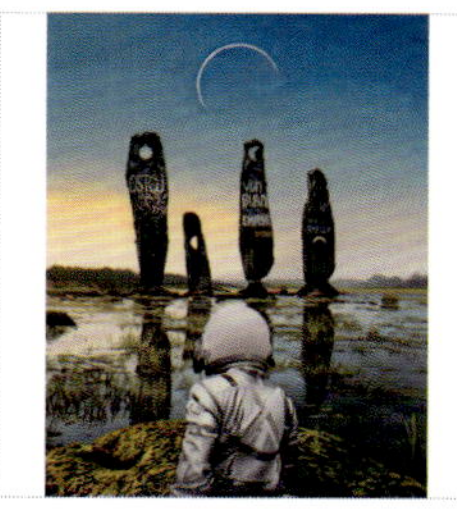

711
FOUR STONES

2024
oil on canvas
20 x 16 in.

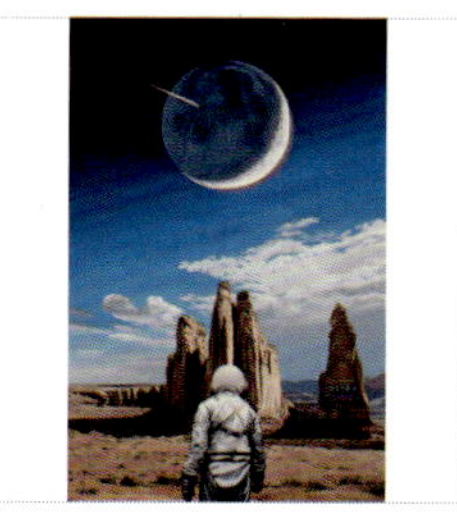

712
THE PLAINS

2024
oil on canvas
30 x 20 in.

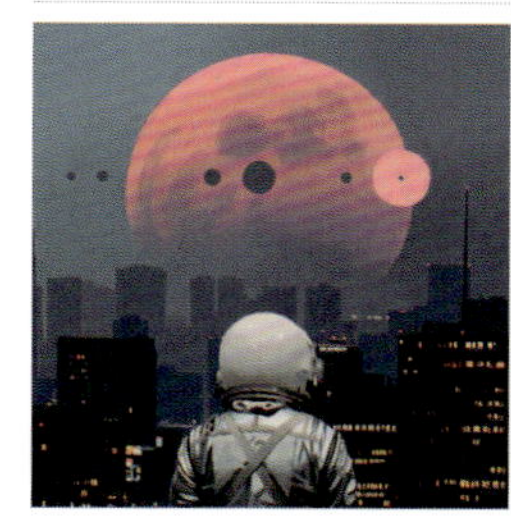

713
ORBITALS

2024
oil on canvas
10 x 10 in.

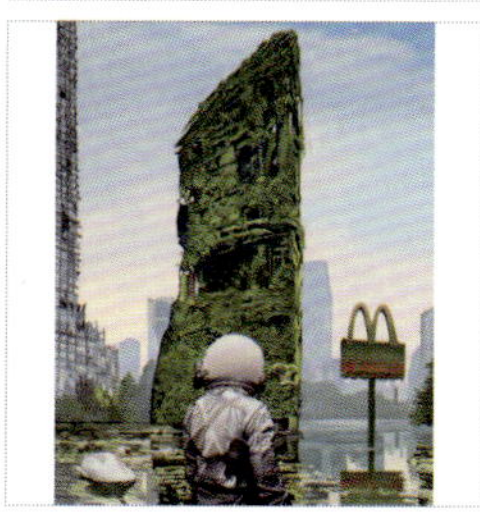

714
MAIN STREET

2024
oil on canvas
20 x 16 in.

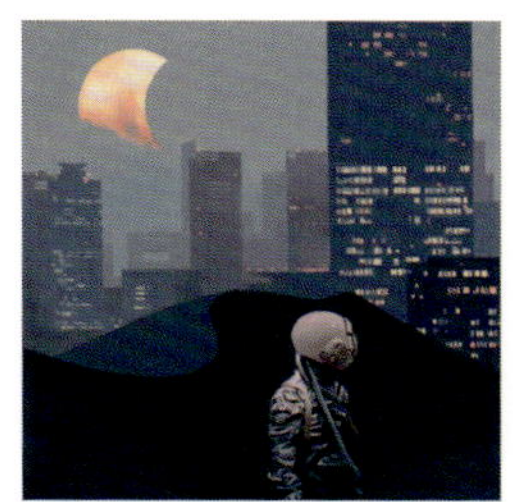

715
BLUE DUNE

2024
oil on canvas
10 x 10 in.

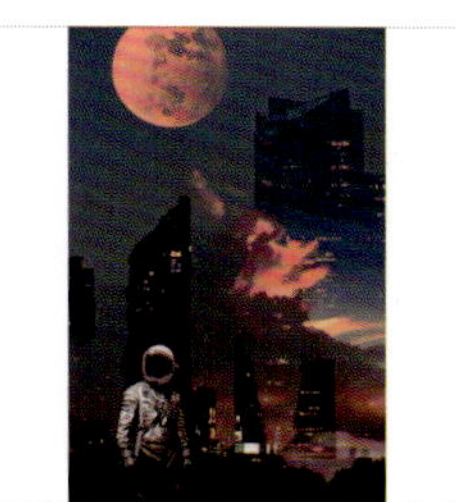

716
FOG OF WAR

2024
oil on canvas
30 x 20 in.

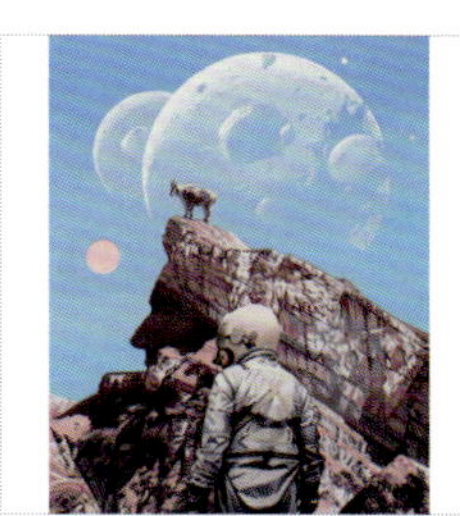

717
OLD MAN OF THE MOUNTAIN

2024
oil on canvas
20 x 16 in.

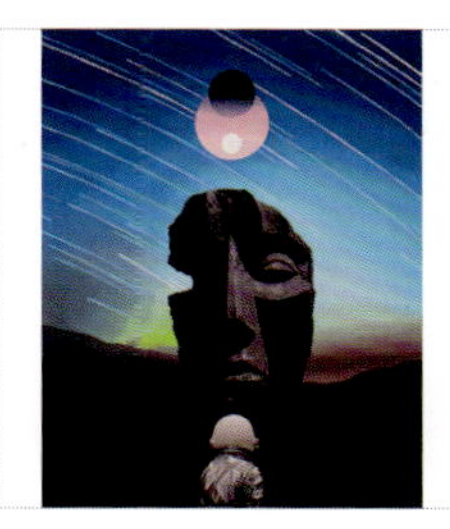

718
THE FACE WITH ONE EYE

2024
oil on canvas
20 x 16 in.

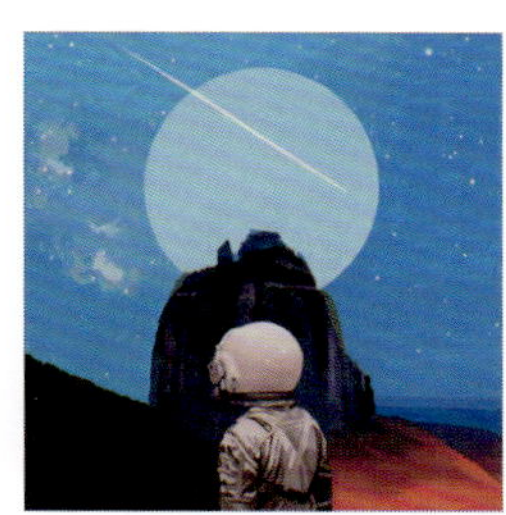

719
BLUE MOON

2024
oil on canvas
10 x 10 in.

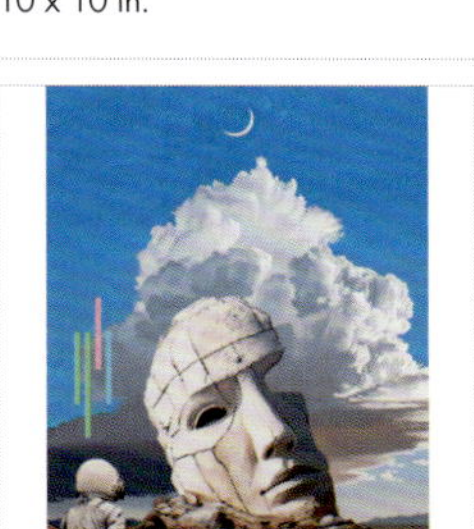

720
ULTRAVIOLET SPECTRUM

2024
oil on canvas
20 x 16 in.

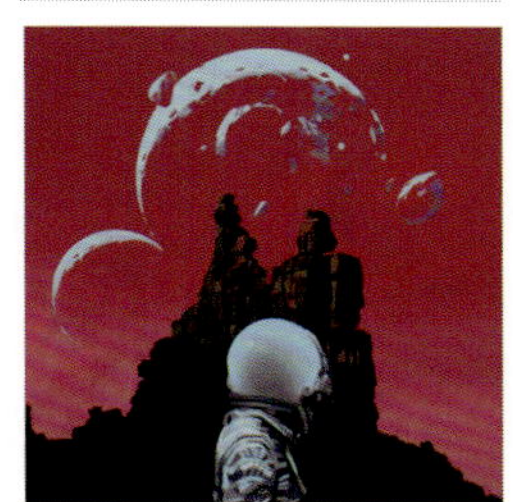

721
MAGENTA SKY

2024
oil on canvas
10 x 10 in.

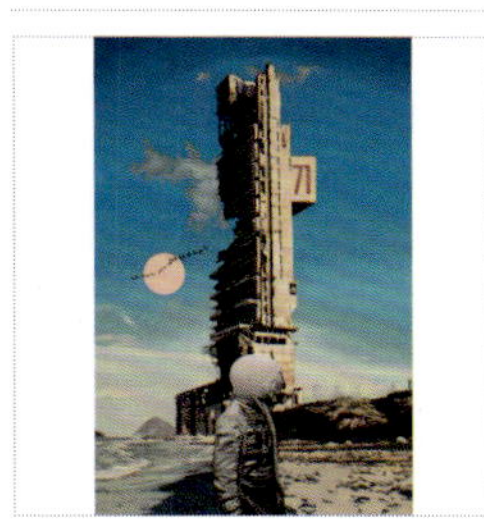

722
BUILDING 71

2024
oil on canvas
30 x 20 in.

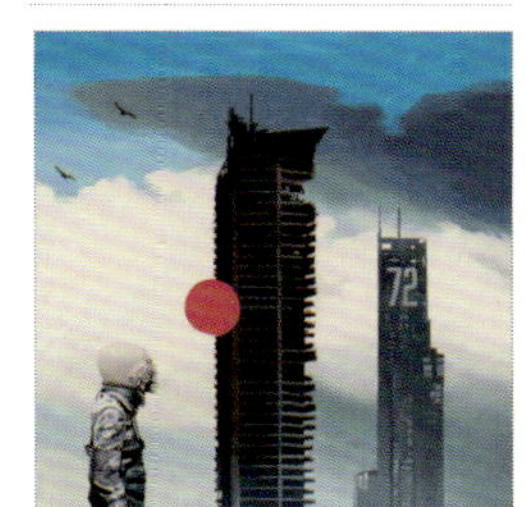

723
BUILDING 72

2024
oil on canvas
10 x 10 in.

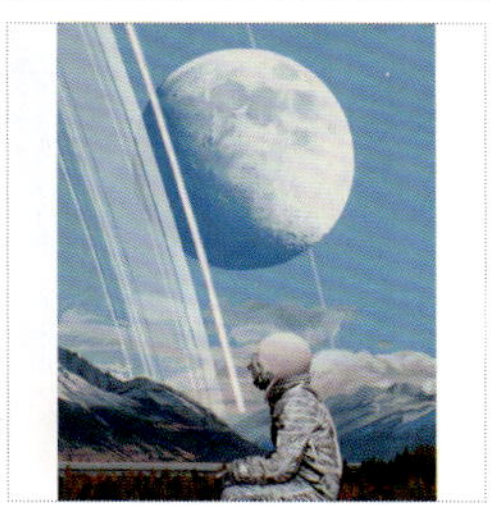

724
MOONFALL

2024
oil on canvas
20 x 16 in.

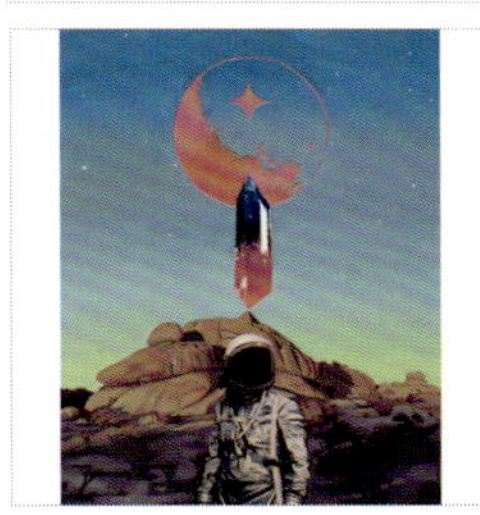

725
CRYSTAL ORACLE

2024
oil on canvas
20 x 16 in.

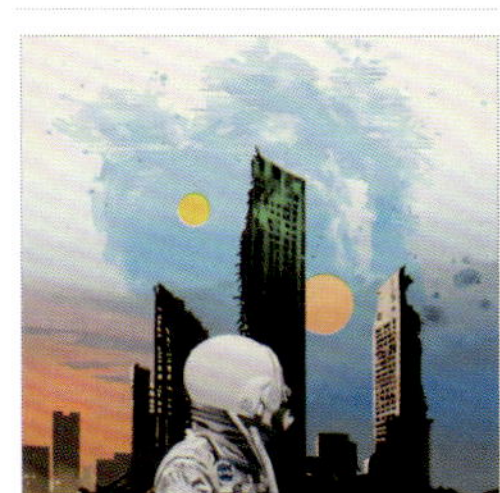

726
CHEMICAL SKY

2024
oil on canvas
10 x 10 in.

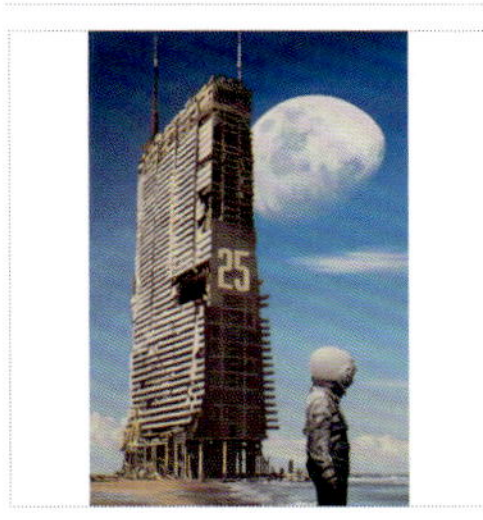

727
BUILDING 25

2024
oil on canvas
30 x 20 in.

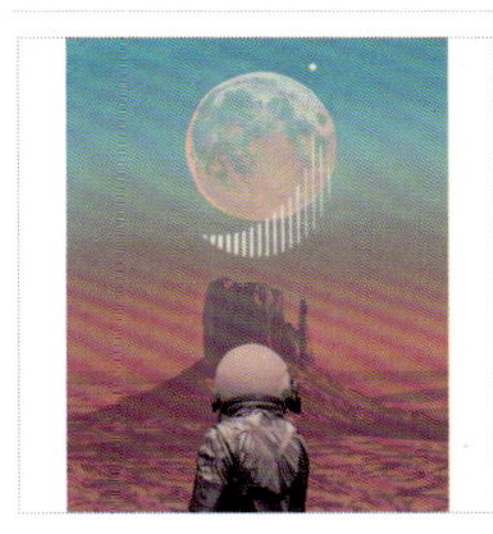

728
PINK MOONSCAPE

2024
oil on canvas
20 x 16 in.

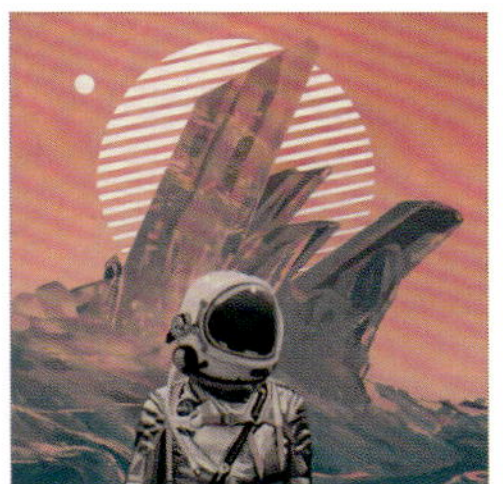

729
CRYSTAL MOUNTAIN

2024
oil on canvas
10 x 10 in.

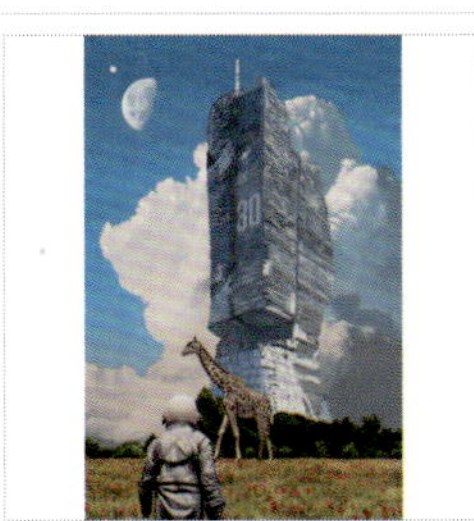

730
BUILDING 30

2024
oil on canvas
30 x 20 in.

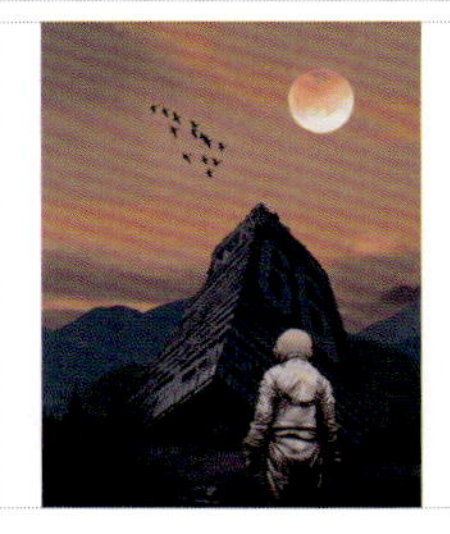

731
THE REMAINS OF BUILDING 66

2024
oil on canvas
20 x 16 in.

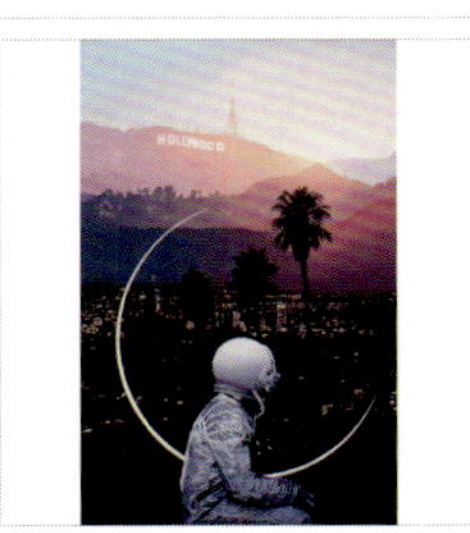

732
DAY & NIGHT

2025
oil on canvas
30 x 20 in.

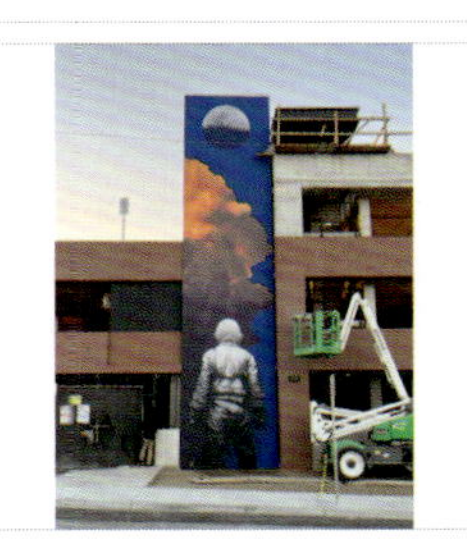

733
EL SEGUNDO MOON

2025
mural
42 x 10 ft.

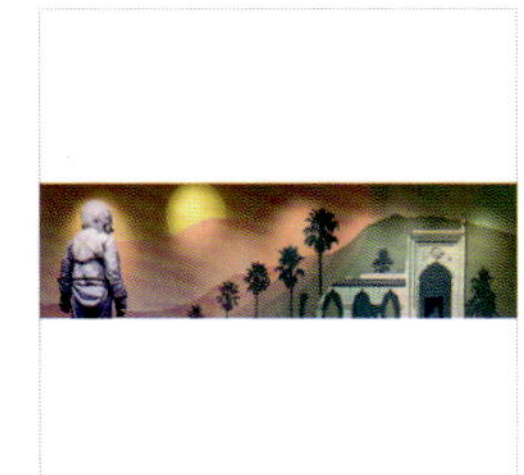

734
WHAT REMAINS OF THE BRAND

2025
mural
10 x 36 ft.

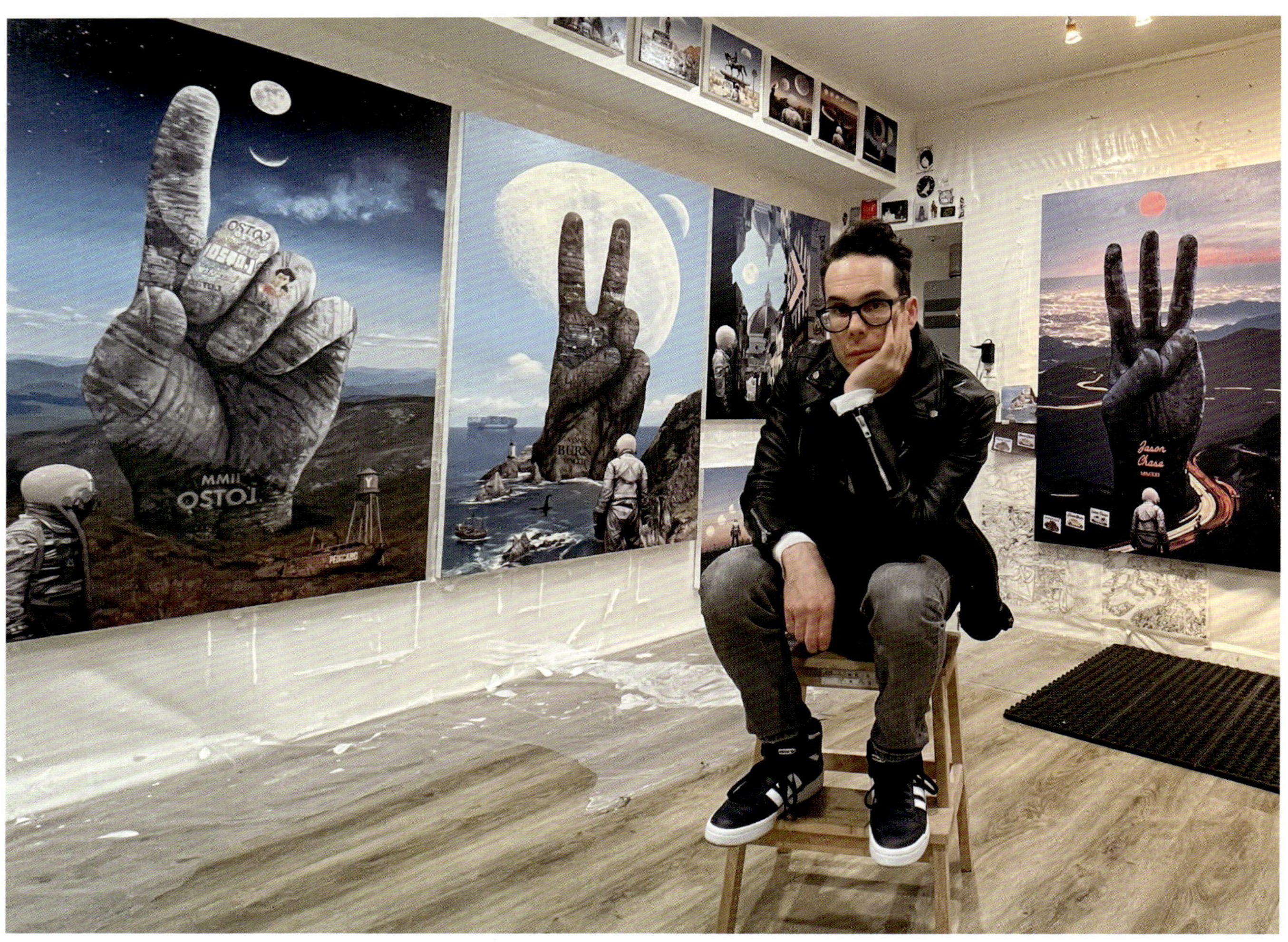

ABOUT THE ARTIST

Scott Listfield is known for his paintings featuring a lone exploratory astronaut lost in a landscape cluttered with pop culture icons, corporate logos, and tongue-in-cheek science fiction references. Scott grew up in Boston and studied art at Dartmouth College. After some time spent living abroad, Scott returned to America and, after watching *2001: A Space Odyssey* for the first time, began painting astronauts and, sometimes, dinosaurs. He now lives and works in Los Angeles.

Scott regularly exhibits his work in galleries and museums around the world, and his paintings have been profiled in *Juxtapoz, Wired Magazine,* and *The Boston Globe*. In 2018 the first book on his work was published by Paragon Books. This is his second book.